The Timeless Land trilogy b..... blend of fact and fiction, comprises ... Land (Book I), **Storm of Time** (Book II) and **No Barrier** (Book III).

It is a compelling saga of colonial Australia, from its difficult beginnings at Sydney Cove under Governor Phillip to its emergence as an established community under the leadership of Governor Macquarie.

Book I, **The Timeless Land**, is the story of the first white settlement and its confrontation with the aborigines who had lived undisturbed, in harmony with their land, for centuries.

Book II, **Storm of Time**, takes up the story of the settlement three years after the departure of Phillip, through the governorships of Hunter, King and Bligh.

Book III, **No Barrier**, follows the fortunes of the settlement through the years of Macquarie's administration.

Though linked by the common theme of the developing colony, each book is complete in itself.

STORM of TIME

BOOK II
of the
TIMELESS LAND
TRILOGY

Eleanor Dark

ANGUS & ROBERTSON PUBLISHERS

ANGUS & ROBERTSON PUBLISHERS
London • Sydney • Melbourne • Singapore • Manila

*This book is copyright. Apart from any fair dealing for the
purposes of private study, research, criticism or review, as
permitted under the Copyright Act, no part may be reproduced
by any process without written permission. Inquiries should
be addressed to the publishers.*

First published 1948
This Arkon paperback edition 1980

© Eleanor Dark 1948

National Library of Australia
card number and ISBN 0 207 14285 8

Printed in Australia by Hedges & Bell Pty Ltd

PREFACE

THE fictional characters in this book are the Mannion family and household, the Prentices, Mark Harvey, Matthew Finn, Tom Towns, Dan Driver, all the natives with the exception of Pemulwy, and a few others barely mentioned. Governor Phillip's *protégé*, Bennilong, did have a daughter named Dilboong, but the records suggest that she died in infancy.

The story of the colony given here is historically as accurate as I could make it, though there are certain incidents the full truth of which will probably never be known. For example, the exact details of what happened on January 26th, 1808, are obscure, though the main facts are clear enough. At a time of violent factional struggle, when party feeling runs high, truth is apt to be cavalierly treated by both sides—as our own unrestful generation well understands. The accounts given by different participants in the affair, and the evidence at Johnston's Court-martial in 1811, are full of conflicting statements about times and events. The historian, confronted by a mass of confused and contradictory evidence, can simply give both sides, and leave it to his readers to form their own conclusions; the novelist must tell a definite story, and therefore can only choose the evidence which, in his opinion, seems most plausible, taking into account the characters of the various witnesses, and the surrounding circumstances. Here one passage from Bligh's address at the Court-martial is worthy of note: ". . . of all the witnesses I have called, not one has his character embarked with mine, nor is his testimony biassed by the knowledge that in protecting me he screens himself. Not so with the witnesses of Col. Johnston. *If he be guilty, which of THEM does not share his crime? If he be worthy of punishment, which of them can hope for impunity?*"

It has been necessary, also, to adapt, eliminate and condense, using such devices as, for instance, the telescoping of a quarrel between two Governors, which in fact spread over months, into one interview; borrowing phrases and expressions actually used in memoirs or correspondence for dialogue; or altering the circumstances—without disturbing the fact or the spirit—of a French officer's gift to a colonial orphanage. Such devices, I hope, make a more coherent story, without doing violence to its essential historical truth.

The name of that "hero of the fleece" who looms so large in the colony's early history was invariably spelt "McArthur" in the records of his time, but the alternative spelling, "Macarthur," is so consistently used in later histories, and so much more familiar to present-day Australians, that I have used it here.

My grateful acknowledgments are due to the trustees of the Mitchell Library, Sydney, for permission to quote from manuscripts in their possession.

E.D.

BOOK I

GOVERNOR HUNTER

1799

THE settlement lay as if beaten down into submission under a fierce sun-light, to which the smoke from surrounding fires lent a sullen, orange glow. Denuded of its native trees, exposed to the merciless glare of midsummer, it huddled up the slope from the water's edge, its little houses and the fences which enclosed them filmed with dust, its tiny patches of garden scorched brown, its narrow, haphazard streets almost deserted. The few larger buildings—the Governor's house, the gaol, the hospital, the granary—served only to emphasise the general appearance of poverty. The arms of the windmill hung motionless, and inside its protective paling the Tank Stream, the colony's water-supply, was disturbingly low. Only the harbour and the sky looked clean—two blue, brilliant, polished plates, between which the imprisoned air shimmered with heat.

After so dry a spring and summer, earlier hopes of a bountiful harvest had been disappointed. The pastures were parched, the cattle skin and bones; ponds were either dry or mere muddy shallows; great tracts of forest were blackened by fire; and still, in the outlying districts, the nights were pricked by the glow of creeping flames, and the days hazy with smoke.

Thanks to the relentless, blazing sky that spread over them day after unendurable day, the colonists knew now that the price of wheat would not be lowered after all; dysentery reduced them to a weakness from which they felt no incentive to recover; almost everyone from the Governor down to the children—restless over their pothooks in the makeshift school-rooms—suffered from a painful inflammation of the eyes; there was never enough to eat, and what there was did not tempt the appetite in a tem-perature which had stood as high as 107° in the shade.

It was the 26th day of January, 1799. The little township of Sydney on the shores of Port Jackson had attained its eleventh birthday, but no celebration marked the event. Few of its inhabitants, indeed (though there were a few among them who would allow the country some virtues), regarded it as an occasion for rejoicing. It was merely another day of exile and suffering; another day to be endured.

The Governor, John Hunter, elderly and harassed, paused for a moment as he emerged from the Court House door to read the order he had issued yesterday, and which now hung on the wall facing an empty and indifferent street. He did not really want to read it, for it was the fifth that he had proclaimed upon the same subject, and in his heart he did not expect it to be more observed than the others had been. But it gave him a moment's respite between leaving the comparative cool of indoors, and facing the cruel, yellow heat, and the walk to Government House. He was sixty-two, and tired—not only with the weight of advancing years, but with the burden of a responsibility for which he was beginning to admit (to himself if not to others) that he was inadequate.

From that September day in 1795 when he had returned to the colony

as its second Governor, he had not known an hour's freedom from anxiety.
The three years between Governor Phillip's departure and his own succession had so altered the character of the little community that each day
confronted him with a fresh shock. For those years had been, under the
Lieutenant-Governors Grose and Paterson, a military dictatorship; and
not all the polite greetings of the officers of the New South Wales Corps
could for ever blind him to the fact that a dictatorship, once firmly
established, does not willingly relinquish its power.

He learned that he was expected to grant himself land, employ convicts
in clearing and cultivating it, and thus acquire, as many others had done,
a valuable farming property: when he made it clear that he had no such
intention, and that he expected his duties as Governor fully to occupy his
time, the air grew colder still. It was much more difficult now than it
had been in Phillip's time for the Governor to keep his watchful eye on
the whole colony. Then it had been small, compact, an area to be
inspected easily from end to end in a few hours. Now it had grown. A
group of farms on the banks of the Hawkesbury were some thirty miles
from Sydney as the crow flew; a chain of them extended for twenty miles
along the river, and more were scattered among the various arms of the
harbour. A tour of inspection was now a matter of days—tiring days
for an elderly man who could find among his entourage no energetic and
capable lieutenant in whom he could place undivided confidence.

He had found to his dismay that many of the minor officials and
tradesmen were completely useless. It would be better, he had thought,
to promote the more deserving of the emancipated convicts to some small
posts of responsibility, than to pay salaries to such drones. Had not the
notorious pickpocket, George Barrington, aquitted himself satisfactorily as
chief constable at Parramatta?

No new land, he discovered, had been cleared for public purposes
during the military interregnum, and that already in cultivation was
producing little, either from the poor quality or the exhaustion of the
soil. Since labour had been recklessly diverted to large private landowners, it was not surprising that the farms of these individuals were
flourishing; but the cultivation of crops had far outstripped the erection
of buildings, and Hunter was dismayed by the inadequacy of barns,
granaries and storehouses. Indeed, except for these oases of private
cultivation, comfort, and prosperity, the whole colony had seemed to be
dying on its feet. Its few boats were battered and decaying, its houses
and buildings in disrepair; huts which had been built in earlier days for
Government purposes were now leased to private individuals, clothing was
in rags, the stamp of bitterness and hunger was on the faces of convicts,
ex-convicts and the poorer settlers.

Before a year passed he had realised the full difficulty of the task that
confronted him. Captain David Collins, ex-Judge Advocate of the colony,
and Mr. Palmer the Commissary, returning to England about this time,
would, no doubt, give to the authorities there a first-hand account of the
trials under which he laboured. They, in personal interviews, would
surely paint a more convincing picture than he could do with his pen.

They would tell—he hoped—how he was surrounded by schemers, mischief-makers, restless, ambitious, designing people who saw in his arrival a threat to their opportunities for self-enrichment. They would bear him out that the only kind of Governor who would be welcome here would be one who was prepared to fall in with all the plans of such people, be complaisant to their every demand, permit them to help themselves from the public store, and supply them with labourers to be fed and clothed at the Government's expense. Mr. Palmer would relate—or would he?—that as custodian of the stores he had not dared to refuse to any soldier, either officer or private, whatever he might demand. . . .

Standing now on the Court House verandah, the Governor focussed his absent stare on the proclamation on the wall. He read idly:

"The filthy condition which the spring water in the tanks is so often reported to be kept in, by those who live near having repeatedly broke down the paling which surrounds them, or left it open when broken by accident, for the admission of hogs, this notice . . ."

A sharp, decisive footfall on the steps behind him, and a long streak of shadow across the stone floor, made him turn. He confronted a man in the uniform of an officer of the New South Wales Corps—a man with a direct, challenging stare, with a long, rather supercilious nose, with a mouth whose lines suggested a truculent self-assertiveness, and whose collar lifted his chin even higher than natural arrogance would have demanded. They faced each other for a moment, warily hostile. The newcomer bowed with a coldness which was matched by the Governor's voice, as he said:

"Good day, Sir."

Captain Macarthur responded with no greater warmth:

"Good day, Your Excellency."

His eyes flickered from Hunter's face to Hunter's proclamation on the wall; the Governor's nerves were raw, and he fancied that he saw a hint of derision in that glance. He enquired with frigid civility:

"I trust Mrs. Macarthur is well?"

"I thank you, Sir; I am happy to say that her health is excellent."

Hunter, passing with a faint inclination of his head, stumped down the steps and out into the sunlight. A sudden heat of anger in his body made him almost indifferent to the heat of the day, but when he reached his house he was puffing slightly, and he made for the chair at his desk in the cool, dim room as for a haven.

He at all events (though the knowledge caused him no particular elation) remembered that this was an anniversary. As he sat alone, relaxed, recovering not only his breath but his composure—which the mere sight of Captain Macarthur was enough to disturb—his memory went back to that day, eleven years ago, when he had assisted at the founding of the colony which he now governed. The thought of those years nagged at his mind, the fear of his own failure haunted him. As if to quiet it with written words, with statistics, with an official record of visible achievement, he reached for documents in which he had set forth for the enlightenment of the home authorities a statement of the colony's laborious progress.

It seemed little enough to show for so much effort and privation, but to-day forced him to comparisons. Not only comparisons between a land in which, eleven years ago, agriculture was totally unknown, and in which, now, thousands of acres were producing; but also, less comfortably, between himself then, a subordinate of whom no more was required than a loyal and faithful obedience to orders, and himself now, from whom the orders must come. From there he was forced to a further comparison —a worried suspicion that his predecessor, Arthur Phillip, had been able to command some quality as an administrator which he himself lacked. He stirred restlessly, pushed aside his return of livestock and land under cultivation, and, with his head propped on his hands, studied the statement of work executed in the previous year.

To look at it, he thought wryly, one might imagine the place to be a hive of enthusiastic industry. The tally of blacksmiths, carpenters, cutlers, coopers, sawyers, shipwrights, bricklayers, shoemakers and thatchers was accompanied by an exhaustive description of the duties they performed, and the labours they had accomplished. Even the activities of two barbers "shaveing all the servants of Government," and of a single ropemaker "makeing cordage out of curryjong," were faithfully chronicled. Nor were the executioner and his assistant forgotten, though their grim function was left tactfully undescribed.

It was easy enough to set it all out on paper; difficult beyond words to keep it moving in fact—to correlate human effort and material supply, to adjust community production to community need, to allow for the fact that though a man may appear as a docile unit in an official return, he is apt to be, in life, a recalcitrant individual. Though the paper might say, with misleading simplicity, "three men splitti'g shingles," he, as administrator, was only too well aware that he must deal not with the cypher 3, but with Tom, an incorrigible idler, and Dick, a troublemaker, and Harry, too physically wrecked to do more than three days' work in five.

He was roused from his gloomy reflections by a servant who came to tell him that the Reverend Mr. Johnson had arrived, and begged the indulgence of a few words with His Excellency.

His Excellency sighed. Mr. Johnson, he thought, was a worthy man, very rightly and properly shocked by the licentiousness and immorality of the colony; but he sometimes seemed to imagine that the Governor could produce chastity, sobriety, industry and godliness with the wave of a wand. He rose with a kind of depressed courtesy to greet his visitor.

Mr. Johnson, too, looked dejected. He began:

"I am hesitant to trespass upon Your Excellency's valuable time . . ." Hunter bowed him to a chair.

"You are always welcome, Mr. Johnson," he said, not altogether truthfully. "In what way can I be of service to you?"

"I wish to see you, Sir, upon a small matter in connection with our temporary place of worship. I have but just come from there, and I find that one of the doors has been broken from its hinges—by design, I should suppose. If Your Excellency would be so good as to give orders that it be repaired before our service to-morrow . . . ?"

The Governor was thankful that nothing more troublesome was demanded of him. He could deal with doors; human beings were more difficult. He responded cordially:

"By all means, Mr. Johnson. I shall have a carpenter directed to the work immediately." He added a civil enquiry: "I trust your health is improved?"

Mr. Johnson passed his handkerchief wearily across his hot brow. The eleven years of his sojourn in New South Wales had dealt hardly with him. Now, at forty-two, his face was sallow, and less rubicund than formerly. He had lost weight during the last few months of intolerable heat, and restless nights had smeared a darkness under his eyes. He answered heavily:

"Unfortunately I cannot say that it is, Sir, nor do I expect it, so long as I remain in this climate. I am in hopes that my application for leave of absence may be granted."

Hunter looked at him thoughtfully.

"You have indeed earned a rest, my friend. As I sat here before you arrived I was reflecting upon this day eleven years ago, when you and I were among those who witnessed the beginning of the colony." He added gloomily: "Much has happened since then."

Mr. Johnson folded his hands upon his knees and looked solemn.

"The circumstance had not escaped my memory, Sir. In my home this morning special prayers were said for the future of our little com-munity. I prayed earnestly that grace might descend upon the profligate and the ungodly, and I most particularly entreated that the Lord in His mercy would support and strengthen Your Excellency's endeavours."

The Governor coughed with slight embarrassment.

"Very good of you, my dear Sir. I trust your intercession may bear fruit." He fiddled with the papers on the table. "You, I think, are one of those who recognise the trials I have been subjected to in my attempt to perform my duty." A faint flush darkened his face. "So strongly do I feel upon this subject, Mr. Johnson, that I confess I was tempted into expressions to His Grace the Duke of Portland which, had they not been justified by extreme provocation, might almost have laid me open to a charge of blasphemy."

Mr. Johnson looked stern.

"You surprise me, Sir."

Hunter raised his hand reassuringly

"You will acquit me, Mr. Johnson, of any such intention. It was no more than my duty to describe at length the state of affairs existing in this place, and I freely admit that the recital of the iniquities of certain people—and of one in particular whom I am persuaded I need not name to you—so inflamed my indignation that I concluded by assuring His Grace that the Saviour Himself, were He to appear in this colony, would not be safe from their intrigues and calumnies. 'There are people here,

I said, 'who would most readily prepair for His sacred head another crown of thorns, and erect another cross for His second crucifixion.' And I told him plainly, Sir, that none more so than the person to whom I had had occasion to allude so frequently in my letter."

Mr. Johnson meditated profoundly for a moment before answering. His memory, like the Governor's, could go back to Phillip's regime, but, unlike the Governor's, it could continue from there through the fateful years during which the officers of the New South Wales Corps had governed the colony in what he had once described to Hunter as "a kind of military manner." He had come to this land, an earnest young man, deeply convinced of the importance of his mission; he had lived in it a confused, disillusioned and frustrated man, bewildered by the apparent ineffectiveness of his spiritual weapons—not only against the depravity and brutality of human beings, but in the face of an environment which seemed to set aside, with a monstrous indifference, every standard and custom to which he had been bred. Yet after Phillip's departure, faced by the startling changes which had then burst upon the colony, he had felt some changes take place, too, within himself. He had had to contend, before, only with a kind of spiritual inertia, a passive resistance, an official neglect of his function which sprang rather from Phillip's intense pre-occupation with the mere effort of keeping the colony alive, than from any active opposition. Through all his confusions there had remained with him the conception of himself as the shepherd of his flock. The wolves which had threatened it then had been abstractions—ignorance, violence, immorality—and against these he neither knew, nor felt it necessary to know, any weapon save prayer. But gradually, as the colony lapsed into confusion, as the civil authority vanished, as the scramble for wealth and power became every day more open and shameless, as the poor suffered and complained, as the wealthy grew more arrogant and rapacious, he began to see the wolves in the shape of men. He had no comprehension of the forces which drove them; he believed in society as it existed, and he saw evil very simply as the devil working in unregenerate souls. Yet when he observed the devil working to such purpose that suddenly the dignity and authority of the Church were being treated with contempt, a flame of indignation and resistance was lit in him. Even now he felt his cheeks flush with anger when he remembered how the drum had beat one morning in the very middle of his discourse, and the soldiers had got up and marched away, leaving him no congregation but half a dozen convicts. The Sabbath had become a day of rioting, drunkenness, and gambling. He had even, upon one occasion, been denied access to two condemned men when he went to assist them in reconciling themselves to God. He had complained bitterly, he had even exchanged heated words with Major Grose. Nor had Captain Macarthur, as commanding officer at Parramatta, shown any regard for religious observances there, and Mr. Johnson well recalled with what indignation his colleague, Mr. Marsden, had described that gentleman's offensive reception of his complaints. Those years were like a wound in his mind—but what more could he have done? He had prayed and he had protested. He knew of nothing else, and yet, like the Governor, he was sometimes tortured by self-doubt. He looked up rather sadly from his clasped hands, and said:

"I have good reason to know, Sir, the nature of the provocations you have received. Yet when I was myself moved to complain with some warmth in a letter to my good friend the Reverend Mr. Newton, of the conduct of Major Grose, he replied with an exhortation which you, Sir, might also consider. I have the letter here. I keep it about me as a continual reminder of my duty as a Christian. Allow me, Sir . . ."

He unfolded a deeply creased sheet of paper, and read with grave emphasis: " *'You take the best method of relieving your own mind from the remembrance of his injurious treatment, and the best method of retaliation, by praying for him.'* " He put the letter away, and said humbly: "I have endeavoured to act upon that noble sentiment, Sir. May I recommend it also to Your Excellency's attention?"

He stood up and prepared to take his departure. Hunter escorted him to the door.

"It is indeed a noble sentiment," he said non-committally, "and admirably expressed. Good-day, Mr. Johnson."

But he was frowning as he went back to his desk. He did not feel like praying for Captain Macarthur.

*   *   *   *   *

He had returned to this place with a feeling that he was to step into an environment which, however hard, was at least familiar; he was to inherit a function for whose performance Phillip had bequeathed him a precedent. He had left a community which was poor, which suffered hardship and deprivations, but which was cohesive, and passably disciplined; he had come back to chaos.

He had found convicts whose terms were expired hanging about the two settlements at Sydney and Parramatta, eking out a precarious livelihood in casual labour for officers or farmers. Others had taken to the woods, where they joined the natives and incited them to plunder settlers in the more isolated districts. He had found vast numbers of women who, deserted by husbands or lovers, were now a serious problem for the Government stores, and his kindly nature here conflicted painfully with his duty of maintaining the colony with as little expense as possible to the mother-country. "*If we estimate their merits,*" he had written with a touch of wistfulness, "*by the charming children with which they have filled the colony, they will deserve our care; but it will become a matter for the consideration of Government whether, after the father has withdrawn himself from the service of the public, his children are to continue a burthen on the public store.*" The soldiers, too, had numerous children whom the pay of a private was quite inadequate to support; these, too, he must feed. "*I cannot,*" he wrote helplessly, "*see their infants in want.*"

Yet he knew that all these confusions sprang from a common ill, a root evil which even now, after four years of struggle, still defied his efforts. Here was a garrison town, threatened by no enemy. Here were soldiers—but no battles to fight. The officers of the New South Wales Corps, with time hanging heavily upon their hands, and with the whole colony under their undisputed sway, had not been slow to seize their advantage. The organisation which they had built up for themselves revealed itself as so strong that the Governor hardly knew where to attack it first. It was not difficult to understand, he thought sourly, why, after Phillip's departure, they should have occupied their farms and embarked upon their agricultural pursuits in the "high spirits" which Collins had described to him. For their land was freely granted; their tools and implements were supplied from the public store; they were each allowed the labour of ten convicts—fed and clothed at the Government's expense —and could hire as many more as they wanted at those times when the gangs were not occupied with public work. Nor was money required to pay even these. For it was evident that Collins had not exaggerated when he described the prevailing desire for liquor as a mania. Where life was hard, sordid and monotonous, where freedom was a dream, where culture was unknown and nine-tenths of the people the product of poverty and oppression, rum was an escape. It was the only luxury. Those who could supply it need offer no other wages.

And the officers could supply it. Since no restrictions were placed on trading, either in liquor or in other commodities, they could buy the cargoes of American merchantmen calling at the port, or charter ships to bring from abroad goods which they bought and resold at fabulous profit. The small settlers and emancipated convicts, having nothing else to pay with, paid with their livestock, their tools, their labour, even their whole farms, and the wealth of the colony flowed steadily into a few increasingly well-lined pockets. To that small group in a poverty-stricken community which could afford the price of purchase, liquor thus became more than merchandise—it became an instrument of power. It opened a back door to gambling, robbery, blackmail, and murder. It reduced Phillip's tight, Spartan organisation to a state of utter demoralisation. It confronted Hunter with a condition in which, as he complained: *"all is confusion, disorder and licentiousness, and a total inattention—nay, I might almost say, a direct disobedience—to Public Orders."*

He was a peaceable man, and he had tried to effect his reforms peaceably. Yet his restoration of the civil authority, and his reinstatement of the magistrates, had been sufficient to teach him with what inveterate enmity he would be treated by those who saw their power threatened by his measures. There was no doubt that they were not entitled to the labour of so many convicts supported at the public expense; yet perhaps he himself could not have said how far the arguments he advanced to His Grace in favour of allowing them this indulgence a little longer were dictated by conviction, and how far by his anxiety not to offend them. More than half the last harvest, he explained, had been raised by the industry of these gentlemen, and the withdrawal of their convict labour would surely result in a poor crop for the coming year, and hardship for all. Moreover, he urged—having already learned something of their methods—would not those who did succeed in producing some grain take advantage of the scarcity to raise the price?

But all his tentative efforts at appeasement did not make them less hostile. He was shocked and genuinely astonished by their greed. Why could they not be content with the farms they had acquired in such advantageous circumstances? Why should they condescend to sully their hands with trade, beyond the proper disposal of their produce to the Government?

And he, the Governor, attempting to push forward with those multitudinous public works, so neglected, so urgently necessary, had found himself without labourers—hardly able, as he had plaintively informed His Grace, "*to call together twenty for any public purpose at Sydney.*"

His black brows came together in an angry frown. He was jealous of his authority as Governor—the more so, perhaps, because he felt in himself no indomitable personal strength to augment it. His resentment smouldered continually against those people who, during his absence, had not only enriched themselves by this shameful trade, but had thereby won an influence which they did not hesitate to pit, covertly, against his own. He remembered angrily the anonymous paper dropped in the streets of the town not two years ago, which had actually hinted that he himself, and his servants, were implicated in this iniquitous traffic, and his own suspicion at the time—which had now hardened into certainty— that it was no convict, no disgruntled member of the lower class who had written it. There was contempt mixed with his resentment. Soldiers, he held, should be soldiers—not tradesmen. "*This spirit for trade,*" he had written bitterly to Under Secretary King eighteen months ago, "*which I must ever consider in the manner it is carried on here, to be highly disgracefull to men who hold in their hand a commission signed by His Majesty, has been carried so far that it has now reached all the inferior appointments, so that it has absorbed all their time and attention, and the public duty of their respective offices are entirely neglected . . .*"

He had thought, as he wrote, of Captain John Macarthur, and he thought of him again now. Indeed, when he confronted his problems, they were apt to become personified in his mind as the figure of that busy, arrogant, self-opinionated man, with whom, before he had been six months in the colony, he had already guardedly crossed swords. And not for the last time. By the middle of the next year Macarthur had become his openly avowed antagonist, and his letters to England returned again and again to condemnation of "this meddling person," "this speculating individual," this "man who has employed the whole of his time in this country in sowing discord, and inriching himself by means truly disgracefull," this "man whose restless, ambitious and litigious disposition has been so often experienced in this country." The turbulence of the colony he ruled he felt as a continual reproach, and he strove to combat the influence of stronger-willed men than himself with a delegated authority. He clutched the King's commission about him like a cloak, but the wind of commercial greed blew coldly beneath it. His pen continually expressed his resentment against Macarthur in bitter phrases. "There is not a person in this colony," he wrote angrily, "whose opinion I hold in greater contempt than I do this busybody's."

He stood up and went across to the window, from where he could see the lately returned *Norfolk* lying at anchor in the cove. When fears of

his own capacity as an administrator beset him, he could find some comfort
in what had been accomplished during his regime in the way of exploration. It had given him great satisfaction to learn beyond a doubt from
Mr. Flinders and Mr. Bass that New Holland and Van Diemen's Land
were separated by a strait; his worried expression grew benign for a
moment as he gazed at the leaky, twenty-five ton sloop, built at the island
whose name she bore. Yes, exploration was a simple matter, not involving
the clash of opposed interests, the bewildering conflict of personalities,
the underground machinations of greed and jealousy. By land or sea
you plotted your course, and went; and nothing impeded you but weather,
thirst, exhaustion, wild country or rough seas. He sighed. He had not,
indeed, been able to undertake many of these journeys himself, pleasant
as they would have seemed to him in comparison with the irksome duties
which he must remain to perform at the seat of Government. Nor had
he—to his indignation—found among the officers of the colony any who
were willing to forsake their own private and profitable concerns for such
arduous undertakings; and he remembered with a touch of nostalgia the
excursions of the settlement's early days, when not only Governor Phillip,
but himself, and Tench, and Dawes, and White had struggled on foot
over miles of monotonous forest to find those places where now settlers
dwelt on their farms.

No, he had been, for the most part, merely the instigator and not the
leader of these more recent explorations. Yet they represented solid
achievement in the midst of so much failure. George Bass and Henry
Hacking had done useful work in exploring inland. There had been dis-
appointments and setbacks, but the colony's horizon had expanded, nevertheless. The ex-convict, Wilson, and his companions had made a not
inconsiderable journey. Farms fringed the river now, below Richmond
Hill. All the way from Sydney to Parramatta they were scattered, and
again from Parramatta to Toongabbee, and from Toongabbee to where
they curved like a green horseshoe about the foot of Prospect Hill. A
herd of wild cattle—descendants of two bulls and four cows lost nearly
eleven years ago—at large on the rich river flats now known as the Cow
Pastures, had seemed to act as a magnet to the feet of exploring parties,
and on this route, all the way across the river to Mount Hunter, there
were patches of country which, in good time, would repay settlement.

The colony progressed. He tried to reassure himself with this thought,
but was unable to subdue the knowledge that its progression was rather
like that of a bolting horse, and himself a driver whose arms ached with
fruitless sawing on the reins. He remembered with bewilderment that
Phillip had been able to maintain a curious, serene faith, based on no
logical reason which he himself could discover. He remembered a stray
phrase of the first Governor's which, at the time, had seemed meaningless,
and seemed so still. "We must allow the country some influence in the
moulding of affairs, Mr. Hunter." The country? He looked at it with
knotted brows. Trees, rocks, water. . . . Moulding? Surely the opposite
was true? Surely the country, with its vastness, its impassivity, its
droughts and its floods, was only something else to be coerced and

mastered? He saw his war with environment as a just war. He was charged with building a community, and it must conform, by Heaven, to a pattern laid down for it on the other side of the world. He did not feel himself arrayed against a law of Nature, but merely against human wilfulness and material obstructions. Though ·the effort kill him, he must (until the happy day when Captain King arrived to release him) continue to squeeze and hammer the colony into a reproduction of an English community. They were English people, and in any latitude must remain so for ever.

Yet he was forced to admit—because the fact obtruded itself brutally upon his consciousness in every waking hour—that the community, in spite of his squeezing and hammering, was becoming not more, but less like an English community every day. The outer forms of English social organisation were there, but they were like an ill-fitting garment, uneasily worn. The urgent life beneath burst indecent holes in it, and split it vulgarly at the seams. He patched and mended and implored a more seemly deportment—in vain. He was forced into continual and unwilling compromise. Time-honoured forms of legal administration showed sudden inadequacies; social conventions, temporarily stretched to meet local conditions, alarmingly remained stretched; the immemorial layers of the English hierarchy showed a disconcerting tendency to lose their clear definition, to melt into each other like alternating stripes of wet paint. What, for instance, could be more confusing, more disruptive, than the metamorphosis of His Majesty's officers into merchants and traders in rum? And was it to be approved that free settlers should take convict women to wife, or that emancipated convicts should wed free women? Or that the officers, both civil and military, should flaunt their mistresses quite so openly? Did not all this cause a blurring of the sharp, salutary line which should ever exist between the officer and the tradesman, the immoral and the respectable, the felon and the free? But where women were scarce, and human nature clamorous, could one do more than advocate lawful union, and wink at illicit intercourse? Yet what place in an orderly pattern could be reserved for the offspring of such unions? Did they not, with their feeble infant hands, tear large rents in the fabric of accepted social convention? Did they not—these helpless babes—fly in the face of age-old precedent by tying together classes which should have remained separate? And he was forced to stand by and see the majesty of the King in his palace, and the authority of his Parliament undermined by a morsel of humanity in a cradle . . .

Suddenly the complexity of his problems combined with the heat of the day to make him conscious of his bodily fatigue. There was a lethargy in his limbs, his head ached, his sixty-two years claimed a respite for self-indulgence. He would sleep for a couple of hours; later, in the cool of the evening, he would work. He turned away from the window, left the room without looking at his desk, and plodded wearily up the stairs.

* * * * *

One March evening, in the house of Mr. Richard Atkins, Acting Judge Advocate of the colony, a supper party was mounting in a crescendo of conviviality to that climax which Mr. Atkins' parties invariably reached sooner or later. No ladies were present, and the six men, now that the cloth had been removed, had settled down to serious drinking. The long, heavy, rather lugubrious face of Surgeon Balmain wore an unaccustomed smile; it seemed to have arrived there without his knowledge or conni- vance, and to have made a sheepish smirk of itself in consequence. His large, light brown eyes, however, refused to co-operate; they were more mournful than ever, and rather bewildered, like the eyes of an anxious dog, and his heavy chin, with the hint of a cleft in it, was sunk deep into the folds of his neck-cloth. Young Matthew Flinders, his dark eyes snapping with excitement, was inclined to be argumentative; his friend, George Bass, sprawling his six feet back in his chair, his handsome face slightly flushed, was limiting his conversation to a sleepy remark now and then in corroboration of Matthew's tales. Captain Waterhouse was leaning forward and interrupting Flinders at every opportunity. Mr. Stephen Mannion, who prided himself upon being, as an Irish gentleman, able to hold his liquor, was sitting ostentatiously upright. The immaculate white ruffles of his cravat showed no signs of dishevelment, and the brightness of his blue eyes was the only sign that he had drunk glass for glass with the others. Mr. Atkins' eyes, however, though eloquent of *bonhomie*, were opaque and bleary; his greying hair was disordered, his hands unsteady, and he was already having some trouble with his speech.

Widely differing as they were in age and temperament, they were temporarily united by the mere fact of being fellow-exiles in a small and strange community. They were all—except Mr. Mannion—bound to its affairs by duty; spectators of and sometimes participants in its endless feuds and turmoils. Tidings from the world they had left, the great European world, came only at long intervals. Events which rocked that world were memories by the time news of them reached this isolated outpost months later. Their violence had shaken or shattered more than one established society during the brief eleven years of the colony's history; a French king had fallen, Napoleon was on the march, England had been six years at war with France; Ireland was in turmoil; and as an undertone more menacing than any bark of gunfire, sounded the universal complaints of people to whom the invention of machinery and the acceleration of industrial production had meant only more bitter poverty and oppression.

These clamours reached the colony as echoes. They came less as recorded tidings in months-old newspapers than as spoken comment from the mouths of living people. Officers brought with them tales of im- poverished French aristocrats, of Pitt and Fox at loggerheads, of the fashionable world turning a deaf ear to the murmurings of the poor, of a restless and seditious spirit manifesting itself in the crew of His Majesty's ships—all the current gossip of anxious and unrestful times. Shiploads of convicts told of foetid, overcrowded gaols, of soul-and-body-destroying labour in factories and mines, of laws growing ever harsher to subdue an ever-growing discontent. Some, whose crime had been the raising of a rebellious voice, brought their resentments with them, a faint spark of intransigeance, smothered but not dead.

Into the new land they came, bearing the problems of the old; against a different background there remained the same problems, but a new environment, a new set of circumstances, a new social pattern demanded a re-focussing of the spiritual vision. Life was life still, but all its customs, all its concepts, all its traditional shibboleths and contrivances here underwent a slight distortion, and an involuntary process of adjustment coloured every thought and action.

Already, in eleven years, the ill-assorted units from an older society, straggling haphazard into the new one in the making, had fallen into place; and if the places of some were curiously different from those they would have occupied in their homeland, that was merely part of the distortion which gave the whole business its vaguely macabre air, its atmosphere of unreality and impermanence.

Not one of the six men who sat around Mr. Atkins' hospitable board thought of this life save as an interlude—a curious, temporary exile from the real world which each would turn to account for his own advantage in his own way. Captain Waterhouse, though he was not yet thirty, could look back to the foundation of the colony; he had taken part in the landing of the First Fleet, seen the first trees felled, and the first wattle-and-daub huts erected, yet even to him the life he had lived here was an incident. Mr. Balmain, too, had assisted quite literally at the birth of the colony, for he had delivered the first child to be born on the First Fleet before it had even left the shores of the motherland. But neither he, nor Mr. Atkins, with seven years' residence behind him, regarded the colony as more than the scene of a task to be done, a professional assignment. Mr. Mannion, who had so strangely come as a visitor in 1790, and as strangely stayed, asserted more persistently than any of them, his detachment. He had bound his fortunes to the land, but not himself. He would make wealth out of its soil—but he would spend it elsewhere. This was still, after nine years, his purpose, and it had not yet occurred to him that his sons—one of them born in the colony—might think of it as home. To the two younger men it was adventure. It was inexhaustible, unexplored territory, endless uncharted seas. Neither Bass nor Flinders would accept for more than a little while any restriction of their horizon. This paltry little colony was a mere *pied-à-terre*, a base from which they could discover the secrets of an interminable, unknown coastline, and challenge the mysteries of an ocean.

Yet here they all were, and here they must remain for the present. The life of the little community closed about them, and they found themselves studying it, speculating about it, participating in it, contributing to it—for there was nothing else. It was so small that any clash became an uproar. Every pebble of disturbance troubled the whole pool. A brawl between two private soldiers became matter for comment even in Government House; two officers disputing could set the whole colony by the ears; the always increasing hostility between the Governor and the New South Wales Corps kept the atmosphere charged with tension. And the war between the free population and the convicts was a continuous subterranean rumble that flashed into explosion now and then with out-breaks of insubordination, and savage punishments.

On the fringe of this unstable, emotionally overcharged society, the natives moved like troubled spectres, their dark, inquisitive eyes, once clouded with bewilderment, now merely observant, alert, and calculating. They had long ago accepted it as a fact that the Bereewolgal, the men come from afar, had come to stay. They had also long ago given up whatever hope they might have cherished in earlier days of learning to understand the white man's law. It consisted, so far as they could make out, in taking what he wanted if he could get it—and this they would have found comprehensible enough if he had not simultaneously denounced stealing as a mortal sin. Faced by such a paradox, they could only regard him as a moral outlaw, in their dealings with whom no code of ethics was applicable. They applied, instead, a simple logic. He took their hunting grounds; they would take from him in return whatever wheedling, force, guile, or theft could procure. He fought his own kind, and stole from his own kind; they would range themselves impartially upon any side which could promise them an advantage. They haunted the settlement like black wraiths, bartering fish or curios or an hour's desultory labour for whatever they could get; and then they vanished to the silence of the forests, to their camp-fires which shone like fixed points of sanity in a disintegrating world, to their own tribes where conduct was exactly ordered, and the Law exactly understood. They left the miseries and the hatreds of the white settlement to the white men; but the white men, even with the help of alcohol and parties, could never quite escape from them.

*   *   *   *   *

Flinders and Waterhouse, having spent the morning serving as members of the Court of Criminal Judicature, in session to try the case of one Isaac Nichols, accused of receiving stolen goods, felt that they had earned an evening's dissipation. In the dreary knowledge that they must to-morrow and probably for several days thereafter return to this uncongenial duty, they were now ripe for relaxation. Captain Waterhouse said belligerently:

"I have heard of this animal before. I have been assured on the most unimpeachable authority that it barks like a dog."

"Barks like a dog!" Matthew Flinders gave a contemptuous snort of laughter, and appealed across the table to his friend and fellow-voyager. "Tell this obstinate fellow, George, that the creature makes no sound but a kind of hiss . . ."

Bass nodded lazily.

"No sound but a hiss." The sibilants betrayed him, and conscious that he had said "hish," he frowned and repeated with careful distinctness: "A hiss, Henry. I assure you, a most unmistakable hiss."

"Not," Flinders hastened to explain, "that it is a savage or venomous animal. On the contrary it appeared of the most placid disposition. It suffered George to nurse it in his arms like a babe . . ."

The company found this amusing, and Flinders, his dark eyes a-twinkle, embroidered the anecdote.

"Upwards of a mile he carried it, gentlemen, dandling it like a mother, laying it over his shoulder, crooning lullabies to it . . ."

Bass let out a good-natured growl of protest which was drowned in the hilarity. Mr. Mannion said:

"There was a creature washed down the river near my property in the recent floods, Mr. Bass. I had no opportunity to dandle it—indeed I was unable to observe it at close quarters at all—but it would not surprise me if it were one of these whombats of yours."

Mr. Atkins roused himself to a conversational effort.

"Floods." He looked owlishly at the table, tapping it to claim their attention. "There is no moderation, my friends, in the habits of this climate." He fixed on Flinders an eye which seemed to accuse him of responsibility for the vagaries of the weather. "We suffer a drought, Sir, a drought which pershish—which persists for months; we fry, Sir, it is not extravagant to say that we fry beneath a pitiless sun; we look for rain, we long for rain, we pray for rain—and what do we get, Sir?"

"Rain," said Flinders, and roared with laughter. Mr. Atkins cried excitedly:

"We do indeed get rain! We get torrents of rain, we get floods, the Heavens open, Sir, and shed a deluge upon us . . ."

"I was not aware, Mr. Atkins," Mannion said dryly, "that the Heavens had bestowed upon you here at Sydney more rain than you could use. In my part of the country, now . . ."

The surgeon, with a spark of interest in his lethargic eyes, leaned forward across the table.

"I am told, Mr. Mannion, that the natives of your district foresaw this flood, and warned the settlers of its approach. Have I been misinformed, Sir?"

Mr. Mannion shrugged.

"There were reports to that effect. I pay no great heed to them, or to any tales from ignorant and superstitious savages to men hardly less ignorant and superstitious than themselves."

Mr. Balmain shook his head heavily.

"The natives are undoubtedly ignorant of all the arts and practices of civilisation, Mr. Mannion, yet I believe they possess a certain rude intelligence. Our late Governor, I think, would be dismayed if he were to see the decay of those friendly relations with them which he made many efforts to establish. Don't you agree, Captain?"

Waterhouse looked doubtful.

"I confess I see no remedy for it. They're an unstable and untrustworthy people. You and I, Sir, both recall the occasion when Governor Phillip was wounded by them. He always attributed it to a misunderstanding." He shrugged. "He may have been right, but for myself I feel that their response to such indulgences as they received from him was, to put it mildly, disappointing. Consider the case of that turbulent rascal, Bennilong . . ."

The surgeon made a gesture of impatience.

"Bennilong! I'm tired of dressing his wounds and putting bandages round his thick head . . ."

"Does he not," Captain Waterhouse asked, "furnish an illustration for my contention? No native received greater kindness or consideration; yet instead of acting to secure friendly relations between our people and his own, he has now placed himself out of favour with both, and is a continual source of ill-feeling."

"Well," Balmain remarked, "we see little enough of him now. I don't recollect even hearing any report of him since some six months back, when I was told he had again been dangerously wounded by his country-men. It's inevitable that his ungovernable temper will bring about his death in the end—either from our muskets or from the spears of his own people. Do you find them troublesome at the Nepean, Mr. Mannion?"

"There have been incidents among the settlers farther down the river. The few that come about my property seem peaceable enough."

Captain Waterhouse enquired:

"Your farm suffered no damage, I trust, in the recent floods?"

"None at all." Mr. Mannion glanced with some distaste at their host, who was pouring wine impartially into his glass and upon the table. "I think I may say that I chose the site for my home and outhouses with some foresight, and the whole of my property is upon a rising ground. I have no fear that any flood will ever discommode me. Many of the settlers farther down, however, had to be taken off from their roof-tops in boats. And much valuable livestock and produce were swept away."

"There was no loss of life, I believe?" Flinders asked.

Mannion, taking the bottle which Atkins was hospitably proffering, poured himself a glass with a hand which, he observed with satisfaction, was still quite steady. He answered indifferently:

"A convict was drowned. He was one of those who came out in the *Sugar Cane* from Ireland; I imagine the colony suffers no great loss."

Mr. Atkins, with his glass half-way to his lips, put it down again on the table so sharply that the wine spilled on his hand. He stuttered warmly:

"The Irish! D-d-damned rogues, Sir! A set of seditious scoundrels! A lawless . . ."

He stopped dead, blinking round the table at four pairs of eyes which held an uneasy warning. He looked vaguely at Mr. Mannion, fidgeted, reddened, belched, and stammered anxiously:

"Your pardon, Sir! No offence intended, Sir, towards your beautiful country, I assure you . . ."

Mr. Mannion, his blue eyes frosty, said:

"I am no friend to sedition, Mr. Atkins, whether in my countrymen or in yours. And we must not forget, Sir," he continued smoothly, "that we have had among us, in Messrs. Palmer, Muir, Skirving, Margarot and Gerrald, notorious representatives of English and Scottish sedition."

Mr. Atkins conceded hastily:

"Very true, Sir! Very true indeed. Though it must be acknow-ledged," he continued clumsily, "that these gentlemen have lived very quietly among us—very retired and respectable indeed, as I've heard His Excellency remark . . ."

"Nevertheless," Mr. Mannion insisted coldly, "such people cannot, I think, be regarded with too much suspicion. In a colony of this kind, isolated as it is, and filled with desperate characters, it is doubly necessary to be on guard against the irresponsible murmurings of discontented people. "Nor," he added, "am I always disposed to regard the frequent abscondings of convicts as lightly as the Governor appears to do. What is to prevent such men from joining themselves into formidable bands, and proving some day a serious threat to law and order in the community?"

George Bass allowed the front legs of his chair to descend upon the floor with a bang; he laid his folded arms on the table and said:

"I will tell you, Sir. Hunger. When I fell in with those seven miserable wretches who had been marooned by their companions on an island down the coast, I assure you their sole desire was to return to the settlement. They had had their fill of liberty in a land which offers no sustenance. They had contrived to exist for three months, but they were nought but scarecrows—indeed, the two I took into my boat were at death's door. The other five . . ." he shrugged, ". . . well, I did what I could for them. There was no room for them in the boat. I conveyed them to the mainland, and left them with a musket, ammunition, and fishing lines—and the knowledge, Heaven help them, that the settlement was five hundred miles distant." He tilted his glass, staring sombrely into its ruby depths. "If they are still alive, Mr. Mannion," he concluded grimly, "they are in no mood for sedition."

Mr. Mannion frowned.

"There is some truth in what you say, Mr. Bass. Nevertheless these absconders do sometimes survive—and not merely survive, but flourish. "I . . ." he broke off, drummed on the table with his fingers, and finished abruptly: "I am convinced of it."

It was not what he had intended to say. The words he had bitten off were "I know." For there had been a strange day nearly seven years ago when, across the flooded river near his then newly-acquired property, he had seen a convict die to save a native woman and her child. A convict who had escaped three years earlier—and who was certainly no scarecrow. It was a memory which never failed to cause him a pang of uneasiness; there had been something about the whole business which he did not understand. For this man, long supposed dead, had been the husband of Ellen Prentice, the woman whom he had taken for his house-keeper and his mistress; the father of her rebellious, red-headed, eight-year-old son, Johnny. And quite as mysteriously as the father had re-appeared, the son had, almost simultaneously, vanished. There had been nothing to perturb Mannion in that; he had heartily disliked the child, as everyone had disliked him except his mother. But from time to time in the years that followed there had been curious—indications. They came mostly from the natives. Two girls whom he had experimentally introduced into his household for domestic services had shown a strange familiarity with various household tools and utensils. They had seemed quite accustomed to hammers and nails, for instance; they had understood the use of a plane without being shown; they had even manipulated with confidence door-keys, and the latches of windows . . .

He had concluded, at first, that they must at some time have visited the other settlers' homes farther down the river. But no; they denied this, and the settlers, when approached, denied it too. Other natives, drifting casually about his farm, had exclaimed over his melons, his maize, his cucumbers, nodding their heads, pointing away up the river as if to say that there they had seen such things before. One, indeed, had even startled him with a word. "Kookumba," he had said cheerfully. They had other English words, too. They said "food," and "give," and "derink," and "cow," and once, to his amazement, pointing to the sky, "God." And all through their gibberish there recurred a word whose significance he had only lately, with a shock, suspected. "Dyonn-ee."

Johnny! Great Heaven, he had thought, is it possible that that child survived? He told himself that it was not possible. Johnny had been last seen at Parramatta, a full twenty miles from the Nepean. There was no reason to suppose that he had ever been near the river. Johnny was a common name. He dismissed the thought. Yet the knowledge that there had been one lonely, unsuspected white man's life out there in the forbidding, inhospitable forests, was like a continual warning whisper in his mind that there might be more. And if there were more? If there were many . . . ?

He said harshly:

"There's a dangerous feeling abroad. We live in times of great unrest. I observed its terrible effects in my own country during my late visit there. Have we not seen them also in England and Scotland, have we not witnessed the springing up overnight of clamorous associations of disaffected people, and do we not see the same poison spreading even to this remote quarter of the globe? Was not the Governor compelled only last year to take stern measures with regard to a body at Norfolk Island, calling itself the Fraternal Society? I tell you, gentlemen, I lay much of the blame for this state of affairs at the door of that infamous, blasphemous atheist and scoundrel, Tom Paine. That vile pamphlet he published some eight or nine years ago has done incalculable harm. And if I remember rightly, Sir," he added, fixing his host with a contemptuous eye, "this same Mr. Muir whom you consider so quiet and respectable, was one of those who advocated the spreading of its poisonous doctrines among the lower classes. And they did spread. I've been told—and I believe it— that two hundred thousand copies of this *Rights of Man* were sold in a single year." He tapped the table impressively. "Make no mistake, gentlemen, these seditious associations springing up like fungus growths— the "Friends of the People," the "United Irishmen," the "Defenders," the "London Corresponding Society," and all their pernicious off-shoots— constitute a real menace to order and tranquillity. And when we consider the appalling consequences of the revolution in France can we doubt that such associations must be resolutely suppressed before they bring us to a like calamity?"

He looked round the table. His hearers nodded, but rather mechanically. Mr. Mannion's eyebrows lifted; he emptied his glass and set it down carefully on the table. He felt, for the thousandth time, a contempt for them which fed his own self-esteem. They were, he thought, good enough fellows, but penned within the circle of their own little interests and concerns; a man such as himself, of wide experience, of breeding, of culture, of cosmopolitan outlook, could not with any real pleasure or advantage converse with them. He must condescend to their littleness, he must narrow his spacious ideas to the compass of their parochial gossip. He added dryly:

"Nor are our seditious neighbours all so quiet, Mr. Atkins. I have heard contrary reports of Mr. Margarot, at least."

Atkins mumbled a confused assent. Captain Waterhouse remarked with sudden animation:

"A turbulent rascal. Not even well-liked, so I hear, by his fellow rebels. Such people," he added with growing heat, "are the curse of this colony. When I returned with these gentlemen" . . . he nodded at Bass and Flinders . . . "in the *Reliance* some eighteen months ago, I was astonished and concerned—profoundly concerned—by the state of chaos which I found."

Five heads moved in acquiescence—Mr. Mannion's with a rather weary inclination, Mr. Atkins' with a solemn wagging. Here, at last, Mannion thought cynically, was the topic to their taste, the topic to which all their conversation finally turned. Here was the juicy subject, rich with its anecdotes of perfidy, its tales of personal grudges, of insults received and resented, of machinations and counter-machinations, of factions plotting against each other, of scandals, of quarrels between wives, of buying and selling, of transactions carried out in secret, of letters written and their contents basely betrayed, of the tyranny of the Governor, the weakness of the Governor, the martyrdom of the Governor . . .

He yawned. Captain Waterhouse continued earnestly:

"I was in a position, gentlemen, to compare the situation with that which had obtained in Governor Phillip's time—when, indeed, we had our little differences and contentions, but when such utter lack of all order and morality would not have been tolerated. I was convinced, and I assure you I am still convinced, that we shall have an uproar in this place which will shake it to its very foundations! I said as much in a letter I wrote to my father at that time. 'Something serious will happen here shortly.' Those were my very words, Mr. Mannion, and the disorder of the period since then has but served to confirm me in that belief." He lowered his voice a little and leaned forward across the table. "And I make bold to say that when the troubles and miseries of this unhappy place produce a cataclysm at last, the chief instigator of it will be found to be Captain Macarthur . . ."

Mr. Atkins woke up in earnest. He banged the table with his fist so that the glasses jumped. His already flushed face darkened to an almost apoplectic tint with anger, and his dull eyes blazed.

"Do not mention the name of that man in my house!" he commanded fiercely. "The scoundrel has inshul . . . insulted me repeatedly! He has cast the basest ashpershions upon my character, gentlemen. He has not scrupled to accuse me of being unfit for my duties. I shuffer no man to calumniate me, and so I told him plainly—in a letter which I believe no man could read, and not blush for his basheness!" His trembling fore-finger indicted an imaginary Macarthur. "'A staymaker,' I said to him, 'an honest and industrious staymaker is a more honourable and useful member of shociety than such a man as I take you to be'!" He glared round the table belligerently. "'Let me ask,' I said, 'who has been the incendiary—who has been the promoter of all the feuds and animoshitics in this colony? You, Sir!'" The glasses jumped again. "I called him a viper, gentlemen—and a viper he is! I called him a leper in reputation, and declared he should be driven from the shociety of all honest men, lest he infect them! I marvelled that he should dare to accuse me of injustice, oppression and peculation—he, out of all men on this earth to make such charges! '*You*,' I said—with every expression of contempt and abhorrence which my pen could summon—'you, who four years ago, was only a lieutenant, penniless but by his pay, and is now reputed worth £8000!' I called him a liar and a scoundrel, gentlemen—and moreover I bid him, if he could find other epithets more opprobrious, to consider them as applied. You, Sir," he added fiercely to the surgeon, "have also suffered under the abominable interferences and audacities of this person . . . !"

Mr. Mannion moved restlessly, and sighed as the conversation reached a pitch of animation which was almost clamorous. This was the tedious aspect of life in a raw, small, undeveloped society. He was jealous of his position in it, his aloof independence as a gentleman of means who was neither a civil, naval, nor military officer. He liked to feel himself above and beyond its turmoil, free of the obligations which bound other men, able to stand aside from the seething intrigues and personal enmities which continually set the place in a ferment. He had watched the bitter feud developing between the Governor and the New South Wales Corps, but he had maintained his right to dine at Government House, and from there to return home via Parramatta, pausing to drink tea with Captain and Mrs. Macarthur. He remained an audience to both factions—but so far an open partisan of neither.

Yet he was conscious of a faint, disturbing conflict in his thoughts. The Governor was the Governor, the representative of those ruling classes the challenge to whose authority he had just so bitterly deplored. Such challenges, when they came from convicts, from impudent Irish peasants, from a ragged, revolutionary, free-thinking rascal like Tom Paine, or from an illiterate French rabble, left him whole and certain in his hostility. But here, when they came from men who, bearing His Majesty's commis-sion, were gradually establishing themselves as the landed aristocracy of the colony, he felt his disapproval tempered by a certain wry admiration. Macarthur, for instance, he could not for an instant recognise as his social equal, but the fact remained that in this grotesque community where all normal standards were overthrown, the man was a power. His control over the buying and selling of the colony's produce had been such that it was the merest policy of expediency to remain on good terms with him. Mr. Mannion, as the scion of a family which had been landed gentry for generations, was not slow to recognise the efficiency with which the foundations were being laid in this country for a whole crop of such families; he wondered now, with idle, speculative amusement, whether in, say, a hundred years' time, there would be Balmains, Marsdens, Johnstons, Macarthurs, living upon their ancestral acres? Or—he glanced round the table—descendants of Mr. Atkins, who had a handsome grant at Parramatta, or of Mr. Bass, at Banks Town, or of Captain Waterhouse, at Liberty Plains? Mr. Flinders, he reflected, had so far taken the ocean for his domain—but perhaps he, too, in time . . .

The discussion, he observed, had degenerated into a perfervid if rather incoherent monologue by Mr. Atkins (with occasional gloomy interjections from Mr. Balmain) upon the iniquities of Captain Macarthur. Bored, he awaited a pause, and filled it with polite regrets.

"I ask your pardon, Sir, if I interrupt this most happy occasion by my departure. I return to-morrow to Beltrasna, and I must be on my way betimes. Moreover, my good host, Mr. Johnson, and his worthy wife, retire early, and I should not wish to disturb them. You will excuse me, gentlemen?"

He drew a deep breath of relief as he stepped out into the mild autumn evening.

*　　　*　　　*　　　*　　　*

He set out early next morning on the first stage of his ride home. The road took him southward for a mile or so, and then swung west through that district known as the Kangaroo Ground—where Major Grose, Captain Johnston, Colonel Paterson and Major Foveaux owned properties —past the Field of Concord, and so on again through almost deserted country till it reached the outskirts of Parramatta.

It was a pleasant, gently undulating highway, and he rode without haste, enjoying the crisp freshness of the morning, and observing that already the country showed signs of revival after the recent rains. He meditated anew upon the strangeness of a land in which it was not winter, but the fires of summer, which stripped the trees bare, reducing them to a temporary death, from which it still surprised him to see them resurrected. He looked at the naked trunks—mere towering columns of charcoal—marvelling that there should be life in them yet, and that it would, in time, send bursting out of those charred stumps, tight bunches of tiny, rosy leaves. That ground, now bare and blackened, would clothe itself again, and adorn its gentle monotint of green with shy flashes of colour. That was the way of spring here—to drift in almost unnoticed after the mild winter, and not, as in his homeland, on a swelling tide of brilliant green, an exultant crescendo of awakening. He hummed to himself as he rode, conscious of an idle contentment which made him feel tolerant of a country whose reticent, and sometimes macabre beauty compared so ill with the lush, emerald landscapes of his nostalgic memory.

Nearing Parramatta, he observed in front of him a gig, jogging along towards the township, driven by a man whose sober black coat and hat he recognised. Overtaking it, he reined in for a moment to salute his fellow-wayfarer.

"You are abroad early, Mr. Marsden."

The Reverend Mr. Marsden acknowledged his greeting with a genial bow. At thirty-five he was already inclined to stoutness, and his white cravat disappeared beneath an ample double chin. His nose was fleshy, his brown eyes opaque, and in repose the corners of his tight mouth turned downwards; but he cultivated a cheerful—even a jovial—manner in his social intercourse, and now replied briskly:

"I might say the same of you, Mr. Mannion. I have been visiting a poor wretch who is not long for this life, I fear."

"No doubt," Mr. Mannion responded with his customary adequacy, "you were able to offer him valuable spiritual consolation, my dear Sir. It is a constant regret to me," he continued glibly, "that our situation on the river makes it impossible for me and my sons to attend Divine Service as often as we could wish." Having done his duty, he lifted his whip in a gesture of farewell. "Which serves to remind me that I have far to go, and I wish to call upon Captain Macarthur on my way. Good-day, Sir. You will be so kind as to convey my best respects to Mrs. Marsden?"

He cantered off. Mr. Marsden continued to jog along, his eyes on the diminishing figure in its cloud of reddish dust. A mere day or two of sun, he thought, was enough to make the rain-soaked roads dusty again; but beneath that idle, surface reflection, his mind was pinioned by the name of Macarthur. It was one which chimed well enough with the memories which had preoccupied him before his meeting with Mr. Mannion. He had been reflecting that it was just five years this month since he had arrived in the colony as assistant to Mr. Johnson, and remembering his first Sunday, when he had walked abroad to inspect his new field of labour. . . . Only, alas, to find people at work who must be—and were—sternly reminded of the evils of Sabbath-breaking. *"My mind was deeply affected,"* he had written, *"with the wickedness I beheld going on . . ."*

Little he had known then of wickedness! Now, sitting behind his ambling horse, the reins slack in his hands, he told himself that the trials of the voyage had been merely the Lord's way of preparing him for what he had to face.

Would he ever forget that voyage . . . ! It had been difficult too for his poor wife, who at last, near the end of it and in stormy weather, had given birth to their first-born, Anne. And yet it had been only an introduction to wickedness. He remembered how, upon landing, he had found himself almost immediately sitting opposite his colleague, Mr. Johnson, and listening to such a tale of evil that his heart froze in his breast.

"More than five years, Mr. Marsden, and there was still no building of any kind erected for a place of worship. I have preached in the open in all weathers, and my health has been gravely affected. It was in desperation, I assure you, my friend, that I at length took matters into my own hands, and caused our poor, rough shelter to be built. And for this Major Grose has represented me to the authorities at home as a troublesome, discontented character! Nor have I ever been able to claim from him that respect which is due to our cloth, or his support in my efforts to combat the disgraceful neglect of religion in this place. The inhabitants are lost to all sense of virtue, sir. Gambling—robberies— drunkenness—licentiousness . . . ! Indeed, all common morality, and even all common decency are strangers to this colony. During Governor Phillip's term of office I complained more than once of having no roof over my head while I preached the word of God, but . . ." he threw out his hands in a gesture of despair, ". . . there was at that time some order kept, some decencies of conduct observed. Now there is no authority in this place but that of the military. Not even," he added bitterly, "the authority of God."

And Mr. Marsden, taking up his abode and commencing his labours at Parramatta, had swiftly discovered how justified were his colleague's complaints. He had found himself subjected .by Captain Macarthur to all the mortifications of which Mr. Johnson had warned him. And now, with Mr. Mannion's utterance of that name, he remembered how last year, requested by Governor Hunter to report upon the state of the colony's morals during the military interregnum, his pen had raced, pouring out not only a recital of iniquities, but a catalogue of his own grievances. *"Your Excellency cannot be ignorant of Captain Macarthur's attempt privately to assassinate my character . . ."*

In the agitation of his memories his hand twitched on the rein, and the horse quickened its pace. He sighed, and flicked it to a trot. After all, things were a little better now, since Hunter's arrival. At the beginning of last year he had secured a lease of some fine land at Parramatta; and very shortly he expected a grant of another hundred acres in the same neighbourhood. He had ideas about farming. There might be compensations, after all, for living in exile in the midst of wickedness . . .

*   *   *   *   *

Captain Macarthur, freshly shaved and brushed, resplendent in his uniform, stepped out into the morning sunshine and stood before his house looking down across sloping fields to the river. In less than six years he had made great changes here at Elizabeth Farm. Those changes—the fertile fields, the orchard, the vineyard, the gardens, the strong brick house behind him, and even the family within it—were to him projections of himself, visible evidence that the passion of self-confidence he had always cherished was not misplaced. In nine years he had altered the whole face of his fortunes, and he was still only thirty-two. He liked to remember now that he had once been considered by his acquaintances in England too arrogant, too ambitious for a young man whose expectations were negligible; and he felt a fierce pride in recalling that he had never wavered in his conviction that he was one who could shape men and circumstances to his will.

His exchange into the New South Wales Corps, bound for an outpost which was not only remote, but embryonic, had not seemed to him, as it had seemed to his friends, a sentence of exile and stagnation. His ears were always open; he had heard rumours of a new colony very much in the eye of Government, of flourishing wheat, of a land where opportunity surely beckoned, because competition was not yet too keen. He never doubted that there he would not only find means of prospering, but would know how to turn those means to the fullest advantage, and wring the last drop of profit from them.

Fortune, indeed, had smiled upon him—but he expected that. The chain of circumstances which had left the colony to three years of military administration after the first Governor's departure, seemed to him only a natural provision of the goddess who might be fickle to others, but never to him. Nothing could have suited him better, for instance, than that Grose's absence in England should have left in temporary command a man such as Major Paterson, who detested strife above all things. Captain Macarthur did not pause to analyse the effect upon an amiable and conciliatory nature of one ruthless and dynamic; he only knew, with satisfaction, that the Major was easily swayed. He did not reflect upon the curious paradox that a man hedging, dodging, compromising and procrastinating to avoid trouble, becomes a most effective tool of trouble-makers; he only knew that his superior officer would yield to strong pressure, and that he himself, single-minded and aggressive, could press more strongly than most.

So deeply did he feel himself under Fortune's especial protection, that the faintest chilling of her warm benevolence enraged him. The most casual disagreement with his opinions stiffened his spine, froze his expression, wakened a cold, implacable hostility. Active opposition was an outrage never to be forgiven or forgotten. His temper was violent, but cold; his enmities bitter, cherished—strong currents running steadily beneath the ice of an outward self-control. He never hesitated to make enemies. The measures of his confidence in himself were his determination to say and do what he liked, and his ability to see any animosity which such a course provoked as the unworthy jealousy of smaller men.

There was plenty of such animosity. He knew it, and the knowledge, like the sight of his broad acres, warmed him. He was a military officer, not only by profession, but by nature. Life was a war; in its battles, its skirmishes, its reverses, its wary reconnoitrings and its heady victories, it was for him to plan the strategy, issue the orders, and blast with the power of his infallible ego any attempt at insubordination.

Yet he had his allies too, and they were all—save one—here in the house behind him. Often during his early morning stroll he missed the companionship of his eldest son, the ten-year-old Edward, now absent in England. But his thought never failed to return warmly to the rest of his family; to his wife, Elizabeth, and their elder daughter, her namesake; to little John, and toddling Mary, and the baby, James. Here were the only people in the world who saw him just as he saw himself—his loyal and loving partisans. Here, since he was allowed to be the sun, whose radiance banished all lesser luminaries from the sky, he shone with a warm and undisturbed benevolence. Those others in the colony who had

ranged themselves with him, who had shared his triumphs and his prosperity, who had closed in to form with him the tight, united front of
privilege, were mere mercenaries. He would use them, and they would
try to use him. It was part of his policy, once away from the haven of
his home, not to shine too brightly; it suited him there to be merely one
—though of course the brightest—of a constellation.

He began to walk slowly up and down the path, his restless brain
hard at work behind his dark, observant eyes. Not even the most favoured
son of Fortune could have expected more than had been bestowed on him
during those three good, rich years when not only land, trade, and labour,
but also the law, 'had been military monopolies. Those halcyon days
were over. Grose and Paterson had been complaisant—but with the
advent of that stupid old woman, Hunter, weak but stubborn, it had
become necessary to fight, plan, intrigue, to preserve the indulgences so
bountifully bestowed by Fortune . . .

His stride checked, his head went up, his eyes scanned his domain
with an angry challenge. Did the system he had fostered need any other
justification than these smiling, sunlit fields? Was he not conducting
important experiments in sheep-breeding, whose results might well bring
prosperity to the whole community? Was he not labouring devotedly to
change a barren, worthless country into a fertile one, to lift it from
penury, to make it self-supporting, and relieve the home Government of
expense?

And how had his efforts been rewarded? Had not Hunter, at first
friendly in his manner, by degrees grown cold? Macarthur's stare became
fixed and abstracted as his memory went back over the four-year development of his relations with the second Governor. He was not the man to
avoid a contest, nor had his ingenuity been taxed to find pretexts for his
passages at arms which would satisfy himself. It was necessary that they
should satisfy himself. He did not admit, even in his most private
thoughts, that the root of his antagonism was the threat which Government
orders offered to a system which had served him well. He was a soldier
—the bearer of a commission from His Majesty—and as such must proclaim
himself a zealous upholder of the very authority which so embarrassed
him as a trader and a farmer. His disagreements with the Governor,
therefore, must seem to arise from other causes. The years of the military
administration, the years of rum, had reduced the community to a condition which bred quarrels—and Captain Macarthur never functioned with
greater confidence, subtlety, and *élan* than in an atmosphere thick with
belligerence. He had not had to wait long for an occasion to pit his strength
against Hunter's.

A quarrel between a carpenter and a private was merely a spark
which he fanned to a bonfire; by the time he had finished developing it,
the Governor and the Commanding Officer of the Corps were involved,
and it had become an issue between the civil and the military power. A
later affair of some stolen turnips had been manipulated with similar
adroitness, but such squabbles were only froth on the top of a boiling
cauldron. Captain Macarthur was sounding the Governor, measuring

his adversary—and he was encouraged. He had resigned his appointment as Inspector of Public Works, complaining that "want of support," and the loss of His Excellency's confidence, made his continuance in that office impossible. He smiled to himself now, remembering with what asperity Hunter had replied. *"Your complaint of want of support can only have proceeded from my choosing to have some opinion of my own . . . !"* Opinion! Macarthur's smile grew colder, frosted with contempt for the doddering old fool who imagined that his "opinions" could contend with John Macarthur's implacable certainties. He had held that letter in his hand, smiling as he smiled now, reading weakness into that sharp, goaded retort, conscious that he himself would never need to use so trivial a weapon as asperity. He had resolved to attack boldly through no less a person than the Secretary of State; a brief, challenging note informed Hunter that Captain Macarthur proposed to write to his Lordship upon the state of the colony.

He had sat long over that letter one afternoon in the spring of 1796, looking up from it now and then to watch his wife playing with the children, meeting her fond glance, warmed by the confidence in her eyes. But his attention was on his task, and his mind, always alert and attuned to the foibles of authority, taught him which note to strike first.

"From a persuasion it is important that this settlement be enabled to maintain itself in food of its own production . . . that the heavy expences may be lessened which it is the cause of . . ." Show him the Government that did not want its expenses lessened! And now a hint—the merest hint to begin with—of maladministration. *". . . to point out some errors in its present management which, if not soon corrected, will create more difficulties . . ."* He wrote calmly and steadily. Figures, facts. He had his thoughts in order, his evidence arranged, his plans for the future of the colony clear in his mind. What could *he* not do with it if he had a free hand! If Hunter could be recalled . . . ! *"I hesitate not to say, further, that the interest of Government is utterly disregarded, its money idly and wantonly squandered, whilst vice and profligacy are openly countenanced . . ."* He could not know what doubts he had sown, but still his patient, scheming, tenacious brain was alert for further opportunities.

A child's voice, shrill with excitement, interrupted his reflections.

"Papa! Papa, look! Look what we have found!"

He turned quickly, the intent, calculating expression of his eyes softening, and held out his arms to the five-year-old boy and the six-year-old girl who came racing towards him round the corner of the house. He sat down on the broad stone step of the verandah, and drew the boy to his knee.

"And what is it you have found?"

The little girl opened her hand carefully, slowly.

"It's an egg, Papa, but very tiny . . ."

"So it is, my love."

"And it's blue, Papa. Look, Mama, what John and I have found in the garden!"

Mrs. Macarthur, smiling and comely, stepped out from the doorway, nursing her youngest child in her arms, and peered between the children's bent heads.

"It is very pretty, my dears, is it not?"

The little girl asked:

"Did it fall, Papa? Did it fall out of a tree?"

"It must have done so, Elizabeth."

"Why didn't it break, then?"

"Perhaps it fell into some soft grass, my love." He looked up at his wife. "I fear it is the egg of that small bird that plunders our orchard in the . . . Ah, Mr. Mannion!"

Mr. Mannion, appearing round the bend of the path, paused for a moment to contemplate an idyllic picture of domestic bliss. He bowed ceremoniously to Mrs. Macarthur.

"Forgive my intrusion at this early hour. I was passing on my way home from Sydney, and could not deny myself the pleasure . . ."

Mrs. Macarthur smiled at him over her baby's downy head.

"You are very welcome, Mr. Mannion. Pray take a seat. You will join us, I hope, when we breakfast presently?"

Macarthur set his son down and drew a chair forward for his guest.

"Indeed yes, Sir, we insist. Elizabeth, child, run indoors and tell Sophy that we shall have a guest for breakfast."

"I shall go myself," Mrs. Macarthur interposed. "Children, come with me. You will excuse me, Mr. Mannion, if I leave you to attend to household matters. Come, John, do not plague your Papa. Yes, Elizabeth, you may take the egg to show Mary if you carry it carefully . . ."

Mr. Mannion stretched his legs comfortably in the sunshine, and glanced at his host with a faintly amused curiosity. Was this the man, he asked himself, about whom most of the colony's quarrels revolved? Was this the stormy petrel? Was this the promoter of feuds and animosities against whom Mr. Atkins had so fiercely inveighed? Here, in the bosom of his family, he seemed all serenity. Here he was the devoted husband, the indulgent father. Mr. Mannion had observed this strange, apparent contradiction before, but it never failed to intrigue him. He remarked amiably:

"You are to be envied, Captain. To a lonely man, the picture you presented as I came down the path—sitting here on the threshold of your charming home, surrounded by your delightful family—was, if I may say so, most agreeable."

Captain Macarthur leaned back in his chair, stretched out his arms as if to embrace not only the sunlight, but all it shone on, and then, locking his hands behind his head, uttered a deep sigh of satisfaction.

"This is my haven, Sir. Here I'm able to forget for a little while the troubles, the injustices and the gross stupidities which abound in this unfortunate colony. Here I endeavour to put away from my mind all thought of the calumnies that are directed against me—and the coldness, to call it by no harder name, with which my efforts are met in quarters where, one would suppose, I might reasonably expect support."

He shot a glance from narrowed eyes at his visitor.

"You have seen the Governor in Sydney, Sir?"

Mr. Mannion replied imperturbably:

"I paid my respects at Government House yesterday. His Excellency was kind enough to promise a visit to my home on his next excursion to the Nepean."

Macarthur, his face slightly clouded, said: "H'm!"

He was not sure of Mr. Mannion who, as a gentleman of substantial independent means, and large properties in Ireland, was in a different position from himself and his adherents. Macarthur was a man who claimed from his associates not so much friendship as partisanship; and Mr. Mannion had so far refrained from committing himself to any expression of opinion regarding the Governor's policies. He asked:

"What news, Mr. Mannion, upon the trial of Isaac Nichols?"

"I have no knowledge of the matter," Mannion replied, "beyond the gossip of the town. It's said that the Governor thinks well of the man."

Macarthur shrugged.

"I'm to give evidence myself to-morrow. There's no doubt in my mind but that the fellow is guilty. Integrity, it would appear, can no longer claim the countenance of authority, Mr. Mannion. The conduct of affairs in the colony . . ."

Smiling, Mr. Mannion raised a hand in protest.

"I'm entirely absorbed, Captain, in the conduct of my own affairs. My property is so far removed from the centre of government that I confess I hear but the echoes of strife. My attention is fully taken up with the management of my farm; and I can only observe with admiration . . ." but his glance at Macarthur was less admiring than amused, ". . . that you are able to combine the duties of a soldier and a landowner with an active participation in public matters."

Mrs. Macarthur, appearing again in the doorway, provided him with an opportunity, promptly seized, for turning the conversation to an uncontroversial topic. He rose briskly.

"My dear lady, I have just been envying your husband his lot. To a solitary man like myself, the spectacle of so happy and united a family . . ."

She shook a playful finger at him.

"Come, come, Mr. Mannion! You cannot persuade me that you are so downcast, for you have your two fine sons—what a handsome boy your Miles is, to be sure!"

Mr. Mannion said suddenly:

"You shall be the first to know my secret, madam. Who better, indeed, than a devoted wife and mother, as the recipient of such a confidence? If I do not seem downcast, it is because I know that my loneliness is soon to be remedied."

"To be remedied, Mr. Mannion?" Mrs. Macarthur's grey-blue eyes lit up eagerly. "You cannot mean . . . ? Indeed, I believe you *do* mean . . . ?"

"Before another year is out," Mr. Mannion assured her, "I hope to have a wife to share my home, and to be a second mother to my sons."

In the joyful exclamations which instantly overwhelmed him, curiosity was almost stronger than congratulation. Surely there could be no young lady in the colony suitable to become the wife of Mr. Stephen Mannion of Beltrasna?

"My bride to be," he explained, "is the granddaughter of a neighbour of mine in Ireland—Sir John O'Connor. I was happy enough to be able to persuade her to share my life when I went home two years ago, but her grandfather considered her at that time too young for an immediate marriage. So I have possessed my soul in patience and kept my secret. Now my reward is not far distant. I entreat—and indeed confidently anticipate —your friendship, dear Mrs. Macarthur, for a young lady far from home, and embarking upon a life which will at first seem very strange to her . . ."

"You may do so, Sir," Macarthur assured him. "There is no warmer heart in the world than my wife's—and, I may add, no woman possessed of greater good sense. We rejoice in your happiness, believe me. And now, my love, are we to have our breakfast?"

As they passed into the house Mrs. Macarthur, still excited by the anticipation of so romantic an event, cried triumphantly:

"Ah! Now we know, Sir, why this new, handsome house of which we have heard so much, is being built upon your property at the Nepean! What a fortunate young lady she is, who will be mistress of the finest house in the colony! May we not know her name, Mr. Mannion?"

"By all means," responded Mr. Mannion agreeably. "Her name is Conor Moore."

*   *   *   *   *

Pemulwy of the Bideegal reached the crest of the hill first, and turned to look down at his companions scrambling up the rocky slope some thirty yards behind him. He squatted on his heels with his back against a fire-charred log, and rested his spears against his shoulder in the crook of his arm. His lean body was naked, and his dark skin shone with grease and sweat; many years ago a wound had injured one of his eyes so that now nothing but the white showed between its scarred lids, and it was this facial blemish, even more than a certain lowering grimness of expression which made him appear a sinister figure.

Below him the farms of the Hawkesbury settlers fringed the river banks; the dwellings on them looked small from here, and their chimneys sent a few threads of blue smoke spiralling upward into the golden, sunset haze. The sound of shouting came very faintly to his ears; he could see people moving about like ants near the hut of the slain man, and as he watched a horse was brought out and mounted, and galloped away towards the ford.

Pemulwy's one good eye watched the commotion stolidly, and turned from it to the two white men and the four natives who were straggling up the slope towards him. His countrymen were naked like himself, and talking rapidly among themselves, but the white men in their tattered clothes and bursting boots were silent. One had a knife stuck in his belt; it was brown at the edges with the dried blood of the settler he had killed. The other carried a couple of dead fowls by the legs, and two of the natives dragged a sack of potatoes between them.

There had been no pursuit. They had chosen a hut isolated from the others, made their kill, seized their loot, and vanished into the scrub-covered hills before the body was discovered. Pemulwy had hoped to do some killing himself, but the victim had appeared alone suddenly and unexpectedly round the corner of the hut, to be despatched before the native could even raise his spear.

Now he was morose, feeling himself cheated of a climax which he had eagerly anticipated when he set out. He was not interested in the meagre spoil they had collected; to him a raid on one of the outlying settlements was an act of war, an expression of hostility and defiance towards the Bereewolgal. He was not of the same tribe as the other natives, for his towri was on the sea coast near Botany Bay, but he went far abroad nowadays, to any place where there were white men to kill. To most of these he was no more than a name—but a name they heard and spoke with increasing frequency. There were some who remembered that even in Governor Phillip's time he had killed a white man, and that a punitive expedition had been sent out to capture him. But he had never been captured. Though he spoke so seldom that he was called the Silent One, it was known that he despised the natives who frequented the white men's settlements. His one eye glared coldly at Bennilong, who had lived among them, and voyaged over the sea in one of their ships, and returned to become a source of conflict among his countrymen—black-tempered, quarrelsome, craving the white men's fiery drink, a stranger in his own tribe, an unwelcome visitor in others, a man with no abiding place among any people . . .

This, thought Pemulwy, was what friendship with the Bereewolgal could do to a man who had once been gay and well-liked, a valued tribesman, a celebrated hunter, and an even more celebrated maker of songs. For himself, he was none of these things—since the injury to his eye he had lost some of his skill at hunting—but with the passing of the years the very qualities in him which had made him unpopular before the white men came, had gained him an increasing influence.

He had always been a difficult fellow—not explosive and unpredictable like Bennilong, but gloomy. Among a people who loved laughter, and were as inquisitive as monkeys, he laughed seldom, and betrayed no curiosities. Among a people who sang and danced as naturally as they breathed, he was oddly inept; it was as if the sense of rhythm were lacking in him, and this was counted a kind of spiritual deformity. He had always performed his tribal duties, and obeyed his tribal laws—but this was not enough. He seemed merely acquiescent in his dull way, contributing nothing. He gave no spark from his inner self to enrich the communal life—no gentleness, no gaiety, no wit, no particular wisdom, no gift of song or image-making. His people never said: "Ah, for *this* we need Pemulwy!"

Yet lately it had seemed that he had some value after all. That same quality of stubborn, uninspired, unvarying consistency which had bored his companions once, now appeared as something which, for the first time in their lives, they needed. Before the Bereewolgal came they had never known a Problem—only problems. Every day brought its problems—of food, shelter, ceremonies, entertainment, ritual, battle, and personal relationships—which arose only to be solved by knowledge, wit, wisdom, resource, or creative skill—all the qualities in which Pemulwy was so curiously lacking. Life had been fluid, restless, and yet unchanging, like the sea. It had been bright, wayward and mobile as a butterfly. Now they had begun to realise with a strange spiritual foreboding that a kind of rigidity had settled upon it; it was becoming enclosed, stifled, dominated by the presence of the white men. Here was a problem not met, solved, and shed, but persisting. It followed the tribesmen into sleep, and woke in their minds, even larger and more oppressive, with the opening of their eyes at dawn.

It had taken them years to adjust their thinking to it, nor was it completely adjusted even now. As they had confronted recurrent problems, so they attempted to confront the recurrent symptoms of an unending problem, disposing of each temporarily, and assuming that the matter was ended. A quarrel with a white man, a theft, a blow, a killing, another encroachment on their territory—they struggled through each incident as it arose, and tried to forget it. But slowly they began to see that the white men were not mere incidents in their life; they were growing into it, capturing and distorting it.

And so by degrees Pemulwy came into his own. The wisdom of the wise men could offer no solution to this endless problem: the Law, which for centuries had provided for everything, made no provision for this; valour as they knew it was useless, for the white men would not meet it with valour, but with the magic of their fire-breathing weapons; wit, comedy, and the corroborees of the song-makers could temporarily buoy up spirits which threatened to sink into bewildered dejection, but they could not point a way to peace. Pemulwy, going about his business with his customary stolidity, was the one man who had never wavered in his surly refusal to concede so much as a passing gesture of amity to the invaders. Others might visit their settlements, mingle with them, and return full of breathless tales of astonishing possessions; Pemulwy squatted by his mia mia, silent as ever, sharpening his spears. To the tribal conclaves which had raged about the camp-fires in the early days of the invasion, he had contributed but one word: "Wee-ree." Bad. Bennilong and others might boast of the honours that had been heaped on them; the womenfolk might chatter of shining gifts bestowed; the whole tribe might talk of the miraculous properties of the fire-breathing weapons; comedians might mimic the absurd antics of the strangers, and provoke side-splitting mirth—from all but Pemulwy. He, crouching in his sulky way by the fire, his shoulders hunched and his white wall-eye lit by the flames, would say nothing but: "Wee-ree."

Of course he was dull-witted; that was understood. In no normal kind of life could he conceivably have had any particular influence over his countrymen, to whom the human mind at its best was a thing of many

sparkling facets, incapable of long, changeless brooding. Yet now, feeling
something fixed, threatening and implacable set against them, they felt
that only in Pemulwy was there something equally stable, equally immovable. They began to see that it was no use hating and resenting the
white men in the normal way; they began to learn with a dark, oppressive
anguish that now they must hate all the time. They must carry this
intolerable load of hatred in their hearts even while they hunted, even
while they sang, and danced, and feasted. Through the years as they
watched the incredible customs of the white men, saw them in their moods
of anger and greed, in the savagery of punishment, in drunkenness, in
sexual promiscuity, their hatred grew—and was fed not only by the
knowledge that their land and livelihood were in danger. Worse than
that was the terrible suspicion that their very concept of life, their concept
of themselves as human beings, was threatened. They became afraid of
a humanity which they could not deny that they shared with these people.
Pemulwy's one word was echoed more and more. "Wee-ree," they said,
"wee-ree."

Where the Bereewolgal lived together in the big settlements, the
natives offered no hostility. The magic weapons, the gooroobeera, were
too numerous there; armed with them, the red-coated ones could decimate
a tribe before it came within spear-throwing distance. But as the huts
of settlers began to spring up in ones and twos and threes in solitary
places, they thought again. The very fact of this isolation was another
bewilderment, and another challenge to their faith. A man does not live
alone, they said. A man lives with his tribe, in his community. If he
withdraws from them, he has surely been cast out, and his tribe will care
nothing for his fate. But leaving his own towri thus, he invades yet
another part of our hunting grounds, and since he takes from us, we will
take from him. They plundered the lonely farms at night, stealing a
sack of grain, a fowl, a few vegetables—and learned that, isolated as he
was, this white man was still a member of his tribe.

They now perceived that violence was no longer the manifestation of
a moment's anger. It was like the chains that the white men used; it
was many angers, each complete in itself, and yet joined to the one behind
it and the one before it, to form one terrible, endless expression of enmity.
Pemulwy, sitting on the hill overlooking the Hawkesbury, was reflecting
that perhaps there were other forms of violence besides killing which
could be used against the white men. There were so many of them—
and so many more arriving continually in the winged boats from across
the sea—that the slaying of one here and there did little to weaken their
fabulous, apparently innumerable tribe. He looked down at the cultivated
land, thinking that a firestick in those fields at the proper time would
probably harm them more than the death of a few lonely settlers; and
with that thought in his mind, he once more turned his watchful, impassive
eye upon his companions.

         *   *   *   *   *

The white man with the knife was a little ahead of the others; he
reached the log and sat down on it near Pemulwy, smearing the sweat

from his forehead with his forearm. He was breathing heavily; exhaustedly; Pemulwy could see his heart thudding beneath ribs which showed through his tattered clothes. His hollow cheeks wore a thick stubble of fair beard, and his eyes were bloodshot. He muttered—but not to Pemulwy:

"No . . . no . . . no!"

He began to shiver a little, looking down from those excited, red-veined eyes at the huts, recalling how he had felt those last, strangled words, that insanely protesting "No!" vibrate beneath his arm as clasped round the man's throat from behind—how the blood had spurted and shone as he pulled his knife out. . . . This was not the first man he had killed, nor the second, yet now, as upon the two previous occasions, he felt a sense of outrage—a wild, amazed resentment that such a thing had happened, and a conviction that he was not the author of the happening, but its tool.

He was twenty-five, and four years ago he had caught a fish in a stream which flowed through a certain nobleman's parklands. From that incident had followed everything that had happened to him since; the man lying dead down there had died because of it; the self which even now he frantically claimed as his real self had retreated farther and farther beyond his grasp, until it could make itself heard and felt only in such moments as this. Sometimes he tried to remember that he had once been a studious lad, but there was no conviction in the memory. Sometimes he told himself that he had dared to dream in the humble cottage where he had been born, of some day becoming a clerk; that in his wilder flights of fancy he had even seen himself as a village schoolmaster—but it was as if he were telling himself stories about a stranger. Reality held him prisoner. He was a runaway felon, and now thrice a murderer.

The other natives had reached the log, and squatted near Pemulwy, but the white man with the fowls stood with his back to the plain, and burst out savagely:

"Ye bloody fool, Tom Towns! Ye'd no call to kill him!"

Towns thrust away into its lonely obscurity the self which was shivering, and retorted harshly:

"No call, eh? He'd have give us food, would he?"

"We'd have took it," the other man insisted. "We'd have took it an' got clear away without him knowin' we was there if you'd waited . . ."

Towns snarled at him inarticulately, and put his hand on the knife at his belt; he saw the other man retreat a pace, and felt his hardihood return. Three—why not four? Now that he was no longer shaken by that shivering, he felt his three murders as a strength. The other man said on a sharp, weak note of protest:

"Look at 'em! Raisin' the alarm! Where're we goin' for food now? They'll have soldiers posted down there—they'll be armed an' waitin' for weeks . . . !"

Towns said disagreeably:

"Ye can go back, Hobbs, like others have done. Ye can go back to Parramatta an' give y'self up. Am I keepin' ye?"

"Go back?" Hobbs' voice was shrill. "Go back, after this day's work?" Towns interrupted him violently:

"Shut y' mouth, ye white-livered fool! No one saw us but him that's dead. Ye can go back if ye want—but . . ." his eyes were so bright and malevolent that Hobbs shuffled uneasily and looked away from them, ". . . if ye speak of me, ye'll go the same way *he* went!" He jerked his head in the direction of the hut, and stood up, looking at Pemulwy.

The halt was ended. They set off down the opposite slope of the hill, Pemulwy leading and Towns bringing up the rear. He watched his white companion with a sour contempt. Since he had absconded from Parramatta more than a year ago to throw in his lot with the natives, he had seen several of his countrymen join the tribes for a while, and then return, defeated, to the settlement. He did not know what drew them back, but he was conscious, sometimes, of being drawn himself. They were hungry, perhaps; he too was often hungry, for the food which seemed adequate for the natives was not always sufficient to maintain his strength, and even for the natives there were lean times nowadays, so near the towris of the Bereewolgal. Yet hunger almost to the point of starvation had been his lot in the settlements too. He thought it might be some craving for a personal relationship which sucked these temporary absconders back to the life they had tried to leave—a woman, maybe, or merely the longing for their own tongue and their own kind—for the interchange of communal news, grim and bitter as it was. Or perhaps, even, they found their only emotional luxury—hatred—becoming blunted when they were away from the source of it, and returned to whet it on the sight of misery, the sound of orders, the taste of servitude . . .

He held his hand over his labouring heart for a moment, frightened by its thudding into a sharp realisation of the precariousness of his life. One craving and one fear contributed to his own restless, intermittent urge to return—but he knew that there the craving would never be assuaged, and the fear would be supplanted by another, greater than itself. His desire was not for the settlement, but for what it represented; he hated it, but was drawn to it as part of a civilisation from whose outer fringes he had once glimpsed glories which would not be altogether forgotten. He had heard the call of learning, and it still called, even here in primordial forests; he had guessed—hardly more—that there was treasure buried in his mind, and he still thirsted to seek for it, even here among Stone Age savages; he had dreamed himself a quiet man, living studiously, and the dream still haunted him, even now when he knew himself an outlaw and a murderer. His fear was of death alone in this place which was not only physically but—more terribly—spiritually alien to him. Here there was nothing of his own culture—not even speech, save for a few weeks or a few months when some runaway made the tribe his temporary home. Bad as it was to live in such solitude, the thought of dying in it was worse. Yet he was known as the author of many thefts, and at least one of his murders; nothing awaited him in his own world but the gallows.

Hobbs would go—and then he would be alone again. It was not

Hobbs he would miss, but the sound of his native tongue, the company of one who had seen cities and English countryside, who could speak of streets, and shops, and snow, and autumn leaves; who knew what a book was, even if he could not read one; who could hum a familiar tune, crack a joke, tell a bawdy tale, curse the Governor . . .

He walked stubbornly, his hand against his side, his head bent, pushing his tired mind on from that thought of solitude to another which often troubled him. Among the tribes there was a rumour, strangely persistent and constantly recurring, of a white man who lived somewhere in the hills much farther up the river. Towns had learned a few words and phrases of the native tongue, and the natives knew a little English, but he had never been able to understand their accounts of this mysterious white man. When he had first heard the tale, soon after his escape, he had been interested—even excited—wondering if he could not find this fellow-runaway, and join forces with him. He had a hut, the natives said. They meant, of course, Towns thought, a native hut—a bark mia-mia. But no, they protested, it was not a mia-mia, but a hut like the white men's huts, with a roof, and a door; they even made motions with their hands which suggested the turning of a key. His excitement mounted. There was no settlement beyond the river up there; this man, if he existed, must be an absconder like himself. And then, into his wild and growing hope, they dropped one shattering word: "Bo-ee."

Dead? He was dead, this man? Yes, he had died; he had drowned in the river. How long ago did he die? They explained by a pantomime which reduced young men to children, that it had been long, long ago— and Towns' heart sank. Yet surely the hut might still be there? And in it, perhaps, still something of use to himself . . . ?

But soon afterwards had come a messenger from one of the river tribes to make arrangements with the Bideegal for an intertribal corroboree, and he had spoken once more of this man—and not as a dead man. Dyonn-ee, they called him. Towns asked, mystified:

"Bo-ee? Dyonn-ee bo-ee?"

No, the messenger assured him, Dyonn-ee was not dead, but very much alive. Towns struggled with the inadequacy of his few native words. Had not this man been drowned, then, many years ago? Yes, he was serenely informed, Dyonn-ee had been drowned. Then he was now dead? No, he was not dead. The native became quite exasperated by the absurd catechism of the white man, and Towns flung away angrily, cursing him for a superstitious savage. He forgot about Dyonn-ee until a chance incident whetted his curiosity again.

A young woman, stolen from one of the river tribes by a raiding party of the Bideegal, was brought back in triumph as a bride for one of its members. She wore about her neck a string twisted from strands of human hair—and one of the strands was red. It was greatly admired by the natives. It was, they explained to Towns, Dyonn-ee's hair. Towns, frowning over it, decided that it meant nothing except that there had once been a red-headed white man in the neighbourhood; but he kept at the back of his mind the thought that where one white man had lived another could live—and the hut might still be there . . .

And then, only a few weeks ago, there had been another intertribal gathering to which members of the river-tribes had come, and one of them had shown Towns a small carving. It was roughly and crudely done, but the white man felt his excitement mounting again as he stared at it. At peacock . . . ? Surely a peacock, with its vast semi-circle of tail-feathers outspread—and where could a native of New South Wales have seen a peacock? But wait—there was said to be a native bird with a spreading tail . . . ? He asked, pointing: "Med-ee-ah?" The native did not understand the word, which was of a different dialect from his own, but he understood the pointing finger and the raised eyebrows. He answered promptly: "Bee-kuk." Towns drew a long breath and examined the carving again closely. It was not old; the carving looked fresh. He asked eagerly: "Dyonn-ee?" The native nodded.

Towns sat staring at it, not daring to cherish a fresh hope, and yet, in the face of this new evidence, unable to doubt. He asked again—almost humbly in his anxiety to understand—if it were not true that this Dyonn-ee had been drowned many years ago, only to be once more assured that it was. Towns ran his fingers distractedly through his hair, and tried again. Dyonn-ee was dead after this drowning? Certainly he was dead, the native answered impatiently. "Bo-ee." Who, then, had made this carving of the bee-kuk? Staring at him as though he were demented, the native repeated emphatically that Dyonn-ee had made it, and demonstrated the manner of its making by holding it in one hand, and with the other making the movements of whittling with a knife.

This puzzle throbbed at the back of his mind as he walked. It might be months, he thought, before he saw another native from the river tribes, but he must wait. Even after a year in the woods he was afraid of the endless, monotonous country, and he remembered tales in the settlements of expeditions which had crossed the river and found themselves in a tangle of hills and gullies where a man might wander till he perished. His health was bad, and growing worse. He had been lost once for two days when he strayed from a hunting party, and the fear he had felt then had never left him. He dared not move without a native guide. But when an opportunity came, he resolved, he would go in search of this fabulous Dyonn-ee who had died—and was yet alive.

*   *   *   *

Mr. Stephen Mannion's new house on the banks of the Nepean was more than half completed. The stone for its massive walls had been quarried from his own property; already the design of spacious and well-proportioned rooms was evident, and on the great semi-circular verandah which looked down from the hilltop upon the winding reaches of the river, slender stone pillars reared upward in readiness for the roof.

Twice, now, ships had brought from England handsome pieces of mahogany furniture which, tenderly packed and swathed, had made the rough journey by bullock-waggon from Sydney. They were conveyed by sweating convicts to a temporary haven in the wooden cottage which

Mannion had built four years ago; but Ellen Prentice, when she polished their curves, flutings and convolutions, and rubbed their smooth surfaces to a lustrous patina, did not deceive herself into imagining that such superior objects could be intended to give pleasure to herself, though she had ordered Mr. Mannion's household for nine years.

She was able to form her own conclusions. Three years ago when he had sailed for Ireland on a visit, taking his two sons with him, she had begun to fear that her period of security was over; it was only a matter of time, she thought, before he would marry again. So she had learned without surprise when he returned that he proposed to build a new house, and with tight lips and sullen eyes, keeping her own counsel, she had watched it grow. It was not for her, Ellen Prentice, ex-convict, to live in such a house. There were moments when she would have liked, instead of polishing those shining surfaces, to scratch and mutilate them. Sometimes when Mannion was absent upon business in Sydney or Parramatta, she would walk up the hill to the unfinished house and stand in the roofless rooms looking about her with a quiet, half-contemptuous bitterness.

At such moments she reviewed her life, but the years before her arrival as a convict in this still alien land were no more than a dark, half-forgotten dream. Only one thread bound her to it—the memory of her first child, Johnny, red-headed and black-tempered, like his father, born in England, transported with his parents to New South Wales, and now . . . where? Where? Her hatred of the country was nourished by that question. It had simply taken him, as it had taken so many others, and lost him. One moment he had been in the garden at Parramatta where they had lived for a time, and the next moment, gone. Gone not for an hour or two on some unlawful errand, to return with oaths on his lips and rebellion in his eyes for a punishment stoically endured—but gone for ever. Ellen never looked across the river at the hills climbing towards some unknown hinterland without thinking that somewhere this country guarded a secret which she was entitled to share. She would never share it. She knew better than to stand on her rights with human beings, and instinctively she transferred that knowledge to her relationship with nature. Neither man nor nature would ever give you anything they could withhold; there remained to you cunning, patience, enmity . . .

Thoughts of her life, then, began with the day eleven years ago when she had come ashore from a convict transport with Johnny on her knee, and another child already quickening in her body. She did not know who Maria's father was, nor did her ignorance disturb her. In the stinking darkness of convict quarters on a transport, one could recognise a man's desire—but not a man. Such things were incidents. Once landed, there had been her husband again; Andrew with his stubborn savagery of pent-up hatred for authority; Andrew with his open hostility to herself, who had incited him to steal, and got him into this hellish place; Andrew with his brooding secretiveness; Andrew, who, like Johnny —but much earlier—had just vanished.

She had never regretted his disappearance. Because of it she and her two younger children, Maria and Andy, had been promoted from a convict hut to the undreamed of comfort and security of her protector's house-hold. The strange story of Andrew's reappearance, and his death in the flooded river, had moved her not at all; so far as she was concerned he had already been dead for nearly three years. Her mouth had twisted sceptically over the tale that he had been drowned while rescuing a native woman and her child. She did not believe it. Andrew had never in his life considered anyone more important than himself.

She had not been surprised when at last her sentence was pronounced; she was, indeed, relieved to learn that it was to be not so bad as she had expected. The evening meal was over, the lamps lit, Mr. Mannion seated before the fire. She had gathered up the last of the dishes, and was turning to leave the room.

"One moment, Ellen."

She knew every inflection of his voice, and was able to adapt herself instantly. There were times when he spoke with a kind of absent-minded detachment, and she knew then that he was merely thinking aloud, requiring nothing of her but silent attention, or even the semblance of it. There was another note which told her that she must earn the roof he kept over her head and her children's, the food they ate. But this was his master-tone, and immediately she became the servant, standing with the dishes in her hands, her face impassive, waiting for orders. He turned the pages of a book, looking at it, not her.

"You have no doubt realised," he began in a business-like tone, "that our present association could not remain permanent."

He frowned slightly. Not only his association with her, but his association with the country, had already lasted far longer than he had anticipated. He shied away from examination of this fact, partly because his first decision to remain in the colony had been made at a time and in a mood which he preferred to forget, and partly because of a strange remark uttered years ago by the first Governor. During that dreadful summer after his wife's death while he had waited week after week for a ship that did not come, he had plunged into a relationship with Ellen which had seemed at the time a mere temporary expedient. So completely, by now, had he recovered his calm that he would not admit to himself that he had ever lost it. His remaining in the country when he could, at last, have left it—which had been in fact the result of a psychological crisis, a collapse of morale—he now preferred to see as an instance of sober fore-sightedness.

For there was, undoubtedly, a future for this colony. His property held him and absorbed his interest. It was only when he remembered his interview with Governor Phillip that this fact threatened to disturb him. For the Governor, looking at him with an offensive amusement (Mr. Mannion was not accustomed to being regarded as comical), had said: "You intend to exploit this land. Have a care, Sir, that it does not end by exploiting you!"

Mr. Mannion had thought it a ridiculous remark; he thought it so still. Far from being exploited by the land, he was steadily imposing upon it the imprint of his own. Had he not introduced into its primitive wildness the tools and methods of civilisation? Was not the very room in which he sat, with its books, its pictures, its silver, its massive furniture, proof of his mastery? And yet . . .

Yet though he had returned to Ireland intending that thereafter the colony should claim him only for visits of inspection, something had altered his plan. He still told himself that it was not altered—that with his wedding to Conor Moore postponed, he had felt that he might as well return to Beltrasna, and gratify her naïve desire for travel by allowing her to join him there for a year or two. Only for a year or two. He knew, nevertheless, that the urge to return had been strong in him before he met Conor, and that she had only provided a heaven-sent excuse for a course he really wanted. It had something to do with a change in himself. He had begun something, and left it unfinished; he had embarked on an enterprise which made demands upon him, and gave him a sense of strength and merit which he would not admit to be novel. For to admit it would be to admit two other things—first, that he had not been perfect before; and second, that there might have been, after all, some sense in Phillip's cryptic observation. For if the land were dragging out of him some qualities which had hitherto lain dormant, was not the land exploiting him? Was not the mark which he laid upon it, whatever it might be, ultimately its own mark?

All this was confusedly behind the frown that creased his brow at his own utterance of the word "permanent." Who could say, warned something in him, what was "permanent"? He could dismiss Ellen from his house, but he could not blot out the years she had lived with him; he could shake the dust of this place from his feet any time he chose, but he could not erase from his mind the effects of nine years spent in it; he could send his sons, Patrick and Miles, home to Ireland, but he could not banish this land from their memories, or deny that for the younger it was the land of his birth.

It was for the sake of his sons, he told himself, that he had always asserted the impermanence of this life. He was by training a determined upholder of the conventions, and though it had at first irked him that they should live under the same roof as his mistress, the fact remained that there was nowhere else for them to live. In this crude colony, isolated from a civilisation which provided circumspectly for such situations, he had been forced to compromise, but as the years passed, he had known there must be a change. He had taken them back to Ireland intending that they should remain; that he, too, should remain except for occasional visits—when Ellen's presence would still provide some consolation for what he was resolved to see as exile. But Conor had altered his plans . . .

He cleared his throat.

"During my visit to Ireland I made the acquaintance of a young lady who has done me the honour to promise to be my wife."

His glance at Ellen was not unmixed with annoyance, for it flicked his pride that he should have to make explanations to an ex-convict. He threw down his book, rose, and stood before the fireplace where, with his back turned to her, he announced coldly: "I expect her arrival within the year."

Ellen said tonelessly:

"You'll not be needing me longer, then."

He drummed on the mantelpiece with his fingers. He was remembering the big book-lined room where, on going to pay his respects to his neighbour, Sir John O'Connor, he had found the old man reading by the fireside with a dog at his feet and whisky at his elbow. The book he had laid aside, Mannion remembered, was that iniquitous pamphlet, *The Rights of Man*, and Sir John's bitter denunciation of its author had led them into a discussion upon the disturbed state of the world, the perilous influence exerted by such ranting agitators as this infamous Tom Paine, the far-reaching effects of the revolution in France, the secession of the American colonies, and the alarmingly rising tide of discontent in their own country. From that they had passed to the Militia regiments formed to uphold threatened law and order, and thence to the *cause célèbre* of the moment, in which an officer of one of those regiments was involved. Neither Sir John nor Mr. Mannion was acquainted with Sir Henry Brown Hayes, ". . . an old and respected family, I understand, Stephen, though latterly closely connected with trade . . ." but Sir John was well primed by friends in Cork with the latest details of this spicy scandal, and he had described to his guest the sensation caused by the impetuous Sir Henry's midnight abduction of an heiress.

"He's still at large, I am told. It is said that should he be brought to trial the death penalty will he ordered—but I should suppose that influence might be exerted on his behalf to have it mitigated to transportation." He had laughed amusedly. "You may yet welcome him to Botany Bay, my dear fellow!"

And so they had drifted into conversation about the colony, and the long, idle afternoon had passed, and at length Mannion had risen to take his leave.

"I fear I've been over-garrulous, Sir, on the subject of my activities in New South Wales . . ."

"No, no! I have been deeply interested, I assure you, in what you tell me of this new colony. I shall hope to hear more at . . . ah! Come in, my dear . . . !"

And then the afternoon had changed from idleness to a sharp, singing excitement. It had not been absent from Mannion's mind that he might look about for a suitable wife, and he had already given some thought to a handsome young woman with an even handsomer dowry. She was forgotten now. He had not reckoned upon being captured by a chit of sixteen with grey-blue eyes, smooth black hair, and a complexion which had instantly reminded him of the petal-fairness of Miles' cheeks in babyhood.

"Allow me to present Mr. Mannion, my dear. Stephen, you will perhaps remember my granddaughter, Conor? Though she must have been quite a child when you left upon your adventures."

"Indeed, yes," he had said, staring, "quite a child . . ."

He was thinking that she was quite a child still. The straight, unembarrassed candour of her gaze almost put him out of countenance for a moment—but only for a moment. He knew that he was a handsome man, and he felt no need to suppose that any woman's scrutiny would leave her quite indifferent. Yes, she *was* still a child; so much so that he had made but little demur when the old man insisted, later, that he must wait at least two years for her. Two years, in fact, would suit him very well. His present *ménage* in the colony, unconventional as it was, could be left undisturbed for another two years. By that time Patrick would be approaching fifteen . . . by that time he could have his affairs in better order . . . by that time he could have a new house built . . .

"I am in your hands, Sir," he had assured the old man. And to the girl, wandering in the garden beside him, he had said:

"In the colony there are often fires that burn vast tracts of land—your eyes are the colour of the smoke that goes up from them."

And she, apparently not interested in the colour of her eyes, had asked eagerly:

"What makes the fires, pray?"

He had felt a little disconcerted—and then on second thoughts not ill-pleased that her innocence should be so unresponsive to lover-like advances.

"I don't know—the natives, perhaps . . ."

"What are they like—the natives?"

"They are ignorant savages—inhuman, brutalised creatures." Her very unawareness of his ardour tempted him again. "Let us not talk of them, Conor. Let us talk of ourselves . . ."

She had given him one of her quick, direct looks.

"But indeed I'm greatly interested in them, Mr. Mannion. And in everything about this colony. I like to hear of it."

"I fear . . ." he began.

"Pray tell me, Sir, will it always remain? I mean, will it really become a new country for white people, and grow bigger and richer and more important? Or is it to be always but a small settlement—a place for felons?"

He had glanced down at her sideways, a trifle puzzled. He had been on the point of responding to her girlish desire for information by regretting that the colony would offer few opportunities for social pleasures. He had assumed that she would thirst for tales of balls and routs and dinner-parties—but she was enquiring about destinies. He replied rather flatly:

"There is no fear that the settlement will be withdrawn. But it *is* a penal colony, my love. Of that unpleasant fact I cannot honourably refrain from warning you repeatedly. There will be little, I regret to say, of such gaieties as you have the right to expect. But it will not be for long, and we shall endeavour . . ."

"There was such a colony that Philip of Macedon founded, was there not, and called Poneropolis, or Rogues' Town? I read of it only recently in an old book of my grandfather's. How strange," she continued thoughtfully, unconscious of his astonished stare, "that this one too should have been founded by a Phillip! It is curious—don't you think so, Mr.

Mannion . . . ?" she flashed a rather sad and absent glance at him ". . . that after so many centuries there should still be felons?"

He laughed with a trace of impatience.

"You are quite a scholar, my dear! Felons there have always been, and no doubt always will be—but it is not for such pretty heads or such tender hearts as yours to fret for them. Forget them, I beg. They will not obtrude themselves upon you, never fear—I give you my word. There is no need for you to be alarmed on that score."

She looked at him in surprise.

"I am not alarmed."

He chose to interpret that in his own way.

"You may have complete confidence in my protection. In that know-ledge, my dear, I beg you to tell me that you will be glad to come to New South Wales—to me?"

She replied without hesitation:

"I have always wished to travel, Mr. Mannion—to see the world. I have never been away from Ireland."

She seemed not to have heard the latter part of his question. He repeated it jealously:

"You will be glad to come to me?"

Her brows knitted over the faint uncertainty in her eyes, and she answered as though she were remembering and repeating a lesson.

"Indeed, Mr. Mannion, I shall be . . . I am sensible of the honour you do me. Are they like the negroes—these natives of New South Wales? I saw a negro once . . ."

Recalling that interview now, Mr. Mannion's fingers beat more rapidly on the mantelpiece. Away from the intoxication of her beauty, he had found himself more than once thinking of his bride-to-be with a flicker of uneasiness. He remembered that her mother, a spirited beauty only a year or two older than himself, had caused the raising of eyebrows by a more than usually indiscreet elopement. True, Conor's father, Desmond Moore, had come of an old and distinguished family, but he had been its black sheep—a wild fellow, given to writing scandalous lampoons upon respect-able people, and even suspected of sympathy with the American rebels . . .

Behind him Ellen was silent, unmoving. He said at last:

"The lady I am to marry is—very young. She will, of course, bring her maid with her, and I expect her to be accompanied by a relative of my own—an elderly lady . . ."

He paused for an instant and sighed inaudibly. Cousin Bertha would undoubtedly be a bore. His father's cousin, widowed in early woman-hood, she had lived as a poor relation in his home ever since he could remember. Pathetically eager to please, she had performed all the more tiresome tasks of the household, and pleased nobody. Rheumatism and increasing deafness had made her almost useless of late years, but his mother, planning Conor's journey with her usual ruthless efficiency, had found one last use for her. It was obvious that Conor must have a chaperone during the voyage; highly desirable that she should have a respectable female companion in this isolated spot from which her husband must absent himself occasionally for several days at a time. His mother and sisters had said with one voice: "Cousin Bertha!"

Well, her presence must be suffered; her age and infirmities encouraged the hope that it need not be suffered for long. He sighed again, and continued:

". . . but it will be necessary for her to have some assistance in the management of the house. The conditions here are not those to which she has been accustomed."

Ellen said nothing. He went on:

"I have already made enquiries for some such person in Sydney. I found only two who seemed in any way suitable. And these, upon reflection, I have decided to be not quite . . ."

He turned and looked at her; she stared back at him steadily. Their looks told each other that despite the cessation of an intimate relationship, he would still have need of her, and she of him. She knew why these other women fell short of his requirements. They would be timid creatures, afraid of the loneliness of Beltrasna, afraid of the natives, ignorant of the thousand small details of management she had learned so thoroughly. He needed her to act as a buffer between his dainty lady wife and the harshness of her new home. She needed him because he still represented security. She had no wish to be flung back into the bog of life in Sydney or Parramatta to subsist by casual labour and casual prostitution. To find another permanent protector, or even some ex-convict or settler for husband would be a long step down from the comfort she had known in Stephen Mannion's house. But it was for him to ask. She kept her eyes on him and her mouth obstinately shut. He said:

"We shall, of course, take up our residence in the new house when she arrives. I have already informed you that I have engaged a tutor for my sons; I expect him shortly. I see no reason, Ellen, why you should not remain here in the cottage with your children, and continue in my employment as housekeeper."

He had said it; she answered laconically:

"I reckon there's no reason."

He scowled.

"I can rely upon your—discretion, I believe?"

"I'm not one," she answered with a shrug, "to speak out of my place."

"That is settled, then. Our manner of life will be changed somewhat —no doubt my wife will wish to entertain occasionally, and extra servants will be needed. Mrs. Marsden has recommended a young girl of eighteen or thereabouts who was for a time in respectable employment in Parramatta, and whom I shall engage as housemaid. Her name is Emma . . . Emma. . . . I forget her surname. . . . No matter! She will be accommodated in the new house. Maria is now eleven years old, is she not? She may be given some light but regular duties, and it has occurred to me that in Sydney or Parramatta I may find a young native girl who could be trained for domestic tasks . . ."

Ellen said harshly:

"Natives! There's no good in any of them—a pack of sly, dirty savages! There's been three of them here already, and . . ."

He silenced her peremptorily with a lifted hand. He had not forgotten Conor's interest in the natives, and it was his fond whim to present her with one, as he might have given a doll to a child. Yet there was no reason why this doll, being human, should not earn the privilege of living in his household. He said coldly:

"Those were girls taken straight from the woods—from the local tribes. I shall make no further experiments of that kind. But in Sydney there are girls who have lived the greater part of their lives in or about the settlements, and who have already received some training in civilised customs. If I am able to find one—a girl of some nine or ten years of age, perhaps—I shall expect you, Ellen, to instruct her in household duties, in personal cleanliness, in civility, possibly in needlework . . ."

"It's too young." Ellen's voice was sullen.

He rebuked her sharply.

"That is for me to say. I look to the future. An older girl—even a girl of thirteen or fourteen—would be, according to the ideas of these people, of marriageable age, and would be inclined to restlessness and discontent. It is essential that I find someone who will become accustomed to her situation here, and sensible of its advantages, before she—before the time arrives—er—in short, while she is still a child. Allow me, Ellen, to know best in this matter."

She lifted her shoulders again in a faint shrug which enraged him. He returned to his chair, picked up his book, and said shortly, without looking at her:

"That is all. You may go."

*　　　　*　　　　*　　　　*　　　　*

The hut which Mr. Mannion had built for the accommodation of his convict labourers was a long, low room whose only ventilation came through the rough-hewn logs of which it was made. Throughout the colony, assigned convicts worked for their masters the same hours as those employed by the Government, and were free at other times to sell their labour elsewhere for what they could get, but a well-to-do settler could afford to employ his servants beyond the allotted hours. Since regulations did not permit them to travel from one district to another without a magistrate's pass, they moved on an invisible chain, and strict confinement was unnecessary. Here, however, in this isolated spot with the woods crowding about it and the unknown mountains rising towards the sky on the other side of the river, Mr. Mannion was accustomed to observe regulations when they suited him, and adjust them to his convenience when they did not. His labourers were shackled at night, and slept under lock and key. It made but little difference if the bell which called them to, or released them from their Government hours of labour rang early or late; they still worked for Mr. Stephen Mannion, and their payment for the extra hours was a little added to the daily food ration.

There had never been an escape from Beltrasna. It was a record upon which its owner prided himself, since of all properties in the colony this would have seemed, from its solitude and its proximity to the mountains, the most favourable to absconders. But Mr. Mannion, in accepting the felicitations which his fellow-landowners frequently offered him on this account, always pointed to the safeguard which his acumen had provided. He was, happily, not compelled to rely, as so many others were, upon overseers hardly more trustworthy than the convicts—nor did convicts supply his only labour. From his estates in Ireland he had brought two reliable overseers, Toole and Merrett, who had grown up in the service of his family; and he had also imported some free labourers. "Without these men," he would explain, "my house could never have gone up so fast, nor would my farm have reached its present satisfactory state. Convicts! They are well enough for the ruder kinds of toil, and under strict and incessant supervision, but I should be sorry to be entirely dependent upon them!"

He had taken some pains to see that most of the prisoners assigned to him were Irish—not from a sentimental desire to be surrounded by his countrymen, but because his recent glimpse of his troubled homeland, and the tidings which letters had brought him, made him profoundly mistrustful of them. Government, he considered, was incredibly lax in its dealings with such dangerous rogues; it were better that he, who did not make the mistake of underestimating their roguery, should have as many as possible under his own eye and discipline.

Yet even the sagacious Mr. Mannion had failed to take into account the demoralising influence of this new and painfully evolving community. He, who liked his own bottle, held strong views upon the subject of drinking among the lower classes, and strictly enjoined upon his overseers that no liquor was ever to touch the lips of any of his convicts. But here liquor was more than liquor: it was currency, and Toole and Merrett had soon discovered a method of augmenting their wages.

*　　　　*　　　　*　　　　*　　　　*

Dan Driver, skulking through the woods in sight of the starlit waters of the Nepean, was burdened with two demijohns whose weight dragged his meagre shoulders down, and slowed his tired, stumbling feet. It had been his task again, as it had often been before, to slip away from Beltrasna at sunset when the convict gang ceased work, and to trudge—halting and sweating at every sound—to a certain secluded and well-hidden hut farther down the river where rum was illicitly distilled. The operator of the still was an ex-convict whose real name was by now forgotten, but who was known as Sailor Joe.

His trade, begun several years ago, had flourished and increased. Five quarts of a diabolical brew which he could sell for six shillings the quart could be made from a bushel of wheat which would have brought him but ten shillings at the Commissary's store. Besides—as he and many other small settlers had discovered—it was by no means certain that he could sell his wheat to the public store even if he wanted to. More than once he had found himself excluded by some wealthy landowner to whom he had at last been forced to sell his grain at half its price—only to see its new owner immediately resell it to the store for its full value. There were better ways, he had decided, of using grain; and he had by now discovered that

he could live and thrive without the labour of growing it himself at all.
He dealt mainly with the settlers in the Hawkesbury district, from whom
he exacted payment in wheat which he manufactured into his potent
liquor, and to whom he sold it back not only for more wheat, but for
anything else he could get. Tools, food, clothing, even an occasional lamb,
heifer or sow, found their way to the hut in the darkness of the night,
and from there travelled to Parramatta, where they were bartered for any
other goods which Sailor Joe might desire. The plot of land which had
been granted to him at Toongabbee upon his emancipation bore little
evidence of husbandry; but it was whispered that the cottage upon it was
furnished with a comfort beyond his station, and that he had dealings with
more than one respectable and influential gentleman.

There were nights when the boat moored to Mr. Mannion's landing
stage, rowed by one of Mr. Mannion's faithful overseers, and laden with
Mr. Mannion's grain, made a quiet excursion down the river, and returned
as quietly before dawn began to lighten the sky. It was simple for Toole
and Merrett when they visited Parramatta upon their master's business, to
receive payment from Sailor Joe or one of his many agents at an appointed
rendezvous, and to proceed, armed with this liquid and easily negotiable
currency, upon their own occasions. It would buy anything from a meal
to a share in a harvest; it would buy a dog, a horse, a woman, or whatever
else might be for sale; it would cement an alliance, or intimidate an enemy;
it would still a tongue or loosen one. But sometimes there was too long an
interval between visits to a settlement where such transactions could be
arranged, and the issue of spirits which Mr. Mannion considered adequate
for the refreshment of his overseers seemed niggardly. Then liquor was
merely liquor, and Dan Driver was pressed into service. The silence of the
convicts was assured by allotting them a share; nor could the miserable
Dan evade his task, penned as he was between the overseers who could
change his life from a mere burden to a martyrdom, and his fellow-prisoners
who lived for their infrequent orgies.

Toole and Merrett had chosen their messenger shrewdly. There were
other convicts who had volunteered—even pleaded—for the assignment,
but the overseers knew that, once free, they might vanish for ever. Dan
was the perfect tool—stupid to the point of imbecility, so morally weak
that he could always be bullied into a dumb, hypnotised obedience, cowardly
and superstitious as only the very ignorant can be, so that it was not
difficult to play upon his terror of darkness and solitude with bloodcurdling
tales of native atrocities, and even of ghosts and spirits that haunted the
eerie woods. Free in those woods, he was still the prisoner of his own
abject fear. It stretched like a taut line between the Beltrasna hut and the
hut of Sailor Joe; it was like a path to his feet. So completely had the
last spark of independence been battered out of him, that not even the
horror of the life he knew could compare with the horror of the thought
that some day he might have to act alone, to make a decision, to rely on
himself, to think.

It was a cold night at the end of June. Rain had been falling up till
a couple of hours ago, but the clouds had broken and the blue-black sky

was powdered over with a frost of stars. Dan had been soaked to the skin, but his clothes had dried on him and his body was warm—even hot—from the exertion of his long trudge, but his hands, gripping the demijohns, felt numb and frozen. He was weak with hunger, too, for he had missed the evening meal, and the thought of it, miserable as it was, set him craving now so that his mouth watered.

He looked about forty. Undersized, undernourished, lame, his hands calloused with work, and his shoulders always cringing with the memory of a flogging six months ago, he moved more like an animal than a man, in short dashes from shadow to shadow and from tree to tree, pausing to turn his head with the sharp, lifting motion of a creature which can not only see and hear, but smell danger. He knew there would be no mercy for him if he were caught. He might be flogged at Beltrasna, or haled before a magistrate at Parramatta—perhaps (for he had always been unlucky) Mr. Marsden, who flavoured the severity of his sentences with religious exhortation which did nothing to modify the torture of the lash. He dreaded the dark, overcrowded hut to which he must return only less than that; he hated the men who helped to bully him into this dangerous task only less than he hated his official masters; yet that hut was home, and those men his fellows. There they might hate each other, but they combined at least in reserving a special and darker hatred for those in authority over them. Beside that hatred their own private feuds became mere gestures. Dan accepted all this because he knew no way of resisting it. He was twenty-two years old, he had been a convict for seven years, and his sentence was for life. This was that life. Behind it there was a vague, half-remembered childhood in England, and a terrible voyage out in the *Royal Admiral* in 1792—but there was nothing ahead. Nothing but struggling through each day as it came, digging, sawing, dragging logs, killing the nights with carousal or with the exhausted sleep that was never so deep and sweet as at that dawn hour when the overseer's voice shattered it. He was afraid of everything—but of nothing more than the thought of freedom. That was a concept which reduced him to breathless, heart-hammering dread; there was only one way he could bear to think of it, only one form in which its menace could be hidden—the form of sleep. If he were free, he would sleep, sleep, sleep all the time. His symbol—the mystic image which he conjured up to defend himself against this terrifying thought of freedom—was a certain vast tree at the edge of a field where he had worked in the summer of 1794, and to whose cool, dark shade his eyes had turned whenever he straightened his back to wipe the sweat from them. So fierce and strong had been the desire of his seventeen-year-old body for rest, that he had never since freed himself from the conception of liberty as a condition in which one could sprawl all day beneath a tree. Sometimes, half-heartedly, he added trimmings to this vision; but labour, either of body or mind, had no place in it. Sensations were what he craved—the bodily delights of sex, of clothing that was not rags; of food that could please the palate as well as fill a void in the stomach; and one crude, perverted spiritual desire—some day to have the power to bring hurt and harm upon another human being.

He had come in sight of the Beltrasna hut now. He halted among the trees at the edge of the clearing, scanning it suspiciously for any sign of life or movement. There was none, and he made a dash for it; his lame gait, his stooping posture of concealment, and the weight of the demijohns gave him the appearance of some simian creature—an ape scuttling for safety.

Exhausted, his heart thudding and his breath gasping, he leaned against the door and scratched it furtively. Toole was waiting; it opened, and he yielded up one of his two burdens to the dark figure that brushed past him with a threat and a curse. He was inside, the door shut and locked behind him, his lungs, accustomed to the freshness of the winter air, revolted by the foetid atmosphere, so that he leaned dizzily for a moment against the wall.

Among the convict population of the colony the various employers were exactly graded. The best, which meant the less brutal and oppressive, were merely hated. But hatred could swell till it became almost a hideously corrupted love, and the man who inspired it an object about which the mind played endlessly with lustful dreams of revenge. Such men acquired a kind of preciousness in the eyes of their slaves; they provided a focus for the sadistic visions of retaliation, the luxurious murder-impulses, the power and release fantasies which were often all that remained of feeling. They died a mystic death of agony and humiliation every time a convict's eyes rested on them.

Mr. Mannion, though not in a place of honour, was well up the list. His rank had been less exalted at first, for though he worked his labourers hard and treated them harshly, he also fed them better than they were fed by most employers. But in the last few years, since the influx of Irish prisoners into the colony, the atmosphere in the Beltrasna hut had changed. The hatreds of their unhappy country still tasted sour in their mouths when they arrived in this distant colony, and found themselves once more at the mercy of a man whose tyranny seemed the blacker because he was their countryman. They had seen and shared the sufferings of an Irish peasantry whose landlords lived abroad and drew wealth from their labour; and to the hatred they felt for Mr. Mannion on their own account was added a hatred which they bestowed on behalf of hungry families in thatched cabins on the other side of the world—whose toil and want, they knew, were providing the money for this lavish colonial enterprise. Their own toil, in turn, would reinforce the wealth and influence by which their master held the tenants of his Irish estate in bondage; they felt themselves helpless cyphers in a sum which added up inexorably to more and more power for Mr. Stephen Mannion.

Dan stood near the doorway recovering his breath, and finding after his first recoil that the smell of close-packed and unwashed bodies, and of the single, smoking tin lamp was, after all, reassuring—the smell of his lair. A sound greeted him, and a movement from the semi-darkness which the feeble light from the lamp seemed only to emphasise. Shapes stirred; voices muttered at him; there was a kind of surge—not towards him, but towards that which he carried, and his only emotion was thankfulness that he could now set it down on the floor and become again an inconspicuous unit in a crowd.

Crawling from their recesses the convicts converged as near to the centre of the hut as their chains would allow. Someone moved the lamp. Passed from hand to hand, it seemed to Dan to float towards him in the air, lighting a shaggy head here, a bald one there, showing him a phantasmagoria of gaunt faces and avid eyes until it came to rest on the floor near the demijohn. Then there was a pale circle of light with the liquor in its centre, and before this object of almost devotional adoration the smoke from the untrimmed wick went up like incense, and there was a moment of pause, almost of contemplation, and a mutter of sound like a prayer.

From beside him Dan heard an elderly man named Taylor utter a thin cackle of laughter.

"There's the fear o' death in Toole to-night!" He pinched Dan's ankle, peering up at him intently so as to miss no shadow of the terror his news would arouse. "The master's been around!"

Dan's legs gave way under him. He crouched on the floor beside Taylor and stared at him, saying nothing, the stare a sufficient question. Taylor told him with relish.

"There's Toole outside, an' we inside—all except you, me young cock! An' suddenly we hear the master's voice. . . . 'Ah well?' 'e says, an' we hear Toole say 'Yes, Sir,' an' then the master bids 'im open the door. We 'ears Toole a-clatterin' the keys—an' Doolan there, 'e grabs a bundle o' clothes an' shoves 'em in your place to look like you was lyin' there, an' then the door's open an' the master says: 'Shine me your lantern in so I can see the fellows,' an' Doolan, 'e sits forward so as to hide the bundle a bit, an' Toole 'e takes care not to turn 'is light there, an' 'is lordship says: 'H'm! Seems all in order,' 'e says, an' 'e goes out, an' Toole locks the door agin . . ."

Dan's breath shuddered out of his lips; his forehead was wet. Taylor laughed thinly. "But Toole's 'ad 'is fright, the rat! Gone off to 'ide 'is liquor in such a takin' that 'e forgot to put the irons on ye! Ye'll sleep easy to-night, like the King in 'is bed!"

Still Dan said nothing. The warmth of exercise was fading; he began to shiver, partly with cold and partly with terror of so narrow an escape. He knew his share of the treasure he had brought would not be enough to give him the oblivion he wanted, but even that seemed unimportant now beside the fact that he was safe again. To be shouldered aside was a comfort; to be cursed for being so long was companionship. He heard the faint clink of pannikins, the murmur of voices, a laugh now and then—not of mirth but of excitement—and he crawled to his own recess and crouched there, almost content.

He saw his neighbour, Doolan, lift a pannikin to his lips, his fingers shaking with eagerness, but though he was passionately relieved that someone had had the presence of mind to outwit the eye of authority, it did not occur to him to be grateful. He knew the unwritten law of solidarity among outcasts. Bitter as your lot might be, you shared it. If

you forgot that—if you thought to win favour by informing, if you failed
to cover up for one of your fellows, if you ranged yourself even for a
moment by any act or omission of an act on the side of the oppressors—
you learned that there was something worse than to be an outcast from
society, and that was to be an outcast from the outcasts. There had
been a few who learned that too late. Dan took the pannikin which
was at last grudgingly thrust at him, and drank.

The crude, fierce liquor burned his throat and set him coughing, but
almost at once he began to feel happier. Fragments of talk rolled about
his ears like balls; bursts of laughter, cautiously stifled, made him smile
foolishly. Somewhere in the semi-darkness a voice began to sing in a
monotonous undertone:

> "Oh can ye see, alannah,
> The shinin' o' the sails?
> They're sendin' me across the sea
> From Cork to New South Wales . . ."

A pannikin was passed back towards a man lying face downward
against the far wall; someone spoke a few words of rough, jeering
encouragement, and there was a groan. Everyone laughed at the groan,
but less with amusement than with a grim, sardonic acknowledgment of
the agony which caused it. Taylor, calling into the shadows that a man
who had been flogged but once had little to groan about, turned his bony,
naked shoulders to the light so that a newcomer might admire the scars
of half a dozen punishments. For the last two, he declared, he had to
thank His Reverence, and a sound like a snarl rose and split into
argument. Names were spoken—Grose, Paterson, Mannion, Macarthur,
Marsden, Johnston—and each gathered about itself a garland of bitter
anecdote and blasphemous invective. Let them wait—these vultures who
fed on misery! There would come a day . . . !

"What day?" Taylor's high, jeering voice struck a pause of uncertainty into the subdued clamour, but it rose again more fiercely. The
day when the Governor, weak old fool that he was, could no longer wink
at open defiance . . .

"Will they hang, then?" Taylor asked contemptuously. "Will they
be strung up for a Botany Bay dozen like we are if we so much as squeak?
Not those fine gentlemen, with their uniforms an' their pockets full o'
gold!" He lowered his voice; it rasped across the silence in a husky
whisper: "Where did that paper come from that was dropped around
the streets o' Sydney a year gone, an' put His Excellency in such a takin'?"
His tone made the title an insult. "Where did it come from, my lads,
if it didn't come from them—plottin' together to get 'im sent back so
they can 'ave the colony to themselves like they did before? But what
does 'e do, the old . . . ?" A lively and scandalous description of Hunter
brought a wave of groaning laughter. " 'E puts up a notice offerin' a
reward! An' they sits snug in their fine 'ouses laughin' at 'im! Who's
goin' to inform on them—answer me that! Us?"

But there was no answer, and in the uncertain silence that fell the voice from the shadows was crooning absently:

> "An' there the rich grow richer
> From what the lowly lack,
> An' there the poor man labours
> With stripes across . . ."

Dan, bemused by the potent liquor on his empty stomach, startled himself no less than the others by saying with sudden incoherent violence:

"They bided their time! I seen it! When the first Guv'nor gone 'ome in 'ninety-two, it was . . . !"

Someone sneered at him:

"You seen it! Y' mother's milk weren't dry on y' lips!"

Dan said excitedly:

"I seen it! Just arrived, we were, an' we seen the old ways change all in a month. I weren't but a lad, but I mind how at first some says it were a good thing—the way Grose give out land, an' put the pris'ners to workin' for the officers instead o' the Guv'ment . . ."

A voice said sharply:

"A good thing for the officers, faith, an' they buyin' up everythin' in the colony for a few gallons o' rum!"

From an angry chorus of agreement another voice rose, full of bitterness:

"An' it's not starvin' they are now neither, for all the proclamations an' orders! There'll be no day o' reckonin' for them, boys, if so be we don't make it ourselves. I got scores to pay, I'm tellin' ye! I'm one o' them that came out on the . . . *Britannia* . . ."

There was a brief pause before the name, and a long one after it which held and deepened, as if in acknowledgement that some words have associations before which the mind halts and the tongue is paralysed; words which, like infections, must be quarantined; words which must be isolated in a little pool of silence; words which become outcasts from the society of other words, and must be spoken on a different breath. And presently the speaker sealed that silence with a malediction uttered as softly as a blessing: ". . . an' may all the devils out o' Hell torment ye, Captain Thomas Dennot, ye black, stony-hearted murderer . . . !"

A breath of sound like an amen endorsed his petition. It was a ritual now; they had performed it many times, and having performed it they put past suffering behind them and closed their minds to the dark procession of to-morrows. Here and now they had the means to wrest an illusion of enjoyment from intolerable life, and a few joined in the song as it began again:

> "A day will dawn, alannah,
> When tyrants are cast down,
> An' they with names for cursin'
> In Cork an' Sydney Town . . ."

The thick, slurred voices died away raggedly; the sounds in the hut were the sounds of orgy, muffled and muted—an oath, a laugh, a hiccough, a groan, a burst of quarrelling. Diminishing as the still, wintry night slid towards a grey dawn, they changed—became snores, heavy breathing, words muttered in sleep, a moan of pain, a sharp cry of nightmare. The lamp guttered and went out.

*   *   *   *   *

Young Mr. Mark Harvey stood restlessly on the steps of the Court House at Sydney, awaiting his employer. Although it was early July, midwinter in this Southern land, his freshly-coloured face was sunburned, for he had spent the last few days since his disembarkation from the *Albion* in exploring the environs of the settlement. Despite the sensational rapidity of the passage—only three months and fifteen days—he had been thankful to find firm earth beneath his feet again, and to feel himself hovering on the outskirts of a community life once more. True, it was an odd community—exiled, still struggling, and not at all respectable—but in this very strangeness there was a flavour of adventure, and Mr. Harvey was young enough to feel that adventurousness was welcome. Or so he had felt four days ago. Since then the strangeness had, in a dozen small ways, come closer, and he was discovering, as many another young man had done before him, that the brightness of adventure was apt to become tarnished near at hand.

He had found word from his employer awaiting him. Mr. Mannion would be unable to make the journey from the Nepean for some days; Mr. Harvey might, therefore, employ this brief leisure in exploring his surroundings, and hold himself in readiness to accompany Mr. Mannion to Beltrasna on the third day of July.

Mark was nothing loth. He had been civilly greeted by a number of the principal inhabitants of the colony. He had paid his respects at Government House, and had dined both with His Excellency and the Rev. Mr. Johnston. He had joined a charming boating party and picnicked with several ladies and gentlemen upon a delightful beach across the harbour. All this had been most pleasant; he had found the manners and customs of his homeland intriguingly transported to an unfamiliar environment, and the convict gangs setting off to work in the morning had seemed as remote from his own life as had the dwellers in the foul back streets and alleys of London.

The rest of his time he had spent in solitary excursions, in completing a long letter to his mother, and in studying with a lively curiosity the appearance and activities of the natives who frequented the township. He thought them miserable looking creatures, with their lean, scarred bodies, matted hair, and bright, restless eyes. Some of them carried fish in nets slung over their shoulders, and bartered these among the townsfolk for scraps of food or clothing; but for the most part they merely stood or sat in the sun, talking rapidly among themselves, quarrelling sometimes, and laughing frequently. From several harbour beaches, crescents of sparkling white sand, he had watched them skimming about over the surface of the water in their crude, bark canoes, and from his pockets he had produced such trifles as he could find to entice their children near him. The weather which, so he had been informed, had been wild, wet and tempestuous during the previous month, was now clear and sunny, and there had been moments when—basking in delicious idleness on the warm sand—he had felt a pang of regret that his duties were to take him inland, away from this halcyon scene.

Into this beatific mood, however, there had burst a few shocks of alarm and repugnance. He had seen a native man suddenly begin to beat a native woman about the head with a club. Someone casually mentioned that a convict had been brought in to the hospital with a spear-wound in his body. He had heard shrill screams, and was informed that a convict-woman was being flogged for stealing food. And then, this very morning, the news of a horrible murder had run like wildfire through the town; Mr. Samuel Clode, a missionary, had had his brains beaten out by a soldier who had owed him some money, and his body had been discovered in a sawpit.

All this was disturbing to a young man who had been gently if poorly reared by a widowed mother, and it was, therefore, not altogether with regret that he had learned of his employer's arrival, and hastened to wait on him. But it seemed that their departure must be still further delayed, for Mr. Mannion had business to transact in the town.

He was, Mark thought, a personable, even a handsome man. In early middle age his hair was only lightly sprinkled with grey; he seemed even taller than he was because of the erectness of his carriage, and there was authority, the confidence of position, in his noticeably blue eyes. He told Mark briskly:

"We shall go by boat to Parramatta, Mr. Harvey, and lie there for the night with friends of mine who have been kind enough to offer us hospitality. I have horses awaiting me there, and we shall set off for Beltrasna early to-morrow morning."

He looked narrowly at the young man, and, on the whole, approvingly. Sir John O'Connor had chosen wisely, he thought. This lad had a frank and agreeable expression, and he bore himself well—with a suitable respect, but without servility. If his mental attainments were as satisfactory as his appearance, he would do well enough for a few years as tutor to Patrick and Miles. Mr. Mannion enquired:

"I assume, Mr. Harvey, that Sir John gave you a full account of what were to be your duties in my household?"

Mark assented.

"He explained to me, Sir—by letter, you understand, for I was at that time teaching Mr. Denis O'Connor's sons in England—that you required a tutor for your two sons, the elder a lad of about fourteen, he thought . . ."

"Patrick is now fifteen."

"I have a good knowledge of the classics, Mr. Mannion, and I have taught Sir John's grandsons for two years with, I think I may say, some success . . ."

Mannion nodded amiably.

"I am sure I may rely upon Sir John's recommendation. You will have Patrick as your pupil, however, for a year or two at most; he will then return to England to complete his education. But my younger son, Miles, is overdue for some instruction—he is eight years old. In addition, Mr. Harvey, I shall require some assistance from you in the writing of letters and the keeping of accounts. My farm grows, and my responsibilities with it. For a week or two we shall be busy with our removal to my new house, which is just completing. And now," he added, "I must be off about my affairs. They will occupy me for a couple of hours, and we shall meet upon the Court House steps at twelve o'clock. I must ask you to be punctual."

"Certainly, Sir," Mark had assured him. "I shall be there."

So here he was. But in those two hours he had added another odd and disquieting experience to his brief sojourn in Sydney. He had left his bags at his lodgings and set off rather forlornly to fill in the time with yet another walk. The interest of the town itself he had long ago exhausted, and so—because it was in a direction exactly opposite to that in which the murder had been committed, rather than for any other reason—he had climbed the hill and turned along the track towards the Lookout Post on South Head. He had fallen in presently with a couple of young officers who pointed out to him the distant, shadowy line of hills at whose foot, they told him, Mr. Mannion's property was situated. He had stood, after they left him, staring westward and feeling lonely. How dull, he thought, how queerly negative and monotonous was the colour of these woods! Or was it that against the profound and startling blue of the sky, no other colour could compete? He stood for so long that he decided at last there was no time to go farther; but before returning he left the path and scrambled downhill some distance to where he could see a great expanse of the harbour spread out before him. He wondered if there were another track skirting the shore, so that he might be saved the exertion of climbing the hill again; and wondering this, came suddenly upon a solitary figure sitting on a rock and staring out across the water. He approached and began civilly:

"Would you be so kind, Sir, as to tell . . . ?"

The expression of the face that turned towards him halted his thought, and set him stammering.

"I—I ask your pardon . . . I do not . . . I had no thought to intrude . . ."

For he had never seen so closed, and brooding, and despairing a face. Its owner was a man past middle age, neatly dressed, and as he looked at Mark his eyes seemed to be making a painful effort to return from some bleak, inner contemplation. It was an effort not wholly successful, for though they told him there was a stranger before him whose presence demanded speech, the thought behind them still anchored him to the past, and his words, coming out of that past, fell incongruously:

"The time is now come when you must either gather round the fabric of liberty . . ."

Mark, his mouth slightly agape, turned hurriedly to depart. This must be a lunatic . . . ! But the voice which had uttered those astonishing and irrelevant words, lost its curious, tranced note of quotation, and spoke again, normally:

"One moment, young Sir . . . !"

Mark turned doubtfully. The man had shifted his position, and sat leaning forward, his elbows on his knees, his hands clasped, looking up from beneath his brows. He said slowly:

"You asked me something? I was occupied with my thoughts . . . of two friends who died some three years ago. . . . May I be of service to you?"

Mark responded awkwardly:

"I fear I startled you, Sir. I am . . . may I presume to offer my condolences on your bereavement? I . . . I was merely about to ask, Sir, if there is a path from here to the town?"

"You will save time in the end by following the track at the top of the hill. You are newly arrived in this country?"

"Only a few days ago, Sir, on the *Albion*."

"Ah. You had a fast passage, I hear."

"Yes, Sir, we were so fortunate."

The man, looking down at his clasped hands, asked in a neutral voice:

"And how is England?"

Mr. Harvey stared, his brain floundering for an answer. *Was* there an answer? England was—England. The man spoke again, and this time, through his carefully colourless tone, a note of bitter passion sounded.

"Still enjoying her 'happy constitution and government'?"

It was a quotation again. Mark felt his cheeks flush with a faint antagonism. He replied stiffly:

"I believe so, Sir. I'm grateful for your assistance, and I wish you . . ."

But the man looked up at him now, and interrupted restlessly:

"Have you ever heard, Mr. . . . ?"

"My name is Mark Harvey, Sir."

"Have you ever heard, Mr. Harvey, of William Skirving, and Joseph Gerrald?"

"No, Sir, I fear I . . ."

But he stopped, his brain searching for echoes of a sensation which had penetrated even to the remote English countryside where he had lived. Skirving . . . Gerrald. . . . His memory found associated names—Muir, Palmer. . . . The man said harshly, staring hard at him:

"My name is Palmer. Thomas Fysshe Palmer. Have you ever heard that name?"

Mark met his eyes as he might have met those of a tiger or a snake. Remembered phrases flicked him to alarm. Mr. Denis O'Connor, storming over the newspapers. . . . Himself, reading them hastily to discover the cause of such fierce denunciations. . . . ". . . causing a spirit of unrest . . " ". . . dangerous to the public peace . . ." He could not take his eyes from the elderly man with the grizzled hair and the unrestful, bitter eyes, and the slow, bitter, cultivated voice. Sedition! That was a crime. This was a criminal. In this country one went for a walk, and found a criminal sitting by the wayside . . .

He stammered:

"Yes, Sir, your name is known to me, but . . ."

"But you feel no desire that *I* be known to you." There was a hint of sardonic but not unkindly humour in the man's eyes now. "Ah, well . . . ! Yet I'm no monster, young man. I have even been, in my time, highly respectable. I, whom you now see, exiled and disgraced, have been a Senior Fellow of Queen's College, Cambridge—an ordained minister of the gospel—a teacher—a man of letters, with some knowledge, and indeed a great love for the fine arts. What was my crime? I advocated Parliamentary Reform, Mr. Harvey. So, once upon a time, did Mr. Pitt. That same Mr. Pitt who later expressed himself as satisfied with the justice of my punishment for expressing views not so different from those which carried *him* to the highest office in the land—but which carried *me*, my young friend, to Botany Bay."

Mark said nervously:

"I know little, Sir, of politics . . ."

"I do not speak," Mr. Palmer said, "of politics. I speak of liberty and justice; and I think of my two friends Skirving and Gerrald who, for that same crime, died here in this place three years ago. And I wonder what our sufferings and our exile have achieved, and whether the oppressions we fought, and whose seeds are already sown in this new land, will flourish here as they have done in the old world." He paused, as if waiting for comment, but Mark was speechless. "Keep your eyes open, Mr. Harvey. You are young—and I think you are honest. You will see oppression and extortion at work here; I have suffered under them . . ." He rubbed his hand suddenly over his eyes and spoke sharply. "I am much alone with my thoughts. I fear my friends in England have forgotten me. You have heard me thinking aloud, Mr. Harvey, and perhaps you find my words wild and disturbing . . ."

Mark blurted out:

"When I first came upon you, Sir, you did utter some words. . . . I thought they sounded like a passage from a book . . . ? 'The time is now come . . .'?"

Mr. Palmer smiled.

"No, no. Not a passage from a book. A passage from what my indictment was pleased to describe as a seditious and inflammatory writing . . . shall I repeat it?"

Mark hesitated. He looked about him. The quiet woods enclosed them, the harbour lay before them, blue and still, there was not a soul, not a building in sight. In the solitude of that remote and unfamiliar scene he felt himself so far from his normal life and his normal self that even the ugly word "sedition" lost its menace. He replied quickly:

"If you would be so good, Sir . . . ?"

Mr. Palmer recited slowly:

"'The time is now come when you must either gather round the fabric of liberty to support it, or, to your eternal infamy let it fall to the ground to rise no more, hurling along with it everything that is valuable and dear to an enlightened people.'"

Mark said shyly:

"Thank you, Sir." He added with naïve candour: "I cannot see, I confess, anything very seditious in that."

Mr. Palmer looked at him with a faint smile.

"No? Nor I, Mr. Harvey. Yet . . ." he made a tired gesture with his hands, ". . . here I am."

Those words brought Mark back to reality. Here was he, also, with an appointment on the Court House steps at twelve o'clock. He said hurriedly:

"I must leave you, Mr. Palmer. I am honoured," he added, slightly surprised to discover with what truth he uttered the conventional words, "to have made your acquaintance. Good-day, Sir."

And he had left Mr. Palmer still sitting on his rock and staring at the harbour.

Now, waiting at the appointed rendezvous, he realised that in the last few days he had asked too much of his feet—accustomed during the voyage to no more than a desultory pacing of the deck. They felt bruised, swollen, aching. He longed to sit down on the steps and take his shoes off, but there had been something about Mr. Mannion which suggested that he was a stickler for the proprieties, and Mark had no wish to displease him at this early stage by being discovered in an un-dignified situation. So he shifted unhappily from foot to foot, and read, and re-read a notice affixed to the Court House wall.

"*The continual complaints which are made to the Governor of the refractory and disobedient conduct of the convict women call aloud for the most rigid and determined discipline among these troublesome charac-ters, who, to the disgrace of their sex, are far worse than the men, and . . .*"

Mark turned away to watch for his employer, and then, after a moment, turned back to read again:

"*. . . most particularly recommended to the magistrates in general that upon proof before them of any improper conduct in these dangerous and mischievous characters, or any disobedience of orders, or neglect of such duties as they may be directed to perform, they be ordered such exemplary punishment, either corporal or otherwise, as the nature of their crime may merit . . .*"

Mark had been trained to set a very high standard of behaviour as desirable—indeed, indispensable—to womanhood, and to believe that no rare piece of porcelain should be treated more gently; these grim phrases made him feel as nothing else had done—not even the murder—that he had come to a land in which his ideas were to be rudely assailed. He saw three convicts, chained together, crossing the street with an armed guard, and suddenly words leapt to his memory: "*. . . the fabric of liberty . . .*"

He looked away hurriedly, and found himself thinking with wonder and uneasiness that only a few years ago there had been nothing here . . . nothing. . . . No streets, no ships, no buildings; he almost added "no people," for indeed the natives seemed less inhabitants of the place than projections of it—growing from it like trees and falling back into it like seeds. And now there was—this. A township, an exile, a murder, three men in chains, an ominous decree gently flapping on the wall behind him . . .

". . . the fabric of liberty . . ."

He found, to his consternation, that his heart was beating a little faster than usual. He passed his hand across his brow, as though he could wipe away the thoughts behind it, and stared anxiously up and down the street, wishing Mr. Mannion would come.

*　　　*　　　*　　　*　　　*

The *Albion*, which brought Mark Harvey to Sydney, had brought, also, despatches from the Duke of Portland to the Governor. He read them seated in a chair drawn close to the fireplace, for last month's cold, wet weather had set up a rheumatic aching in his shoulder; his knitted brows, and the faint, nervous twitch of his mouth, however, were caused less by pain than by what he read.

Not that His Grace did not begin graciously. He expressed approbation of the measures taken for enforcing obedience; he assured the Governor that in all such measures he might count on the support of His Majesty's Government; he approved, too, of Hunter's arrangement for dividing the colony into districts with wardens, constables and magistrates to preserve order. But later the tone became a little austere.

"*I must next advert to the evils which you represent as arising from the speculation and traffic in grain, livestock, and spirits, into which the officers of Government, and particularly those of the Military Department, have entered, contrary, as you very properly observe, to the nature of their institution and the duties annexed to it. . . . With respect to the sale of spirits, it is certainly in your power, as it is your duty, to prohibit by the most positive orders, all officers of Government, civil or military, from selling any spirituous liquors to the convicts or settlers.*"

Hunter laid the pages on the table beside him and stared gloomily into the fire. A few dead leaves, still clinging to a bit of wood, burst into flame, and a sharp, smoky scent filled the room; a curious ruby-red gum boiled out from a cracked log, and trickled in a bubbling stream on to the hearth. The Governor's mind caught and struggled on those thorny words: "*it is certainly in your power.*"

He felt hemmed in on all sides by covert opposition and hostility. He had known for nearly a year now that when the time came for his own recall, Captain King was to replace him, and his lips thrust downward in a sardonic grimace as he wondered whether his successor would find the correction of abuses so simply "in his power." He was ready enough to be relieved of this tiresome office, but he had no wish to be recalled under censure, to spend his declining days in obscurity, to forfeit his chances of promotion. He was already beginning to be uneasy about his acquiescence in an arrangement made between the leading inhabitants of the colony, both civil and military, to combine in buying the merchandise offering on ships entering the port. He had been assured by the officers that such a course would be of immense benefit to the whole community, and he had believed them—perhaps because believing them was less arduous than opposing them. Yet he could not but be aware that it conflicted with the principle he had so often laid down, and which Portland had just so firmly endorsed—that it was no part of the duties of Government officers to engage in trade.

As for the sale of spirits . . . ! He stood up and lumbered across to his desk. His files of General Orders, he thought, with angry self-justification, were surely in themselves a record of his struggle against rum! He thumbed them over impatiently. First—far back in January of 1796—he had attempted to reason, to point out the danger of liquor *"the quality of which is of so poisonous a nature as must in a very short time ruin the good health of the settlement."*

But reason had gone unheeded. In March he had appealed for co-operation—with no better result. He had by then begun to realise that it was a species of traffic highly profitable to those whose co-operation he invited to suppress it. By June his sense of helplessness had lent a querulous note to a pronouncement that *"it is high time a trade so pernicious to individuals, and so ruinous to the prosperity of His Majesty's colony, should be put an end to."*

But it continued. He did not know how to prevent it. In July he had railed against *"the shocking consequences of the abominable practice of drinking to excess,"* and had known that scolding was even more futile than threats.

He stood staring down at the papers, his fingers fidgeting among them. What means had he of keeping order, he argued angrily to himself, but this very New South Wales Corps whose behaviour was his worst problem? Had he not sent home by David Collins a despatch in which he pointed out that far from being, as they should be, men of the very best and most orderly kind, these soldiers—recruited from the military prisons, characters regarded as not good enough for other regiments—were often more hardened in infamy than the worst of the convicts? Yet these soldiers of the rank and file were not by any means his most dangerous opponents. He was learning all the time, and learning bitterly. By August he was hinting in his home despatches that there were *"some persons in the colony (whose situations are probably respectable) extremely inimical to the necessary influence and authority of the civil power."*

To know it was one thing; how to deal with it? He was conscious at every turn of their machinations, but they were, as he had explained to Portland, neither so bold nor so imprudent as to oppose him openly; he fought with shadows. His isolation from the source of his authority depressed him. Months must elapse before his complaints, his warnings, his appeals could reach that source; more months before he could feel himself strengthened by its support. And too often it seemed to him that, in spite of his laborious explanations, his difficulties were not, and could not be, understood in so distant and different a world.

He toyed reluctantly with a dark doubt. Were they even trying to understand them? England was at war. Was a tiny colony on the other side of the globe of sufficient importance to claim more than a desultory attention from the Secretary of State at such a time? It had been founded for a special purpose—to drain off from the overcrowded prisons of England the felons whose presence there had become an embarrassment. But now the exigencies of war had temporarily modified this scheme of transportation. Did they know—or care—what new problems this fact presented to a Governor charged with administering a colony in accordance with set instructions, and a rigid policy? For this was intended to become in time not merely a penal settlement, but a community of peasant farmers. Expirees and emancipated convicts, as well as the comparatively few free settlers, were to be given small holdings. Yet with so irregular a flow of convicts and immigrants—sometimes thinning to a trickle, sometimes descending upon him in a deluge—the Governor could not know from one year to another for how many he must provide, how many he must victual, how many he would have available for public works, or how numerous would be the applicants for land.

Nor did they realise at home, apparently, that the close ring of monopoly, formed in the three years of the military administration, had already set the colony upon a road never intended in that inflexible official policy. Small farmers could not survive in the face of rising prices which enriched the few who had money available to monopolise commodities as soon as they arrived. There were two distinct and conflicting interests in the colony—that of the whole community, which Hunter was struggling in accordance with his instructions to mould as a peasantry; and that of a few private individuals who, obeying nothing but their own avarice, were well on the way to establishing themselves as large landowners. It was for him to care for the former against the opposition of the latter— among whom could be included almost every man of those who were ostensibly here to support him.

He sighed, still fiddling with his papers. He was an easy-going man, a man who, from choice, would take the line of least resistance, hoping that time, virtue, reason, better counsels, chance, piety—any abstraction, in fact, which might lift the burden from his own shoulders—would dispose of his problems. He was a humane man in so far as the customs of his time and his office allowed; and within the same conventional limits, a religious man. It was upon a Monday, he remembered, a Monday in December, 1796, that he had penned the Order that his eyes were now doubtfully reading. Mr. Johnson had been eloquent the day before at Divine Service. His discourse had dealt—as indeed it usually did—with the evils of drunkenness and profligacy, and the Governor, listening, had found it difficult to believe there could be hearts so stony and unregenerate as to ignore the fearful consequences of depravity which the clergyman described. That mood, he suspected, had coloured the next day's order.

"*The dangers attending too great an indulgence in the use of spirituous liquors are so truly melancholy that we would willingly and anxiously hope such distressing examples might kindle up in the minds of the inhabitants of this colony some sparks of reflection and remorse . . .*"

Vain hope! Now—two and a half years after those words had been written, he was no nearer to a solution. He took a sheet of paper from

the desk and returned wearily to his chair to make notes for the reply he
would send to Portland. He wrote slowly: *"Where I must depend for
the executing of my Orders on persons interested in their failure, how
little can I expect from such Orders."*

That was it. That was the core of the matter. What was his
machinery for enforcing orders? The military forces and the civil courts.
Who composed those forces—those courts? Was not the whole of his
little society tainted with this trafficking? He did not dare to ask himself
how many men there were among those whose positions made them
eligible for authority, who had never at any time disregarded the laws
they were being required to enforce. He did not dare to ask it; he
dragged his mind away from so dark a thought, fastened it upon simpler
matters, scribbled perfunctorily: *No cloathing by Barwell or Buffalo—
labouring men working in fields literally as naked as natives—inclement
weather has for lack of cloathing reduced people to great distress . . .*

A sound of distant shouting distracted his attention; he rose and went
across to the window.

Down by the water's edge near the foot of the Government House
garden, one of those brief, explosive brawls which often disturbed the
peace of the township, had flared out in a few insults, a few threats, a
few blows—and was now over. Two privates, he observed, and a native
seemed to have been the central figures; a handful of bystanders was
scattering, the soldiers had turned to walk up the hill with angry backward glances at the native, now limping down to the water with a fishnet
in his hand.

Hunter, too, followed that figure with his eyes, for it was one he knew
well. It was not often, now, that Bennilong was to be seen in the town,
but when he did appear it was usually in that condition which his unsteady
gait now proclaimed all too clearly. Drunk or sober, Hunter thought,
turning away from the window, he had always been a quarrelsome rogue
—touchy, self-assertive, unpredictable. He found, as he returned to his
chair, that the mere sight of the fellow had stirred in him a curious
regret, something like nostalgia, and he fell into a brown study, staring
at the jumping flames.

Somehow he could never see or hear of that black reprobate without
feeling himself transported back to the early days of the settlement when
Bennilong, as the first Governor's protégé, had seemed a symbol of the
relationship between the white men and the natives. There had been,
then, despite all hardships, some germ of unity. Hatreds, quarrels and
despair had not been unknown, but beneath them there had been a queer,
persistent feeling that all the diverse and hostile elements which this
adventure had brought together, might beat their way, finally, to a compromise, an understanding. Civil officers, marines, convicts, natives, had
then seemed but parts, however awkward and recalcitrant, of some pattern
which might one day absorb them all. Now the pattern was broken up,
the parts scattered. Now that drunken figure, stumbling bemusedly away
from the place where once it had so confidently swaggered, seemed to
Hunter an intolerable confirmation of his fear that what had once been

possible, was possible no longer. There was no united effort here; there was no attempt, however inept and fumbling, to find a common ground . . .

He felt lonely. His thoughts, still influenced by Bennilong, went back to the little group of men who had founded the settlement eleven and a half years ago. Perhaps it had been the possible danger and the certain strangeness of the land which had welded them together . . . ? He thought of the officers of the Marines who, in those days, had been called upon to perform many duties not strictly military, but upon whose energies the colony as a whole had had the urgent and the only claim. Now. . . . His mind paraded the officers of the New South Wales Corps for inspection, and found no comfort. Lieutenant-Colonel Paterson—its Commanding Officer since the departure of Colonel Grose over four years ago —was not even here; he had been away in England for nearly three years. Captain Abbott was in England too. Major Foveaux was very busy with his land grants. Captain Johnston seemed more concerned for the welfare of the Norfolk Island pines which he had planted on his estate, Annandale, than for the welfare of the colony. Land, land, land—they all wanted land . . . ! The junior officers too—all landowners first, traders second, and soldiers only as an afterthought . . .

And Macarthur . . .

The Governor drowned an involuntary expletive even from his own ears by turning it into a noisy clearing of his throat. There was no longer any room for service in this place, he thought bitterly—no room for anything but the mad scramble for advancement. If only the authorities would sanction the scheme he had more than once put forward for the establishment of a Government store, would not many of the evils of this private trading be circumvented? A store from which clothing, hardware, tools, sugar, soap, tobacco and such articles could be bought by the public, and paid for in grain or livestock . . . ? He must try that line again. He leaned forward over the table and made another note: *"recur to my letter on the subject of a public store on account of Govt.—observe that as 100% is least demanded by those who bring articles here for sale, and from that up to 1000%, conceive that such a store . . ."*

He looked up impatiently. The servant in the doorway said:

"Mr. Mannion asks permission to see Your Excellency."

Hunter threw his pen down and gestured at the smouldering logs.

"Mend the fire, and then show Mr. Mannion in."

He awaited his visitor with a certain pleasure. Mr. Mannion, a gentleman of birth and fortune, could be trusted to accord to him that ceremonious, unvarying deference to which his office as Governor entitled him. Hunter revered birth and position, and he was rather naïvely gratified that birth and position should treat him with a respect in which (being a simple man) he never detected an undertone of amused condescension. He greeted his guest cordially.

"You are very welcome, Mr. Mannion. I did not know you were in town." He added with a heavy attempt at humour: "We may, perhaps, use the phrase 'in town' when referring to our modest little settlement?"

Mr. Mannion bowed, and made, as usual, the perfect rejoinder.

"Under your wise guidance, Sir, it is fast becoming worthy of that title."

Hunter, already conscious of a warming return of self-esteem, said hospitably:

"Pray be seated. May I have the pleasure of your company at dinner, Sir?"

"Your Excellency is most kind. I'm engaged, however, to reach Parramatta this evening, and I must be on my way by midday. It is always my pleasure as well as my duty to pay my respects and enquire after Your Excellency's health when my business brings me to Sydney. To-day I have also to express my gratitude, Sir, for the notice you have been pleased to take of the young man who has come out to act as tutor to my sons."

"Ah, yes!" Hunter nodded benignly. "Mr. . . . Mr. . . . ?"

"Mr. Harvey."

"To be sure—Mr. Harvey. The name escaped me for a moment. A worthy young man, I think, Mr. Mannion. I trust he will fulfil his duties to your satisfaction. Your farm prospers, Sir?"

"In the main things go along very well. There is one matter which I feel bound to bring to your attention, however. I have reason to suppose that my convicts are securing liquor . . ."

Hunter's face clouded suddenly; was there no respite? Mr. Mannion continued:

"I have them working on a new field, Sir, felling timber and clearing it from the ground, and when I went down to inspect their progress recently I observed one of them lying on the edge of the field. My overseer informed me he was ill, but . . ." he shrugged eloquently, ". . . when I had approached no nearer than the width of this room I was satisfied that he was in a disgraceful state of intoxication."

"You questioned the overseer?"

"I dismissed him on the spot, Sir. He had lied to me. He was a fellow I had picked up here—not one of my own men brought from Ireland. He denied, of course, all knowledge of how the man had come by the spirits, but I conceive it my duty, Sir, to inform you that there are rumours abroad of an illicit still operating somewhere between my property and that of the settlers farther down the river. The convict I sent to Parramatta, where he came before Mr. Marsden, and has suffered for his misbehaviour. Your Excellency's well-known determination," he added suavely, "to stamp out this evil, has encouraged me to feel that you would not wish to be kept in ignorance of such insolent disobedience to your repeated orders."

Hunter said gloomily:

"I am indebted to you." His eyes wandered to his page of notes, his fingers reached out and tapped it nervously. "This whole business of the sale of liquor, Mr. Mannion, is causing me great concern. Very great concern, Sir."

Mr. Mannion remained attentive, polite, and unresponsive.

"You can hardly conceive," the Governor went on, "the difficulties I meet with—and I regret to say from the very quarters where I might be supposed to seek support." His guest, recalling how often he had heard just such words from Captain Macarthur, kept his smile to himself, and suppressed a yawn. "At the Nepean," Hunter was continuing, "you are far removed from our troubles, yet you cannot but know how I'm opposed. It would be enough," he exclaimed with sudden warmth, "to be charged with the supervision of convicts, the most infamous, degraded and intractable set of characters under the sun, without . . ."

But Mr. Mannion had no intention of being embroiled. He knew how to interrupt so smoothly and adeptly that he could carry forward into his own remarks that part of an unfinished sentence which suited him, and jettison the rest. He did not want to hear a diatribe against the officers, but it was quite safe to deflect the conversation to convicts.

"You use a kindlier word, Sir, than the one which has been much in my mind of late. 'Intractable,' you say. 'Seditious' is the word I should employ! And since you have introduced the subject . . ." he observed with amusement that Hunter, slightly bewildered, was wondering whether he really had introduced it, and continued imperturbably: "I will confess that the number of such ill-disposed persons that have come to the colony in recent years causes me grave disquiet."

"With reason, Mr. Mannion." Hunter rose and stood with his back to the fire. "I have not been blind to the dangers, I assure you. I have repeatedly made representations in my despatches to the effect that if a disproportionate number of such people are sent out, they will infect the rest with their wild and lawless notions."

"My concern," Mannion told him, "is not unaffected by the fact that many of these desperate characters are my countrymen. The tide of rebellion has risen so high in Ireland, Sir, that a loyal Irishman must be aghast to imagine its consequences. The lower classes are seized by fantastic notions—fathered in France, of course—of a state in which the poor shall become rich, all shall wear silk and eat venison, there shall be neither rents, tithes nor taxes . . ." He made an impatient and contemptuous gesture. "Such visionaries would be laughable, Sir, were it not that they are prepared to support their clamours with excesses of the most outrageous nature. If this colony is to be made a repository of all such turbulent and dissatisfied people—of "Defenders," and "Friends of Liberty," and "United Irishmen" and the like—of madmen who seek anarchy under the guise of reform, of all infatuated dreamers who conceive impossible Utopias—then, Your Excellency, England may become a more tranquil place, Ireland may become less tumultuous, but New South Wales, Sir, will become a place compared with which the nethermost parts of Hell could be called Arcadian!"

The Governor blinked. He had said all this himself to Portland, but not quite so eloquently. He nodded acquiescence, and his guest, having steered the interview past the threatening shoals of the particular into the smooth waters of generality, and transformed a risky conversation about respectable people into a safe conversation about rascals, rose to take his leave.

"My comfort, Sir," he concluded urbanely, "is that we have at the helm a man of broad vision and immovable purpose. I don't doubt that you will deal firmly with this and all other situations as they arise."

His words paid tribute to Hunter, his bow to Hunter's position as the King's representative. He left the Governor still standing in front of the hearth, and feeling a warmth and comfort for which the fire was only partly responsible.

*　　　　*　　　　*　　　　*　　　　*

Mr. Harvey at last saw, with relief, his employer striding towards him. But he was not alone. Trotting as his heels, rather as a docile little dog might trot, was a thin, native girl-child who looked barely eight years old, clad in a shapeless blue frock, and carrying a bundle tied in a red handkerchief. Mr. Mannion looked pleased with himself, as if his business had gone well. He greeted Mark with genial condescension.

"I fear we have kept you waiting, Mr. Harvey. If so, I beg you to blame this small creature . . ." As he turned to indicate the child with a wave of his hand, she seemed to shrink—not to shrink away, but somehow to diminish in size, to contract, to fade, as if life had taught her as it teaches some insects, that safety may lie in inconspicuousness. Mr. Mannion continued:

"I have had some difficulty in finding her. My housekeeper requires the assistance of a young native girl to be trained for certain domestic duties—those we have taken from the Nepean tribes have proved completely useless. They vanish like smoke, and return to their savage life in the woods."

To Mark's already disturbing accumulation of strange experiences was now added that of feeling himself somehow in the same category as a small, black child. Were they not both new employees of the same master? Were they not embarking together on a new life in new surroundings? He wondered, looking down at the child's face, in which only her bright eyes betrayed nervousness, whether she felt as tense, as anxious as he did himself. Mr. Mannion was studying the diminutive figure beside him with a slight frown.

"She is rather smaller than I had intended. But she has the advantage of having been reared from infancy among white people, and she comes with the recommendation of the good Mrs. Johnson." He added explanatorily: "Of course these people are normally incorrigible thieves, and quite inconceivably dirty in their personal habits."

Mark said:

"This one, at all events, looks clean, Sir."

Mr. Mannion nodded complacently.

"It was what finally decided me to take her. Time, after all, will remedy her excessive youth." He laughed appreciatively at his own wit, and Mark produced a dutiful smile. "She is a protégée of Governor Phillip's—the daughter of a certain black rascal called Bennilong, whom he took into his favour during his term of office. His kindness proved misplaced, for the fellow turned out badly; a drunken, troublesome rogue. But it appears that the Governor recommended the child to the protection of Governor Hunter, who has consequently felt himself in some degree responsible. During the last year or two she has been employed by various respectable women in the town, so we may hope . . ." he glanced again, not very hopefully, at the small figure, "that she has acquired some civilised habits, and perhaps even some Christian principles. Her name is Dilboong."

He looked at Mark's modest baggage standing in readiness on the step. "These are your belongings, Mr. Harvey? We may set out, then. A boat is at the wharf, yonder, and my men should be awaiting us there."

He strode off briskly across the shore, the child scuttling at his heels. Mark, hastily gathering up his two bulging bags, hurried after him, trying not to limp.

    *   *   *   *   *

Dilboong, riding pillion behind Mr. Harvey along the road between Parramatta and Toongabbee, peered round that young gentleman's back so that she could keep her eyes on the summit of the hill ahead. There had been a number of such hills, and—travelling thus into the unknown— she had mistrusted each as they came to it and held her breath as they neared its top, having no idea what might lie beyond, but fearing because she had never yet in her short life journeyed more than a mile or two from Sydney.

To Bennilong's daughter the land seemed less hers than the white men's. She had opened her eyes to life not in a bark hut, but in their hospital. She had lived in their houses, knowing no other kind of habitation, and yet conscious that she did not belong there as they did. Already there was at least one member of the race of Murri who saw herself as an intruder into their life, and had no conception of them as intruders into hers.

She did not know where she was going, or why; the Bereewolgal had always disposed of her. Her fear was not of them, but of the journey, and of the great beast upon which she rode. Some atavistic instinct told her that to leave one's own towri was no light matter—but if one must leave it one should go on foot, as part of some tribal migration, and not alone, casually, as though one place were no different from another.

Yet although they had travelled so far, the world looked much the same except that there was no more harbour. Each hilltop spread out before her anxious eyes the same endless vista of undulating country, its grass winter-brown, its dull green trees always different and yet always familiar, and the rough road going on and on to disappear over yet another hill. She grew tired and sleepy, for last night she had been too bewildered and alarmed to sleep soundly. In the house where they had stayed the servants had been very busy preparing the supper when they arrived, and Dilboong had been set to washing dishes and doing small tasks about the kitchen. When all the bustle was over, she had been given a plate with some scraps of food on it, and a piece of bread, and she had crept out into the dusk to eat it alone.

She was always more at ease out of doors. There was a step upon which she could have sat, but years of familiarity with stools and chairs had not taught her to be comfortable seated above ground level. She preferred the earth, and squatted there with her bare legs doubled beneath her, eating hungrily, and licking her fingers when the platter was empty. She murmured to herself incessantly, for she liked words, and her greatest pleasure was to fit them together into long, rambling tales, or into short phrases which she could repeat to a rhythm beaten out on her knee. She was happy enough for the moment, her hunger appeased, chanting to herself; but when the dusk gave way to dark she became frightened. She had never heard the tales of her people, nor learned of the evil spirit who prowls at night beyond the glare of the camp-fires, but instinctively her fearful eyes sought the comfort of the lighted windows, and she stole into the house again through the kitchen door. Here there was more bustle going on, and more dishes to be washed, and by the time she had finished the tasks that were set her it was late, and she was very sleepy. The two servants whose quarters she was to share had quarrelled over her. One declared she would not sleep with a black heathen, and vowed the outhouse would afford the dirty savage better shelter than she deserved; but the other opposed this view with such shrill and profane violence that Dilboong, standing on one leg and hanging her head, feared her champion almost as much as her enemy. In the end room was grudgingly made for her on the end of the bed, and she was even given a shawl to cover herself, so she had curled into as small a space as possible, and slept fitfully till the dawn aroused her.

*   *   *   *   *

Mark rode silently. It was not for him to initiate a conversation, but to answer respectfully such questions, observations and comments as Mr. Mannion saw fit to make. They had been few, and Mark was the better pleased, for he had much to look at, and still more to think about. They had lodged the previous night at the house of the Rev. Mr. Marsden, and Mark, captured by the clergyman's wife, had been treated to a homily which perplexed rather than reassured him.

"You may perhaps find your life somewhat solitary at the Nepean, Mr. Harvey," she had told him earnestly, "but believe me, solitude is to be preferred for a young man to the kind of society in which you would be in danger of finding yourself if you remained in the settlements. Your dear mother has been spared to you, Sir?"

"Er—yes, Madam, I am happy to say that she was well when I left England."

"Her thoughts and prayers will be always with you, I don't doubt. It is well for her peace of mind that she cannot fully comprehend the kind of place to which you have come. I beg you to be warned by me, Mr. Harvey, and to exercise the greatest care and discretion in choosing your acquaintance. Mr. Marsden, I assure you, will be always at your service should you require advice in spiritual or in worldly matters."

Mark, somewhat taken aback, had stammered politely:

"You are very kind, Madam—er—I'm greatly obliged—but I must own that I have so far been received everywhere with much kindness . . ."

She lifted a plump forefinger.

"An outward kindliness, Sir, can cloak the most shocking depravity. I say no more. It is no subject for a gentlewoman. Yet, as a mother, I should be doing less than my duty did I not warn you. There are strange—*very* strange—characters at large in this colony."

Mark, remembering Mr. Palmer, coloured slightly. He was relieved to see his hostess withdraw, and to be summoned by Mr. Marsden to a seat nearer the fire.

"You have a new neighbour, I believe," Mr. Mannion was saying from his chair on the opposite side of the hearth. "I'm told Mr. d'Arcy Wentworth has recently been appointed to Parramatta."

Mr. Marsden pursed his lips and replied austerely:

"I cannot say that I find it a matter for rejoicing. The manner in which Mr. Wentworth arrived in this country does not prompt me to regard him very favourably."

Mr. Mannion shrugged.

"Come, come, my dear Sir! He was acquitted of the charges that were laid against him. It so happens that I myself, being at leisure in London at the time, attended his trial at the Old Bailey. He and I," he added reminiscently, "reached Port Jackson almost simultaneously in 1790."

"Nevertheless, Sir," Mr. Marsden answered stiffly, "despite what you say—and upon which I offer no comment, being ever disinclined to give ear to rumour—I cannot regard Mr. Wentworth as a desirable addition to our community." He abandoned a subject which was evidently distasteful to him, and added:

"We are to have the pleasure, this evening, of a visit from the good Mr. Cover. Mr. Cover, Sir," he explained to Mark, who quickly withdrew his gaze from Mr. Mannion's face, over which there had passed a swift shadow of *ennui*, "is a missionary who was compelled to flee with his fellows last year from the island of Otaheite—in consequence of the violence of the natives. I fear he has found this so-called Christian society no less plunged in wickedness than the heathen one he left. You will find his conversation both interesting and elevating."

Interesting Mark had certainly found it for a time; but since it concerned, during the first hour or so, nothing but the details of the recent murder of his colleague, Brother Clode, he could not regard it as elevating. Nor, as it passed from this instance of specific villainy to the subject of villainy in general, was it so remarkable for elevation as for eloquence. Mr. Cover, Mark learned without surprise, was in the habit of delivering lectures. The one which he delivered last night which reduced Mr. Marsden to a hypnotised silence, valiantly punctuated with weighty nods of agreement, Mr. Mannion to glassy-eyed boredom, and Mark to a swimming sleepiness. He had felt himself nodding, and straightened guiltily to hear Mr. Mannion slip a wily comment into one of the missionary's pauses for breath:

"You are well pleased with your grant of land, Mr. Cover?"

From that moment, Mark realised now, no one had been bored or sleepy. Mr. Cover's harangue had been succeeded by the most lively and animated conversation, to which he himself had listened with breathless interest. Moralities had been forgotten; the discussion now was of more mundane things—crops, soil, livestock, wages, climate, prices, labour. One word had predominated—a refrain which sang in Mark's mind now as he rode, and made him see the countryside about him not just as country-side, but as acres—virgin acres, ownerless acres, acres that clutched at men's minds, and stirred them to avid desire.

Land—land—land . . .

Land not inherited, not even to be bought, but to be acquired by a scratch of the Governor's pen! How much of it? No one knew. Mark's eyes went to the mountains ahead, and he recalled last night's tales of expeditions and failures, conjectures of what might—or might not—lie behind those hills which looked so low, so gentle, so softly blue, and which had yet proved so forbidding.

"It is a matter for Government," Mr. Mannion had said.

Mr. Cover laid the tips of his fingers together and nodded.

"Doubtless, doubtless. Yet the reports so far have been discouraging."

"Most discouraging. I heard from the lips of Mr. Dawes himself, who made the first attempt many years ago, that nothing was to be found but endless crags and chasms, inconceivably rocky and unfertile. Paterson, you remember, endeavoured to penetrate the country in boats up the Grose River, but was forced to abandon the attempt. Later on—in the following year, was it not?—Mr. Hacking met with no better success. Even Mr. Bass, bold and indefatiguable explorer as he is, was defeated."

"I am satisfied," remarked Mr. Cover, "that where Mr. Bass failed others would have small hope of success. I was assured that he scaled the most formidable cliffs—having his hands and feet equipped with iron hooks for that purpose—and caused himself to be lowered into virtually bottomless ravines; and all in vain. Ought we not," he enquired piously, "to regard the lack of reward for such hardihood as the clearest indication by Divine Providence that we should be content with what has already been so bountifully bestowed?"

"That fellow Wilson," Mr. Mannion interposed, "who made an expedition only last year, claimed to have penetrated a hundred miles to the south-west. Who knows? For myself . . ." he bowed with gentle irony to Mr. Cover, ". . . I am content to await the pleasure of Providence. In my view there is ample land this side of the mountains to serve the colony many a year."

And indeed, Mark thought, remembering this conversation, there seemed to be plenty of it, for a name had been barely mentioned last night before the land its owner had acquired, or hoped to acquire, was men-tioned too. Not only settlers, but soldiers, sailors, doctors, clergymen, missionaries, tradesmen and civil officers all wanted land—and apparently all got it. Not in paltry roods and perches, either, but a hundred or more acres at a time. Even Mr. Cover and his fellow-missionaries, Mr. Oakes and Mr. Hassall, had not been too preoccupied with Heaven to secure for themselves a hundred acres each of earth. To Mark it had sounded as if the world were being given away, for the tales last night had not only been of abortive inland expeditions, but of voyages along an interminable coastline, so that he had gathered an impression of a country so huge that property might some day be measured in square miles. He felt queerly exhilarated; here was a spaciousness that was exciting. He was roused from a daydream of fabulous estates of his own by his employer's voice:

"I must make you acquainted with your surroundings, Mr. Harvey. Ahead of us there, to the left, is Prospect Hill—excellent country. Beyond Toongabbee the road branches off in that direction . . ." he flourished his whip to the north-west, ". . . towards the Hawkesbury settlement."

"You consider the country promises well for agriculture, Sir?"

"In parts, decidedly. Our last harvest was poor—and small wonder with the drought we suffered, and the whole countryside ablaze with fire. However, the recent rains promise us better fortune this season."

"No doubt," Mark suggested diffidently, "the more fertile parts are already settled, Sir?"

Mannion shrugged.

"Who knows the extent or possibilities of this land? There are those who hold that it is a veritable Canaan, and others who maintain that beyond this coastal strip lies nothing but barren desolation. For myself, I am content for the present with what I see and hold. Yet I'm disposed to believe, Mr. Harvey, that without going beyond the already explored boundaries, there are thousands upon thousands of acres which will repay cultivation. In some neighbourhoods the soil is highly fertile. Thirty bushels of wheat to the acre may be expected in a good season. Upon my own property I grow both wheat and Indian corn, and vegetables of all kinds in the greatest profusion. My orchard already bears plentifully."

Mark's glance at him was tinged with envy and admiration. An exciting and unfamiliar sensation had invaded that sober acceptance of his respectable but modest station in life which training had implanted in him. He was beginning to succumb to the magic of a virgin land, ripe for plundering. He was seeing himself not as the retiring lad he had always been—modest, shy, content to be unnoticed—but as a man rather like this fine gentleman who rode beside him, full of the confidence of possessions and authority, mature, handsome, and successful . . .

Mr. Mannion announced:

"We are approaching the township of Toongabbee. You are fatigued, Mr. Harvey?"

"No, Sir, thank you." Mark looked about him. Here were signs of cultivation again; a score or so of convicts, almost naked, were clearing a field to the left of the road. At a distance some were felling trees; nearer, a log was attached to a long pole dragged by six men abreast, and Mark could see the sweat-streaked skin stretch tight over their ribs as they strained and strove. He asked:

"Is it a large town—er—settlement, Sir?"

Mr. Mannion smiled indulgently.

"You will find it very small, I think. The total population of the colony, so I'm informed, is not much over five thousand souls—and of these about half are at Sydney, and something over a thousand at the

Hawkesbury settlements. We are a small community. How small I am continually reminded when I reflect upon the proportion of felons and disaffected people. To say nothing of the savages."

Mark digested this, curiously conscious of one very small, meek savage behind him. Feeling his expansive mood contract a little, he enquired:

"Have you had any trouble, Sir—from either quarter?"

"I have been fortunate—so far. Yet I don't deceive myself . . . ah! they are at work upon this bridge at last . . . !"

The few scattered buildings of the settlement were in sight now, and fifty yards ahead a gang of convicts was repairing the rough, wooden bridge by which the road crossed a small stream. Mr. Mannion, to whom convicts were no more to be regarded than the stumps of felled trees by the wayside, rode ahead, continuing his conversation over his shoulder as they approached: "No, I don't deceive myself. A country populated with rogues and heathens requires an unceasing vigilance on the part of those in authority." As his horse picked its way down the sloping mud bank, splashed through the shallow water and up the other side, he added: "We shall halt for a few minutes, Mr. Harvey. I have a message to deliver for the worthy Mr. Cover; he proposes to preach here next Sunday . . ."

Mark, following and glancing at the convicts as they passed, felt what remained of his mood of optimism shrivel under the dark bitterness of their stare. He heard the missionary's name muttered to the accompaniment of a few blasphemous words; a smothered, sardonic laugh was cut off short by a shouted order from the armed overseer. He rode on quickly without looking back; he had never known before how ugly could be the sound of laughter.

Near the military guard-house he dismounted with his employer, and lifted Dilboong to the ground; she remained exactly where he placed her, moving not so much as a toe. Mr. Mannion, leaving them beside the tethered horses, went up to speak to the soldier on duty. Mark stared round him curiously at the few thatched and whitewashed huts, at a dog scratching fleas in the sunshine, at a couple of ragged children who peeped and pointed at Dilboong from behind a sagging fence—and then stiffened suddenly.

The sound was one which, though he had never heard anything like it before, seemed somehow shockingly familiar. Not quite a scream or a shout; something more like a howl such as a mortally wounded animal might make, and yet dreadfully proclaiming its human origin by an intermixture of speech. There were words in it; what words Mark could not tell, but the sound of them was defiance, agony, hatred, denunciation. The savagery of their protest rent the air, but Mr. Mannion and the soldier talked on, unperturbed; the children went on peeping and whispering as if deaf; only the dog stopped scratching for a moment and whimpered faintly, and Dilboong showed the whites of her eyes in a frightened glance over her shoulder.

Mr. Mannion came briskly down the steps, but instead of returning to the horses, set off along the lane between the huts in the direction of

the soldier's pointing finger. In the direction, too, whence that sound
had come. Mark, shaken but nervously inquisitive, followed him. As
he came round the corner of a building, he found himself almost jostled
by a group of men carrying something away, but his startled attention
was on the ground at his feet, for it was spattered with blood. His first
confused thought was that they had been slaughtering a pig, and that he
must have imagined the sound of words in that terrible shriek. He
raised his eyes with a strange, slow reluctance—as if some wiser and
worldier self were warning him—to confront a bloodstained post, and a
man who walked away after the others, shaking the knotted thongs of
his cat so that a few crimson drops splashed suddenly and horribly on
Mark's carefully polished boot. But he could not take his eyes, now, from
a small, circular hollow on the ground near the post, for it was full of
blood. He stared at it incredulously for a few seconds, and then turned
to stare after the flogger, strolling away unconcernedly, his left foot dyed
red . . .

Mark stumbled back round the corner and collapsed on to one of a
pile of boxes stacked against the wall. His head was swimming with
nausea, and he took it in his hands and leaned his elbows on his knees,
and shut his eyes so that they should not see his bloodstained boot. It
was less than an hour ago that this land—so wide and inviting under its
clear, golden sunlight, had stirred him to enthusiasm; now it filled him
with horror.

Land . . .

These alluring acres of land must be cultivated. One cannot cultivate
a hundred acres quite alone. One must have labour. Convicts were
labour. Land must be cleared, dug, harrowed, sown, tended and reaped
by men such as those dark-faced, thin-bodied, semi-naked, bitter-voiced
men he had seen by the stream—or that other whom he had barely
glimpsed being carried away . . .

He opened his eyes hazily. He leapt to his feet and hurried, almost
running, back to the horses. He knelt and pulled a handful of grass,
tried to wipe his boot, and found his fingers sticky with blood. He threw
the grass down and turned with a feeling near to panic in his heart to
find the round, solemn eyes of Dilboong regarding him. He stared back
at her. Felons and savages. As they had been joined in Mr. Mannion's
condemnation, so now they were joined in Mark's agonised and guilty
flood of pity. He stammered, hardly knowing what he said:

"Are you . . . do you want . . . would you like a drink, Dilboong?"

He almost knew that he was offering it not to her but to whatever
was left of the man they had carried away from that place of torture.
He almost knew that it was less water as a drink that he was offering,
than water as a symbol of compassion. Her eyes brimmed over suddenly
and her face puckered; she gave the ghost of a nod.

He looked round desperately. He did not know where to get water,
but it had become a matter of profound necessity that he should not fail
to provide what he had offered; he could have brought no more passionate
determination to the task of procuring a coach and six for her than to the

task of finding her´ a few mouthfuls of cold water. The two children
were still peering round the fence. He called to them:

"I want some water for this child . . ."

They giggled; the boy made a face. The rage that boiled up in Mark
was not really against the children, but he took a threatening step towards
them and shouted furiously:

"Be off with you—bring me a cup of water immediately!"

They vanished into a nearby hut. It was the girl who emerged alone,
sidling apprehensively towards him, carrying a brimming pannikin. As
he gave it to Dilboong Mark was shocked to see that his hand was shaking
so that the water spilled. She drank it thirstily, staring at him over the
brim of the cup, and he thought vaguely that her great, black eyes were
beautiful—and that he was, after all, tired.

Mr. Mannion's voice, with a note of irony in it, startled him.

"You are quite ready, Mr. Harvey?"

He answered mechanically:

"Yes, Sir."

"Then we need waste no more time."

"No, Sir." But still he did not move, and Mannion said testily:

"What ails you, Mr. Harvey? Are you indisposed?"

The young man came to himself with a start.

"No—no, Sir. It was . . . I witnessed a . . . a punishment . . ."

"There have been two floggings this morning, I understand. You
must realise that you have come to a penal colony where corrective
measures must be severe if they are to be effective. Lift the child up, if
you please, and we shall be off again."

They rode towards the declining sun. Mark looked at the wide,
waiting country now with a kind of shrinking resistance. He did not
want land any longer. Never, never, he thought, so long as he lived in
this terrible colony, would he feel that lure again.

*   *   *   *   *

Rather more than a year ago Patrick Mannion had begun to keep a
journal. It was common—even customary—he had observed, for gentlemen to keep journals, and his father had not only approved, but had
procured for him just before they returned from Ireland a handsome
leather-bound book with the word JOURNAL stamped upon its cover
in gold letters.

Patrick's education had been sketchy. A few lessons with the Reverend
Mr. Johnson when they had lived at Sydney, a few more at Parramatta from
a young man who had not, however, remained long enough in the colony
to impart any great store of knowledge to his pupil, and a little desultory
instruction during his visit to Ireland, had been all his formal teaching.
Since their return there had been no more lessons until Mr. Harvey's
arrival three months ago; but when the ships came in there was usually
something on board for Mr. Mannion—furniture, table-linen, agricultural
tools, clothing, and, not infrequently, books. These books were the cargo
in which Patrick was interested, and from them he learned. His spelling,
indeed, was odd, but the same might have been said of many illustrious

persons, including the Governor himself, so Patrick had addressed himself
to his task without misgivings.   He had begun by inscribing his name very
carefully upon the front page:

"PATRICK JOHN FRANCIS MANNION,
BELTRASNA, NEW SOUTH WALES,
MAY 23rd, 1798."

Beneath this he had written:
"*Haveing just returned from Ireland with my Papa, Mr. Stephen
Mannion, in the 'Barwell,' and haveing been presented by him with this
Journal, I shall write in it of my expeariences in this Coleny where I have
now resided for eight years.*"
For the first page his pen had flown:
"*I came to this Coleny with my Parents when I was but six years old,
but my brother Miles was not born then.   A very sad Circumstance ocured
soon after our arrival, and that was the Death of my dear Mama.   I do
not remember very much about our Life in Sydney, for I was quite young
at that Time, but I remember some things, and one is seeing the convicts
landed from the ships, and one is talking to Mr. Dawes, and I also remember haveing Lessons with Mr. Johnson, but most of all I remember
Johnny . . .*"
He had paused then, for a moment, a little astonished to discover how
clearly, through all that had happened since, he did remember Johnny,
and how strongly there still lived in him the awe he had always felt for
that rebellious, self-sufficient, incomprehensible child who depended on no
one, asked no quarter and gave none, ran away and lived with the black
people, was haled back to the settlement, fought, stole, lied, cursed,
bartered and intrigued, and saved up his ill-gotten money to . . .
Even now Patrick felt bewildered when he thought of that secret
hoard of Johnny's which he had once inadvertently discovered.   Even
now he remembered the shock, the embarrassed incredulity with which he
had heard Johnny's confession of an ambition which that money was one
day to realise for him.   "*I'm goin' to be gentry, like you!*"
Rather more slowly, Patrick had continued:
"*Johnny was a convict child, and his mother, Ellen, is my father's
Housekeeper, and he knew some of the Indians, and ran away to live with
them.   But he was brought Back.   He was not a Respecktable kind of boy,
because the convicts are not Respecktable, but once he got bitten by ten
soldier ants and he did not cry, so I think he was brave, and sometimes
he would play Games with me, though my Papa did not think him a
proper Companion for me because he was a convict.   Of course my Papa
was quite right, but Johnny knew some good games to play, and other
Things, though he did not know his Station in Life.*"
That, he had found, was as near as he could come to referring in his
Journal to Johnny's incredible ambition.   But he had confided to its pages
something which he had not confided to anyone else.
"*For some time before we came to live here at the Nepean we resided
at Parramatta, and Johnny said to me once that he would like to go to*

see the Nepean the next time my Papa went, because my Papa was at that time prepairing to build our House here. So I asked Papa if I might go with him, because I thought if I were Permitted to go Johnny might be too, but Papa said No, it was too far, and I told Johnny we could not Go. Because at that time my Papa had no horses in the Coleny, and it was a long way from Parramatta to where my Papa's Property is. But I think that perhaps Johnny did go, all the same, because he Dissapeared, and nobody has ever seen him since, and everybody thinks that he must have died from Hunger or been killed by the Indians, but I think the Indians would not kill him because of what he told me about them when he lived with them before. So I think that Johnny may be still alive because he was clever and looked after himself like a grown Man, although he was only eight years old at that time, but my Papa says that the convict children are old in Wickedness."

Now, upon a late September evening, Patrick had turned back to this year-old entry, and was staring at it with a worried frown. He had settled himself to write at a table in the little room where Ellen sat sewing in the lamplight. Outside he could hear his brother playing in the gathering dusk with Ellen's children, Andy and Maria, and he knew—though he heard no shouts from her—that the little black girl, Dilboong, was there too, silent, solemn, following the handsome and masterful Miles, as faithful and unobtrusive as his shadow.

Patrick turned back to his new page, upon which he had written, as yet, only a few words. His glance from them to Ellen's impassive face was troubled. He had never been able to feel quite at ease with this strange woman. She was a convict—or an ex-convict, for her time was now expired—and as such, an inferior. Yet his memory of his own mother was vague, and Ellen had been Miles' foster mother, and had given to himself such woman-care as he had known since his mother's death. She had given him no love, nor would he have expected it—though he sometimes thought that her eyes and voice softened for Miles —but she had attended to his needs. She conformed, as he did himself, to what they both regarded as a natural line of cleavage between her social status and that of her protector and his family; she observed the rules laid down for her. She was officially Mr. Mannion's housekeeper, whatever she might be in fact, and as such she occupied the housekeeper's room while the large drawing-room, its hearth cold, remained unused save when the master inhabited it.

As for the children, they accepted in theory and constantly violated in practice the arrangements decreed by the god-like authority of Mr. Mannion. It was understood that Maria and Andy—and, lately, Dilboong —should keep themselves to the back parts of the house, where Miles was occasionally permitted to join them when in need of companionship. But it was also understood that Miles was a superior being, whose condescension must not be presumed upon. Miles never dreamed of questioning this convention, but having been reared in the wilderness, he was sufficiently unspoiled not to suffer, or make others suffer for his privileges. He lorded it over the other children less because his birth gave him the power to do so than because he was by nature lordly. He played with them—or, more accurately, allowed them minor rôles in the terrific and extravagant pageants, battles, feats of arms, and romantic adventures which his fertile imagination spawned incessantly, and in which he was consistently a central figure quite as satisfying to them as to himself. He failed, as they did, to see anything odd in the fact that his clothes were handsome and expensive while theirs were poor and ragged; that he should have a tutor, while for them learning was presumably unnecessary; that he, Patrick, their father and Mr. Harvey should eat with some ceremony in the dining-room, while Ellen and her children ate with none at all in the kitchen, and Dilboong, on the doorstep or in the yard, munched the scraps that were left.

All that was as far beyond their comprehension as it was beyond their control. What mattered was that sometimes Mr. Mannion went away, and then, by a subtle consent, never mentioned, or even consciously considered, all rules relaxed. The scion of an ancient Irish family, the children of a convict, and a small, black, heathen girl ranged at will about the house and fields. Ellen saw, heard, and held her peace. Mr. Harvey saw, heard, wondered, hesitated, and finally decided to remain blind and deaf. Patrick himself, still anchored to a childhood which had also known its small subterfuges, took it for granted, and to-night made his own gesture of rebellion by preferring the little lamplit room with its litter of needlework on the table and Ellen stitching beside it, to the solitude of the more formal rooms.

Yet he was almost sorry that he had done so. He found it difficult to write what he must write, with Ellen there. It was as if he feared that the very sound of his pen scratching on the paper would be a voice that she could overhear . . .

She was Johnny's mother, he said to himself. His *mother*. It seemed monstrous to know what he knew, and to tell it, not to her, but to the unresponsive pages of his Journal. He looked down again, furtively, at the words he had already written.

Sept. 26th, 1799.

"*Yesterday I had a very astonishing Expearience which has greatly disturbed my Mind . . .*"

His disturbed mind turned it over anxiously. The day before yesterday, just as his father and Mr. Harvey were about to leave for Sydney on business, a man had arrived at Beltrasna on horseback with a message from the Governor. His Excellency had already set out from Parramatta upon an expedition to inspect the herd of wild cattle up the river, and if Mr. Mannion should feel himself inclined to join the party he would be very welcome. Directions followed as to the place of rendezvous, and Mr. Mannion, knitting his brows in perplexity, had looked at last at his tall son, and seen a solution. He was unwilling to decline so gracious an invitation, but even less willing to defer the important business which awaited him in Sydney; Patrick, he thought, could well deputise for him. And so Patrick, nothing loth, had set out with the servant, had duly fallen in with the Governor's party, had conveyed the ceremonious message of regret entrusted to him by his father, and had then proceeded to enjoy the expedition hugely.

They had camped that night, and crossed the river yesterday in the early morning, and there had been exciting moments when they encountered a herd of about twenty cattle, so fierce and wild that only for the yapping and snapping of the dogs which accompanied them, they would have been attacked. A few natives who had joined them promptly climbed trees. The cattle, harassed by the dogs, had at last fled into the surrounding hills—all but a young bull calf which, perhaps mistaking the horses for its familiar herd, had persistently run between them, bellowing loudly in its confusion and distress. Then one of the party, fearing that its clamour would cause the cattle to return, put a bullet through its head, and they had all feasted magnificently on roast veal. After that they had crossed the river again, and explored the country some more; and when the time came for the Governor to return, and for Patrick to take his leave and make his way back to Beltrasna, the boy had felt for the first time that he was really a participant in this strange adventure of exploring and settling a new country.

Having been genially patted upon the shoulder by the Governor and bidden to convey His Excellency's compliments and regards to his father, he had ridden to the crest of a little hill to watch the party out of sight, and then turned his horse's head northward towards home. Mostly the way was easier at some distance from the river; but in the late afternoon he had found himself upon its banks again, and dismounted for a drink. He had wandered downstream a hundred yards or so, and sat for a while with his back against a great rock, resting and re-living the events of the day. He was not accustomed to camping out of doors upon the bare ground, and he had had but little sleep the previous night. That, together with the excitement of the expedition and the long day in the open air, had tired him, and he was feeling drowsy when a sudden movement on the opposite bank startled him wide awake.

For a moment or two he was not sure that he really was awake. There were five natives—three on the bank, and two in a rough bark canoe. Had the canoe come from up or down the river? He had heard nothing; he must, surely, have been asleep. Perhaps he was asleep still, or half-asleep, for he had thought . . .

The canoe was out of sight now, screened by the rock against which he sat, so he had jumped up and peered over it, and in that second the natives saw him. They must, he had realised, have come from down the river, for otherwise they would have seen his horse, and obviously, from their startled manner they had been quite unaware of a stranger in their neighbourhood.

He had gripped the rock, his mouth and eyes wide open, staring at one of the figures in the canoe. It was Johnny—it was, it *was*! He was naked like the others, and carrying spears, but he was a different colour —a sort of reddish brown—and his hair, catching a glint of sunlight through the trees, flamed fiery red. Patrick gulped once, and cried out:

"Johnny! Johnny . . . !"

  *   *   *   *

Sitting now at the table, pen in hand, he found himself stealing another glance at Ellen from beneath his brows. He was torn between the conviction to which his whole upbringing had conditioned him—that Johnny, as the child of two convicts, had no business to be ranging at large instead of taking his lowly and appointed place in the white community—and a deeper conviction from some unknown inner source, that to mention this strange encounter would be an act of betrayal. Had not Johnny escaped once before, only to be brought back, shrieking and protesting?

But Ellen? Surely she was different? Patrick dipped his pen in the ink again, but did not write. One problem he had now fought out to its conclusion; he would not tell his father about Johnny. He would not tell anyone except . . . perhaps . . . ?

Suddenly out of the turmoil of his thoughts a word broke loose and shattered the silence of the room.

"Ellen . . ."

She looked up at him enquiringly. He stammered:

"Nothing. I wondered . . . do you think my father and Mr. Harvey will return to-morrow?"

She put her sewing down, yawned, and rubbed her eyes.

"He said he would, Master Patrick. You heard him yourself. By sundown, he said."

And then, her attention caught by some expression of tension on his face, she added dryly: "You're missing your tutor, maybe? You want to get on with your lessons, I reckon. You were always one for books, Master Patrick."

He shook his head unhappily.

"No. No, it isn't that. I don't know if . . ." He shut his journal and leaned forward towards her, his arms folded over it, his eyes bright with a half-fearful resolve.

"Ellen!"

"Eh?" She stared at him, puzzled, a frown beginning between her dark brows.

"There's something I . . . listen, Ellen, can you keep a secret? Will you promise not to say anything to my . . . to anyone, if I tell you something?"

She was startled, wary, sensing possible danger to her security. Her voice was sharp as she answered:

"I won't, indeed! Nothing of the kind! If you've been getting into mischief, Master Patrick, you tell your father. It's none of my business."

She picked up her sewing again and began to stitch fast, as if this scrap of domestic needlework were a talisman against even so faint a threat to her peace. But Patrick whispered:

"It's about Johnny . . ."

Her hand, with a long thread half drawn out, stopped in mid-air. She met his eyes, her face suddenly pale. She stared at him steadily; with his flushed face, his strong body and his fine, neat clothes, he looked so handsome and so invulnerable that she was swept by a rage of hatred such as she had not known for years. She was seeing in her mind's eye a skinny, ungraceful body, a pale, hunger-sharpened face, a pair of dark eyes incessantly watchful and invincibly rebellious; and a seven-year-old pain, never quite allayed, stopped her breath and set her hand trembling so that she lowered it, and clasped it hard on the edge of the table. She said slowly in a voice which had dropped to match his own whisper:

"My Johnny . . . ?"

He nodded impatiently. "Of course!" She demanded fiercely:

"What is it? What did you hear about him? Tell me!"

"I didn't hear." Patrick shot a nervous, instinctive glance at the door behind him. "I *saw* him!"

Her face seemed utterly blank for a few seconds. Then she made a sound which was half a sigh, and half an exclamation of impatience.

"How could you see him? Don't talk so silly, Master Patrick." Suddenly she was angry. "Upsettin' me like that, you've got no heart!" She interrupted with increasing bitterness his attempt to protest: "How'd you know my Johnny even if you did see him? You wasn't much more than Master Miles' age when . . . when he got lost . . ."

Patrick hit the table with the palm of his hand.

"Don't be stupid, Ellen! Of course I remember Johnny! Didn't we play together at Parramatta? I tell you I saw him! I *talked* to him!"

Now she believed him, and Patrick, who had always been too sensitive for his own comfort, was shocked and a little awed by the hungry look in her eyes. He found himself feeling astonished that she should be so affected—and then guilty because he was astonished. For, after all, did not mothers as a matter of course love their children? In a few seconds of silence he floundered to a realisation that he had not been quite sure that the rule applied to convict mothers. He had seen convicts landing from the Second Fleet when he was six, and the impression he had formed then—that they were an entirely different race of human beings from himself—had left its mark. Why, he found himself remembering with an indignant attempt at self-justification, Ellen had never *seemed* to love Johnny! She used to beat him often, and scold him nearly all the time! He thought: "I didn't ever see her kiss him . . ."

Kiss Johnny . . . ? Ridiculous! And rushing together in his mind were pictures of eight-year-old Johnny, sly, alert, malicious and detested Ishmael of the settlement, and fifteen-year-old Johnny as he had seen him yesterday, surprisingly tall, surprisingly robust, naked, harshly confident among his native companions.

No. Not for the past Johnny or for the present Johnny could one imagine endearments, even from his mother. And yet that mother was now staring across the table with an expression which she might have worn if she were starving, and he were withholding food from her. He stammered out:

"I did, Ellen, I swear it! Coming back yesterday. I saw him with some natives across the river. At first I thought he was a native too, because he had no clothes, and he was carrying spears like the others, but then I knew it was Johnny, and . . . and . . ."

She said bitterly: "Them Indians! Always off with them, 'e was!

Ever since that Arabanoo!" She urged impatiently: "Go on, go on, what
else?"

"When I saw it was really Johnny I called out to him . . ."

Patrick stopped, his brow wrinkled. Through the limitations of class
and circumstance which were none of his making, he had always admired
Johnny, and tried to be friends with him. It had been, therefore, with a
sense of hurt, of indignation, that he had seen yesterday how deeply and
with what animosity Johnny now mistrusted him. He had cried out:

"Johnny! Johnny, don't you know me? I'm Patrick Mannion!"
And then, with angry incredulity: "Where are you going? Don't go
away!"

For the canoe was already at the opposite bank, and Johnny was
clambering out of it, followed by the other natives.

Outraged and unbelieving, Patrick had seen then that though Johnny
halted at his call he did so behind a rock which would afford him cover,
and the natives took the same precaution. He had cried indignantly:

"What's the matter? What are you hiding for? I'm not going to
shoot!"

And then, unconsciously following the procedure of the settlement's first
Governor, he had laid his musket on the ground, and held his hands up,
empty. And by degrees Johnny, still gripping his spears, had come out
from behind the rock and advanced to the bank. Not more than forty
yards of green, deep, slow-flowing water separated them; they stared at
each other across it, and across a gulf of seven years. Patrick repeated:

"Don't you remember me, Johnny?"

But when Johnny spoke he felt another shock. Something in the
quality of the voice, the intonation, was purely native. The words
themselves came awkwardly, forming disjointed sentences. Johnny had
all but forgotten his own language.

"I know," he said, and paused with his head slightly on one side, as
a bird pauses after song. He seemed to be listening to his voice making
such unaccustomed sounds, and perhaps searching his memory for more.
He found them, and uttered them aggressively: "You go. Not come.
Not want white people." Memory, stimulated, sent up a sudden little
flood of profanities which fell so glibly from his lips that he looked at
once startled and pleased by his own achievement. He added, waving
his spears authoritatively: "Go way!"

Patrick's astonishment became indignation.

"I won't go away! I *live* on the river! My father has a house down
there, and . . . why, Johnny . . ." the thought had dawned on him
suddenly, ". . . your mother's there too!"

Johnny shook his spears with a gesture of rage.

"I *know*!" he shouted angrily. "I see—often. I see you, father,
all . . ." with an impatient movement he sketched the height of children
with his hand to supply a missing word. "I see all . . . every . . .
Don't want. You go way!"

But Patrick had persisted obstinately:

"Where have you been, Johnny? What happened to you? Everyone thought you were dead long ago. Have you been living with the Indians?"

Suddenly Johnny seemed to come to a decision. Gesturing to his black companions to remain where they were, he slid the canoe into the water again, jumped into it, and paddled swiftly across the river. He did not land, but nosed his craft into the soft mud of the bank, and kept it there with an occasional expert flip of his paddle. He looked up at Patrick standing on the bank above him, and there was an old contempt in his eyes—an old, implacable hostility. Patrick said uncertainly:

"Why don't you come home with me, Johnny? My father would give you employment—I'm sure he would. Wouldn't you like to live in a house again?"

Johnny said shortly:

"I got a house."

Patrick stared.

"I got a house!" Johnny repeated fiercely, reading unbelief in the blue eyes that looked down at him. "I got a house—table—chair—gun . . ."

"Gun?" said Patrick incredulously. How could an escaped convict child have a gun?

"I got *two* guns," Johnny said, his voice rising with anger.

Patrick, dumbfounded, looked at his spears, and disbelieved him silently. He felt suddenly frightened. Across the river stood four dark, motionless figures, looking queerly intimidating, the sharp points of their tall weapons catching the slanting sunlight over their heads. His own musket lay on the grass a dozen paces from him. Looking down at Johnny he felt again, as he had felt long ago in their childhood, that there was something about this boy which belonged to a grim world from which his own circumstances had sheltered him, and of which they had kept him in ignorance. Johnny had never trusted his awkward, fumbling attempts at friendship; he did not trust them now. He trusted nothing in the white man's world—but in the black man's world he felt secure. An emotion which he could not analyse had swept Patrick then. There was anger in it—anger that conditions could exist which made his goodwill suspect; anger that he had been denied some knowledge which, he vaguely felt, would have pierced the darkness of his bewilderment with a ray of comprehension; anger that there should be between him and Johnny a barrier whose very invisibility, whose very intangibility, made it insurmountable. What was it? This emotion in him felt like a ladder on which he could climb to scale it, and yet there were things that dragged him back. Images of convict huts at Sydney; images of chained convict gangs; images from long ago of creatures who looked hardly human being brought ashore from the transports. Memories of his father saying: "You are to have no dealings with the convicts, Patrick; they are not fit for you to associate with." Glimpses from his own world of another where men lived differently, and learned to look, as Johnny was looking now, out of eyes which . . .

Eyes which said with passionless conviction that a man would get nothing unless he took it. That life was a war—win or be defeated, kill or be killed, expect no mercy and give none, trust nobody . . .

Patrick's surge of emotion ebbed to an unendurable sadness, but he was no longer afraid. Friendship was what he had wanted to give—always that, even in those far-off childhood days—but now they were older, and he understood that Johnny had never cherished any illusion that such a thing was possible.

Still searching for understanding, he asked nervously:

"But why *did* you run away, Johnny?" He remembered his father's tale of the elder Prentice's death in the flooded river, and thought with excitement that here, perhaps, was the explanation. "Was it to go to your father? Did *he* take you away?"

Johnny stared at him blankly for a moment while he digested these questions, and then, with a native exclamation of disgust, spat over the side of the canoe. Evidently he had wasted no more affection on his father than on his mother; Patrick felt safe in saying:

"He was drowned—your father. Did you know? My father saw it."

Johnny's face was as a mask of indifference. His father might have been flogged, hung, drawn and quartered for all he cared. Patrick, who had been moved by that tale of sacrifice, said with a touch of indignation:

"He was trying to save a native woman and her baby from the river when it was in flood. He *did* save them, but he drowned himself. My father saw it all from the opposite bank. Don't you believe me?" For there was something in Johnny's expression which said that he would accept no story from the lips of one who belonged to the oppressor class of his own race, and Patrick, still fighting instinctively to establish his own good faith, searched his mind for corroboration. "Surely you must have heard, Johnny—from the natives? You've been here all the time, haven't you? Johnny, you might *know* this woman. My father said she had a necklace on—he couldn't see it very clearly, but he said it was made of big round things—brassy-coloured—like metal . . ."

The indifference was gone, the cold incredulity shaken. Johnny's eyes were suddenly startled and intent. His hand went up with pointed forefinger, and sketched a semi-circular line slowly on his breast to indicate how a necklace would hang; his brows frowned heavily over the question in his dark eyes. Patrick nodded eagerly. And suddenly, without a word, Johnny had swung his canoe round, shot across the river, and pulled it up on the other bank. Patrick saw him point towards the south-west. Then, with movements no more conspicuous than the flutter of tree-shadows, they were gone without a word or gesture of farewell, without a backward look.

Patrick had picked up his musket and walked slowly back up the river to where his horse was tethered; he had ridden homeward in the twilight, feeling lonely, bewildered and depressed.

*　　　*　　　*　　　*　　　*

Now, looking at Ellen, he began to be sorry that he had told her. He began to feel that in sharing a secret from his father with a convict woman he had taken a fateful step which cut him off from his care-free and irresponsible childhood. But it was too late now. She was waiting, and he told her all—or nearly all—he knew.

"He said he had a house."

She brushed that away contemptuously. Johnny had always been a liar, a weaver of any fantastic tale that might serve his ends, or increase his self-importance.

"And he said he had a gun—two guns."

Her eyes were narrowed at that. It was not impossible that he should have a gun. Soldiers had been lost. Had he been with natives when they killed a soldier? Had he, perhaps, incited them to kill . . . ? She thought of a gun not as a means for his defence, but as an instrument for crimes, actual or potential, which might make him a hunted creature if his existence became known, and bring him back to a death on the gallows. Patrick, meeting her eyes, saw in them the same bitter mistrust and hostility which he had seen in Johnny's. Her words came slowly, and he understood that the menace in her voice was beyond her control; it was an undertone to the pleading, almost cringing note of the servant with which she was striving for his goodwill.

"A—a secret, you said, Master Patrick . . . ?"

He hesitated. Ellen said harshly:

"He's thought dead. He's doin' no harm. You're a young gentleman, Master Patrick, and you'll be goin' home to Ireland soon, and you'll live a fine life there and forget this place . . ." He looked at her. She insisted vehemently: "You'll forget . . . *everything* . . . eh?"

Patrick knew that he would never forget—not the place, nor Johnny, nor the strange confusions of his own mind in which they had involved him. But he would pretend to forget. He would write everything down in his journal, and remember to lock the big cedar chest where he kept it, and he would pretend to forget . . .

His decision, and his sharp movement as he rose from the table, interrupted the beginning of a further plea. He spoke with something of his father's authority:

"It's a secret, Ellen. I do not wish you to speak of it to anyone, not even to me. I shall not speak of it myself." He picked up his journal; the sound of its pages clapping together as he shut it was the closing not only of the book, but of the subject. As he left the room he heard her go to the window and call the children in, and he thought there was a new note in her voice which he had never heard before—as if she had come alive.

*   *   *   *   *

In the hills above the Wollondilly River a native woman was dying in the hut which the escaped convict, Andrew Prentice, had built eight years before. Cunnembeillee lay on a pile of possum skins spread on the earth floor, and listened to the rain pattering on the shingled roof. Rain or no rain, she would have preferred to die in a bark mia-mia, for though she had grown accustomed to the hut by now, the approach of death re-awakened in her a nostalgic desire for a way of life which was whole, logical, and orderly; which provided in its rituals for such solemn moments as the passing of one's spirit; which offered the support of age-old customs, and the promises of age-old legends to her growing fear of the unknown.

There was no place in the ancient, everlasting faith of her people for a hut, a table, a bench, a door, a key. At this moment when, with her body failing her, she needed spiritual reassurance, the white man's dwelling was a persistent discord, shattering the harmony towards which she groped. It reminded her, with a frightening shade of accusation, that her life had deviated from the pattern of a woman's life which was laid down in the laws of her people; that ever since the moment when she had left her tribe to follow the red-headed An-droo, there had been confusion and mystery where all should have been clear and comprehensible.

An-droo had died. Long, long ago he had saved her and their child, Billalong, from the flooded river, and died himself—for a very little while. Almost immediately she had found him again, transformed by some magic which she could accept without even an attempt at understanding, into an eight-year-old boy. He had been quite clearly recognisable; his face was the face of An-droo grown young again; his hair was An-droo's strange red hair; the key of the hut hung around his neck as it had always done. His name, indeed, was different, but that was only to be expected, since the names of the dead may not be spoken. An-droo or Dyonn-ee, her place was as his side, and at his side she had stayed ever since, here in the hut to which she had guided him—for his temporary death seemed to have wiped from his mind all memory of their previous life together.

Here they had lived—she and Dyonn-ee and Billalong, and Milbooroo, whose wife she had become, since obviously one cannot be the wife of an eight-year-old boy. Here there had been born her second and third sons, Gooradoo and Balgundra, and their little sister Gooburdi—now five, and four, and two years old. Here she had been happy enough, though always on the edge of a vague uneasiness because her past association with a white man had made her different from other women of her race, and her present association with the boy to whose body that white man's spirit had returned after death, laid a mist of magic over all her thinking.

And not only over her own thinking. She was alone now because that fear in herself had communicated itself to the other native women who had been visiting her, and who had tried to work a spell upon her sickness. Dyonn-ee had gone down the river two days ago, as he so often did (and had so often done in his previous life) to watch from a hiding place on the opposite bank the doings of the white men; and Billalong had gone hunting with Milbooroo. The women who came to visit her, finding her ill, had done their best. They had sung, they had repeated the necessary words, they had performed all the usual rituals— but Cunnembeillee had been conscious that in them, as in herself, there was doubt, uneasiness, and fear. She read doom in their hesitancies, their sidelong glances, their awkwardness, the dreadful lack of confidence in their eyes. Here, within the four walls of the white man's hut, sur-rounded by his possessions which challenged the inevitability of their own way of life, and troubled in their hearts by the mystery of his reincarna-tion, their tribal magic grew thin and shadowy. The spirits and the sorceries of their own faith which, in their own ageless and untouched environment filled the air with power, could not function here. Doubt was an evil more terrifying than anything in their experience. Only through the free spirit, certain and unquestioning, could sorceries be performed; but here their spirits could not lift, they could not range out into the world of magic in search of healing; their words faltered, their movements baulked, and there was no release; they were bound to their own bodies by this doubt.

What can it be that opposes magic save a stronger magic? Evil was at work, binding their spells—white man's magic whose abiding place was this hut, and . . . perhaps . . . ?

They spoke rapidly to each other, pointing to Cunnembeillee's throat, about which hung a necklace of buttons from the coat of a dead soldier whose body she had found many years ago. Could one expect to perform a successful magic for a woman upon whose breast lay so alien an object? Might it not be this very thing which was frustrating their efforts? Fear came into the dim hut. A woman reached out her hand towards the necklace and drew it back sharply. Cunnembeillee, only half conscious, heard their words through a fog of delirium, and remembered the soldier's coat when it had been a brave scarlet, when the buttons had adorned it, when An-droo had given it to her. . . . She moaned and cried out: "An-droo . . . !"

A quavering chorus of horror went up from the other women; they shrank, shivered, scrambled to their feet, backed towards the door, snatching up Cunnembeillee's children as they went. The name of the dead had been spoken. Now to their vague fear of white-man magic was added the clear, definite terror of their own. They pushed the door, huddled through it, and fled; the bar of grey daylight narrowed as the door swung shut. Cunnembeillee had swooned for a little while, and opened her eyes heavily at last to semi-darkness and solitude.

She was not able to think clearly, but she knew that she was dying, and she knew that she was alone. Solitude was a terrible thing; among her people one did not live, and still less did one die alone. She too had felt, before she lapsed into unconsciousness, that the spells which were being woven to save her were without that potency which naturally belonged to them; and now, struggling back to a dim awareness, she was oppressed again by the roof over her head, and by the enclosing walls.

She had only one need, with death looming above her like a monstrous shadow—to return completely to her own Law. Somehow she must free herself from the influence of the white man, whose intrusion into her life had confronted her with mysteries which confused and diminished the power of her own. Somehow she must repudiate every-thing which had separated her from her own people; and in this dark hut the air breathed not of them, but of him.

She rolled off the possum skins and began to crawl weakly towards the door. She reached it at last, trembling, and laboriously pushed it ajar. With the first breath of wet, fresh air she revived a little. The rain on her burning flesh was cool and sweet; she wanted no shelter from it. She lay on her back feeling it splash on her body, and spatter her dry lips, but she was frightened by the pounding of her heart. She was not yet released. Something still impeded her re-union with the certainties of her own faith, and she came gradually to a knowledge of what it was. Within one's breast dwelt one's life; she could feel her life labouring there, thudding, struggling, leaping, striving to break free. But upon her breast lay the necklace, the white man's charm which denied it free passage into the spirit world. To her, as to all her people, the spiritual life was rich in symbolism; to free her mortal body of a white man's symbol was quite simply and surely to free her spirit of his influence. With shaking and uncertain hands she pulled it over her head and threw it aside. Instantly she felt its magic fail. Now there was nothing between her and the life to which she belonged, the life whose true frame and setting were about her—quiet, rain-wet trees, hard, rain-wet earth, aromatic, rainy scents which linked the first breath she had ever drawn to the last which was now flickering at her lips. Here all the magic to which she could tranquilly yield herself gathered powerfully about her; she felt her body drop away as her spirit, released, rushed out of it, and upwards to the sky.

*   *   *   *   *

Johnny found her there when he returned. He stood in the rain looking down at her with a grief which was more than half anger because she had not stayed alive just long enough to answer the questions which had been teeming in his mind all the way home, since his encounter with Patrick Mannion. His memory of that long-ago day when she, weak and exhausted from her struggle with the river, had clambered up with Billalong in her arms to the fire beside which he sat, would have been dimmer than it was but for the corroboree which the natives of the river sometimes performed. He had watched it half a dozen times, more interested in it than in any of the others, only because the black people seemed to believe that it concerned him. No name was given to the central character, whose black locks were always obliterated beneath red clay, but his activities, as expressed in elaborate pantomime, were obviously the activities of a white man. He swung an axe, he dug the ground, he fired a gun, he sawed and hammered and milked. Then the performers ranged in two lines, enacted the flowing of a great river, waving their arms with long, sweeping movements, and making strange sounds like the rushing of water. Between their ranks two other actors portrayed a woman and a child battling with the flood; and as the clay-crowned figure leapt to their rescue, and then sank out of sight beneath the flood of swift-waving arms, the sounds changed to wild chanting, and mystery invaded the legend. It was at this point that Johnny, never more than a spectator, felt himself somehow become the centre of the drama. He understood that for some reason best known to themselves they identified him with the clay-bedaubed actor; but never, until Patrick had uttered those amazing words about the necklace, had he suspected that the red clay represented the red hair of his almost forgotten father.

Now the mystery which had always surrounded this fantastic, impossible hut which the natives had practically forced him to regard as his own, began to lift. Standing beside Cunnembeillee he looked slowly from her to it with a resentment in which there was a trace of superstitious fear. He had escaped from his white man's life, put it behind him, repudiated it. To him his father was no more than one of the dim but hated memories of that discarded life, and he did not like the sudden knowledge that the elder Prentice had performed a similar act of repudiation. He had thought—or felt—that he had won his own freedom and independence; now he began to feel that he had merely inherited it. His father—that brutal, lowering, red-headed ogre who had once threatened to skin him alive—had been here before him. Part of the life he thought he had escaped had been merely waiting for him to walk into it again. He had come to the hut as an eight-year-old child by whom miracles could be accepted; but its association with his father altered it. It had made him Johnny Prentice again; he preferred to be merely Dyonn-ee.

Now he began to understand the superstitious awe with which the natives had always regarded him. His father must have made that fire, his father must have dropped that key where he himself had found it. He knew now why Cunnembeillee, finding him there, a replica in miniature, of his father, and wearing the key which symbolised ownership of the hut, had shrunk and cowered in fear. He was the dead returned to life.

It occurred to him suddenly as he stood there that Billalong might be, then, his half-brother; and with that thought it was as if a mist cleared away from the eyes of his memory, and he realised that Billalong was not, in appearance, all native. His skin was lighter, his features were different, his legs were less thin . . .

He looked down at Cunnembeillee again, and beyond her he saw the necklace lying on the ground. He picked it up and examined it with a vague feeling of wonder. This was his only heirloom. He hung it round his neck and went to look for the tribe; it was their business to perform the obsequies. But when he found them they would not come. Something had alarmed them—something about a name. His father's long-forgotten name rose from the depths of his memory. Andrew Prentice. He shut his lips on it. He knew their customs, and conformed to them. This was the name of a dead man. He looked round the circle of dark, watchful faces, and his eyes came to rest on Milbooroo and Billalong.

Would not Milbooroo return with him to perform the appointed ceremonies at his wife's grave? No, Milbooroo would not; the place was tabu. Would not the children, Gooradoo and Balgundra, return to look for the last time upon their mother? The women snatched them jealously and chorused an angry and frightened refusal. With a curious constriction of fear at his heart Johnny looked at Billalong with a question in his eyes; the boy was instantly at his side.

They returned together to the hut. They got out the rusty spade and mattock and dug a shallow grave. When Billalong brought green boughs to line it after the native custom, Johnny looked at him for a moment and then brought more himself. Silently, in the drizzling rain, they laid Cunnembeillee's body in it, and filled it in. Billalong was unhappy and a little frightened. Johnny pointed authoritatively from the grave to the sky between the weeping trees, and the child was comforted.

*   *   *   *   *

Small as was the township of Sydney, it was yet the metropolis of New South Wales, and Mrs. Marsden conceived a visit to it to be worthy of her best bonnet with the white satin ribbons. It was early November, and the *Walker* from England had but a few days earlier anchored in the Cove. To an exiled and news-hungry community the arrival of a ship was still an event, for there would be letters on board, packages, merchandise, reminders of a far-distant civilisation. This time there was more than that. Lieutenant-Colonel Paterson and Captain Abbott had returned with their wives, but even this notable addition to the female society of the colony was eclipsed. Mrs. Marsden, drinking tea with Mrs. Johnson, was all agog.

"You have seen her, then? Pray tell me what she is like?"

Mrs. Johnson's mild, rather harassed eyes turned reluctantly to her guest's face. She had been trying to see through the window what the children were doing outside; there was a silence highly suspicious. She replied vaguely:

"She seemed an amiable young person—quite the lady."

Mrs. Marsden bridled. Anyone less naïve, she thought, than poor Mrs. Johnson would have comprehended that the gentility of Mr. Stephen Mannion's bride was not in question. She herself, an heiress, and the great-grand-niece of a famous and titled Admiral, could not but feel a pitying condescension towards such unworldliness. She said gently:

"That we may assume, my love. She is, I understand, the granddaughter of Sir John O'Connor, whose estates in Ireland are *very* considerable. I spoke of her appearance. Is she handsome?"

Mrs. Johnson hesitated. She was a kind-hearted woman, and her glimpse of Conor Moore had stirred a vague maternal uneasiness in her. She said slowly:

"She would be allowed so, undoubtedly. Her features are pleasing and her complexion admirable, but . . . there is a—a softness, an unworldliness—a frankness almost confiding . . . I should not have expected . . ." She rose and went to the window. "Henry! What are you doing with that mud, child! Milbah, you are not watching the little ones! Mrs. Marsden, I fear your Anne's frock will be sadly soiled . . ."

Mrs. Marsden raised her brows resignedly.

"The trials of a mother in this colony are something which could hardly be believed at home. We intend, of course, to send Anne back to England in a year or so. Our position," she continued, plying her fan vigorously, "when I come into my fortune under the will of my great-grand-uncle, Sir Cloudesley Shovell, will be such that I cannot contemplate my daughter growing up a hoyden. But tell me, my dear Mrs. Johnson, your impressions of Miss Moore. You were saying . . . ?"

Mrs. Johnson, whose thoughts habitually strayed and ambled like sheep, made an effort to muster them. She had gained, in fact, only one impression, and she voiced it simply:

"She seems *very* young."

Mrs. Marsden nodded comprehendingly.

"The *ingenue*, perhaps? You are right, my love; it is hardly what one would expect. Dignity is wanting . . . ? That . . . that *air* which one would have supposed a gentleman of Mr. Mannion's station would require in a wife?" Her plump shoulders under a drapery of scarves, lifted in a faint shrug. "However, it is not as though she were to be moving in a fashionable society. We are in the wilderness, are we not, where a few small gaucheries may pass?"

Mrs. Johnson agreed innocently. She had been studying Mrs. Marsden's bonnet all the afternoon, for though she had hardly varied her own sober and matronly style of dress in all the long years of her exile, ribbons, feathers, frills, fans and lacy parasols were the substance of her secret dreams. Mrs. Marsden continued:

"And the other ladies? You must tell me what news they bring from England?"

"Spencers," replied Mrs. Johnson with sudden animation, "are being much worn. The high-heeled shoe is almost totally discarded, and morocco slippers are all the rage." Mrs. Marsden's feet withdrew quickly beneath her skirts, but Mrs. Johnson was guiltless of malice. She continued happily, unconscious of her guest's heightened colour: "They say that the tax Mr. Pitt has put on hair-powder has almost ended the fashion for it."

Mrs. Marsden said rather tartly:

"It is still worn, I'm told, in the best society."

Mrs. Johnson looked vague.

"No doubt. But only imagine, my dear Madam, the supporters of Mr. Pitt were wearing red waistcoats, and those of Mr. Fox yellow! And jewels are becoming quite outmoded—it is all corals now, and cameos, and they say that caps are going out too, and muslin fillets are being worn instead. I am happy to learn," she added, suddenly recalling her position as the wife of a clergyman, "that there is a greater decorum in ladies' dress now than a few years past. I have been told that in Paris there were women—I cannot call them ladies—who appeared in public wearing but *one* garment, and that almost transparent, and . . ." she lowered her voice, ". . . pink tights beneath!"

"That," replied Mrs. Marsden coldly, "was Paris. I have been in England more recently than you, my love, and I assure you that no such mode was ever favoured there—at least not in any society which I frequented. I understand that the hair is being worn quite short now." She touched the brown curls about her own shoulders complacently. "I should be sorry to see so unwomanly a style become popular."

"Miss Moore still favours ringlets," Mrs. Johnson assured her, "and she was wearing a bonnet not unlike that most elegant one of yours, dear Mrs. Marsden."

"She is staying with Mrs. Paterson, is she not?"

"For the present, I understand. My husband is to perform the marriage ceremony next week."

"She brought her maid with her, no doubt."

"No—she had no attendant, I believe."

"No attendant?" Mrs. Marsden looked shocked, and Mrs. Johnson hastened to explain:

"Oh, she was not unaccompanied, of course. Her maid fell ill just before they were to sail, and was left behind. But a relative of Mr. Mannion's—a cousin, I believe—made the journey with her."

"Indeed? Have you met her, dear Mrs. Johnson? What is her name?"

"I have not met her, madam. She is an elderly lady, I am told, and not in good health. Her hearing is gravely impaired, and she has lived for some years in considerable retirement. Her name is Mrs. Herbert."

"I see." Mrs. Marsden was only partially mollified. "It seems strange for a young lady of Miss Moore's birth and position to travel without a servant—and even more strange, perhaps, for one elderly and infirm to do so. However, I am happy to know that the poor young thing will have a mature and respectable female companion when she goes to the Nepean, for I declare it is no suitable environment for a gently born young woman, and what I would never countenance for one of my own dear girls when the time comes for them to enter the married state." She glanced narrowly at her hostess. "You have heard no other news, Madam, since the *Walker* arrived?" Correctly interpreting Mrs. Johnson's blank stare as a negative, she sat forward in her chair.

"You will not breathe a word, my love, of this? You have reason to know how rumours agitate the peace of this colony. It is said that His Grace the Duke of Portland is seriously disturbed by reports of the Governor's administration here." The white satin ribbons nodded within an inch of Mrs. Johnson's nose. "You and I, my dear Madam, know the plottings and schemings that go on against His Excellency." Her voice dropped to a whisper. "They say that an anonymous letter has reached the authorities at home! It is even hinted—I rely upon your discretion, my love—that he may be immediately recalled!"

Mrs. Johnson uttered a dismayed tut-tut. She said earnestly:

"It would be an evil day for this colony, Madam, if it again fell into a similar condition to that which prevailed after Governor Phillip left. I have been here since its foundation, and though it must be admitted that the convicts and lower orders of the people are profligate and ungodly . . ." her brows knitted for a moment in distress, ". . . I have sometimes wondered if that state were not aggravated by the oppressions they suffered at that time. And indeed, still suffer, though the Governor has undoubtedly introduced some greater degree of order . . ."

She looked doubtfully at her guest, whose husband had already acquired a reputation for severity as a magistrate, and to whom, therefore, mention of the sufferings of convicts might seem tactless. But Mrs. Marsden was not thinking of convicts. She pursed her lips and confided weightily:

"There are—certain influences at work. I say no more, my love. To you it is not necessary. Captain Macarthur is a man from whom neither your husband nor mine has been able to claim that respect to which their calling entitles them. And it is only too well known, is it not, that his relationship with the Governor is far from cordial? Gossip is what I abhor, madam, and ever set my face against, yet I assure you I have heard it whispered in more than one quarter that his ambition is such that he would be satisfied only by being himself made Governor. I say no word against Mrs. Macarthur—an agreeable lady, and a devoted mother—but if there is mischief afoot, mark my words, Captain Macarthur will be found to be at the bottom of it!"

Mrs. Johnson stiffened slightly. She had not forgotten the report which had reached her ears by the devious paths of gossip in those early days when she and the Captain's wife had been the only ladies in the settlement; the memory of a cool little phrase which had described her as a person in whose society Mrs. Macarthur could reap neither profit nor pleasure, now made her sallow cheeks flush faintly, and she answered with reserve:

"This colony has indeed suffered from both avarice and uncharitableness. Had more attention been paid to religion . . . oh, la, Madam! Are the children in mischief again?"

For Mrs. Marsden, from her seat near the window, was craning forward eagerly. She beckoned to her hostess in a manner less dignified than might have been expected from the great-grand-niece of Sir Cloudesley Shovell, and hissed excitedly:

"It must be she! Pray look, my dear Mrs. Johnson—walking over there with Mr. Mannion!" Flinging decorum to the winds, she rose, concealed herself behind the curtains, and frankly peeped. "Her back is turned—how unfortunate! I do not think her dress very particular, do you, Madam? And I cannot say that I admire her bonnet. Mr. Mannion seems most attentive, does he not? How provoking—they are passing up the hill out of sight! I wonder," Mrs. Marsden pondered, resuming her seat with a sigh, "where they can be going?"

*   *   *   *   *

Mr. Mannion was himself rather ruefully wondering the same thing. Already, though she had been but a few days in the colony, Conor had covered an astonishing amount of ground. She was possessed, he observed —at first fondly and then with a growing dismay—of a degree of curiosity about places and people which was, to say the least, unusual in a young lady. In these few days Mr. Mannion had already walked more than in the past six months; and now, as they passed, all unconscious, beyond the view of the deeply-interested Mrs. Marsden, his recollections not only of walks but of conversations with his Conor were causing him a faint uneasiness. He had imagined these days before their marriage as their first real opportunity for courtship; she would sit in Mrs. Paterson's parlor, or perhaps upon a pile of cushions and beneath a parasol in some sunny spot out-of-doors, and listen to his wooing. But no.

"Pray where does that road lead, Mr. Mannion?"

"To the look-out post on South Head, my love. Can you not learn to call me Stephen?"

"Indeed yes—I forgot. Let us go there, Stephen."

"It is too far, my dear Conor. It would fatigue you."

"No, I assure you. I am most fond of walking."

And next day:

"Could we not procure a boat, Sir, and go across the harbour?"

"There is nothing to see there, believe me. Merely more woods, and views of bays and promontories quite similar to those you saw yesterday."

"But there are people living there. Mrs. Paterson told me."

"None with whom you would wish acquaintance, my dear."

"Is it not in that neighbourhood that Mr. Palmer lives? Some of the ladies I met were speaking of him and his associates—they declared Mr. Gerrald was a cultured man who might have been welcome in any society had it not been for his wrong opinions. And they said Mr. Muir used to have a little farm across the water before he left the colony—Huntershill, was it not?—and that Mr. Palmer lives near by . . ."

He smiled indulgently.

"You have come to a strange society, Conor, but not so strange that you should need to number Mr. Palmer among your acquaintances."

"But Mr. Palmer is a gentleman, Sir, and a scholar. I have heard my grandfather say as much . . ."

He replied firmly:

"In my view, Conor, those facts but make his crime the more deplorable."

"What *was* his crime, Stephen?"

He answered more harshly than he had ever spoken to her before.

"His crime was sedition. I make all allowances, my dear, for the fact that a young lady has small knowledge of the world; yet even you have seen something in Ireland, and heard something from France, of the horrors and excesses perpetrated by rabbles incited to violence by unscrupulous schemers and infatuated visionaries . . ."

"Pray, Stephen, which is Mr. Palmer?"

He said angrily:

"I do not care which he is! Let it suffice that he is a man who has forfeited the regard of all respectable people."

"Nevertheless I should like to go across the harbour, Sir. We need not go near Huntershill, if you prefer it."

Prefer it? He had ordained it. He was a little nettled that in accepting his decision she had made it appear a concession by herself; but they went across the harbour.

And now, into his already slightly troubled thoughts, she shot another embarrassing question.

"Who is that lady walking with the children?"

"Her name is Mrs. Dawson, I believe."

"She looks agreeable, I think. Will you not present me to her?"

"It is out of the question, Conor."

"Why?"

"She is—er—housekeeper to one of the medical gentlemen."

"All the same . . ."

"Do not press the matter, I beg of you. You are in novel surroundings, my love; pray be guided by me."

She looked at him, and from him back to the woman with the two fine children. She flushed faintly and sighed. He reassured her kindly:

"There will be companions for you, never fear. Mrs. Paterson and Mrs. Abbott, and that excellent soul, Mrs. Johnson . . ."

"But they will all be so far away, Stephen."

"We shall make frequent occasions for you to visit them. And Mrs. Marsden at Parramatta . . ."

She made a little *moue*.

"I am told she is rather tiresome. And her husband, I confess, makes me want to laugh, with his fat face, and his bulging eyes . . ."

He shook his head in gentle rebuke.

"You are over-censorious, my dear. But we must not omit Mrs. Macarthur from your list of acquaintances."

"Tell me, Sir, is Captain Macarthur a very remarkable man? Everyone speaks of him."

Mr. Mannion replied dryly:

"If to be much spoken of is to be remarkable, then Captain Macarthur is remarkable indeed. There's little which goes on in this colony, I assure you, that he is not concerned in, and no man of my acquaintance makes foes so ardently, or leaves such a trail of commotion in his path. However, the turmoil and the animosity which attend all his public actions are remarkable only for their excessive violence. In this colony, my love, what is really remarkable about him is the impeccable virtue and tranquillity of his private life."

"He must be," she said thoughtfully, "a strange man. When he came to call upon Colonel Paterson the other night I heard him speak several times, with considerable warmth, of his efforts for the progress and prosperity of the colony . . ."

Mr. Mannion smiled.

"It is a favourite subject with him. Believe me, his efforts are directed towards the progress and prosperity of John Macarthur. Nothing else. Should any thing or any person stand in the way of that—be it the opposition of his fellow-colonists, or the law, or the Governor himself . . ."

"Ah, the Governor . . . !" She turned towards him quickly. "I found His Excellency so unlike what you had led me to expect, Stephen. You spoke of him as genial, and kindly, though a little lacking in determination. But he was so silent when Mrs. Paterson presented him to me —so absent in his manner—almost morose . . ."

"You are unwittingly trespassing into the realm of colonial politics, my love. In my opinion His Excellency has reason to be morose. I'm told that Paterson brought him despatches from England, and I hazard a guess that their contents were not to his taste. Indeed, the very ship which brought me my heart's desire . . ." there was no one in sight, so he bent over her ardently—"may well have brought His Excellency a rebuke whose consequences will be serious for him."

"Rebuke?" She looked up at him frowningly, evading his caress. "Why should he be rebuked?"

Mr. Mannion withdrew his disregarded arm and said rather sharply:

"Indeed, Conor, these are matters with which you need not trouble yourself. You are in the happy situation—how happy you will speedily discover—of being in no way connected, even remotely, with the problems of the colony's administration. I am an independent man, my dear, and I have been at some pains to avoid being embroiled in disputes. I do not doubt your good sense and discretion, but I entreat you to guard your tongue."

"But I need not guard it with you, Sir? Pray tell me why the Governor should be rebuked?"

"I did not say that he should be rebuked, but I have small doubt he was. He is in the unenviable position of having to enforce a law which all those who should support him find it in their interest to evade. Fortunes have been made in this place within three years—not from farming, as I, who am a farmer, well know—but from a trade which the law forbids. Flourishing farms there are, which will repay their owners handsomely in time, and which even now, in many cases, yield a not inconsiderable return, but . . . now surely, my little Conor, these are tiresome matters for your pretty ears . . . ?"

"No, no, Stephen, indeed I am vastly interested."

"The basis of these fortunes is trade. Trade in many things which come to the colony, but above all, in rum."

"Rum? But Stephen, surely it is rum which is the cause of so much —so much misery—and degradation . . . ?"

He said testily: "What do you know of misery and degradation, Conor? Such things, I trust, are and will always be quite outside your experience."

"But I do know, Stephen. I have heard Captain Abbott and Colonel Paterson speak of the dreadful intemperance among the convicts and settlers. On every hand I have heard of it. Surely His Excellency cannot permit . . ."

"I have already explained that he does not 'permit.' But with or without his permission, rum continues to be the main currency of the colony."

"But cannot he enforce . . . ? Has he not the courts to try offenders? And the military? And are there not constables . . . ?"

"The courts, the military—what are they but associations of people? I assure you, I should not like to be called upon to name more than half a dozen in the whole colony who have no hand in this traffic. And among them I think I should—yes, I should—name the worthy Governor himself."

"The *Governor*, Stephen . . . ?"

"There have not been wanting hints that he is implicated. Reflect, my love, how convenient it would be for some who wax rich on this illicit trade to have the Governor recalled, and another period, perhaps, like that when Grose and Paterson held sway . . ."

"But Colonel Paterson . . . indeed, Stephen, I cannot believe . . ."

"I make no accusations against the worthy Colonel save that he is too amiable. In the goodness of his heart I make no doubt that it gave him considerable pleasure to follow a course laid down by Grose, and hand out to his friends land and labour like a prince distributing largesse. And indeed . . ." he laughed amusedly, ". . . they have lived like little princelings, these people, on their new estates!"

"During the voyage," she said slowly, "Mrs. Paterson told me that her husband had been ordered to rejoin his regiment so that he might correct certain abuses. And rum was mentioned, but I assumed that its sale was conducted merely among the lower orders of the people. Surely it is for those in responsible positions to set an example . . . ?"

"My love," he said wearily, "I beg you not to tease me with incessant questions. You have no knowledge of the world, and . . ."

"I am most conscious of that," she answered him quickly, "but how am I to correct my ignorance if I do not ask questions? And of whom should I ask them, if not of you?"

"Have I complained of your ignorance?" he asked tenderly. "In my eyes, dearest, you are perfect. It is my task to protect you from all such knowledge as could bring the faintest frown to that lovely brow. This colony and its sordid concerns need not occupy our thoughts. We shall be here, as you know, for a few years at most, and then you will return to circumstances more suitable to your birth and station, and your sojourn here will be but a dream. It is my hope to make it a lovely dream, my Conor. Its ugliness shall not touch you."

"But you will be visiting the colony sometimes to supervise your estate. Shall I not accompany you?"

"I think not, my love. You will have other matters to occupy you by then, doubtless." He gave her a glance of tender meaning to which she responded promptly:

"Indeed I hope so, Stephen. But many wives accompany their husbands upon long voyages, and rear families quite successfully as well. How great a waste," she pleaded, "would be the building of this beautiful new house you tell me of, if I were to occupy it only for so short a time! And I am told by everyone that the climate is highly salubrious, and that children thrive . . ."

Mr. Mannion passed his hand exhaustedly across his brow.

"We are gazing far into the future, are we not? Let us be content to think of the present, my dear—or at all events look no farther into the future than next week, when our happiness will be complete, and we shall journey back together to our home. I am all eagerness for you to see it. I have spared no pains, and no expense, I assure you, to make it worthy of you. The rooms are large and handsome, and from the verandah one looks down across fields to the river, and across the river to the hills . . ."

"Does not the Governor contemplate any further exploration of those hills? I've heard so many conjectures. It is said that there may be great tracts of fertile land beyond them. Why, Stephen," she cried in sudden excitement, "would it not be possible for *us* . . . ?"

For the first time in his life Mr. Mannion raised his voice in speaking to a lady.

"NO, Conor, it would *not* be possible! I have already sufficient property for my present needs. I keep an open mind about the future of this colony, and should rich country be discovered at some later date beyond the mountains, be assured I shall not remain idle. But pray disabuse your mind of so wild a thought as that I should permit my wife to hazard a journey which has already daunted many men. I am astonished, my love," he added austerely, "that you should entertain so infatuated a notion, even for a moment!"

Conor looked at him, and sighed again.

"No doubt you are right, Sir."

"You may rest assured of it, my dear. And now," he added firmly, "it is time for us to retrace our steps. I cannot allow you to become fatigued."

"Indeed," she replied mischievously, "I believe it is yourself, Stephen, who finds our little excursions fatiguing!"

Mr. Mannion experienced an actual shock. She was laughing at him! For the first time he realised that he was middle-aged. He said stiffly:

"You are quite mistaken."

A sudden vivid flush of compunction swept over her face. She touched his arm timidly.

"It was a foolish jest. I fear I am very thoughtless."

He forgave her magnanimously. He was gratified to find that during the walk home she was all gentleness and docility. And, even better, that she asked no more questions.

1800

On January 11th, 1800, two ships cast anchor in Sydney Cove. The *Minerva* transport from Ireland brought rebels to the exile which the law had decreed as their punishment; but the presence of the *Thynne*—sedately as she rode in the sunshine with the Danish colours fluttering at her mast—was in itself a rebellion. To Governor Hunter, staring gloomily at them from his window, the covert and gentlemanly law-breaking symbolised by that little square-rigged vessel was more disturbing than the arrival on the *Minerva* not only of some hundred and eighty Irish convicts, but also of several notorious disturbers of the peace, including Joseph Holt, Father Harold, and the Reverend Henry Fulton.

Both ships carried clothing, shoes, hats, linen, tea, sugar, casks of beef and pork—articles for which the hungry and shabby colony hungered—but both also carried spirits. Hunter, clasping his hands beneath his coat tails, paced the room restlessly, well aware that the officers who had chartered the *Thynne* without his knowledge, and who now blandly presented him with a *fait accompli,* would not tamely submit to having their profitable cargo withheld from them when it lay practically within their grasp. He could, of course, forbid its landing. What then? Where were the officers whom he could trust to see such an order obeyed? He stumped about the room angrily, helplessly. Forbid as he chose, that cargo would be landed. Somewhere, somehow, in one of the secluded bays of the harbour, it would be smuggled ashore. Somehow, some time, it would seep through the community, and in its wake would follow not only drunkenness and depravity, but more financial turmoil, more extortion, more rapacity, more debts, more lawsuits, more chaos. He was Governor of a penal colony, but his thought hardly halted upon the new prisoners committed to his care. The arch-criminal of his community was Rum—and can you, he thought rather wildly, put chains and handcuffs upon Rum, and pen it in a gaol? The very wildness of the thought provoked a wilder one—that perhaps the handcuffs and the chains were on the *wrong people* . . . ? He saw a momentary, fantastic vision of respectable citizens and officers labouring in the fields with good broadcloth, with gold-braided scarlet upon their backs, and shackles on their feet. His mind fled from it in terror; this accursed country, he thought, with its hardship, its solitude, its intolerable heat, came near at times to robbing a man of his sanity. He mopped his brow with a hand that shook slightly, having seen for one second all civilisation as he knew it challenged and destroyed.

*　　　*　　　*　　　*　　　*

From the deck of the *Minerva* Mr. Joseph Holt contemplated the country of his exile. He stood still only long enough to exchange a word occasionally with two of his fellow-passengers, Dr. O'Connor and Captain

Alcock, for he was a man whose energy and impatience expressed itself in physical restlessness, and he left them from time to time to pace the deck and observe from some fresh vantage point the harbour and the swarm of small craft which had surrounded the transport within half an hour of its anchoring.

He was far from being depressed at his situation. He did not see himself as Joseph Holt, political exile, but as "General" Holt who had tasted adventure and power; who had been hunted, hated, feared, courted, and adored; who had shivered and starved in the Wicklow mountains, and dined with the nobility. While he could see himself thus his vanity was well-nourished, and while his vanity was well-nourished he was content. His compact, vigorous body, a little above the average height, was not poorly clothed—though all clothes now seemed poor to him in comparison with the green-faced, gold-epauletted scarlet jacket in which he had entered Dublin Castle less as a prisoner than as a condescending guest. He and the little group of rebels who had accompanied him on this voyage were not lower-class felons; they had passed the voyage in comparative comfort, and confidently expected to pass their exile without undue suffering. Mr. Holt had made friends during the voyage with Mr. William Cox, paymaster of the New South Wales Corps, and saw no reason to suppose that he would not find other congenial and respectable company in the colony. His small dark eyes stared with a lively curiosity from beneath their bushy eyebrows at a distant islet from whose rocky summit rose a gibbet where the skeleton of a convict hung in chains; but it was the surface curiosity of one who observes the world only as the scene of his own personal encounter with life. Returning to his companion, he favoured Dr. O'Connor with a genial slap on the shoulder.

"You look glum, my friend!" The wind ruffled the curly hair receding from his high, round forehead, and he caressed the beard which (as the mark of the fraternity of United Irishmen) he wore beneath a well-shaven chin; his eyes twinkled inquisitively at the doctor. He who had been a storm-centre of that stormy year, 1798, in their country, was far from comprehending the origin of the whirlwind he had ridden. As the son of a comfortable farmer, and still more as himself, to whom all was well so long as Joseph Holt was well, he had been swept up, uncomprehending, into a revolt whose incidents afforded him opportunity for posturing, but whose cause was only less obscure to him than its aim. About others who had been similarly engulfed he entertained, therefore, a naïve, blank curiosity, while congratulating himself that, whatever their motives may have been, they had cut a far less dashing figure than himself. The whole business, he had long ago decided, had been a lamentable mistake; a mistake from which he, with a price of three hundred pounds upon his head, had managed to extricate himself quite adroitly. The laws of the land, he now proclaimed with solemnity, were good laws; reform was needed, not of them, but of individuals who, for reasons entirely unconnected with politics, stirred up the spirit of revolt by their persecutions and oppressions. His eyes, malicious, more than a little contemptuous, stared at the doctor who leaned silently against the rail. He continued, faintly jibing:

"Do you not now regret, Sir, that you forsook the selling of herbs and pitch plasters for the thorny path of disaffection? Would you not rather at this moment be feeling a lady's pulse, or repairing her decayed beauty with your admirable lotions, than confronting your fate in this remote and extraordinary land?" He laughed heartily, but continued to eye his companion with that hint of genuine, blank wonder. "I confess," he continued, "that I am at a loss to understand why a man such as yourself, in the most comfortable circumstances, should scald his fingers in the burning pitch of politics!"

The doctor's faint shrug gave him no answer. He turned his bright, speculative eye upon Captain Alcock.

"And you, Sir! Were you not on full pay? Have you not a private fortune of three hundred pounds a year? Indeed, I am puzzled to know what can have created disaffection in *your* mind! For myself, as all the world knows, I was deeply wronged, my house burned to the ground, my dear ones rendered homeless, myself made fugitive, bound by an oath taken in the heat of anger at my persecution—*I* was the victim of circumstance!" Charmed by the sound of his own voice, he continued rhetorically: "Ah, Fate, how strange it is! By what varied paths did we go forward until we found ourselves entangled in the meshes of rebellion, unable to recede for fear of having no friends on either side! Yet though we went in by different routes, we come out by one, and find ourselves —here! How does the prospect strike you, pray? For myself, I don't doubt that I and my family will be very comfortable . . ."

The sound of a shot and an outburst of shouting interrupted him. One of the soldiers on board, acting with an excess of zeal upon his instructions to keep the boats away from the side of the transport, had fired upon one which did not withdraw quickly enough, and killed a young man. Conversation was temporarily halted by this exciting incident, and when there was no more to be seen Mr. Holt withdrew to his cabin where his wife, nursing their six-months-old infant on one arm, and watched by their twelve-year-old son, was busy packing the family effects. She observed her husband's buoyant step and lively manner without enthusiasm. She was beginning to feel that the notoriety of being the wife of the picturesque "General" Holt hardly compensated for the constant anxiety she felt about their future livelihood; she enquired sharply:

"You have made plans for us, Joseph?"

Plans! He, Joseph Holt, who had planned for an army, need feel no dismay at the prospect of planning for a family! He smiled upon her benevolently.

"Never fear, my Hester! I have already had some conversation during the voyage with our worthy friend Mr. Cox. Are we not both the children of farmers, my love? And is this not a flourishing agricultural community? Excellent prospects lie before us!"

She looked dubious.

"You have not been accustomed to labour, Joseph. How shall you obtain subsistence for us, pray?"

"Government," he replied airily, "will not let a good soldier starve."

Her brows wrinkled. Farmer—soldier. That was the trouble with Joseph. One was never quite certain what he really was. And would Government exert itself to care for one who had so long and so effectively defied it, even if he had—somehow—made his peace with it at last . . . ? She turned back to her boxes and remarked rather dryly:

"They'd sooner give you a rope than a breakfast."

*   *   *   *   *

Mr. Harvey, accompanied by Toole, had been sent post-haste to Sydney upon news of the *Minerva's* arrival, for Mr. Mannion had lost two convicts recently—one by death, and one upon the expiry of his sentence—and these must be speedily replaced.

It was Mark's first opportunity to observe the procedure by which felons were disembarked and distributed, and—thanks to Captain Johnston of Annandale, who professed himself delighted to be of service to Mr. Mannion—he and the overseer were allowed on board the day after the vessel cast anchor. They found themselves among a small group which included the master of Annandale and Mr. Nicholas Divine, Superintendent of Government labour in Sydney. The convicts, their irons removed, were drawn up on deck in three rows; gaunt and pale from long confinement, they stared about them at the bright harbour with sliding, sideways glances which always returned sharply to the Captain—standing with documents in his hands, and barking questions in his loud, military voice. Names, trades, causes and particulars of their convictions—the interrogation seemed endless, and the sun was hot. The Captain grew more and more irritable as he shuffled his papers, pausing now and then to swear at a convict for a stumbling or inaudible reply, to roar at another for moving unbidden, or to confer for a moment with Mr. Divine. Mark, watching the prisoners, was glad that it would not fall to him to make a choice of two from among so many. To Toole, more experienced in such matters, the selection would be left, and he asked curiously:

"Which ones have you set your eye on? They look poor creatures to me."

Toole tilted his cap forward to screen his eyes from the sun, and squinted down the rows contemptuously.

"An' that's the truth, Sir. A bunch o' rogues, take my word for it. They say there's many'll be sent straight to Norfolk—an' it's the worst sort go there. Divine yonder, he'll have first pick o' the rest for the Guv'ment labour. Then the officers get their turn, an' the Captain'll see I'm gettin' in early for his Honour. There's two I'm watchin', if so be I can be gettin' 'em . . ."

Mark's bewildered eyes swept along rows of what seemed to him uniformly unprepossessing faces.

"Which two?"

"Yon big rascal down there at the end o' the first row. An' the young one with the black hair just opposite the Captain."

Mark stared at them.

"Why?"

"Cattle," said Toole briefly. "Bullocks. Plenty o' work an' no throuble in either o' them. Whisht, now, there's Divine after choosin' his lot, and please Heaven we'll not be here much longer, an' meself with a thirst that'd drink the harbour dry . . ."

Mr. Divine wanted tradesmen. He wanted carpenters, stonemasons, blacksmiths, sawyers, bricklayers, weavers. Mark heard his companion click his tongue in annoyance as the black-haired young man was called, and fell out from the line to join the group Mr. Divine had chosen. By the time those destined for Norfolk Island, and those selected by various officers had been withdrawn, there remained not more than a score or so when Toole's turn came. The big man at the end of the row was still there, and the overseer having signed to him to fall out, appraised the rest frowningly. He chose, at last, a broad-shouldered and powerfully-built fellow of medium height, and turned away with an irritable mutter which suggested that he was not well pleased with his luck.

It was next day before the convicts were disembarked, and Mr. Harvey was down at the wharf among the crowd which had gathered to see them come ashore. In the noise, confusion and excitement of this brief interlude between the discarded discipline of the ship, and the not yet established discipline of the colony, there was actually a kind of liveliness that made him wonder. How quickly, he thought, the human spirit responded to an occasion! There could be but little of gladness, surely, in such an event as this, and yet it was clothed in something of a holiday atmosphere. To those on shore it was a break in the monotony of life; some were discovering friends or relatives among the new arrivals, and all were shouting for tidings of a far-away and long-lost world. The prisoners themselves, bitter as they knew their future might be, were yet caught up in that sense of climax which makes a festival of a journey's end. To be released from the ship, to know the perils of the ocean left behind, to feel space and clean air about them, to see new faces and to set their feet once more upon the earth—these things were enough to re-awaken hope, and to print a strange, dazed, doubting joy upon their pallid faces.

It would not last long. They were exchanging one captivity for another, one monotony for another; and already, as they marched away towards the Parade Ground where His Excellency would favour them with a brief homily, the shadow of that knowledge was in their eyes.

Mark followed them up the hill and remained to listen to the Governor's address, but when that was over he had further business of Mr. Mannion's to attend to in the town. It was not until next morning that he met Toole again at the wharf whence a batch of convicts was being despatched to Parramatta.

He asked as they waited in the sunshine:

"What becomes of the women? I heard they were to come ashore to-day."

Toole gave him a sidelong glance and a slow grin.

"Sure, Sir, there's always been a lack o' females in the colony. The officers get their pick o' what they want for servants, an' I'll be tellin' ye it's the young an' pleasin' ones go first, the way ye'd be thinkin' a broom an' a dish-clout couldn't be handled but by a lass with a neat shape an' a bright eye. An' then the privates are after havin' their turn, an' next the free settlers, an' then it's the convicts with their time expired that get the leavings. But sure, they're glad enough, an' all o' them wantin' a wench—that bein' the nature o' the way God made us, Sir. And there'll be some, maybe, with husbands here already that'll get tickets o' leave, an' some'll be put to weavin' linen, or cardin' wool an' the like. An' find time for mischief in between, make no doubt of it, for they're at the bottom o' half the devilry in the colony . . ."

He broke off to point at the men lined up on the wharf, and now beginning to step one by one into the waiting boat.

"There's our precious pair, yonder. Divil take me if I like the look o' that second rogue I had to pick! He'll bear watchin', that one . . ." He pulled a crumpled bit of paper from his pocket and studied it. "Henry Donnelly, labourer . . . that's the long one, an' it's fourteen years he's got for stealin' a piece o' linen, but there's no harm in *him*. . . . It's the other I'll be keepin' a sharp eye on. Will ye look at the rascal, Sir, an' him with a glare in his eye would shtrike us dead if it could! Matthew Finn, labourer. . . . I'll give him labour, I promise ye! Sure, it's only by the King's mercy he's here at all, an' not underground where he belongs. It's him an' his like that's been raisin' the divil in old Ireland, Sir, an' I tell ye I saw it in his face before ever I was readin' it in his papers . . ."

Mark, staring at the man, met for one instant a sharp, searching gaze that disconcerted him; he felt that the overseer's claim might not be exaggerated. Toole yawned and stretched.

"Well, it's a life sentence he's got himself—an' there's no place he can be doin' less harm than at Beltrasna. It's a quare thing, Sir," he added ruminatively, "the way ye can get to know the temper that's in a man from a glance when ye've been dealin' with rogues as long as I have. That Finn, now. . . . Not a word out o' him, mind ye, but to be answerin' the questions . . . but I know. . . . There's throuble in that rascal. Ye can see it in horses, an' ye can see it in men . . ." He shrugged, and spat into the clear water. "It's no matter—I've broke both before now . . ."

Mark said shortly:

"They're ready to leave."

"Aye. It's a nice little water trip they'll be havin' this fine day, an' let them be makin' the most of it, for it's the last day they'll be idle. Well, Sir, our pair's safe off our hands for a while, the way they'll be lodged safe in the gaol at Parramatta till we fetch 'em to-morrow. Will ye be done with his Honour's business by ten in the mornin', Sir, for the master was after wantin' us back by sundown . . ."

Mark was still watching the boat as it pulled away across the blue water, its oars dipping and flashing in the sun. Beneath Toole's surface respect there had been, throughout this expedition, an undertone of familiarity and condescencion that irked him. The overseer had been too

plainly the expert and the mentor, emphasising by his manner the youth-
fulness and the inexperience of which Mr. Harvey was uncomfortably
conscious. And he was still oddly disturbed by that momentary glance he
had intercepted from the convict Finn; still uneasily aware of words
echoing in his mind: "*I've broke both before now* . . ."

He said curtly, turning away:

"I shall not be ready before ten-thirty. You may wait for me near
the store."

He stalked off with a brisk air of purpose which disguised uncertainty and bewilderment. In his lodgings, in the streets, and over his
frugal meals he had found people very willing to talk, and his brain was
full of confusing fragments of information and opinion. It was common
gossip that the small 'settlers felt themselves on the brink of ruin, and
everywhere the blame was laid at the door of the large landowners and
monopolists. Mr. Harvey's knowledge of agricultural economy was rudi-
mentary, but even he could understand the plight of a small farmer forced
to purchase his supplies from these all-powerful gentlemen who demanded
so fantastic a profit; forced to employ labourers who, in their turn, were
compelled to raise the price of their labour if they were to exist. What,
he had enquired tentatively, was being done to remedy this situation? His
Excellency, apparently, had attempted to adjust matters by fixing the price
of labour as well as the price of grain, but it seemed that this expedient
was not successful. Mr. Harvey even gathered the impression that the
Governor's regulations were considered in some quarters as not worth the
paper- they were written on; but the conversations to which he listened
taught him less than the manners, gestures and expressions that coloured
them. A shrug, a jeer, a short, unmirthful laugh, a fist crashing on a
table, a pair of hands flung out despairingly, had driven him to apply his
own logic, and toy with disconcerting conclusions. Of what use to say
that a man must not receive more than nine shillings for felling an acre
of forest timber if nine shillings would not maintain him? And, tramping
the narrow, winding, dusty, hilly streets, Mr. Harvey found these problems
somehow joining in his mind with the memory of the convict Finn, who
had rebelled against the laws of his land, and was paying for that rebellion
with servitude for life. The alarming thought flickered about the edge of
his consciousness that in such circumstances laws became merely a set of
repressive restrictions to be evaded, circumvented, ignored, or openly
defied. For men will live—within the law if they can, but beyond its
pale if they must.

*   *   *   *   *

In April the *Speedy* arrived, bringing Captain Philip Gidley King to
succeed Hunter as Governor. Jane Dundas, scuttling up on to the deck
with a cloak for her mistress over her arm, halted a moment, staring across
the water at the shores of Sydney Cove. This was her second arrival in
Port Jackson, but because she was a practical woman whose imagination
never ran ahead of her daily experience, she was quite unprepared for the
strange sensation which now arrested her hurrying footsteps. She had
first seen this place on a summer's day in 1788, and though her surface

thought was: "Mercy on us, how it's changed since then!" there was a deeper thought which invited her pleased contemplation of how she herself had changed.

Then she had been a convict. But not one of the silly, flighty ones who had succumbed to fate, and drifted down to those depths of disease, drunkenness and degradation of which she knew very well. She smoothed her neat, dark gown with a gesture of complacency. No. She had kept her head. A convict woman who could behave in a sober and seemly fashion was so rare a creature that advancement would surely be her lot. And she had found herself, sure enough, after some two years of careful propriety, employed in no less exalted a situation than that of housemaid to Governor Phillip himself. She had watched his departure from an upstairs window, and descended to make ready for Lieutenant-Governor Grose. Two years later she had seen him, too, embark for England, and had transferred her conscientious services to Colonel Paterson and his wife. Her unformed thought had been that Governors come and Governors go, but housemaids remain; it had seemed to her at last that Government House was less theirs than hers. She had known a certain nostalgia for it, even during her visit to England, and now, returning with the new Governor and his lady, her eyes flew eagerly to the plain, whitewashed building on the hillside, and her mind teemed with domestic plans.

Five months at sea! Five dreadful months, cooped up on board with never a place to call your own; with gales that set the ship floundering and sent the water splashing into the cabins; with a fire started in the gunroom so that they had all expected to be blown up; with the dreadful tropic heat that set your skin itching and prickling; with the master suffering from the gout, and the mistress near distracted with tending him and the little Elizabeth . . . ! Jane looked across the water at Government House as she might have looked at the gates of Heaven.

It was autumn, and there was a nip in the breeze that blew down the harbour. She shook herself away from her daydreams, and bustled along the deck to where her mistress was standing beside the Governor-elect, her hand through his arm.

"La, King!" Jane heard her say excitedly. "The place is vastly grown, is it not? See the verandah on Government House! I declare it gives it quite an elegant appearance! And that large brick building is new—what would it be, now—a storehouse, no doubt . . . ?"

"It's the granary, Ma'am," Jane told her. "Now here's your cloak, Ma'am, put it on, do, or you'll get your death with this nasty wind . . ."

Mrs. King motioned her away impatiently.

"I don't want it, Jane. I'm going below, and you must go with me and help me finish my packing." Her brown eyes were so bright with excitement that her rather plain face seemed less plain than usual. "My love, you will be going ashore immediately, no doubt, to deliver your despatches to Mr. Hunter?" King nodded without taking his eyes from the shore. His wife chattered on: "How I long for the time when we shall leave this odious ship! When shall we see Mrs.

Paterson, I wonder? I trust it will not too greatly discommode her,
having us all in her house—but there, she is the kindest creature! Jane,
there will be a great deal to do at Government House—I cannot suppose
that Governor Hunter will have had the time or the inclination to effect
much improvement there. Poor man, the ordering of a house is no part
of a bachelor's task! One cannot expect it. We shall hang the red
curtains in the parlour, Jane, unless—oh, la!—unless they have been
spoiled by the sea-water! Which box were they in? I must open it
again and satisfy myself. King, I beg you to move out of the wind—
you will be prostrated with the gout. . . . Jane, why are you loitering so,
come with me, there is a multitude of things to be done."

King, left alone, stood with his hands on the rail and kept on staring
at the tiny township from which he was to govern an expanding colony.
For the moment, however, he was not thinking of it, but of his wife.
Like most husbands of his time, he subscribed to the convention that a
lady was a delicate creature, timid both physically and intellectually; but
unlike most he was prepared to re-examine his conventions when he
observed the facts refuting them in one particular instance. True, he
thought with a ghost of a smile, his Anna Josepha never hesitated to
proclaim herself the most arrant coward. She had quaked and trembled
and twittered upon many occasions during their nine years of married
life. Upon that evening long ago at Norfolk Island, for instance, when
mutiny had threatened; and half a dozen times at sea upon their various
voyages, when the ocean had seemed about to overwhelm them. Yet
she had borne three children in unfavourable circumstances at the island,
and another at sea on the way home to England. She had seen one
daughter die, and had left a boy and a girl behind her when she embarked
upon this voyage with him. She had nursed him devotedly during his own
periods of illness. Not lack of fear, he reflected, but the capacity to
ignore it, was the sign of courage. He was not ill-pleased that his wife
should turn to him for reassurance in moments of physical danger, but
he could admit that feminine flutters might mask a moral fortitude not
unworthy of masculine respect. Not all women, he thought, could have
learned with such good sense and magnanimity of the existence of two
illegitimate sons for whom their father admitted affection and responsibility. Those sons, Norfolk and Sydney, were safely bestowed in England,
and on their way, he hoped, to a respectable and useful life . . .

His eyes, still on the shore, focussed and became attentive again. He
was a man of character and determination, and he faced his task not only
without serious misgivings, but with enthusiasm. He cherished no illusions
that it was to be an easy one, for it was well-known in England that the
colony had lapsed into a state of chaos from which it appeared that
Hunter had been unable to rescue it. Mr. King, however, had confidence
in Mr. King. He was vain and slightly pompous, and he flared easily
into irascibility. He possessed a sharp and sometimes malicious sense of
humour, and could turn, on occasion, an ironical phrase which might be
witty, but did not stop short of wounding. He saw no reason why he
should not succeed where Hunter had failed. After all, he told himself,

he had had some experience of colonial administration; his years at Norfolk Island would now prove to have been a useful apprenticeship for this more important command. Nor was he to be among strangers; most of the people whom he would meet when he stepped ashore would be old acquaintances—some of them old friends.

Nevertheless his brow wrinkled faintly as he thought of one of those old friends. It was but a year ago, when he was still in England, chafing at the misadventures which had already delayed his departure so long, that he had spoken of Colonel Paterson in a letter to Sir Joseph Banks. His regard for the Colonel, who had shared his life on Norfolk Island for fifteen months, was quite sincere; for his Anna Josepha's sake, too, he hoped to preserve cordial relations with one whose wife would greet her as an old friend in a country where ladies could not easily find the companionship of their own sex. All the same, he frowned. Support—firm and wholehearted support—from one who was to be his Lieutenant-Governor would be essential, and Paterson, he was forced to admit, was not remarkable for firmness. Moreover, he was a military officer, commanding the New South Wales Corps, and King was not naïve enough to imagine that he himself would be spared the opposition from this quarter which had so harassed Hunter. He had hoped for a civil rather than a military Lieutenant Governor, and something of his doubts had crept into his description of Paterson to Sir Joseph when he had qualified: "A man who would do what is right and honourable" with "if he acts from himself, without attending to intrigues . . ."

Intrigues . . . ! His lips made an impatient sound, his open hand hit the rail in a gesture of exasperation. He had had some experience also of intrigues. Jealousies, scandals, whispered hints, quarrels, plottings and manœuvrings had disturbed the peace in Phillip's time, not only at Sydney, but at Norfolk Island, and he knew that since then they had swelled to open animosities and come near to open rebellion. He deplored them, but believed that he could deal with them. Phillip had dealt with them, and King, for all his admiration of the colony's founder, considered his own qualities to be not inferior.

He stirred, shifting his position, leaning his arms upon the rail, thinking of his meeting with Hunter, now so imminent. It would not be a pleasant task to hand over despatches from Portland which, he had no doubt, would contain a severe censure along with the order of recall. Once that was over, and Hunter gone, he could settle down to his task. For a few years, at all events, he would have personal security. His financial affairs had never ceased to be a worry, and with a family which—if one included, as one must, Norfolk and Sydney—now numbered five, he was continually apprehensive of the future. Governor Phillip had supplied him with a letter making over to him his share in the cattle lost in the first year of the settlement, and since discovered to have multiplied so remarkably; and that, he reflected, might prove a valuable addition to his worldly goods. He stared at the township, feeling that at last he was in possession of an assignment which would not only try his mettle, but bring him prosperity and advancement.

*   *   *   *   *

His first sight of Hunter caused him a slight shock. "Why," said his thought, prisoned behind an expression of civil greeting, "the fellow's an old man!"

Indeed, Hunter had aged. His face was more deeply lined, his movements slow, and there was a note of querulousness in his voice.

"I'm happy to see you again, Mr. King. Your health is improved, I trust?"

"I am well at present, Sir, though I have been troubled by the gout." King glanced round the familiar room where, with the other officers, he had sat one evening nearly ten years ago, listening to Phillip explaining the desperate straits to which the colony was reduced. Things had looked black then, but it had survived. Hunter was asking formally:

"You had a good passage, I believe?"

"Passable, Sir, passable. My wife found the heat of the tropics distressing."

"You bring with you a Mr. Caley, I understand—a *protégé* of Sir Joseph Banks?"

King permitted himself a smile.

"Yes, Sir. He is a young man of somewhat fiery and impatient disposition, but Sir Joseph thinks well of him as a botanist. From what I remember of this country there will be ample to occupy his time."

Hunter said: "Yes, yes," rather absently. He was not really, King thought, in the mood for this small-talk. There was a kind of remoteness in his gaze, as if he could not even for a moment detach himself from his anxieties and grievances. His mouth had developed a slight nervous twitch, and his fingers were never still. King felt a momentary qualm. He had thought of Hunter as a phlegmatic man, a practical Scot, an honest, capable, limited, plodding naval officer who would do his usually adequate best, and be content with that. What sort of experience was it which could reduce him to so obvious a condition of self-mistrust? For his whole demeanour, the faint edge to his voice, even the unnecessary asperity with which he had rebuked a servant for a moment's clumsiness as he ushered King into the room, proclaimed a man at war with himself. And King, who had been Phillip's friend, who had glimpsed without understanding it the first Governor's strange preoccupation not only with his colony but with the unknown land which was to be its cradle, felt as if he had been suddenly warned.

There was more here, he thought soberly, than administering a colony. There was the problem of meeting the effect of the land upon the minds, the emotions, the avaricious impulses of men who were not content to inhabit, but longed to possess. There was the problem of its effect, too, upon the minds of those whose fate had always been captivity, either by want or by fetters. What did the land say to such people? What but different—*different*—DIFFERENT . . . ? There was an intoxication, perhaps, in space; hope lifted in a new country, ambition enlarged, and hands stretched out to grab. Here was no vast, elaborate structure of government, rooted in centuries of tradition, to quell the murmuring masses and exact a scrupulous support from the more privileged in return for indulgences.

Here was nothing but a modest brick house, a worried elderly man, and a flag, flapping in the sun. What was that to set against the lure of a country whose extent and possibilities were beginning, dimly, to be suspected?

He cleared his throat and asked:

"I'm told, Sir, that you have had some reason to fear insubordination on the part of the convicts at various times?"

Hunter looked at him queerly from tired, red-veined eyes.

"I have. And not only from the convicts."

King said carefully:

"I hope to hear more at some other time—when Your Excellency's leisure will permit—of the affairs of the colony. For the moment I have wished only to pay my respects, and to deliver the despatches which have been entrusted to me."

He laid a bulky package on the table. Hunter looked at it, and there was a pause during which those papers so dominated the thought of both men that they were held motionless and speechless in a painfully extending silence. The Governor jerked out at last:

"I thank you, Sir. And now . . . you are doubtless anxious to make arrangements for disembarking your family . . ."

King rose quickly.

"Yes, Sir. We shall be temporarily under the roof of Colonel Paterson. I shall be at your command, Sir, at any time."

Hunter watched him go, and turned to the papers on the table. A sudden agitation set his heart pounding so that he drew out his chair and sat down, feeling breathless and shaken. He did not mind being recalled; he hoped never again to set eyes upon this scene of so much struggle and humiliation. But the knowledge of foes working in the dark to bring about not only his recall, but his disgrace, had tormented him for too long; and since that November day five months ago when Paterson had returned, bringing him a disturbing communication from Portland, he had known that he was fighting a losing battle. He could not contend with anonymous letter-writers who attacked not only his administration, but his character. He could do nothing but protest, and explain, and appeal, and protest again. Protest his innocence of any participation in the trafficking he had been instructed to suppress; protest that he ought hardly to be supposed capable of bringing disgrace upon the high position which he had served forty-six years to attain; protest in long, impassioned periods, and in one brief, stark assertion whose very starkness lent it dignity. "*I have no turn for traffic, my Lord; I never had.*" Explain all over again, with dogged and desperate persistence, those measures which he had taken to enforce obedience—guards on all the ships, constables and watchmen posted along the shores, rewards offered for information and discovery—and all of no avail. Appeal for the protection of his reputation from the poisoned shafts of slander. Protest that from his irksome and exhausting, if exalted, position, he had won nothing to his personal advantage but the miserable savings from his salary; that burdensome as the position was, he would prefer to die discharging it, rather than submit to the ruin of his "fair, unspotted character."

He had sat far into the hot November night writing that vehement, outraged letter; but now, staring at the papers on the table before him, he knew that his fate had been decided even then. He pulled them towards him, broke the seals, and began to read.

It began badly enough with complaints that insufficient returns of stores had been forwarded, that expenses were too large, that certain irregularities in the Commissary's department called for His Grace's decided disapprobation. But Hunter's eyes skimmed nervously down the paragraphs to halt with sick apprehension at Portland's sharp comments upon his action in endorsing the trading agreement made between the officers and the colony's principal inhabitants. He had always been uneasy about that, staunchly as he had tried to justify it both to Portland and to himself. And here was his uneasiness fatally translated into uncompromising words. "*A sanction to officers engaging in traffic.*"

A chill of hopelessness descended on him. He could not read all the rest until he knew that worst which, he now felt sure, was lurking somewhere in the pages. He turned fumblingly to the end and found it there: read it slowly, attentively, his head in his hands:

"*. . . I feel myself called upon by the sense of duty which I owe to the situation in which I have the honour to be placed, to express my disapprobation of the manner in which the government of the settlement has been administered by you in so many respects—that I am commanded to signify to you the King's pleasure to return to this kingdom by the first safe conveyance which offers itself after the arrival of Lieut. Governor King, who is authorised by His Majesty to take upon him the government of that settlement immediately on your departing from it.*"

Hunter got up and stood for a moment looking blankly at the opposite wall, his shoulders bowed and his hands unsteady on the back of his chair. He saw, in that tired moment of defeat, that the best he had—his genuine goodwill, his sincere humanity, and his plodding, stubborn honesty—were inadequate equipment with which to contend against the lust for wealth and privilege which had opposed them. Goodwill shrivelled in an atmosphere of financial intrigue; humanity was a luxury denied to the Governor of a penal colony; honesty could be assailed by the innuendoes of an anonymous pen. He was a failure.

And yet, even now, some resilient remnant of his stubbornness challenged that admission. There was failure here—but was it all his? Was he not being made the scapegoat for a failure whose origin was elsewhere? In this psychological crisis his mind achieved a flash of unaccustomed perception in which it passed over the handful of men whose greed had corrupted the colony, passed over the Home authorities who had left it for three critical years to the mercy of such men, and clutched at the fleeting ghost of an idea that everyone concerned in this venture, from Portland himself to the lowest convict, was the victim of some profound social misconception which damned them all. His brain caught at it as ineffectively as his fingers might have caught at a shadow; when he tried to examine it there was nothing there—nothing but the sudden, testy knowledge of a tired, elderly man that he was cold, and the fire was nearly out.

He went across to the hearth and bent stiffly to knock the logs together. He thought bitterly:

"King will learn!"

*   *   *   *   *

Mark Harvey, from his chair at the table set upon the Beltrasna verandah, looked up from Miles' slate at Mrs. Mannion. Unconscious of his stare, she stood beside one of the tall stone pillars, still gazing down the hill towards the rough road leading to Toongabbee and Parramatta, along which her husband had ridden out of sight a few moments since. The handkerchief with which she had waved him farewell still fluttered in her hand, and the smile which had been for him, though he could not see it, was still on her lips.

She turned away at last, and stood hesitating for a moment as though, having sped her husband as a dutiful wife should, she were not sure what to do next. She began to stroll up and down the verandah, studying her home and her surroundings with eager eyes. She was still new enough to the sensation of being mistress of so fine an establishment to spend much of her time in this way, but this morning she felt a trifle restless, and would have welcomed some more active pastime. She was a little shocked to discover in herself even so faint a feeling of rebelliousness, and entered the front door with a sudden air of purpose which, however, carried her no farther than the wide entrance hall.

What now? After all, she knew it by heart already. To the left a door opened into a fine drawing-room which was connected in turn with a dining-room and a small parlour—all looking out from long french windows with tall wooden shutters across the verandah to the river and the hills beyond. A small room to the right of the entrance hall served as Stephen's study, and next door to it, on the south-west corner of the house, was a bedroom, now occupied by Mr. Harvey—both of these, like the reception rooms and the fine bedroom which she shared with Stephen, opening through long, shuttered windows on to the verandah. A passage, shooting away to the north, led to Cousin Bertha's room, and to another which—so Stephen had tenderly suggested—would some day make a pleasant nursery; and beyond these again was the large room which Patrick shared with Miles. Another passage led to the kitchen and those meaner regions of the house where three small rooms would provide quarters for the additional servants they would have soon, and dark, narrow steps plunged down into a subterranean cellar. From this passage, too, opened the small housekeeper's room where Ellen and the maid, Emma, sat late into the night, sorting and mending linen; and beside it, with a window opening on to the east verandah, was yet another bedroom to accommodate a guest.

She knew it all—and she had nothing to do in it. This morning she did not even feel inclined to go and stand in the doorway of the nursery and imagine the children who would some day inhabit it. She returned slowly to the verandah and paced it idly, throwing an absent smile to Mr. Harvey and the boys as she passed their table, and looking out over the broad, sunlit fields. To the north-east were the stables and the barn and a few outhouses. To the south-east the low roof of the convict hut could just be seen at the bottom of the hill. Those were all outside her domain, but she paused for a moment and looked rather wistfully at the small detached storeroom separated by a few yards from the kitchen door, and stoutly built, like the rest of the house, of stone. She would have liked to go in there and explore the bales and casks and bins of household goods—but it was kept locked, and Ellen had the keys, and somehow she found Ellen rather forbidding . . .

Another time . . .

She stared down the hill at the little cottage standing about midway between the convict hut and the river which had been the Mannions' first home here, and which was now occupied by Ellen and her children. She sighed and walked back towards the front of the house past the studious trio at their table, and Mr. Harvey's eyes followed her.

He was, for the first time in his life, deliriously—and yet most respect-fully—in love. He desired no more, at present, than that he should continue to live under the same roof with her, be able to look at her, have the bliss of opening a door or drawing forward a chair for her; he had hardly even reached the stage of being jealous of Mr. Mannion, whose birth, wealth, and prepossessing person seemed only husbandly attributes to which so exquisite a creature had an undoubted right.

Seeing her move away, and walk down the path which curved out of sight round the house, he sighed, and turned again to his duty, to find a black head close beneath his elbow near the yellow one which Miles was bending over his task. He said severely:

"Dilboong!"

He caught a momentary glimpse of the whites of her eyes as she flashed up at him one frightened, guilty glance, and then she was gone. He did not turn his head to see how far. He knew from experience that some-time or another he would find her there again. He never saw or heard her come; her bare feet on the stone flags were soundless. Suddenly, repeatedly, persistently, she was simply there, her hands clasped behind her back, her eyes fixed in a trance of absorption upon Miles' laborious writing. It was for her own sake that he dismissed her so sternly. He knew that a hundred tasks awaited her, and that Ellen's hand was heavy. And Mr. Mannion himself—long ago, soon after Mark's arrival—had forbidden her presence when lessons were going on.

He wondered uneasily how many times she had been beaten for dis-obedience—for just this one disobedience. In other matters she was docile. She was quick and deft; even Ellen had been heard to admit, grudgingly, that for a worthless, ignorant heathen she did well enough, considering her age. But there was hardly a lesson-hour when she did not materialise as if out of thin air for a stolen moment or two of wonder which she evidently thought worth a beating. Mrs. Mannion (tender-hearted as she was beautiful, thought the infatuated Mark) had once attempted to intercede for her.

"She does no harm, Stephen. Mr. Harvey, she does not interrupt the boys at their lessons, does she?"

His stammered negative had been drowned by Mr. Mannion's decisive reply:

"That is hardly the point, my love. She has other duties, and she must learn to attend to them. The greatest fault of these people is their total disregard for all regularity in their labour. They will be industrious for ten minutes, and then, for a whim, leave their task unfinished and revert to idleness. I intend to train this child in habits which will be of value to her, no doubt, should she ever be employed elsewhere. Dilboong, be off about your work immediately!"

It had sometimes seemed to Mark that she had some sixth sense, some primitive awareness inherited from ancestors who, for centuries, had lived by their alertness, their capacity for reacting in a flash to the faintest stimulus, their acute sensitivity to anything which menaced them, either physically or spiritually. He had known her to vanish from a room moments before Ellen entered it, and to disappear like a shadow before he had even heard the hoof-beats which heralded Mr. Mannion's return.

Suppressing a yawn, he bent over Miles' exercise. The boy was intelligent enough, he thought, but idle—unlike his elder brother, who brought a studious concentration to all his lessons. He said firmly:

"You must take greater pains with your spelling, Miles. Here is a word I corrected in your exercise only yesterday, and you have made the same error again. Now spell it."

Miles, smiling up at him amiably, intoned:

"B.E.L.I.E.V.E."

"Again . . ."

"B.E.L.I.E.V.E. But I think it looks just as well the other way, Mr. Harvey. Why can I not . . . ?"

"The other way is incorrect. Now write it down in capital letters three times, and then it may not escape your memory again. Say them aloud as you write them, if you please."

But it was not only Miles' voice which said them. From the background, faint as a distant echo, Dilboong chanted in time with him:

"B.E.L. . . ."

Mr. Harvey looked round at her in despair. She was so intent that she was unconscious of his forbidding regard; he thought she was not even aware that she was speaking aloud. When he addressed her she jumped, and backed away a few feet, startled and apprehensive.

"Dilboong, have I not told you again and again that you must not loiter on the verandah while Master Miles and Master Patrick are at their studies . . . ?"

Miles, pleased by the diversion, turned in his chair and smiled upon her benignly.

"She wants to read," he explained. "Dilboong, you want to learn to read and write, do you not?"

Mr. Harvey snapped:

"Nonsense! Attend to your work, Miles." To Patrick, who had lifted his eyes from his book, and was studying the child thoughtfully, he said: "Yes, Patrick?"

Patrick's serious blue eyes turned to him.

"Could natives learn to read, Mr. Harvey?"

Mark, baffled, said hastily:

"I—er—I don't know. I think their mental attainments would probably be entirely unequal . . . in any case, Patrick, it would serve no useful purpose. You have learned the passage I set?"

"No, Sir, not quite."

"Then continue with it. Miles, I must insist that you go on with your work. Dilboong . . ."

He glanced round for her. She was gone. And at that moment Ellen emerged from the house. She looked coldly menacing.

"Excuse me, Sir, if you please—has Dilboong been here?"

Mark, angrily conscious that he was colouring beneath the bland, enquiring gaze of Miles, answered:

"She was here—some little time ago . . ."

"Thank you, Sir."

She went indoors again. Miles, resting his arms akimbo on his slate, announced magnificently:

"I shall teach her to read and write."

"Then," retorted Mark rather tartly, "you had best set about learning yourself."

*   *   *   *   *

Ellen went out into the scullery and found Dilboong where she was supposed to be—kneeling upon the floor with a pail of water and a cloth. The child did not look up—only shrank a little from the sharp slap that set the side of her face tingling, and hardly heard the "idle, deceitful brat!" that Ellen hurled at her as she passed through the room. She felt that she had got off lightly, and she had brought back with her from her unlawful excursion to the verandah something for which a slap was a very small price to pay. The floor was made of planks stoned and sanded smooth; she began murmuring to herself, moving the cloth across it rhythmically, in time to her chant.

> "Bee-ee, ee-ee,
> Ell-ll, eye,
> Ee-ee, vee-ee, ee."

It was undoubtedly magic. She knew nothing of the sorceries of her own people, but her mind was atavistically receptive to the idea of magic: it mattered little whether the stories she learned of witchcraft, of invisible beings, of supernatural influences, of an unseen Father-of-all, were those of her own race, or those of the Reverend Mr. Johnson and his tribe. Baiame or God, it was all the same to her. She had never heard of Gnambucootchaly the evil spirit, but she had heard of Satan. She had never seen her people clamouring about their dead to speed his passing spirit to the sky, but she had learned from Mrs. Johnson that it was to the sky one went after death. She did not know about Nangali the cloud-man who gave a wand to the tribesmen by virtue of which they could summon him to appear in the heavens and bring rain; but she knew about Moses, who used a wand to smite a rock, and procure water for his tribe. No one had ever told her of Iltdana who opens graves and prowls the darkness clad in the rattling skeletons of the dead; but more than 'one shivering servant-maid had whispered in her presence of ghosts that haunt the graveyards in clanking chains. She understood magic very well, and of all the magic which the white people performed, none seemed so wonderful to her as that which they produced by making small marks like those which Miles formed upon his slate. She herself had known Mr. Johnson to cover a paper with such marks and bid her carry it to Mr. Atkins; and when she had done so Mr. Atkins had merely looked at it, and it was as if Mr. Johnson had spoken to him, though he was far away. All the magic over which Mr. Johnson presided on Sundays, when his tribe gathered about him and performed their rituals, was bound up with this magic of marks upon paper. For everyone held little books in which the mysteries were kept, and by looking at them they knew which words should be said upon different days to repel the evil spirits and propitiate the good. People who had mastered this magic could even take a closed box, or a package, and by looking at the marks upon it could tell before they opened it what was inside . . .

Dilboong crooned contentedly, swishing her cloth about, thinking of this mystery. It was the sight of the shining wet line it made on the floor which tempted her. She stopped crooning and was silent, still, her eyes growing round and her heart beginning to thump. She moved to a dry place and slowly, greatly daring, made a large, wet B with the cloth, and hastily smeared it out again. Nothing happened. She looked over her shoulder nervously into the dim corners of the room, but everything was quiet; no angry gods or spirits appeared to punish her for attempting the white man's magic. She crawled a little farther and repeated the B. Then she made an E, and an L, and an I; and then, faster, another E, and almost in a panic, a V—and then she stopped. She dared not add the last E. So long as it remained incomplete it was, perhaps, an impotent magic. Her hands were trembling a little, and she was almost crying with fright, but she was full of a wild, excited pride, too. The letters were large and clear and beautiful—those which Miles made upon his slate were no better —but already the first one was drying, disappearing before her eyes. Squatting back on her heels she watched it fade, and felt a kind of despair; there was something terrible and sad about the impermanence of an achievement which had cost her so much courage.

* * * * *

Conor walked down the hill towards the river. The summer was over, and she thought of that as she walked, and wondered that its passing should leave the land so unchanged. It was as if not only every other attribute of the civilised world had to be brought here, but the very seasons themselves;

for it was only in the cultivated fields, and the fruit trees, and the young oak outside the parlour window, and the row of little poplars flanking the house, that she could see evidence of autumn. The air was cooler when one was indoors, but the sun burning on her cheeks made her remember guiltily that she had forgotten her parasol again. She had promised Stephen to remember it; he had not shared her amusement one night when her mirror had reflected a delicate complexion darkened with sunburn, and a shapely nose quite frankly red. She sighed, half turned back, hesitated, and went on. She told herself that it was dull in the house when Stephen was absent for the whole day; but she missed him less for his own sake than because when he was there he was visible evidence of the reason for her own presence in a place where she still felt, sometimes, an interloper. It was a pity, she reflected, that Mr. Harvey's conversational powers seemed to be so limited—that her every word and look should throw him into such remarkable confusion. Of course he was in love with her—but why should that make him behave so oddly? Stephen was in love with her too, but he never blushed and stammered. She herself, she never doubted, was in love with Stephen—but she was not robbed of her senses and her composure by the fact.

Nor was Cousin Bertha, poor dear, a stimulating companion. She was kind and gentle, but her rheumatism had increased so much during the voyage that she was now often hardly able to do more than hobble with the aid of her silver-headed stick from her bed to her chair, and from her chair to her bed. And she was so very deaf, and forgetful and inattentive, and apt to fall asleep; and the kind of unimportant, gossipy comments and observations which were always itching on the end of Conor's busy tongue, sounded foolish when they were shouted . . .

All the same, she was glad that Cousin Bertha was here. The old blue eyes were vague, but they were loving, and there was even a ghost of merriment in them sometimes, though it faded abruptly when Stephen was near. Strange! She seemed almost afraid of Stephen! But the old, thought young Conor wisely, are full of fancies. This was but a foolish fancy, for dear Stephen was invariably civil to his aged kinswoman. But even as she thought of that civility Conor felt oppressed by a faint, uneasy bewilderment; its coldness and its emptiness touched her like a breath of warning.

To feel in herself a warning against Stephen was too disturbing and ridiculous; she evaded it quickly by transferring it to Ellen, in whose manner to herself she had felt this same cold and empty civility. A singular woman, silent and unresponsive, who would say nothing but "Yes'm," and "No'm," and who did not even thaw when Conor took some kindly notice of her two unprepossessing children . . .

As she walked this first shadow of loneliness subdued the high spirits which the crisp and lovely morning invited. She had led a secluded life, it was true, with few young people to afford her companionship, but she had found company in the books that lined her grandfather's study, security in his love, and that of her old nurse, more friend than servant, and pleasure in the goodwill of every other member and frequenter of the household. She sighed, gathering her skirts about her ankles to walk through a patch of tall, coarse grass. Miles, she reflected ruefully, whom she had warmly and romantically hoped to mother, seemed to need no mothering. He had done without it all his life, and appeared none the worse. Only Patrick seemed to promise companionship. He was, after all, but three years younger than herself, and she felt, wistfully, that if she had been able to go with him when he went riding and exploring along the river, time would have passed more pleasantly. Stephen, however, had forbidden such excursions unless he were there to act as her escort, and indeed, she admitted ruefully, Patrick himself did not seem anxious for her company.

In the evenings things were better, for then Stephen would usually withdraw with Mr. Harvey to his study, and there become absorbed in business matters, and she and Patrick and Miles would spend a couple of hours together. Sometimes Patrick would read aloud while she toyed with a scrap of embroidery, or re-arranged the ribbons on her best bonnet, and Miles listened, interrupted, and laughed. Sometimes they would just talk—about Ireland, about their voyages, about the colony, about the river and the mountains; and Miles would make wild plans for exploring them, and vow that somewhere he would discover gold-mines and diamond-mines. Then Patrick would remind him soberly that even the famous Mr. Bass had failed to cross those hills, and she would champion Miles till she remembered that she must not encourage him in wild fancies; and Miles, throwing his handsome head back, would laugh at her hasty admonitions until she laughed too.

Indeed, she thought, walking briskly, it was ungrateful in her to repine, even for a moment; she was most fortunate, and very, very happy. Stephen was a truly indulgent husband. She was the mistress of what was undoubtedly the most elegant house in the colony. She had only to express a wish, and (provided, of course, it were not something of which Stephen's superior judgment could not approve) it was immediately granted. And upon this thought she saw in the distance an overseer standing upon the river-bank, gesticulating to someone hidden from her sight.

She walked on until she could see two convicts labouring below him in the river-bed, and paused, wrinkling her brows, wondering what they could be doing, for she knew that all the labourers were needed in the fields. She went on till she too stood on the bank, but farther down-stream, and observed that the convicts were dislodging large, flat stones, and dragging them out to the foot of the bank.

Of course! She flushed with pleasure. She had conceived the idea —only yesterday morning—that she would like a rose-garden. It would be, she had explained eagerly to Stephen, planted around a stone-paved circle with a fountain in the middle—and dear Stephen, omnipotent and ever-indulgent, had already found time in the midst of his serious pre-occupations to set about accomplishing her desire! These, without doubt, were to be her paving stones! She looked delightedly at a pile of them already lying clear of the water at the foot of the bank; they were perfect, she thought, admiring their exquisite colouring—some pale yellow, some grey, some with a warm tint of reddish brown, and all very large and flat, with rounded edges and a smooth, water-worn surface . . .

All *very* large . . .

She became conscious of the convicts who, up till now, had been mere moving automata, disregarded. One was a small, wizened man who limped badly as he walked, and whose skinny arms, narrow shoulders and flat chest made him look almost like a child until he turned, and his lined face became visible. The other, stocky and thickset, seemed stronger, but she observed that even he struggled and sweated over his work.

The overseer swept his hat off in a deferential salute. She called graciously:

"Good morning, Toole."

"Good morning to ye, Ma'am, and a fine morning it is, to be sure!"

Her presence inspired him to display his zeal in her service. He bellowed to the convicts, gesturing towards the river:

"'Tis not pebbles we're wanting, ye lazy rascals! Fetch me up that yaller one—there—no, are ye blind? Farther down . . ."

She saw the two men, standing in the shallow water, pause and turn to lift their faces for a dumb moment towards him. The morning sun shone down on them with a light so searching that Conor felt a shock of repugnance for their sweat-streaked, unshaven ugliness, their gauntness, their strange expression of exhaustion and dammed-back revolt.

She felt a little frightened of them, and was glad that Toole had a pistol. They made suddenly real to her that hitherto vague menace, the rebellious lower classes, tidings of whose ravages, lawlessness and atrocities had disturbed the peace of her homeland for so long. They re-awakened memories of a hundred phrases heard but not fully realised—made them true, and perilous. *"They're burning houses in County Wicklow . . ."* *"No woman is safe with these miscreants at large."* Echoes of Stephen's voice said: *". . . the horrors and excesses perpetrated by rabbles . . ."* *"It would appear that our notorious countryman, Holt, has come to dwell among us . . ."* *"I must insist, Conor, that you do not walk or ride abroad unattended . . ."* And she remembered with a new comprehension that old warning which he had uttered soon after their betrothal: *"It IS a penal colony, my love . . ."*

But while she watched them the strange moment of tension passed. They turned away, and, with their backs to her as they waded through the shallows towards the yellow stone, became depersonalised again, no longer ominous. The smaller man walked bent, stumbling a little; the other carried a crowbar; she watched him drive its point beneath the stone and begin to drag down on it. The stone did not move. Toole yelled to the other man who was standing motionless in a curious, limp attitude, with drooping head and hanging hands:

"Ye worthless idler, it is a spectacle we're making for to entertain ye? Get on to it, the two of ye together! Finn, ye fool, stand back and make room for him on the bar . . . !" She saw Finn look at his companion, who looked back at him; there was another infinitesimal pause, and then the lame man stumbled to his position. The two pairs of arms strained downward; the stone moved a little, and a thread of muddy water ran out from beneath it and was lost in the clear rapids. Finn, stooping, dragged a smaller stone to place beneath the crowbar; crouching, with his hands feeling beneath the water, he was partially hidden from Toole by his companion, but not from Conor, to whom it appeared that he was taking longer than necessary, purposely delaying, glancing up now and then at his fellow-convict whose hand had crept up to his labouring chest. Her forehead creased with the sudden thought that he was, perhaps, ill— that the man called Finn was trying to gain time for him to recover his breath and strength before the next effort—and now the time was up, the moment no longer to be postponed, and she saw them both pull down on the bar, throw their whole weight on it, lift the stone's edge clear of the water . . .

And then the smaller man collapsed. His hands fell away, and he dropped to his knees uttering a queer sound between a grunt and a groan; with his weight gone from it the crowbar shot upward again, the stone sank back into its bed, Finn staggered a little and recovered, and Toole began to shout angrily.

She heard the shouting, but only as a background of noise adding confusion to the intent labouring of her mind as she watched Finn. He stood over his crouching companion, motionless, his head slightly bent but his eyes fixed on the overseer, and again there was something in his expression which was frightening. There was doom in it, there was fate in it; there was hatred and contempt, but there was also a kind of detached, intelligent observation. It was implacable, but it was also patient. To Conor, that look—unconscious of her as it was—asserted that she was wrong to see this merely as a painful incident. Into her distress and dismay shot the thought that it was not happening only *here*, but everywhere— not only *now*, but long ago, and far, far into the future . . .

The thought flashed and vanished, like lightning. She was blind again, but with the memory of having seen. She knew nothing but that she had grown angry herself, and that every bellow from Toole was making her angrier. She called out sharply:

"The stone is too large, Toole."

He whipped off his hat again to address her.

"Sure, then, Ma'am, there's no great weight in it. The lazy rascals'll have it out for ye, never fear, or me name's not . . ."

She cried angrily:

"I do not wish it out. It is . . . too large for my purpose. Kindly see that none is larger than . . . than those already on the bank."

She was conscious only for a second of his surprised face, whose angry mortification showed through the thin smear of a hasty smile; she was confronting that steady stare of Finn's again, now fixed upon herself so disconcertingly that she turned quickly away. Her departure, for all its dignity, for all its carefully unhurried pace, was a flight.

She walked downstream along the high bank, watching the river, watching the birds, watching a floating stick, watching tiny fish darting in the shallows, watching the butterflies in the grass about her feet—but thinking of none of them. Stephen had said to her: "*It IS a penal colony, my love . . .*" but she had only just begun to realise what that meant. It meant that she, Conor Mannion, had *enemies*. It meant that she, herself, was an enemy. She had been brought up to feel herself surrounded by love, and the thought shocked her. She was bewildered by the knowledge that her moment of sharp, personal compassion for those two men had not been enough—not nearly enough—to exorcise a vast, impersonal enmity towards her which she had felt, and which was still making her heart beat a little faster than usual.

She sat down on the bank with her hands clasped about her knees, and worried about it. Stephen was right—Stephen, of course, was always right —this was a strange place she had come to. She fumbled for a word to express her anxious thought, and found "barriers." There were no barriers here; things came close about you—close, clear, demanding, not to be ignored. She had always thought the lower classes set apart as by some act of God—naturally, inevitably, finally. She had always believed that she would spend her life among people, conventions, situations tailored by custom to fit her. And here—not only at Beltrasna, but throughout the colony—it was as if that way of living had been wrenched askew. It existed still—but it was no longer all that existed. She had once thought that it was life itself; now it seemed only a garment—one of many garments, perhaps?—that life might wear. Why had the man stared at her like that? Hatred! She plucked a long blade of grass and twisted it nervously in her fingers, trying to believe that what she had seen was not the stare of an enemy, but merely the naturally forbidding expression of a degraded and ill-favoured felon. For why, she asked herself, flinging her mangled grass-blade away petulantly, should he hate her? She armoured herself hastily in the truth that she had never personally oppressed any member of the lower classes, and that it was, therefore, unjust, outrageous, and unthinkable that they should regard her with animosity; but the thought gave her strangely little comfort. Her own dislike, at this moment, was directed not at them, but at Toole, who was, she unwillingly acknowledged, on her side. She, in a fleeting and isolated incident, could champion them against him—but they were not deceived. Ultimately, in some wider and vaster warfare which was no incident, but the whole of life, it was for him to champion her against them . . .

She stood up, brushing grass-seeds from her skirts, and began to walk back, slowly, along the bank. She could not forget the undersized convict whom she had last seen on his knees, clutching at his chest as if in pain, and it was with relief that she observed, when she reached her vantage-point again, that he seemed to have recovered.

But perhaps not altogether; for she thought that as they rolled a stone from the creek to the bank, it was Finn who really took the weight, while the other man did little more than rest his hands upon it. As she watched they began, in response to a shouted order, to shift the pile of landed stones up the steep bank. Some were small enough to be carried between them, but others had to be dragged, rolled, levered, manœuvred through the mud inch by inch up the slippery slope. They had one half-way to the top when Finn's foot skidded, and he fell heavily, sprawling downhill to the pile of stones below. The smaller man held on for a frantic moment to his burden, teetering on its edge, but its weight defeated him. Conor saw it began to roll, saw Finn on his hands and knees attempt to scramble clear of it, and heard his cry, and the crash as it met the pile, pinning his leg from the knee down.

Suddenly she was blind with anger again. Life, outrageously harsh and inimical where it had always been benevolent before, had made her responsible for this. Her thought was one wild protest. Had she asked that men might suffer to make her rose-garden? Hardly knowing what she did, she descended in a fury upon the overseer who, having levered the stone clear, was bending over the injured man and trying to drag him ungently to his feet.

"What are you doing?" she cried fiercely. "He cannot walk . . ."

"We'll see . . . !" said Toole, dragging; and then, catching her eye, he emerged sufficiently from his temper to adjust his tone to one of suitable respect. " 'Tis nothing, Ma'am—a scratch—do not distress yourself, Ma'am, I beg . . . a small mishap which . . ."

She repeated vehemently:

"He can neither walk nor stand—you hear me? You will go immediately and summon men to carry him to his quarters."

Toole, straightening, looked at her in amazement and apprehension. Mr. Mannion, he was thinking uneasily, would be ill-pleased to find one of his strongest men incapacitated. Agitated, but still obsequious, he said cajolingly:

"Sure, Ma'am, 'tis not necessary . . ."

She stamped her foot, and felt it sink over her shoe-top in mud.

"You will do precisely as I bid you, Sir! You will take this other man with you, for he is not fit to work, and is to do no further work to-day. I shall remain here until you return . . ."

He protested in real horror:

"Whisht, Ma'am, is it leaving you here I'd be, with a rogue the like of this? His Honour would have me blood, Ma'am, and rightly! If you would be so kind, Ma'am, as to send word to . . ."

She looked down at Finn, lying grey-faced, and with shut eyes.

"You talk like a fool!" she said contemptuously. "I can be in no danger from an injured man."

"Your pardon, Ma'am, but it's years I've been working for His Honour, and I well acquaint with all the tricks of scum like these. They're all malingerers, Ma'am, and the master . . ."

Her sharp gesture froze him into silence.

"The master is away, as you well know, and during his absence you will receive your orders from me. Go!"

But when they had gone her anger ebbed, and with it her confidence. She felt unfamiliar to herself. She was alone on the bank of a wild, remote river in a country still strange to her, with a convicted felon. She was standing ankle-deep in mud; the hem of her skirt was soiled and heavy with it; she had been afraid, and she had been angry; she was a stranger to herself. She looked down at the man and saw that his eyes were shut, that there was grey in his hair and his stubble of beard, but that his eyebrows were black and thick, and his lashes long, so that she was strangely reminded of Miles as he looked when he lay asleep. Before, when there was anything to be done, she had always rung a bell, and servants came to do it. Now she felt that there was much to be done, but she stood motionless, helpless, doubtful, uncertain what it was. His injury should be dressed and tended. She glanced swiftly at the bare foot and ankle protruding from a ragged and filthy trouser leg; the flesh was swollen and purple, a dark streak of blood already clotting on it. She looked away again hurriedly, clasping her fingers together hard. His head, perhaps, should be more comfortably pillowed—but on what? Was he unconscious? For swooning there were hartshorn, and vinegar and burnt feathers—but not here. Should she dash water in his face? There was, at least, water . . .

She picked her way down the bank through the mud, and bent, holding her skirts gathered about her, to dip a handkerchief in the river. Returning to him, she felt her hands baulk and hesitate before they would approach him. He was, she thought with a little shiver of dismay, so incredibly dirty, and the smell of dried sweat from his body and his clothes filled her with nausea. She dabbed the wet handkerchief hastily over his face, and then laid it on his forehead. The opening of his eyes startled her so much that she drew back abruptly, slipped, and found herself sitting in the mud, meeting his gaze with a fascinated alarm.

He pushed himself up on his elbow, put his hand to his brow, felt the handkerchief, took it in his hand and looked at it, and from it to her again before he replaced it. The tightness and the stress of pain were on his face but no other expression. He turned his head, looking up the bank.

"They have gone," she explained hurriedly, "to summon men who will carry you . . . the other man was not strong enough. . . . I fear your leg must be extremely painful . . . indeed, when I asked Mr. Mannion for a rose-garden I did not . . ."

She stopped, horrified and confused. What did he know of her rose-garden? Was she making excuses—*apologising*—to a convict . . . ? He looked at her again, incuriously, as though he had not heard her, and lay down with his head pillowed on his arm.

His indifference annihilated her. His utter lack of response to her attempt at ministration made her feel at once unhappy, astonished, and annoyed; should he not have been humble, grateful, overwhelmed by her condescension . . . ?

The sun, climbing higher, shone down on them hotly. She began to wish for her parasol. Flies buzzed about the prostrate man, and he lifted his hand from time to time to brush them from his face. They swarmed about the clot of blood on his ankle. Conor, fanning them from her own mouth and eyes, felt herself near to tears. That he should choose this moment when she could see only through a dazzle of moisture to look at her, disturbed her so much that she rose quickly, snatched the handkerchief from his head, and turned away.

"I will wet it again." Crouching over the water, she regained her composure and returned to him with dignity. He was sitting up, craning forward, trying to drive the flies from his leg. She waved them away, placed the handkerchief over the swollen flesh, and asked recklessly:

"You would like a drink of water, perhaps?"

Even before he had answered with a short, expressionless "Yes" she had realised that she had no drinking-vessel—no means of giving him what she had offered. She had realised that she must cup water in her hands and let him drink from them. Close to panic, she peered over the top of the bank, hoping for Toole's return; but there was no one in sight.

She went down to the river again and brought him a few mouthfuls in her hollowed palms; it was only by the fiercest effort of will that she did not snatch them away from the incredible touch of his unshaven cheeks and chin, but she asked him, nevertheless:

"Shall I bring you more?"

Again he assented; again she nerved herself to endure his touch. When he had drunk he looked at her drying her hands on her skirt, and surlily said:

"It's well enough I'll be doing now, Ma'am, till they return. There's no need ye should be waiting here, and the sun hot on ye . . ."

She replied nervously:

"I do not find it too warm." But the sound of his voice, its brogue, the familiar intonation of her native countryside, was vaguely reassuring. She asked:

"What is your name?"

"Matthew Finn, Ma'am."

"And the other man—he who was working with you?"

"Dan Driver."

"From what part of Ireland do you come?"

"From County Wicklow, Ma'am."

"I," she offered uncertainly, "have relatives there—I often visit—used to visit them . . ."

He glanced at her, and away again, as if the information could have no possible interest for him. Pride would not allow her thus to be silenced. She asked more coldly:

"Your leg is paining you, I fear?"

"It is that, Ma'am."

Her remorse, her feeling of personal guilt, swelled in her till it forced an outlet in a few incoherent words.

"Indeed I wish it had not . . . I am greatly distressed . . ."

He felt a sudden stab of pain that goaded his long-disciplined deeply-buried anger to the surface. It lit his face for an instant like a glare of lightning, so that she moved back from him a pace, and thought wildly that Toole had been right—she should not have remained here alone with a creature who looked so villainous, so full of hatred. He cried out at her loudly, violently, on a breath that ended in a gasp:

"Distressed, is it? Let ye be keepin' y' distress for y' spoiled gown, and y' shoes with mud on them . . . !"

Blank astonishment mingled with her flash of fear; rage killed them both.

"How dare you address me like that!"

He was silent for a moment, breathing heavily. His face darkened; the watchful, patient enmity settled down on it again like a cloud, dimming its brief blaze of reckless hostility.

"There's times," he muttered, not looking at her now, "when a man goes so low in misery that he can go no lower; and then he'll dare anything."

She was still breathless with shock. Never—*never* in all her life— had any member of the lower classes spoken to her save with respect . . . not even the servants of her grandfather's household, privileged as they were . . . and now a convict, a felon!

She said fiercely:

"There are punishments for insolence which I think could bring you even lower in misery than you are now!"

He uttered a sort of laugh—harsh, mirthless, defiant.

"Is it a flogging ye threaten me with?"

She came to her senses then, aghast, frightened by the ugliness into which her moment of temper and hurt pride had betrayed her. She stammered:

"Indeed I threaten you with nothing. . . . I would not wish . . . and I understand that—that the pain of your injury caused you to speak unguardedly . . ."

He retorted quickly, angrily:

"I spoke me mind, an' 'tis not a bruise that would be making me speak it."

That he should make light of his suffering gave her, suddenly, a key to this incomprehensible situation. It made him a mere man, touchy, as all men are about their physical hardihood, eternally unwilling to admit that pain might even for a moment govern their actions or their tongues. Grandfather, in his attacks of gout, had been just the same. She discovered that in thinking of him as a man, and not as a convict, she felt less confused, for it gave her a status in relation to him which she could recognise. She fell quite naturally and easily into the tone with which women indulgently rebuke the little vanities of men.

"It is more than a bruise, I think."

That tone, with its sureness, its hint of dry reproof for an obvious lie, brought a response from him. He glanced at her sideways with eyes which for the first time saw her not as the master's wife, but as herself. He looked a little startled, and more than a little sheepish, but a spark of unexpected liveliness, awkward from long disuse, flashed in his answer.

"Faith, Ma'am, I think so too."

It was a confession; it was an agreement; it was a kind of truce declared. She had hardly begun to savour the ease and relief of it when she heard voices, and rose hurriedly to peer over the bank. Toole was returning with two convicts. She said over her shoulder: "They are coming." And suddenly, knowing this bewildering but most interesting incident about to close, she realised that she still had many things to say—to ask. . . . She realised that she had been holding a phrase in her mind ever since he had uttered it—holding it awkwardly, fearfully, measuring it with alarm and incredulity against her own bright existence. "So low in misery . . ."

She crouched beside him and enquired urgently:

"What did you mean when you said . . . I did not know that my husband's labourers . . . are you in truth so low in misery that you would dare anything?"

He answered without looking at her, his face forbidding:

"The life of a convict is not a kindly one, Ma'am."

"But—but it can only be made worse by. . . . Are you not afraid of —of the punishments that could be inflicted on you?"

Still he did not look at her; his words seemed less an answer to her than a reluctant admission to himself.

"Aye, I'm afraid of them, Ma'am, as any man would be, and him with no more than human flesh, and the nerves in him shrinkin' from pain, and the pride in him cryin' out against humiliation . . ."

"And yet," she insisted, speaking hurriedly in the knowledge of those approaching figures, "you would dare it for—for what . . . ?"

He looked at her now, wary, suspicious of her sudden catechism, but obsessed like herself by the excitement of this stolen moment of honest communication. His eyes darted from her face to the bank, and back again, but his answer seemed spoken to himself rather than to her.

"For freedom . . ."

"But you would *not* be free!" She was almost whispering. "You would be less free than ever, would you not?"

He put his hand up to his head exhaustedly:

"I? Yes . . . an' that's the truth, Ma'am. But freedom is not mine —not mine alone—*nor yours* . . . !"

She did not know what he meant, but there was a startling challenge in his eyes and his tone as he hurled those last two words at her. For a second they stared at each other, their awkward attempt at spiritual contact slain by the reality of the war between them. She, hardy in her ignorance, reckless in her youthful curiosity, would have sought to re-establish it, but the moment was past, and they were no longer alone. She turned away from him, scrambled up the bank, ignoring Toole's deferential offer of assistance, and set off across the fields, walking fast and blindly.

*   *   *   *   *

Mr. Mannion, hearing of the incident, was displeased. "You will relieve my mind, Conor, by giving me your assurance that you will not again venture so far from the house alone."

She evaded that with a question:

"The man's injury is better, Stephen?"

"He will do very well."

For the next few days she felt restless. She opened a novel which Stephen had brought her from Sydney, but it bored her; she tried to alter a dress to the new mode with puffed sleeves, and failed; she stitched desultorily at an embroidered bandeau for her hair; she played piquet with Cousin Bertha, and was relieved when the old lady fell asleep; she began a letter to her grandfather, and put it aside. She watched the convicts going to and fro between their hut and the fields, and was haunted by Finn's words. "*So low in misery . . .*" She seemed to notice things as she had not done before. Their drab colouring and their shapelessness which made them look like mere moving clods of the earth, had a new meaning. She had seen one of them at close quarters, touched, smelt him, and she knew that these things meant dirt, sweat, rags, the degeneration of unwashed and untended bodies. She took to rising early and standing on the verandah to watch the men going to work. In that first quiet hour of daylight she felt their ugliness and their servitude as she had never felt it before. The scene which enclosed them then underlined their maimed humanity; in the untouched purity of the crisp air, in the diamond glitter of dew on the grass, in the long soft shadows and the long pale shafts of sunlight, in the river, cool and placid, in the quiet hills and the silence, she felt an innocence and a cleanliness through which the convicts moved like an offence—like a blasphemy. She found herself thinking of them all day. She heard Toole speaking to her husband. A man called Geraghty . . . insubordinate . . . he would appear before the magistrate at Parramatta . . .

She thought: ". . . *and him with no more than mortal flesh, and the nerves in him shrinking from pain . . .*" She found that the palms of her hands were damp, and wiped them on her handkerchief. She wandered out on to the verandah, paced up and down, blind to the anxious and devoted stare of Mr. Harvey, and then suddenly, as if driven, went rapidly inside to her husband's study, and entered.

He was writing, and his upward glance at her was surprised rather than welcoming, but he rose courteously.

"You wish to speak to me, my love?"

"Yes, Stephen." She stood opposite him, playing nervously with a paper knife which lay on the table. "How . . . how is he?"

" 'He'? Who is 'he'?"

"The convict . . . Matthew Finn." She spoke rapidly, with a slight breathlessness. "The man whose leg was injured."

He frowned.

"Toole tells me it will yet be a day or two before he can work again. It was most unfortunate. But have no fear, your garden shall go forward, nevertheless. I have had two other men directed . . ."

She interrupted sharply:

"I do not want the garden!"

"You do not *want* . . . ?" He stared at her in astonishment. Her face was flushed and her eyes looked near to tears. His frown deepened. It was not the first time he had found her youth, with its urgency, its undisciplined emotions, its sudden and unpredictable shiftings from one mood to another, a trifle tiresome. He was not a young man, and he desired tranquillity. His Conor, for all the loveliness which had ensnared, and still often delighted him, was not tranquil. He sighed. It was his duty—having married her—to mould her, to guide her development from this rather gauche and over-emphatic girlhood into a serene and gracious maturity. He set about it.

"My dear, you have been—very naturally—distressed by the incident you so unfortunately witnessed, but I have every confidence in your good sense. A gentlewoman, my love, maintains her poise in all circumstances. To say that you no longer want your garden because of a mishap in which, believe me, I should not have had you involved for worlds, is not worthy of you. It is childish. We shall say no more of the matter. Now there is a more pleasant subject . . ."

She drew a quick breath and blinked her eyes hard.

"I do *not* want the garden, Stephen. I should take no pleasure in it. And I am anxious to know that he—that the convict, Finn, is receiving proper attention for . . ."

He interrupted coldly:

"That you may leave to me, Conor. I am indeed astonished—I will even say displeased—that you should intrude into matters which don't concern you in the least. Now, if you will be so kind as to give me your attention, I have here . . ."

She said stubbornly:

"It is my understanding of marriage that my husband's concerns are also mine. I have no wish to intrude, Stephen, but I beg your assurance that the man's injury has been properly tended and . . ."

He walked past her to the door and shut it. He drew a chair forward for her with some ceremony, and waited until she had seated herself, tensely upright, on its edge. Under his cold, angry gaze she felt burdened by her youth, her ignorance, and her inexperience; she hated the tears that were scalding her eyes, and the nervousness which seemed to be closing her throat; she knew that she had only to succumb, to let the tears flow, to admit herself wrong, to say "Of course you know best, Stephen"—and this horrible scene would be over. He would be gentle, forgiving, indulgent, and playfully chiding; he would wipe her eyes and kiss her . . .

She said almost inaudibly:

"I ask only for that assurance, Stephen."

He replied at length. His cool, controlled politeness chilled her courage as no scolding could have done. His knowledge and assurance shamed her. Did she not realise that labour was of the first importance to his affairs? Did she suppose him so foolish as to neglect an injury which was holding one of his most valuable servants idle? She was very young, and consequently permitted her natural and admirable tenderness of heart to govern her judgment; but he would remind her that for those whose duty and privilege it was to protect her, there could be no romanticism in dealing with convicts. "These are felons, Conor. They are criminals. This man in whom you interest yourself has been guilty of plotting to bring the whole fabric of civilisation crashing to the ground.

That is why he is here. He has plotted in Ireland, and—have no doubt of it—he would plot again if the opportunity presented itself. Did you not hear at home of rioting and violence—of houses burned to the ground? Answer me, if you please."

"I—yes, Stephen."

"Do you wish to hear of the same thing in this country?"

"No—oh, of course no, but . . ."

"I have endeavoured to shield you from even the rumour of such things. But I must now inform you that in Sydney and Parramatta at this moment they are causing grave concern to those in authority. There is the same spirit of unrest at large here as has already manifested itself —with what hideous results you know—in our own country. It has not been absent among my convicts, and I have good reason to believe that it is nourished by the seditious utterances of this very man for whom you show what is, believe me, a most inappropriate concern. You find that incredible?"

She looked up at him, but did not see him. She saw, instead, Finn's face as she had seen it when he stared at the overseer . . . when it had frightened her . . . when she had felt glad of Toole's pistol. . . . No, she did not find it incredible. Her face was white, and her eyes reflected a dazed uncertainty. She shook her head, slowly, unwillingly. He continued, some of the coldness gone from his voice:

"I have thought it advisable, my love, to be thus frank with you. Your inexperience of life may, if you are not forewarned, lead you into indiscretions. Rest assured that this man will receive such attention as is necessary to enable him to perform his duties—but banish from your mind, I beg of you, any concern for a criminal who would show you no mercy if he were ever able to achieve his villainous designs." He turned to the table and picked up a sheet of paper. "And now, my dearest Conor, pray let us speak of happier things. See, I have a little surprise for you!"

"A surprise, Stephen . . . ?"

He put the letter in her hand. She read; realised that though her eyes had seen the words, her mind had not grasped them; read again:

> "Gov'r Hunter presents his Comp'ts to Mr. and Mrs.
> Mannion, and requests the honour of their Company
> at dinner on Friday, 23rd, at Gov't House. 3 o'clock."

"We shall leave to-morrow, and pass a few days at Sydney . . ." Mannion was saying when she suddenly put her face down in her hands and wept. He was all concern; he consoled her tenderly. "You have been pale of late, my dearest—I have observed it. Our life here is something tedious, I fear, but this little excursion will restore your liveliness. You need the companionship of your own sex. Mrs. Paterson extends her hospitality to us. Dry your eyes, I entreat you, my love, and make your preparations for our modest festivities . . ."

She said: "Yes, Stephen," and escaped, bewildered by her own sudden tears.

*   *   *   *   *

But Sydney was not very festive. At first it seemed to Conor as they left Beltrasna behind and rode towards what passed for civilisation in this distant land, that she was waking up from a disturbed and dreaming sleep. From Parramatta, where they halted to dine with the Macarthurs, she looked back at herself as she had been doing the previous week, feeling that vague wonder with which, in health, one looks back on the twilight time of illness. In Sydney, where Mrs. Paterson swept her into the midst of such society as the colony afforded, she almost succeeded in forgetting that she had ever been anything but light-hearted. Captain and Mrs. King made much of her; Governor Hunter—though he seemed apt to be even more gloomily preoccupied than before—exerted himself to treat her with a ponderous gallantry. She renewed her acquaintance with her fellow-voyagers, the Abbotts. Major Foveaux, Captain Johnston, and many other gentlemen were presented to her, and a certain amusing Captain Piper was agreeably attentive. His Excellency's nephew, Lieutenant Kent, who commanded the *Buffalo*, escorted her with a party of other ladies upon a tour of his ship. Mr. Robert Campbell, a young merchant who had established himself in Sydney some two years previously, talked to her with a seriousness which she found flattering. There was a delightful boating party, at which the gentlemen vied with each other to place cushions for Mrs. Mannion, arrange her parasol, and ply her with refreshments.

It was all so much more like the world to which she had been accustomed that she was nearly beguiled by it into a feeling of security and reassurance. All these gentlemen talked to her of the beauties of the harbour, the quaint customs of the natives, the diversions and amenities of a far-away society nostalgically recalled—and, as gentlemen will, of themselves. But she heard them talking, also, to each other. Then—and when the conversation was no longer tête-a-tête, but general—there were different matters for discussion, and she found the small-talk, the trivialities, the courtesies and the compliments flowing over the surface of her mind, while its depths were disturbed by under-currents.

Because this community was so small, she was able to see it, though not to understand it, in its entirety. Here was the great world in miniature, and very close. The matters which she heard discussed were happening within a score of miles from where she sat. The policies of Government, which she had hitherto known only as remote abstractions, were here in the making at her very elbow; criticisms of them were not criticisms of distant powers, unknown and unimaginable, but attacks upon an elderly and bedevilled Governor at whose table she had dined. In the life she had known before her marriage, food, clothes and wine had flowed in a mysterious but utterly reliable stream from some unknown source; she had never speculated about the labour which produced them, or the financial manœuvrings which attended their marketing. Now she found herself trying to piece together from scattered remarks a picture of the system by which they all lived. She had thought of soldiers as crusaders who fell on the field of battle in defence of their country, and she was more than a little astonished to find that the conversation of these soldiers was concerned almost exclusively with buying and selling. She had thought of them, too, as supporters of authority, and she had seen and accepted authority as vested in the Governor. Yet it needed only a word here, a sharp phrase there, a shrug, a sneer, the intonation of a voice saying "His Excellency," to teach her that some conflict existed where she had assumed unity. Yet these people who combined against the Governor were not, she discovered with increased amazement, entirely at one among themselves. She was even the abashed and unwilling recipient of whispered confidences: "This fellow is a rogue." "That fellow is not to be trusted." "I declare, my love, it is openly said . . ." "Mrs. Mannion, pray pay no attention to that shameless mischief-maker . . ." "I have it on the best authority that he bribed . . ." "There is a rumour abroad that he and the Governor . . ." "A man utterly without scruple, I assure you . . ." "When you consider his origins, my dear, his pride and insolence are intolerable . . ." "They say . . ." "I am told . . ." "I have heard . . ."

Yet they combined. She was conscious that apart from all their personal feuds they had a common purpose, and common enemies. For it was not only the Governor's name which brought the hard light and the acid tone of antagonism to their eyes and lips. She learned, for example, that they regarded with great disfavour the Mr. Campbell whose conversation she had found so interesting. And at the mention of the lower classes—convicts, emancipists, the poorer settlers—they became almost wolfish in their enmity. Feeling their hatred of these people, she felt in it an element which was less evident in their hatred of the Governor—fear. The word "rebellion" was used until, by mere repetition, it became ominous. They muttered "insubordinate," and "seditious," and "lawless," and "conspiracies," and "revolt," until she began to catch the infection of their alarm, remembering the river bank, and the bitter face of a convict, and his strange, hostile, defiant words. Yet under a growing uneasiness she felt curiosity stir; with the mounting of a tense expectancy, the ebb of gaiety from her heart passed almost unnoticed. She thought—and was young enough to feel apprehension shot with excitement—"Surely something is going to happen . . . !"

She was not alone in this disquiet, this sense of events waiting to be born of pregnant circumstances. From her seclusion, and from the false serenity in which Stephen had enclosed her life, she came late, and suddenly, to a situation whose menace had been present since the foundation of the colony, mounting for years, sharply increasing in the last months. Unrest was growing stronger every day. The despair of convicts was more and more reinforced by the despair of emancipists who found that emancipation bestowed few practical benefits, and by settlers who became ever more embittered as the prices of commodities soared farther beyond their resources. Among them were now heard the rebellious doctrines of those who already, in a different scene, had raised voices, and sometimes weapons, against oppression. They worked in sullen and resentful minds like yeast in dough. They whispered that in this place the oppressors were few, and that rebels would be no longer leaderless. Were there not men among them who had led insurrection in the very strongholds of privilege . . . ?

Revolt was in the air of this distant land as it was in the air of the great world outside. Like the smell from the smoke of burning forests, it crept across the country, drifted through the streets of Sydney and Parramatta, filtered into the huts of convicts, into the soldiers' barracks, into the gaols, into the settlers' modest dwellings, and—most disturbingly of all—into the homes of the wealthy. All through the year 1800 people whispered, muttered, shook their heads. Mrs. Paterson, seated at her escritoire on a hot February afternoon, had already recorded the sense of general uneasiness in her delicate, pointed writing: "*The Minerva arrived about a month ago with the first cargo of rebels—they are already begun to concert Schemes. I fear they will be a troublesome set. I cannot say I like the place near so well as I did before . . .*"

To Hunter at Government House had come rumours that Irish convicts were holding secret and unlawful meetings. He had caused an investigation to be held, and discovered—nothing. Yet the smell of revolt, like the smell of smoke, was unmistakable; a smoke meant a fire, and somewhere, he knew, the fires of rebellion were smouldering.

He thought with a certain dour satisfaction that his own escape was near. It was even in his heart sometimes to hope that King, so impatient to take control, would have this problem to deal with besides all the others which had made his own period in office a long nightmare. For relations were not happy between the Governor and the Governor-elect. The latter's presence in the colony at this time, when Hunter, smarting under official censure, was preparing to leave it, was a continual irritation to the older man, a pin-pricking of his pride, a threat to his consequence. Beneath King's stiff deference and his careful civility, Hunter read criticism. Behind every formal approach made to him in his official capacity, he guessed at a hundred informal approaches made to King. He felt himself consulted as a mere matter of routine, deferred to as a mere matter of convention; Government House had become the empty shell of authority, while the powerful and the influential manœuvred and jockeyed for position with King.

Hunter held on to his dwindling importance with a stubborn, bitter persistence. He knew that King spoke openly of reforms which he intended to effect upon his accession to the Governorship, and he knew also that throughout the colony the impression grew that his successor, and not himself, was now the man whose ear was to be sought. As the weeks after King's arrival stretched into months, the relationship between them, strained from the beginning, grew taut under the stress of an emotion which was irritation rather than personal enmity. It betrayed them both into moments of asperity; words and phrases crept into their ceremonious letters to each other which were mere outbursts of temper, born of nervous reaction to a long-drawn-out and intolerable situation.

King, suffering the disappointment of knowing his accession still further delayed, had planted a barb in one of his earliest letters to Hunter which rankled all through the months that followed. For he was s of delays. His dormant commission as Governor of New South Wales in the event of Hunter's death or absence had dated from May, 1798, and from that time until the departure of the *Speedy* in October, 1799, he had been obliged to cool his heels in England, keeping himself and his family in constant readiness to embark. He had actually sailed once, in the *Porpoise*, a ship which, already twice disabled, had been once more compelled to put back into port. Again he had been forced to maintain his family in expensive lodgings; he had spent his savings, and even anticipated his future salary to the tune of some four hundred pounds; he had found many of his belongings, stored for fifteen months on the *Porpoise*, damaged and useless; he had arrived in Port Jackson at last with the feeling that a bad dream of frustration and adversity was behind him. He was ready, eager, agog to begin his task.

There was no doubt about the instructions sent to Hunter. He was to return to England "*by the first safe conveyance which offers itself after the arrival of Lieut.-Governor King.*" That knowledge had been maddeningly clear in King's mind as he penned his first letter to Portland at the end of April—already aware that it was to be four months before Hunter proposed to sail. "*I deliver this,*" he wrote, "*to Governor Hunter for his inspection and forwarding by the* Friendship, *which. proceeds from hence to Bengal to load for Europe the 3rd or 4th of next month.*" But it was less to Portland than to Hunter himself that he addressed the next sentence. "*Agreeable to Your Grace's direction, I have to inform you that the* Friendship *is the FIRST . . .*" his pen scored a heavy underlining, "*. . . safe conveyance that has offered since my arrival; but the time appearing too short to Governor Hunter to arrange his business, he informs me that it is his intention to take his passage in the* Buffalo, *and to sail about August. Perhaps no other safe conveyance may occur before that period; but should His Majesty's commands for Governor Hunter's return by the first safe conveyance not be attended to (which I have no reason to suppose can or will be the case) I shall not fail to follow my instructions.*"

Hunter, reading that, felt his cheeks darken with a fierce flush of rage. He snatched a pen and copied it down. More than once in the ensuing months he read it, always with a boiling indignation.

*   *   *   *   *

King, in the meantime, kept his eyes open, and his ears attuned to the sounds of varied colonial conflict. He was not simple enough to imagine that the cordial welcome he had received from the officers on his arrival was a guarantee of enduring tranquil relations. "*Many,*" he wrote sardonically to Sir Joseph Banks, "*will change their tone when their nefarious proceedings are arrested.*" He saw the havoc wrought by the liquor traffic; he noted that the children lived in an environment of misery, vice and prostitution; he was startled and shocked by the exorbitant prices demanded for the most common necessities. His wife, aware of trouble brewing for her husband, naïvely felt that once formally established as Governor, he would be armoured against it; she pined, too, for the amenities of Government House.

"I declare, King," she protested, "it seems vastly unjust that you should be kept so long out of your authority. It has been said to me more than once that many would gladly see you at Government House even before Mr. Hunter . . ."

He interrupted her impatiently.

"Impossible, my dear Anna! I have myself been approached by officers, both civil and military, to take the command, but I assure you it cannot be contemplated."

"You are the best judge, my love. Yet to me it appears madness that the colony should remain in so wretched a state for want of determined direction . . ."

"Determination," he replied, speaking as much to himself as to her, "will not alone suffice. Patience, patience. My task will call for much of that quality—and by Heaven . . . !" he added restlessly, ". . . by the time this delay is ended I shall have learned to command it! There can be no half-measures in a situation of this kind. A total change must take place, and *will* take place when I am left to myself. But there must be no reckless haste, no violent or sudden measures. For I shall have enemies, never doubt, when it is observed that I propose to alter the present course . . ."

"But on all hands," she exclaimed, "I hear condemnation of the present course! Surely you can look for support from . . ."

"I can look for support," he assured her grimly, "from no one but myself. Those who should support me will be my enemies, for the success of my plans will mean the downfall of their own. Has not Captain Johnston—who, as the Governor's aide-de-camp, should surely be above reproach!—just now been put under arrest for selling liquor to a sergeant of his company?" He laughed shortly. "You have no great facility in matters of business, my love, but you can well understand, I should suppose, how profitable it is to buy liquor off the ship at ten shillings the gallon, and dispose of it at twenty-four shillings. And has not this same individual in the great goodness of his heart permitted a large number of the Government stock to run upon one of his farms—and has he not at another more distant farm calves belonging to the Crown which enjoy his most generous hospitality? Nor is he the only one. Reflect, my love—shall I endear myself to them when—even with the most handsome thanks for their past magnanimity—I withdraw all Government stock from the control of private individuals? Do not deceive yourself, my dear Anna. I, who am now hailed as the deliverer, will soon enough be dubbed the tyrant!"

She sighed.

"I declare the place is so full of rumour and gossip, and everything so disturbed by ill-will, that I scarce know how to confront the people that I meet. Only yesterday there was a female in the street—who, I assure you, had never been presented to me—and she eyed me with so strange a look of meaning that I was quite put out of countenance! Mrs. Paterson told me she was the wife of one of the Scottish rebels—a Mrs. Margarot—

though why she should have winked and grimaced at me passes all under-standing . . ."

He shrugged irritably.

"I can enlighten you, my love. I received a most impudent com-munication from her husband—a letter couched in mysterious terms of innuendo, and having the impertinence to suggest that I should make occasion as if by accident to visit him, when he would unfold to me all manner of sinister information, and permit me to read certain documents, which, no doubt, would teach me my duty as Governor! Naturally, I ignored it, and I trust that if you are favoured with any further nods and becks from Mrs. Margarot you will do likewise." He brought his fist down on the table·with an angry thump. "The whole atmosphere of this place stinks of intrigue!"

She reassured him comfortably:

"You will overcome all difficulties—I am confident of it."

He put his hand over hers for a moment before he rose.

"I shall indeed. We shall produce order from this confusion. There are a thousand things to be done. We must have a survey made of the south-west coast—Flinders can undertake that when he returns. I must get Foveaux to Norfolk Island—it is absurd to imagine that the place can be effectively administered without an officer resident there . . ."

She broke in eagerly:

"Foremost among your plans should be the one you have talked of— to rescue the children of this unhappy community from their appalling life of vice and destitution . . ."

"I have already taken steps in that direction," he assured her. "Mr. Kent, who goes home with Captain Hunter, is willing to sell his house and grounds. They will provide an asylum for such children until we can build a better." He stood for a moment frowning, and then burst out: "Did I not suffer enough delays in England? Yet here I am, helpless to do anything but by an application to His Excellency which, civil, humble as I can make it, is yet regarded as an affront! 'You have not yet been long enough in the colony,' he tells me, 'to know what is best to be done. You will learn,' he warns me with a look that tells his satisfaction, 'the difficulties of government with every man's hand working, and every man's tongue whispering, against you!' Am I a fool? Have I not eyes in my head . . . ?"

"Pray, my love," his wife urged him placidly, "do not excite yourself. You will bring on another attack of the gout."

*   *   *   *   *

The uncompromising attitude of the Governor-elect was indeed begin-ning to cause some uneasiness among the trader-landowners. Captain Macarthur's aggressive determination warred with a streak of calculating caution which made him weigh the situation with care, and some mis-givings. Yet his self-confidence—never a delicate growth—had burgeoned with success, and he was fiercely unwilling to see even a modification of the profitable pattern of sale and barter which he and his brother officers had evolved. Yet, unlike most of his friends, he thought not only of the present, or of amassing a fortune as quickly as possible. His personal tastes were simple enough, and to live well was merely to supply himself with a background worthy of his quality; in a community where scandal was incessantly busy with rumours of alcoholic excess and sexual irregularity, no one ever whispered that John Macarthur was other than a sober, abstemious and irreproachable family man. His eyes missed nothing in the present, but looked through it to a future. He desired money less for what it would buy than as an instrument of power; and he desired power less for what he could achieve with it than as a means for exercising and expressing the clamorous urge of his egotism. He must shine, he must tower. His image must be in every eye, and his name on every tongue. His astuteness and his energy exploited the colony and the present with an efficiency that was almost automatic, but his pride would not remain content within so small a compass. His mark must lie on the world and the future.

He knew the sensitive spot in the home Government's attitude to this distant colony; it was costing too much, and affording no return. There had been from the beginning an almost querulous demand that this preposterous country should produce something—anything—which would repay the honour conferred upon it by white settlement, and offset its serious drain upon the Treasury. But so far such natural resources as it provided had done little to compensate for the expense of its maintenance. Flax was cultivated in a small way; there was thought to be a possibility of a trade in whale-oil and sealskins; the vines planted by Governor Phillip had failed after some years of success; Bass had discovered a coal seam on the south coast, but it had proved inaccessible, and Portland's high hopes of exporting valuable cargoes to the Cape were dashed. True, another seam to the northward promised better, and some export to Bengal had already been made—but there seemed little hope for the speedy development of any of these embryo industries. Captain Macarthur, shrewdly summing up the situation, took all this into account—and set against it his own faith that sheep were a very different matter . . .

For he was by now convinced that he possessed in his flocks the means of increasing his fortune and thus consolidating his power even beyond what he had dreamed possible in earlier days. Were not English cloth manufacturers crying aloud for raw material for their craft? Might he not reasonably hope to win official recognition and support if he could supply it? Most of his fellow-colonists—men of little imagination and no daring, he reflected with a curl of his lip—thought of their sheep as carcasses: he thought of them as wool. As long ago as 1794 he had begun his experiments by crossing Indian ewes with an Irish ram. The merino sheep imported by Captain Waterhouse three years since had provided him with material for further experiments, which had proved highly encouraging, and already he had notably improved the quality of his fleeces. By far the greater number of sheep in the colony, he reflected, belonged to him and his brother officers; Government held something over, and the settlers something under five hundred, while the officers between them owned nearly five thousand. His own share of that five thousand was substantial—and would increase in quantity as it had already improved in quality. Some day the nations of the world would clamour for that wool . . .

As for King . . .

He was inclined to think that he had developed a technique for embarrassing Governors. There was nothing in this colony that could not be—manipulated. And that included the prejudices and passions of human beings, their fears and their needs, their private quarrels and their lawsuits. He and his allies had their hands firmly upon everything that could be used as a weapon—land, livestock, grain, liquor, merchandise— and the courts. They were, by virtue of their bright uniforms, the only lawful dispensers of force. Perhaps, after all, the new Governor was not to be greatly feared . . .

Captain Macarthur kept very quiet during this uneasy interval before Hunter's departure, but his eyes were watchful, his ears alert, and his brain busy.

    *   *   *   *   *

During the winter Patrick succumbed to the first illness of his life. Mr. Harvey, despatched to summon the surgeon, dismounted before the gate of Mr. d'Arcy Wentworth's house at Parramatta and strode up to the door in a fine glow of romantic devotion. He had been given an errand to do for *her* (he chose to think it was for Conor rather than for Mr. Mannion, or even for Patrick), and Dick Turpin himself had never ridden his Black Bess harder than Mark had ridden Mr. Mannion's Mor from Beltrasna to Parramatta.

His hand, uplifted to knock, was stayed by the opening of the door. He found himself confronting a small boy who stared up at him from a pair of eyes whose gaze he found slightly disconcerting, for one seemed to be observing his face while the other just missed it, and contemplated the view over his shoulder.

"This is Mr. Wentworth's house, I believe?"

"Yes, Sir." The boy's faint squint, suggesting as it did at first an indirectness and hesitancy, was curiously contradicted by the crisp confidence of his voice.

"I should like," said Mark, "to speak with him if he is disengaged."

"I am sorry, Sir, he is not at home."

Mark drew an impatient breath. The matter was urgent. Not because Patrick was seriously ill—Mark did not, in fact, believe him to be so—but because *she* was distressed, and anxiously awaiting the arrival of the doctor. The whole world, he felt, should hold itself in perpetual readiness to serve her at a moment's notice; he was irritated—even a little shocked—to find that Mr. Wentworth could be unavailable on the instant when she required him. He said blankly: "Oh!" He looked up and down the street, though he would not have recognised the doctor if he had seen him. He said with annoyance:

"That is most unfortunate. I have been required by Mr. Mannion of Beltrasna to request his presence there immediately . . ." He looked down at the boy again, and reminded himself sharply that this *was* a boy, and not—as something in his manner and his self-possession seemed to suggest—a grown man. Mr. Harvey, after all, was accustomed to boys; he was, so to speak, a specialist in boys. He adjusted his voice to a suitable tone of benevolence:

"You can tell me, perhaps, my lad, when he will return?"

"I should not think," the boy replied with composure, "that he will be long away. Will you step inside, Sir, and wait for him?"

Mr. Harvey stepped inside. The room in which he found himself was of a fair size, but its narrow windows gave little light. He sat down by one which commanded a view of the street; the boy remained standing, regarding him with that curious, calm, one-eyed stare until he found himself fidgeting, and spoke for the sake of speaking:

"You are Mr. Wentworth's son?"

"Yes, Sir."

"And what is your name?"

"William Charles Wentworth, Sir."

"Ah!" Mr. Harvey turned in his chair to peer through the window. The boy, kneeling on the settle beside him, looked at Mor, and remarked:

"One of the servants could attend to your horse, Sir, while you are waiting."

Mark said hastily:

"Yes—yes, indeed. I was just about to suggest . . ."

The boy was gone. Mark heard his clear, high voice call: "Thomas!" He saw a man approaching down the street, and half rose—but it was not Mr. Wentworth. A woman went by, followed by two soldiers, at whom she glanced over her shoulder, provocatively. Mark thought of Conor: She will be waiting. She has been quieter of late . . . something distresses her . . . there is an uneasiness . . . she sits alone on the verandah with her needlework, but she is not sewing . . .

William's voice said from behind him:

"Thomas is good with horses. I can ride quite well."

"Indeed?" Mark replied vaguely. He saw the man come round from behind the house and lead Mor away. He said: "I am obliged to you, William."

"Mr. Mannion lives at the Nepean, does he not, Sir?"

"Yes."

"I have never been there."

"Have you not?"

"No. I can ride quite well."

The tutor, temporarily submerged by the lover, stirred and struggled. Mark well knew that the pride of boys in their physical accomplishments demanded recognition, commendation. He replied with dutiful warmth:

"That is excellent, my lad."

William enquired:

"Are you the gentleman who teaches Mr. Mannion's sons, Sir?"

Mark assented, comparing the boy half absently with Miles, making the pedagogue's automatic estimate of his age, and guessing him about eight or nine. He was considerably smaller than Miles, who was barely ten—but

Miles, of course, was tall for his age, and exceptionally robust. This boy did not look particularly robust, and yet he gave no impression of that timidity which was so commonly found in delicate children. . . . And his steady stare was rather disconcerting . . . .

Mark enquired hastily:

"And how long have you lived in the colony, William?"

The seriousness of the boy's face wavered under a smile which held, actually, a hint of indulgent superiority.

"I was born at Norfolk Island, Sir."

"Indeed?" Mark was suddenly conscious of himself as a newcomer. "But you will go home, no doubt, some day . . . ?"

William looked faintly puzzled.

"I am to go to England soon, Sir—perhaps this year—for my education." He paused, his crooked stare fixed on the opposite wall in a kind of absent contemplation. Mark, looking out into the street again, heard: "But of course I shall come home when it is completed."

He did not look round. He was thinking again of her, of her beauty, of her anxiety, of the way she had put her hand upon his arm for a moment when she sped him on his journey. *"Pray make haste, Mr. Harvey!"* She had actually touched him! He was remembering that—so bemused by the sweetness of it that he was only conscious of something in the boy's last remark upon which his mind had caught for a second, as his fingers might have caught on a knot in a smooth string. There was a long silence—so long that Mark forgot his companion, and started when he spoke again.

"I trust Mr. Mannion is not ill, Sir?"

"No," Mark said. "No, it is one of his sons . . ." He looked at William. "Are you acquainted with Mr. Mannion's sons?"

"No, Sir," the boy replied, "but I have seen them . . ."

Mr. Harvey jumped up hurriedly.

"There is a gentleman coming in . . . I think it must be your father returning . . ."

Mr. Wentworth entered. Through their greeting, and his own hurried explanations, Mark's impression was of a glum man, hardly yet of middle age, but seeming older by reason of a certain watchful, unyielding reserve; a man whose manner was a wall which he erected about himself, as though he would say "You cannot approach me" to a world which he knew would not approach him if it could. He said, looking at Mark appraisingly from under his brows, matching his stolid calm against the younger man's nervous impatience:

"I am at Mr. Mannion's service, Mr. . . . . Mr. . . . . ?"

"Harvey. I cannot too strongly urge, Sir, that the matter is of the most pressing importance . . ."

"Yes, yes. I shall require a few moments only for my preparations. William, you will kindly tell Thomas to saddle my horse. Pray be seated, Mr. Harvey; I shall not detain you long."

Mark watched his far-too-unhurried exit and sat down again on the edge of the settle; he heard William's voice pleading in an urgent under-

tone from the passage outside: "Papa, may I not go with you? I have
never been . . ." He drummed with his fingers on his knees. He sighed
and fidgeted. He rose to inspect a picture on the opposite wall, and
returned to his seat without having seen it. Every moment of delay was
another moment of distress for her. He went outside and paced the path-
way in the sunshine, fuming and dreaming.

When they set out at last they were accompanied by William. Mr.
Wentworth rode at a jog trot, refusing to be hurried. He conversed—
or rather delivered, intermittently, a curious, disconnected monologue to
which Mark made an absent-minded rejoinder now and then. He spoke
at some length of education, and Mark, who at first regarded this choice
of a subject as a civil attempt to find a topic of interest to his companion,
came finally to the conclusion that it was chosen because to speak of
education was one way to speak of William. Mr. Wentworth trusted
that Mr. Harvey found his young pupils diligent. His close, guarded
smile, his glance which half included, over his shoulder, the boy trotting
happily a few yards behind them, said that be they never so diligent, they
could be no match for William. Mark's store of worldly wisdom was
limited, but what he had learned he had learned well, and the fondness
of parents was no new thing to him; he responded with a well-practised
if slightly weary courtesy to this latest manifestation of it, and pursued his
own thoughts. Yet he could not be entirely unconscious of his companion
and his preoccupation was disturbed by memories of comments he had
heard about Mr. Wentworth. Not a convict—no—but in the eyes of the
colony's self-appointed aristocracy, so near to it as made no difference.
A man living a life of exile only half voluntary; a life which, so far as it
was his own life, had been resigned to defeat, but which still, in bitter
pride, had its purpose and its justification in William. Something like
that, Mark reflected, was the sum of the impression he had gained. Mr.
Wentworth might dine—and had dined—at Government House, but he
knew that it was not there that a man's social status was determined; he
might transact—and did transact—business with the rich and the powerful, but he remained aware of a line, sharply drawn in their minds, which
set him apart from them. He acquiesced in his obscurity; his purpose
demanded it. He must keep himself in eclipse so that William, some
day, might be enabled to shine forth more brightly. And William would
shine. He said ruminatively: "The Army is in my mind, of course, Mr.
Harvey . . . yes, no doubt the Army . . ." He spoke of his younger
son and namesake, d'Arcy—but he returned to William. "A boy of
unusual intelligence, Sir, and with a firmness of character beyond his
years . . ." Mark murmured suitable noises of congratulation. The miles
grew tedious, speech grew tedious, thought shut the three of them away
in a prison of silence, broken only by the sound of hoofbeats. Mark
thought of Conor; Mr. Wentworth thought of William; and William
thought of what he saw. His thought of it took no account of any
future; he made no plans; he observed the land, and because no knowledge
of any very different landscape intruded a memory between him and the
acceptance of this scene, it came direct through his vision to his heart.

He saw a lonely, spacious harmony of fields, and trees and sky—saw it as beautiful without strangeness, and took it as his own without reserves.

*   *   *   *   *

To Ellen, busy in the kitchen, came her young mistress, pale-faced and anxious-eyed from a long vigil at Patrick's bedside.

"Surely Mr. Wentworth should be here soon, Ellen?"

"Yes, Ma'am."

"Master Patrick seems no better, I fear."

"I have seen many," Ellen answered in a cool tone which belied her soothing words, "worse than he is, Ma'am, and they soon recovered."

"But he is in a high fever, Ellen, and he is so hot and restless, and he talks so strangely . . ."

"It's what they all do in a fever, Ma'am."

Conor looked at her unhappily; her expression almost pleaded for some sign of assurance, but Ellen kept her eyes on the silver she was polishing, and her face was impassive as ever.

"He speaks of the natives," Conor said anxiously. "Is that not strange? And he calls out to someone called Johnny, as if . . . what is it, Ellen? Can you see Mr. Wentworth coming?"

For Ellen had turned sharply towards the window, and now she turned back again slowly, not meeting her mistress' eyes.

"No, Ma'am. I thought I heard something—but they are not in sight yet."

Conor asked:

"Have we not some limes, Ellen? A little of the juice might be refreshing to Master Patrick."

"They are in the storeroom," Ellen replied. "Shall I fetch them, Ma'am?"

"I will fetch them myself," Conor answered. She was unused to illness, and to busy herself with some small task for the boy who lay so hot and feverishly restless on his bed promised to allay her feeling of helplessness and inadequacy. "Give me the key, Ellen, if you please."

Ellen unhooked the bunch of keys which dangled at her waist.

"It is this large one, Ma'am."

Conor crossed the few feet of pebbled yard which lay between the kitchen door and the storeroom. She fitted the key in the lock, turned it, pushed the heavy door open into a cool semi-darkness. The walls were so thick that the two small, barred windows were set in embrasures two feet deep. Here were stacked boxes and bales, harness, horseshoes, tools, nails, coils of rope, sacks of grain and potatoes; there was a strong and not unpleasant smell—a mixed smell of earth and leather, of new rope and fruit. She found the limes and came out again into the sunshine, pulling the door to behind her. She locked it, and tried to pull the key out, but could not move it. She left it there, returned to the kitchen, and said, placing the fruit on the table:

"I cannot get the key out of the lock, Ellen."

"I know, Ma'am," Ellen assented. "You have to lift it upward as you pull it out, and it comes easy enough. Toole keeps saying he will fit a new lock, Ma'am, but no one uses it but him and me and Merrett, and we know the trick of it. I'll fetch it in, Ma'am."

She hurried out and retrieved the keys; returning, hooking them on to her belt again, she shot a quick glance at Conor.

"If I might make so bold, you should not be all the time in Master Patrick's room, or you'll catch the fever yourself, Ma'am. If you'd take a rest, Ma'am, on your bed, I can see well enough to him till the surgeon arrives, and give him a drop of the lime juice if he fancies it . . ."

Conor looked up at her in surprise. She had never heard so long a speech from Ellen before. She had been reared among servants from whom she had learned to expect a solicitous and indeed a devoted care, and Ellen's cold aloofness had always worried her. This first and most unexpected hint of concern for her took her unawares, and brought a sudden lump to her throat. She replied hastily:

"Indeed I do feel a little fatigued, Ellen. You will call me, will you not, if Master Patrick should seem worse?"

"Yes, Ma'am."

"Or if you should see Mr. Wentworth coming?"

"Yes, Ma'am, to be sure."

Ellen took up her post beside the boy's bed. She kept her eyes sharply on his flushed face as he tossed and babbled, and her head bent to catch his words, but they were a meaningless jumble now, and she did not hear the name for which she waited half in longing and half in dread. Ever since he had told her of his encounter with Johnny she had watched him jealousy. Where did he go when he rode away alone up the river? Had he ever seen her son again? For months after she learned of Johnny's survival she had half expected him to come to her, and she had been torn between her desire for his coming and her fear of it. She told herself that he was safe from the law of the white world if he did return, for he was not himself a felon after all, whatever his parents might have been; his classification as a "convict-child" was social, not legal, and his absconding at the age of eight was not a crime to be punished, but a childish escapade, long-forgotten, and unlikely to be held against him now. Nevertheless she was afraid. She feared Johnny himself; she feared his stiff-necked intransigeance which had never allowed him to go softly, taking what he could get from a society which exacted and expected obedience and humility in return. He was neither humble nor obedient; no scolding could silence his shrill voice, no beating could teach him docility. She felt sure of one thing—that while he lived secretly with the natives he was safe, and she was safe, and Andy and Maria were safe; but if he returned there would be trouble for them all. She did not know or conjecture what kind of trouble it would be. She only knew that contact between Johnny and his own civilisation meant collision. Experience had taught her that no individual of her class, be he never so indomitable, could survive that collision; but her knowledge that he was alive, living independently of it, had given her more than once a dark thrill of pride and satisfaction. He could not vanquish it—but he could outwit it. It seemed to her that merely by continuing to exist without its sanction or assistance, he had achieved a kind of victory.

She looked down at Patrick's face, her own ugly with fear and mistrust. Had he seen Johnny again? Did he, perhaps, see him frequently? Not Mr. Mannion himself could have more deeply resented the thought of friendly contact between Johnny and Patrick than she resented it. One might with less danger make friends with a tiger than with a gentleman. One might—as indeed Johnny had shown—step into a community of savages with greater security than one could intrude even an inch into the far more alien world of the gentry. She turned it over in her mind that Master Patrick would be going home to Ireland soon—quite soon, she had learned, from hearing her master talk. She hoped that he would never return.

She sat still, listening, watching, brooding, until the sound of hoofbeats announced the arrival of Mr. Harvey with the surgeon. She summoned her mistress, and hovered, an unobtrusive presence in the background, while Mr. Wentworth made his examination and prescribed his remedies, but the time came when she must leave the room to supervise the preparation of the evening meal, and while she worked she worried lest the name of her son should be spoken again—and arouse a perilous curiosity. From the window she could see Miles with Mr. Wentworth's son, but for once she felt no softening of the heart as she looked at him. Maria and Andy were there too, instead of being about their work as they should have been, and worse still, Dilboong was there, standing with one skinny leg curled about the other, her dark face lifted eagerly, her black eyes fixed adoringly on Miles. Ellen could see that, as usual, Miles was doing all the talking, and the others were hanging on his words—all except Mr. Wentworth's son, who stood gazing across the river at the hills—and Dilboong was holding the back of her hand up to her mouth as if to suppress her giggles, for she had learned to feel guilty about laughter. Ellen flung the window open and called harshly:

"Dilboong! Come in, you worthless brat! Andy! Maria!"

She felt a sudden rage against them all, and leaned on the sill with tears burning her eyes. So many years since she had seen Johnny, and yet they were nothing! In her heart he was still a child, an eight-year-old as she had seen him last, and she felt something that was almost hatred for all other children who tortured her by being there before her eyes while the one child she longed to see was absent. As she closed the window, Miles was still talking volubly, and Mr. Wentworth's son was standing with his hands clasped behind his back, staring up at the mountains.

*   *   *   *   *

To Governor Hunter and his successor, time, far from being a healer, was becoming increasingly an irritant. During June and July they exchanged letters in which civility succumbed steadily to acrimony, and when Captain King waited upon His Excellency one bright winter morning, their tempers, ridden upon a tight rein for many months, boiled up to an open quarrel. King's complaint that he had been unable to obtain the necessary information for a set of muster books, his request that such books be made out, and orders given for a general muster of the colony's inhabitants before Hunter's departure, was innocent enough in substance; but matters had reached such a pass between them that King could no longer speak without an undertone of injury, nor Hunter hear without resentment. The Governor replied haughtily:

"It has never been my wish, Sir, that information should be withheld from you. I intend that a muster shall take place; it has been delayed only on account of the Hawkesbury settlers being occupied in sowing their ground."

His mention of the Hawkesbury was unfortunate. King retorted promptly:

"As for these settlers, I'd told that upwards of seventy of them are shortly to be served with writs for debts which they have incurred through the unbridled rapacity of certain individuals—and by the exorbitant price of spirits . . ."

Observing unmistakable signs of rising anger in his companion, he endeavoured to introduce a placatory note. "Your Excellency's humane feelings will, I trust, excuse the liberty I take in suggesting what a glorious example it would be if these—these assassins of public liberty were obliged to relinquish their claims, and confine their profits to a hundred per cent."

But Hunter was not mollified.

"No one," he protested angrily, "has had cause to complain of want of humanity since I have been in authority here, Sir." He made, in his turn, a grudging attempt at conciliation. "If you can suggest any means within the law of lessening these exorbitant demands of creditors, I have to request that you will state it."

"An ordinance might be established," King replied curtly, "similar to that which I laid down during my term at Norfolk Island, whereby the price of spirits might be fixed at 20/-, and all claims for a greater price invalidated. I do not know with what approval you would consider an instruction to the civil court prohibiting cognisance of any debt contracted for spirits above that price. I," he added grimly, "shall have no hesitation on that score when the command is left to me."

"You will find," Hunter told him hotly, "that the imprisonment of many of the settlers for debt is a misfortune you cannot prevent any more than I have been able to do, unless the courts of justice are to be entirely shut up. You have not been here long enough to know what a little more time will give you a more perfect acquaintance with."

King's hand made an impatient gesture.

"I have no wish to see the courts of justice shut up," he answered irritably, "but I will not permit the unwary to become the dupes of a set of villains, nor allow the commissioned or other dealer to prey upon the public. This, Your Excellency, is what fills the criminal courts with culprits. Forgeries, robberies, destitution! All these evils arise from the quantity of spirits with which the colony is inundated! Inundated, Sir!"

"I have not spent five bitter years in this place," Hunter said, his voice shaking with anger, "to be taught by a newcomer what I know very well! You have conspicuously manifested, since your arrival, Sir, an indelicate impatience to possess my office; and I confess myself no less eager to relinquish it than you are to grasp it." His face was flushed, and his hands moved restlessly among the papers on his desk. "Your noisy and ill-considered threats of what you would do when I am gone have not only affected my authority as Governor, but have been injurious to my character as a man and an officer. It has been believed, Sir—and whether you have been the originator of that belief I shall leave your conscience to determine—that you possess the power to annul my authority, and render me a mere cypher. You have consistently spurned my offers to afford you every information in my power, preferring, it would appear, to seek such information through other channels which— I warn you, Sir!—are far from reliable!"

King held on to the remnants of his composure; the effort suffused his cheeks with a choleric tint, and made his eyes bulge slightly. He was human enough to repel with the greatest warmth that part of Hunter's accusation which struck home with a sharp stab of truth.

"I have declined to take the command until Your Excellency's departure," he snapped, "which surely is sufficient indication that I have been guilty of no such impatience as you impute to me. As for my 'noisy threats,' Sir, they have been directed towards, and frequently uttered in the presence of notorious dealers in spirits, in the hope that they may abandon their nefarious practices before I am in a position to compel it . . ." Hunter uttered a brief, contemptuous snort of laughter, and King said fiercely: "You may jeer, Sir! You have heard me utter my threat in public, and I now repeat it. I will send home the first officer who disobeys my orders respecting this traffic."

"You will be responsible for your actions," Hunter retorted, "as I have been responsible for mine. I require no support but truth and justice. I resent, Sir, your insinuation that oppressed people must appeal to you for redress. Such people are well aware that I am never deaf to any just complaint."

"Rightly or wrongly," King interrupted, "my aid and intervention was solicited, and I should have held it criminal in myself not to have acquainted Your Excellency with the facts. No man has a higher sense of your many virtues than myself," he continued, with a last clutch at amiability, "and I have no hesitation in assuring you that I possess no power whatever to annul your authority, nor have I ever attempted to suggest . . ."

But Hunter, who had been rummaging among his papers, now produced and flourished in King's face the copy he had made of that paragraph which had so incensed him months ago. His accusing voice shook with fury.

"Here are your own words, Sir, which, if they mean anything, can only convey a suggestion that I may be disposed to disobey His Majesty's commands, and that you possess some mysterious power which you have not seen fit to communicate to me." He read aloud, tapping the paper fiercely with his forefinger. " 'Should His Majesty's commands for Governor Hunter's return by the first safe conveyance not be attended to . . . I shall not fail to follow my instructions.' What is that, Sir, but an open insult, and a veiled threat?" He blundered heavily to his feet, and took a few nervous paces about the room. "It is not useless and empty parade, nor personal compliment and attention that I wish to be shown; it is the necessary authority of a Governor's situation which I cannot with indifference see treated in a way which must draw contempt upon the office, and upon the person who holds it . . ."

King rose, stiff and tense with anger.

"I have never so treated it, Sir. My actions have at all times been governed by what I conceived to be the welfare of the colony, nor is it likely that I should attempt to lower the consequence of an office in which I shall myself shortly need all the authority it can bestow."

"Can you deny, Sir," Hunter challenged him bitterly, "that these sentences in your letter which I complain of are designed to produce in the mind of the Secretary of State an impression disadvantageous to my character as a faithful and obedient officer—and to convey a very opposite impression of your own?"

King, his hat under his arm, bowed brusquely.

"I do deny it," he said, "and since your remarks, Sir, suggest to me that my presence can only be abhorrent to you, I request Your Excellency's permission to withdraw."

"Good-day, Sir!" replied His Excellency, glaring.

*   *   *   *   *

But Hunter was not to escape without seeing the unrest of his colony break out in something more serious than a personal squabble at Government House, and the fourth day of September found him seated at his desk, gloomier and more harassed than ever, drafting a letter.

"Sydney, September 4th, 1800.

"Gentlemen,

"Having received information that certain seditious assemblies and consultations of the people have been held in different parts of the colony, to the great danger of His Majesty's Government and the public peace, I have to desire you will meet and call before you all such persons as you shall be of opinion can afford you any information how far these reports are well or ill-founded, and to suggest such steps as may appear to you necessary for the preservation of order.

"I am, etc.,

"Jno. Hunter."

The gentlemen to whom this letter was addressed—three military officers, the Judge Advocate, and Surgeon Balmain—assembled promptly and proceeded to an interrogation of suspected persons which spread over eight anxious and rumour-filled days. From it there emerged by degrees much that could not but be disquieting to Authority. It was confessed

that there had been a plot afoot to confine Hunter and put King to death.
It was even alleged that there were many of the soldiers who would have
been ready to join the plotters.   It was said that people at the Hawkesbury
had planned to march on Parramatta and take it with the aid of confederates there, and to descend upon Sydney before daylight and storm
the barracks.   Authority, though disturbed, was incredulous and more
than a little scornful.   How was such a thing to be accomplished by
unarmed men?   That question was answered with tales of pikes made and
concealed, with claims that the insurgents would have had the settlers'
arms, and many of the soldiers'; and the next question came sharp and
threatening.   Where were these pikes?   But to that there was no reply.
Those who would speak did not know, and those who knew would not
speak.

He remembered that one witness had spoken of a meeting of men at
Mr. Cox's farm, where that fellow Holt was overseer.   'General' Holt,
forsooth!   How in God's name, fumed the Governor, was he expected to
preserve the tranquillity of the colony while the Home authorities continued to unload upon its shores all the rascals who had proved too
embarrassing for its own management?   Muir, Palmer, Skirving, Margarot,
Gerrald; Holt and the Reverend Henry Fulton; Father Harold and his
fellow-priests, Dixon and O'Neill . . . !   Such political prisoners were,
he held, a far greater problem than the highway robber and the pickpocket, and he had not been surprised to hear the assertion of one witness
that Mr. Margarot had been involved in this deplorable affair.   His
Excellency thought it only too probable, and spared a moment to count
himself lucky that Mr. Thomas Fysshe Palmer had lately completed his
sentence and left the colony.   Hunter brooded glumly over that suspicious
remark said to have been made by Holt to one of the witnesses: "*You are
an Irishman, Kennedy, and we will all go home in one ship together!*"
There was mischief brewing, he felt, in that sly fellow who was the
more difficult to handle because his status was not that of a transported
felon, and who had already demonstrated his ability to save his own skin.
He would profit, perhaps, by a sharp lesson . . .

So to the farm of Mr. Cox came eight soldiers with fixed bayonets
in the small hours of the morning, and plucked Mr. Holt, all injured
innocence, and loudly protesting, from his bed.   Confronting his ques-
tioners boldly, prosperously attired in a fine blue coat with a black velvet
collar, he declared that he had no intimacy with the Irish convicts; that

he had been informed by a certain man, whom he named, that "the business was gloriously going on," and that upon enquiring what business, he had received the reply that his informant had been sent to know if he would lead the men. What answer had he made to that? He had answered: "Surely, my God, does not everyone know where I live, and one moment is enough for me!" A reply, he hastened to explain, his sharp eyes slyly upon the stern faces before him, designed merely to discover what was afoot, for he well knew, and had warned his companion, that nothing could be accomplished . . .

For the moment he suffered nothing worse than removal to the house of the head-gaoler—but others were not so fortunate. Before mid-September it was judged that a sufficient number of scapegoats had been secured to terrify those still at large into docility. Sentences of one hundred lashes, five hundred lashes, and deportation to remote parts of the colony were mingled with offers of clemency to informers who would come forward with suitable expressions of contrition. The symptoms of revolt having thus been scotched in the time-honoured manner without disturbing the cause, Hunter drew a long breath of relief. Yet as one last precautionary measure he formed a volunteer force of civilians to reinforce the military in case of need. With this body—the Sydney and Parramatta Loyal Association—in being, he permitted himself to believe that the dark forces of sedition were routed, and order secured. The devil's brew in the colonial cauldron, having threatened to boil over, subsided again temporarily to an ominous simmering.

But the lull was very brief. Almost immediately there were fresh alarms—but now Hunter was upon the point of boarding the *Buffalo*, and it was for King to deal with them. Throughout another disturbed week the air was filled with tales of plots, and Mr. Marsden was kept busy at Parramatta interrogating suspected persons. Again the whereabouts of pikes and weapons was not to be discovered. "*They are an unaccountable set of beings*," the reverend gentleman wrote plaintively to King. "*It is difficult to prevail on any of them who are accused to say a single word.*" Such words as they would say were disappointingly inconclusive, as the four officers appointed by King to study and report upon the depositions soon discovered. They all agreed there could be no doubt that a wicked and dangerous plot subversive of all order and tranquillity had been hatching—but it was another matter to find proof. "*No act and fact being clearly established by proof to amount to a capital conviction,*" they declared, "*we submit to His Excellency Governor King the expediency of bringing them to severe corporal punishment . . .*" They recommended that five of the prisoners should receive one thousand lashes each, and eleven others varying lesser amounts; this, followed by hard labour in some remote spot, might be sufficient, they respectfully suggested, "*to reduce them to due obedience, subordination and order.*"

It might do that artful and designing rogue Holt no harm, King reflected, to witness one of these punishments. And so one day Mr. Holt was taken back by boat to Parramatta, and on a warm, windy spring morning marched to Toongabbee to observe with his own eyes the fate of plotters. Blood and bits of skin spattered his face as he stood fifteen yards to leeward of the two floggers—one right- and one left-handed—but the Governor had misjudged him. Mr. Holt soon recovered from a momentary squeamishness. Set at liberty again after this salutary exhibition, he repaired home to Parramatta, and over an excellent dinner in a tavern the same night described the scene to an audience which hung upon his words. "Not a syllable could they get out of young Paddy," he declared. "They cut his shoulders to the bone with the first hundred, and gave him another hundred lower down, and the third on the calves of his legs. I swear to you, gentlemen, the lad never whimpered, and when they ask him where the pikes are hid he shouts out at them: 'Ye'll get no music out of my mouth to make others dance on nothing!' A fine fellow, and he no more than twenty! My friends, I declare I never saw two threshers in a barn move their flails with more regularity than those two man-killers did!" Mr. Holt shook his head and carved himself another slice. "A terrible sight indeed! This beef, Sir, is excellent, and the wine very passable."

* * * * *

The *Buffalo*, meanwhile, still lay at anchor in the harbour. Hunter had gone abroad one Sunday morning at the end of September after reviewing the New South Wales Corps and delivering—with bitter mental reservations—an address of farewell in which he praised its past conduct and exhorted it to similar laudable endeavours in the future. Attended by the civil and military officers he had passed, as his predecessor had done, down a road lined on either side by the soldiery, to the wharf where his boat awaited him; but unlike the first Governor, his mood was darkened by a consciousness of defeat. Nor was he even now to depart in the glory of official farewells which, however formal, might have served to clothe his inglorious recall in some illusion of dignity and consequence; for three weeks were to pass before the *Buffalo* set sail.

* * * * *

King spent that evening letter writing. In his new-found sense of relief and exhilaration his pen flew. He spoke of cultivation, of articles required; he reiterated his determination to end the traffic in spirits; he spoke of Captain Johnston, going home in the *Buffalo* under arrest for having participated in this traffic, and then he paused for a moment, frowning. Johnston had objected to being tried by a General Court Martial in the colony, and King was inclined to think that Hunter had blundered in admitting this objection, and sending him home. Would it not constitute a precedent? Would it not place him, as Governor, in an embarrassing situation if in future all officers were to decline a local Court Martial? For King knew Captain Johnston was not more censurable on this charge than his confreres, and sooner or later he would have them to deal with. "*I am persuaded,*" he wrote, "*that there is not an officer in the Corps or colony (except Governor Hunter and Colonel Paterson) who has not been guilty of similar transactions, by which the greater part of them have made sufficient fortunes to be indifferent about what happens to them.*" These nabobs, he reflected, were no longer dependent upon their military pay.

Mrs. King, occupied with her own correspondence, looked up and enquired:

"You are writing to Sir Joseph Banks, my love?"

"No—to the Under-Secretary. I shall write to Sir Joseph presently."

"Do not forget to tell him about Mr. Caley and his infatuation. I declare it is the strangest thing that he should have fixed upon a woman with a family, and be so determined to marry her! He is such a head-strong young man, is he not? I trust this business will not interfere with his botanical researches, or Sir Joseph will be sadly disappointed!"

King yawned.

"Paterson thinks he will settle down if he has his way. We shall establish a botanic garden for him, and no doubt that will help to keep him tranquil. He sends two boxes of specimens to Sir Joseph by the *Buffalo*, and there's the box of stones from the Coal River, and two waratahs, and a box of fleeces, and a cask with the water-mole in it . . ."

"La, won't Sir Joseph be pleased with the mole!" cried Mrs. King delightedly. "Do you not recall how you showed the drawing of it to Colonel Paterson and Governor Phillip and several others when we were waiting for the *Porpoise* to sail, and they all agreed that no such animal had ever been seen, and indeed most of us conceived such a creature could hardly exist, which was most natural to be sure, since no one could be expected to imagine anything so strange, and I declare when I first set eyes upon it I . . ."

King grunted complacently.

"It will cause brows to be raised at the Royal Society, I have no doubt. Sir Joseph shall see that we don't forget him."

He bent over his desk again, and the room was silent save for the scratch of two busy pens. The relief of knowing his long wait ended lent a warm and lively optimism to King's words. He did not despair, he assured Sir Joseph, of getting things on a very tolerable footing before long. He wrote of his plan for a mining settlement at Port Stephens.

"Unfortunately we have only one miner in the country, who is now a convict for life. He is very clever, and is now boring over a seam at the head of George's River . . ."

He thought restlessly: We have not yet begun to know this land! If I can preserve order and produce prosperity in this place—if I am not continually embroiled in fruitless disputes, and can devote my attention to exploration and development of the country—who knows what we may not discover, and achieve? Who knows . . . ?"

Mrs. King, looking up from her own paper from time to time to watch his scribbling pen, permitted herself no doubts. He was the Governor, and she the Governor's lady; at last, she thought with the serene confidence of a fond wife, this turbulent colony was to become a very pattern of colonial administration.

*   *   *   *   *

The *Buffalo* was ready to sail at last. Captain Kent had come aboard; Captain Johnston had come aboard—a very different man from the twenty-four-year-old lieutenant who had stepped ashore with Phillip more than a dozen years earlier. The Reverend Richard Johnson with his wife and children had come aboard, and among their brood came Patrick Mannion, half excited and half forlorn. Like all the children of the colony, he had been bred in an atmosphere of nostalgia, and like all those of the wealthier class, at least, he had been accustomed to hear the colony spoken of as a place of temporary exile; but unlike the others he had already paid one visit to his parents' homeland, and could remember that he had been conscious of nostalgia there, too. He was sixteen now— almost a man, and anxious to behave not only as a man but as a gentle-man. Agog for the voyage, and the new life which awaited him on the other side of the world, he was unwilling to admit the faint desire to stay which clouded his eagerness to go.

When the hour for departure arrived, and his family, waving from the shore, disappeared from sight as the *Buffalo's* sails bore her down the harbour towards the Heads, he stood alone on the deck and felt a curious dejection settle on his spirits. A hand descended on his shoulder, and he heard the voice of his erstwhile tutor.

"Come, come, my lad," Mr. Johnson admonished him with kindly severity, "do not look so cast down! To part from your dear parents and your brother is no doubt something of an ordeal—yet consider to what a wider and richer life you are going, and thank Divine Providence for the opportunities which now unfold before you!"

"Yes, Sir," said Patrick, gulping slightly. He looked up at the frowning cliffs of the Heads as they approached, remembering himself dimly as a six-year-old child who had passed inward between them one wild, wet morning long ago. It had not seemed to him then that anyone could possibly live in a place which looked so strange, so lonely and deserted; and yet there was a life here, and he had shared it, and it had woven bonds between itself and him so softly and imperceptibly that he had not noticed them until now, when they began to tug at his heart.

"Consider," Mr. Johnson was continuing, "consider, my boy, the great privilege which is being bestowed upon you—to study diligently in order that your worthy father may take pride in you! In order that your dear brother may be in turn inspired by your example! There is no future for a young gentleman in this land, Patrick, and but few associates of your own age in whose company you could find profit . . ."

His voice went on, but Patrick heard no more. That last sentence had carried his thoughts to Johnny Prentice, the one associate of his own age with whom he had ever established . . . what? Not friendship— that was in some mysterious and irrevocable way, impossible. But a sort of intimacy. And suddenly all his vague nostalgia for the land he was leaving became concentrated in the thought of that harsh, intractable boy who had snatched his own life into his own hands, and run away with it. Who, with an astounding temerity and a breath-taking contempt, had spat in the face of his heritage, and left it. Who had found or made for himself a hidden life in this land, and who had emerged from it just once to look at Patrick with an old, mistrusting scorn, and disappear again.

For he had never returned. Never, never, though Patrick had gone often to the river bank where they had met. Never, though he had searched and called, using the long-drawn "Coo-ee" of the native people. Somewhere in the dark, wild hills beyond the Nepean he was even now occupied with the unguessable adventures of his incredible existence; and suddenly Patrick was resentful of Mr. Johnson's tireless enumeration of the blessings and advantages of being a gentleman, and for one mad moment he thought that he would rather be with Johnny . . .

". . . and now," Mr. Johnson was concluding, "our long exile is ended, is it not? We have done our duty, and are to have, I hope, our reward. Ah, the green fields of England! Eh, my lad?"

"Yes, Sir," said Patrick, staring at the low, quiet hills.

*   *   *   *   *

And Governor King, having watched the vessel out of sight, drew a deep breath and squared his shoulders.

"Now . . . !" he thought.

BOOK II

GOVERNOR KING

BOOK II

GOVERNMENT EXPO

MRS. KING stepped out on to the long, sunny verandah of Government House, holding little Elizabeth by the hand. It was a bright November morning with a promise of heat in the sun climbing above the hill; a fresh breeze whipped the harbour into tiny, white-crested waves, and turned the lazy arms of the windmill across the cove. Elizabeth, not yet four, tugged urgently at her mother's hand. She wanted to go down to the foot of the garden where the water splashed in among the rocks and sucked out again, where crabs scuttled in crevices, and dark seaweeds swung. Mama was not to be dragged.

"Not now, my love; Jane shall take you presently."

But she allowed herself to be pulled a little way down the path, and from there turned to survey the unpretentious, white-washed house which was now not only the seat of Government, but, for the first time, a family home. She studied it with all the critical eagerness of a long-frustrated housewife. La, what a state it was in! Roof, windows, doors—all in the most shocking state of disrepair! Yet it had its virtues, and, being a woman who was willing to make the best of inconvenient circumstances—having had, indeed, much practice in doing so—she reflected that its rooms were really very well-proportioned, commodious, and excellently suited for the entertainments which she planned. The drawing-room, fifty feet long, had two fireplaces, and four fine windows looking out across the harbour. A door led from it into a thirty-foot dining-room, and beyond this again was a parlour. Upstairs there were the bedrooms—and always from the windows there was the great sweep of blue water to be seen, and the quiet, tree-clothed hills.

But she must not stand here idling—pleasant as it was in the sunshine; there were still some boxes to be unpacked, and a thousand things to do. She called:

"Jane!"

But there was Jane coming out on to the verandah, and behind her Mrs. Paterson, the kind soul, run up doubtless with a little gossip! Elizabeth, committed to Jane's care, set off down the path to the water's edge, and the two ladies entered the parlour where a large box, half-unpacked, awaited the attention of the Governor's wife. Mrs. Paterson sank upon a sofa, fanning herself.

"Pray, dear Mrs. King, how have you found your things? No more of your gowns have been spoiled, I trust?"

"When I reflect how long our boxes lay in that abominable *Porpoise*," Mrs. King replied ruefully, "I must own that it might have been worse. But some excellent calico muslin is quite ruined, I fear, and many other things sadly marked by the salt water."

"In this place," Mrs. Paterson lamented, "even small losses are great losses—for who knows when they can be replaced?"

"My Spode tea-set," Mrs. King assured her, "is arrived safely, I'm happy to say. Let us hope we may have tea to drink from it! King has ordered tea and sugar and thirty-six dozen of port wine to be sent to us each year, and we can only trust they will reach us. But tell me, pray, what you hear of our Orphanage Fund? Have there been further subscriptions? Almost six hundred pounds, was it not, at the last meeting of the Committee? We shall miss Mr. Johnson sadly as our secretary . . ."

"It was most handsome of His Excellency," Mrs. Paterson declared "to direct that his fees from land grants should be paid into the fund— most truly benevolent! And the shipping charges, too. We shall have our Orphanage established speedily, I make no doubt of it."

Mrs. King replied rather dryly:

"I imagine we shall gain more revenue from the fines for smuggling and drinking after hours." She sank into a chair opposite her friend, clasped her plump hands together in her lap, and confided earnestly:

"I declare, my love, that now the time has come for King to take on the command, I find myself somewhat apprehensive." She glanced quickly at her friend, busy with the thought that it could do no harm to impress upon the wife of the recalcitrant New South Wales Corps Commanding Officer that the Governor intended to stand no nonsense. "Of course," she added quickly, "I have no fear that his efforts to reform the colony will be unsuccessful, for he is a man of the most determined character, dear Mrs. Paterson. But no doubt some will do all in their power to lessen his authority, and I fear we shall have much animosity to contend with. I cannot tell you," she concluded tactfully, "what a source of satisfaction it is to him to know that he may rely upon the support of the Colonel!"

Mrs. Paterson smiled and sighed.

"I've often thought," she confided, "that William is more suited to some retired and scientific pursuit than to a military career. He is of that quiet and placid disposition that abhors strife. You can't conceive how much pleasure he finds in the study of botany, and I believe nothing would content him more than to be able to roam the countryside, like Mr. Caley, in search of specimens." She leaned forward, and her gentle blue eyes became anxious. "But indeed, dear Mrs. King, my own apprehensions are of the convicts and the lower orders. Have they not been daring and insolent of late? When I heard of those ruffians seizing the *Norfolk* in the Hawkesbury and making off with her, I was appalled! Can we sleep safe in our beds with such miscreants at large?"

"They will not be long at large," Mrs. King assured her soothingly. "They will be recaptured, never fear. And even if they should escape from here they will surely perish at sea, for King tells me the vessel is leaky and its sails rotten, and they have no compass, chart or quadrant. I cannot think how they should be mad enough to undertake so desperate a venture!"

Mrs. Paterson shook her head unhappily.

"It is that which perturbs me, my love. Their recklessness passes all comprehension. I won't conceal from you that I fairly quake when I imagine what excesses it may lead them into." She sighed. "Do you not often recall the happy times we spent at Norfolk Island years ago when your Phillip was a baby?"

Mrs. King recalled not only happy times, but many anxious ones when her husband was ill, the convicts mutinous, and she herself enduring pregnancy and childbirth in peculiarly difficult circumstances, but she answered brightly:

"Indeed I do! And how we used to go and visit dear William Chapman at Phillipsburgh—and how he played with the children, and how merry we all were together! I wish William were with us now."

"I declare," mourned Mrs. Paterson, "I could weep for the changes that have taken place. You have heard, have you not, that our old servant James has left us—he that was with Sir Joseph Banks? Yes, I assure you! To become a baker, if you please! He wishes to be independent!" Eyebrows, shoulders, and delicate hands lifted together in dismay. "Upon my word, servants no longer seem to know their place! How fortunate you are, dear madam, that your excellent Jane does not conceive some romantic notion of bettering herself!"

Their laughter came faintly to the ears of Governor King where he sat drafting an Order regarding the colony's new currency. Behind all the administrative detail that claimed his attention, he was incessantly conscious of his major problem, and as he wrote down his table of guineas, Johannas, half-Johannas, ducats, and Spanish dollars, one part of his mind was weighing soberly his chances of success.

He found himself with some advantages which his predecessor had not enjoyed. Captain Johnston's departure had removed—at least temporarily—one of the leading monopolists; Mr. John Palmer, lately returned from England to resume his post as Commissary, was not, as his deputy had been, a complaisant tool of the officers; and Colonel Paterson . . .

King, adding Dutch guilders, rupees, and English shillings to his neat column, reminded himself once more that Paterson was the kind of man whose actions would be determined by the amount of pressure which could be brought to bear on him. Hitherto, that which had come from the officers had been stronger than any which Hunter could apply; but King hoped that in the tiresome months of waiting he had been able to convince not only the Colonel, but also Major Foveaux, now in command at Norfolk Island, that their hopes of reward and promotion would best be served by their affording him a dutiful support.

Yet he detected more and more a general atmosphere of hostility towards himself; with almost every order he issued, he felt it grow. He had directed that not more than two assigned servants working for any officer might be fed and clothed by Government; he had limited the profits which could be made by private retailers of imported cargoes; he had forbidden the landing and selling of spirits without a permit, and fixed a maximum price; and he knew that these orders were less gestures of authority than declarations of war.

On that thought his pen halted for a moment and he stared gloomily in front of him. He did not know that already he was falling into the same habit which had possessed Hunter—of linking the thought of opposition automatically with the thought of Captain Macarthur. The Captain, he reflected, had been very quiet of late. Two days after assuming command, King had received from him a brief note offering his farm and stock to the Crown for the sum of four thousand pounds—"*in consequence*," so the note explained, "*of my wishing to return to England as soon as I can obtain leave*." What was behind that, the Governor wondered now, tapping his pen thoughtfully on the table. Had his own prompt measures, his freely expressed intention of ending the trading privileges of the monopolists, convinced Macarthur that New South Wales was to be no longer a suitable scene for his activities? Had he decided to retire ere he be routed? King had a well-developed self-esteem which would have welcomed such an explanation—but he also had a shrewdness which made him regard it warily. Whatever the motive, nothing would please him better than the disappearance from his domain of so turbulent, ambitious, and unduly influential a character, and he had recommended to the Duke of Portland that the offer be accepted. He could advance sound reasons for accepting it, quite apart from his own inclinations, for the breeding of livestock was an important part of his plans, and Captain Macarthur's stock was good, his property well cleared and cultivated, his barns and buildings in excellent repair, and his grasslands the best in the colony. The Governor sighed and re-focussed his eyes on his paper. He must await Portland's reply—and in the meantime Macarthur was still here, quiet at present, civil in his stiff, unbending, arrogant way, but ominous.

Somehow it was all ominous. The new Governor was more oppressed than he would admit by the hostility he could feel about him, and by the suspicion that intrigue was so rife, personal jealousies, rivalries and ambitions so interwoven into the administrative structure of the colony, that he could make no move, and barely utter a remark, without the fear that it might have sudden and surprising repercussions. His recognition of a determination in himself which could match that of the first Governor had given him a confidence which, already, was slightly shaken. What he did not recognise was his own lack of that serenity, that simplicity of character which had been Phillip's armour. Vanity lent to his manner a hint of arrogance, a shade of self-satisfied complacency; he could not confront hostility as Phillip had done by noting it, dismissing it, and passing on. It made him irritable, suspicious, and jealous of his consequence. The fact that he had as yet been provided by the Home authorities with neither Commission nor Instructions—that he was, indeed, no more than an Acting Governor—irked his pride in spite of the realisation that it left him free to pursue his own methods. Yet here again the burden of responsibility which he must assume sharpened his temper and made him more sensitive to criticism.

*   *   *   *   *

In this uneasy mood one welcome surprise was to cheer him and his lady before the year ended. From Norfolk Island, early in December, came a vessel bringing despatches from Foveaux, and their bearer was no other than Mr. William Chapman, the Kings' old-time friend and favourite. He was an amiable young man; he was blessedly free from involvement in all the complex plots and machinations of the mother-colony; he adored Mrs. King, and accorded to His Excellency a devotion in which the familiarity of a privileged *protégé* was nicely mixed with a very proper deference. His reception at Government House, therefore, took the form of a joyful and enthusiastic reunion, and Mrs. King contrived during the afternoon to draw him aside for a confidential chat.

"I cannot express, my dear William, how happy I am to see you! It was but lately that I said to Mrs. Paterson how much I wished you could be with us here!"

Mr. Chapman was gratified, but not altogether surprised. He possessed an easy and agreeable manner, a fresh and comely face, and a temperament which seldom made him enemies. From the time he had journeyed out with the Kings to Norfolk Island as a lad of seventeen, he had been surrounded by genial and indulgent affection, so that by now he was accustomed to regard himself as one whose presence was always welcome. He smiled charmingly at his hostess.

"You cannot be more happy than I am, Madam, for I assure you not a day has passed but I have thought of you and the Governor, and longed to see you again."

She leaned forward and put her hand on his sleeve.

"Now listen, William. Would it not be agreeable to you to remain here . . . ?"

"But Major Foveaux . . ."

"Yes, yes, I know the Major has need of you at the Island, for my husband tells me he said as much in a letter to him. But we have need of you also, and . . ."

"It is most kind of you to say so, Madam, but . . ."

"William, you are such an old friend that I will speak frankly to you. The Governor meets with much opposition here, and he has scarcely a person about him he can trust, except perhaps Captain Mackellar who is his Aide-de-Camp and Secretary, and of course there are not the bonds of old association and friendship even there which exist between *us*. And also, William," she urged, "you know his habits, and you are accustomed to his—his *manner* when he is troubled by affairs, or when he is indisposed, and I assure you he is still greatly afflicted with the gout from time to time, and you will recall how we all agreed long ago at the Island that it is but natural he should speak a little sharp at such times . . ." Her fingers tightened on the young man's wrist for a moment, gave it a little pat, and released it. "I can only tell you that it would immeasurably sustain him to have you here, and I won't deny that it would greatly relieve *my* mind, dear William, were I to know that he had even one person at his side in whom he could place confidence . . ."

Mr. Chapman, thus wooed, listened attentively to the proposals which His Excellency set before him the same night. He learned that he might have the office of Deputy Commissary, and, in due course, that of Secretary to the Governor also.

"With a salary of ten shillings a day, William. And should the office of Commissary fall vacant I don't doubt you could fill it with credit, in which case your salary would be twenty shillings a day. Pray consider it, my lad, and you can return to the Island in the *Porpoise* to settle your affairs there, and then rejoin us, and we shall be a happy family again as in the past."

The battle in the breast of Mr. Chapman was neither painful nor prolonged. Against the fact that he had his way to make in the world, that the patronage of the Governor was not to be despised, and that, in truth, his affection for the Kings was sincere, he had only to set a certain nostalgic attachment to the little Island where he had spent so many years. He answered:

"Believe me, Sir, any advantage I might derive from remaining at Norfolk Island would be as nothing compared with the privilege of assisting you, and the happiness of renewing my association with your family."

"Capital, William, capital!" The Governor slapped him heartily on the back. Mr. Chapman withdrew to begin a letter home, acquainting his sister with this change in his fortunes.

1801

Tom Towns, holding on to the trunk of a slender gum sapling, watched Jeegala vanishing, reappearing, vanishing again among the trees far down the slope.

It had been blowing hard all this fierce February day—a hot, dry gale that made the exhaustion of rough walking more exhausting still—but it was only now, in the shock of loneliness and approaching night, that Towns heard a sound of threat and torment in the wind. It was the quietness of this accursed country that he had always feared; a thousand times its intolerable silence had set his nerves on edge. He had been schooling himself to meet that, and this wild, loud, tempestuous voice with which it now challenged him, took him by surprise, and dried his mouth with sudden panic.

It was unfortunate for his precarious self-control that the red rim of the sun should have dropped behind the hills almost simultaneously with the departure of his guide. Only a few moments ago it had been sending its last long shafts of brilliance to warm this lonely spot with reassuring daylight; now the dusk was already cheating his vision, and Jeegala was less a shape than an occasional flicker of movement far down the shadowed valley. Towns, straining his eyes for that movement, realised that he was watching the outline of a wind-blown shrub, and knew that he was quite alone.

Daylight gone, not even a black savage for company. . . . He clutched the sapling tighter, for his legs were weak, and he was dizzy with illness and fatigue. Three native guides had brought him, acting in relays within their own towris, a member of the Boorooberongal taking him over from Mungala of the Bideegal, and passing him on to Jeegala when they crossed the river. From the second afternoon he had been ill, sleeping little at night, and walking by day in a trance of feverishness, so that he had noticed even less than he usually did the landmarks of their journey. Now his brain was trying to work, but hampered by curious flashes of thought distorted by fear into fantastic and irrational shapes. The loss of Jeegala and the loss of daylight seemed intermingled; one left darkness, one left solitude, but he thought that if Jeegala returned, daylight would return too, and the sound of threat in the wind be stilled. Then he remembered Dyonn-ee, and clutched at the thought because he knew he had long held that name in his mind as a hope, a future, a reason for effort and endur-ance. Yet he could not reach its comfort because he was haunted by a dreadful fear that he was seeking a ghost—that there was no such person as Dyonn-ee—that he had been following a legend . . .

He said aloud, his forehead tortured with the strain of thinking:

"Dead. . . . What am I doing here? They said he's dead. Long dead . . . drowned . . ."

He terrified himself with the words, and began to tremble, half with fright and half with fever. When he was whole and sane he could scorn the superstitions of the natives, but now—ill and alone in their country—he felt himself surrounded by its mysteries, and yelled aloud suddenly:

"Jeegala! Come back! Jeegala! Coo-ee! Coo-oo-oo-ee!"

The sound of his own fear-maddened voice contending punily with the wind startled him into a flash of coherent thought, and he stared wildly round him, at the narrow gorge at whose mouth he stood. Jeegala had refused to go farther. He had pointed up the gorge, describ-ing by gesture rocks which narrowed on either side of the little stream to hem it in—and then, waving his companion on, he had turned to go. Towns had tried to urge him forward, for he was afraid of being left alone before he had found Dyonn-ee, but Jeegala was not to be persuaded. He would go no farther. The place, he declared, was a bad place. Someone had died there. Towns, still holding on to his tree-trunk and swaying on his feet, thought semi-deliriously that perhaps it was Dyonn-ee who had died again—Dyonn-ee, who had died once before, and yet lived—Dyonn-ee, who might die many times . . .

His fingers, aching from their nervous grip, unclasped themselves from the sapling, and as if this loss of support set his feet moving again of their own accord, he began to stumble up the gorge. When he came to the little stream which tumbled in a series of cascades down its rocky bed, he knelt to drink, dashed water over his face, remained kneeling for a few moments, collecting his strength, and feeling his thoughts grow steadier.

He had been five days on the journey—not because the distance was great, but because he was ill, because the country was, during the last couple of days at least, wild and hilly, because so much time had to be spent by his guides in finding or killing the meagre food they ate, and because no native could ever understand that there was any need to hurry. Kneeling there by the creek, Towns wondered dully just how ill he was.

He had attacks of shivering and vomiting, and his heart pounded climbing hills. He thought that his dull, grinding headache might be partly due to hunger, for his stomach had rebelled at the half-raw food that Jeegala offered. He knew that unless this legendary hut and its legendary owner existed, he would die; and perhaps he would die in any case.

Fear throve on the knowledge of his own ineptitude, but resentment throve on it too. This was not the life he had wanted—why should he excel in it? He lacked the skills of the savage, and in two long years had failed to acquire them, but he knew with bitterness that he had once been capable of other skills. He had learned to read, and to write as fair a hand as any gentleman; the pen in his fingers (as if it had a life of its own) had drawn pictures, too—fine, delicate pictures whose memory had tormented him in these last years when the urge to draw grew too strong to be resisted, and he scratched crude sketches with bits of charcoal on flat rocks—and in his heart despised the admiration of the natives who watched him.

He pushed himself to his feet and began to struggle up the creek again. He muttered as he clambered over rocks and slipped on mossy stones—a harsh, violent indictment of this hated land, a prison-land in truth, its whole length and breadth a prison where a man needed no shackles on his feet to be a captive; a gaol that yawned wide open to receive him when he fled from the servitude of chains, and which clamped on him instead the servitude of hunger and privation; that penned him in not with doors and bolts, but with the mazes of its endless forests . . .

The creek-bed grew steeper and he went more slowly still, pausing now and then to splash his hot forehead with water, keeping his eyes on his clumsily blundering feet, so that it was not until he felt a sudden darkening about him that he realised he was walking into a kind of cavern. Rock walls towered above him on either side, showing only a narrow slit of fading light above, and ahead the creek took a sudden turn. When he reached it he stopped dead, staring at what he saw through the confusing twilight, unsure whether it were real, or some cheating hallucination born of his fever and his hope.

No native had built that hut. No native had made that strong log fence about the little yard, or that patch of cultivation. He forgot in his almost insane relief that he had planned to approach this place—if it existed—warily, in the knowledge that its owner might not welcome intruders. He plunged forward, clambered out of the creek bed, staggered across the clearing, and leaned on the door of the hut, shouting in what he did not know was a whisper. No one answered. He turned the handle of the door and pushed. It was locked. He could stand no longer, and, collapsing on his knees, he heard a snapping and snarling from within before he fainted.

A hand, shaking his shoulder roughly, seemed to shake the world, and a bright, leaping light hurt his opening eyes. Even through unconsciousness some hope must have remained with him that the next human being he saw would be a white man; but it was a native child who stood before him—a boy of about nine, holding a flaring stick in one hand, and a wooden coolamon in the other. It was someone else who was shaking his shoulder—but it was quite dark now, and the uncertain light from the child's torch showed him only another naked figure—another savage. His head fell forward; he swooned again, and passed from swooning into a restless, dream-ridden sleep.

    *   *   *   *   *

Pale sunlight through an open doorway roused him, and he sat up, clutching his head and staring. He lay on the earth floor of the hut, and in one of its corners he could see the naked savage and the child busy with something at a rough, plank table.

Savage . . . ?

He rubbed his hand across his sleep-bleared eyes and looked again. Red hair! His heart began to thud painfully, and he put his hand out to steady himself on the floor. A native dog thrust its wolf-like head through the doorway, a growl rumbling in its throat. The taller figure at the table spun round and faced him.

Towns thought hopelessly: "But this is a *boy* . . . !" He floundered among memories of the tales he had heard. He had been told of a *man* —a man who had built a hut many years ago, and who was drowned in the river, and who was yet alive. But if this were Dyonn-ee, he was not a man even now. His body, though it looked strong and wiry, was lean and immature; his face was beardless; he could not be more than sixteen. His sharp brown eyes under their thatch of red hair stared at Towns with a wary, hostile curiosity.

The convict thought: "A boy . . . a boy . . . !" He looked at the child. Two boys—and the younger a native. . . . No one else? If not. . . . He had grown accustomed to thinking first of violence as the solution to all problems, and his hand instinctively sought the knife at his belt. It was gone. And there were three native spears leaning against the wall within reach of the elder boy's hand.

A word was shot at him suddenly:

"Ooaryu?"

He thought at first that it was a native word, and then his brain, slowly disentangling its sounds, made three words of it—three English words curiously run together, and uttered with a native intonation: "Who are you?"

He answered cautiously:

"From the settlements. From Parramatta. Tom Towns."

The boy stated sharply: "Convick." Towns muttered: "Lost. Lost my way . . ."

He was not sure if he had been understood. Indeed, from the strange expression of mingled bafflement and anger that confronted him, he gained the impression that the boy was not sure himself; but the next word warned him not to lie too much.

"Jeegala." The boy took a step towards him, tapping his breast angrily, and gesticulating in the direction from which the intruder had come. "Jeegala," he repeated accusingly. "See Jeegala, Jeegala say . . ." he hesitated, and pointed at Towns, ". . . say man come . . ."

He looked so angry and threatening that Towns' alarm increased. He toyed with the thought that if he could entice the lad near enough he might overpower him even without the aid of weapons. He had said: "Give me a drink," before he realised that he was in no condition to overpower anyone, and that there were now two native dogs at the door, both snarling. For the present his only hope was to allay this hostility, and he said quickly:

"Ye've no call to fear me, lad. Who are ye? What's y' name?"

No answer. The anger that had flamed in the dark eyes seemed fading to a grim watchfulness. Towns risked the name that had been haunting him; it might, he thought, mean something to the boy—establish some kind of relationship . . .

"Dyonn-ee . . ." he said, and watched tensely for a reaction. What was the expression that flickered over the boy's face? Anger—bewilderment—embarrassment . . . ? The silence was so long that Towns began to think the word must be unfamiliar, and his heart sank. But Johnny was struggling between his white self and his native self, and here, in the presence of another white man, he had felt suddenly ashamed of his native name. He burst out emphatically:

"*Johnny!*"

But even now the habit of years governed his tongue, and the word came out awkwardly so that for yet another instant Towns stared uncomprehendingly. Then he understood. He knew now that if he had not been misled by a preconceived notion that this was a native name, he would long ago have identified it as "Johnny." He asked eagerly:

"Where's Johnny, eh? Where?"

The boy stared, scowled, and began to tap himself on the breast again.

"Johnny," he said fiercely, as if claiming something which the other denied him. "Johnny, Johnny!"

"*You* . . .?" Towns said incredulously. He put his head down between his hands and tried to think. It was no use—he could not understand. But he must accept the fact—or the fancy—that this was the fabulous Dyonn-ee he had come to seek. He would unravel the mystery later. What mattered now was that this incredible boy should not turn him out; what mattered now was to have food, and shelter, and sleep. He looked up and asked wearily:

"How long have ye been here? How long?"

Again Johnny looked embarrassed, searching his mind for the almost forgotten conception of time, and for the words—weeks, months, years—to express it.

"Big . . ." he began, and hesitated. "Long . . ."

"Who else is here?"

No answer.

"Somebody lives with you?"

No answer.

"Other men here? More people?"

The red head jerked towards the native child.

"Only him?" Towns took the silence for assent, but could not believe it. "No white men?" he persisted, and when Johnny shook his head impatiently Towns asked, sharply suspicious:

"Who made this hut then?" He gestured at the surrounding walls. "Been here a long time, it has. Who made it? Not you—never tell me that!"

He realised that the question had angered the boy again and, fighting for his goodwill, shied away from the subject with an inspired remark:

"But you made a peacock—come, now—a little wooden peacock—eh?"

At this, the boy did a surprising thing. He turned quickly, and from a shelf nailed to the wall took down several small objects and brought them carefully on the palm of his hand to Towns. They were four more small carvings, crude but recognisable—a kangaroo, a cow, a man, and a tiny, masted ship.

The convict took them with hands that shook a little under the impact of two conflicting emotions. The boy was now within his reach—unarmed. Towns might have risked the dogs, risked his own weakness and gambled upon being able to overpower this lean stripling by his greater weight and size, had it not been for an old, familiar fear. For, after all, where was he? His terror of the lonely country and of his own incompetence paralysed him. He could not recognise landmarks, nor trails of beasts; he was neither agile nor robust; he had lived on the charity of his native hosts, and without it he would have died. That was the first check to his murderous impulse; but as he held the small carvings in his hand and looked at them he became aware of another—not sudden, but slow, not fearful, but strangely warming. For was not this boy, half-native though he seemed, a fragment of his own civilisation, incredibly existing in the middle of that primitive life which had held him only because there was no alternative? Was not this someone who could speak —however haltingly—his own tongue? And yet who evidently knew how to exist here, and with whom he need not starve? At all costs he must placate this strange youth. He touched the small ship with his finger and said:

"That's fine, that is . . . !"

Johnny's head was slightly on one side, as if he were listening; he frowned and gave it an almost imperceptible shake. Puzzled, but conciliatory, Towns tried again:

"A rare likeness, ye got, lad . . ."

Still that frown, that dissatisfied, listening intentness.

"A grand little ship it is . . ."

A breath, a sudden clearing of the brow beneath the red hair, a word spoken several times rapidly—a forgotten word, now jealously recaptured. "Ship, ship, ship . . ." Towns stared at the boy wonderingly, his mind beginning to grasp the thought that this Dyonn-ee wanted something he could supply. He wanted the dim memories of his white life clarified, explained, interpreted; he wanted confirmation and recognition of a non-native self that he had always felt; he wanted his language back . . .

And that being so, Towns was no longer an empty-handed mendicant.

He had something to bargain with, and he began to bargain for food with words.

"I'm hungry," he declared, pointing to his mouth and clasping a hand over his stomach. "Hungry—eat." Johnny nodded quickly. "Food," said Towns urgently. "Water." He made the motions of drinking, and Johnny gestured to the child. Billalong immediately placed a lump of half-cooked meat and a coolamon of water on the floor beside the convict. Beef, Towns thought in amazement, tearing at it ravenously; not kangaroo meat, but *beef* . . . !

Johnny watched him for a few moments before crossing the hut to gather up his spears. He took Towns' knife from the table and gave it to Billalong. He reached up to the wall for something dangling on a loop of kangaroo-hide string from a nail, and hung it round his neck. Towns saw that it was a key. Johnny summoning the child to accompany him, went to the door, and from there turned to speak to his visitor peremptorily:

"Stop," he commanded. "Not go. Stop here. Johnny come more."

They went out, closing the door behind them. Towns heard the key turn in the lock, and stared in stupefaction at the one window whose shutter stood wide open, admitting a streak of sunlight. Lock the door on him, and leave the window open . . . ? He was too tired to wonder any more. He finished his meat, drained the water from the coolamon, and stretched himself on the floor to sleep.

*   *   *   *

Towards June of that year Governor King planned further explorations. Nothing, he felt, could be more arduous and exacting than the work he performed here in Sydney—the administrative work which kept the colony functioning—but it was not spectacular. It was the kind of thing that the Home authorities would take for granted. An announcement of the discovery or development of new territory or resources would be far more convincing proof of his zeal.

His thoughts turned to the river some sixty miles northward which young John Shortland had found five years ago during an expedition in search of escaped convicts. He had named it the Hunter, but most people still called it after its most interesting characteristic—coal. That the colony possessed this useful commodity had long been known; four years ago the crew of the *Sydney Cove* had reported large quantities of it on the inhospitable shore where their vessel had been wrecked; Bass had examined a seam in the cliff face south of Botany Bay, and suggested that it might prove to run through the whole Blue Mountain range; Caley had more recently expressed the opinion that immense veins existed throughout the colony. And the Duke of Portland had long ago pointed out to Hunter the desirability of sending coals to the Cape from Sydney rather than from England.

King had not failed to let His Grace know that the matter was receiving his attention. But he had also suggested more than once the advantage of having another settlement established—not too far, and not too near— to which the more troublesome convicts might be despatched, and the existing communities thus freed from their subversive influence. Port Stephens, he urged, would be extremely suitable. *"The harbour is safe,"* he wrote, *"and the land about it good, but its greatest recommendation would be the vicinity to the places where there is such an abundance of coal."*

He pursued the subject informally one evening with Paterson while they toasted their feet by the fireside at Government House, and their ladies chatted with William Chapman, now installed as His Excellency's secretary. King, watching his guest with a half-impatient tolerance, reflected that Paterson's attitude to himself rose and fell like a barometer with every change in the psychological temperature of the colony. Left alone, he would have remained friendly and amenable; but he was not left alone. As Lieutenant-Governor his allegiance was to King, but as Commander of the New South Wales Corps he was never permitted by his brother officers to forget that certain of King's policies bade fair to embarrass them considerably. The Governor leaned forward to spread his palms to the fire, and remarked casually:

"The *Lady Nelson* should be ready soon, Colonel. Are you of the same mind about joining an expedition to the Coal River? You recollect our former conversation on the subject?"

Paterson's dark, rather depressed countenance lightened, but his reply was correctly framed to convey that not his own preference, but the service of the colony was to be considered.

"Should you be of the opinion, Sir, that my presence on such a journey would prove useful, I'm most willing . . ."

"My friend," King assured him genially, "it is indispensable that I should have someone upon whose account I can can confidently rely. It is decided, then. Excellent! I shall send along our miner who was there before, and perhaps Mr. Harris, and certainly our young friend Barrallier —he acquitted himself admirably with the surveying on the last voyage to Bass Strait . . ."

"Why, Sir," cried Mrs. Paterson, "what is this I hear? You propose to steal that amiable young man from us again?"

"I propose, Madam," replied King with mock sternness, "to steal your husband from you—but I hear no complaints on that score!"

Mrs. Paterson protested blushingly while they laughed at her:

"Indeed it was my wifely duty only that kept me silent, for I well know how William will welcome the opportunity for the voyage. As for Mr. Barrallier," she added with a pout, "it is your own daughter, Sir, who will be inconsolable! I declare that she quite lost her little heart to him, and he bows over her hand as though she were the Queen!"

"They are old friends," Mrs. King reminded her. "Many a time he has carried her on the deck of the *Speedy* during our voyage here. When do you propose that the expedition should sail, my love?"

"As soon as all can be got ready," King answered. "Early next month, perhaps. That would meet your convenience, Colonel?"

"I'm entirely at your disposal, Sir," replied Paterson impeccably.

King leaned back in his chair, crossed his legs, and folded his hands over his comfortably rounded waistcoat; no one saw his brief, faintly satirical glance at his second-in-command. A little vacation for the Lieutenant-Governor, he thought—a little respite from the steady, implacable pressure of his military confreres—would not come amiss.

Yet he was to wish many times during the next turbulent months that Paterson had not chanced to be absent at just that time. For upon the same day that the *Lady Nelson* cleared the Heads upon her journey north, the *Earl Cornwallis* transport anchored in the harbour, and set in train a series of events which were to bring Captain Macarthur from his unnatural retirement.

Its commander, the colony learned, had been drowned at Rio de Janeiro, and his personal possessions, upon the vessel's arrival in Sydney, were duly advertised and sold at a public auction. Tongues immediately began to wag. Lieutenant Marshall, they whispered, who had come out on the ship, had purloined certain articles belonging to the late Lieutenant Crawford, including a valuable gun, and some bedding. And since the echoes of all wagging tongues found their way eventually to Captain Macarthur, Marshall found himself confronting that gentleman—now, during Paterson's absence, temporarily in command.

Looking back at it all later, irritated almost to frenzy by the boiling feuds and the endless legal disputes which so small a matter could arouse, King realised that he had sent Paterson away just too soon. True, Captain Macarthur asserted that he had handled the affair with the utmost delicacy. The Governor smiled wryly. Marshall had been foolish; he had substituted certain of Crawford's possessions for certain inferior ones of his own, by way of adjusting a small debt which Crawford had owed him. That was indiscreet, reprehensible, irregular, and he had been duly reprimanded for it by King himself. And there the matter might have rested—would, surely, have rested had the charges been laid by the mild Paterson rather than by the turbulent Macarthur. Gossip raged about the colony, and came even to Beltrasna.

"It seems that our impetuous friend Macarthur is again in trouble," Mr. Mannion told his family over the candle-lit dining-table. "This business of Lieutenant Marshall's threatens to become a storm."

"I had understood, Sir, that all was settled," Mr. Harvey replied, and Mannion shrugged.

"I have noticed," he remarked dryly, "that little breezes of discord among us are apt to blow themselves out if the worthy Captain is not involved. Yet since it is seldom that he is not involved; most of them become whirlwinds which he rides for his own purposes. Marshall, so I hear, is now to be tried for assault and battery upon Captain Abbott."

"Mercy on us!" Conor exclaimed impatiently. "What has this affair to do with Captain Abbott, pray?"

Her husband began to laugh.

"It appears that Marshall insulted Macarthur, who sent Abbott to call him out." He laughed more heartily than ever. "Here is the jest, my love, since you seem bewildered by my amusement. Marshall named a certain Jefferies as his second—the fellow is a purser, I believe, on the

Earl Cornwallis—and as such he proved unacceptable to our colonial aristocracy in the persons of Abbott and Macarthur." He wiped his eyes on his handkerchief. "You are at a loss, Mr. Harvey? Don't you know rumour has it that Macarthur is the son of a linen-draper, and was at one time apprenticed to a staymaker? Hence the nickname that I have more than once heard whispered from lip to lip—'Jack Bodice'! But the gentility of Jack Bodice does not permit him to appear on the field of honour with a purser—so Marshall cooled his heels for an hour, awaiting his adversary in vain! You must allow that the situation has its comical aspects!"

"But the assault, Stephen? The trial?"

"Marshall is said to have waylaid Abbott and struck him. And then last Thursday, so Minchin and Hobby tell me, he confronts Macarthur on the Parade Ground and menaces him with a cudgel. And Macarthur draws his sword and threatens to run him through, and delivers him over to the soldiery to be lodged in the Guard House. And there he awaits his trial—which," added Mr. Mannion, addressing himself to his meal again, "if I may hazard a guess at the composition of the Court, will go unfavourably for him."

It was a joke for Mr. Mannion, but not for his Excellency, who, as the trial progressed, felt the subtle machinations of Macarthur working to draw him into an affair upon which, as Governor, he must maintain a rigid impartiality. Macarthur, giving evidence, called into play all his histrionic gifts.

"Let me entreat you, gentlemen," he cried, "to look upon this man—view his gigantic stature—examine his tremendous club—imagine that you seen him advancing intoxicated with fury, breathing mischief, and looking destruction to the object of his search, and you will be enabled to form some idea of the danger of my situation. For . . ." he added—over-modestly, since he was able to observe with satisfaction that his eloquence had produced a tense hush in the Courtroom—". . . I have neither language nor ability to give you a just description of it." He gazed about him with dignity, and continued in a careful tone of scrupulous truth-fulness: "It is true that I was armed with a sword to oppose him . . ." He sent a dark glance of ineffable disdain at Marshall. ". . . a weapon as appropriate to me as an officer and a gentleman as a bludgeon was to him as a ruffian—but what could a sword have availed in my defence if this monstrous mass of matter, this second Goliath, had been animated with one spark of spirit, one atom of courage?"

He knew the strength of his own personality, and the almost hypnotic influence of his unassailable self-confidence. Once again he was using an incident to gauge the quality of a Governor, for King, he knew, was not satisfied with this trial. Marshall had objected to a Court of whose seven members five were military officers whom he claimed to be prejudiced against him, and Paterson, by now returned, was one of the five. This business, Macarthur thought, might serve to set the Governor and the Lieutenant-Governor at loggerheads. Yet for the moment all this was in the background; his immediate task was to annihilate the insolent nobody who had presumed to cross his path.

"Who is there who saw him advance," he continued dramatically, "armed as he was, and who had witnessed or heard of his attack upon Captain Abbott, but supposed I must be immediately crushed beneath his arm? Such, gentlemen, was my own expectation, and great was my astonishment to observe my drawn sword instantly operating on this ferocious savage like the wand of a necromancer, or the talisman of a magician! To see it in a moment taming him . . ." the sneer in his voice was deadly, ". . . from the excess of offensive fury, into unconditional surrender, and coward-like submission!"

It was such a scene as was meat and drink to him, but no personal quarrel could obscure his cold calculations. Feeling ran high among the officers, and in the ensuing weeks he exploited it industriously, inciting them to a display of hostility towards the Governor. King found himself remembering his first interview with Hunter:

". . . *you have had some reason to fear insubordination on the part of the convicts . . . ?*" "*I have. And not only from the convicts.*"

How much more difficult, he thought, was this kind of insubordination than the crude and foredoomed rebellion of felons! But no one save his Anna Josepha, in the privacy of the conjugal bedchamber, saw the full force of his anger. She sat with a shawl clutched round her shoulders and watched him pace the room, waving a bulky sheaf of papers, and exploding verbally as much to himself as to her.

"It passes my understanding how Paterson can permit himself to be made the tool of this mischievous villain! The man is a fool!"

"My love," Mrs. King urged anxiously, "I feel sure that the Colonel would not . . ."

"Fiddlesticks!" cried her spouse irritably. "The Colonel will sway like a reed to every poisonous breath this destroying wind in human form chooses to blow upon him! I have written to the Under-Secretary of this affair. I have spoken my mind. I have uttered a warning about Macarthur." He shuffled his papers, and read aloud to her in emphatic tones of ominous prophecy: " '*One thing I shall remark, that the arts and intrigues of a man you have heard so much about (I mean Captain Macarthur) will one day sett this colony in a flame.*' Can I speak more plainly?"

"Indeed no," she replied soothingly, "but I entreat you to cease fretting and come to bed. You will catch your death of cold, pacing the room like that . . ."

"He has spared no pains and no ingenuity," King raged on unheedingly, "to involve me in this dispute! He has had the audacity to insinuate that he has throughout the affair acted on my advice, and in such a manner as to receive what he is pleased to call my 'entire and perfect approbation.' Approbation! When it's common gossip that he has been urging his fellow-officers to shun me like a leper! Paterson himself has told me that the fellow pronounced himself offended—offended, forsooth! —because the Colonel declined to withhold his visits to me! And that he threatened to noise abroad certain private correspondence and conversations, with the sole object of creating a dissension between me and my second in command! I tell you he will stop at nothing! I should have clapped him under arrest, and Marshall and Abbott as well—and by Heaven, if I had known the uproar that was to follow this business, I should have done so!"

His unwary pacing brought him too close to a chair, and he stopped short and swore violently. His wife cried in dismay:

"Oh, la, now you have hurt your bad foot again! Pray do calm yourself and take some rest, or I declare you won't be fit for your journey to the Hawkesbury on Monday."

"Ha!" barked His Excellency, thus launched upon another train of thought. "The Hawkesbury! The settlers starve because of my mismanagement, do they?"

"Gracious Father!" cried Mrs. King distractedly, "I'm sure no one says so, my love, for it must be plain that . . ."

"No one says so?" He laughed harshly. "Oh, yes, indeed, our good Colonel says so . . ." he quelled her distressed attempt at intervention with a testy wave of his hand, ". . . oh, not the Colonel by himself, or of his own volition—but taught and tutored by that benevolent philanthropist Captain Macarthur, whose fatherly care for the poor has always been so touching!"

Mrs. King asked faintly:

"To whom did he say such things, pray?"

"To Sir Joseph Banks. I have seen the letter—I have an extract from it here, and I don't need the evidence of corrections in Macarthur's handwriting, I assure you, to envisage him standing behind the Colonel's chair as he wrote. *I cannot help observing,*' he says—and indeed I believe he could not, the poor weak cypher, with those basilisk eyes upon him!—'*that the Governor has carried his economy too far. There was a time when wheat might have been had (which he refused to take). The consequence was that many of the settlers had no way of disposing of their grain than to feed their stock with it, and hundreds of bushels have been used for that purpose.*'" He glared at his wife, tapping the paper fiercely with his forefinger. "Economy! Where would have been the economy, pray, in purchasing grain while the storehouses were already full, and the vermin eating it before it could be issued? Should I have purchased and left it to rot in the streets? No doubt it would have suited those like the worthy Captain, who had vast sums due to them from the unfortunate settlers for their monopolising and their rapacious dealings . . ."

Mrs. King cried despairingly:

"Indeed it is all most difficult to understand! If the storehouses are so full, my love, why are some of the people in want, as I am told . . . ?"

"I am responsible for the expenses of this colony," he said angrily. "I might have bought the grain, the vermin might have eaten it, and the weather might have destroyed what the vermin left; but I, and only I, would have had to explain to my superiors why the cost of grain for the last three quarters amounted to twenty thousand pounds instead of some seven thousand. But this is a good enough stick with which to belabour me. Paterson admits that it has been freely discussed among the officers, and used to agitate their minds as well as his against me. Those words I have read to you were not his words—they were extorted from him . . ."

He continued to rage, but his wife was now pursuing her own melancholy reflections. How provoking were these male quarrels, and how they threatened her own relationship with Mrs. Paterson and Mrs. Macarthur! It was so unpleasant, she thought mournfully, when the husbands of the very few ladies in the colony indulged in animosities. This three-cornered duel could not fail to cast a blight upon the cosy friendship of Mrs. King with Mrs. Paterson, and Mrs. Paterson with Mrs. Macarthur; wifely bosoms could not fail to swell with reflected indignations. She looked up to find her husband's eyes upon her with a faint glimmer of dry, unexpected humour.

"We shall send out cards of invitation, Anna."

"Invitation, my love . . . ?"

"To the officers. To celebrate the anniversary of His Majesty's coronation. Most timely. To every officer, civil and military, except Captain Macarthur. We shall see how successful he has been in attempting to send us to Coventry. Pray attend to it to-morrow morning, my dear, before Divine Service."

*   *   *   *

Mrs. King, having sped His Excellency on his trip to the Hawkesbury at about one o'clock on Monday afternoon, was to see him back at Government House late on the evening of the same day. For he had gone no farther than Parramatta when he was overtaken by news which brought him post-haste back to Sydney, to be greeted by his wife, pale-faced, and with traces of tears about her eyes.

"I have been with Mrs. Paterson," she told him unhappily. "The poor soul is near distracted . . . it's feared the Colonel's wound may prove fatal, and . . ."

He walked past her with a nervous gesture, pulling off his greatcoat as he went. The night was chilly though it was mid-September, and a brightly burning fire on the hearth flung up a welcome warmth to his face, haggard with worry, and still stinging from the sharp wind that had nipped it on the long journey home. He sat down and stared sombrely at the jumping flames. His wife followed him to the fireside, and he asked heavily, without looking up:

"His life is in danger, you say? I've not yet had the surgeon's report . . ."

"I fear so, from his poor wife's account—though in her distress she may be seeing it worse than it is . . ."

"What do you hear of this affair, Anna?"

"What I hear is but gossip, my love, that flies about the town and comes to my ears through our good Jane—and what I can discover from my unhappy friend. But she is so beside herself that I dare to hope . . ."

"What does she say?"

"She vows that Captain Macarthur so basely abused their hospitality,

and so wounded her feelings and the Colonel's, that he had no alternative
but to call him out. She says Macarthur repeated conversations of a
private nature that took place when he was a guest in their house, and
. . ." Mrs. King's pallor was invaded by a sudden flush of indignation,
". . . my name has been drawn into it too, for he is said to have made
use of a letter written by Mrs. Paterson to Mrs. Macarthur, and interpreted its contents to insinuate that I would use my influence with you to
injure him." She clasped her hands over her temples, and shook her head
despairingly. "I do declare, King, the rumours and intrigues and quarrels
of this place are such that I cannot tell whom to trust, or what to believe,
and all is in such a coil that I dare not think what the consequences may
be . . . !"

He stood up with a violent movement and went across to his desk.

"I shall provide the consequences," he said grimly. He snatched up
a pen and wrote:

"*Government House, 14th September, 1801, 8 p.m.*
"*Lieut.-Col. Paterson, Commanding Officer of the New South Wales
Corps, now suffering under a wound he received this day from Capt. John
McArthur of the New South Wales Corps, Ensign and Adjutant Minchin
will inform Captain Abbott, next in command, that it is my order Captains
Piper and McKellar, seconds to the above officers in the rencontre, be put
under arrest, and a centinel placed at each of their barracks until further
notice.*

"PHILIP GIDLEY KING."

The Governor slept little that night, and was back at his desk by eight
o'clock next morning. He summoned Piper and McKellar to Government
House to write their separate accounts of the duel. Macarthur, he had
decided, should be sent to Norfolk Island, and in the meantime ordered
into close arrest until Paterson's life was declared out of danger. He sat
frowning over the reports of the two seconds when they were brought to
him—a long and circumstantial one from McKellar, and one from Piper
whose brevity and nonchalance gave His Excellency's touchy pride a stab.
He awaited dourly the inevitable protest from Macarthur, and the following
morning brought it. The Captain proclaimed himself entirely at a loss
to understand why he should have been placed under arrest, or why he
should be transferred to Norfolk Island. "*My part, Sir,*" he wrote
austerely, "*is obedience; but I think it incumbent upon me to require information whether these to me apparently extraordinary measures are
intended as punishment for some supposed offence, or whether it is only to
be considered in the ordinary course of duty?*" For to Captain Macarthur
it was a spiritual necessity not only to be always in the right, but to be
acknowledged so; not only to be guiltless, but to be injured and persecuted;
not only to be thus wronged, but to appear loftily magnanimous under
injury and persecution.

He had further opportunities. The eight days' limit for a military
arrest having expired, with the Colonel still in danger, King ordered the

three culprits to be released on bail, and to give an undertaking to keep the peace. The seconds complied, but Macarthur—hugging his chains and his conception of himself—responded only with a letter to the Adjutant, desiring him to inform the Governor that he declined coming out of arrest, *". . . but that from a solicitude not to impede His Majesty's Service I am willing to do my duty wherever I may be ordered, provided it be admitted I am . . . doing duty under an arrest, and that I am to be brought before a Court Martial as soon as the public service will admit it."*

This document brought His Excellency near to an apoplexy. He stamped about the room muttering: *"'. . . solicitude not to impede His Majesty's Service . . .'!* He sets the place by the ears for weeks, he spares no effort to create discord between the Corps and myself, he seeks to undermine my authority, he provokes a duel with his Commanding Officer —and then he speaks of not wishing to impede . . . ! *'Solicitude' . . . !* Damnation take the fellow and his intolerable impudence!" He flung himself into his chair, breathing heavily and reflecting upon the curious fact that those human beings whose characters were such as to preclude their ever becoming martyrs, were often most jealously anxious to claim martyrdom. He stared with almost unbelieving fury at the concluding words of the Captain's missive: *"I am the person who has been betrayed, who has been exulted over, and who has been treated with the basest ingratitude, and the blackest treachery."*

And there, thought the Governor, was perhaps one inadvertent spark of truth, for he made bold to guess that there were indeed many people in the colony at that moment exulting in the predicament of Captain John Macarthur. Yet he had his supporters too. King scowled darkly at the letter, remembering that Captain Piper, for one, seemed to have fallen completely under Macarthur's spell; the Governor recognised the man who possessed a personality so capable of swaying his associates as a force to be reckoned with. Yet how? It seemed impossible to try him on the spot upon a charge of creating dissension, clear though the evidence was, for King could hardly order a Court Martial, appear himself as the prosecutor, and—again as the prosecutor—approve the sentence. Most of the members, moreover, who would compose the Court for such a trial were themselves so compromised that they could no longer be considered as impartial. And it would also be necessary to call them as witnesses

He worried over the problem for a few days longer, and then wrote an order which caused him at once some satisfaction and a certain doubt. *". . . His Majesty's Service requires that Captain John Macarthur do prepare himself to embark for England in the arrest he has thought proper to continue himself under."*

The prospect of being rid of him provided grounds for satisfaction. But the Governor had, by now, a bitter respect for his enemy's gifts of persuasiveness and self-justification, for the plausibility of his arguments, and above all for the strength of his personality. There was always power in perfection—and Macarthur's egotism was perfect. In this small community where its impact had fallen heavily, he might be disliked, mistrusted, feared —but he still commanded that power. In England, where nothing was known of him, what might not be its potency? What tales might he not relate of colonial maladministration, and into what influential ears might he not pour them?

King fingered the bulky stack of documents which had accumulated during this tiresome affair. Written testimony from various people of Macarthur's efforts to create discord was not wanting, and would, he trusted, carry some weight with the authorities at home. Yet he would add his own.

Early in November, about a week before the departure of the *Hunter*, upon which Macarthur was to sail, the Governor settled himself at his desk and unburdened himself to the Under-Secretary in a private letter.

"*I need not inform you,*" he wrote, "*who or what Captain Macarthur is. He came here in 1790 more than £500 in debt, and is now worth at least £20,000. . . . His employment during the eleven years he has been here has been that of making a large fortune, helping his brother officers to make small ones (mostly at the public expence), and sewing discord and strife. . . . Experience has convinced every man in this colony that there are no resources which art, cunning, and a pair of baselisk eyes can afford, that he does not put into practice to obtain any point he undertakes. It is to these odds and the independance of his fortune that I have to oppose my exertions for the tranquility of this colony, the welfare of the publick, and my own reputation. Had I allowed Captain McArthur to direct the concerns of this colony, and Col. Paterson had allowed him to command the regiment, this perturbator would have so far remained in silence as first to turn the surrender to his own advantage, but not without scenting an opportunity to throw the colony into that confusion he has so lately failed in doing. However, as a very different course was pursued by me, persecution and opposition became Captain McArthur's system. If the records of this colony, now in your office, are examined, you will find his name very conspicuous. Many and many instances of his diabolical spirit has shown itself before Gov'r Phillip left this colony, and since, altho' in many instances he has been the master-worker of the puppets he has set in motion. . . . If a Governor —nay, a series of Governors are to be thus treated . . . unhappy must be the lot of both Governor and governed.*

"*Judge, Sir, from all this (which is no imaginary statement) how uncomfortable it is for any man to do his duty, goaded and perplexed as I have been, either with satisfaction to himself, or advantage to the public interest; and had I preferred ease and quiet, and chosen to continue Captain McArthur arbiter of the colony, you would have heard nothing of this. . . . I shall close the subject by observing that if Captain McArthur returns here in any official character, it should be that of Governor, as one-half the colony already belongs to him, and it will not be long before he gets the other half.*"

* * * * *

For Conor that winter had passed none too happily. It was late in May that she first suspected she was to have a child, and at first life had seemed—for this and other reasons—to take on a brighter colour. It was pleasant to have so amiable a lady as Mrs. King at Government House, and there were occasional excursions to Sydney for visits and dinner parties. But almost at once Stephen began to hint that in her delicate condition long rides would soon be undesirable, and it was with a forlorn suspicion that this jaunt would be her last for many months that she had set out with her husband early in June to celebrate His Majesty's birthday at the Governor's levee.

She was young enough to find excitement in the little ceremonies of the day. She enjoyed the martial spectacle of the New South Wales Corps drawn up under arms to hear a Royal Proclamation read; she admired the new flag fluttering bravely over Dawes' Point, and found the salute of twenty-one guns fired from the *Lady Nelson* at noon vastly impressive. To her—reared in such strict seclusion in the Irish country-side—the scene at Government House where His Excellency waited to receive the compliments of the colony's *élite*, seemed one of gaiety, and even of some importance. She was naïvely pleased by the assurance which she read in many male eyes that no lady present could match her youth and beauty; and by side-long female glances which told her that none was more elegantly attired. Stephen, too, with his handsome face, his beautiful blue coat, his snowy ruffles and his glossy boots, with his assured and polished manners which made so many of these colonial officers seem clumsy and boorish, was a husband to be proud of. She sighed contentedly as she sank into a chair and prepared to be civil to Mrs. Marsden.

This lady's conversation, she had found in earlier encounters, was not particularly diverting; but a few quickly-stolen glances now assured her that here was a suitable recipient of the great secret which she had been cherishing alone—for one's husband hardly counted in such a matter. Mrs. Marsden heard her shy whisper with gratifying excitement, and from her superior wisdom as the mother of three and another imminent, waxed solemn.

"Dear Mrs. Mannion," she murmured, "I am indeed happy to know you are to be blessed with a child! The crowning joy of a woman's life, my love! I myself . . ." she leaned closer confidentially, and Conor, warned by a quick feminine instinct, permitted her eyebrows to express the astonishment she did not feel. Mrs. Marsden nodded. "In October! I flatter myself you would never have guessed!" Her eyes wandered speculatively to Conor's waist. "And you . . . ?"

"Oh, not until December, Mrs. Marsden."

"The summer heat is most trying in this country. I fear that you will find the last months very difficult to support. Indeed, my child—if I may call you so, since you are so young—I feel deeply for you, situated as you will be so very far from civilisation in this delicate state of health."

"But my health is excellent, Mrs. Marsden, I assure you."

"I make no doubt you will endure your trials with the greatest fortitude, my love. A woman's life in this country is not easy. But tell me, pray, are you not alarmed by the thought of these dreadful savages?"

"The natives, madam? We see very few of them at Beltrasna, and I have always thought them poor, miserable, inoffensive creatures . . ."

"Inoffensive . . . !" Mrs. Marsden lifted her hands. "My dear Mrs.

Mannion, have you not *heard* of the excesses they commit? We have had trouble with them at Parramatta—killing the sheep, and even threatening to murder all white men they meet! And at Prospect, too. There was a stockman called Conroy murdered in the most shocking manner only recently, and a settler most severely wounded. Why, my love, it's barely a month past that His Excellency was compelled to issue an order permitting them to be fired upon in those districts, should they venture near the settlers' dwellings . . ."

Mr. Mannion, approaching, found his wife a trifle pale. She asked him as they rode homeward past the farms round Prospect Hill:

"Has there not been some trouble with the natives in this district lately?"

"I believe so."

"Is there—you would not expect that they would prove hostile near us, would you, Stephen?"

He shrugged.

"I would not expect it, but I am at all times prepared for any emergency. Your task, my dear, is to preserve your good health and spirits. All the rest you may confidently leave to me."

But she found that it was not easy to preserve either in the lonely and inactive life which now closed upon her. The walks which she had once taken by the river were curtailed, not only by a remnant of the uncertain fear which Mrs. Marsden had aroused, but by her husband's firm pronouncement: "It is necessary to spare yourself all fatigue." She was suddenly as fragile and precious as a porcelain vase. "My dear, the ground is damp; pray remain indoors to-day." "You would be well-advised, Conor, not to sit by that open window." "The wind is a little bleak for your constitutional this afternoon, I think."

She did not believe that all husbands made such a to-do of pregnancy, and sometimes she wondered how poor women managed to bear children at all; but she knew nothing of such matters, so she acquiesced. Yet she could not subdue the restlessness of her young, healthy body, and enforced inactivity began to weigh heavily on her spirits. She entered upon a strange period of psychological confusion—a mixture of moods, all heightened by the one underlying emotion of approaching motherhood. She felt a new surge of feeling towards Stephen which brought her nearer to loving him than she had ever been, or was ever to be again, and made her desire to please him; but she felt, also, a hostility towards him because he was the author of this demanding parasite which claimed her body and condemned it to idleness.

It was in some ways pleasant to be so pampered; and yet the legend spun about her that she was now something more than herself, something mystically sacred, like an idol, wakened strange impulses of waywardness and tyranny. They made her sit and be served—well, let them serve! All tears, all tempers, all brooding and wilfulness were now condoned as evidence of her maternal sanctity, and having no other outlet for her boredom, she used them to enliven the long, dull days with illusions of something happening. Yet Stephen's indulgence, the dog-like devotion of Mr. Harvey, and the impassive ministrations of Ellen—in which she seemed to read a faint contempt—only heightened her inner turmoil. They were making her, she felt desperately, into something which she was not. She wanted to be, at this time, gay, happy, busy, loving and beloved; but she was miserable, cross, idle, treated as one loved not for her own sake, but endured for the sake of the child she carried. Now more than ever she wished that Cousin Bertha were not so old, so deaf, and so tired. Of all the household, only she seemed to take this business entirely for granted.

There was nothing one might do, it seemed, but sew, and read, and rest. Conor sewed until the sight of her needle, her little ivory winders of silk, her gold thimble, her work-box inlaid with mother-of-pearl, and brimming with trifles of lace and ribbon, snatched her back to childhood on a wave of absurd, hot-eyed, tight-throated rebellion. She had thought she was grown up. She had escaped from Nurse's: "Whisht, now, Miss Conor, dear, there's your sampler to finish!" only to be condemned to Stephen's: "Shall I not fetch your needlework, my love?"

She read till her whole being revolted against the romantic adventures of a series of heroines—barren substitutes for adventures of her own. She rested, lay on couches, reclined in chairs, accepted cushions from Stephen, and shawls from Mr. Harvey, until at last a kind of inertia possessed her, and she found that the more she rested the more fatigued she felt.

She had too much time to think, and too little to think about. Her ignorance of the world was like a wall through whose chinks she saw only fragments of a bewildering and incomprehensible whole. From the settlements there came little news save when infrequent visitors arrived, and when Stephen or Mr. Harvey returned from an errand to Sydney or Parramatta, but she seized upon what came, and plagued her husband fretfully with questions. "More quarrels! What is it that causes all this animosity?" A second insurrection had threatened, pikes had been found in readiness, the plan had miscarried, the culprits had been flogged and sent to the chain-gangs on the roads. "But Stephen, what can these people hope to gain from such conduct?" It was not Stephen who answered that question, but the ghost-voice of a convict who had once answered another like it. *"Freedom . . . ?"* She tossed and turned in her bed at night, thinking of her husband's convicts in the hut which she had seen only from a distance; inviting and shrinking from the thought that she, tended and cherished, was also a prisoner; struggling with the problem of freedom—physical freedom, spiritual freedom—finding her own confused unhappiness rush out to receive those other remembered ghost words: *"so low in misery . . ."*; and then retreating, shamed by the knowledge of clean linen against her skin, fine clothes in her closet, foods carefully chosen to tempt her capricious appetite. She blushed for even imagining herself miserable.

Mannion spoke of desperate and diabolical characters sent from Ireland, and still sedition-bent. "But what have they *done*?" She learned nothing from his answer. They were infamous plotters against the peace of the realm; provokers of strife; opponents of lawful Government. "La,

Sir, are there not others already here—people in high positions of respect-ability—who disturb our peace, and provoke strife, and plot against the Governor? Have you not told me so yourself? What is the difference, pray, between them and these men who come here in chains?"

He grew impatient, but she no longer met his impatience with docility. He had decreed that her whims were law, and her present whim was to be answered upon pain of tantrums. Rumours of the depredations of the blacks continued to find their way to her. "Would it not be better, Stephen, to *give* them food? Or could we not teach them farming, so that they may support themselves? Could we not teach them many things which would be useful? Why could they not learn? How do you know that they have not any intelligence? It seems to me that Dilboong is not without some aptitude . . ."

Mr. Mannion was tempted to believe that he had not enhanced his felicity by introducing so absurdly importunate a young creature into his life. She had become, indeed, extremely trying, and even her physical charms were waning. Her once exquisite complexion was sallow from indoor life, her hair no longer glossy, but lank and lustreless, her figure distorted by pregnancy, her once gay and charming disposition sometimes positively shrewish. She had become sulkily unresponsive to his ardours. He found his eyes and his thoughts turning again to Ellen.

By the end of August Conor was exhausted. It was Emma, fresh from gossiping with a man arrived from Parramatta to mend Mr. Mannion's harness, who told her of the tragic death of Mrs. Marsden's three-year-old son.

"Thrown from the gig, Madam, with his mother. They say a man with a wheelbarrow came out suddenly and frightened the horse, and . . ."

Conor stared at her in horror.

"But Mrs. Marsden, Emma . . . ? She is . . . she was not also . . . ?"

"No, Ma'am, only the child."

"She was . . . she is expecting to be confined shortly too . . ."

Emma looked at her lugubriously.

"Yes, Ma'am."

Conor went away and thought about the terrible precariousness of the life within her body. A slip, a fall, an accident. . . . For the first time in months her thoughts of her child were tender and protective. Only my body to shield it. . . . She found a kind of still, waiting patience again—not happy, but serene. She had no energy to spare for the healing of a wordless estrangement that had come between herself and Stephen, so she turned to Mark Harvey, in whose company she found a soothing, inarticulate companionship.

In the evenings of that early spring when the shadows had stolen up to the spot on the verandah where Cousin Bertha's chair was placed to catch the last rays of the setting sun, the old lady would waken from her nap, and rub her knotted fingers in their woollen mittens, and say to Conor:

"The evening draws in, my love, does it not?"

"Indeed yes, Cousin Bertha; it is time for you to go indoors."

"I fear so. It is pleasant here, and the view so charming, but . . ." she would give her ghostly little chuckle, and grope for her stick, ". . . but the fireside is the place for old bones, my love." Hobbling to the long windows on Conor's arm, she would repeat: "Old bones!" And again, with a sigh, sinking painfully into her chair by the firelit hearth: "Old bones!" Almost immediately she would be nodding again, and Conor would return to the verandah and sit there alone, listening to the murmur of her husband's voice from the study, and the rustle of Mr. Harvey's papers. After a time they would come out and stand beside her in the gathering twilight, and she would wait, tense and rebellious, for Stephen's admonition:

"You will take cold, I fear. The evening air is quite sharp still."

"I am warm. I shall go indoors presently."

"Pray do so, my dear. I shall take a turn for an hour before it grows dark."

She would watch him go, and Mark would sit down on the edge of the verandah with his back against one of the stone pillars, and they would remain thus, breaking long silences with occasional trivial remarks.

"How loudly the crickets chirp!"

"Yes, indeed, Madam."

"I think I can smell smoke. Surely there are no fires at this time, Mr. Harvey?"

"No, Madam—they have been burning logs in the field by the river."

"What curious clouds, are they not?"

"They say such clouds are a sign of wind."

"How does Miles progress with his lessons, Sir?"

"Well enough, Madam, though I'm bound to say he shows less application than Patrick."

"It grows dark so quickly! And cold . . ."

"Shall I fetch your shawl, Madam?"

"No, thank you. I shall go indoors now."

Scrambling to his feet to offer a ceremonious hand in assisting her from her chair, he would have his brief reward in the touch of her fingers on his own. He was disturbed by her quietness now, as he had been disturbed earlier by the moods so foreign to her natural gaiety of temper —but to him, too, she was at present less a human being than a female idol. He would watch her disappear with her heavy, languid step into the lighted doorway, and return to his own loneliness.

*   *   *   *   *

One dark evening at the end of October, when rain clouds were blowing up from the east, Mr. Mannion rose late from the desk in his study to retrieve a paper which had blown to the floor, and to shut the windows and draw the heavy curtains across them. The paper was a letter from Patrick, brought by the *Minorca* from London a couple of weeks earlier, and he read the clear, round boyish script again as he stood there.

"My tutor is pleased with the progress I have made in my studies, but he will write to you himself concerning this. I have been giving some thought to my future as you bade me do, Papa, but I still do not think that I am well suited to the Army. Though you were kind enough to say that no decision need be reached immediately, I feel I should acquaint you with my not having altered my mind about this. I mean entering the Army. I am aware that you hoped I might find myself disposed to a military career, and I would not wish to cause you displeasure in this or any other regard. But Papa, I do not think that the military life would be agreeable to me. You have often stated your intention of returning to Ireland and leaving your estates in the colony to the care of your agents, but would it not be much better, Papa, if I were to come home and undertake this duty for you, for surely I should be able to care for your interests better than a stranger? And from the circumstance of having lived so much of my life in the colony, I am already well acquainted with it, and do not doubt that in a few years' time I should be capable of relieving you in order that you and Mama and Miles may return to Ireland as you have always wished. You say but little in your letters, Papa, of how things go on at Beltrasna, and I am wondering if there have been any more floods, and whether your new barn is yet completed.

"I trust you are well, and Mama also, and I send my love to my brother, and Cousin Bertha and Andy and Maria and Dilboong, and my respects to Mr. Harvey, and subscribe myself, dear Papa,

"Your affect. and dutiful son,

"PATRICK JOHN FRANCIS MANNION.

"P.S. I have written an essay about life in the colony which my aunt has shown to several ladies and gentlemen, and they have been kind enough to speak highly of it."

Mr. Mannion was frowning slightly as he finished this letter. There was a certain naïveté about the lad, he reflected, which was very well in a child, but should be yielding to a more worldly attitude in a youth of seventeen. It was hardly becoming, he felt, that Patrick should bestow his love so indiscriminately. Nor was he pleased by this anxious and persistent unwillingness for an army career. He stood by the open windows, looking out into a dark, restless night, faintly lit by gleams from a young moon between black, scudding clouds. The wind was rising. There had been heavy rain, and by the look of it would be more. Mr. Mannion, staring out the windows, felt a sudden hostility to this harsh land with its intemperate moods. Drought, fire, floods . . . ! The very people who found themselves exiled in it, he thought, seemed to take their temper from it—to match its violence with their own, to borrow from its enigmatic aloofness a habit of watchful and secretive mistrust, to respond to its heat with their own flaring animosities, to its floods with their own periodical surges of discontent, to its more beguiling moods with . . .

He uttered a faint, irritable exclamation. He himself had felt more than once—however faintly, and however sharply quelled—the insidious temptation of those moods when the sunlight, shining through miles of clean, unpolluted air, and upon miles of silent, virgin land, destroyed his memory of the real, civilised world, and left him instead a world where time and effort and tradition meant nothing. Now he felt a mood rising in him to match the mood of the unrestful sky, and all the time his mind turned the phrases of Patrick's letter, and his eyes watched the light from Ellen's window. *"I do not think that the military life would be agreeable to me."* Agreeable? What did the boy want? *"Would it not be much better, Papa, if I were to return home and . . ."*

Home! The word and its implications struck suddenly upon his consciousness for the first time. He made an angry gesture of repudiation. The lad was a booby! He had grown up so far from the civilised world that he was unable to appreciate its advantages. A colonial farmer! Not for a time, for a whim, as he himself had been, but permanently—as a career! Preposterous! His mind addressed Patrick sternly. You are a Mannion. You have a position to fill, a tradition to inherit. It is in order that you may have ample means to carry on that tradition in a dignified and fitting manner that I have exiled myself for so many years in this colony . . .

He checked for a moment on that, knowing it to be untrue, and yet angrily unwilling to admit that though an irresponsible impulse had brought him to this place, he had remained because it held him. It had held him not by a challenge, but by an indifference more goading than any challenge. He had stayed because he would not leave it unmastered. And now, suddenly, there seemed to blow in to him out of the windy night that damnable, persistent echo of Governor Phillip's voice saying: *"You intend to exploit this land; have a care, Sir, that it does not end by exploiting you!"*

The meaningless words had a meaning now, and his hands tightened on the window-frame as he confronted it in the image of his elder son, whose careful, tentative phrasing held a hint of nostalgia, and whose pen had so far betrayed him as to write "home." His younger son—born here—what of him? His child as yet unborn, in whose lungs this air would be the first breath, and whose eyes would open upon this scene . . . ?

He thought: "I was a fool—a fool! I should never have returned here after that voyage to Ireland . . ." He saw a picture of his life with Conor as it would have been there—serene, orderly, gracious, securely walled off from disturbances—and contrasted it bitterly with the memory of months just passed. Anger against himself became anger against her, and merged into the desire which she could no longer satisfy. His fingers began to tap nervously on the window. It was intolerable, this existence with an ailing, silent, moody wife—exiled in a paltry colony rent with petty conflicts—in a land which offered bounty with one hand only to snatch it back with the other—and the wind, blowing harder and harder, piling up black, swollen clouds—and Patrick's letter in his hand—and the whisper of Phillip's prophecy in his ears . . .

The branches of a small tree between him and Ellen's window whipped to and fro, making a hypnotic movement of light and dark; he stepped through the windows, closed them behind him, and began to walk quickly down the hill towards it. As he reached it the rain began to fall heavily.

*　　　*　　　*　　　*　　　*

Before mid-November summer had descended on the colony, and the red earth road from Toongabbee was thick with dust. A dray, laden with wheat just harvested from the Beltrasna fields, lumbered into Parramatta one Saturday morning, and halted before the building where Mr. Marsden, as magistrate, presided over the claims, disputes and punishments of the week. Mr. Mannion, who had ridden ahead, was awaiting it impatiently, switching flies from his face and cursing the heat; he watched Merrett descend and order out the two convicts, but he was in no mood for the tedious formalities which must attend their appearance before the reverend gentleman on charges of idleness and insubordination. That they should so appear at all was merely a gesture which he conceded to legality when it suited his convenience. True, His Excellency had issued an order a year or so ago forbidding the summary punishment of convicts by their employers, but Mr. Mannion was not alone in feeling that too strict an observance of such an edict was unnecessary. To him, indeed, so far from those centres where the law functioned, it would involve an intolerable interruption of his affairs; why should he lose the services of an overseer for a full day merely for the sake of having a convict flogged at some twenty miles' distance, when the business could be so expeditiously despatched by Toole in the little yard behind his own convict hut?

Yet it was well to make the gesture from time to time, and this occasion—when there was his wheat to send, and he himself desired a word with Captain Macarthur before that gentleman's departure for England—seemed opportune. He waited, therefore, only long enough to give Merrett a few orders about their return, and to see the two convicts, chalky-faced and wild-eyed, shamble away with the chains clanking on their dragging feet, and then rode on through the hot sunlight to Elizabeth Farm.

Captain Macarthur received him cordially.

"A pleasure I had not anticipated, Mr. Mannion. Be seated, pray. You will forgive the slight disorder in which you find me . . ." he gestured at the room, where boxes stood open on the floor, and papers littered the table. "You are no doubt aware," he continued with an ironical smile, "that I am about to embark on a voyage at His Majesty's expense."

Mr. Mannion matched the smile.

"I have learned of your departure, Captain. Condolences, I assure you, freeze upon my lips, for I cannot feel that a journey home—even in the delicate situation in which you find yourself—can be regarded as a misfortune."

Macarthur replied grimly:

"I shall do my best to ensure that it is at least not an unmixed misfortune, Sir." He scowled. "I have been most scurvily treated, Mr. Mannion. For doing no more than my duty I have been publicly assaulted, my honour has been impugned, and I am placed under an arrest. The

good name of my regiment is dear to me, Sir, and I make no apology for
having openly resented the scurrilous assertion of that poltroon, Marshall,
that the military officers on the Criminal Court were so biassed as to
prejudice the justice of his trial . . ."

"A bold assertion, in truth . . ." murmured Mr. Mannion ambiguously,
tapping his boot with his riding whip.

"So monstrous an assertion," Macarthur continued angrily, "that one
would hardly have expected to see the Governor himself lend it countenance. Yet the honest and manly resentment which has been aroused
among the officers as a natural result of this infamous libel has been
attributed to *my* influence! I am accused of creating dissensions! The
mind of my commanding officer is so inflamed against me that he calls me
out—and for defending my honour I incur His Excellency's displeasure!
In me, Sir," he concluded sombrely, "you see a scapegoat."

Mr. Mannion, feeling a smile twitch at his lips, covered his mouth
hastily with his hand, and cleared his throat.

"Your absence," he remarked, "will be a severe trial to your family,
I fear."

For the first time an expression crossed the Captain's face which, in
its natural, unguarded sadness seemed to emphasise more strongly those
histrionic masks in which his features frequently clothed themselves. He
said slowly:

"I shall feel this parting deeply, Sir. Though I take two of our
children with me, and shall find our eldest boy awaiting us in England,
I . . ." He stopped, as though mistrustful of this vulnerable self which
he was exposing; the mask of martyred dignity concealed it again.

"I took pains to enquire of the Governor whether I might be permitted
to walk abroad in my own grounds for the benefit of my health." His
full underlip thrust out in a sneer. "I must suppose that the granting of
this is to be judged a great indulgence!"

Mr. Mannion changed the subject tactfully:

"You take specimens of your fleeces home with you, Captain?"

Watching his host's face, he seemed to see again half of a real expression—but only half. To speak to Captain John Macarthur of fine wool
was to speak of a love as deep as his love for his family, but less simple.
No one opposed that simpler love; no conflicting motives blurred it to
himself; he did not have to scheme for it, or spend himself in different
and irreconcilable functions to serve it. Now wariness veiled the light
that sprang to his eyes at the mention of his fleeces. Not only love was
here, but strife and policy.

"I do, Sir," he replied. "And I am sanguine that there will be those
in England who are not blind to the possibilities they open up for the
advancement of this colony."

Mr. Mannion urged smilingly:

"And for your own advancement I trust! You have been the prime
mover in this matter, and your efforts should not go unrewarded."

"Naturally," Macarthur said, "I shall expect some recognition." He
lifted his shoulders deprecatingly. "You may find that expectation oddly

optimistic, Sir, in view of the treatment I have received here. I confess myself embittered—as any man of sensibility must be, who has been made the victim of gross persecution—but I am not despondent. I am serene in the knowledge of the justice of my cause."

"In that case," responded Mr. Mannion briskly—for he was beginning to find this tiresome—"pray accept congratulations rather than condolences. I trust your representations may have the beneficial results you anticipate for—er—for the colony."

Macarthur leaned forward in his chair.

"I have given much careful thought to them. The authorities at Home must necessarily rely for their information concerning this country upon those who have had personal experience of it, and form their plans accordingly. Whether the information has been reliable, and the recommendations made sufficiently bold I need not, surely, enlarge upon. Of this, however, I am sure; the plans that have been made in the past are totally inadequate—nay, they are worse—they are ill-judged, and would in the end prove disastrous."

"You think so, Captain?"

"I am convinced of it. Reflect, Mr. Mannion. For thirteen years—for almost fourteen years—Government has poured money into this place without the smallest return! Nor will they see a return, Sir, until it is able to produce some raw material suitable for export in large quantities. It is folly to imagine that so small a population (and the bulk of it felons and worthless idlers!), situated as it is at so vast a distance from the civilised world, can ever support itself without some such commodity."

Mr. Mannion nodded reflectively. It occurred to him that he might do worse than watch attentively the manœuvrings of this shrewd and ambitious man. The fellow was, of course, a pushing upstart—but if, for his own ends, he pushed a way to come conclusion by which other land-owners in the colony might also benefit—well, let him push! He asked:

"And this commodity is wool?"

Macarthur slapped his palms down on his knees and rose restlessly.

"Undoubtedly it is wool, Sir! What else can be produced with so little labour and expense? Is it not in continual demand, and are not the manufacturers of England importing from Spain that which could with better advantage be imported (and no whit inferior, Sir!) from here? Will it not withstand the long voyage without spoiling? What else but wool, pray?"

"Your enthusiasm is inspiring, Captain," Mr. Mannion said politely. "I shall observe your progress with the deepest interest, believe me. And now, Sir, may I solicit your aid in a small family matter?"

"Delighted, I assure you."

"My elder son, Patrick, is, as perhaps you know, in England. He attends a school out of London, but spends some of his time with my sister, whose town address you will see upon this small package. Would it be presuming too much upon your kindness to beg you to deliver it to her? It contains merely some letters to various members of my family, and to my man of business in London."

"I shall be most happy, Mr. Mannion."

"My heartfelt thanks. And now I must return to the township where Mr. Marsden is, I trust, meting out a salutary discipline to two of my labourers. We shall have trouble with these rogues some day, Captain —do you not agree?"

Macarthur shrugged, escorting him to the door.

"I think there's no occasion for any great apprehension. A company of our lads, and a volley or two, and they would soon come to their senses. A rabble, Sir, leaderless and undisciplined, is never to be feared."

Mr. Mannion shook his head.

"The accounts I heard during my stay in Ireland a few years ago, and the letters I received after my return, do not altogether bear out your contention, Captain. True, the disturbances were eventually put down, but not before they had created great havoc. As for leaders—does not the self-styled 'General' Holt live but a few miles from this spot?"

The Captain smiled contemptuously.

"I imagine he is too occupied in building his fortunes—at some expense to his employer, I have no doubt—to make mischief of that kind."

"He is still superintending Mr. Cox's farm?"

"I believe so. He is an impudent fellow. Hardly more than a week after his arrival, I'm told, he and the now most respectable Mr. Barrington were entertained by no less a person than Mr. Atkins, and all got merrily intoxicated together! A fine company, and one typical of the chaotic community in which we find ourselves—a seditious rebel, a pickpocket —and the Judge-Advocate of the colony!"

"In my opinion," Mr. Mannion said, settling his hat carefully upon his head, "the Governor was not wise in remitting the sentence of exile that was passed upon Holt after that business last year. Such dangerous characters should be removed to where they can do no harm. However," he added, "the responsibility, I am happy to say, is not mine . . ." He looked past his host at the little girl who sidled out of the door and stood behind her father, staring at him over a pile of clothes tightly clasped to her breast. Macarthur laid a hand fondly on her head.

"Have you no greeting for Mr. Mannion, Elizabeth?"

"How do you do, Sir?" she said shyly.

"I am well, little Miss Elizabeth," Mr. Mannion replied benignly. "And you, I imagine from your burden, are preparing to set out and see the world . . . ?"

"Yes, Sir," she replied solemnly. "I am going to England with Papa. John is going, too."

"Run along, child," her father interposed, "and give those fal-lals to your Mama before you drop them all upon the floor."

Mr. Mannion stepped down from the verandah into the hot sunlight, and offered his hand to his host.

"Farewell, Captain, and *bon voyage* . . ."

"I shall walk a little way with you, Mr. Mannion," Macarthur replied, and added dryly: ". . . since His Excellency has been pleased to permit it . . ."

Elizabeth watched them stroll off along the path together, and then ran back into the house. She hurried importantly into the bedroom where her mother bent over an open valise, and laid her pile of clothes tenderly on the bed.

"That's all, Mama, except for the petticoat that Sophy is doing, and she says it will be ready soon."

"Very well, my love. Who was that talking to your Papa?"

"It was Mr. Mannion, but he is gone now. Have you finished packing John's clothes, Mama?"

"Almost, child. You will remember, will you not, Elizabeth, that the sea-air is treacherous, and you must wear your cape. And recollect, my dear, that you're older than John, and must take care of him . . ."

"Yes, Mama, but you must tell him to mind what I say, because he always. . . . Mama . . . ?"

"What is it, my dear?"

"Mama—are you crying?"

"Of course I'm not crying, you foolish child!"

Mrs. Macarthur hastened to a cupboard whose open doors concealed her while she whisked a handkerchief across her eyes. She returned to the bed and sat down, drawing the little girl to her knees.

"Elizabeth," she said earnestly; "I am *most* glad that you are going to England, for have I not often told you of its beauties, and of the opportunities it affords for education in all those accomplishments a well-bred girl must be mistress of? We have been very happy here, my love, but I would be a poor Mama indeed were I to deprive you of such advantages."

"But you do look sad, Mama."

"I am a little sad, I confess, at parting with my dear girl and boy."

"You have James and Mary and William still."

"If I had a score of others I would still miss you and John. You will not forget your Mama, Elizabeth . . . ?"

The child's face puckered suddenly; tears sprang to her eyes, and she flung herself into her mother's open arms. Mrs. Macarthur, stroking her head with one hand, and applying the handkerchief to her own eyes again with the other, chided brightly:

"Come, come, there is nothing to cry about! You are a big girl—eight years old! How shall I entrust your brother to you if you weep like a baby? And you must take care of Papa also, and be a help and comfort to him. See, my love, I have packed all your warmest clothes, for in England it is colder than here. How strange it will seem to you to see London! I declare there will be so much to interest you that you will hardly know what to look at first! Fine streets and great houses, many horses and carriages, more people than you can imagine! Look, child, here is your Papa—do not let him see you in tears. That is Mama's good girl! Now dry your eyes and run to Sophy for your petticoat, for we must have everything in readiness by to-night . . ."

She watched the small figure disappear through the open doorway where Macarthur stood, and the sternly suppressed tears filled her eyes again. He came to sit beside her on the bed and took her hands down from where they had flown to cover her face.

"My dearest wife," he said gently, "I understand your distress. Be assured that in parting from your husband and these two children you suffer no more than I in leaving you and our three others. Elizabeth and John will have my tenderest care, never fear."

"Indeed I know it," she sobbed. "Yet I cannot but reflect that this parting must take place so often. First our dear Edward, whom already we have not seen in seven years—now Elizabeth and John—and some day Mary, and James, and William . . ."

"In laying such trials upon you," he said earnestly, "Providence has also given you the fortitude to endure them. There can be but few women in the world who combine as you do, my Elizabeth, all the female virtues with so masculine a strength and steadiness of character. I have been fortunate indeed in the partner who has shared my successes, and now with such resolution shares my ill-fortune . . ."

She lifted her face at that and dried her tears energetically.

"Your ill-fortune will not long continue," she said quickly, and he, as quickly, agreed.

"I am certain it will not. You have been the confidante of all my plans, and you know, do you not, that it is not my habit to rest until I have achieved my purpose?" He rose in the excitement which contemplation of his own inflexible will always aroused in him, and began pacing the room as he talked his dreams aloud. "We are established, my dear wife, in a land where I can find scope for the abilities I possess . . ." As he spoke of it the land swung before the eyes of his mind, and his mind subtracted from it ruthlessly all but that which he wished to see. Imagination did not paint for him the progress through it of the rum which had so materially assisted his fortunes; nor follow it into huts where food had been bartered for it; nor to plots of ground uncultivated for want of the tools which had bought it; nor to hospitals where men and women fought the death in it had hastened; nor to dark corners where the law was cheated to obtain it; nor into the desperate minds and hearts of people confronting a life so base that they could trade every human decency for an hour or two of the oblivion it brought. He saw no shabby little settlements stretching their poor cottages along dusty streets; he saw no convicts dragging half-starved bodies to another day of exhausting labour; he saw no lonely huts standing in a few acres of painfully tilled soil where small settlers staved off bankruptcy from month to month; he saw no bewildered hordes of dark-skinned people retreating, dispossessed, before his dream. He saw only land, land, land—empty land, sun-drenched and grass-covered, its green slopes dotted with thousands upon thousands of woolly, moving shapes—a land virtually untouched and unrealised. A land for plunder . . .

His wife heard his words, and because she was a woman of intelligence one part of her mind attended to them, but with another she was storing her memory with pictures of him against their long separation. How handsome he looked, she thought fondly, flushed and animated, his dark, narrow eyes so bright, his lower lip outthrust with that truculence which carried him past all obstacles . . .

He paused, and stood before her, his arms akimbo.

"The fleeces I take home with me," he told her emphatically, "are indeed golden fleeces, my dear! Never doubt that when they are inspected by those qualified to judge them our battle will be half won. A rosy future awaits only the sanction and encouragement of authority for the labours of such people as ourselves . . ." He sat down beside her so impetuously that she smiled, thinking how boyish he could be, for all his thirty-four years. He grasped her hands again and continued earnestly:

"Turn your mind, I beg, from the difficulties of our present situation! Let your imagination play upon the future! Picture these dear children now being torn from you as inheriting a fortune founded upon our labours and our sacrifices! Never permit yourself to dwell upon the obstacles which have been thrown in our way, or those which we shall yet have to overcome. Have confidence in me. Hunter opposed us—and he is gone. King opposes us—and I make no doubt calumniates me in the despatches he will send home—but I also have a tongue, my love! A tongue—and our golden fleeces . . . !"

She smiled at him, returning the pressure of his hands.

"I have complete confidence in you," she assured him serenely, and lifted her face for his kiss.

*   *   *   *   *

Mr. Mannion rode back to the township, where he was fortunate enough to encounter Mr. Marsden returning homeward with something less than his usual buoyancy of step. He gestured a greeting, and the clergyman, bowing in acknowledgment, stood back in the shade of a wall and mopped his brow with his handkerchief while Mr. Mannion dismounted and crossed the road to speak to him.

"Good-day, Sir. May I enquire after my two wrongdoers delivered into your charge this morning?"

Mr. Marsden took off his hat and fanned himself with it.

"A suitable punishment was ordered, Mr. Mannion. The weather grows uncomfortably warm, does it not?"

"We must expect it, I suppose, at this time of the year. This is the first opportunity I have had, Sir, to offer my condolences on your most tragic bereavement. Mrs. Marsden and her infant are well, I trust?"

"I am truly thankful to say they are, Sir. In my wife's precarious state of health so terrible an accident might well have cost both her and the child their lives. You are staying the night in Parramatta, Mr. Mannion?"

"No, I am on my way to Sydney, where I shall stay with Captain Piper. Those miscreants of mine will be fit to be sent back to Beltrasna to-morrow, I presume?"

"Oh yes, I see no reason to suppose otherwise. I ordered them but twenty-five each. I trust it may prove salutary, but my experience has shown, Mr. Mannion, that many of these men are so hardened that punishment has but little effect upon them. I recall the incredible obstinacy of those fellows who were involved in the attempted insurrection about a year ago, when we endeavoured to discover where the pikes were hidden, and who else had been concerned in the business." Mr. Marsden shook his head gravely. "There was one young man who, I am convinced, would have died upon the spot rather than tell a single sentence. Three times he was taken down, Sir—punished upon his back, and also on his bottom when he could receive no more upon his back—but he was in just the same mood when taken to the hospital as he was when he was first tied up."

"They are obstinate rogues. And unless I am mistaken," added Mr. Mannion, glancing across the street, "you are at present being saluted by one who was perhaps not so innocent in that affair as he would have us believe?"

Mr. Marsden's plump face became tinged with an angry pink; his eyes followed the jaunty figure of Mr. Holt with disfavour.

"That insolent fellow! When he was first arrived, Sir, it was I who, as a Christian duty, received him, and showed him the house where he was to live. But when I warned him—as was also my duty—that for one in his situation to undertake the management of Mr. Cox's farm was something presumptuous, he behaved in the most impudent fashion!"

Mr. Mannion nodded.

"You don't surprise me, Sir. But I must not detain you. However, before we part, may I beg your assistance . . . ?"

"You have only to command me, Mr. Mannion."

"I wish to arrange for a midwife to come at the earliest possible moment to Beltrasna. My wife's time is drawing near. A Mrs. Blake, Sir, has been highly recommended to me—can you direct me to her house?"

Mr. Marsden did so. "You will have no difficulty in finding it. A worthy woman, in whom you may place confidence. I trust Mrs. Mannion's health gives you no cause for alarm?"

"She is somewhat low in her spirits. The heat, no doubt, and the unavoidable seclusion of our life. And of course as we married men know . . ." they exchanged a patiently resigned smile, ". . . ladies at such times are apt to be—shall we say a trifle capricious?"

"My wife will regret that owing to her own family ties she is unable to visit Mrs. Mannion. In ordinary times, Sir, I believe she would make nothing of the journey to the Nepean, for she is a capital horsewoman. However, she is not yet completely restored to health—her confinement having followed so closely upon the terrible misfortune that she suffered . . ."

"Naturally, my dear Sir. At some later date we shall eagerly hope for a visit from you both. Good-day, Mr. Marsden."

Mr. Mannion re-mounted and proceeded upon his search for the midwife.

In Sydney he collected, willy-nilly, further gossip. It was whispered that warnings had come to His Excellency's ears that his despatches concerning the Paterson-Macarthur duel would not reach England. Mr. Mannion shrugged that aside contemptuously. The Governor knew his business well enough to ensure that copies of his correspondence were kept, and duplicates forwarded by different ships; no one in his senses would think to suppress evidence by the mere stealing of a despatch case. Yet when he reflected he felt his old, wry admiration of Macarthur stirring again. It could be only rumour that what the Governor's despatches urged upon the authorities was nothing less than that gentleman's permanent banishment from the colony—yet His Excellency's sentiments were well enough known to lend it conviction. Captain Macarthur's ambitions were no less well known, and Mr. Mannion had the evidence of his own eyes and ears that the Captain saw his future gloriously linked with that of the infant colony. Might not the situation, then, resolve itself into a race for the ear of authority? Which would have the advantage of first audience—the indictment of Macarthur, or Macarthur himself, armed with his self-confidence, his quick, intriguing brain, and (not least) with a plan for making this expensive and troublesome colony pay? And his fleeces to back his argument! The indictment, borne away by Lieutenant Grant in the *Anna Josepha* more than a fortnight ago, had a good start, for Macarthur himself was not due to leave yet for several days. Yet Mr. Mannion was too old a resident of the colony not to be aware that it harboured many ingenious gentlemen to whom the picking of a lock was no problem. He began to think that the elaborate precautions which the Governor was said to have taken to safeguard his precious documents might well have been prudent—and fruitless.

Mr. Mannion found Captain Piper so full of the affair as to be, for once, almost tedious. This genial young man, not yet thirty, had already been in the colony for ten years, with interludes at Norfolk Island and in England; and in a society where the friends of to-day were often the enemies of to-morrow he had enjoyed the distinction of being almost universally well-liked. He wore his worldliness innocently over a kind heart. Amiable and gregarious, he preferred horses and dogs to more profitable livestock, saw money as something to be transformed into the amenities of social life, and found his interest in the spending of it rather than in amassing it for the power and privilege it could bestow. He had received small grants of land from Grose and Hunter, and had added a little more by purchase, but he was continually in debt, and his property barely served as a means to help him out of continual financial embarrassments. His more ambitious brother-officers, therefore, were not compelled to see him as a rival, and his modest position as a junior officer had at first saved him from becoming too deeply embroiled in the civil-military intrigues which made up the politics of the colony.

This happy detachment had been rudely interrupted by his dramatic involvement in the Paterson-Macarthur duel. He would have been hard-pressed himself to explain just how it had happened, though his promotion the previous year to the local rank of Captain had undoubtedly brought him into closer contact with Macarthur. And to a young man who loved the smoothly-polished surfaces of life, Macarthur could not fail to be an exciting and admirable figure. Captain Piper had found him so admirable that his conversation with Mr. Mannion threatened to become an endless panegyric.

"I assure you the letter I received from him while I lay under arrest by the Governor's orders almost moved me to tears. His sole thought was to cheer and hearten me in case I should be sent home to England, and he assured me in the most generous terms that should I find myself in any pecuniary difficulties he would see it as no more than his duty to assist me. He uttered no complaints on his own behalf, Sir, and urged me to have no apprehensions for him. 'Do not care for me,' he said, 'for I am now so deeply in that the game begins to be amusing.' And he took the trouble to write out a letter for me to send the Governor, counselling me not to alter a word of it, and you may be sure I did not. 'Settle all your money concerns,' he bade me, 'and let me know what they are.' He well knew—for he seems to know everything—that I was in pretty deep with Cox, but he urged me not to be downcast about it—'for,' he said, 'no man shall call after you for a shilling.' I give you my word, Sir, I was deeply affected by his concern for me."

Mr. Mannion eyed him with a mild amusement in which there was a shade of resignation. He had enjoyed the company of this young man because up to the present he had been able to report and discuss the affairs of the colony amusingly and without undue heat. Now, apparently, he too had become a partisan. Mr. Mannion, as a man of the world, was well aware of the manner in which the great secured adherents, and of the silken chains of obligation in which they bound them. Again he paid half unwilling mental tribute to Macarthur—this obscure captain of a third-rate regiment who was learning so adroitly the techniques of his betters.

"A remarkable man," he observed dryly. "I should have no anxieties on his behalf were I you, Captain. He will vindicate himself in England, never fear."

*　　　*　　　*　　　*　　　*

Conor's rose-garden was not a great success. The stones from the river had been duly set in place; beds had been dug; Mr. Mannion had even caused the whole plot to be enclosed in a ring of young cypress trees, destined some day to protect it from the winds; he had had an arbour built, in which, theoretically, Conor was to recline, sniffing the scent of a thousand roses.

But of the many bushes sent from Ireland less than half survived the voyage. These, thrust into a strange soil, lived listlessly, or died. Only a hardy pink rambler planted beside the arbour seemed to thrive, and one hot November morning Conor sank into the chair Ellen had set for her in the shade, with her fan, and her needlework and a book on a little table beside it, and thought that the profusion of rosy blossoms over her head only emphasised the dusty barrenness of her ill-fated garden.

The cypress trees were still very small, and she could look over the fields from which Mr. Mannion was harvesting his wheat; he had kept men posted there night and day for weeks, alarmed by tales from other settlements of natives who set fire to the crops. It was Pemulwy who was the moving spirit in these depredations, so everyone said—Pemulwy and two escaped convicts. Only recently Mr. Harvey, returning from Sydney, had told her of the Governor's order offering rewards for their apprehension. Dead or alive . . .

Conor looked past the fields to the undulating, tree-clothed country which harboured, so it seemed, a different world. So close! If she could be spirited suddenly from this spot, and set down among those dull green trees only five miles away, what would she find? But most likely nothing. For the natives were not very numerous, and the land very large, and full of—nothing! That was how it had seemed to her on the few occasions when, escorted by her husband and several other gentlemen, she had penetrated a little way into these strange and silent woods. You looked round and tried to say what you could see—tree-trunks, shadows, fallen bark and twigs; you went on a little farther and tried again—tree-trunks, shadows, fallen bark and twigs. It was a different place, and yet eerily the same; after a time you began to feel that you were not moving from one place to another at all, but through an illusion, a kind of static, changeless dream. It was withdrawn, it held no communication. There seemed no human imprint on it, and no human legend to bind it to one's life . . .

And yet, she wondered, might not its own people feel some affinity with it—a closeness and confidence such as she herself had felt in the Irish countryside? Might it not be legends, songs, tales, the spiritual imprint of generations, even more than the imprint of their hands and tools, which made a homeland? She began to remember stories woven into her childhood—tales of the great Cu Chulainn, and Cormac, and the wise man Sencha mac Aillela; of sad Dierdre, and of Conor, that high king of Ulster whose name had been so strangely bestowed upon her; and of the heroic Finn mac Cumaill . . .

Finn . . .

Her wandering thoughts caught on the name for an instant as her skirts might have caught on a thorn. She pulled them free and passed on, saying to herself a trifle hurriedly: "Yes, that is it—we are strangers here, with no stories behind us . . ." And then, feeling a faint shock, she thought: "We are ourselves the first stories!" The thought disturbed her. What kind of stories . . . ? Yet in those Irish legends of her childhood there was violence too—strife and bloodshed and sorrow—but grown dim with the passing of time, so that their ugliness was veiled by an illusion called romance. She thought of the books she had read in her grandfather's study, and how she had dreamed over past centuries as though they had nothing to do with her own time. But was not all time one? She began gropingly to shape the idea that one must hold fast to history no less than to one's own small lifetime; walk there not with ghosts but with men and women; sift its mass of accumulated legends as one tried to sift the crowding events of personal existence. She looked at the countryside again, thinking that, empty as it seemed to her, it must surely be peopled for the natives with the uncountable legions of their forefathers.

To them this unresponsive land must speak. She felt the movement of her child, and for the first time saw her motherhood not as a personal matter but as a link between the present and the future. Would this land speak to her children—her grandchildren—her great-grandchildren? Would they, looking back at her, perhaps through some old letters, or a miniature, or some strangely surviving trinket—a fan, a brooch, this gold thimble on her finger—see her only as a picture, bloodless, and emotionless? Would they never know her as the living creature she had been? She felt forlorn, and faintly indignant. Yet she knew that she had seen her own ancestors thus, and she began to wonder again about the natives, to whom their forefathers were no less real than themselves. It seemed necessary, she felt vaguely, to hold all time together, saluting your ancestors and your descendants as though they were living friends beneath your roof. And the natives, whose roof was the sky above their land . . .

Her idle train of thought seemed to have led her back to Pemulwy, thrusting his blazing firestick into the fields of the invaders. Pemulwy and his black companions—and his white . . .

Now she confronted a question which her thoughts had been merely skirting. Why are we here at all? Was not the answer to it in those white companions of the black Pemulwy? Or—was it elsewhere . . . ? It was too vast a question for her. It abandoned the natives who, in spite of her groping effort, seemed creatures of a different clay, and took her with one fierce stride into her own world. And there, though not a stranger, she was a child, untaught and uncomprehending.

She sighed and took up her needlework, but her fingers were sticky with heat, and she stitched only for a moment or two before laying it down and looking out dejectedly again across her rose garden.

It was perhaps her own fault, she thought unhappily, that it had been a failure. Tears came easily to her eyes of late, and they came with sharp unexpectedness as she looked at the paving stones. Where were the lovely colours she had seen on them when they lay submerged in the clear water, or wet and shining on the river bank? They were dull and dusty now; the weeds which grew up between them, dry and yellowish under the hot sun, had scattered untidy fragments over their smooth surfaces. And to achieve this shabby desolation two men had suffered, and one walked to this day with a limp.

She thought: "They are water-stones. They belong in the water. I should have left them there . . ." She thought of the fountain she had planned, and for a moment her interest stirred again. Perhaps if it could spray over them . . . ?

But the fountain was now a very distant dream. True, Stephen had ordered it to be made in England, and despatched to the colony; it was to be most elegant—a white marble naiad holding up a vase from which the water would gush—but he had also explained how much time and labour and money must be expended before this could be pumped from the river, and in these last miserable months his zeal to please her had waned. And she herself had never felt the same about her rose-garden since that incident on the river bank . . .

So she sat here in her shady arbour, and fanned herself, and waited for the long morning to pass. She tried to combat a growing sense of loneliness and exile by remembering the voice of her old nurse reading tales so familiar that even now their words welled up in her memory without effort: *"On a certain day when Finn mac Cumaill rose at early morn in Almu in Leinster, and sat on the grass-green plain, having neither servant nor attendant with him . . ."*

She saw a man come round the corner of the house—a man in shapeless convict clothes, with shackles on his feet, limping, carrying a spade over his shoulder; the sight, breaking into her fairytale, was like a bitter jest. She flinched from it, startled, angry, but not sure whether her anger was against reality for breaking into a daydream, or against the daydream for beguiling her. She had been spinning Ireland from fine threads of memory, and now they were in tatters. This was not Ireland—it was a far continent where her tales meant nothing. It tossed aside her vision of Finn mac Cumaill, and showed her Finn the convict . . .

She felt a sudden agitation, and made a movement as if to rise. Time had pushed that episode not out of her mind, but to the back of it, where it lay darkly and uneasily. She had seen him but seldom since, and always at a distance, always with a gang of other convicts, so that she had been able to divest him, partly, of the alarming individuality which she had once glimpsed. Now he was here alone, close to her. Yet not so close that he need intrude upon her solitude. He had not seen her; he was working at the opposite side of the garden, digging among the woebegone bushes with his back turned to her. If she ran away. . . . She caught herself up angrily on the unwary phrase that had slipped into her mind. If she rose, and went indoors, he might see her—he might think . . .

Mercy on us, what does it matter what he thinks? I shall stay here! What *does* a convict think . . . ? Does he have thoughts, as I have, sitting here? Surely his hair is more grey than it was—then . . . ?

She picked up her book and pretended to read, watching him over it. He worked with a dull, mechanical steadiness, turning the clods of earth over, stooping to pull out tussocks of weed and throw them on the stones, digging again, stooping, digging . . . The patch of freshly-turned earth showed up, reddish brown, divided from the rest by a straight, neat line along which his spade moved with stubborn patience. She thought of her own attempts at work—a scrap of embroidery tossed aside when she became weary of it; a sketch-book full of half-finished watercolours; even a whim, once, to cook, which had proved so tiresome that she had abandoned it to Ellen . . .

Work which could not be so lightly left? Work which had to be done whether you were weary or not, bored or not, ill or not; in rain, in wind, in blazing sun; work not chosen, but imposed upon you—to be performed on pain of . . . ?

She sat quite still and watched him until Mrs. Blake came, all clucking solicitude, to escort her indoors. He had paused only to drag his arm across his sweaty forehead, and he was still digging as she glanced back from the doorway.

She remarked to her husband that night:

"You are having some work done in the rose-garden again, Stephen."

"Even though your interest in it has ceased," he replied, "I dislike to see any part of my property in such a state of neglect. Now that the harvest is nearly in I can spare a man for a few days." He glanced at her. "It is that fellow Finn."

"I know," she answered. "I saw him at work this morning. . . . He . . . he still limps badly, does he not?"

Mannion frowned slightly.

"Since the sight of him may have unwelcome associations, my love, it might be advisable for you to avoid the arbour while he is employed there. I set him to the task partly because he was, in his youth, a gardener, and partly because . . ." his frown blackened for a moment, ". . . I think it wise to separate him as much as possible from his fellow-rogues. He is too ready with his tongue. But we must preserve your tranquillity at all costs, my dear Conor. Mrs. Blake shall place your chair on the verandah for a day or two."

She made no reply to him, but the next morning she said to the midwife:

"I shall have my chair in the arbour."

Mrs. Blake paused, books and cushions under her arm.

"But the master said, Ma'am . . ."

Conor repeated sharply:

"I shall have my chair in the arbour."

Finn had dug more than half of the garden. Sooner or later his work would bring him within a yard or two of where she sat. She thought that he had seen her, but if so her presence seemed of no more interest to him than the presence of the arbour itself. The morning was hotter than ever, with not a breath of wind. Even in the shade she felt a moisture on her brow. The roses were fading, and their petals floated down silently, one by one, to the ground; a thin, pink carpet of them lay among the dust and weeds. There was no sound at all but that made by the thrust of his spade into the earth, the clink as it struck a stone, the little clatter as he threw the stone on to the pavement. He moved out of her sight, hidden by the side of the arbour, but the sounds of his digging came nearer. He coughed now and then. It was nearly mid-day when he reached the patch of garden directly before her, and she said:

"Good morning, Finn."

His reply was as mechanical as his work—a glance, a mutter, an automatic gesture of his hand to his forelock. No hint of surprise—or interest. He had known she was there as he had known the roses were there; her greeting fell on him as unimportantly, and perhaps as incongruously, as their petals fell on his bent shoulders.

She was annoyed because this contact, which clearly meant nothing to him, should mean so much to her. She did not know, or attempt to discover, why it should mean much to her. She only knew that in these last months with the child quickening in her body, dissatisfaction with herself had grown till it was a perpetual torment. She was a woman, and about to be a mother, but she had never escaped from her childhood. It was the task of everyone she had ever known to raise walls about her. For her protection—yes, of course, for her protection. . . . Protection—from what . . . ? These walls, she thought, do not only protect me—they shut out my view. I'm safe. But I can't see. What is outside? And she was driven on by the knowledge that once, through this man, she had seen a glimpse of what was outside. She said, keeping her eyes on her needlework:

"The master says you have been a gardener, Finn?"

He answered briefly, with no pause in his digging:

"Aye, Ma'am—and many other things."

"What other things, pray?"

His glance seemed to say that he found her questions tiresome; that they interrupted some train of thought which he was impatient to pursue. He muttered:

"Thatcher—weaver—gravedigger—stableman—labourer—anything that would be bringin' me a crust, Ma'am."

Stitching industriously, she thought: "Gardens. In the garden of some great house, perhaps . . ." That brought her pictures of such gardens, and the strange idea that their beauty could be made and tended by such men as this. She stole a glance at him. He was so ugly. So dirty, drab, grotesquely clothed; so brutal-looking, so degraded—and yet she must think of him as one who had grown flowers . . . ! Some of her wonder, her incredulity, found its way into her naïve question:

"Do you like flowers, Finn?"

His head lifted for a moment, and she found herself looking at his eyes. Bodies can be starved, distorted, battered by life; hair can be matted and unkempt; cheeks can be dirty and unshaven; mouths can set in ugly lines, and teeth decay—but eyes remain truth-tellers. The eyes she saw might once, in childhood, have been large and clear and grey; now they had retreated behind a defence of lowered brows and narrowed lids; their whites were slightly bloodshot, and their colour indeterminate, but there looked out of them something which denied the depersonalised exterior which life had forced on him. It looked out of his eyes, and it spoke with a faint but still bitter contempt in his voice:

"I can see a colour, Ma'am, and smell a scent, like any other man."

She felt her cheeks begin to burn almost before she realised that she had been snubbed. She had meant to be kind, and was rewarded with this thinly-veiled insolence! Yet she knew that it was not only benevolence, but the nervous, restless itch of her curiosity which had prompted her to question him, and her annoyance, as she reached for her book, was mainly because a door seemed to have slammed in her face.

She would read, and ignore him. She picked the book up from the table, but she was not as calm as she would have liked to be, and she dropped it clumsily on the floor. He was digging again, with his back to her. She leaned from her chair to reach for the book, but it lay beyond her stretching finger-tips. La! what a provoking thing it was to be so heavy, so clumsy, so helpless! It put her in a sudden rage, and she said peremptorily:

"Kindly pick up my book, Finn!"

He drove his spade into the earth, came into the arbour and bent down for the book. It was true, she thought, looking at the top of his bent head, he was much greyer than he had been a year ago. She noticed that as he handed her the book he turned it slightly with an automatic movement as if to read its title. It was not until he had been digging again for five minutes that her curiosity once more vanquished her pique.

"Can you read, Finn?"

"Yes, Ma'am."

"Who taught you, pray?"

"A good friend I had, Ma'am."

"Where is he now?"

"He was hanged, Ma'am."

That struck her speechless for a moment or two. He did not hear the faint "Why?" which she uttered at last, so she enquired again, with sudden and unnecessary loudness:

"Why? What had he done?"

" 'Twas said he picked a pocket, Ma'am."

"Do you . . . do you believe he did so?"

"I don't know, Ma'am," he answered indifferently.

"If he was your friend," she insisted with a touch of indignation, "you could not, surely, believe such a thing of him?"

He glanced at her. His look said as clearly as if he had shouted it aloud that such ignorance as hers was not even worthy of contempt. He pulled his spade out of the earth and began to walk away. To walk away! Leaving a question she had asked him unanswered! Her temper flared again.

"Where are you going, Finn?"

He halted and looked back at her darkly, unwillingly.

"There's the other side to be dug, Ma'am."

"You have not yet finished here."

"No, Ma'am."

"Then do so."

She would almost have been glad to see some hint of anger in his face. It was expressionless. He began to dig again, and she to read, conscious all the time of emotional turmoil, half hated and half welcomed. The echo of her own voice, sharp almost to shrewishness, disturbed her; here again was a situation which was making her seem something she was not. She said at last, with an attempt at dignity and calm:

"I had asked you a question. Can you believe that this good friend of yours was a thief?"

His spade struck into the earth with violence, as if he hated it; there was a goaded irritation in the movement of his head as he half turned it towards her; his voice was blurred and thickened as if with anger painfully controlled.

"It's many a thief I've had for friend, Ma'am . . ." the control slipped a little, and fury edged his voice more sharply, ". . . aye, and murderers too!"

She said breathlessly, hating him for the knowledge she had demanded, and which he was now flinging at her like stones:

"You have been both yourself, perhaps?"

He was still now, resting his thickened, ugly hands on the spade, staring at her with an attention which she found even more disconcerting than his indifference. Yet he seemed to be speaking less to her than to himself.

"Not a murderer—yet. But many times a thief, and I living in a world that says to me steal or starve . . ."

She said quickly, with querulous anger:

"There are charitable persons, and charitable institutions which . . ."

And then, still not moving, he burst out savagely, unbelievably:

"For the love of God cease your silly chattering . . . !"

After that there was a silence which seemed to Conor long and terrible. She felt something strange happening to her face—a slow tightening of the skin as her colour ebbed, and a hot suffusion as it swept back in a flush of outraged anger and astonishment. She saw sudden fear obliterate the momentary rage which had broken his impassive expression; a convulsive, hunted movement jerked his hands and body as that fear warned him: "Run! Escape!"; stiff, tense immobility descended upon him as reason told him there was no escape. They remained motionless and silent, staring at each other in a kind of bewildered horror.

He broke the spell. She saw that his hands were shaking violently on the spade as he turned his back on her and began to dig again. She tried to rise, but her legs felt weak, and the clumsiness of pregnancy made the business of getting out of her low chair an effort which brought childish tears to her eyes. She struggled to her feet at last, knocked blindly against the table, turned to look at him, and found him staring at her over his shoulder, his face sick-looking in its pallor, and streaked shinily with sweat. She knew what was in his mind—not a question, not an appeal, but merely recognition of her as the author of torture and humiliation in store for him; and suddenly she found herself shaking her head violently, repudiating that thought, protesting against that misconception of herself. She said desperately:

"No, no, I shall not speak of . . ."

But she could manage no more words. She stumbled away up the path to the house, holding her handkerchief clenched against her mouth. She met no one. Her room was cool and dim, and there she threw herself face downward on the bed to weep.

*   *   *   *   *

She went no more to the arbour until his work there was finished. She tried to compose her mind; to forget not only Finn, but all convicts; to distract her thoughts with scraps of news from the townships, plaguing Mr. Harvey with questions when he returned from a visit to Sydney late in the month.

"What new matters are afoot, Mr. Harvey?"

"The Governor has got a cargo of salt pork from Otaheite lately, Ma'am, and he hopes . . ."

"Pork!" cried Conor petulantly. "Come, Sir, have you nothing more diverting than pork to tell me of?"

Mr. Harvey blushed and tried again.

"It seems the settlement at Coal Harbour is doing well, and a great abundance of coals is being procured . . ."

His glance at her face showed him that he had failed again. Despite his unhappy knowledge of his own inadequacy, he still treasured these half-hours in her company when her couch was set out on the stone verandah in the comparative cool of the evening, and she lay there fanning herself, and demanded to be entertained. He did his best, but her moods were strangely wayward. If he offered trivial gossip she grew impatient and protested that such nonsense was of no interest to her; if he spoke of more serious subjects she pouted, and vowed that he made no effort to amuse her. Yet all the time he was aware of unhappiness in her, painfully sensitive to the abruptly changing inflections of her voice, and the restlessness of her hands.

And she, for her part, knew that she was tormenting him. She would have a gentler moment, and then flare into irritation when she saw eager relief in his eyes. What right had his eyes to shame her? She would smite the relief from them with a sharp word or a brittle laugh, and then fall into self-loathing and despair because their sudden hurt accused her still more clearly. She said now, twisting a scrap of ribbon round her fingers:

"You have told me nothing of my friends. His Excellency is well?"

"He was recently indisposed, but he seemed well when I saw him, Ma'am, and begged me to convey his respects . . ."

"Oh, la, yes, his respects . . . ! And Mrs. Macarthur? Is she not very lonely without the Captain?"

"I am sure she must be, Ma'am, but she is so much occupied with the management of their affairs . . ."

"It would seem," interrupted Mrs. Mannion tartly, "that some ladies are capable of useful employment in their husbands' interest. Would it not, Mr. Harvey?"

"Er—yes, Ma'am." Mr. Harvey shot an anxious glance at her, and passed on a trifle too quickly to what he hoped was safer ground. "Her youngest child, little William, is a fine boy now, a year old or thereabouts, and he . . ."

"I have had a very full account, I assure you, of little William in the letter you brought me from his mother. What of the ships that have arrived recently? Are there no new people of interest in town?"

Mr. Harvey, who dared not even guess by now what might or might not be of interest to this capricious lady, ventured doubtfully:

"On the journey home from Parramatta, Ma'am, I fell in with a party travelling to the Hawkesbury, and rode some distance with them. There was a young man who came out on the *Minorca*, and is to be clerk to the storekeeper there—a very talkative fellow, Ma'am, who told me that his name was James Vaux, and for upwards of three miles gave me the most astonishing account of his life . . ."

Mr. Harvey's voice trailed off suddenly into an embarrassed silence. The account had been astonishing indeed, and his own lively interest in it had for a moment made him forget that it was one not altogether suitable for a lady's ears.

"Well, Sir?" Conor's voice was impatient. "What was so entertaining about this gentleman's life?"

But Mr. Harvey was dumb. Theft and petty fraud, profligacy, mistresses, intemperance, card-sharping, cock-fighting—indeed it had been but a sordid tale, and he blushed that he had found it so enthralling.

"I—I fear that I can recollect but little of it," he stammered at last. "He was at one time in respectable employment as clerk to an attorney, but confessed that his own folly had brought him to his present state . . ."

"Oh," remarked Conor coldly, "a convict."

"Yes, Ma'am. It was the theft of a handkerchief, Ma'am, which of course he denies, but . . ." He observed with dismay that Conor was delicately stifling a yawn; escaping from one unpromising subject, he rushed clumsily into another. "And there was a good deal of talk in town about another young man sent out on the *Minorca* . . ."

"Another convict?" Conor's voice was sharp. "I do not wish to hear of convicts, Mr. Harvey."

Silence fell. Mr. Harvey's conversational powers were exhausted, snubbed out of existence. He sat moodily on the edge of the verandah plucking at the leaves of a lavender bush growing beside him, touching his fingers absently to his nostrils to sniff its scent. And presently she said rather sulkily, as if speaking against her will:

"Well, Sir? What of this young man? What is his name?"

"Redfern, Ma'am."

"Did you speak with him, pray? And what is he?"

Something warned Mr. Harvey that he had embarked upon the wrong topic again; he threw down the leaves he had been crushing between his fingers, and answered nervously:

"I saw him, Ma'am, among the—the other prisoners, but I had no words with him. It seems that he is a medical man—at one time Assistant Surgeon on H.M.S. *Standard* . . ."

Again a silence, into which Conor's low voice crept warily:

"And now—a convict . . . ?"

"Yes, Ma'am."

"Did you learn—what his offence was, Mr. Harvey?"

"Mr. Grimes the Surveyor was my informant, Ma'am. He said that the young man protested against the quality of food provided for the men on the ship—declaring that their health could not be maintained on such a ration."

"Is that," her voice asked on a note of half-frightened incredulity, "a crime?" Mr. Harvey stammered:

"The circumstances, Ma'am—a matter of discipline as I understand— it was some four years ago, at the time of the mutiny at the Nore you recall, Ma'am, when there was much murmuring and discontent in the Navy, and Mr. Redfern—so it seems—expressed sympathy with the mutineers, for which he was condemned to death . . ."

"To death . . . ?" cried Conor, and Mr. Harvey hurried on:

". . . but clemency was extended to him on account of his youth, Ma'am, for he was then but nineteen years old . . ."

It seemed to Mr. Harvey that there was a kind of wildness in this new silence; he glanced at her imploringly as if begging her to break it, for he could not. And she did break it with words whose tone of weariness and defeat struck at his heart.

"Will you be so kind as to call Mrs. Blake, Sir? I—I should like to go indoors now . . ."

As he passed into the house on his errand he saw a tear fall on her tightly clasped hands.

    *   *   *   *   *

Early on the morning of Christmas Eve the labour pains came upon her; all that day and the next night she groaned and strove, snatched a few moments of exhausted sleep from which ever-fiercer pain woke her to groan and strive again, watching the sweat run down her wrists from hands that gripped the bed-post. It was a sight that interested her; long afterwards in the confused memories of that ordeal she remembered it, and clearly remembered also that two words had obsessed her. Work. Labour. They meant the same thing. This was labour, this was work . . .

On Christmas morning while a glaring sun reddened by smoke beat against the curtained windows of her room the midwife laid her daughter beside her.

" 'Tis a good omen, Ma'am—a Christmas baby, and as fine a little maid as ever I saw! Come now, Ma'am . . ."

But Conor was still stupid with exhaustion, and she only said thickly: "Girl? Silly. . . . Silly chattering . . ."

The midwife was accustomed to the foolishness which women talked at such times. She did not even raise her eyebrows.

1802

In the first month of the year 1802 Johnny Prentice celebrated, un-known to himself, his eighteenth birthday. Since the hot February night nearly a year ago when he had found Towns unconscious at the door of his hut, he had been feeling his way back from his native life to his white heritage. His almost forgotten language had returned to him quickly, and with it memories long overlaid by the incidents of a very different existence had taken shape again. For years they had been only dim pictures, unreal and unrelated—the cove, the wattle-and-daub huts, the ships anchored off the shore; but under the stimulus of Towns' stories he began to understand something of why they had existed, and what had been his own place there.

For years he had remembered fear and hatred only as dark things from which he had escaped; now, in the bitter words of his new com-panion, he found reasons for that fear, and objects for that hatred. He had no need to remember hunger, for that was something he had often experienced for short periods during his native life, but there had been some bad memory always linked with the feeling of hunger which was now made clear to him. For hunger, here, was an emptiness of the belly and a challenge to action—no more. You took your spears and your knowledge, and went out into a world full of food to measure your skill, your quick eyes, your patience and your strength against it. If you hunted well, there was feasting; if you failed, it was your own failure. But there hunger had been a kind of captivity. Food had been doled out —enough to keep life—but not zest—in your body, and you could not get more save by stealing the share of someone else. Your eyes watched avidly for it, and when it came it only whetted the edge of hunger . . .

He had not really forgotten that life, but he had remembered its emotions more clearly than its events. He thought of it as the natives thought of evil; something in him shrank from it, hated, recoiled and pre-pared to resist. The tales he heard of it from Towns had to pass this barrier set up by his native self before his white self would receive them. He listened silently, trying to link words to mental pictures grown so dim as to be almost shapeless, yet knowing that they described some way of life which had once been his. Often these tales went back to a legendary place called England where his memory could not follow, but to which, nevertheless, he knew himself bound.

Somewhere in that unknown life there must have been an event which sent him and his parents to this country, but he had never known what it was, and he wearied of Towns' persistent questioning. When he mentioned his surname for the first time a quick gleam of interest wakened in his companion's eyes, for there was no convict in the colony who had not heard and cherished the story of Andrew Prentice. Towns had tried to probe the relationship, and the circumstances of Johnny's own escape, but the boy was surly on that point, and obstinately silent; it was a dim, difficult and hurtful memory.

Often as he might leave Towns alone in the hut, and go off to occupy a day or two in the pursuits of native life, curiosity drew him back, eager to hear more of the life he had deserted. Indeed he had deserted more than a life—he had deserted an ambition, and only now did he realise how faint and far away, how absurdly unreal it had become. He had once resolved to climb from the abyss of felony to the heights where the gentry lived, and though he had hugged the resolve for years, it had become more and more a fantasy—a favourite daydream. Steadily and imperceptibly the native habit of living for the day had worn down his grim, unchildlike plan for the future. For the land imposed its own philosophy on those who lived close to it, counting a single lifetime as too brief to be measured, promising æons ahead to match those past, offering through its silence, its immensity and its solitudes, not time, but eternity.

In this bewitchment ambition had grown shadowy. He came back to it by slow degrees, painfully, and with reluctance. He had submitted himself to the simple logic of native law, and his mind had lost the knack of accepting chaos. He listened, and every sentence was a tale of sense-less confusion. Hunger . . . why? Chains and floggings . . . why? Wealth, oppression, misery, servitude . . . why? Yet the lure of *things* shone through this lunacy and beckoned him. He, whose birthright was a ship, had only a bark canoe; he, who was born to woven cloth, went naked; he, whose world was full of the marvels of a restless and exploring civilisation, had counted himself rich in the possession of a log hut, a few worn tools, a battered pail, two rusty muskets . . .

Towns rarely left the plot of cleared land about the hut, for he had never fully recovered from the illness and exhaustion in which Johnny had first discovered him. He was a little less thin since he had lived on fresh meat and milk, and the few vegetables which Johnny's erratic labours produced, but he seemed to have no strength or energy, no desire to do more than sit in the sunlight beside the stream, or crouch on winter days beside the fire. He coughed and spat, and sometimes his sputum was tinged with red.

Johnny provided for him as a matter of course. The tribe naturally provided for its young, its old, and its infirm. They were a tribe of three —one young, and one infirm, so Johnny was the hunter, the leader and the protector. Soon, Billalong would be old enough to assume tribal duties, for he was twelve now, but Johnny had adopted the native attitude of indulgence toward the young, and if Billalong brought back a fish or a bird, or tracked a bee to its nest, it was but a game.

Yet Towns, as Johnny soon discovered, could earn his shelter and his food. He held the key not only to the lost world of white-man events and actions, but also to the undiscovered world of learning. Johnny had never even begun to explore that world, but during his brief childhood association with Patrick Mannion he had begun to know that it was there, and now his mind leaned towards it as the trees in his creek-bed leaned towards the sunlight. Towns' own scholarship was meagre, and had been hardly won; his spelling was crude, but his work-distorted fingers possessed the gift of form, and the letters he made, and taught Johnny to make, had the disciplined beauty of long, flowing curves. For hours at a time the boy and the convict squatted on the flat rock opposite the hut, covering it with charcoal copperplate, and washing it clean like a slate with water from the creek.

Most of all, Johnny liked to write his name; he was native enough to feel the mystical sacredness of identity, and these two words were set apart from all others because they were himself. He wrote them over and over again in every idle moment—with charcoal on rocks or bits of wood, with a sharp pebble on the dusty ground, with a wet finger on a dry stone, with a stick in the damp sand. "*Johnny Prentice,*" "*Johnny Prentice,*" "*Johnny Prentice.*" All over his towri he left his signature; and all over his towri the land quietly obliterated it with wind, and sun, and rain.

So the months had fled past him while he strove to rediscover himself. Primed now with knowledge which was not new, but only newly-sharpened, he began to make more frequent pilgrimages to the place where Cunnembeillee had found him many years ago, following an easy route he had learned across the tableland between the river which the black men called Wollondilly, and that which the white men called Nepean. He came upon it near those rich flats to which, long ago, his father had followed a handful of wild cattle, and where now their progeny roamed. Here he was always wary, for the white men liked this place, and he watched the ground sharply with native-trained eyes for signs of their passing. A few miles down the river, concealed in the scrub near a great pool, he kept a bark canoe, and in this he accomplished most of the remainder of his journey. A mile or two above the spot where Mr. Mannion's domain began, he landed on the west bank, concealed his light craft again, and so came at last to an unremarkable overhanging rock where once the pattern of his life had changed. No white man would have known in passing that it was a place often frequented; no native could have failed to know it. To Johnny it had always seemed a place undeniably his own; he came to it with confidence and finality, as a man enters his house. He did not know whether his own thought or the natives' had made it thus, but it seemed natural to him that he should have, as they had, a kind of sacred place whose identity was interwoven with his own.

Yet now his acceptance of this, like his acceptance of so many native ways, was disturbed. It was no longer simply Dyonn-ee's birthplace, but also the place of Johnny's death. Here he had passed from white man's life to black man's life. He stood in it uncertainly, his white self clamouring: "*Return! Return!*" But it was his native self which, with the symbolism of the primitive mind, insisted that it was only from here, where he had left his own life, that he could begin the journey back. So he would sit alone beneath the rock, not so much thinking as waiting. He had long ago forgotten that a day was divided into hours and minutes; that these hours and minutes should be filled with appointed tasks, that contemplation must be disciplined by the ticking of a clock. He knew nothing of time save that the sun rose and the sun set, and between its rising and its setting one must hunt and eat, and between its setting and its rising one must sleep. But he was aware that something was happening to him, and he came to his own place and squatted there, waiting for it to reveal itself.

Return? To what? All through the years of his exile he had often gone a little farther down the river from here till he could see across it, and across the open fields, a stone house, stately on its hilltop, a cluster of lesser buildings, green squares of cultivation, gangs of labouring convicts, an incessant stir of purposeful activity.

Years ago children had played sometimes down near the river bank; they had been the most familiar to him of all the dwellers in that other world, so near, and yet so incredibly remote. He had watched them grow as he grew, and noticed that as time passed they came more rarely than before. His knowledge that the tow-headed girl and the red-headed boy were his sister and brother seemed to have no personal significance, but he had always watched with a faint feeling of tension for rare glimpses of the woman he knew to be his mother, and theirs. The tension increased to a kind of frozen violence when he saw Mr. Mannion, for all his old angers seemed concentrated in that one figure—the one which had loomed largest in his life when, at the age of eight, he had found that life intolerable, and walked out of it. Mannion was the symbol of oppression, frustration and punishment, but even more and even worse than that. He was the symbol of something Johnny could not name—something that affected his mother—something so bad and ugly that the boy had never dared to dwell upon it . . .

Sometimes he had remained till it was quite dark, and he saw the night suddenly pierced by yellow light from the windows of the great house, and those of the small cottage where his mother lived. Yet he had felt no nostalgia; to look at these things had been no more than an obscure need for a spiritual link with his own tribal past—the same need which his native friends satisfied by telling and hearing tales of their ancestral heroes.

But now his impulse had become less simple. His past was somehow merging with a future. The angers and hatreds which his childhood had left him only as emotions were being shaped by conscious thought. He was gathering them together and looking at them, not only as legacies of the past, but as possible equipment for the future.

It was dark on that night of his eighteenth birthday, when he first crossed the river and set foot on the Beltrasna fields. He floated silently over the black, idly-flowing water in his canoe, and stepped out on to the muddy bank with two spears in his hand. He had said nothing to Towns of his intention, for there was nothing to say. He was only moving a little nearer. He was only drawn by the desire to see the inside of a room, and not merely a chink of light from its window. The big house had been long in darkness; the fields were black and silent, no one moving on them but Johnny—and Mannion's second overseer, Jake Merrett.

Between them lay the goal of both—Ellen's cottage—and from the curtained window of her room a narrow streak of lamplight marked the way for her son. As he approached he even played with the thought that he might make his presence known to her, but the tension and excitement that he felt were born only of his sense of danger. He knew that she had once had an importance in his life which was, somehow, like the importance of his overhanging rock. She was his place; where she was, was home. For the rest, she was merely the first authority in that monstrous hierarchy which had oppressed his childhood, yet he knew—with more bitterness than hope—that he had a claim on her. He reached the window, crouched, listened, raised himself warily, and peeped between the curtains.

It was as if the intervening years burst like a bubble on the water. He was eight again—a convict child, a sly, violent, rebellious urchin, tormented by his knowledge and his ignorance, full of hatred because hatred was invisible, the only kind of injury you could inflict upon your enemies without being caught. He felt the ugly, forgotten sex-knowledge of the convict huts rise about him like a flood of foul water, and the incomprehensible but iron-hard sex-taboos of his own society force themselves back on his mind like fetters. Memories of sly looks, lewd jokes, religious denunciations, insults imperfectly understood, but wildly resented, flashed through his brain—thin lightning-shafts that struck him down in the agony of that emotion he had never dared to face—shame. He fell back from the window and crouched in the darkness, trembling all over, while the old torments and confusions roused the old defiance, and hatred burned up in him like a bonfire, and his hands ceased shaking as they recognised the feel of his spears.

Every nerve of his body and every drop of his tumultuous blood denounced Mr. Stephen Mannion. Now, on the edge of manhood, he fiercely endorsed the uncomprehending hatred of his eight-year-old self for this cold, remote, magnificent master of his servant mother; he felt the gulf between his white self and his native self contract, their emotions run together and meet at a point where both were savage. The white Johnny, breathing murder, could now fuse gratefully with the native Johnny, exulting in the possession of weapons and techniques for vengeance.

The light in the window went out. He began to move softly round the house, all doubts and indecisions gone, nothing left but a clear purpose. He was going to kill Mr. Mannion. He might have to wait long, but he had learned how to do that, and to be as still as a rock in waiting. Yet as he crept to the corner he was halted by a stealthy sound of movement near the door, and froze against the wall, listening and peering. So soon . . . ?

Merrett had come softly up to the door on the other side of the house. He had understood for a long time—ever since Ellen had made it known that his visits were no longer welcome—that his rival was one whose rivalry it were wiser not to resent. He had thought that now the mistress' child was born, the situation might have re-adjusted itself, and

Ellen be once more prepared to answer his soft knocking signal on her door. But a man's voice from within, even though so low as to be unrecognisable, was sufficient warning to him that it would be the part of discretion to withdraw as silently as he had come.

He had turned away and taken three noiseless paces before the first spear struck him in the side. He uttered a strange cry, and staggered; the second spear was not thrown, but thrust, and he went down on his back with its shaft standing upright in his chest. Johnny was half-way to the river before the door opened, and Mannion, shocked, raging and alarmed, stared down at the body of his overseer, lying still in the path of lamplight.

*   *   *   *   *

The harvest had been the most plentiful in the colony's history, but the Governor would not permit himself to feel over-satisfied. He was developing a defensive attitude in response not only to the incalculability of the society he governed, but of the land itself, and his mood was that of a man who walks a dark road, keeping warily in the middle, and watching the shadows for assault.

He allowed himself to believe that his regime had already produced some gratifying results. True, the lower orders of the population went in rags, but a new supply of clothing from England would soon remedy that; in the meantime, as he remarked to William Chapman with one of his flashes of sharp humour, they were not only *sans culottes*, but *sans chemises*. Neither clothing, food, housing nor agriculture, however—important as they were—agitated his mind as did the omnipresent problem of rum.

He had not suppressed the liquor traffic, but he had hampered it; his vanity betrayed him into imagining it more hampered than it was. Farms, farm produce, and livestock still drifted into the hands of those who could offer liquor as payment, and it was still clandestinely brewed in secluded spots. Men still gathered round a bucket of spirits with their quart-pots, and drank themselves into insensibility, or into maniacal frenzies ending frequently in bloodshed. There were still smugglers who knew how to use a dark night, and the long, lonely miles of harbour foreshores.

All this His Excellency realised, and all this he tried to crowd into the back of his mind, filling its foreground with brighter pictures of his minor victories. He dwelt less upon the still strong and deeply entrenched power of the trading organisation which opposed him than on the more welcome reflection that Johnston and Macarthur had been, at least temporarily, ousted from the colony. He congratulated himself that he was pursuing the policy laid down by his superiors of settling as many small farmers as possible, and he was pleased with the progress he had made at a new settlement some eight miles from Parramatta, which he had called Castle Hill. Here he had set aside a large area for a Government farm, and had promised himself that he would have two hundred acres sown by the end of the year. He had sponsored important discoveries, too, in Bass Strait and at the Hunter River—yet in spite of all these achievements he remained nervy. The harvest might be good, but there was winter ahead; Macarthur might be gone, but his influence remained, and the Governor turned over in his mind the phrases of a letter he must write to the Under-Secretary, pointing out yet again the inadvisability of allowing that author of discords to return. It would be, of course, a private letter, but its contents, he trusted, would be discussed in the proper quarters. "*If Captain McArthur is allowed to return here, and some notice is not taken of the other officers' conduct, my recall or permission to return will be absolutely necessary, to prevent such steps being taken by me as will not much tend to the quiet of the colony. . . .*" Somehow they must be made to understand that, even in the light of Flinders' recent discoveries, the continent of New Holland was not big enough to contain both Captain Macarthur and Governor King. "*. . . for to serve under such a set as will then be in the colony is what neither my pride will stoop to, nor my situation allow of . . .*"

He could do no more, for the moment, in the matter of these adversaries, but to turn from their defiance was merely to turn to the always threatening rebelliousness of the convicts. They were quiet enough at present, but King's ears were so sharply cocked for sounds of rebellion that murmurs reverberated in his head like shouts. The Irish prisoners in particular—many of whom had arrived without so much as a paper to show with what offence they were charged, or for what term they had been convicted—were a source of continual uneasiness to him; there were more than enough of them already in the colony, he thought, without the substantial reinforcements which he had been bidden to expect this year.

Reports which reached his ears at the beginning of April galvanised him, therefore, into action so prompt that it suggested an underlying panic. The proclamation which he issued for the intimidation of deluded people transported for crimes which he felt safe in describing as diabolical even without documentary evidence, not only reminded them of existing British law, but, with a fine abandon, adjusted it to colonial needs. Where the motherland permitted no more than fifty persons to assemble without official sanction, Governor King permitted no more than twelve. Where twelve might in England be required by a magistrate to disperse within an hour, two might be separated on pain of death in the colony—and not necessarily by a magistrate, but by any free man. Transportation being the penalty for the taking or administering of unlawful oaths, such a crime here—committed by miscreants already transported—was to be punished by one thousand lashes, and a term served out to its bitter end in the gaol gang. That, he thought, should surely terrify them into docility; but by way of example he ordered two suspects to receive five hundred lashes each, and, that the example might be widely noted, directed that Sydney, Parramatta, and Toongabbee should each be privileged to witness a third of the punishment.

Yet he was still apprehensive. Racking his brain for further safeguards, he commanded a general search of all dwellings for unauthorised weapons, and Captain Piper, paying a visit to the Mannions at Beltrasna, waxed satirical.

"He is always exercised in his mind over something! I suspect that it enlarges his consequence in his own eyes to be continually discovering plots which he can put down. He's like an ill-trained watch-dog, whose yelpings and yappings do more to disturb the barnyard than to protect it." He shrugged elaborately. "Picture it, Mrs. Mannion, I beg! The descent of the searchers upon innocent householders before they have even rubbed the sleep from their eyes—the confusion, the poking and prying! His Excellency was in ill-odour with the housewives that morning, I'll wager! And for what? A few muskets, Sir, and a pike!"

Mannion replied:

"You're a soldier, Captain, and naturally inclined to make light of rebellious rabbles, unarmed and untrained. Yet at the risk of being dubbed an alarmist, and joining the Governor in your disfavour, I must point out that a few muskets and a pike may be the prelude to many muskets and many pikes. We have had sharp and terrible warnings, Sir, of what rabbles may accomplish. America. France. And my own unhappy country. And of these last incendiaries—whom I don't willingly call my countrymen, I assure you—we have many here. I have one in particular among my own labourers, a man by the name of Finn, who belongs to that pestilential tribe of trouble-makers who rouse their fellows to unrest. He is a talker." Mr. Mannion smiled and spread his hands in a disarming gesture. "That's a failing to which we are said to be prone, we Irish. And indeed I know enough of the persuasiveness of the Irish tongue to regard it with suspicion in a man convicted of plotting against the peace of the realm. I don't doubt the Governor shares my misgivings concerning villains of this kind. No, Sir, I cannot agree with you that his precautions are unwise."

"You may be right, Sir," Captain Piper conceded amiably, "and I venture to guess that His Excellency sees Irishmen in his dreams, for he's continually vexed and harassed by their claims that they are being wrongfully detained—which he has, in many cases, no means of disproving . . ."

"I know it very well," Mannion interrupted emphatically. "I have had two in my own employ who came out in the *Anne* without documents of any kind, and it has afforded them a fine excuse for discontent. The Governor has told me that he has applied to have records sent, and I have written personally to Lord Pelham on the matter; but in the meantime, my friend, the absence of a bit of paper does not dispose me to see these rogues as other than rogues. They were not sent here for nothing. They complain that they have had no fair trial, that they received summary sentences from magistrates at proceedings of which no record was kept—but who, I reply, threw the country into such an uproar and anarchy that the customary processes of the law were disturbed? Those who seek anarchy will seek it anywhere, believe me, and upon the smallest pretext. I was even assured when I was in Parramatta that when some of the Irish heard of the arrival in port lately of the French ship, they threw down their tools and began to assemble, seized with an infatuated notion that their brother revolutionaries of France were come to free them . . ."

Conor looked up quickly.

"A French ship in port? I had not heard of it. What ship is it, pray?"

Piper gave her one of his wide, good-natured smiles.

"What version will you have, Ma'am? To the Irish it seemed a ship of deliverance; some say it is sent to spy out the land for the French Government so that they may dispossess us, or at least form a rival establishment somewhere along the coast. I believe His Excellency is not without some apprehensions on that score. But the less romantic truth would appear to be that it is merely *Le Naturaliste*, one of two vessels despatched on a voyage of scientific discovery."

"Is it still here, Captain?"

"It sailed a week or so ago, Ma'am, but I understand from Captain Hamelin—whom I found a most agreeable fellow—that they propose to cruise off the coast until the arrival of the second ship, *Le Géographe*, which is daily expected."

Mr. Mannion asked idly:

"Flinders fell in with them, did he not, during his latest voyage?"

"With *Le Géographe*, Sir, in Encounter Bay. *Le Naturaliste* was already here when Captain Flinders put into port early this month. And by the way, I hear that Flinders now proposes a voyage northward, since the winter is about to set in. It has been in my mind, Ma'am," he continued with a smile at Conor which did not quite contradict the ruefulness of his tone, "that a sailor's life is happier than a soldier's. Here I sit, still in disgrace over that accursed duel, waiting to hear my fate from home, when I might—had I chosen my career with greater foresight—be bound with Flinders for who knows what adventures in tropical climes . . . !"

She answered rather dryly:

"I cannot believe a sailor more free of troubles than a soldier, Captain, or that misfortune is a stranger to tropical climes."

He looked at her in surprise. It was not the first time he had been disconcerted by this note of seriousness from one whose youth, beauty and position should surely have combined to make her gay and carefree. One could not be sure, he thought, faintly aggrieved, that she would respond lightly to the kind of nonsense one naturally talked to ladies . . .

Mr. Mannion was saying:

"Captain Bligh of the *Bounty* would agree with you, my love. From what we hear, it was precisely the allurements of tropical climes which brought disaster upon him. And there again, Captain, in that affair of the *Bounty*, we may find this dangerous spirit of unrest, this insidious discontent, breaking forth in open mutiny . . ."

"Mercy on us!" Conor made a sudden, sharply irritated movement. "Must we talk always of rebellion? I declare it seems you gentlemen can speak of nothing else! Mr. Mannion goes on about it, Captain, till I am near distracted, and even the Governor gives it all his attention—though you would imagine, would you not, that after the shocking murder of our overseer, he would be more concerned about the natives . . . ?"

Piper, slightly astonished by this outburst, noticed with interest that his host's expression had become austere. No doubt he was displeased that his wife should criticise him; was he also nettled by her reference to the murdered overseer? The Captain answered pacifically:

"Measures are being taken against the natives also, Ma'am."

Mannion said sharply:

"The two subjects are not unrelated. It's well known that absconding convicts have joined the Indians and incited them to acts of violence. I'm not without suspicions that the native who murdered Merrett may have been taught by some escaped rogue of our own colour, with a grudge against overseers."

Captain Piper's lively dark eyes shot a quick glance of curiosity from wife to husband. Like all those whose interests are mainly personal, he dearly loved gossip, and preferred it with a spice of scandal. The colony had learned with even more interest than murders usually aroused, that Merrett had been speared by a native on the doorstep of Mannion's house-keeper, where Mannion himself had discovered the lifeless body. It was well known that in previous years this housekeeper had been more than a housekeeper, so gentlemen had exchanged glances and ladies had whispered to each other: "How *came* he there, my love, at after midnight . . . ?"

Piper was conscious of constraint. Young Mrs. Mannion's mood was uncertain, to say the least. He observed carefully:

"A most shocking occurrence! You found the poor fellow yourself, Sir, so I'm told?"

Mr. Mannion gave him a cool stare.

"I did. My housekeeper, hearing a noise outside, opened her door and observed the body lying there with a spear thrust in it. I was walking over the fields, as I frequently do at night to assure myself that all is well, when I heard her scream, and hastened to the spot. I sum-moned assistance—but it was too late. The man must have died instantly. The spears were native, of course, and the prints of bare feet were found."

The Captain made suitable shocked noises. He had not imagined that he would learn anything from Mr Mannion's account, but his glance at Mrs. Mannion's face was more rewarding. She was looking straight before her, sombrely, her fingers tapping briskly on the arms of her chair. He thought admiringly: "A spirited little baggage, on my word!" And then, ruefully indignant: "Damme if *I* would have been prowling in the dark after that sloe-eyed slut . . . !" She looked at him, and he said too hastily:

"I fear this must be a distasteful subject for you, dear Mrs. Mannion . . ." She kept on looking at him, and he began to stammer, deserted for once by his poise. "I—I mean, of course—naturally such violence and brutality are hardly fit for a lady's ears . . ."

She said coldly:

"A lady's ears cannot be over-delicate in this colony, Sir. I have heard much of brutality—and upon the first occasion when I witnessed it, an overseer was its perpetrator."

He guessed that this remark, though addressed to him, was aimed at her husband; he left her husband to deal with it. Mr. Mannion proceeded to a demonstration of how husbands might retire from dangerous ground by introducing not only a new topic, but one in which few ladies could participate—and certainly not this lady who sat so still in the warmth of the fading autumn sunlight, her hands idle on her lap, and her face wearing a curious expression half-angry and half-bewildered. Captain Piper's kind heart was disturbed, and he listened absently to his host's words. Mr. Mannion spoke of crops; he spoke of prices; he compared the fertility of the soil in different parts of the colony; he shut her away from them with a wall of words.

She was painfully conscious of being excluded, but not only from their conversation. She had known at once that her husband's presence at the scene of the murder was not accidental, and at first she had been too amazed to discover how little the knowledge pained her to give it any other thought. Then she grew angry. The revelation that there was, after all, no love in her marriage, did not seem to matter, but she was conscious of suffering nevertheless. She was shut out of something, and she was seeking it all the time. She was seeking it now, not only in thought, but through her senses, measuring the loveliness of the mellow afternoon against her own hurt, feeling that beauty observed should be matched by some beauty of inner experience, knowing herself close to her solution, but still baffled.

* * * * *

Early in June Pemulwy met his death. The two settlers who shot him saw the incident as a stroke of luck, for now, as the reward promised by the Governor, each would have the free labour of a convict on his farm for a whole year. Pemulwy's head—even uglier in death than it had been in life, with its heavy features and its sinister wall-eye—was conveyed to His Excellency who, recalling the desire of Sir Joseph Banks for such a specimen, immersed it in spirits and sent it to his friend and patron. He spared a line or two in his next letter for a laconic obituary: "*Although a terrible pest to the colony, he was a brave and independent character.*"

But in the tribes around Parramatta it was as though something had stopped. Had there been a halt in the seasons or had the waves on the harbour frozen suddenly into stillness, it might have seemed like this. Suddenly they felt themselves at the end of something. Life looked the same, but it had lost movement. Pemulwy had been the heart of their resolve, their impetus to steady and relentless action. He had fed their anger when it flagged, and without him there were times when they forgot it. It was a disaster, and yet, when the first shock had passed, it was a kind of deliverance too, for he had been urging them against the deep-flowing current of their philosophy, against the belief in life's changeless rhythms which the unchanging centuries had bred in them, against their volatility and their light-heartedness, against the childlike inquisitiveness which lured them towards the white men's settlements.

Now they relaxed with something of the relief of children leaving a too-stern authoriy to return to their playmates and their childhood world. They would, of course, hate the Bereewolgal still; steal their grain and animals when food was scarce; kill them when the opportunity presented itself. But in the meantime the white Governor had assured them that with Pemulwy dead, they would once again be made free of the white men's towris. There would be peace and time for gaiety, and life would not be made solemn and sinister all the time by that grim voice saying implacably: "Wee-ree! Wee-ree!"

And they could now perform the new corroboree, which Pemulwy had sourly disliked, about the unknown land beyond the mountains. It was not the first of these, by any means. Many had been made before—notably that great epic created by Wunbula long ago, which told of the spirit who made his home there, and sent the fierce, cold winds raging down over the plains. But now, with the Bereewolgal before their eyes —more strange than any spirit, and more disturbing than any wind—the imagination of one youara-gurrugin had peopled that mysterious country with beings of a similar kind, who dwelt not beside a harbour, but beside a great lake, and built their stone habitations, and tended their animals, and grew their alien plants and trees, and spoke the same tongue as did the invaders whom they knew.

It made a fine corroboree, with great scope for improvisation, for mimicry, for drama, and the few runaway convicts who had joined the tribes and heard of it were deeply impressed. A settlement of white people, they enquired, on the other side of the mountains . . . ? There could be little intercourse in words between the natives and these outcasts. The few phrases they mastered in each other's tongues were quite inadequate to express the difference between fantasy and fact, or to convey how very shadowy and trivial, to the native mind, such difference could seem. Rumour spread out like a mist from the tribes to the convict huts, and throve on the ignorance it found there. For how should convicts know the size or the nature of a land which even Captain Flinders was but learning? How could they guess the policies or the activities of the far-off Government which had snatched them up like so much cargo from their native soil to dump them here, and which might—why not?—have dumped others elsewhere with no greater ceremony?

The word "escape" was never absent from their minds, but in this land another dogged it like a shadow. "Where?" There had been so many escapes, and so many failures. So many had been dragged back, already half-dead of privation, to punishment. And those who had never returned? Who could tell? The recaptured absconders, with the quaver of an old anguish in their tones, and the strain of an old horror branded on their gaunt faces, told of a country in which merely to keep alive was an effort almost beyond human strength. To be risked, perhaps, if one could look through it to an end—but here there was no end. Their minds baulked at endlessness. They had come from a country in which to go from one place was to go to another; but here you could go, and go, and go, driving your failing body, every step a struggle, day after day till time blurred, and still you arrived nowhere. You could not even make yourself a goal that did not cheat you with its unendurable same-

ness. That hill—that creek—that distant valley. . . . There I may find
something . . .

But it was always a hill like any other—dry, stony, smelling sharply
of its aromatic plants under the sunlight, sprinkled with sparse shade,
rustling underfoot, barren, silent, lonely, indifferent. In the creek there
might be water, or only a faint smell of damp that maddened your
intolerable thirst, but it led to nothing different. And in the valley when
you stumbled down into it, sliding drunkenly in your fatigue, slipping
on the dry, fallen leaves, you met only the silence again—a little deeper;
and the shade—a little darker; and the same waiting, secret, annihilating
solitude. Nothing beyond? Climb one more hill? Give up here, when
from that next crest I might see . . . ?

But from that crest nothing that you have not seen a thousand times
before, in every waking moment and in nightmares, and in fits of
delirium. Hills—nothing but hills, merging into each other, marking
nothing, leading nowhere, repeating and repeating themselves in lunatic
confusion till they died out on the horizon, and the sky itself took up the
torment with shadowy clouds, like hills again, fading to infinity.

Not even an interplay of colours to relieve your jaded, desperate eyes
—no copse of brighter green, no splash of autumn gold, no open patch
of grass, or sudden drift of flowers. One colour; one quiet, slaty, impassive grey-green that changed only as sunlight burnished it on a hilltop,
or shadow dimmed it in a valley, so that the flowers it harboured seemed
enfolded in it and subdued, revealing themselves only when your foot was
almost upon them, or your hand brushed their leaves. And with the
coming of night there fell a silence so deep that it was like a weight on
the chest, and a loneliness that turned the mind back in vanquished terror
to the bitter companionship of the convict huts, and a feeling of age and
immensity so awful that to move in it with the paltry steps of a man
seemed sacrilege.

"Escape?" they said bitterly to their more hopeful fellow-prisoners.
"Where?"

*　　　　*　　　　*　　　　*　　　　*

The days grew shorter, the mornings and the evenings crisply cold.
Frost lay sometimes on the fields before the sun climbed high, and bitter
winds came down across the mountains. That was all, in this land,
which Nature told of autumn sliding into winter, but Conor felt it, too,
in an increased loneliness, for visitors came now less often to Beltrasna.

When they did come, much of the news they brought was not of a
kind to cheer her growing depression. True, there were some alluring
accounts of the parties and other little social pleasures arranged for the
entertainment of the French officers, now recuperating in the colony after
a hard voyage; and once Colonel Paterson brought Monsieur Péron to
view the Nepean, and to admire the beautiful house—and the beautiful
wife—of Mr. Stephen Mannion. Mr. Robert Campbell, whom Conor
had met in Sydney, had been married last year to Miss Sophia Palmer,
sister of the Commissary—a young lady only a few years older than
Conor—and now came tidings of the birth of a son. Messages came

also from Mrs. Paterson, praying that Conor would visit them; and from kind Mrs. King, promising a dinner-party next time Mrs. Mannion should be in town; and several novels from Mrs. Macarthur; and a most charming robe for the baby from Mrs. Marsden. And Stephen promised that a little later they should accept the delightful invitation of Mrs. Paterson, but he would prefer to wait until the carriage he had ordered arrived from Ireland, "for your health is still delicate, my love, and the weather is severe."

But there was more often news of another kind—the old, familiar tales of feuds and rivalries and quarrels. And in late July came terrible accounts of the transports *Hercules* and *Atlas* which had arrived a few weeks earlier, and of the miserable human freight they had carried. In August Surgeon Jamison, who had been a passenger on the *Atlas* during the earlier part of its voyage, had occasion to visit Beltrasna in his professional capacity when Cousin Bertha took a chill, and was confined to her bed; seated at the candle-lit dining-table, he told tales which kept Conor wakeful throughout that night, and haunted her dreams for weeks

"No excuse can be offered," he declared vehemently, "for the appalling conditions which existed on that ship—and on the *Hercules* also . . ."

"But I'm told, Sir," ventured Mr. Harvey quickly, "that the *Perseus* and the *Coromandel* enjoyed a good voyage . . ."

"That is true, Mr. Harvey. They arrived with every soul healthy and fit for immediate labour—which but makes the iniquities practised on board the *Atlas* and the *Hercules* the more marked. His Excellency informs me that he has written in terms of the strongest reprobation to the Captain of the *Atlas*. For my part," declared the surgeon fiercely, "I should conceive the noose as his fitting end!"

Mr. Mannion took up his carving-knife.

"Permit me to replenish your plate, Sir. This duck was shot on the river below the house."

Conor asked:

"Are there not orders given, Mr. Jamison, to regulate the treatment of prisoners during the voyage? Surely the authorities . . ."

Mr. Jamison snorted angrily.

"Regulations, Madam? Indeed there are regulations, but little attention was paid to them by that inhuman monster, I can assure you."

"But," protested Conor, frowning at the tablecloth, "I cannot understand why he should behave in a manner which he must have known would endanger his advancement, and bring censure . . ."

Mr. Jamison uttered a short, grim laugh. Mark, glancing apprehensively from him to Conor, felt a wave of indignation and hostility. Did not this obtuse and heedless person realise that he was causing distress to the kindest and gentlest of ladies?

"Captain Brooks, my dear Madam," the surgeon continued remorselessly, "was at all times alive to what he considered might best serve his advancement. The voyage was, to him, solely an opportunity for engaging in private trade. Every available inch of space on board was given over to the merchandise which he carried for this purpose. The vessel was so deeply laden that it became necessary to keep the air scuttles closed. The hospital was stored with ropes and sails so that the sick were compelled to lie with those that were still healthy. The whole ship, Madam, was suffered to continue in a state of cumulating filthiness which, to spare your sensibilities, I shall not attempt to describe. The hammocks and the bedding were never brought on deck, and from the humidity caused by the confined state of the convicts, the air became so noxious that . . ."

"Some more wine, Sir?" interjected Mr. Mannion.

Mr. Jamison's glass was refilled. He drank. Mr. Harvey began hastily:

"Pray, Sir, do you find the colony . . ."

But he was too late. Mr. Jamison, having set his glass down and wiped his lips, was already addressing himself to his host:

"I intend to lodge a complaint, Sir, to the highest authorities on this matter."

"Very right and proper, Mr. Jamison. Have you visited . . . ?"

"There is no doubt in my mind that the prolonged and circuitous route taken by the *Atlas* was pursued with no other object than to afford opportunities for trade. Some merchandise was disposed of—I make no doubt very profitably—at Rio, but hearing on his arrival there that he could expect no very favourable market in New South Wales, Captain Brooks proceeded to the Cape of Good Hope. And all the time, Sir, withholding from the convicts a considerable portion of their ration, keeping them confined in their noisome quarters, loading their legs with irons . . ."

"Indeed, Sir . . ." said Mark desperately.

"Yes, Mr. Jamison . . . ?" said Conor, staring hard at the surgeon.

"Nor was it uncommon, Madam, to see them wearing irons round the neck, with a padlock which weighed at least a pound and a half, nor will you be surprised when I tell you that these afflictions produced a debility which terminated in scurvy and dysentery, of which many died . . ."

Mr. Mannion intervened firmly:

"Such things are indeed shocking to the minds of all humane persons, Mr. Jamison, but I think we may spare my wife a further recital."

Conor, rather pale, her food uneaten on her plate, said slowly:

"If there are unfortunate wretches, Stephen, who can endure suffering such horrors, surely I . . . can endure to hear them described? Pray continue, Mr. Jamison."

But Mr. Jamison, in some confusion, excused himself. He spoke instead of a very different kind of passenger who had shared this voyage. "A countryman of yours, Mr. Mannion, Sir Henry Brown Hayes."

Mr. Mannion, remembering a long-ago conversation in the library of Sir John O'Connor, brought the palm of his hand down on the table with a slap, and laughed.

"So your grandfather's prediction was a true one, my dear! Sir

Henry has cheated the gallows, and atones for his ill-advised gallantry in a penal colony!"

"I am informed, Sir," remarked Mr. Jamison dourly, "that it was less gallantry than cupidity which inspired his abduction of Miss Pike. She was a considerable heiress, I believe."

Mr. Mannion nodded.

"Very likely, my dear Sir. And pray tell me—how did the fellow impress you?"

The surgeon, with his glass halfway to his lips, put it down and glowered at it.

"No cordiality was wasted between us, Mr. Mannion. Sir Henry was the friend and boon companion of the Captain, whose goodwill he had purchased for the sum of some three or four hundred guineas, and I assure you that he—though a convicted felon—suffered none of the inconveniences I have described. He messed with the Captain, Sir, came and went at his will, and was permitted to occupy a good part of the space allotted to passengers with his baggage. His arrogance and offensiveness defy all description, and I am pleased to say they have already put him in some disfavour here."

Conor asked slowly:

"And the merchandise which this Captain Brooks brought, Mr. Jamison? He will not, surely, be permitted to sell it, since it was the cause of so much misery and suffering?"

Mr. Jamison looked at her for a moment. He lifted his glass, drank, set it down, and replied non-committally:

"I understand that His Excellency does not intend to permit the spirits to be landed, Madam."

"But surely, Sir . . . !"

"My love," interposed Mr. Mannion urbanely, "you will no doubt be glad to return to the drawing-room; even with the fire we are a trifle chilly here. We shall join you shortly."

Conor rose, gathering her shawl about her shoulders. Indeed, she had shivered.

*   *   *   *   *

She was learning that an active mind will find food for its thoughts somewhere. She might have been beguiled from problems too knotty for her if she had been swept into the kind of life commonly provided for young women of her birth and breeding, for she was young, beautiful, and had once been gay. She suffered from the persistence of thoughts which were so predominantly dark and harassing, but she could not banish them. They were bitter fare, but they were all she had, and she found herself brooding over them, examining them, turning them this way and that, wringing the last fragment of enlightenment they had to offer, as a starving man might gnaw endlessly at a bone.

Such enlightenment as she won was less the steady light of intellectual comprehension than the intermittent bonfire-flare of emotion. Her knowledge was too scant, and what there was of it too faulty, for a successful plunge beneath that ugly and confusing surface of life where incidents occurred. Incidents were terrible, and they filled her horizon; she could ask in distress and indignation: "Why?", but she could find no answer save the brutality, the duplicity, the greed and the malice of individual men.

She found some consolation—but not much—in her infant daughter, Julia. It was not to be denied that babies were entrancing, yet it became clear very rapidly that whole weeks and months could not be employed in admiring them. And that was all she was permitted to do, for the worthy Mrs. Blake had recommended a wet-nurse of excellent character, the widow of a settler, and had not taken her departure until this young woman was installed. The buxom and efficient Bessie attended to the infant's material needs; its mother's task was no more than to display it, suitably frilled and beribboned, to admiring guests, and to coo over its cradle now and then. Conor became very bored—and, as time went on, apprehensive. For Stephen was speaking more and more of their return to Ireland.

"For me," he explained, "it will be but a visit this time, so there appears no reason why we should upset the admirable arrangements at home. My mother is quite able to order our affairs there, and Mahon is an excellent steward. You will be free of all anxieties, my love, and my mother and sisters will afford you companionship . . ."

But Conor interrupted him crossly:

"I have told you many times that I do not wish to remain in Ireland if you return here."

She felt, indeed, a kind of terror at the thought. She knew something of his Irish home, ruled with a formal and elegant ruthlessness by his aristocratic mother, and his three elderly sisters, all virgin, and all grim. If the choice lay between that and this, she would choose this, for here she had at least some semblance of authority and independence . . .

But her husband argued blandly:

"Yet you do not seem entirely content here either, my love."

She kept her eyes on her needlework, finding no answer to this save the accusation she did not quite dare to make. For undoubtedly he could not only send her back to Ireland if he wished, but keep her there; and she knew by now that he would so wish if she disturbed the pretence of tranquillity and decorum which her silence ensured.

"You would not, I am sure," he pursued, "wish Julia to spend her childhood in this place?"

She muttered rebelliously:

"Why not, pray? Patrick and Miles have done so, and . . ."

"Patrick and Miles are boys."

She stabbed her needle fiercely into her embroidery. She did not attempt to question the law which decreed different fates for boys and girls, but she thought, with despairing, childish petulance: "Why wasn't she a boy?"

"And even for boys," Mannion went on, "it was, as I now realise, a mistake. The Macarthurs have been wiser in sending all their children home at an early age. I am determined that Julia shall not be the victim of a similar error of judgment—and it is time that Miles went also. He is growing noisy and undisciplined, and his association with Ellen's children and Dilboong has already lasted too long."

She held her peace, and made stormy, secret resolves. "If we must go, we must; and if Julia and Miles must remain there, they must; but I shall not!" For the moment, she waited, punishing her husband in the only way she could punish him—by wilfulness, capriciousness, and a cold unresponsiveness to his reviving husbandly ardours. And Mannion, though his mature sang-froid concealed it, was punished. He had been badly shaken by Merrett's murder, which he could not fail to suspect had been meant for his own murder; he was ready enough now for a reconciliation with his young wife.

But he could not pass the barriers she set up against him, and his pride would not permit him to break them down. She resisted him stubbornly, and confronted her unhappiness alone. She reproached herself sometimes for contemplating without very much grief a possible separation from her daughter, but she felt that they were already separated. Mr. Mannion claimed omniscience in the matter of infant welfare as in all other matters, and when she ventured an opinion, gently pointed to the inexperience she could not deny. Her daughter, Conor felt, was a stranger, shut away from her in the speechless world of babyhood, and her own life still seemed more important to her than Julia's. The more important, perhaps, now that she had nothing else, now that there was no longer love in it, now that she was goaded by that emptiness and lovelessness to look outward at the world and try to understand it. Here, in this harsh, strange colony she felt herself sometimes almost at grips with it; and here she would remain as long as she could.

One evening towards the end of August she came to grips with it again. Her husband was reading on the verandah in the last of the sunlight, but the winter afternoon had been chilly, and she had drawn her chair close to the bright log fire in the parlour, and taken up one of the novels which Mrs. Macarthur had sent her. It was *The Romance of the Forest* by the celebrated Mrs. Radcliffe, and Conor, curled in the capacious armchair, became absorbed in the remarkable adventures of its heroine. She felt that there was some similarity between herself and the lovely Adeline. True, she had not been borne away to a strange and sinister Gothic castle, but she was in a strange land, and often it seemed sinister. She saw no moving lights, heard no mysterious sighs; her mirror reflected nothing but her own face, familiar in all but the forlorn expression which it had worn lately. Yet, like Adeline, she felt her senses excited and her reason bewildered; she too was conscious of an imagination grown restless and turbulent, and felt forces about her which were no less disturbing because she did not conceive them as supernatural.

With the fingers of one hand buried in her ringlets, she read eagerly of her heroine's strange discovery of a prisoner's manuscript—so lost in the tale that it was with a feeling of being dragged rudely into another world that she heard her husband utter a loud exclamation, steps approach along the gravelled path outside, and Stephen's voice say sharply to the new overseer who had replaced Merrett:

"What is amiss, Byrne? Good God, man, you look as though you had been set upon by . . ."

Byrne's voice sounded strange and thick.

"An' that's the truth, Your Honour," he cried excitedly. "I *have* been set upon, Sir, by that scoundrel Finn—like a wild beast, he was, Sir . . ."

Conor's head lifted sharply from her hand. She heard her husband's chair scrape on the flagstones as he rose, and knew that he had moved away to the edge of the verandah. She could hear only scraps of the conversation now, but she listened intently, her face strained and still, her eyes dark with some not clearly comprehended fear. ". . . readin', he was, Your Honour, out of a book. . . ." ". . . so I says 'Get back to your work!' and knocks it out of his hand. . . ." Conor's eyes moved down slowly to stare at the book on her own knee; she heard stray groups of words leap out from the blur of Byrne's voice: ". . . at me like a tiger, he was, Sir, and I all unprepared. . . ." ". . . standin' over me, and black murder in his face. . . ." ". . . would have had me life, Your Honour, not a doubt of it, if Toole . . ."

Stephen's clear voice asked sharply:

"He is confined, of course? Shackled?" And then, in reply to another murmur from Byrne: "Very well. It is time an example were made. Send Toole to me."

She heard the overseer's footsteps receding along the path, and Stephen's, returning to his chair, halt suddenly. He called:

"Byrne!"

"Yes, Sir?"

"Where is it?"

"What, Sir?"

"The book, you dolt! The book this fellow had. You secured it, I suppose?"

"Yes, Sir—oh, yes, Your Honour, I have it here . . ."

"Give it to me."

"Yes, Sir."

There was a brief pause.

Then Stephen's shadow, long and black in the dying sunlight, entered the room before him. Conor looked at him as he followed it, and her fear took shape as she saw his face. He stood sideways just inside the french windows, holding a small, tattered volume towards the light; his expression made him seem a stranger to her, and she stared aghast at fury being transmuted before her eyes into a cold, implacable cruelty. She said his name faintly, as if trying to summon back from some evil bewitchment the Stephen whom she had once imagined that she loved, and he looked up from the book with a start. He saw her, but only as he saw the furniture of the room; anger was blinding him, shaking his hands, freezing his face to a stiff, ugly mask, and her voice had hardly disturbed the concentrated hatred and vengefulness of his thoughts. He stared down again at the book in his hands, and suddenly, with a violence that startled her to her feet, flung it past her into the fire. She felt the wind of it across her face, heard the thud of it against the logs, and saw a cloud of sparks rush up the chimney from the disturbed and glowing charcoal. One word exploded in the still room: "*Poison!*" She stood gripping the back of her chair, trembling, her mouth slightly open, and for several moments after he had gone she remained thus, holding in her mind the echoes of that word, and his rapid footsteps, and the slam of the door.

It was the gentle, fluttering sound of burning paper that drew her blank, shocked eyes at last to the fireplace. The little book was all but consumed, yet it kept, precariously, the shape of a book still, its fine, blackened leaves standing up and curling outward, print still shining on them, the ghosts of dead words. A few loose sheets had come apart from it in the impact of its fall, and they lay scattered here and there, some burning, some lying clear of the flames, but moving and darkening with heat, as if in pain.

Conor looked at them. Poison . . . ? She looked at the door. She gathered her skirts around her and knelt before the hearth, and drew the few unburned scraps towards her with the poker. She picked them up, handling them gingerly, feeling some of them crumble between her fingers for all her care. Holding one towards the flames she read in the firelight between its charred edges: " '*The science,*' says he, '*of the politician consists in finding the true point of happiness and freedom. Those men would deserve the gratitude of ages who should discover a mode of government that contained the greatest sum of happi . . .*"

Wondering, she laid it down, and took up another fragment. She read: "*. . . if you say you can still pass the violation over, then I ask, hath your house been burnt? Hath your property been destroyed before your face? Are your wife and children destitute of a bed to lie on, or bread to . . .*" Beneath a brown scorch which obliterated a line or two, the strange words went on: "*. . . then are you not a judge of those that have. But . . .*"

She read that again, her brows knitted painfully. Had not Stephen, too, deplored the burning of houses? Had he not explained to her that it was the riotous behaviour of people like Matthew Finn which caused such things to happen? She shook her head, drawing her breath in with a sharp sigh, and took up another scrap of paper. "*. . . more worth is one honest man to society and in the sight of God than all the crowned ruffians that ever . . .*" That shocked her a little; crowned ruffians . . . ? It was less the idea than the sight of words in a startlingly unfamiliar association. It was as if she had read of black snow, or icy sun. The only other fragment of any size seemed to be the end of a chapter, for below the print the page was blank save for a few words written in faded ink. Peering at the print, she read: "*O ye that love mankind! Ye that dare oppose not only the tyranny but the tyrant, stand forth! Every spot of the old world is overrun by oppression. Freedom hath been hunted round the globe. Asia and Africa have long expelled her. Europe regards her*

*as a stranger, and England hath given her warning to depart. O! receive
the fugitive, and prepare in time an asylum for mankind."*

She re-read that passage with bewilderment. Tyranny . . . oppression . . . ? Freedom hath been hunted round the globe . . . ? He had
spoken of freedom that day by the river. . . . She held the paper towards
the fire to read the faint, clumsily-written words below. *"Tyranny, like
hell, is not easily conquered."* And underneath: *"I thank God that I
fear not."*

She felt her heart begin to beat heavily. Whose words were those—
his own, or some other's? Perhaps some other's—yet surely still his
own . . . ? Why had he written them here? Were they, she wondered,
shivering even in the fire's warmth, a kind of talisman to him . . . ? To
him, who had once said to her: *"Yes, I fear them, as any man would, and
him with no more than mortal flesh . . ."*

She reached out to her chair for *The Romance of the Forest*, laid the
charred fragments between its pages, and closed the book on them carefully. She was afraid to think, knowing to what horrors thought would
lead, but the feel of the novel between her hands reminded her of Adeline,
who had also found the writing of a prisoner; and instantly her mind
shook and rang and quailed with the clamorous, intolerable memory of
Stephen's voice saying: *"He is confined, of course? Shackled?"* She leapt
to her feet, ran to the door, opened it, hurried along the passage to the
study, and entered like a wind, to stand halted by the annoyed exclamation with which her husband greeted her.

"I am occupied, Conor. I must ask you not to . . ."

The thudding of her heart was so heavy that it seemed to shake her
whole body, and so loud that she thought he must hear it, but she felt
more anger than fear, and she said with a breathless note of challenge:

"I heard. I heard Byrne speaking to you of Finn. What are you
going to do?"

He answered her with that voice in which each word seemed to splinter
sharply against its neighbour, like chips of ice. Once, when she had
thought she loved him, it had frightened her; now, though it still struck
coldly, she heard it with rage that hovered on the edge of hatred.

"The affair is not yours," he said, "and I am at a loss to know why
you should intrude into it. I am capable, I assure you, of dealing
with . . ."

She interrupted fiercely:

"I will not have him flogged!"

At that his face flushed darkly with incredulous anger. He came
round the table with three strides, and took her by the arm.

"Oblige me, Madam, by confining yourself to your own duties, and
allow me to be the judge of . . ."

She wrenched her arm free and turned on him ferociously, very near
to tears, and stammering under the stress of her emotion.

"I have no duties! I am but a—a cypher, and—and ignorant, I confess it . . . yet I abhor cruelty, and here there is nought but cruelty, and
I will not permit this unfortunate man to suffer . . ."

Mr. Mannion exploded.

"*Permit* . . . ? *You* will not permit . . . ? By heavens, Madam, were it not that I'm too well aware of your ignorance, and your inability to control yourself as a gentlewoman should, I might suppose that you had taken leave of your senses! This 'unfortunate man,' as you are pleased to call him, is a villain of the deepest dye, and he *shall* suffer, I give you my word, not only for striking my overseer, but for attempting to in-troduce pernicious, inflammatory and revolutionary doctrines among my labourers!"

She began to see, too late, that she had stormed the position of an enemy without pausing to consider her armoury. She had no weapon. She began to tremble so that she was forced to grasp the back of a chair for support, and she knew, looking down at her white knuckles against the dark, carved wood, that she could protest and rail and rage, she could cry madly that she would not permit—but the power was his.

No weapon . . . ?

She gave a wild, bewildered glance about the room, as though the thought that had come to her were some visible devil. Once she had wielded power—no, not power, but influence. . . . Once—and not so long ago—he had desired to please her. . . . Revulsion from her dawning thought was so strong that she felt it as a physical nausea, yet it offered a chance—the slenderest chance—of saving that poor wretch with no more than mortal flesh from . . .

She said faintly: "Stephen!" She kept her eyes lowered till she had driven the hatred from them, and then raised them, sweetly lying, to his face. "Stephen, I—I fear I have behaved very ill! Oh, pray forgive me, and—and understand that I am somewhat distraught . . ." She saw the blackness of his expression clear a little, and forced her reluctant hand to stretch towards him, to rest timidly on his arm. Tears were not diffi-cult, for they were tears of shame, but she thought that he was seeing in them welcome evidence of her surrender and contrition. She whispered unsteadily: "We—we have been—estranged lately, have we not?" She stood close to him. She placed her hands on his shoulders and glanced up at his face for a moment appealingly; the expression she saw waking there was at once a horror and a triumph. She said softly: "Will you not tell me that I am forgiven? Can we not—can we not be happy once more, as—as we were at first when . . ."

Now she could feel the potency of her weapon, for his hands had covered hers, and were drawing her towards him. Now, for a little while, she need lie no more in words, but even more painfully with smiles, with kisses, with submission to the pressure of his arms and the ardent caresses of his hands, and with silent acquiescence to his whispered words. And presently, summoning the bitterly-learned strategy of her sex, mar-shalling its beguilements, judging with delicate and instinctive accuracy the perfect moment for attack, she breathed:

"Indeed, I have been very foolish! I am ashamed, Stephen, that I have been so tiresome, and that I should have seemed to question your judgment. But you know, do you not, that I have been in low spirits since—since our dear Julia was born, and it has distressed me that you seem to love me less, and I cannot deny, either, that all the—the violence and the suffering and the punishments of this place affect me . . ."

Her head drooped on to his breast. He murmured into her hair:

"I know it, my love, and it is for that reason that I have endeavoured to prevent them from coming to your knowledge."

"Yet since this *has* come to my knowledge," she pleaded, "could you not spare me, could you not so far indulge my foolishness as to overlook for this one time the insubordination of . . ."

He said firmly:

"You do not know what you are asking, my dear. It is out of the question."

She felt her hands stiffen against his chest, and forced them to relax. She looked up at him piteously, and then down again, standing back a little that he might see the sad submissiveness of her expression.

"You must be the judge," she said faintly, lifting a lacy scrap of cambric to her eyes. "But—but—I shall dream of it, Stephen, I shall not sleep, I assure you. I shall pass a night of misery which I—I had hoped would be—so happy . . ."

There was a pause; a pause, she thought with wild hope, meant reflection. He said at last:

"My love, I would not for the world have you imagine me heedless of even your lightest wish. Conduct such as this ruffian's cannot be passed over, yet to please you I will halve his punishment—which," he added, "will make it four times less severe than he has merited. Now dry your eyes, my dearest wife, and we shall count this little incident as fortunate, shall we not, since it has been the cause of our reunion . . . ?"

She knew that she had won as much as he would yield. She allowed him to escort her to the door and close it behind her. She walked slowly along the passage to the parlour, and sat in the chair beside the dully glowing embers of the fire, staring across the darkening room.

Half his punishment. . . . The shame she felt was an agony, yet even for this half-victory she was ready to accept it. She would have preferred a different weapon, she thought wearily—but what other weapon could a woman command? Tyranny, like hell, is not easily conquered.

*   *   *   *   *

The polite society of the colony had been thrown into a pleasant agitation by the presence of the French ships. Monsieur Baudin, it was agreed, was a most amiable and cultivated gentleman, though there were some pointed criticisms of a commander whose crew had arrived in such a state of disease and weakness as to be incapable of working their ship into port without assistance. These, however, merely added to the enjoyment of gossip, since it was gratifying to compare the misery of the French vessel's company with the hearty well-being of the *Investigator's*. The colony, indeed, liked Monsieur Baudin the better for being a less successful commander and navigator than Captain Flinders.

It was agreeable also to conduct the gentlemen of the French expedition about the country, to receive the rapturous congratulations of Monsieur Péron, and to accept with a deprecating smile and an inward satisfaction his professions of astonishment at what he never tired of describing as *l'état florissant de cette colonie singulière et lointaine.*

True, there had been a few small unpleasantnesses, not only between the English and the French, but between the Frenchmen themselves: it was clear that the relations between Monsieur Péron and Monsieur Baudin were not cordial. But it made a pleasant diversion for the civil and military élite of the colony, surfeited of each other's company, to play hosts to these genial gentlemen in the little retreat near the barracks, where an evening could be so amusingly passed at cards or billiards.

The ladies, too, were in a flutter, for there were many parties, dinners, and outdoor diversions to be planned for the gallant and attentive visitors. And was it not a fortunate circumstance, they exclaimed happily, that a peace should have been concluded between France and England, and that this welcome news should have reached them so soon after the arrival of the French ships? Not, of course, that it would have made any difference; civility and humanity alike required that hospitality be extended to a scientific expedition, even if it came from an enemy country—but it was so much pleasanter that they should not be enemies!

The guests, in turn, expressed delight at the kindness of their reception. Monsieur Péron, in particular, displayed an admiring interest in everything. He travelled indefatigably about the country, even to the outlying farms of the Hawkesbury; he endeared himself to Mr. Marsden by expressing stupefaction at the thriving condition of the reverend gentleman's farm; he visited the humble homes of the settlers; he was eager to be instructed on the colony's methods of administration. He enquired the strength of the garrison, the number of the convicts, the proportion among them of disaffected Irish, and even studied the habits and disposition of the natives. His appreciative comments—those of a true scientist—upon Colonel Paterson's garden, caused that gentleman's dark, melancholy countenance to brighten, and he was thereafter the Lieutenant Governor's constant companion. Charming excursions were arranged to different parts of the harbour, where Monsieur de Freycinet never wearied of exploring the shores, and during *al fresco* meals Monsieur Péron was inspired to further floods of questions. Was not the climate highly salubrious? Did not the population enjoy a peculiarly robust health? Were not the children born here remarkably strong and healthy? And was it indeed true that a most interesting increase in the fertility of the womenfolk had been observed?

Almost daily the Frenchmen stretched their legs beneath the hospitable board of *Monsieur le Gouverneur.* Mrs. King, in a delightful orgy of entertaining, waved aside their rueful apologies for the inordinate appetite with which they fell upon her fresh food.

"La, messieurs," she cried, "you have been at sea! I know how tedious it becomes to eat nothing but ship's fare!"

"Were it a little later in the year," boasted the Governor, tucking his thumbs into his armholes and beaming on them benevolently, "we might show you a greater variety of fruits and vegetables. But what the season permits we are most happy to offer you."

Monsieur Péron had already noted the different kinds of fruit trees in the Governor's garden—oranges, figs, cherries, peaches, pears, apricots. . . . He had his own private thoughts about this expedition, and he saw no reason why he should not take advantage of the admirable pretext provided by his scientific investigations to learn all he could of this astonishing colony. He had sailed along much of the coastline; he knew that this was a vast country and he did not believe that the English would long be content with a single foothold. Indeed, was not His Excellency already speaking of a new settlement to be established at Port Phillip? Was he not interested in Van Diemen's Land? This beginning that had been made was, he felt sure, only a beginning. The English were already established on the east coast, and Monsieur Flinders had recently been busy upon the south. Yet not only the continent, but New Zealand, the great southern ocean itself and its many islands, lay open to their ambition. Such ambition, thought Monsieur Péron shrewdly, must surely be challenged by the other great Powers of Europe. It might be easy, he ruminated, hiding his thoughts behind the smile that curved thinly on his lips, and rubbing his long nose reflectively, to challenge it—to destroy it —now, while it was represented by this one small, lonely community. But who could tell how formidable an undertaking it might prove in another twenty-five years?

So he was observing, asking questions, making notes. Monsieur de Freycinet, too, while allegedly examining the port as a navigator, had taken the opportunity to mark down spots suitable for the landing of troops, and had paid particular attention to its entrance. There might come a day when such information would be valuable—and surely it should be soon, for *les Anglais* were not idle! Monsieur Péron marvelled for the hundredth time—nor found it necessary to keep his marvellings to himself—that so much had been accomplished in so short a time.

Here, already, he exclaimed to his host, was *la civilisation!* Here was a port crowded with shipping; one saw vessels bound for China, and others, laden with coals, for India and the Cape of Good Hope. Here were to be found ships from England, from Ireland, from America, and at the moment—"our great good fortune, monsieur!"—from France. Here, already, was *l'industrie*, producing bricks, tiles, earthenware, pottery. Here were the wretches, *les condamnés*, not long since outcasts without hope or virtue, now being transformed and reclaimed by the wise and just rule of the estimable Monsieur King! Here one might observe the spirit of science at work upon the study of the land's fantastic plants and animals—*ces bizarreries de la nature!* Here were fine buildings, gardens, flourishing farms, residences which might vie with the country seats of Europe!

"*L'ouvrage de quatorze ans!*" cried Monsieur Péron enthusiastically. "*Ces routes, ces habitations, ces champs, ces moissons, ces vergers, ces troupeaux . . . ! C'est incroyable!*" King's chest expanded.

His chest expanded, but his shrewd mind was alert. The French ships came with a passport from His Britannic Majesty. There was no reason to suppose their mission other than it claimed to be. Nevertheless he preserved—well hidden beneath the genial demeanour of the host—the wariness of the colonial governor.

* * * * *

Pervasive if inconspicuous, the spring of this southern land came to the colony without drama, but not without effect. Through the strong scent of the native forests, and the salt breath of the sea, the alien flowers and fruit blossoms in the gardens sent a sweet, nostalgic perfume. Sunlight searched out the young leaves of the sober-tinted gum trees so that they wore a rosy nimbus, and stood transfigured. The air was still warm by night, and by day laden with a faint, feverish sense of growth and wakening. With dawn there came—like the voice of that glad, unrestful fever—the magpie's song, rich and liquid with a wild joy that seemed to quiver on the edge of pain.

In this balmy season the colony bestirred itself. The ladies ventured forth more frequently to visit each other, and to exchange gossip about their families, their fortunes, and the current scandals of the settlements. Mrs. Macarthur was too occupied for many parties, but where she went it seemed that her husband was an almost visible presence at her side, and her words but an echo of his voice. "Macarthur tells me," she would say, "that he is constantly engaged upon the matter of wool." The image of him stood clearly in all minds; the phrase "constantly engaged" chimed neatly with all recollections. Never had there been a man more constantly engaged, more subtly and relentlessly busy, more capable of imbuing his observers with the conviction that all matters to which he turned his mind and hand were not only high matters, but bound to be successful. Impossible to remember that he had departed for England under arrest; impossible to picture him as one humbly awaiting the verdict of outraged authority. And the more impossible just now, when Major Johnston, who had also left the colony under a cloud, had returned apparently unchastened. The ladies shrugged and whispered.

"It is said they won't try colonial cases at home—they have sent him back for Court Martial here."

"You are quite misinformed, Madam, for I have it on the best authority that he is not to be tried at all."

"Mercy on us, that will not please the Governor! What is the reason, pray?"

"Oh, la, it is some tedious legal matter of the composition of the Court which my poor head will not compass . . ."

"There are not enough officers, Madam. You may believe me, ladies, that the whole matter is to be dropped. I had it from Mrs. Paterson, who had it from her husband, who was written to direct from London. They do not believe that any good purpose would be served by continuing the proceedings. And His Excellency summoned the Major to Government House and released him from his arrest and ordered him back to his duty. And there the matter ends. But tell me, pray, has anyone heard . . . ?"

The growing coolness between the Governor and Colonel Paterson was discussed.

"Upon my word, their wives will now barely speak to each other!"

It was hinted that His Excellency was more than ever out of favour with the military since his refusal to permit the landing of spirits from the *Atlas*.

". . . but they say the French officers have been accommodated with as much as they desire!"

A passing word and a titter were bestowed on Mr. Caley, now roaming abroad with redoubled zeal in search of new specimens and plants.

"I'm not surprised, I assure you, when I consider his ménage!"

The Governor's plans for a new assault upon the mountains made idle conversation for a few moments.

"Ensign Barrallier is to go, they say. I quite fear for the poor young man, and I declare I cannot see the purpose of it, since that country is said to be so barren and worthless . . . !"

But all these matters which provided the ladies with tea-table gossip presented the Governor with problems. It was to the last of them that he was at the moment giving his most serious attention.

It was unfortunate that an expedition arranged for the previous autumn had been made impossible by bad weather, and that a more recent attempt by young Barrallier had been rewarded by no very important discovery; but the fever-magic of spring inspired His Excellency too, and lent him a fresh optimism. They must try again. This time a series of established depôts to provision the journey had been planned, and King was sanguine of success until he met obstruction from Colonel Paterson. Conscious that one of those recurring waves of hostility to himself was gathering to a crest, he suspected that his Lieutenant-Governor was again being made the mouthpiece of a resentment which had its origins elsewhere.

Paterson, approached with fair words, remained sulkily unco-operative. To give Ensign Barrallier leave of absence for such a purpose, he stiffly informed the Governor, would be contrary to his instructions. King fumed, but was helpless; for the moment it was checkmate. But was it . . . ? His sharp brain and his derisive humour combined to present him with a solution. Was he not entitled to an aide-de-camp—and, since the departure of Captain Mackellar, without one? The corners of his mouth bent downward satirically as he composed a carefully formal letter to the Lieutenant-Governor, requesting in the politest terms the services of Ensign Barrallier in that capacity. The Colonel was peevish. If Mr. Barrallier were to be detached from the regiment, he complained, the duty of the remaining subalterns would come more often. The Governor snorted at that, and renewed his request with some asperity. "Whenever the officers of this garrison cannot afford two nights in bed," he wrote tartly, "I shall instantly dispense with his services."

Mr. Barrallier was delivered to him. The little triumph put him in a good mood, and tempted him to improve it with a garnish of astringent humour which, he trusted, would prick the sullen dignity of Colonel

Paterson. Ensign Barrallier, somewhat embarrassed by the tussle for possession of his person, was summoned to receive his instructions.

"As my aide-de-camp, Sir," King informed him solemnly, "I propose to send you upon an embassy. You will journey into the country, deliver my compliments to the King of the Mountains, and assure him of my regard." He shouted with laughter and slapped his ambassador on the shoulder in enjoyment of his jest. Mr. Barrallier was dismissed to make his preparations and spread the tale.

*   *   *   *   *

It was not only at Government House, however, that spring suggested another challenge to the mountains. Into the convict huts also came an increasing fever of restlessness—a renascence of hope, and a wild temptation to set that hope against the fear which held them paralysed. Escape . . . ? Escape . . . ? *Where?* But now the rumours they had heard seemed to offer a fantastic answer, and the warmer weather promised better fortune to absconders. A settlement of white men somewhere beyond the hills . . . ? A goal, a destination! What kind of settlement? Did it matter? No unfamiliar devil could seem worse than the devil they knew, and the excitement of conjecture became a madness so compelling that the Governor grew alarmed.

He had set out early in October upon a tour of the outlying settlements, and everywhere he had found signs of this unrest. It filled him with the same irritated wonder which had disturbed the first Governor more than ten years ago; but King's wonder, unlike Phillip's, was all projected outward. It did not turn him to uneasy examination of his own mind and conscience, nor to a perilous questioning of his own function. His brain, as he drafted an Order to deal with it, merely punctuated his written words with exasperated mental comment.

"*The Governor has for some time been informed of a report as wicked as it is false, and calculated to bring the believers of it to destruction, that a settlement of white people exists on the other side of the mountains . . .*"

Preposterous! What fantastic delusions would not ignorance harbour! He slapped irritably at a moth hovering about the lamp, and wrote on:

"*. . . and that several of the prisoners were so far deluded as to concert means for reaching that settlement, in consequence of which several have lately absconded . . .*"

Imbeciles! Would they never learn? Ten years ago they had been babbling about China—China a mere hundred miles away, and to be reached on foot! And now a mythical settlement beyond the mountains! All the same, these worthless fools must be saved from the consequences of their folly! Liberty—bright beacon! Yet it was no beacon, he thought impatiently, but a will-o'-the-wisp, shining, fluttering in those impenetrable fastnesses beyond the river—and he must quench it.

"*A few simple and ill-informed people have been led into these ridiculous plans . . .*"

And to what end? To starve—to die at the hands of the natives— to be recaptured and flogged! And in the meantime to burden him with unnecessary worries! Words—threats to dissuade them from such frantic and foredoomed attempts . . . ! His pen scribbled swiftly across the paper.

"*Nor is there a doubt that if the present adventurers could have reached the mountains, they must have languished and died for want of food before they could have got a mile into them . . .*"

And, as he wrote, one who had reached the mountains was dying there, precisely as the Governor in his wisdom warned, not more than a few miles beyond the river. He had set out with three companions; they had stolen food and clothing from settlers' huts, and left their own betraying convict garments hidden in the scrub. Two days after their escape he had seen his companions retaken by a detachment of soldiers returning from the Hawkesbury, and had avoided capture himself only by jumping into a pond and hiding under its bank in the stagnant water and the long, green weeds. With them had gone most of the food, and he had been weak already by the time he reached the river. He had eaten grass and drunk water while he searched along its banks for a place to cross; he had almost drowned when he swam it, and had lain for the rest of that day and the next night recovering his strength. He had eaten the few mouthfuls of sodden bread and salt meat which remained, and set out for the foothills . . .

He had walked and walked, paused to rest, and walked once more, not realising in the bemusement of fatigue and hunger that he often walked in circles. Here in the hills there was no grass, so he gnawed the leaves of shrubs, and counted himself lucky to find a dead lizard, and walked again. Then there was a day when he ate nothing at all, and found not even a creek; thirst began to seem more terrible than hunger, and to climb a hill was to crawl up it on hands and knees, cursing his own weakness, crying with pity for his own exhaustion, seeing tears on his hand, and licking their salt moisture.

And he had come at last, partly walking, partly sliding, partly crawling, down into this little gully where a narrow stream trickled between banks of green ferns; and its water was all that had passed his lips for three days and three nights. He was now so near to death that he had ceased to fear it, and imagined that he was merely resting. The few pictures, half thought and half dream, that wandered through his mind were still of another effort he would make presently, and of a hilltop where he would stand before long, and look down upon his goal.

There Johnny Prentice found him the next morning. He stood looking down at the emaciated body, the dirty, outflung hands, the sunken, bearded cheeks, the wide-open, sightless eyes, and felt nothing but perplexity. He had no precedent for dealing with this kind of death. He had lived for too long as a native to be capable of seeing the end of a life as an isolated affair; in the absence of relatives, friends, fellow-tribesmen, the dead body of a man seemed like the dead body of an ant—something to glance at, and pass by.

Yet Johnny stood and stared. He was bothered by a death which was enclosed by no rules and acknowledged by no rituals. But for these there must be the dead man's tribe about him. There was always some one person who, by virtue of relationship, was responsible for directing the ceremonies which ensured the safe passage of a man's spirit from life into the eternal dream-time, and though Johnny lacked the centuries of ancestral teaching which made these matters so simple to the natives, he had lived their life long enough to feel baffled by the death of a tribeless man.

No father, no brothers, no sons . . .

Slowly, through his native thinking, there came to him vague memories of burials he had seen long ago. There had been—hadn't there?—some ceremony . . . ? Some man had spoken words . . . ? There had been people gathered . . . ? He knew with a sudden, painful unwillingness, that he and this dead man were of the same blood—the same tribe. Yet he could feel no grief, no fear, no uprush of defiant hostility toward death, the dark enemy which had snatched one of his race, and he felt uneasily that there was some lack here, some danger, some fault in a tribe when one of its members did not care that another had died.

That was the voice of his native self; but as he stood and looked and thought the voice of his white self was not silent either. Perhaps this death did not matter to him, after all—not as a loss and a grief, but as an opportunity . . . ? It was only a couple of months since he had learned with anger and astonishment that he had killed the wrong man that night before his mother's door. The tale had come to him slowly, passing from the lips of one native to another, and—at first incredulous—he had gone to his vantage point across the river to watch and watch until his own eyes told him that indeed Stephen Mannion was not dead. And he had resolved that some day there would come another chance—and then he would make no mistake . . .

His sharp, dark eyes were still staring at the figure at his feet, and he was seeing, now, not the man, but the clothes that covered him. Clothes. What separated Johnny Prentice from his own tribe save nakedness? He laid his spears down. He stripped the body and began to put on the clothes, fumbling at them with the awkwardness of inexperience. The shoes were so worn that the soles hardly held to the uppers, but he sat down on a rock and pushed his feet into them. He took the cloth cap and put it on his head where it perched oddly over the unkempt thatch of his red hair. He felt very strange, but excited, and he stood still for a moment or two, holding his arms in the stiff, coarse sleeves out a little from his body, and frowning down with wonder at his shod feet, protruding so unfamiliarly from the ragged trousers.

Suddenly he was eager to be home again. He wanted to walk into his hut wearing these clothes, and confront Tom Towns with the spectacle of Johnny Prentice, the white man, no longer cut off from his own tribe by nakedness. . . . He took up his spears, gave the dead body of the convict one last, indifferent glance, and left it lying there.

* * * * *

It was one day early in November that the natives brought him news of a new expedition, more ambitious than anything before attempted, which the Bereewolgal were preparing. Its leader, they told him, was to be the

same man who had already once intruded into the valley of the Wollondilly, and they had learned from other natives who had fraternised with
him on that occasion, and who proposed to haunt his camps upon this,
that many elaborate preparations were being made for a longer journey
than usual.

Johnny and Tom Towns exchanged glances. Towns had been very ill
during the winter; he lay most of the time now on his possum skins in
the corner of the hut, and coughed and spat blood frequently. Yet,
strangely, as his body wasted and failed, his mind seemed to achieve a
new, restless energy. He had conceived a plan, and infected Johnny
with his enthusiasm. Were there not, he demanded, settlements of white
men down the river, always poor, always struggling, always on the lookout
for anything which would alleviate their want? To achieve wealth and
influence in this colony, he argued, nothing was needed by a shrewd man
save a commodity to sell. And had not Johnny such a commodity? Were
there not hundreds upon hundreds of wild cattle straying in areas which
none knew better than he? And were they not, he added with sly irony,
Johnny's own property?

Johnny, quite unconscious of the irony, agreed. He knew only the
native point of view upon this matter, and since he was eight years old
he had accepted its verdict that the cattle were his. They had belonged
to him in his previous life before he was drowned, and they still belonged
to him. He had inherited his father's possessions—his hut, his key, his
woman, his son—and his cattle. So he listened attentively to Towns,
nodding his agreement.

Cattle, said Towns, meant beef. The first thing to do was to acquire
some casks and some coarse salt. Settlers would pay for salt meat, and
not enquire too closely where it came from. They would pay with what
they had—grain, perhaps, or liquor, or livestock, or tools, or even money.
These things could be bartered again. Johnny had clothes now—and not
convict clothes. He could speak his own language, and even write it a
little. In the Hawkesbury settlements, Towns assured him, there might
indeed be curious glances for a stranger—but no hostility, and no too
searching questions for a stranger who did not come empty-handed . . .

Towns' knowledge of the topography of the country was still vague.
His own journey to this place had been so interrupted during the periods
when his guides changed (and saw their meeting as an occasion for some
pleasant idling and gossip), so erratic in its route, and so confused in
his own mind by illness and exhaustion, that he could not have told
whether the Hawkesbury settlements were twenty miles distant or fifty.
His own morbid fear of the country had never left him; it had held him
like a chain to the neighbourhood of the hut. He knew only that Johnny
seemed to make light of his excursions to that part of the river where the
Mannions lived, which was nearer than the Hawkesbury settlements, but
how much nearer he had no idea. And Johnny, for his part, thought
little of distance, for he thought little of time. No journey could seem
long to one who had, if necessary, a whole life in which to accomplish it.
His customary route over the tableland to the Nepean was by now as

familiar and as easy to him as a highway, and once there he could perform the rest of the journey by canoe down a long waterway interrupted only here and there by shallows and rapids.

The plan had stimulated in him a wild excitement. Towns, who for all his ineptitude in other matters, was clever with his fingers, had repaired the dead convict's shoes with bits of cattle hide, and Johnny had learned to walk in them with confidence if not with perfect comfort. He was proud of his clothes, and liked to pause at still pools to admire his transformed reflection. The ambition which had once been so strong in him, and which during his native life had receded not into oblivion but into that peculiarly primitive form of fantasy in which the dream could be as satisfying as the reality, now clamoured in him again as something which could actually be achieved. Already he had begun to act. He had driven a small herd of cattle over the tableland into the valley of one of the Wollondilly's tributaries—not too near his own, and yet not too far away. It had been a long, arduous and even dangerous task, accomplished only with the aid of a party of natives who had employed their kangaroo-hunting technique to surround the herd and keep it together. But the wild cattle were not kangaroos. They were savage and aggressive; one native had been badly gored, and Johnny himself had but narrowly escaped injury by climbing a tree.

So now, with his plan made, accepted, ready to be carried out, he was alarmed by this news of an expedition. So long as the white men had confined their explorations to the river which they had named at different points the Nepean and the Hawkesbury, he had felt safe enough; he still dwelt securely behind the first line of hills that rose to the west of it. Yet a determined effort to push westward from that part of the Nepean where the wild cattle mostly strayed might bring them perilously close to his retreat. He spared a wondering thought for the almost forgotten father who must have known this fear too—a fear which had kept him from the main valley of the Wollondilly, and drawn him to the fastnesses of this wild little stream falling steeply to the river through its rocky gorges. Only by literally stumbling on it would his hut be found; yet with the Wollondilly known—perhaps settled—someone would stumble on it soon . . .

And Towns, watching him, recognising his fear and sharing it, muttered anxiously:

"Ye better watch 'em, Johnny . . ."

Johnny watched them. On the morning early in November when Ensign Barrallier crossed the river at the ford which the natives had shown him, Johnny, hidden in the scrub of the hills overlooking the waggon, drawn by two bullocks, lumbering down to the bank to halt there while the party inspected the crossing. He saw the animals unyoked and led across, the waggon laboriously unloaded, the stores transferred on men's shoulders through the shallow water, and finally the waggon itself dragged to the opposite bank. There were eleven men—ten white and one native. Five scarlet coats proclaimed soldiers; the other five were convicts. It took a long time to get everything across the river, and Johnny watched the sweating, toiling men with a fascinated intentness. He had forgotten this kind of work; he had forgotten that there were men who laboured as though in desperate pursuit of each fleeting minute, as though time were an adversary they must conquer. The sight frightened him a little, and yet he felt an unwilling affinity with them, and his mind, though fearing their object, endorsed their air of stubborn purpose. The vague sense of impatience which he had sometimes felt for the waywardness, the volatility of his native friends became a strong, restless beating in his blood, a surge of excitement. He knew that these people, having once begun to move forward, would continue to move—slowly, perhaps, but with a deadly determination. He hated them for it, but found that it somehow ratified his own confidence in himself. He, too, having begun to move, would go on . . .

So he watched and followed. They kept south along the Nepean for a time, but then struck westward—joined on the second day by two intimate friends of Johnny's called Bungin and Wooglemai. At a spot known by the natives as Nattai they halted to build a hut, and Wooglemai, slipping away to meet Johnny that night, explained that the waggon and the bullocks and a party of men were to remain here, while the rest went on. When they did go on Johnny's anxiety increased, for they reached the stream of which his own was a tributary, and it passed his understanding how they could fail to see the traces of his frequent passing. But they did fail. The natives, he knew, would not betray him —and indeed as the party passed by, not a mile from his hut, the black men faded away into the bush to rejoin it later, for this was a death-place, and therefore to be avoided.

He breathed more freely when they had followed the stream down to the junction with the Wollondilly, and turned south to trace that river upstream. This time, at all events, they were not going to blunder on his hiding place. Bungin, Wooglemai, and other natives who by now had added themselves to the expedition, fought, chattered and argued about the camps of the white men, showing them how to obtain food, offering them lizards, frogs, shellfish, and parrots, demonstrating the throwing of boomerangs, laughing as the kangaroos fled, terrified by the noisy approach and the scarlet coats of the intruders. One night Barrallier heard the distant lowing of Johnny's cattle, but the natives had no difficulty in persuading him that it was the croaking of giant frogs—a sound which it did, indeed, resemble. And often at night they vanished for a few hours to bring Johnny news of strange foods, strange doings and strange customs. The white man who led the party, they related, spent much of his time upon an occupation which they described in pantomime, and Johnny nodded his comprehension with a pleasant sense of superiority. He too knew how to write. And once when the explorers had left a camp and moved on he came down to it and found a scrap of paper blowing about on the ground. He studied it for a long time, but for all Tom Towns had taught him he could make nothing of it. ". . . *terrain que j'ai parcouru pendant la matinée est composé* . . ." He could not understand the writing, but he cherished the paper. With a splinter of charcoal still warm from their fire, he wrote his name several times on its blank side, and secured it, native-fashion, in his hair. He continued to dog the footsteps of the expedition, bewildered by its apparent purposelessness, by the incredible inefficiency of the white men, by the way they even retraced their steps for many miles to procure more food from the waggon, and then set out again. Were they so clever after all? Why should men make such toil of a journey—encumbered by clothes, burdened with a mass of unnecessary equipment, plodding on and on through burning summer days till they almost sank to the ground exhausted? He became exasperated to a frenzy, but he followed obstinately—far, far beyond the territory which he knew himself. When the expedition at last turned back he went ahead of it; and when Barrallier, after six weeks of arduous exploration, re-crossed the Nepean and vanished eastward towards Sydney, Johnny was there—relieved but still mistrustful—to watch him go.

*   *   *   *   *

At Sydney, in the meantime, the Governor—though not altogether recovered from an illness, and harassed by the knowledge of increasing animosity towards himself and his policy—prepared to speed the French vessels upon their way. It was hardly to be expected that complete accord should have prevailed between visitors and hosts over so long a period in a place where one word could become a rumour overnight, and the smallest indiscretion be magnified into a perfidy; and indeed there had been difficulties. Nevertheless, the Governor and Monsieur Baudin had succeeded in maintaining their relations on a plane of cordiality which was not merely official. Between them there had arisen a genuine mutual esteem, and now that the guests were to depart the drawing-room at Government House was swept and garnished by Mrs. King and her faithful Jane Dundas to welcome them for the last time.

Monsieur Baudin, toying with his wineglass, looked round at the assembled company with a smile which only partly masked his abstraction. The interrupted voyage which must now be resumed had been hard—and sad. The quarrels on board *le Géographe*, the shocking weather, the scurvy, and the death of two of his friends, had combined to make it one he would remember without pleasure. And, he thought—recalling the charts which he had been shown by the commander of the *Investigator*—with little pride. For he had been disconcerted to find how small a part of his own discoveries had not been anticipated by the indefatigable Captain Flinders.

This interlude in a strange colony had amused, interested, and faintly exasperated him. Already, he reflected wryly, these Englishmen had deceived themselves into imagining that *le bon Dieu* had created it expressly for them! He was a man of philosophic temperament and liberal mind; the machinations of power politics aroused in him an interest which was lukewarm, and rather wearily dutiful. He was a Frenchman, a naval commander with a task of exploration and investigation to perform, yet since the ill-fortune of his voyage had compelled him to put in at Port Jackson for succour, it would be but his duty to apprise his Government of its progress. He supposed—on the edge of indifference—that policy might require some measures to counteract what he could not fail to recognise as the germ of considerable English power in this loneliest outpost of the globe. But in the meantime he was a guest. This, Governor, this Monsieur King, had received them with generosity and was a man of some intelligence. He spoke French very creditably, and Madame, though not beautiful, poor lady, had a kind heart and—what was more important—a passable cuisine. Monsieur Baudin sighed in-audibly and sipped his wine. He was over fifty, and he felt tired, though not too tired to turn his eyes instinctively from the homely but beaming countenance of Madame King to *la belle Irlandaise*, Madame Mannion, about whose chair no less than three of his compatriots were hovering. Yet she seemed less interested in their compliments, he thought, than in the conversation taking place between de Freycinet and young Monsieur Flinders, who stood near her, apparently oblivious of her eager gaze. Flinders was smiling, he was polite, but there was an absent air about him, as though his thoughts were far away. With his young wife, perhaps, to whom rumour said he was so devotedly attached? Or already off upon another voyage, impatient of the delays which held his body shorebound? "Captain," Baudin heard de Freycinet say to him, "if we had not been kept so long picking up shells and catching butterflies at Van Diemen's Land, you would not have discovered the South Coast before us!"

It was a jest, received with laughter, but it held the flavour of rivalry; though Mr. Flinders answered lightly his dark eyes were no longer absent, but sharp and attentive. Monsieur Baudin sighed inaudibly. In his private thoughts he had permitted himself some reflections on the subject of colonies, and despite the civil admiration he had expressed for the march of progress in this new country, he had harboured a faint, philosophic regret for the violation of its primeval solitude. He remembered the crash of ancient trees, the smoke that climbed to heaven from their burning trunks and leaves, the roads and fields that scarred the countryside, the strange, black, primitive people moving like spectres on the expanding edge of settlement. He thought: "The woods are doomed; and *les naturels*—they, too . . ."

He became aware that his host was rising, clearing his throat, prepar-ing to deliver an oration; he roused himself to courteous and smiling attention.

Monsieur King spoke eloquently of the imminent departure of the guests whose presence had been so welcome in their isolated society. "We should wish," he proclaimed, "to bestow upon the gallant Commander ..." bows were exchanged, "some little token of our friendship which may serve to recall us to his memory during his future voyagings." To the gallant Commander's bewildered and at first incredulous ears it became plain that he was about to be presented with a piece of wood. Yet he was not long left in doubt that this was no ordinary wood. The tones of *Monsieur le Gouverneur* became solemn, and the faces of his entourage acquired an expression of decorous gravity. This wood was nothing less than a fragment from the whaleboat of Monsieur Bass—the selfsame whaleboat in which he had performed the feat of discovering the strait between New Holland and Van Diemen's Land.

Monsieur Baudin was overcome by that mixture of levity and embarrassment which the sentimentality of the English always aroused in him. *Nom de Dieu,* but they were a strange people! He avoided the eyes of his countrymen—unnecessarily, since they were all carefully downcast. It had been a source of astonishment and amusement to them already to learn that *la chaloupe de Monsieur Bass* was preserved with veneration in the harbour, and that splinters from it (like the bones of the saints, or fragments of the true Cross!) were eagerly sought. Already, he thought in amazement, it is a relic! Already they are creating *les légendes!* He composed his startled countenance, and rose to receive the gift which the Governor was proffering—*"avec,"* thought Monsieur Baudin dazedly, *"une sorte de respect religieux!"* It was, he observed, set in a handsome silver band, about which were engraved the particulars of the celebrated voyage.

He collected his scattered wits and his Gallic politeness. Was it possible, he enquired with gentle reproach, that *Monsieur le Gouverneur* really believed a present necessary to remind them of the hospitality they had received at his hands? Nothing, he protested, could ever eradicate from their minds grateful memories of the kindness they had enjoyed! Yet not only on his own behalf, as a friend of the host who had entertained them so generously, but also as a symbol of that friendship which now happily existed between their countries—and which he prayed might endure for ever—he accepted with the profoundest gratitude, and the deepest sense of the honour done to him, this—this historic—er—object. *Les Anglais,* he pursued, gaining fluency, were men of the most practical temperament, as all who had been privileged to witness the astonishing development of the colony, and who had admired the achievements of Monsieur Bass and Monsieur Flinders, must allow. Yet this gracious gesture proved that they possessed also *la sensibilité*—if, indeed, proof had been wanting to those who had observed the fatherly solicitude of *Monsieur le Gouverneur* towards those placed under his direction. Particularly moving was the care lavished upon those young females who, deprived of parental guidance, had found sanctuary in the Orphan Asylum, where—thanks to the devoted attention of Madame King and the other amiable and benevolent ladies of the colony, they were enabled to live a life of industry, piety, and virtue. Might he, then, be permitted the great honour of begging Madame's acceptance of a trifling sum to further this humane and noble work?

He tendered his gift, bowed low, sat down in a clamour of applause and congratulation, and wiped his forehead. He was suddenly depressed. Monsieur King was indeed his friend; from his heart he desired the peace between their countries to endure; yet over his friendship and his desire he felt the shadow of nations warring for supremacy. Madame was in truth benevolent; yet behind that benevolence stood the ruthlessness which created the need for it. They were all caught up in this warring and this ruthlessness which made a mockery of courtesies and civil words . . .

Across the room he caught the round-eyed stare of little Miss Elizabeth King, enjoying the indulgence of making a brief appearance in this dazzling company. "Are there none save children," he thought a trifle wildly, "who can speak quite without hypocrisy?"

*   *   *   *   *

But *le Géographe* and *le Naturaliste* had hardly cleared the Heads before there burst like a storm about the Governor's ears the rumour that they were bound for Van Diemen's Land to establish a French settlement. They had talked openly of this intention, it was said, to Colonel Paterson and other officers. They had even displayed a chart. But the Colonel, pressed for information, only replied rather loftily that conversation among the Frenchmen upon the subject had been so general that he could not have supposed the Governor unaware of it; and King, his sharp temper made even sharper by illness and worry, treated his wife to another tirade against the weakness, the unreliability of his second-in-command.

She had heard it all a thousand times before, but it never failed to distress her. For she knew—and was well aware that her husband knew also—that the Colonel's main crime was an easy-going nature, a fatal amiability. Strained relations between the Governor and the military faction found him always struggling with a divided allegiance, and relations at present were very strained indeed; nor did it seem that while King persisted in carrying out his instructions they could ever be otherwise. Paterson was a soldier among soldiers, and when the official policy of the Governor conflicted, as it must, with the unofficial policy of the soldier-traders, he leaned heavily towards his brothers-in-arms. So Mrs. King sat plying her needle and listening unhappily to her husband's violent denunciations.

"And he leaves it until the French ships have departed," he raged, "to inform me of this!" He flourished the Colonel's letter at her. "He 'did not consider it anything more than a commonplace conversation'! The man is a fool—a weak fool; but there are those about him who are not weak, and worse than fools!"

Mrs. King laid her work down and announced with decision:

"I do not believe a word of it! Not a word! Monsieur Baudin would have told you if he had had any such intention—of that I am fully persuaded."

But King merely grunted. The gallant Captain had endeared himself to the ladies, and to none more than to the Governor's wife, who had appreciated his attention to the little Madamoiselle Elisabet no less than his benevolence towards her orphan *protégées*. The Governor himself, however, while still entertaining a personal regard for the French commander, was conscious of high matters in which that gentleman might be but a pawn. It was true that Baudin, closeted with him, had been very frank. He had denied in so many words knowledge of a French plan for settlement on any part of the continent. He had shown the Governor his journals and his orders; King had carefully observed that those orders spoke only of exploration and the collection of natural history specimens, and contained no instructions to touch at Port Jackson. It did not appear, therefore, that Baudin had been sent to spy upon the colony; but the Governor could not afford to be too trusting, and it took him no more than ten seconds to decide that a ship must be sent instantly in pursuit of the French vessels. They were bound, he knew, for King Island in the western entrance to Bass Strait, but the chart shown to Colonel Paterson had indicated Storm Bay Passage on the south coast of Van Diemen's Land as the spot chosen for their settlement. The Governor made quick and complicated plans. The *Cumberland*, he decided, commanded by Robbins of H.M.S. *Buffalo*, should be. hot on their heels, and Mr. Robbins should be provided with not one set of Instructions, but two. The first, for his eyes alone, should order him without the loss of a moment to King Island, where he would find the Frenchmen; and the other, to be shown to Monsieur Baudin, should direct him to Storm Bay Passage, there to hoist the British colours and leave a small guard of soldiers. Thus it would be made clear to the representative of France that the representative of England did not propose that His Britannic Majesty's claims should be disputed. And if the appearance of the *Cumberland* so far off her course should seem strange, Robbins could plead an easterly wind which had driven him into the strait . . .

Mr. King wrote his two sets of Instructions and pondered further. He desired in this delicate matter to preserve the amicable note which had up to the present characterised his relations with his guests, and he saw no reason why this should not be possible, provided always they bore in mind that they were—guests. In a personal letter to Monsieur Baudin, he reflected, they could be warned off with civility, courtesy, even friendliness . . .

"*You will be surprised to see a vessel so soon after you,*" he wrote, and, remembering Baudin's intelligent and discerning gaze, wondered for an uncomfortable moment if he really would be so surprised. He dipped his pen in the ink again, considering. He would be quite frank about these rumours; he would disclaim any personal belief in them. He wrote slowly, choosing his words with care, and paused presently to consider his last sentence with a thoughtful frown. "*. . . at present totally disbelieving any such thing ever being thought of . . .*"

Totally disbelieving. And yet . . . ? He discovered in himself a fierce and jealous sense of almost personal possessiveness. It occurred to him with a shock that it was nearly fifteen years since he had first come with Governor Phillip's fleet to these shores. He had twice left them and returned again, and with each return he had felt them more familiar, more identified with himself. He was not a man who often paused to examine his own emotions, but he recaptured now with astonishment the vague memory of a time when this had seemed an incredible country— fantastic, unreal, impossible. A time when he had looked at everything with sharp, amazed inquisitiveness; paused to pick and smell the leaves and flowers which he now passed without a glance; sketched as remarkable human curiosities the natives whom he now took for granted; seen everything between this earth and sky as strange, remote from himself who stood outside, staring at it. At what unobtrusive and unnoticed stage had he begun to forget that it was strange . . . ?

He shook the momentary sense of wonder away from him impatiently. The present fact was that French ships were cruising round the shores of a British colony—perhaps as innocent as they seemed, and perhaps not. This land was large—growing larger year by year as the feet of the explorers pushed inland, and the sails of Captain Flinders' ship moved like a white speck along the coastline. He blinked down at his half-written letter and added to its frankness a line or two not so frank. "*I consider it but proper to give you this information in case the Cumberland should fall in with your ships.*"

But he was thinking that there must be no "in case" about it. Monsieur Baudin, as a Frenchman, must be informed without delay that no part of this expanding continent was for him; as Monsieur Baudin, however, he should find these tidings softened by a cordiality which, the Governor hastened to tell himself, need not be the less sincere for being diplomatic also.

"*Myself and family,*" he concluded, "*join with me in the kindest wishes for your health, and shall long remember the pleasure we had in your society.*"

Yet as he pushed his chair back and rose with the letter in his hand, he felt a momentary inexplicable dissatisfaction like a sour taste in his mouth.

1803

When business called the gentlemen of the colony to Parramatta, their favourite rendezvous was the establishment of a French Jew called Larra. An ex-thief and forger Mr. Larra might be, but he had endeared himself to his distinguished *clientèle* by providing excellent food and wine, and Mr. Mannion, riding into the town from Beltrasna one hot January morning, decided to break his journey to Sydney, and take some refreshment at this hospitable inn.

In the street, however, he came upon Mr. Jamison and Captain Kemp seated upon a log, and convulsed with laughter over a scrap of paper which Lieutenant Hobby was displaying to them. Somewhat curious, he reined in and dismounted, calling a response to their hilarious greeting.

"You are in high spirits, gentlemen! May I ask what it can be that so entertains you in this insupportable weather?"

Mr. Jamison explained, offering him the paper:

"The Muse of poetry has been busy among us, and we were enjoying her latest effusion. Pray share our poor seat, Sir, and our rich jest."

Mannion declined the seat, but accepted the paper, and his eyebrows rose as he read. It was no secret that the Governor's unpopularity with the Corps had reached new heights, but he had been unaware till now that its members had discovered what was at once an amusing diversion, and a new method of discomfiting their enemy. His reluctance to identify himself too closely with a class of colonial landowners and nabobs whom he regarded as upstarts could not quite blind him to the fact that his interests were the same as theirs. Though his isolation from the settlements afforded him better opportunities for quietly ignoring tiresome official edicts, he too had been inconvenienced sometimes by the Governor's measures, and he was not altogether ill-pleased, therefore, to find that His Excellency had become the target of anonymous 'pipes.' The lifting of his brows was accompanied by a broadening smile as he read this latest product of the lampooner's art. "*The great King*," he noted, was roundly described as "*a wicked, oppressive, notorious man*," and the point of a reference to "*Queen Josepha*" was sharpened by a satirical footnote explaining that this was "*one of the names of a great King's lady.*" It was a crude effort, he thought, and barbarously rhymed, but it made up in venom what it lacked in wit.

> "Then,' says K-g, 'I soon shall be put to the rout;
> But damn me, while powerful I'll do what I can
> According to what I proposed as a plan,
> To make all subservient, humble and poor,
> Take women and children from off of the store,
> Crush all independence, and poverty plant,
> Ruin, tense and distress, and make everyone want . . .'"

He nodded as he read, and smiled more broadly. Though the naïve respect he had received from Hunter had caused him some lofty amusement, he had in his heart considered it but his due, and the rather arrogant self-confidence of King amused him not at all. An opinionated fellow, who paraded his authority all too offensively! A mere colonial Governor who did, indeed, seem disposed to see himself as King in function as well as in name! Mr. Mannion finished his perusal and handed the sheet back to Hobby. He drawled:

"A truly interesting document, my dear Sir! Pray, who is its author?"

Hobby shot a sly glance at his companions and answered promptly:

"Damme, Mr. Mannion, who can tell? It was found by my servant in my chaise this morning, before I was out of bed."

"It is addressed, I see," observed Mr. Mannion, "to Johnston. Has he seen it yet?"

"Not this one—though I should be astonished, on my word, if others had not come his way."

Mannion's eyebrows rose again.

"There have been others?"

Captain Kemp laughed.

"They're falling about the ground thicker than autumn leaves, Sir!" He felt in his pocket. "Here's a copy of one which was found in the yard of my barrack but a few days past. It begins:

> *'Dejected, here forlorn, by all despised,*
> *By every human turpitude possest—*
> *He sinks beneath those sins, to none disguised,*
> *A wretch to whom all pity is bereft.'* "

"And there was another, was there not, Hobby, found in the barrack-yard of the Corps, and addressed to Captain Abbott, which is said to have come to our illustrious Governor's own eyes. And I trust," he added, "that it will teach him how his tyrannies are regarded by honest men. You are sending this one down to Annandale, Hobby?"

Mr. Hobby took the paper back from Mr. Jamison and folded it lovingly.

"In good time, my dear fellow, in good time! But I have made a copy of it, never fear!"

Mannion enquired urbanely:

"Will you not do me the honour, gentlemen, of joining me in a little refreshment?" He stilled their chorus of acceptance with a gesture of mock warning. "I shall not drink any seditious toasts—but should you lift your glasses to the confusion of an unnamed tyrant I shall not deny my thirst, I assure you, for I've had a long and a plaguey hot ride."

But as they made their way towards Mr. Larra's inn they encountered the Deputy Commissary who, buttonholed by Lieutenant Hobby, listened with evident delight while that gentleman read aloud from his cherished document. Captain Kemp said jovially as they passed on:

"It's but a ceremony, Hobby, to hold the thing up before your eyes, for you know it by heart already!" And Mr. Jamison interrupted hurriedly:

"My dear fellow, there's Wentworth across the street with a face as long as His Excellency's flagstaff. It would be but an act of charity to afford him a little entertainment!"

Hobby protested:

"Confound it, my throat's dry with all this reading! Mr. Wentworth shall be indulged with the loan of my copy for a little while, but we must not detain Mr. Mannion. Walk on, pray, and I shall rejoin you in a moment."

Mr. Mannion, as he strolled down the street with his companions, looked back to see a sheet of paper pass from Hobby to Wentworth; he reflected that though no one seemed to know who wrote these interesting rhymes, there was no lack of people eager to read them.

In Sydney a couple of days later, he presented himself at Government House to enquire after His Excellency's health. It was the merest formality, for he had already learned of the Governor's recent recovery from a severe attack of illness, and had in his pocket at that moment a copy of another lampoon, one verse of which celebrated precisely that event:

> *"To every loyal and Christian feeling heart*
> *The earnest news I hastily impart;*
> *Congratulate you all, Te Deum sing,*
> *Escaped from death and gibbet is our K-g!"*

The doggerel was running in his head as he stood at the long window looking out over the harbour. The *Venus* brigantine lay there at anchor, and the sight of her recalled to Mr. Mannion his conversation that same morning with its owner, Mr. Bass. How many and varied, he reflected, were the enterprises already budding in this infant colony! Mr. Bass, he had learned, was shortly bound for South America, from whence he hoped to bring cattle—both alive, for breeding purposes, and salted down for food. He had plans, too, for pork and sealskins, and was negotiating with authority for an exclusive fishing lease of the waters round the south of New Zealand. "For if I can produce food from the sea, Mr. Mannion," he had argued, "in places now useless to the world, am I not exclusively entitled to the fruits of my ingenuity, as much as a man who obtains letters patent for a corkscrew, or a cake of blacking?"

Mr. Mannion had assured him that he was. Year by year the master of Beltrasna was becoming more firmly convinced that there was great wealth to be won in this land. Macarthur had put his faith in wool, and had no doubt done wisely, but there were other avenues to be explored, and as the country opened up who knew what other treasure-trove might be revealed? Minerals—gold—precious stones . . . ?

He had long ago forgotten that his presence in the colony was the result of an obscure and freakish impulse. He congratulated himself now upon his foresight and acumen, and as he stared idly at what was visible of the township, he even toyed with the thought that the few acres of land he had recently purchased on its outskirts might in time become a valuable asset. He had bought it with the idea that he might some day build another house; in years to come, when he was visiting the country, it might be pleasant to have a place to which he could repair from his country estate for a change of air and scene—and convenient, also, for the transaction of business in the metropolis. A "town house"! He smiled at the ambitious phrase, and then ceased to smile, remembering how the straggling settlement had grown and grown in its planless, persistent way, its narrow streets developing rather than being formed, its houses becoming every year more like houses and less like huts, shops and warehouses appearing almost overnight, as it gathered to itself all the trades and activities which made up a civilised community . . .

He thought with quick excitement: "It *is* a town!" He even found his fancy racing ahead into a fantastic future. A bigger and bigger town. . . . A city . . .

But that was too far away; it was a town, and the headquarters of a colony. The colony in turn was the headquarters of a continent. Wise government was needed here, he reflected, if the endeavours of the wealthy to develop it were not to be circumvented. But Government, it appeared, was more concerned with indulging the small settlers who ineptly scratched and muddled on their few paltry acres than with affording countenance and encouragement to those whose resources enabled them to work grandly on a large and profitable scale. It was with this thought in his mind that he turned to greet his host.

The brusque salutation of King contrasted unpleasantly with his memory of Hunter's mild and deferential courtesy. The Governor's roundish face, he noticed, was a little flushed, but it seemed less the ruddiness of health than the flag of a quick, goaded temper flying over a sallow skin. His small, tightly pursed mouth looked tighter than ever, and his expression was grim.

"Mr. Mannion!" he barked. "Good-day, Sir. Pray be seated."

Mannion bowed distantly.

"I thank you, Sir, but I shall not detain you. I called only to pay my respects. I heard of your recent illness with grave concern, and am happy to see you recovered."

"I am far from completely recovered," King replied shortly, "but I am well enough, I trust, to discharge my duties." He stared hard at his visitor with angry eyes, and added: "Foremost among which will be the bringing to justice of those who have been seeking to overthrow my authority and assassinate my character while I lay at death's door. You understand me, Sir, I don't doubt?"

Mr. Mannion became more distant still; such crude forthrightness was not to his taste. He replied coldly:

"As Your Excellency must be aware, I do not concern myself with the politics of the colony, or . . ."

"Nevertheless," snapped King, "I could wager that you have read the scurrilous attacks that have been made upon me. The villains who have so industriously circulated these contemptible anonymous papers shall not escape, I promise you. I have in my possession at this moment a copy of one which I have reason to believe was spread abroad in Parramatta two days ago, Ensign Bayly having had it of Major Johnston, and Major Johnston of Lieutenant Hobby, and all in turn making copies and disseminating its foul calumnies still farther. You, Sir, as a private individual, may be said to be in a different position from those who hold Commissions from His Majesty, and yet seek to undermine the authority he has vested in me. But I have to require of you as a citizen such information on this scandalous affair as you may possess. I am informed that Mr. Wentworth was among those to whom Lieutenant Hobby showed this paper; have you any knowledge of that, Sir?"

Mr. Mannion, unaccustomed to being browbeaten, was quite pale with anger. He said sharply:

"I must decline all interference in . . ."

"Very good!" The Governor made a violent gesture which swept Mr. Mannion contemptuously from his calculations. "I shall make my enquiries of Mr. Wentworth himself. I propose to issue warrants for the Court Martial of those principally concerned—but make no mistake, Mr. Mannion, I'm fully conscious how little impartiality I may expect when offenders are tried by those of their own Corps, who may not themselves be guiltless of the same crimes. Yet such infamies cannot be passed over, Sir, and you may inform any of your friends who might be interested that a full report on this matter shall be sent to Lord Hobart in due course . . ."

But Mr. Mannion was tired of being harangued.

"Your Excellency will pursue such methods as seem best to you," he replied curtly. "For my part I shall attend to my own affairs. I shall not trespass further upon your time, since it appears to be fully engaged."

But the Governor had one more shot to fire, and it brought Mr. Mannion up sharply halfway to the door.

"Speaking of your own affairs, Sir, I am informed that you have on several occasions caused corporal punishment to be inflicted on your labourers at your own property, without first bringing them before a magistrate. You are no doubt familiar with the law on this matter?"

Outraged astonishment held Mr. Mannion speechless for a moment, and in that moment His Excellency said harshly: "Good-day, Sir!" and stalked out of the room without even the pretence of a bow.

*   *   *   *   *

Yet his uncompromising demeanour hid a secret dismay which grew during the ensuing weeks while he sought legal redress for the insults that had been levelled at him, and found himself hampered and circum-vented at every turn.

From Paterson no firm support was to be expected. Indeed, by the end of January the Colonel had announced that the state of his health compelled his complete retirement from all public business. It was true that a never very robust constitution had been damaged by the wound he had received from Macarthur; but a temperament which shrank from taking sides in any conflict had been even more sorely tried. The Governor strongly suspected that the Colonel was hugging an ill-health which provided him with an excuse for doing nothing.

It was with Major Johnston, therefore, that His Excellency must deal. The chaos which was produced in the colony by the overlapping of functions, by the influence of intricate factional manœuvres, and the cross-currents of personal animosities, had never seemed so mad, so unmanage-able, so unsusceptible to any processes of law, or even of common-sense, as they did at this time. Testy, gouty, bitter and bewildered, King struggled among the coils of intrigue, slander, rumour, and legal techni-calities which enmeshed him. He recalled wryly that it had been the objection of the military group to Mr. Atkins (and was not the origin of that far back through the years in a feud with Macarthur?) which had first persuaded him to make a gesture of conciliation by appointing Surgeon John Harris of the Corps to act as Deputy Judge Advocate upon Courts Martial. Yet the fact that Harris was friendly to him, and had to some extent supported official measures against the liquor traffic, had speedily drawn upon him the displeasure of his fellow-officers. Now it ill-suited them that one whom they regarded as unsympathetic should officiate at the proceedings which the Governor instituted against Hobby, Bayly, and Kemp.

King was hardly surprised, then, that Johnston's counter move should be to arrest Harris on a charge that he had disclosed the votes of the members of the Court Martial in the case of Hobby; with one stroke further proceedings were blocked, and two enemies discomfited. The very document setting forth the charge now became a source of scandal, for in naming the date upon which the surgeon was alleged to have made his wrongful disclosures, the word "ultimo" was used instead of the word "instant"—thus providing a legal flaw which King's enemies were swift to assert had been purposely introduced to nullify the proceedings. Manœuvres and machinations became ever more complex and more frenzied. Mr. Atkins, the erstwhile foe of the military, was now, by reason of his irresolute and amenable character, acceptable to them in a function where they had previously opposed him. King's appeal to him for a decision upon the legality of Johnston's action brought merely the timorous reply that in so purely a military matter he could offer no opinion.

The Governor swore; he raved and brooded and racked his brains and pored over a treatise on Courts Martial. Constant attacks of gout, which he feared was developing into an acute rheumatism, did nothing to preserve the remnants of his equanimity. The tone of his correspondence with Johnston became more and more acrimonious, and its volume mounted until he snappishly informed the Major that he would soon be obliged to continue it on brown paper. He might have added that his store of patience, even more than his store of stationery, was becoming exhausted. He realised that against this combination of ruthless obstruction and vacillating weakness he could do nothing. Forced at last to appoint Atkins in place of Harris, he was unsurprised, but bitterly resentful, when the proceedings ended in the acquittal of the officers. He hit back with an order for the release from arrest of Harris (now derisively known as "Pat Ultimo"), but he could not pretend that it was a victory. After the complications of such an affair it was a relief to turn to so simple a matter as the drafting of instructions to Lieutenant Bowen for his journey with the *Porpoise* and the *Lady Nelson* to establish a settlement in Van Diemen's Land.

*   *   *   *   *

At Beltrasna life had settled down, outwardly at least, to a more tranquil rhythm. No more was heard of Conor's return to Ireland, though Mr. Mannion spoke often, as if in duty bound, of the necessity for a more civilised environment for Miles. Conor listened, saying nothing, studying her husband with a new, cold detachment. There had been a night some weeks after her intercession for the convict Finn when, without warning, she was overwhelmed by a doubt so monstrous that she started up in bed and cried out faintly, and then clapped her hand over her mouth in terror lest Mannion should have wakened. But there was no movement, and presently she lay down again, trembling. How did she know that he had really halved Finn's punishment as he had promised? The fact that she could harbour such a doubt—that she could for a moment believe her own husband capable of such duplicity—was a final revelation to her that not only had love departed, but that its place had been taken by mistrust, dislike, and even contempt. For the thought, once formed, could not be dismissed. She could not believe him incapable of cheating her. From that time she had felt so far from him that the contact of their lives seemed accidental, and she began to live her own without any reference to him, save to evade him as an obstruction in her path.

When she found that he was, for the present, prepared to defer the question of her return to Ireland, she realised quite calmly that he no longer saw her as a nuisance, no longer wanted to be rid of her now that she was docile again, and prepared to fulfil her wifely obligations. She could be acquiescent in this new, frozen indifference, but she could not be gay. That, she observed, still calmly, did not worry him, and she understood that her vitality, her high spirits and her curiosity had seemed tiresome to him. He was better pleased with a silence which he could interpret as tranquillity, and a movement of the lips which he could count a smile.

She learned a kind of wisdom which tasted bitter, but brought her some small triumphs. She was pleasing him; he must be taught that modest as was her price for pleasing him, there *was* a price. She began to walk abroad again with Miles, or alone. When he protested she said gently with her unsmiling smile that if she were not to be permitted this small diversion, perhaps he would provide her with another? She had seen but little of the colony, she explained, and now that they had the carriage it would please her extremely, and greatly benefit her health, if she could go driving now and then. The Morgans, father and son, who had come from Ireland to be his coachman and groom were, she pointed out, steady and reliable servants. She would be completely safe, would she not, in their charge?

He frowned.

"The road to Toongabbee, my love, is scarcely worthy of the name, since Government has seen fit to direct all its energies to the making of roads towards Hawkesbury and Green Hills and Castle Hill. A carriage drive is as yet a matter of necessity rather than pleasure, surely? I propose to put some of my own men to work improving our route into Toongabbee as soon as I can spare them from more pressing tasks, and I strongly advise you to wait until . . ."

"I shall not mind the roughness, I assure you. And my expeditions would be mainly along those roads to the settlements you speak of. I'm told the scenery in the neighbourhood of Green Hills is charming. I look forward to seeing it."

He could never have suspected that there might be even the shadow of a threat in her gentle words, but he could foresee, with irritable and uneasy apprehension, the consequences of a refusal. He did not want more pining, more caprice, more tantrums . . .

So the handsome equipage of Mr. Stephen Mannion was fairly frequently to be seen turning north from Toongabbee. Sometimes Conor sat in it alone beneath her silk parasol; sometimes Miles sat beside her; sometimes the nursemaid, Bessie, dandling the year-old Julia, was her companion; occasionally Mr. Mannion himself accompanied her, or rode alongside. The carriage paid toll at the floating bridge which Andrew Thompson had built across South Creek, and Conor thought innocently: "He was a convict, and is now a man of substance and respectability—it is not always so hopeless, then, for convicts." She drove into the little village of Green Hills and saw the log granaries, the brick stores, the weatherboard house with the shingled roof where the district's commanding officer lived, and the official business of the settlement was transacted. She thought of the hut she had heard about once, where the settlers came, maddened by their desire for liquor, leaving their land uncropped to barter anything they possessed for a few mouthfuls of destroying spirits. Where was it, she wondered—still here? That man plodding across the field—those others talking in the shade of the young willows—had they drunk there . . . ?

She drove the long, rough roads, trying to pierce the surface of what she saw. Always there were convicts felling trees, and the hot, afternoon sunlight was often amber with smoke from the fires that burned their fallen trunks. Yonder was the property of the romantic Baron Verincourt de Clambe, a French gentleman whose flight from the revolution had led him at last to this distant country. He lived, so she had heard, in such retirement that even a visit from Monsieur Péron last year had not been entirely welcome, occupying himself with his farm, and with experiments to induce his cotton plants to yield coloured cottons. How strange a turn of fortune! She pondered confusedly the meaning of revolution. Grim word, already so often on men's tongues in a new land! Would the French aristocrat, having escaped one, meet another here?

The fields in those early months of the year were parched with drought, and red dust flew up from the carriage wheels to settle on Conor's delicate gown and white gloves. Sometimes she passed a gaol-gang working on the road, and felt her gaze shrink involuntarily from the sullen eyes upturned to stare at her. Sometimes a hill, a corner, a sudden downward slope, showed her settlers' huts, mean and dingy among their half-tilled fields, and her eyes searched those fields while she remembered what she had been told—that the potato crop was very poor this season, and that indeed all vegetables were like to fail from want of rain. Sometimes a woman peered from a doorway, or a few ragged children ran to a gate to stare. She drove on, taking with her the strange thought that perhaps the failure of a potato crop was more than an item of news, told casually and quickly forgotten.

Sometimes from a hilltop, when there were no huts and no unhappy human beings visible, she looked across the countryside and found her bewilderment touched with an irrational hope. Even in drought there was a hint of promise in this landscape—a promise which seemed to lie in spaciousness that led the eye on to the blue challenge of the mountains, and up to the blue infinity of the sky.

It was one day in the middle of February that she heard galloping hooves behind her carriage, and turned quickly to look back along the road they had come. A party of soldiers went by in a cloud of dust, but a young officer called to a couple of his men, and reined in to speak to her.

"Your servant, Madam. You are returning home?"

"I am, Sir," she replied in surprise.

"If you will permit me," he said, "I shall direct these men to escort your carriage to your house. There are dangerous rogues at large, Madam

—we know not quite where, but in this neighbourhood, and making, as we believe, for the mountains."

"What men are they, Sir?"

"Fifteen of them, Ma'am—convicts who came out on the *Atlas*, and who were put to labour on the Government farm at Castle Hill."

"They have escaped?"

"Yes, Ma'am, but not without committing some terrible acts of violence, for which reason I beg you to accept the escort I offer till you are safe within your own home."

She thanked him quietly, and watched him ride away. Morgan, half-turning, muttered rebelliously: "An' is it children he thinks of, Ma'am, meself an' Shawn here, an' we with muskets handy the way His Honour bids us?"

She shook her head at him absently, and he flicked the horses with his whip, still muttering. She was thinking: "They came out in the *Atlas* . . ." She was remembering the words of Surgeon Jamison, spoken across her dining-table: ". . . *withholding their rations* . . ." ". . . *the sick must lie with those that were still healthy* . . ." ". . . *heavily ironed* . . ." ". . . *necessary to keep the air scuttles closed* . . ." ". . . *a cumulating state of filthiness* . . ." ". . . *the air became so noxious* . . ."

And now they had escaped—after committing terrible acts of violence . . . What stored-up hatreds, what black memories, what bitterness had been the fatal ingredients of that violence? Clasping her hands tightly together in her lap, sitting very straight and seeing nothing, she came back to Beltrasna in her carriage with a red-coated soldier riding on either side.

*   *   *   *   *

It was not until more than a month later that Mr. Harvey returned late one evening from a journey to Sydney to find her seated by the parlour fire with her embroidery on her lap, and Miles whittling at a piece of wood, and scattering chips in the hearth. It was a dark evening of heavy cloud, and the first warning of autumn was in the air. She looked up to greet him with a smile that was kind enough, but he thought with a pang that her eyes were sad.

"You are late, Mr. Harvey, and you must be fatigued. And cold. Pray come to the fire."

"I made the journey from Sydney to Parramatta by passage-boat, Ma'am," he replied, "and you know how tedious that can be. We were to have left at eight in the morning, but it was near eleven when the boat appeared, and already growing dark when we arrived at Parramatta."

"That's nothing to complain of, Sir," Miles told him, "for I heard Papa say the passage has sometimes taken as long as twelve or thirteen hours. Did you bring the paint-box, Sir, and the pencils?"

"I did, Miles, but first I must assure myself that I have forgotten none of the commissions your Mama entrusted to me. A dozen yards of white satin ribbon, Ma'am—one hundred of the best White Chapel needles—one dozen lawn handkerchiefs for Mrs. Herbert—tape—thread—these I bought of Mr. Bevan, but he was unable to supply silk twist of the colour you described, so I enquired of Mr. Simeon Lord in the High Street, and was fortunate enough to obtain it there. And he begged me to tell you, Ma'am, that he has a supply of elegant shawls, and some very superior jaconet muslin. And I procured some writing paper also, and here is the Dutch sealing-wax, and there were some very diverting cuckoo clocks, Ma'am, which I ventured to suggest you might like to see when you are next in town, and Mr. Lord says he will be honoured to put one aside for you . . ."

She was turning the packages over as he talked, and his eager rush of words faltered before her air of listlessness. He drew a small bundle of papers from his pocket and offered them to her with a kind of nervous hopefulness.

". . . and I brought these, Ma'am . . ."

"What are they?" she asked idly.

"They are copies of the new weekly newspaper, ma'am—*The Sydney Gazette and New South Wales Advertiser.*" He added awkwardly: "I fear I have been but an indifferent bearer of news in the past, Ma'am, but now you will be able to read of all that goes on yourself, and . . ."

Miles scrambled to his feet.

"Show me, Mr. Harvey! Pray, Mama, show me!"

"Gently, Miles—you are so impetuous, my love! See, here is one for yourself, and I shall look at the others while Mr. Harvey has some supper —of which he must be greatly in need! You will join us again, Mr. Harvey, when you have supped? Mr. Mannion is writing letters, and does not wish to be disturbed."

When he had gone, she picked up one of the papers and began to glance at it. There was a column of General Orders which her eyes skimmed only half-attentively. She passed on to the third column, devoted to an address from the Editor to his public. *"The utility of a PAPER in the COLONY, as it must open a source of solid information, will, we hope, be universally felt and acknowledged. We have courted the assistance of the INGENIOUS and INTELLIGENT. We open no channel to Political Discussion or Personal Animadversion . . ."* She turned the page with a sigh and glanced at a column of Public Notices, paused for a moment over a reference in the Ship News to the *Castle of Good Hope*, *". . . the largest ship that has ever entered this port, and measures about 1000 tons . . ."* Then, passing to the third page, she found herself looking at a column headed "FUGITIVES," and bent with sudden attention over the poorly-printed sheet.

"On Thursday, 15th ultimo, Fifteen Labouring Men fled from the agricultural settlement at Castle Hill, after having committed many acts of violence and atrocity . . ."

"Mama," announced Miles from his seat on the hearthrug, "there is a rhyme in this paper."

"Is there, Miles?"

"They at first forcibly entered the dwelling house of M. Declamb, which they ransacked and stripped of many articles . . ."

"It is a riddle, Mama."

"Indeed, my love?"

"*They next proceeded to the farm houses of Bradley and Bean at Balkham Hills. Mrs. Bradley's servant they wantonly and inhumanly discharged a pistol at, the contents of which have so shattered his face as to render him a ghastly spectacle . . .*"

"Would you not like to guess it?"

"In a moment, Miles . . ."

"*In Mrs. Baines house they gave a loose to sensuality equally brutal and unmanly. Resistance was of no avail, for their rapacity was unbridled . . .*"

"I shall read it then—pray listen, Mama."

"*Two of the depredators were taken into custody upon the second day after their flight near the Hawkesbury Road, by Mr. Jamison, Jnr., assisted by A. Thompson, Chief Constable at Hawkesbury, and a party of military who had been despatched in pursuit of them . . .*"

Miles cried impatiently:

"But you aren't listening, Mama!"

"*On the 23rd ultimo eleven more of the desperadoes were secured by a party of military and constables between Hawkesbury and the mountains . . .*"

Miles knelt beside her, pulling at her sleeve, half-laughing and half-indignant.

"Mama! Don't you want to hear?"

She said vaguely:

"Why yes, my love, of course . . ."

He read out:

> " '*We are little airy creatures*
> *All of diff'rent voice and features,*
> *One of us in GLASS is set,*
> *One of us you'll find in JET.*
> *T'other you may find in TIN,*
> *And the fourth a BOX within.*
> *If the fifth you should pursue,*
> *It can never fly from YOU.*' "

She heard nothing until the last lines chimed with her thought, and made her look up at him strangely. Pursuit, flight. . . . She thought: "Between Hawkesbury and the mountains. . . . They were fleeing to the mountains, but people die there, it is well known—did they not know? They discharged a pistol in the face of a man . . . sensuality . . . rapacity . . . what kind of men are these, are they men or beasts, and how do men become beasts . . . ? If my carriage had met with them in the road . . . ? A pistol discharged in Morgan's face, Shawn overpowered, and I . . . ? They came out in the *Atlas*. . . . Was I wrong to pity them . . . ?"

Miles was saying impatiently:

"Well, can you not guess? It is easy!"

"Guess, my love . . . ?"

"The riddle, Mama!"

"Ah, yes, the riddle . . ." She stood up, letting the papers slide from her lap to the floor; she went to the fire and stood before it, holding her hands out to the blaze and rubbing them together nervously. "But I am . . . very bad at riddles, Miles. Tell me the answer, love."

He came to stand beside her, and she looked with a kind of wonder at his ruddy, handsome, laughing face. "Vowels, of course!" he cried triumphantly. "Don't you see? A is in glass, and E in jet, and . . ."

"I see," she said.

When Mr. Harvey returned and Miles had retired to bed she took up her embroidery frame and spoke slowly, keeping her eyes on it.

"I learn from these papers that they have captured the absconders from Castle Hill, and that the trial has already taken place."

"Yes, Madam, they were tried a week ago or thereabouts. Some were acquitted on one charge, but detained on another, and all were finally condemned to death." He added quickly: "Doubtless some of them will be reprieved."

"One declared—so this paper says—that his reason for absconding was that he hoped to cross the mountains, and so be reunited with his family." She looked up at him—a quick, bewildered glance. "Could that be true, Mr. Harvey? Could he be so ignorant as to imagine that?"

"They *are* ignorant, Ma'am—yet it may have been no more than a crafty attempt to win compassion. Who can tell?"

She put her work down suddenly and cried:

"Is there no end to misery and cruelty and punishment . . . ?"

Startled, he answered:

"Madam, indeed I understand and honour the tenderness of the female heart, and I will not deny that sometimes I myself. . . . But these are felons who, though Heaven knows objects of pity, must for the safety of society be . . ."

She interrupted as if she had not heard him:

"I have been much shielded from the sight of suffering, but I have seen something of it here, and the thought of it has—greatly agitated my mind. And I have felt—though no doubt you will think me fanciful, Mr. Harvey—that in so new and large a land there should surely be decent subsistence for all, and even . . . freedom for all . . . ?"

"Freedom?" he repeated in astonishment. "For felons?"

"Ah!" she cried with sudden vehemence. "What *are* felons? I thought I knew, Sir. I thought they were breakers of the law. Yet here do we not know—is it not openly acknowledged—that people in high situations of trust and responsibility daily flout the law? Yet they are at liberty, they are held respectable, they are even wealthy and esteemed . . ." She looked at him again with a smile that hurt him. "It is a riddle, is it not? I have just told Miles that I am not good at riddles."

In the long, heavy silence that followed he felt again the burden of his inadequacy. He longed for a flow of convincing argument to comfort her, but knew of none; and after a time, busy with her needle again, she asked:

"Do you think that freedom hath been hunted round the world, Mr. Harvey?"

He stared at her in amazement. Long ago—when he had encountered the enigmatic Mr. Palmer—he had seemed to hear this same note of quotation in a voice, and he stammered uncertainly:

"I hardly . . . indeed, Ma'am, I should hope . . . why do you ask?"

"I read it," she sighed. "It was written in a little book which my husband—which I saw once. It said: *'Ye that dare oppose not only the tyranny but the tyrant, stand forth!'* And then it said that freedom hath been hunted round the globe."

He said slowly:

"That is strange. I met a man once who said something of the same kind, Madam. He said: *'The time is now come when you must either gather round the fabric of liberty to support it, or to your eternal infamy let it fall to the ground . . .'* I forget the rest." He studied her bent head uneasily and asked: "What was this book, Madam? Who was the author?"

"I do not know its author," she replied, "but there were the words 'Common Sense' at the top of one page. Do you think that can have been the title of the book? It seems a strange one, does it not?"

Now he was really disturbed. He said:

"That was the name of a book by the notorious Thomas Paine, Madam." He felt oddly guilty and a little afraid. What were they doing—he, a respectable if poor young man, and she, the most gently-born of ladies—sitting here repeating to each other the words of two outcasts? Tom Paine—rebel, atheist, the most reviled of men, a veritable monster— and Thomas Fysshe Palmer, exiled for sedition, for plotting against the peace of the realm . . . ! He said hastily:

"But it could not, surely, be the same book. Mr. Mannion would never give you . . ."

"He did not give it to me," she said simply; "he threw it in the fire. I could only find some small pieces unburnt. I think I have heard of this Thomas Paine, Mr. Harvey, but I had thought of him as a very evil man. Yet he wrote of happiness and misery and tyranny in words which seemed to me noble and enlightened."

Agitated, Mark rose and began to walk about the room. He must have been quite a small child, he thought, when he had first heard the name of Tom Paine. Even then it had been associated with head-shakings over the rebellious behaviour of the American colonies. And yet he had a memory of having heard later of Mr. Paine in England, respected, almost fêted. . . . And then again, later yet, when the earth still seemed to be trembling with the reverberations of the Bastille's fall, and alarm spread through an unrestful England, people had begun to talk of a book which spoke disturbingly of the rights of man. And Mark remembered, too, that he had once actually seen a scarecrow effigy of Tom Paine burned in the market-place to the accompaniment of hoots and maledictions.

What was the truth? Why was a man in one short lifetime so condemned —then courted—then loathed and feared? Why had he been hailed almost as a saint in France, and then imprisoned? Mr. Harvey returned to his chair, wondering how it was that the fierce and demanding spirit of such a man should find its way incongruously into this quiet room at the world's end, into the minds and the conversation of himself and Mrs. Stephen Mannion.

"I have not read his works, Ma'am," he said at last, "but there was much talk of him in England in the years before I left. And it would seem that he created public unrest, and that he was an atheist . . ."

She shook her head.

"I do not think he can have been an atheist, Mr. Harvey, for one scrap of paper I read spoke of God in a way which I think was no atheist's way. Though it spoke also of kings," she admitted with a faint sigh, "in a manner which was surely—unbecoming."

She put her work aside and made a movement as if to rise. He was immediately on his feet, gathering her scattered trifles from the table and the floor. She said gently:

"I thank you, Sir. I am a little tired." Halfway to the door she glanced back at him. "I fear I am—very ignorant. Good-night, Mr. Harvey."

She was gone, and he sat there alone, pondering with distress upon her words and her tone. He had heard many women confess their ignorance —but smilingly, coyly, as if inviting their hearers to recognise it as the crowning touch of perfection to their helpless and alluring femininity. She had spoken of hers sombrely, with sadness and a painful note of shame. His desire was only to serve her—but could he help her here? He realised with humility and frustration that for all his Latin, he was hardly less ignorant than she.

*   *   *   *   *

Miles Mannion, seated between his tutor and his stepmother in the Church of St. John in Parramatta, stared round at the congregation with so frank and lively a curiosity that his father leaned across to whisper a reproof.

"Pray sit still, Miles!"

He said "Yes, Papa," and obeyed for a few moments, but it was interesting to see so many people all at once, and since most of them were behind him, how could he see them without turning his head? He turned it. It was a great occasion, this first celebration of Divine Service in the imposing new church. The soldiers were there, stiff and splendid in their scarlet, and the orphans, dim and decorous in their black, with downcast eyes and their sharp-eyed preceptresses beside them. All the foremost citizens of the colony were there, the ladies in their best gowns and their newest bonnets, and the silence was a rustle with faint sounds of movement—the flutter of turned pages, the whisper of silks, the scraping of shoes, occasional carefully-muted coughs. The Reverend Mr. Marsden claimed Miles' attention for a few moments at least. *"Behold, Heaven and the heaven of heavens cannot contain Thee,"* he proclaimed, *"how much less this house that I have built."*

Miles was impressed. He asked clearly of his tutor:

"Did Mr. Marsden build it, Sir?"

"Sh-h-h!" said Mr. Harvey.

Miles sighed and stared round him again. He did not see why God should not dwell here, for the building seemed quite large and splendid enough, and why else was a church called the house of God? But he never spent undue thought upon problems, and was content to enjoy the novelty of a ceremony such as he had never attended before.

Mr. Mannion, seated on the other side of his wife, was thinking with annoyance that his younger son was no better than a barbarian. The years had flashed by, and the infant whose life had been bought with its mother's death was suddenly a lad of thirteen, handsome, robust, undisciplined, and incredibly naïve. It was, his father reflected, precisely because he had always been so perfectly happy at Beltrasna, that he had been—overlooked. Not even to himself would Mr. Mannion use the word "neglected," but this first excursion of his son into polite society had made him realise that the boy was indeed most shockingly unversed in its manners and customs. Nursed and tended by a convict woman, having no playmates save her children and a native girl, he had grown up in almost total ignorance of those conventions by which the gently-born governed their lives, and it was high time he was sent to England to learn them. A glance showed Mr. Mannion that Miles' head was again incorrigibly craning for a better view of the soldiery, and through his irritation shot a gleam of paternal pride. For whatever the lad's shortcomings might be, no one could deny the handsomeness of his fresh, tanned skin, his fine, black eyebrows, his shining, fair hair, and his vividly blue eyes.

"My love," Mannion whispered to his wife, "can you not prevail on Miles to sit still? His behaviour is outrageous."

Conor's gloved hand rested on the boy's knee for a moment. He looked up at her, met her reproachful eyes and the slight, admonitory shake of her head, and smiled dazzlingly. He tried to whisper, but he was accustomed to shouting in the Beltrasna fields.

"Where does the other gentleman talk, Mama? The Roman gentleman?"

Heads turned; eyes stared; Conor blushed, and Mr. Mannion, his face a trifle red, gazed sternly straight in front of him. Yesterday, when they had visited Mr. Marsden, that gentleman had spoken at some length, and with considerable indignation, of the permission granted by the Governor to one of the exiled Roman priests to perform the Catholic service. He had not expected, he declared austerely, to see the kingdom of Satan strengthened in this manner. But who would have supposed Miles to be attending to such a conversation . . . ? Mannion shot an exasperated and rather apprehensive glance at his son who, he suspected, was quite capable of enquiring loudly whether they might not sample the discourse of the Roman gentleman next Sunday; but Miles, to his relief, was wriggling round in his seat again to observe the congregation. Far better, thought his father grimly, that he should be guilty of a little indecorous fidgeting, than that contemplation of Mr. Marsden should inspire him to further embarrassing questions. But there remained no doubt at all that he must be speedily removed from a life which afforded him no opportunity to learn the behaviour of a gentleman.

From Parramatta they went on to Sydney, for the opening of the church had been merely the preliminary to a social round. At the home of Colonel and Mrs. Paterson Miles continued to find his holiday both novel and enjoyable. He liked to go shopping with the ladies in Chapel Row, for while they examined silks, tapes, thread, stockings and snuff-boxes, he could stand at the door and watch the people going by—sailors from the ships in port, and soldiers, and waggons loaded with bricks from the kilns, and men pushing wheelbarrows, and convict gangs going off to work, and women with baskets who stopped to gossip with each other, and sometimes a few natives, clad in odd scraps of clothing, who glanced sideways with bright, dark eyes that were like Dilboong's.

There was the harbour to look at too, and sometimes to cross in rowing-boats when a little picnic party was arranged; and there was the great day when Captain Kent gave a fête on board the *Buffalo*. Miles was not, of course, permitted to attend, but he saw the ship dressed with colours, its yards manned, and the Governor and Mrs. King going aboard to a salute of fifteen guns. At night he saw Colonel and Mrs. Paterson and Mama and Papa and several other ladies and gentlemen depart for the festivities, and glowed with satisfaction because, for all the magnificence of his uniform, the Colonel was not nearly as handsome as Papa; and Mama in her new gown of blue satin was far lovelier than any of the other ladies. He saw the ship, gay with lights, lying off the shore, he heard the sound of music coming across the water from the band of the New South Wales Corps, and he felt for the first time the excitement of belonging to that exclusive world of gentlefolk for whom such splendours and delights were reserved.

But the most enjoyable incident occurred unexpectedly during a visit to Government House which, at first, seemed to be taking the same shape as some others which he had suffered, when he was expected to sit quietly on his chair, speak only when he was spoken to, and wring what interest he could from the interminable conversations of his elders.

On this occasion, however, little Miss Elizabeth King was present, and kept plaguing her Mama to allow her to go and see someone called Robert. Miles, though maintaining a suitable condescension towards a little girl less than half his own age, became intrigued. Under cover of a burst of laughter from the ladies and gentlemen, he asked her in a whisper:

"Who is Robert?"

She looked up at him in surprise.

"His papa makes the *Gazette*, and sometimes Robert helps."

Miles was more intrigued than ever. He was a faithful reader of the *Gazette*, but he never paused to wonder who made it, or indeed to realise that it was "made" at all. It was one of those things like clothes, or carpets, or silver forks, which simply appeared. He nudged Elizabeth.

"Ask your Mama again. Ask if I may go with you."

Elizabeth, at six, had learned that the desires of guests were readily attended to. She pulled at her mother's sleeve and renewed her request in an adroitly amended form:

"Mama, the boy wants to go and see Robert."

And thus, within a few minutes, Miles found himself conducted by his small hostess to the doorway of an annexe at the back of the house, and staring into a most strange and interesting room. It was wildly untidy, and rather dirty, and it smelled of ink and paper. Miles' attention was instantly captured by the sight of a boy of about eight, wearing a leather apron round his waist and several inky smears across his cheeks, energetically manipulating a wooden screwpress, and paying no attention whatever to the loud exclamations of protest and despair which were filling the room. These, Miles observed, came from a man who was seated at a littered table, running one hand distractedly through his thick, brown hair, and with the other irritably flicking over the pages of a sheaf of papers which lay before him.

"Am I," he was enquiring rhetorically of the room at large, "forever to find whole passages torn from my copy, leaving my sentences bleeding like mangled limbs, and the sense of them utterly destroyed? If my prose is to be dismembered, disembowelled and rent asunder," he cried, rising and shaking the pages dramatically above his head, "can it not at least be done with some regard to the rules of grammar and syntax, or must I myself . . . ?"

The sight of his young visitors stopped him in mid-sentence. He came and stood before them, his arms akimbo, and Elizabeth piped up:

"Good-day, Mr. Howe."

He answered rather heavily:

"Good-day to you, Miss Elizabeth." He turned his brown eyes to Miles; with the fading from them of excited indignation, they looked tired and mournful. "Good-day, young Sir. You have come to watch us at our labours?"

Elizabeth had already slipped past them to stand beside the boy at the press, who continued his work with no more than a glance at her, so Miles responded:

"Yes, Sir, if you please." He added simply, without tactful intention: "I read the *Gazette* every week."

"Indeed?" Mr. Howe eyed him solemnly from beneath his brows. "And what is your name, young gentleman, if I may enquire?"

"Miles Mannion, Sir."

"Ah. And what portion of the *Gazette* do you find the most enjoyable, Master Miles?"

Miles considered this seriously.

"It is all interesting, Sir, but I read the rhymes first—like the one about the Irishman who fished under the bridge when it was raining, because he thought the fishes would go there to get out of the wet." He laughed heartily. "And I was greatly interested in your account of the gentleman who rode into town from the Hawkesbury in three hours, Sir, for I live near the river myself."

"I am happy," Mr. Howe remarked dryly, "to find so enthusiastic a reader." He glanced down at the papers in his hand, and his eyes began to snap again. "The task of producing a newspaper is no light one, and it is gratifying to know that one's efforts are appreciated." He took a few restless steps up and down, and the conversational note of his voice faded once more into the declamatory. "I flatter myself that I am a skilled tradesman, young Sir, having served from boyhood as my father's apprentice—as my son Robert will serve me. But I have many difficulties to contend with, I assure you. My supplies of paper are scanty and uncertain, my press is inadequate, my subscribers do not always discharge their financial obligations as promptly as I could wish, my salary is niggardly, and my copy . . ."

He paused before Miles again and thrust the papers beneath the boy's nose, tapping them fiercely with his finger.

". . . my copy, prepared with the most loving care, and couched, I venture to assert, in elegant and cultivated language, is subjected to a rigorous official scrutiny, and frequently returned to me so mutilated that all is to do again! But do I complain . . . ?"

"Yes, Sir," replied Miles truthfully. Mr. Howe looked sharply at him, as sharply from him to Elizabeth, and became suddenly taciturn.

"No, my young friend," he said sombrely, "I do not complain. I endeavour to discharge my duties so as to provide elevation and enlightenment for all, and give offence to none." He turned back to his desk with a sigh, saying over his shoulder:

"You would like to watch my son at work, perhaps? Despite his tender years, I trust he will shortly be my permanent assistant."

Robert did not seem to share his father's loquacity. He continued to work, paying no attention to his respectful audience of two. For ten absorbing minutes, before a servant came to conduct them back to the drawing-room, Miles stood and watched the sheets of the *Gazette* come wet and inky-smelling from the press, and found himself envying the lad who was engaged upon so important and interesting a task.

* * * * *

To return to Beltrasna after this exciting interlude might have seemed to some boys a trial. But Miles, throughout his long life, was to possess the gift of putting yesterday behind him, of ignoring to-morrow, and of living ardently in a to-day which never failed to entertain him. Moreover, he was almost at once informed that his stay at home would be brief; he was to go to England as soon as a passage could be arranged.

"Your grandmama and Aunt Frances," explained his father, "have both mentioned several times that they expect me to send you home soon. Indeed, your aunt was kind enough to say in her last letter that she looks forward to receiving you in her home in London, as she has done for your brother. I propose that you shall go in the first vessel available."

"Yes, Papa," agreed Miles willingly. "What vessel will it be?"

"I understand that the *Venus* is to sail shortly, and Mr. Harvey is at present making enquiries in town . . ."

"Will Mr. Harvey come too, Papa?"

"Pray do not interrupt, Miles. No, I shall still have need of Mr. Harvey's services for a time, so he will not accompany you. Meanwhile you must pay particular attention to your studies, and endeavour to mend your manners. You would not, I suppose, wish your aunt and your brother to find you an ignoramus and a barbarian?"

Miles answered dutifully: "No, Papa." But to so robust and self-confident a nature the suggestion that anyone might regard him with disapproval was not convincing. Nor was his father entirely justified in his fears that the colony could provide no means at all of schooling a youth to recognise his superior station in life, and conduct himself accordingly. Miles had learned much from his sojourn in Sydney.

His preoccupation with the present made him receptive of its impressions; he not only observed events, manners, and customs, but absorbed their implications, and even the much-despised colonial society had sent him back to his old environment with a new attitude. He understood now that his home was not merely a child's playground of spacious fields and flowing river, but a farm—an enterprise. He had observed the importance of wealth, and noticed that there were subtle grades not only of gentility, but of servitude, and he applied his new knowledge to the household of Beltrasna. Cousin Bertha, he now perceived, was a grade lower in importance than Papa and Mama and himself and Julia, but a grade higher than Mr. Harvey. Here gentility ended, but in the lower realm of servitude Ellen, as housekeeper, jealously claimed precedence over Bessie, as Miss Julia's nurse. But Bessie, as a free woman, counted herself superior to Ellen, as an ex-convict, and there were sometimes interesting squabbles. Both of them clearly stood higher than Emma, who was merely a housemaid. Miles had always known that Andy and Maria were servants, and Dilboong a creature even lower than they—as low as it was possible to be, and still remain human; but now he felt it too, and his masterfulness, which had once been but the expression of a vigorous and dominating character, became conscious. He had always ordered them about, and they had always obeyed, but now he did so in the knowledge of adult authority and example behind him. He was no bully, and they were no rebels, so the change was less one of action than of atmosphere. Indeed, this adjustment in their relationship had been taking place gradually for a long time, and the new element in it was merely the finality of their acceptance. Maria had been steadily withdrawing—or withdrawn— during the last year or two as she was claimed more and more by household tasks. Andy, for all his immature body and undeveloped mind, was now accounted of an age to make his own way in the world, and Mr. Mannion—having looked him over with repugnance, and decided that he would never be anything but an inefficient drudge—had recently found him employment with a settler at Green Hills.

Dilboong, now twelve, was the only one of the children whose status remained quite unchanged—if one so very lowly could be said to have a status at all. Yet it was to her that Miles still turned when he sought non-adult companionship, treating her with a lordly and good-natured indulgence, as he treated his pony and his dog, and accepting her humble, wordless adoration as natural. She still hovered round his chair sometimes when he was at his lessons, and stole a glance at his books when she could. She had mastered her domestic duties, and performed them, for the most part, well enough, though she was apt to fall suddenly into tranced idleness, staring blankly before her, and singing softly to herself. The most menial tasks of the kitchen still fell to her lot, but when these were performed she had others. Occasionally she was permitted to tend the baby Julia, whom she loved with a passionate devotion. She had become Cousin Bertha's special attendant, fetching and carrying for the old lady, cleaning and dusting her room, standing beside her on summer afternoons to ply a fan, rubbing the knotted, blue-veined hands when rheumatic pains tortured them. "She is a good child," sighed Cousin Bertha. "She has a gentle touch, and she moves quietly."

Dilboong, if not happy, was most of the time content. She had never known, and therefore hardly missed the spontaneous positive happiness which characterised her people; and a kind word from Conor, a pat on the head from Cousin Bertha, a grave smile from Mr. Harvey, an hour or two with Julia, or—best of all—admittance even for a few moments to Miles' company, were her all-sufficient joys. Ellen was her task-mistress, from whom scoldings, and sometimes blows, were to be expected, but during the last year she had become nervous of Maria, and sharply afraid of Andy. The physical and psychological signs of his adolescence had filled her with an obscure dread; he followed her, teased her, pinched her, pulled her hair, told tales on her, and maliciously frustrated her panic-stricken efforts to avoid him. She had wept with relief when he departed.

But Maria was still there—a big, clumsy girl of fifteen who looked older, and who made Dilboong uneasy by being two different people. In the house about her duties she was dumb, hardworking, respectful to her betters, neat and negative in her black dress and her white apron, her tow-coloured hair concealed under a mob-cap, her pale blue eyes expressionless. But in the kitchen at night when the work was done, she changed. The discarding of that starched white armour of apron revealed a body thickening towards an awkward and undisciplined maturity; the staid manner dissolved into a kind of suppressed violence that found vent sometimes in loud laughter, sometimes in storms of tears, sometimes in fierce quarrels with her mother. Between these two there was now a relationship so intense in its alternating moods, so vehement in its contradictory revelations, that Dilboong feared them as her people feared the unpredictable and inexplicable vagaries of the evil spirits.

For Ellen, too, this was a period of readjustment. Her maternal emotions had always been most strongly concentrated upon her firstborn, her lost, rebellious Johnny, and she had resented her employer's high-handed disposal of Andy less because it took him from her than because it underlined once more his authority and her dependence. But into her attitude towards Maria there had crept a tormenting conflict. For her daughter was no longer a child, but a fast maturing girl for whom men loitered round the kitchen door, and at whom they looked more often than at herself. In all her life Ellen had known no rapture, no excitement, no release of tension or taste of sensuous joy save in sexual passion, and now she grew bitter and afraid. She was no longer young—and yet not so old that she could confront with equanimity a life from which that one fiery streak of excitement had faded; she was not ready yet for the sunset of her days. The sight of Maria turning to meet those adventures which were receding from herself, both enraged and titillated her—goaded her to abuse one moment, and to sly innuendo the next, and often kept her weeping far into the night.

Ever since the murder of Merrett she had known that Mannion was done with her for ever. She had cared nothing for the overseer. He was a brute, but he was her own kind of brute, and even at his most brutal he had angered and humiliated her less than the gentlemanly lover whose assumption that he could step into her life and out again as he chose, had stirred her long-cherished resentment to hatred. Merrett's death had left her with no lover at all—and now the men about the farm looked not at her, but at Maria.

And Miles was going away. He had been her foster-child, and something in his beauty had stirred her heart a little. Robbed of the emotional outlet of sex, finding herself deprived by one means or another of all those with whom she had felt some kind of personal bond, her thoughts turned more and more to Johnny. Sometimes a mental picture of him—always as an eight-year-old child—appeared to her so vividly that tears sprang to her eyes, and her hands fumbled at their work. A strange melting of her heart came with this indulgence of a grief which sprang from real love; her mood softened and her bitterness fell away from her with this capitulation to the one deep and genuine emotion of her life. Sometimes she tasted the curiously poignant pleasure of thinking tenderly, and of discovering within herself embryonic pities and perceptions.

Such moods were rare and transient, but she carried something from them back into the harsh and hardened cynicism of her normal attitudes. They taught her, for example, to feel a fleeting compassion for that unhappiness in her mistress which she had long observed with mingled contempt and satisfaction. They brought her the bewildering notion that Ellen, the ex-convict, and Mrs. Stephen Mannion were of sufficiently similar clay to suffer similarly from loneliness. Her hatred of Mannion, and her own hardly-won knowledge of his capacity to wound, made her watch her mistress with a gleam of pitying comprehension. "Rich she may be," thought Ellen, "and young and handsome too, but I wouldn't stand in her shoes! I know where they pinch!"

*   *   *   *   *

Mrs. King peeped round the doorway.

"Are you not done yet, my love? Mercy on me, you have no fire! What was Jane about? You must be half frozen! I shall send . . ."

From his desk the Governor gestured impatiently without turning his head.

"I'm not cold—I don't want a fire. I shall be done shortly, and in the meantime pray don't allow me to be disturbed."

Mrs. King, a sensible woman, withdrew softly without argument, but her expression was troubled as she returned to the parlour and the cheerful blaze of gum-logs on the hearth. For she had seen that her husband was not writing, not reading, not working at all, but merely sitting with his elbows on the paper-strewn desk, staring gloomily in front of him. She sighed as she took up the latest number of the *Gazette*, and tried to fix her attention on an article dealing with the interesting medical experiment of inoculation for the Cow Pock which was being tried by the Assistant-Surgeon upon some of the orphans; but she was distressed, and her ears were alert for sounds of movement from the other room.

There were none. King still sat at his desk, fingering his papers absently, his mind pricked on by a word or a name here, and a sentence there, from one harassing thought to another. For almost the first time in his life he was a prey to serious doubts. Not even to his wife did he express them, save in that manner well known to wives, and explicit as any words—in a sharper temper, in small outbursts of irritation, in moody silences. Indeed, they were largely beyond expression, even to himself. His normal energy, founded less upon robust health than on a restless temperament, a goading ambition, and a touchy pride which made him seek to assert himself by continual activity, had been depleted by his illness during the height of the summer. He was physically tired, and in moments such as this when weariness called his body to a halt, his mind was left vulnerable to a swarm of misgivings.

Ambition had been alarmed by the realisation of how ruthless was the enmity of his military opponents, and pride intolerably wounded by the methods they had recently used to show it. He knew that, formal as outward relationships might appear, not a soul in the colony was unaware that a contest was being waged which had all the savage and rancorous vulgarity of a brawl. He understood now that each new incident in the vendetta was less important for itself than as a pretext to add fuel to the flames. He suspected, for example, that if he had been more generally complaisant towards the officers, there might not have been so bitter an opposition to his appointment of emancipated convicts to form his personal bodyguard; that Captain Piper might not have so haughtily declined to have them under his command; that Colonel Paterson might not have been so peevishly outraged by the sight of them in uniform; that Major Johnston might not have so roundly declared that the Corps would suffer degradation by the admission of ex-felons as soldiers. Under the sway of a Governor who placed no obstacles in their path, these gentlemen, he thought cynically, would still have deplored such an innovation—but the raised eyebrow would have been followed by the shrug.

And he knew by now that his fears for the safety of the despatches he had sent home concerning the Paterson-Macarthur duel had been well-founded. Despite all his precautions, they had been stolen; when the despatch box was opened in London, they were not there. A feeling of hopelessness had descended upon him, and a note of it had crept into a private letter to Sir Joseph Banks. How could one contend with such unscrupulousness? *"The plan was too well laid, and bound with ill-got gold to fail,"* he wrote bitterly. *"Let the villain enjoy the success of his infamy."* He began to feel as impatient to be rid of his command as he had once been to assume it. His fingers, turning over the papers on his desk, paused on a copy of his recent letter to Lord Hobart, into which he had interpolated what was in effect a cry for help. He glanced through it now, anxiously obsessed by the knowledge that the home authorities would not for ever suffer the colony to be rent between two opposing factions. He had explained that only his sense of responsibility, and his consciousness of the uproar which such an act would precipitate, had prevented him from calling out his enemies for personal satisfaction on the field of honour. He had begged that a commission might be appointed to enquire into the state of the colony, and into his own actions. *"To the members of that tribunal,"* he had written almost desperately, *"I shall most readily submit the whole of my conduct, public and private."*

Yet lacking confidence that this request would be granted, he had played his last card. He had humbly implored that if a Commission should be considered inadvisable, he might be given leave of absence to return to England and submit his case for His Lordship's personal consideration. But privately his attitude was less humble than increasingly resentful. He told himself, as Hunter had done before him, that those distant powers were too distant to feel the urgency of his needs. They required of him only that he govern the country according to their instructions, without plaguing them overmuch with requests, complaints, and bills.

Only that . . . ! He threw the letter down with an angry and unmirthful laugh. Obey instructions. Establish agriculture—without ploughs, without trained farmers, without an adequate supply of tools! Make the settlers independent—but avoid conflict with the military trading monopoly which controls their only market, the Commissary's store! Suppress the liquor traffic—but uphold the prestige of His Majesty's forces, which harbour the chief traffickers! Conciliate the natives—but build your towns and settle your farmers upon their hunting-grounds! Maintain harmonious relations with all—while Macarthur intrigues, and Johnston obstructs, and Paterson wavers; while Hobby and his friends circulate scurrilous rhymes; while the Captain of H.M.S. *Glatton* requests pardon for a female convict so that he may cohabit with her on the voyage home, and finds himself bitterly affronted by a refusal; while to please one is to offend another, and friendships are killed by scandals, and the courts of law become an arena for incessant personal feuds . . . !

The courts of law . . .

King set his elbows on the desk and dropped his head on to his hands. He seemed from day to day and from month to month to labour in a maze of legalities, and he knew himself untrained in such matters. Appeals from the verdicts of the Court of Civil Jurisdiction were so frequent that they occupied a formidable amount of his time; nor could he be unaware that Judge Advocate Atkins, upon whom he must rely for advice, was himself far from being a legal expert. How could justice be dispensed, the Governor asked himself bitterly, without the assistance of people properly trained to the law?

The sight of a letter he had just received from that arrogant and troublesome fellow, Sir Henry Brown Hayes, stirred his resentment into a flare of rage. He snatched it up and re-read it angrily. Sir Henry had done nothing but protest ever since his arrival, and he was still protesting. His application recently to establish a Freemasons' Lodge had been refused—and he had attempted to establish it all the same. He seemed to imagine, King thought wrathfully, that his wealth and social standing nullified the fact that he was a convict! Yet even while he glared at Sir Henry's letter, his thoughts were using it mainly as a point of departure towards another problem. The military faction was not the only one whose enmity disturbed him. Not the least tormenting aspect of this fantastic community was the manner in which all social values were upset, and contradictions which challenged all accepted conventions a daily commonplace. There were individuals—like this man, Hayes—whose positions in the colony were such that a kind of confusion was engendered by their very presence. They would not permit society to solidify into the appropriate and time-honoured patterns. They could not be classified. They varied in personal character, in social background, in profession, in creed, and in their attitudes to their fate. Yet in the Governor's mind they formed an awkward and disconcerting group, for (though some were convicts, and some political exiles) none of them was here from choice, and none of them belonged to those lower orders whose involuntary presence in a penal colony seemed natural and fitting.

Their status on the one hand as beings superior to ordinary lower-class felons, and on the other as beings inferior to free men, made them difficult enough. But having penned them within this tiresome and unsatisfactory grouping, His Excellency could not but feel that they were less a group than a collection of unpredictable individuals who, by their mere existence in such an invidious position, threatened the stability of his little world. There were doctors among them, lawyers, scholars, priests, ministers, a baronet, and at least one poet. And it was the poet who had jumped to his mind while he was brooding over legal difficulties, and remained there while the sight of Sir Henry's letter deflected his surface thoughts.

For the poet was also a lawyer, and, King suspected, a better lawyer than the Judge Advocate, whose clerk and assistant he was. The sense of grievance which vexed the Governor was never so strong as when he contemplated these people who embodied in their own persons the bizarre contradictions which made his colony such a nightmare to govern. He felt peevishly that a lawyer such as Mr. Michael Massey Robinson had little right to be a poet; but that he should be a blackmailer also was outrageous, and that necessity should place and hold a blackmailer in a respectable position, quite intolerable. That a gentleman of title and fortune such as Sir Henry Brown Hayes should also be a convicted felon was a shameful blow at the prestige of titles and fortunes. That ministers and scholars should be guilty of sedition, was a foul attack upon the respectability of both godliness and learning. Such people could not but be a bewildering and infuriating embarrassment to a Governor who was expected to build a neat, orderly, and exactly-graded society.

He had not been given orderly and exactly-graded people to build with. And even those who arrived still classifiable were apt to become displaced as if by some malignant magic of the land, so that soldiers were less soldiers than traders, landowners and politicians; sailors became farmers; farmers became destitute and drifted to the towns; ex-forgers flourished; pickpockets became constables; distinctions faded, and new distinctions arose; wealth was no longer related to birth, position, or even respectability; honour left those citadels where it traditionally dwelt, and appeared incongruously in unexpected quarters. And as if all this were not enough, he must also receive these godly agitators, these erudite rebels, these titled felons, these blackmailing, poetic lawyers, these unplaceable enormities, these sociological monsters . . . !

He was never quite sure what they were up to. One thing only he knew of them—that (with the possible exception of Dr. Redfern, whose impulsive youth had so regrettably betrayed him into expressing sympathy with mutineers) they felt no kindliness toward himself, the representative of the Government which held them captive. How much influence did they wield? To what extent were they still propagating their infamous republican sentiments? What transactions were there between that sly fellow, Holt, and the pestilential Mr. Margarot? With whom did they correspond in England, and what accounts of the colony did they send? Had he been unwise in permitting Father Dixon to perform his clerical duties? Might these—and Sir Henry's Freemasonry—be artful covers for the unlawful assemblies which he had so rigidly prohibited? His Excellency, driving his anxious thoughts through a labyrinth of such questions, was tempted to feel that the consistent, organised animosity of the military faction was less nerve-racking than this hypothetical, subterranean plotting about which he could only guess.

He rose abruptly, his mind suddenly invaded by the memory of a letter he had received from Monsieur Baudin. He felt cold now, and scowled at the empty fireplace. It was May, and another summer was past. He went across to the long windows, opened them, stepped out on to the verandah, and stood there rubbing his chilled fingers together and looking down across the garden to where the black water glittered faintly in the starlight, and upwards to where the stars themselves twinkled with a remote and chilly purity in the black sky.

At night, when darkness robbed the town of much of its reality, reducing it to a few straight silhouettes of buildings, and a few points of yellow light, he sometimes felt again the old, half-forgotten sensations of a dozen years ago. Listening. Waiting. Staring into the dark. Wondering and guessing. Listening again. Holding one's breath to listen, for surely no silence could be so profound, so empty as this? And knowing that for all its silence it did hold voices; that for all its emptiness, it was peopled; that somewhere the night hid human beings as dark and enigmatic as itself . . .

And all the time Baudin's letter plucked at his thoughts as importunate fingers might pluck at a sleeve. He had received it after that unfortunate episode when he had sent the *Cumberland* off in pursuit of the French ships, and ever since it had kept on invading his thoughts, returning like a sharp prick of light, not always welcome, into some unacknowledged confusion of his mind. Was it the letter which had made him think suddenly of the natives? Or had his thought of them pushed to the forefront of his consciousness one phrase of that letter which now came like a whispered accusation out of the dark night? *". . . you will presently remain the peaceful possessors of their heritage . . ."*

He turned abruptly and went back into the house. Peaceful . . . ? Peace was very far from this ill-fated spot! His slightly protruberant eyes were fixed in an angry frown as he went quickly up the stairs to his room, and opened a box where he kept his private papers apart from the mass of official documents. He found Monsieur Baudin's letter, unfolded it, laid it on the table, and stood over it, resting the palms of his hands on the polished wood; his expression as he looked down at the ornate letterhead and the rows of small, neat writing, had a shade of truculence.

Above a picture of two sailing vessels and a cluster of objects symbolising the scientific and artistic purposes of their voyage, stretched a scroll bearing the words *Bonaparte Premier Consul*; but it was upon two other words standing isolated on either side of the scroll that the Governor's eyes halted and his mind baulked for a fraction of a second.

Liberté. Egalité.

He moved the paper so that the lamplight fell upon it more directly, and began to read words with which he was already disturbingly familiar.

"Having answered your letter as Governor-General of the British settlements in New South Wales, I now write to you as Mr. King, my friend, for whom I shall always have a particular regard. It is on this ground alone I shall enter into details with you, and tell you frankly my way of thinking."

Strange power in words stretching across a sheet of paper in the lamplight! Words with a voice behind them, with a face and a personality behind them which called insistently to some submerged half-knowledge of himself! Mr. King, accustomed though he was by now to being obliterated by the Governor-General of the British Settlements in New South Wales, made an effort to stand forth in response to what seemed like a summons.

It was less with his imagination than with his alert, practical intelligence that he was coming to suspect something deeply and fundamentally wrong with the society he was trying to govern. He observed only the surface of events, but he observed that keenly. Orders, punishments, regulations and prohibitions might stave off disaster for a while, as the patching of an unseaworthy ship might cheat the hungry ocean for a time, but he perceived that they were expedients. Yet where was the cure? It was not for him to mould society, but nowadays when he observed the mould in which it was cast, he found his thoughts turning often to this letter. A letter, he told himself, such as one might expect a Frenchman to write; a letter from the heart, but filtered through a mind as clear as water, and lit by a humour as mild, and dry and lucent as winter sunshine. A letter that went farther in linking the theory and practice of morality than he could unreservedly approve; which took benevolence beyond such matters as the succouring of an individual in distress, the building of an Orphanage, or even the administration of a colony with as much humanity as might be . . .

Recalling hours in the Government House drawing-room, when Baudin's wit had salted but not obscured a broad and humane philosophy, and brought a touch of cosmopolitan freshness into the all too stagnant atmosphere of a small, isolated community, King recalled also (with less pleasure) a suggestion of sly derision, a hint of amusement so charged with ironic discernment that it was almost bitter, and more than a little sad. He had been made uneasy by that elusive quality in his guest which hinted that this colony, while impressive, was also rather grimly amusing; from that notion had arisen the implication that its Governor's pretensions to dignity and importance might also be comical. That quality was very apparent in this letter. Mr. King had matched his wit against Monsieur Baudin's very pleasantly many times, and was himself often tempted to treat serious matters with levity; but when Baudin directed his quiet satire at the whole principle of colonial expansion, the Governor of a colony could not be expected to approve.

He stared down at the page with a half-exasperated frown. There was nothing funny about acquiring territory in the name of one's King and country; it was a solemn business. It had been his obvious duty to take possession of Van Diemen's Land, despite the Frenchman's gentle gibe which at this moment was looking slyly up at him from the lamplit paper. "... *everyone knows that Tasman and his heirs did not bequeath it by will to you* . . ." Absurd. And that his country's flag, improperly hung, should have been subjected to the twinkle in Monsieur Baudin's eye, still irked him sorely. "*That childish ceremony was ridiculous, and has become more so from the manner in which the flag was placed, the head being downward, and the attitude not very majestic. . . . I thought at first it might have been a flag which had served to strain water, and then hung out to dry* . . ." His Excellency still resented the irony of that description, and suppressed the involuntary smile that twitched Mr. King's lips as he read it again. Ridiculous or not, the ceremony had been necessary. Yet he felt discomfited. Monsieur Baudin had clearly not been at all deceived by his manœuvres . . .

"*I was well convinced that the Cumberland had other motive than to bring me your letter; but I did not think it was for the purpose of hoisting the British flag precisely on the spot where our tents had been pitched a long time previous to her arrival. I frankly confess that I am displeased that such has taken place.*"

The rebuke was mild, but it stung Mr. King with the charge of discourtesy to an always courteous friend; and it stung the Governor to angry self-justification. He had a duty to do, had he not? Was he to stand idly by while the representatives of a foreign power . . . ?

"*I have no knowledge,*" replied Monsieur Baudin's handwriting calmly, "*of the claims which the French Government may have upon Van Diemen's Land, nor of its designs for the future; but I think that its title will not be any better grounded than yours.*"

Title? Title? Mr. King moved his bent shoulders impatiently. What was it that gave title to a territory? Discovery? Certainly not, objected the Governor sharply—for that would mean that by the efforts of Abel Tasman, Van Diemen's Land must have belonged since 1642 to the kingdom of Holland. Even the French expedition of Marion du Fresne in 1772 would have a prior claim to that of the English explorers who had brought the *Adventure* to anchor in Storm Bay a year later. No, not discovery. Possession? The mere fact of establishment? The hoisting of a flag? "*Precisely,*" repeated Monsieur Baudin's writing suavely, "*on the spot where our tents had been pitched a long time previous to her arrival . . .*"

Yet possession was possession. Let him take who can. Monsieur Baudin had not taken, but the Governor-General of the British settlements in New South Wales had. Possession was the fact which could not be gainsaid; possession was the title . . .

But here Mr. King felt his thoughts come full-circle and knit with a little shock to that phrase which had teased him not an hour ago. For had there not been others in possession before all these passing voyagers? The soundless voice of Monsieur Baudin spoke to him again from the page beneath his frowning and unwillingly attentive eyes.

"*To my way of thinking I have never been able to conceive that there was justice or equity on the part of Europeans in seizing, in the name of their Governments, a land seen for the first time, when it is inhabited by men who have not always deserved the title of savages and cannibals which has been given to them . . .*"

Savages and cannibals. Mr. King's memory went back to the time when the natives about this settlement had been, in the first flush of novelty, seen as individuals. As low, brutish variants of humanity, indeed, but still as individuals. Bennilong, merry, vain and violent; the gentle Arabanoo; the grim and sober Colbee; Barangaroo, shrewish and tempestuous; Daringbah, submissive and soft-hearted . . . For a long time now he had thought of them only collectively, as one of his many administrative problems. Except when some brawl, some theft, some killing forced one of them separately upon his notice, he had forgotten them as individuals. Even the ugly head of Pemulwy, shipped to England as a scientific specimen, had seemed less important as the head of a brave and independent character than as the last mortal remains of one who had been a terrible pest to the colony . . .

"*It appears to me,*" pursued the mute voice of Monsieur Baudin, "*that it would be infinitely more glorious for your nation, as for mine, to mould for society the inhabitants of the respective countries over whom they have rights, instead of wishing to occupy themselves in improving those who are so far removed by immediately seizing the soil which they own, and which has given them birth. These remarks are, no doubt, impolitic . . .*"

The Governor, with a movement as if to re-fold the letter, thought with annoyance: "They are indeed!" Mr. King stayed the impulsive fingers, and read on:

"... *and had this principle been generally adopted you would not have been obliged to have formed a colony by means of men branded by the law, and who have become criminals through the fault of the Government which had neglected and abandoned them ...*"

"Nonsense!" said the Governor aloud. "Fantastic!" But Mr. King went on reading.

"*It follows, therefore, that not only have you to reproach yourself with an injustice in seizing this land, but also in transporting on a soil where the crimes and diseases of Europeans were unknown, all that could retard the progress of civilisation, which has served as a pretext to your Government ...*"

A pretext? King, both in his official and his private capacities, shied at that like a nervous horse. Certainly the place was a penal colony. Yet criminals there had always been, and must always be, and were they not here offered an opportunity to reclaim and redeem themselves? Was it not towards establishing those of them who could overcome their criminal tendencies as respectable and industrious small farmers that all his energies were consistently directed?

And as consistently frustrated ...

He left the table and took a restless turn or two about the room. He felt a hot and genuine indignation. It was no pretext! He knew that whatever the Frenchman might believe, the conception of themselves as upholders and spreaders of civilisation was one which lived invincibly in the minds and hearts of his own countrymen. He would not allow for one moment that their service to it was merely lip-service, and he went back to the table and stood over the letter, glaring at it as though it were Monsieur Baudin himself. He knew what had been in Phillip's heart when he governed here, what had been in Hunter's—ineptly as he had striven for it—and what was in his own. They were not monsters, they were not tyrants ...

Yet he knew also that there had always been a gulf as deep as Hell between what they had intended and what they had achieved. Could it be true, as Baudin seemed to hint, that the things they had all struggled against were not incidents, not accidental ill-fortunes, not ignorant or recalcitrant individuals—but inevitable results of a false moral attitude? No, no! For surely a true moral attitude was there, it was laid down, it was explicit in every instruction they had received. The words which had guided this adventure had been noble words; they had invoked justice for the natives, justice for the convicts, reformation, enlightenment, industry, virtue, religion. Where was the failure?

For an instant, recognising the gulf that yawned between the natives and his own people, he clutched at the thought that it was significant—that it was only the widest, and therefore the most obvious, of all the gulfs that separated the sections of his community and his world. From the opposite sides of unbridged chasms, not only white and black, but white and white faced each other as enemies ...

His eyes went on moving slowly down the lines of black writing.

If you will reflect upon the conduct of the natives since the beginning of your establishment upon their territory, you will perceive that their aversion for you, and also for your customs, has been occasioned by the ideas they have formed of those who wished to live amongst them. Notwithstanding your precautions, and the punishments undergone by those among your people who have ill-treated them, they have been enabled to see through your projects for the future; and being too feeble to resist you, the fear of your arms has made them emigrate, so that the hope of seeing them mix with you is lost, and you will presently remain the peaceful possessors of their heritage, as the small number of those surrounding you will not long exist . . ."

King's frown deepened. There was something in that dispassionate and unemotional statement which shocked him. He did not like to have his mind thus thrust into the future, nor to be made to see himself as an instrument of destruction. In that prophecy, certainly, the Governor saw a solution—the grim and simple solution of gaining one's end by the quiet extermination of those who hampered it. Mr. King, however, in a distressful moment of perception, heard a warning in it, and glimpsed an accumulating burden of guilt which the next generation, and the next, and the next must inherit, until a distant posterity should earn, perhaps, by some means which he did not even try to imagine, a sad and belated absolution . . .

He picked up the letter and folded it slowly. As the paper creased over to hide the writing only two words at the top of the page were visible, but his eyes and his mind passed over them, unseeing. *Liberté, egalité*—two words, a catch-cry distorted by emotional reactions, a rallying-call grown dim with repetition, two words, and nothing more. The Governor replaced the letter in his box, settled his cuffs, turned down the lamp, summoned himself back with the aid of trivial, everyday actions from unpractical mind-wandering to the real world of established and accepted facts. A good fellow, Baudin; an excellent fellow—but a Frenchman, and not uninfected, it would seem, by that visionary, democratic fervour which had lately swept his country . . .

He went briskly down the stairs to join his wife in the parlour. He settled himself at ease in an armchair, stretched his feet to the comforting fire, and took up the *Gazette*. Mrs. King, stealing a glance at him presently over her embroidery frame, noticed that he was not reading his newspaper, but staring abstractedly over it into the jumping flames.

* * * * *

Mark Harvey did not quite know himself what impulse it was that brought him one cold, June morning almost before daylight to the spot where he had once encountered Mr. Thomas Fysshe Palmer. He was in Sydney, accompanied by Toole, to arrange for the despatch to Beltrasna of a new convict, but having concluded this business he had still a long list of commissions to execute. So, having seen Toole depart by passage-boat with his charge, he had remained overnight to negotiate the sale of some farm produce, and to make purchases which ranged from a cask of Madeira to smelling-salts for Cousin Bertha, and ribbons for Miss Julia Mannion.

But he had slept poorly in his humble lodgings in Pitt Row. His bed was hard, and its covers inadequate for the winter night. There had been a noisy brawl in the street outside; and though Mr. Harvey, wakeful on his pillow, was reflecting on his own concerns, the young convict whom he had just delivered to the tender mercies of Toole kept peering in on his thoughts like a pale face at a window. He had dozed, wakened, dozed again; and finally, when the room lightened to a grey and cheerless dawn, he had risen and bundled on his clothes, and stepped out into the deserted streets to walk off a sense of despondency and chagrin.

Since the departure of Miles for England three weeks ago, he had felt increasingly restless and disturbed. He was not, he told himself indignantly, a clerk! He was not an errand-boy! It was true that he had been employed in both these capacities occasionally ever since his arrival, but he had been able to console himself with the thought that he was, nevertheless, tutor to Miles rather than general assistant to Mr. Mannion.

Now it was different. He had become part-clerk, part-steward, part-overseer, even part-valet. He could no longer maintain the fiction that he was not directly concerned in the management of his employer's estate, or comfort himself with the reflection that he was really there for the benefit of his employer's son. This new situation was, he knew, a respectable one which many a poor young man might have envied him; his present distress and confusion were caused as much by bewilderment at the repugnance with which he viewed it, as by distaste for the employment itself.

Now he was wholly involved. All the commercial transactions of Beltrasna lay exposed to him in the letters he wrote to Mr. Mannion's dictation, in the accounts he cast, in the lists of food, clothing, tools, seed, and human beings which he compiled in his neat handwriting. Now his duties often took him into the fields and down to the convicts' quarters; now he was brought frequently into contact with Toole and Byrne, and a third overseer named Evans whom Mr. Mannion had recently engaged. Now he had begun to recognise some of the convicts as individuals, and to find himself avoiding their eyes; now he knew the cost of the food which appeared on the dining-table of the house, and of that which found its way to the convict hut; now he saw the meagre rewards of harsh toil and bitter living measured against the rich rewards of gentle birth and well-lined pockets.

He could not question all this with any conviction, far less denounce. He could only suffer a growing restlessness, and find his thoughts turning to the events from which it seemed to spring. To Mr. Palmer and his strange words; to that ugly scene he had witnessed at Toongabbee; to Conor's distress, reaching out towards his own like the hand of one child in the dark to another's; to the words she had quoted—"*freedom hath been hunted round the globe*"; and now to the expression he had seen on the face of that young convict yesterday.

So here he stood in the cold, early morning light, looking at the rock on which Mr. Palmer had sat as if it held some answer to his perplexities, and might speak. His hands were thrust deep into the pockets of his greatcoat, its collar was turned up about his face, and his eyes watered in the icy wind. He was reflecting moodily that he should have returned to England with Miles. He should have explained civilly to Mr. Mannion that family affairs required his presence there—thanked him for his amiability and condescension—bowed over Cousin Bertha's hand—held Conor's, perhaps, one second too long—and shaken the dust of this cruel, crude colony from his feet forever.

Well, he could yet do so. He turned to look at the harbour. The grey sky above it was faintly flushed now towards the east, and against this pale rose-gold the ridge leading to South Head was starkly silhouetted. Just opposite him Clark Island seemed to crouch in the ruffled, lead-coloured water as if huddling low against the wind, but farther up to the westward the slender, rocky spire of Pinchgut reached up through the wintry air towards the slow brightening of the sky. Mark was cold, and something in the outline of that lonely little rock, strong yet vulnerable, stark yet lovely, struck a chill to his heart too. Pinchgut! Was it somehow symbolical that so ugly and bitter a name should have been imposed upon so beautiful a spot? How many men marooned there, desperate and semi-starving, had watched bleak dawns like this alone? How many corpses had hung there in rattling chains? What kind of gift was this civilisation which had already bound a legend of despair upon a place surely designed by nature as a symbol of aspiration?

Something that was almost panic set Mr. Harvey's eyes to an eager scanning of the vessels lying at anchor. There was the *Lady Nelson*, and there *H.M.S. Porpoise*, and beyond them the brig *Nautilus;* and yonder were the *Alexander*, the *Bridgewater*, the *Rolla* and the *Cato*—the last three all to sail soon, so it was said, for England . . .

Suddenly it seemed to Mr. Harvey as if the rock beside him really did speak. It seemed to say in a carefully neutral voice with an undertone of satire: "*And how is England?*"

Homesickness surged up in him, shouting one answer which drowned another, still too hesitant and too unwelcome to be heard. England was in leaf and flower, in midsummer, green with grass and corn, bright with gardens. England was full of years and wisdom, resting on its long history and its hallowed traditions, rich in its ripe culture, calm, dignified, powerful and secure. England had a pattern of living, and towards that pattern young Mr. Harvey yearned, shaken and revolted by the chaos and the crudity, the greed, brutality, strife and suffering of this unhappy infant colony.

But with the dying down of that emotional flare he heard the other answer, faint but persistent, like someone calling from far away. It said with soft relentlessness: "*This is England. Not the land, not the harbour, not the rock pointing at the sky. But the houses, the ships, the gallows on the rock. The greed, the brutality, the strife and the suffering were not born here. They were brought.*"

He stared at the ships which he had seen as a means of escape, and wondered with a sinking heart if escape were possible. And then he came with relief to the simple knowledge that he could not, after all, do more than toy with his dream of departure—for there was Conor. She had said: "I am glad you are to remain with us, Mr. Harvey." The words had lifted him to Heaven only for so long as it had taken him to realise that if she had meant them as he would have liked her to mean them, they would not have been uttered at all. Yet he knew there was some comfort for her in his presence; and for himself no discontent could really be strong enough to set an ocean between them. Only to be near her! Only to see her and talk to her sometimes . . . !

But could he not remain in the colony and yet free himself from this new, exclusive bondage to her husband and her husband's activities which was already tormenting him, and which in time would surely become insupportable? Was not this place frequently described as a land of opportunity, and had he not himself watched men rise from penury to a comfortable affluence? But it was always by land or trade—and Mr. Harvey was almost shamefacedly aware of a certain squeamishness in himself which, he suspected, would impede his advancement by either of these means. He sighed, shivered, and began to clamber up the hill towards the path. He had a copy of the latest *Gazette* in his pocket, and the feel of it beneath his half-frozen fingers reminded him that he had noticed an article about tobacco-growing. Pausing on the hilltop, he pulled it out and stood for a moment to read and recover his breath.

"The quantities of Tobacco growing wild in the streets reminds everyone that this necessary plant may be raised and manufactured in the Colony, without paying sums of money to Americans and others for what . . ."

Perhaps he would not need much land—just enough to raise a small crop . . . ? The sun was just over the eastern hill now, and his eye caught the flash of a sail far down the harbour. A ship coming in! He climbed a high rock to see better, and presently recognised it with a little thrill of excitement. It was Captain Flinders, returning from his latest explorations in the *Investigator*, and for a moment Mark forgot all about tobacco, and imagined for himself an adventurous seafaring life, charting strange coasts and discovering fabulous wealth on some unknown Pacific island.

Here on the hilltop the wind struck more coldly than ever. Not only its chill, but also that honesty which Mr. Palmer had descried in him, and which sometimes struck more bleakly than any wind to the heart of his romantic flights of fancy, made him shrug suddenly, jump down from his rock, and turn his back on the white sails. He knew as he trudged back towards Sydney that even tobacco-growing was too exotic a pursuit for his serious consideration. He would keep his thoughts soberly upon that line of life in which he had already some experience. There would be others, no doubt, requiring tutors for their children. Or perhaps some day he might even establish a small academy for the sons of gentlefolk . . . ?

*   *   *   *

To the Hawkesbury at the end of June came Captain Flinders himself for a few days' holiday, and from there rode up to Beltrasna to visit Mr.

1d Mrs. Mannion. He was in poor health after a hard and anxious
voyage, lean and sallow, distressed by the news he had found awaiting
him of his father's death, and worried about his ship—now so unseaworthy that his plans for future explorations were upset. Conor found
him at first a rather taciturn young man, seeming older than his thirty
years: but later, when he sat alone with her for a time on the sunny
verandah, his mood changed, and he talked more freely.

He spoke with sorrow of his father's death, with tenderness of his
family, with humorous affection of his friend, George Bass, ". . . who
always seems to be elsewhere when I hope to meet him again, Madam . . ."
He spoke of his wife with a kind of guarded longing, as if he hardly
dared to admit even to himself how their long separation hurt him. "She
would have been happy here, I think," he said once, "and she would not
have lacked charming companions of her own sex." He passed his hand
over his head with a rueful gesture. "I grow grey alone, Madam!" And
Conor observed that there were indeed a few flecks of silver in his dark
hair.

He spoke of the progress of the colony, ". . . a spectacle highly interesting, Mrs. Mannion, to the contemplator of the rise of nations." But
observant as his eyes were, and shrewd as were his comments, she thought
that he saw the colony only as a foothold between voyages, and counted
every day ashore as a day wasted. It was true that he was restless. He
was trained to notice, and he noticed his surroundings wherever he might
be. He saw the new brick granary which was being built at the Hawkesbury, and preparations going forward for the erection of a school. He
observed that barley was being widely cultivated against the completion
of the brewery at Parramatta. On his return to Sydney he studied the
new church begun on the hill near the Barracks, and the strong stone
bridge which now spanned the Tank Stream, and watched labourers
enlarging wharves and building vessels. But every opportunity found
him at the Governor's elbow, seeking a solution to the problem of a navigator without a ship, and urging haste. His confidence in himself was
too strong to be disturbed by the presence of rival explorers in his waters;
he saw the activities of the French as an advantage in drawing the
attention of the world to this remote continent, for his own charts, he
thought calmly, would sustain his reputation, and stand comparison with
any others. But he felt the impatience of a man to whom his work is a
vocation; he wanted to be about it without setbacks or delays. Those
short winter days seemed long to Matthew Flinders.

*   *   *   *   *

Early in July the Governor issued a proclamation:

"*Whereas there is great reason to suppose some persons not duly
authorised do make a practice of going to those parts beyond the Nepean
where the strayed cattle resort, for the purpose of killing them, whereby
several are wounded: To prevent which it is hereby ordered that if any
person whatever frequent the Cow Pastures, or pass the Nepean without
a permit signed by the Governor . . . he or they will, on conviction, he
put to hard labour for six months as a vagrant. And if any person what-*

ever, not authorised, shall presume to kill any of the above black catt *male or female, they will be punished to the utmost extent of the law . .*

His Excellency could not know that the person to whom this docume was mainly addressed was a red-headed youth who spent all his ti beyond the Nepean, and knew nothing of proclamations; and it was t merest accident that Johnny ever heard of it. He had killed an occasion animal from the wild herds for ten years past, and he considered hims fully authorised by inheritance, custom, and native legend to do so. H trade in beef, though haphazard and irregular, was by now fairly w established. For months a mysterious young man had been appeari from nowhere among the settlers at Green Hills. The first time he h traded fresh beef for two small casks and a supply of coarse salt; t second time salt beef had paid for a sack of potatoes, a worn coat, government blanket, and a pair of rusty scissors. He had accepted t scissors only because they were, to him, a novelty, but they had prove useful. He had found (as many a white man had found before him that the natives he pressed into service to help him transport his war did not long maintain an enthusiasm for hard work; after his seco journey there had been no volunteers for a third. But when they sa Johnny and Billalong with their wild locks trimmed close, and discovere that this remarkable implement could similarly transform themselves, th were willing to bargain. Even so, their services were liable to be errat but this disturbed Johnny far less than it did Towns. In his illness, whi held him more and more a prisoner in the hut, Johnny's comings ar goings became increasingly important to the convict as a kind of vicario contact with his lost world. He grew avaricious, too, greeting each ne article which Johnny brought home with a miserly joy. He urged the la to insist upon at least some part of his payment in money, and gloated ov the growing hoard of small coins that lay carelessly on a shelf in the hut.

But he found that he must exhort and insist continually if weeks we not to slip by without adding to their possessions. For there were st strong influences of his native life at work in Johnny, and he had not y rid himself entirely of the heretical belief that time was not importan And so, with a cask of beef ready to be taken down the river, he woul seem to forget it; go hunting with the tribes; sit in the sun, whittling at piece of wood; vanish for the day into the Wollondilly valley; lie on th flat rock writing words with charcoal; disappear to attend a corroboree; g off with Billalong to fish.

Towns railed at him. This was no way to acquire riches. Johnn listened, struggling with opposing impulses. He, too, was gripped by th lure of possessions, though the stimulation of contact with his own kin and the excitement of bargaining were even stronger motives for h expeditions. But there were times when he felt inclined to do other thing —or even to do nothing. There was food in the hut; why not eat it, an enjoy oneself? It would be time to labour when that was gone.

But always he returned to his work in the end. Sometimes he coul muster two or even three natives, each with his own canoe, and his ow load of salt beef, but more often he had to be content with a singl companion, who was usually Billalong. It was rarely that he went quite alone, for the small and fragile bark canoes could not be heavily laden, and moreover there were precautions which he liked to take while negotiating that stretch of the river which flowed past the Beltrasna fields. It was important that to any casual eye watching from those fields no curiosity should be aroused by the canoes or their occupants. Johnny knew that his red head was a betraying sign, and that a clad figure would excite instant attention. Naked, his clothes rolled in a bundle on the bottom of the canoe, his hair darkened with charcoal, he was, at a distance, indistinguishable from a native. But occasionally there were men working quite near the river, and then Johnny disembarked on the opposite bank, upstream, and made his way on foot through the sheltering trees, leaving his black companion to tow the second canoe to a meeting place farther down the river, and safe from watching eyes.

He became interested in the variety of things which could be traded for his beef. His most cherished prize was a tinder box to replace the one Andrew Prentice had stolen from Mr. Mannion's store-hut, and which Billalong had lost many years ago. But though he often acquired useful things, Johnny would sometimes accept an article merely because he had never seen one like it before, and there were those in the settlement who said, because of this, that he was half-witted. He caused surprise and sly amusement when he bartered his whole supply of meat, on one occasion, for a stack of damaged writing paper and a couple of pencils. The natives frequently shared his wonder and delight in unfamiliar objects, but Towns swore at him when he returned with a thimble, a candle-snuffer, and some bits of broken glass.

It was Towns, of course, who urged him to secure ammunition for the old muskets hanging on the wall. It was Towns who cleaned them with the oil Johnny brought, and loaded them, and coached the boy in their use, and pointed out how much more safely and expeditiously they could kill than native spears. Johnny tried one of them on the herds at the Cow Pastures, and wounded several animals before he killed one. He thought it an uninteresting way of hunting, but he began to feel a curious sense of power. Nothing—not even his mastery of reading and writing, or his new freedom from the laborious method of fire-making—had seemed so rapidly to widen the gulf which he felt opening between himself and the black men. Sometimes, watching one of them pass far beyond spearthrowing distance, he would think: "I could kill him. If he were my enemy I could kill him . . ."

They were not his enemies, and he did not wish to kill them, but his mind moved on to the thought that he did have enemies. There was Mannion, of course, whom he would kill some day. That he did not immediately set out to do so was because the thing seemed so inevitable that he need only wait for it to happen in its own time and fashion. He thought more of "them"—the white rulers of the white people—who were the enemies of himself and all his kind. So much Towns had taught him, reinforcing the blurred memories of his own childhood; and the possession

of muskets, now loaded and potent, often inspired him to exciting bu
formless daydreams of revenge.

At Green Hills he was not watched or questioned too closely. It wa
well known that he brought his merchandise down the river in canoes, anc
no one chose to conjecture in anything louder than a whisper that unlawfu
depredations were being made upon the Government herd of wild cattle
It had been done before, and was still done occasionally by settlers robust
enterprising, and hungry enough to confront a long journey, and beast
whose ferocity made them dangerous. If this youth with the red hair anc
the restless, dark eyes chose to risk his life and liberty, it was his owr
concern.

Late in July, upon one of the rare occasions when he made the journey
alone, Johnny learned two interesting things. The first came as a warning
muttered by a time-expired convict named Miller, who had brought a pair
of half-worn shoes to barter for meat. They transacted their business in a
secluded spot on the edge of the settlement. The sun had already set
behind the western hills, the quick, cold winter twilight was deepening, and
shafts of smoke were rising from the chimneys of the few scattered cottages
in sight. Between the river and the low, wooden palisade which marked
the boundary of Miller's small holding, a narrow lane, muddy, trodden by
cows and horses going down to drink, by men and women with pails, and
by children bent on play, wound between the bracken down to the willows
on the bank where Johnny's canoe was lying. In the hut from which his
customer had come to join him, a lamp had been lit, and Johnny's eyes
kept straying to the open doorway through which its yellow light shone.
He could hear voices and see the people moving about inside—a woman,
and children. He would sleep himself, to-night, in his own place, his
second home, which to the uninitiated eye bore no sign of habitation, beneath
that overhanging rock where he had been born as Dyonn-ee, and from
which he had begun a pilgrimage which, at this moment, seemed to him
must end with some lighted doorway, with voices, with figures having as
yet no names or faces, but waiting for him there. He was cold, hungry
and impatient. He would have departed without keeping his rendezvous
with Miller if he had not wanted the shoes. He thrust the meat into the
hands outstretched to receive it, snatched the shoes, turned to go, and then
halted—stayed not so much by the hand on his sleeve as by something he
read in the ex-convict's eyes. They were faded blue eyes, set in a lined,
unshaven face, and what held his attention now was that behind their wary
furtiveness there was an almost unrecognisable expression—friendliness.

He stopped and listened with astonishment and growing anger. He
was being told in a hoarse and hurried whisper that the arch-enemy, "their"
leader, the Governor himself, was contesting the right of Johnny Prentice
to kill his own cattle!

"Six months ye'll get in the gaol-gang, lad, if they catch ye, an' the lash
across y' back as well, most like." He was being warned. "Keep clear o'
Forbes up yonder, the rat, an' Harry James across the creek, there, for
they'd inform on ye as soon as spit . . ."

Johnny's sharp, brown eyes darted a rapid glance about him, and Miller

was momentarily startled by a fantastic impression. The lad looked like an
ndian! But the dark eyes whose quick, instinctive searching of the land-
cape for the enemy, for cover, for strategic advantage, had seemed only
n instant ago so reminiscent of the restless eyes of the natives, were now
till, staring, fixed with a peering concentration on a figure walking along
he palisade towards them, leading a cow by a halter round its neck. An
unremarkable figure, moving slowly for all its youth; a thin, sallow face,
ed hair beneath a dirty cap . . .

Johnny whispered with a sharp gesture:
"Who?"

The monosyllable touched off another flash of impression in Miller's
mind that this boy was—different. His speech. . . . It was English, but
English with a difference. His eyes, his attitudes, his movements, his queer
mixture of shrewdness and unsophistication . . .

Staring curiously, he muttered:
"Workin' for Blake—up the river a piece. Prentice, e's called—Andy
Prentice. " 'Is ma's 'ousekeeper—an' some says more—to . . ."

But he was suddenly alone. The twilight was deepening, frogs were
croaking, the boy with the cow had gone slouching past with barely a
glance. Under the deeper twilight of the willows on the bank there was a
stir as if a shadow were moving and presently a faint plash of paddles.
Miller went down to the water's edge and stared up the broad, darkening
stream. Its eastern half still shone like a mirror, reflecting the last light
of the sky, but its western half lay in the shadow of the bank. He saw
the canoe shoot from silvery water to black water, and vanish. What was
the reason for that sudden alarm? He shrugged, and climbed up again
slowly towards his own lighted doorway.

*   *   *   *   *

But Johnny's precipitate retreat had been caused not so much by reason
as by a kind of wild-animal instinct. In all his contacts with his countrymen he was still as nervous as a wallaby, attracted by curiosity, but mistrustful. To find himself without warning only a few paces from his
brother had made him feel that this white world was advancing a stride
to meet him and involve him, instead of awaiting passively his own cautious
approach. Too close—too close . . . !

Yet as he paddled up the river in the dark, past the Beltrasna fields,
and saw the lights of the big house shining on the hilltop, he was already
growing calmer, and wondering whether this incident might not point the
way to opportunities. He had no plans, but his hatred of Mannion rose
in his throat like a sickness as he stared up at those distant lights; the hill
was not really high, but from water-level they looked hardly lower than
the stars. What, Johnny wondered, was his brother doing at Green Hills?
Did he ever come back to this place? And if he did—or could—might he
not be useful . . . ?

Towns had no need to urge Johnny upon his journeys during the next
couple of months. On the contrary, he grew suspicious when the boy not
only went more often than usual, but sometimes remained absent seven or
eight days. He did not even always trouble to take meat with him, or

bring anything back, and the convict became alarmed. What would he do if Johnny deserted him? For he was now very weak, and had grown so accustomed to being fed and cared for that the thought of having to fend for himself again in this accursed country was terrifying.

Johnny never mentioned Andy to him. This was but another symptom of his white-man development and his native decay. As a child in the settlements he had learned very thoroughly to hold his tongue, for words could be either dangerous or profitable—and in either case must be carefully guarded; but in the tribes, where every man's business was the tribe's business, and it was rarely that one felt the need to practise reticence, he had forgotten that old, wary habit. It returned to him now. His visits to Green Hills were frequent, but he used them for watching and listening, and talked little. He discovered, without asking, where Andy lived and worked, but for the present made no attempt to do more than observe him from a distance. In the meantime he began to learn other things. The people with whom he talked were mainly convicts employed by settlers, or ex-convicts making a living as best they could by casual labour, or on small farms which had been granted to them, and they spoke freely before him because they knew that in killing and selling the Government cattle he had put himself outside the law. He accepted this as quite natural, for though he did not know or care what his legal status might be, he took it for granted that the law was his enemy.

So he listened eagerly to those who were also quite obviously its enemies. Their rambling talk of escape, rebellion, and vengeance excited, but sometimes bewildered him. If they wanted to escape, he thought, why didn't they? The river was close, the nights dark, and they were a good deal of the time unsupervised. He found it difficult to realise that the wild, unsettled country so familiar to himself could paralyse their will with fear; or that they dreaded starvation where he himself had never hungered for long; or that his friends, the natives, could be regarded as dangerous and hostile savages. But he was more interested in the talk of rebellion, and imagined naïvely that such talk must be a prelude to immediate action. He grew impatient as the weeks went by, and still nothing happened. He asked: "Why? Why?" They answered him only with a brief, queer glance, or a jibe, or a laugh, or a slap on the shoulder, for they had all decided by now that he was not quite sane. But he began to learn from his listening that for a rebellion arms were needed, and a plan, and numbers, and those who would lead.

He said eagerly:

"I got two guns."

They stared and grinned. They had assumed that he must have a gun to kill the cattle, and besides, he had once accepted some stolen ammunition in exchange for his beef. But they did not take him seriously until, upon his next visit, he actually brought one of his old muskets and gave it to them. Then they thought him madder than ever, but began to feel that, mad or sane, he was a useful ally. They told him that already a few of them had stolen firearms; that there were pikes made and hidden; that they had tidings of similar preparations in other settlements. But his excited

uestions as to when this rebellion was to take place brought, as yet, no
nswer.

    *   *   *   *   *

By August the Governor was informing Lord Hobart that the crops
romised well; that he was sowing forty-acre tracts with clover, sainfoin,
ye-grass and burnet to serve as fodder when the native grasses failed; that
e was encouraging the use of the plough; and that the settlers were exert-
ng themselves in the erection of better houses.

He hinted in passing that those who decided the destinies of the colony
might be moved by the report of Captain Flinders to establish a settlement
n the north coast, and experiment with the cultivation of tropical plants
n that warmer climate.

He reported the arrival of a French ship from Ile de France with a
argo which included a quantity of very bad spirits, and assured His
ordship that he had left the captain in no doubt that such cargoes were
nwelcome.

He touched upon the possibility that this small but growing colony
might not only awaken the covetousness of the French, but interfere with
he trade of the Spanish settlements across the Pacific. "*To defend the
olony against the one,*" he wrote, "*and to annoy the other, it would be
ecessary that some regard should be had to military and naval defences.*"
A couple of artillery officers with twenty men under them, and an additional
alf-dozen twelve-pounder cannon would, he suggested, meet all present
equirements.

It was not only to impress the Secretary of State, but also to reassure
imself that he took pains thus to appear the alert and indefatigable
dministrator, with a watchful eye not only for the detail of the colony's
nternal management, but for its place and possibilities as a pawn in the
game of nations. For tireless as his efforts had been, and substantial as
were many of his reforms, he was conscious of failure. The monopolists
vere still strong and hostile, the soldiers still traders, the liquor traffic still
a major problem, and the atmosphere still thunderous.

He turned from this letter to preparations, half regretfully made, for
he departure of Captain Flinders. In a place where there were few to
whom he could talk in freedom and friendliness, he had valued the company
of the young explorer whose appearances in the colony were too fleeting to
et him actively on one side or the other in this bitter warfare. It had
been decided after long consultations that he would return to England in
the *Porpoise* as a passenger, to submit his charts to the Admiralty and ask
or a new ship. And when the *Porpoise*, followed by the *Cato* and the
Bridgewater, sailed down the harbour one day towards the middle of
August, the Governor accompanied his friend as far as the Heads, and
Mrs. King and Miss Elizabeth waved him an affectionate farewell from
the shore—never dreaming that within a month they were to see him back
again.

His Excellency was at dinner with his family when Jane Dundas—
claiming it as her prerogative to be the bearer of sensational tidings—
appeared without ceremony in the doorway.

"Please, Sir, by your leave, Sir—Captain Flinders is here!"

The Governor stopped with carving-knife poised. Mrs. King stared blankly.

"Captain *Flinders* . . . ?" snapped His Excellency.

"Captain *Flinders*, Jane?" cried Mrs. King. "Have you taken leave of your senses? How could . . . ?"

"No, Sir, I mean no, Ma'am—yes, Sir, if you please, it *is* Captain Flinders—la, Ma'am, I could scarce believe my eyes, but . . ."

King was half-way to the door. The young man whom he found awaiting him was leaner than ever, haggard, unkempt, with three weeks' growth of beard on his strained and weary face. He reported the wreck of the *Porpoise* and the *Cato* on a reef seven days out of Sydney, answering the Governor's flood of questions with the slow care of one whose physical endurance is almost exhausted. Later—fed, rested and made welcome—he described with a kind of grim detachment the outrageous conduct of the captain of the *Bridgewater*, who had made off for Batavia, leaving the crews of the other ships to their fate. Mrs. King, her brown eyes wide with horror and distress, cried unhappily:

"Gracious, Father! How many were lost?"

"Only three, Ma'am," he replied slowly. He told of the landing of tents and stores on the reef, of hurried and desperate plans, of the final decision that the larger of the *Porpoise's* six-oared cutters, with himself in command, should attempt the seven-hundred-mile voyage to Sydney in search of aid.

"We called her," he said, "the *Hope*." He looked at the Governor, a picture of consternation, at Mrs. King, dabbing her eyes with a handkerchief, at Jane Dundas hovering in the doorway, and smiled vaguely. "So here we are, Sir."

*   *   *   *   *

Mr. Howe—not often blessed with so dramatic a tale to tell in his *Gazette*—seized eagerly upon the written report of the affair which Flinders submitted to the Governor, and the colony buzzed with excitement over the calamity at Wreck Reef. Plans must be made immediately for the succour of the ninety-four marooned men, and Flinders was closeted for hours in earnest consultation with His Excellency.

The *Rolla*, a merchant ship bound for China, the *Francis* and the *Cumberland*, it was at last agreed, must sail to their aid without delay. Some of the rescued would go on to Canton in the *Rolla*, some would return to Sydney on the *Francis*, and the remainder would accompany Flinders to England on the *Cumberland*. The Governor knit his brows a little over this arrangement, for the *Cumberland* was a twenty-nine-ton schooner, the first vessel to be built in the colony, and—as Flinders wryly remarked—"something less than a Gravesend passage-boat."

"You agree," King asked, "that she is capable of performing the voyage?"

Flinders shrugged. He was thinking of his first voyage with George Bass along these coasts years ago in the little *Tom Thumb* of eight feet keel and five feet beam, with one boy for crew. He answered soberly:

"Yes, Sir. I must reach England with my charts and journals as soon as possible."

King nodded.

"Very well, Captain. I shall direct the Commissary to make her over to you, and provide her with the necessary stores. When you arrive at Wreck Reef you will select such officers and men as you think fit, see the other vessels provided with what they require, and then proceed to England by whatever route you judge the most advisable."

"Yes, Sir."

"And I shall entrust to you my despatches, which you will deliver to the Secretary of State."

Flinders glanced at him dubiously.

"My instructions before I left on the *Investigator* voyage were that I was not to carry letters or packets other than those given me by the Admiralty or the Secretary of State . . ."

King waved the objection aside.

"We were then at war with France; that is not the case now. I shall have the box delivered to you before you sail. Nevertheless, my dear fellow, the times are uncertain, and I need hardly urge you to ignore any opportunity that might present itself of making a capture—and to preserve the strictest neutrality in case a state of war should exist before you reach England."

"Of course, Sir." Flinders frowned thoughtfully at the table. "With regard to the route, I would point out that the small quantity of stores and water which can be carried on a ship of this size will compel me to put in at every convenient port . . ." His fingers tapped them out one by one on the arm of his chair, ". . . Koepang, Ile de France, the Cape of . . ."

But the Governor interrupted:

"Ile de France? That's hardly desirable, Captain. I'm anxious not to encourage communication between that place and this. Besides, you are likely to meet with hurricanes in that neighbourhood at the time of year when you would reach it." He glanced at Flinders' doubtful face and added: "Of course your actions must be dictated by necessity, my friend, but you will oblige me by making every effort to give Ile de France a wide berth." He stood up and offered his hand. "May good fortune go with you, Captain. I shall provide you with your written instructions to-morrow. You know how heartfelt are the good wishes of myself and my family. This time I trust there will be no unhappy sequel to our farewells."

Many times in the next two years he was to remember with a pang those parting words.

*   *   *   *   *

Now he must turn back to a task growing every day more uncongenial. Chapman's part-time assistance as secretary was not enough to free him from hours at his desk which seemed interminable, yet he found time to ride abroad, and His Excellency with his bodyguard of troopers was a familiar sight upon the roads. One look at the Hawkesbury and its tributaries where settlement was established sent him back to Sydney with a frown between his brows, to harangue his wife and Chapman upon the stupidity of farmers who denuded their river banks of timber.

"Already," he said irritably, "the results of this disgraceful improvidence are to be seen. Acres of ground have been washed away in floods. And not only land, mark you, but houses and stock and stacks of wheat. More than once I saw large trees which have fallen into the water from having their roots undermined—and there they lie, impeding the stream and often rendering water-traffic impracticable."

Mrs. King glanced up from her escritoire, serene in wifely confidence. "You must forbid it, my love."

"I shall certainly forbid further cutting," he assured her. "Remind me, William, to issue an order to that effect to-morrow. But why wait till to-morrow? Pray, my dear, give William some paper and a pen, and he shall make notes immediately." He walked up and down the room dictating, while Chapman scribbled on his knee. "No settler or other person to whom ground is granted or leased on the sides of any river or creek where timber is now growing on any account to cut down or destroy, by barking or otherwise, any tree or shrub. . . . We shall make it a condition of their grants. . . . And should they not observe this regulation, a fine of forty shillings—no, damme, fifty shillings—for each tree cut down. . . . Two rods of timber to be left along the banks, and another rod within for a public road. . . . You have that, William?"

Chapman stifled a yawn, for it was growing late, and his thoughts were turning to his little cottage and his comfortable bed.

"Yes, Sir. But you say there are many who have already cleared the banks . . . ?"

"They are fertile, and tempting for cultivation. Which will avail their owners little if they wake one morning and find them swept away into the sea. Make a memorandum that it must be earnestly recommended to them that they re-plant their banks." He sat down and clasped his hands behind his head. "And speaking of the Hawkesbury, Anna, reminds me that I heard a curious rumour of a young man who sells salt meat in that neighbourhood. No one seems to know who he is, or whence he comes, but I hazard a guess that the wild cattle are the source of his supply."

Mrs. King looked indignant. Governor Phillip's share in those cattle, lost so many years ago, and now so enormously multiplied, belonged to her husband. There were estimated to be somewhere in the neighbourhood of four thousand head—a not inconsiderable asset. She said pensively:

"Who can it be? I have often wondered if the natives do not kill them. Surely they must have learned by now that the flesh is good for eating?"

He shook his head.

"All accounts agree that the natives have always manifested the greatest fear of them. Caley assured me that they immediately climb trees if the cattle approach. And this young man is no native, though it's said that natives sometimes accompany him." He glanced at his wife

with a twinkle in his eyes. "Shall we make an expedition, my love, and
investigate the condition of these cattle for ourselves?"

She looked startled.

"To the Nepean? I? I declare, King, I fear the distance would . . ."

Chapman rallied her gaily:

"Come, come, my dear Madam, where is that intrepid spirit I have
always admired in you?"

She said sharply:

"Have I said that I will not go? Indeed I shall! It will be a most
enjoyable experience!"

She bent over her letter again, her cheeks slightly flushed. His
Excellency caught Mr. Chapman's eye; Mr. Chapman almost winked.

*   *   *   *   *

But it was December before Mrs. King had an opportunity to prove
her intrepidity, and in the meantime the routine of life went on, broken
only by such small incidents as provided gossip for a few hours or days,
and a paragraph for Mr. Howe's *Gazette*. In August Mrs. Marsden's
fourth child was accidentally scalded to death; she wept bitterly over this
second tragedy in two years, but with a fifth child barely two months old
in her arms, had not time to weep long. Late in September Major
Foveaux arrived from Norfolk Island; wheezing with asthma, he gave to
the Governor and his wife and young Chapman tidings of their erstwhile
home. In October the colony was swept by a hot, dry wind that scorched
the fields and orchards, and destroyed the peach crop. Rumours of smut
in the wheat at the Hawkesbury were later confirmed by news that the
crops—not only there, but at Parramatta, Prospect, Baulkham Hills and
Seven Hills—were almost ruined by this deadly blight. In Sydney
labourers were busy in Pitt Row constructing a new gutter for the water
which made a bog of the street in rainy weather—but save for occasional
storms there was little rain that spring, and the colony resigned itself to
another droughty summer.

In November came two important items of news. The *Ocean*, drop-
ping anchor in the harbour towards the end of the month, sent ashore a
bundle of letters for the Governor. She hailed from Port Phillip on the
south coast, where Colonel David Collins had arrived from England some
seven weeks earlier to found the settlement which King had so earnestly
advocated. But the report of it which he now studied, sitting with his
wife on the verandah of Government House, was not enthusiastic.

Anxious to get his people disembarked and settled after a long voyage,
Collins had lost no time in exploring the bay, but his examination had
evidently proved disappointing. In one place he had found fresh water,
but a soil that was mainly sand; in another, better soil, but no water.
And at last he had been compelled to land his stores and some three or
four hundred people upon about five acres of land on the eastern shore,
". . . from which," he explained, "I now have the honour of reporting
my proceedings to Your Excellency."

Mrs. King, meanwhile, had seized upon a letter from Sir Joseph Banks.
She broke in upon her husband's preoccupation with a little shriek.

"Oh, my! Pray listen to this, my love! Sir Joseph says he has received all our packages—how fortunate!—and he goes on: *'among the last was the head of one of your subjects, which is said to have caused some comical consequences when opened at the Customs House.'* That ugly savage, Pemulwy! Can you not imagine their amazement? And it is now in a museum!"

"H'm . . . ?" The Governor dragged his mind from Collins' letter, and looked at her absently. "Pemulwy? Ah, yes. . . ." For one second the thought of that stubborn, vanquished enemy crossed his mind like a shadow, but his attention was too strongly engaged by Collins' news to hold it. His wife, quick to notice his abstraction, enquired:

"How does the Colonel speak of Port Phillip? Is he satisfied with their situation there?"

"He is not," King replied gloomily, "and their situation seems far from comfortable. He thinks but poorly of the timber. He says the bay is dangerous, and a vessel must have favourable wind and tide to enter—and then the water is too shallow to come close in to the shore, so they have had great labour unloading. And most of their stores still lie piled in the open, at the mercy of the weather."

"I declare, it puts me in mind of what you have told me of the first settling here, when there was nought but virgin forest!"

"There was a good harbour," he said, "and good water. There, it appears, they are depending on casks sunk into the sand."

But he had been thinking himself that it was like an echo from the past, and he wondered if Collins, writing that letter, had heard the echo too. The silent, untouched land, offering nothing; the natives, watching from afar, between curiosity and resentment; the confusion of disembarkation and unloading; the anxious weighing of difficulties and advantages; the convicts—some useful, but many useless; the lack of reliable overseers and artisans; the scantiness of the military force; how well he knew it all!

Mrs. King was intent upon Sir Joseph's letter again.

"He is disturbed that Captain Flinders' charts have not arrived." She uttered an indignant exclamation. "He says the Captain's enemies suspect idleness on his part! Idleness! How I hope that the *Cumberland* is making a speedy voyage home so that he may vindicate himself! What else does Colonel Collins say, my love?"

King lowered the letter to his knee for a moment and stared out across the harbour.

"He thinks it would be advisable to remove. And indeed, unless he can come upon a better situation . . ."

He left the sentence unfinished. The thought crossed his mind that perhaps Collins was not the man to have been entrusted with such a task. Something more was needed, he thought, than the previous experience of the country, and the praiseworthy attention to duty which had apparently caused his appointment. Recalling the quiet, mild young man who had so admirably filled the offices of Judge Advocate and Secretary to the Governor during Phillip's regime, and who had so meticulously recorded the events of that bitter time, King wondered if this was the temperament which made bold decisions, and overcome obstacles. Was not this a man whose virtues were humanity, conscientiousness and application, rather than fearlessness, resolve, and audacious optimism? Was he not one who observed rather than acted, who wore down his own confidence by long weighing of pros and cons, who doubted and hesitated under the burden of responsibility . . . ?

He returned moodily to his study of the letter. It had always been his view that a strong, permanent settlement should be established some-where to the southward—and if Port Phillip proved unsuitable, then it must be Van Diemen's Land. Either Port Dalrymple, he thought, or the Derwent—where already his small garrison under Lieutenant Bowen stood guard against any attempt by the French to dispute His Majesty's possession . . .

And Mrs. King, on the end of this thought, exclaimed:

"Mercy on us! Sir Joseph declares the political situation in Europe is troublesome and turbulent in the extreme. Only listen to this! *'The Chief Consul wishes to be at war; and in order to bring about this event he assails us with uninterrupted affronts of the most serious nature.'* La! How tiresome the man is! *'Flesh and blood cannot stand it,'* Sir Joseph says. I should think not, indeed! *'We have already had a message from the King to say that the French are arming, and refuse to say for what purpose, which has put the spirit of this nation very much up. How it will end I cannot foresee, but it cannot go on—well, as long as the Chief Consul lives.'* "

She looked at her husband over the sheets of paper, and her eyes expressed a truly feminine mixture of dismay, bewilderment and exaspera-tion. They demanded of him, as a man, some explanation of man's incorrigible belligerence. He pulled out of his pocket another letter received but little more than a week ago from Ile de France, and un-folded it slowly. Did he, an Englishman, want war? Did Baudin, a Frenchman, want war?

"It but adds weight to Baudin's hint," he said morosely. He read aloud, hardly aware himself that he was reading less to refresh his memory than to refute that implied accusation in her eyes.

"*On prétend qu'actuelment il existe quelques discussions politiques entre votre nation et la mienne; mais j'espère que le nuage qui s'est élévé se dissipera sans que l'on entende gronder le tonnerre. . . .*'" Again it was an impulse which he did not analyse that made him pass from French to English as he read the final sentence; some obscure desire that these words should carry the utmost flavour of validity, prompted him to lend them the conviction of his own tongue. " *'In any case I commend myself to your friendship, and pray you to believe that we shall always be friends.'* "

The brief silence that followed was broken only by the rustle of paper as he re-folded the letter and returned it to his pocket.

"Ah, the good Monsieur Baudin!" sighed Mrs. King at last.

"Yet I fear," remarked her husband, "that the thunder is already audible, my love."

She rose with an impatient movement. Her gesture, as she tossed Sir

Joseph's letter on the table before him, proclaimed that she washed her hands of all this nonsense. She cried crossly: "War, war, we are scarce finished with one before another is threatened!"

      *   *   *   *   *

By the time His Excellency sat down to reply to Collins two days later, he knew that the threat had become a reality. For upon that day the *Patterson*, an American ship, arrived with news of war between England and France. The Governor thought it improbable that this remote corner of the globe would be considered worthy of attack, but he prepared, nevertheless, for emergencies. Collins must get himself established—somewhere. If Port Phillip would not answer, then elsewhere. His own preference was for Port Dalrymple, but he left the final decision to Collins, and turned to the affairs of his own domain. The free inhabitants must, of course, be privileged to place themselves at his disposal for its defence; they must be trained to the use of cannon, and to bearing arms; the Sydney and Parramatta Loyal Association must be re-formed. He bestirred himself. He bustled. Some part of him was almost grateful for a crisis which, while calling for his attention, was yet something for which he could not be held responsible. Yet he was human, and he had his friendships. He thought of Baudin. He remembered with satisfaction that he had urged Flinders not to put in at Ile de France— and then, with uneasiness, that he had made him the bearer of official despatches. And he wondered anxiously: "Where is Flinders?"

      *   *   *   *   *

That summer was hot and dry. The fields of native grass were no longer green, but a pale brown that turned silver when the wind ran over them. Caked mud lay at the bottom of creeks and ponds. Cattle were afflicted by a strange disease, of which some died. By now the stores held such reserves of grain that no serious hardship need be caused by one season of drought, but there were other effects of this implacably fine weather. There was bemusement in so much sunshine. There was almost a throb in the burning light, almost a beat in the air, as if nature had fallen asleep, and nothing were left but the rhythm of her breathing. In her slumber men were not even a dream, and their cultivation no more than an unregarded touch upon her breast.

Against this momentous indifference, this maddening oblivion, human activity almost seemed incongruous. Within this idle sequence of golden days human impulse swung between the lure of acquiescence and the goad of irritation. The white men were both baffled and affronted by a land which could thus withdraw from them—leave them awkward and ignored, like uninvited guests. They wanted to rouse it, to mark it, to shatter its siesta with their commotions; to scar its earth with plough and fire, and raze its trees; to come and go, full of schemes and projects for its subjection; to build and traffic with what they could tear from it; to brandish clocks and calendars in the face of its ageless, timeless calm.

Man's immemorial urge to be identified with his environment was here frustrated. He could, as yet, neither claim this place, nor permit it to absorb him; neither call it his, nor yield to it. Every white man and woman in the colony suffered the spiritual malaise of humanity unrooted —felt a curious sense of impermanence, of illusion, of drifting, almost of transparency, as though they were ghosts, or clouds, or blown shreds of smoke between earth and sky. And so, resist it as they might, and cling as they would to memories of the soil from which they had been torn, they were obsessed by this unresponsive land. They dreamed their various dreams of a contact, a relationship, a union with it—to use it, to know it, to impose a pattern on it, or merely to share its space and its tranquillity; to sow and reap, to explore, to govern, or merely to live with it. There was pain in the slow adjustment of their senses, effort in the attunement of their ears and the re-focussing of their eyes, a struggle between nostalgia for an old, and craving for a new abiding-place. The land slept on through the long summer months, and let them struggle.

This uneasiness of the spirit which, among the free inhabitants of the colony, translated itself either into experimental action of one kind or another, or into a bemused inertia, could find no such outlet among the convicts. For them there could be neither experiment nor idleness, and in the unmerciful routine of drudgery and hardship their imprisoned restlessness mounted towards frenzy and explosion. To dispossess the possessors was the recognised aim of their emotions; revenge and freedom were the desires they saluted in themselves. But behind these acknowledged passions the riddle of the land was, for them too, an itch and an incitement.

In the latter half of November a gang from the Government farm at Castle Hill came plodding along the road to Beltrasna. They walked slowly in single file, an armed soldier riding on either side, and Mr. Mannion, returning from an inspection of his fields, reined in for a moment to watch them. King had decreed that prisoners at public labour, having got in the Government wheat, were to be available for three weeks of the harvesting period to such settlers as might require their services, and Mr. Mannion had promptly taken advantage of this welcome indulgence. For though the drought had destroyed the early promise of abundant crops, sickness had broken out in his convict hut, and several of his labourers had perforce been removed to the hospital at Parramatta. Extra hands were needed—and here they were.

All the same he was frowning slightly as he rode on. He did not like the intermingling of convicts from different parts of the colony. He did not, in fact, like to see any convict speak to another convict—for what could such rogues have to say to each other which was not undesirable and probably seditious? Yet he must have additional labour, and as he rode on up the hill towards the house he was making a mental note that Toole must be exhorted to even sterner vigilance.

Now he could see his vegetable gardens laid out on a gentle slope to the east of the house. Across the red-brown soil stretched fine green ribbons of young plants, brilliant in the slanting sunlight of late afternoon. He had got his lettuces and his cabbages in early this year; at Green Hills, so he was told, they were only just being sown. But if this dry weather should continue . . .

His hand jerked suddenly on the reins, and Mor stood still. Mr. Mannion sat and stared. A solitary figure had come into view between those straight green rows, and some optical illusion—produced, perhaps, by its position on the skyline, and against the golden light of the westering sun—made it look gigantic. A man, stooping, hoeing between the young plants—but a man eight feet—ten feet—twelve feet high! A man whose vast, black silhouette was ringed with fiery radiance, so that it seemed as if he flamed, as if the sunlight with its heat and power were being generated within him, instead of behind him in the blazing sky . . .

Mr. Mannion shrugged and rode on, but he was frowning more than ever. A curious phenomenon! Thus he tried to dismiss it, and yet it somehow underlined with a strange, disturbing emphasis the doubts which had just been troubling him. An ill-conditioned dog, that Finn! A surly, dangerous rascal. It had been a wise policy to keep him away from his fellows as much as possible—a policy even more rigorously pursued since the outrageous incident with that abominable book. Well, he had suffered for that—and several others with him who had seemed in danger of being influenced by his vile, inflammatory doctrines. Since then he had worked alone, with irons on his ankles, for he was the kind of desperate villain who might attempt escape, as it had been attempted at Castle Hill—and here the mountains were temptingly close . . .

Mr. Mannion glanced sideways occasionally as he rode at the distant figure which now, as he came level with it, diminished, lost its illusive immensity and its borrowed radiance. Alone in the wide field with the long downward sweep of other fields behind it, and the empty vault of sky above, it looked small, dwarfed, insignificant. Mr. Mannion turned his back on it and cantered home.

Finn watched him go. From his hilltop he too had seen the convicts arriving from Castle Hill, and when Mannion had vanished he looked down at the earth again, and returned with a stirring of excitement to his endless thoughts.

He thought of escape—but not an escape of the kind Mr. Mannion imagined. Sometimes, indeed, he looked at the mountains and toyed with the idea of that kind of escape, but always he returned to the problem of a liberation which would be not only his own, and which stretched far beyond any hard and hunted life which he could spend in that unknown territory across the river. He thought of liberty which could strike shackles not only from his own feet, but from the feet of all men everywhere. And he thought not only of shackles made of iron, but of others, invisible, which held men's minds imprisoned. He felt them on his own mind—the lack of learning, the weight of bodily exhaustion, the nagging temptation to resignation or despair—and in these long days alone he pulled at them, worked at them, eased them here and moved them there so that he released, from time to time, a thought, a wonder, a question, even a revelation which rewarded his patient striving. Thus he had discovered how solitude could sharpen the senses, and whet the emotions to a keener edge. Thus he had realised that the earth would not be hated—even in bondage to it; that there was a fellowship

which no distorting man-made customs could destroy between his hands
and these plants; that with every root they sent down into the soil, he too
was taking root. And then that curiously poignant discovery turned to
him its dark side—the knowledge that for all his husbandry this earth
was not for him.

What earth was his? Six feet in which to lie some day when he had
gone beyond the laws of man, and nature took back his body and made
earth of it too? Yes, that at least; and there fate would be equitable,
and justice perfect, for what else, what more than this, awaited Mr.
Mannion, or his wife, or Toole, or His Excellency, or the King himself?
And so he came to proof that the bitterness felt for one's own mutilated
life was, by itself, but a barren thing. Were a man's efforts to be
governed and limited by the span of three-score years and ten? Was his
vision to be always halted by the headstone on his grave?

To be so much alone with the earth, and to think so much of the
future was to feel towards a fusion of the two; it was, in this empty,
unknown land, to confront a hypothesis, and a challenge. In the old
world, long-established facts lent to conjecture of the future a kind of
desperation in which hope flared bravely but thinly. There authority
was monstrous and monstrously armoured; there time had laid its sanction
upon custom; there nothing could be changed without first destroying.
To look into the future was to peer with half-blind eyes upon which
generations and centuries had stamped a pattern so familiar that the
forward thrust of imagination was obstructed. But here—what facts?
A huge and empty land. A nothingness. No pattern. No customs. A
sheet of paper with no words written . . .

But upon this eager, racing thought he sternly clamped a sudden brake
of grim qualification. With *almost* no words written. . . . He straightened,
moving his shoulders automatically to ease their aching. The sun was nearly
gone, the day's work nearly over. From this hilltop the fields sank away
to the east, the north and the south, and the dark trees took up their
tale of space and emptiness. To the west the river lay shining at the
foot of the hills, and beyond it those hills climbed to a sky which roofed
the unknown. But close to him were a house, a barn, a stables, and the
long, low roof of a convict hut. The page was not quite virgin, and the
words which had been written on it were the beginning of an old and
too-familiar story.

His face and his thoughts were sombre again as he returned to his
digging. The loss of his book had brought not only physical isolation,
imposed upon him by his master, but a spiritual isolation imposed upon
him by his fellows at night, when, of necessity, he was returned to their
society. He and his book had brought punishment upon them; he felt their
mistrust and their withdrawal. His separation from the book which had
been his talisman and which, with patient and unremitting caution he
had managed to secrete and preserve so long, had seemed the most insupportable of his trials until he had realised that he was not separated
from it after all. It was more potent now than it had ever been, for he
found that his memory still held whole passages of it; and where his

memory failed, and he could no longer turn to its pages, his own thought must labour, and grow stronger with labouring. Now his brain not only received it, but replied to it; now his use of it was less a study than a conversation, less a research than a communion.

It was answering at this moment his thought that the page was not quite virgin. It was reminding him that not only society had been brought here, but Government, and holding up for his contemplation its definition of Government. "The badge of lost innocence . . ." That was true. It was man's confession of failure. Yet to confess failure was not to embrace despair, and in this land, so lightly marked as yet by tradition, new patterns of life seemed possible. That was what he had tried to make his fellow-prisoners see. Sometimes he could strike fire from them, but it was a fire like the flaring of dead leaves—hot, fierce, and quickly dead. It could light and warm their vision of to-morrow, or even of next week, but next year was beyond its range, and the next generation no more than a fairytale. They lived in their half-starved, half-naked bodies, seeing achievement in a few extra mouthfuls of food, assuagement in a pannikin of rum, revenge on the master in a moment's stolen idleness, hope in the expiring of a sentence and a life still black with poverty. He had tried to tell them—his own back raw and bloody —that the menace of the flogging post was in their fear of it; that the invincibility of a red-coat was in their doubts of themselves; that the power of the Governor was built upon their resignation, their fecklessness, their ignorance and their despair. They looked at their chains, gestured at the musket in Toole's hands, and jeered at him.

Yet there was strength in them too. They could repel him with their stubborn disbelief, but very few would betray him. With their own endurance worn paper-thin they could find reserves to sustain one of their fellows in whom, for the moment, endurance had failed, and move quickly to his aid with a subterfuge, a rough ministration, an extra effort of their aching arms, a word to distract the attention of an overseer. . . In the harsh texture of their talking there would sometimes appear a fine, bright thread of tenderness; a word—or perhaps a silence—would tell of a friend who had been valued, a woman who had been loved and not merely used, a child who had been cherished, a hope nurtured, a place remembered. This, too, was a strength. But it was the useless strength of men imprisoned behind high walls. The present hemmed them in. Reunion with *that* friend, *that* woman, *that* child? Fulfilment of *that* hope? Return to *that* place? Their bitter, jibing laughter mocked his assurance of a future when no man would be separated from his woman or his child, when hope would be but the first step to achievement, and the nostalgic exile would have only to turn homeward . . .

A dream, they said. He became angry, and struck his hoe more violently into the ground. Aye, as all things were dreams before they became facts! Dangerous half-virtue of endurance which became a vice without its other half, made up of dreams! Here was the marriage from which achievement was born. And Finn, awaiting the end of the day, thought of the night, of new faces in the convict huts, and of tidings that elsewhere in this grim colony there were others who could dream.

*   *   *   *   *

And indeed there was a different note in the talk that went on in the fitful half-light from the single tin lamp on the floor. Here was a break in the deadliness of the labouring routine, relief from the boredom and the irritation of too close and too prolonged association. Voices spoke more crisply; there was less surliness, and no quarrelling; there were a few flashes of grim wit that brought laughter, and even some singing as the night wore on.

At first the craving was only for news. All Mr. Mannion's care had not entirely prevented the spread of rumour and gossip to the convicts in this outpost of the colony, for sometimes a new prisoner must come to replace one whose time was expired; sometimes an expiree, returning with a drayload of goods for the great house, contrived a few moments' conversation with his erstwhile companions, or one at Green Hills sent a message by Andy Prentice; sometimes, even, a *Gazette* found its way surreptitiously to the huts, and then those who could read had an avid audience. But such infrequent incidents provided only crumbs of news compared with the feast which the uninterrupted society of six new convicts from the outside world could bring. Moreover, the prisoners at Castle Hill, like those at Beltrasna, were predominantly Irish, and there was a stimulating flavour of national reunion in their presence.

One of them was a prematurely white-haired man called Gogarty, whose brother had died in the Beltrasna fields three years ago; another was a talkative little weaver from Belfast, whom his companions called Phelim; a third, John Place, was the sole survivor of three absconders who had attempted to cross the mountains; he had made a second attempt, and the weals of the flogging he had suffered on his re-capture still showed plainly on his bony shoulders. There was, too, a youth with a round and strangely childlike face and a vacant smile, of whom his companions whispered that he had not all his wits about him.

" 'Tis the nature of the way God made him," explained Gogarty, "but it's a voice like an angel he has. Let you be giving us a song now, Paddy, the way we'll be after thinking we're in Heaven itself."

The laughter at that was unmirthful, but the high, true voice, more a boy's than a man's, held them silent. To succumb, even for a few moments, to the nostalgia it awakened, was to return with increased bitterness to present realities, and the song was hardly ended before Phelim asked:

"Is it true, then, what they do be saying, how there's no heed took of the Government orders in this place?"

A chorus said "Aye!" And "True it is!" But Finn denied sharply:

" 'Tis but a part of the truth, and the worse for that. The master has his wits at work, and well he's knowing that without he takes a man to the magistrate from time to time there'll be those must be asking why. When there's a high-up folk come here to visit him it's Government hours we keep—but when there's none to carry tales the bell's after ringing

early for work and late to leave off, if so be it suits him. And what's to
hinder? It's only the birds flying over that do be seeing the post in the
yard outside these walls, and the ground red with blood about it the way
a pig might have been killed there."

He felt a sudden impatience. He wanted to ask in plain words
whether it were true, as rumour said, that rebellion was being planned at
Castle Hill. He longed to be able to urge that there were those in the
Beltrasna huts who would rise to support any general revolt. But he
was no stranger to the techniques of conspiracy; he knew from the bitter
experience which had brought him here that plans less often went astray
from treachery than from rash talking, from the faulty assessment of
character, from over-confidence, and too much said too soon. So for the
moment he attempted no more revelation of his own attitude than might
be guessed from the bitterness of his tone; and he thought that Gogarty
looked keenly at him while he spoke. He thought, too, with a stir of
excitement, that when Place mentioned the name of Cunningham it might
be a kind of hint, an oblique message, a tentative approach. Yet it was
not he, still cautious, who responded, but a man named Lynch who had
come out in the *Anne* transport from Cork nearly three years ago—one
of a hundred and thirty Irish prisoners transported for sedition—and who
had been brought straight from the vessel to Beltrasna. This man broke
in eagerly:

"Cunningham, is it? Well I know him, the wild boy he is!"

Phelim peered at him in the half-light.

"Is it on the *Anne* ye were, then?"

"Where else? And in the thick of the mutiny with a cutlass I was
after grabbing from a sentinel on deck, and he out of his wits entirely
the way I put the fear o' God into him . . . !"

Phelim interrupted sharply:

"It's below the mutiny was, if so be that . . ."

"Amn't I after telling ye," shouted Lynch, "that it was on deck I
was with a score of others for the exercise, and there's Cunningham below
when the Captain goes down with the mate and the gunner, and it's
himself that catches the Captain by the throat and calls out 'Death or
Liberty!' On the deck we hear the alarm given, an' we snatching iron
bars from the caboose an' laying about us when the soldiers come, an' it's
God's truth we'd have held them off till those below could join us, if so be
two white-livered traitors hadn't been losin' heart and releasin' the Captain
and the others, the curse o' Cromwell on 'em! But then it's all over as
fast as it's begun. . . ." The excitement passed out of his voice; he passed
his hand across his mouth nervously. "They get wind that Marcus Sheehy
and Kit Grogan's at the bottom of it. An' Sheehy goes over to the sharks
with a bullet in him, an' Grogan's tied up for a hundred and fifty strokes
with the cat, an' we standing by to see it done . . ."

"Aye," said Phelim, looking at Gogarty.

"Aye," said Gogarty, nodding his white head slowly, "that's the way
Cunningham does be telling it."

"And why wouldn't he," Lynch snapped irritably, "and that the way of it? A fine, wild boy he was, and a high heart in him. It's what I've seen with me own eyes, no less, and Finn here says the same, and himself with Cunningham once in a bit o' business in the Wicklow mountains when Holt was after getting his men together . . ."

Finn saw Gogarty's eyes turn slowly towards him again, intent and considering. He returned the stare with one no less appraising, and his thoughts were grim. Yes, he had been with Holt, and to this day he had never seen clearly through the confusion of that time, or been able to still the uneasy voice of suspicion in his mind. He had been one of the band in the dark, wild Devil's Glen when spies had guided the military to their hiding place and set fire to it; when Holt became the leader of McMahon's men he had joined them; he had helped to make the gun-powder called "Holt's Mixture" from saltpetre and sulphur and ground charcoal; he had been in the Battle of Ballyellis; he had watched new recruits coming in to join them at the rate of thirty or forty a day—some of them deserters from the army, bringing muskets and ammunition with them—and he had known the fierce excitement of effective action, and the exhilaration of success.

And then—what had happened? In the wild disorder of that guerilla warfare, always on the move, what could one know save that a rot began, a decay, a crumbling of spirit that seemed to have its origin in their leader— with a price of three hundred pounds on his head? He came and went, and no one knew his business. Sometimes he was the General, full of fire, imagination, and inventiveness—and then he was someone else, whose eyes were watchful, cautious, calculating. "Can I trust you?" said those eyes. "Or shall I desert you before you desert me?" And one day, after a long absence, he had reappeared with news that he was about to surrender himself—and no one could check the ebb of confidence, or halt the disintegration of his little army. And then, whispers . . . he was being well received by the gentry . . . he was dining with lords . . . he was far, far from them, a stranger . . .

In the fury and frustration of that time mistrust had bred fear, and fear had bred betrayal, and betrayal had meant—for others besides Finn —capture, and the voyage that had brought him here to this moment, and the rumour of another rebellion, and the sound of familiar names . . .

He said slowly:

"Some months since I did be hearin' how Cunningham's in favour at Castle Hill, an' he with a house o' his own, an' made overseer of the stonemasons . . ."

"He is that," Gogarty answered, watching him.

"An' they do be sayin' how Holt lives at his ease in Parramatta, the way he's a free man. An' how it's a hundred acres o' land he has, be it more or less, an' his own beasts, an' money in his pocket. An' how he's Cox's man . . ."

"Ah, whisht, now," interrupted Phelim, "it's more the way Cox is his man, I'm tellin' ye, for Cox is near bein' ruined not a year gone, an' who is it but Holt that saves his money for him at all? It's cunning as a fox he is, an' divil a man I know could be up to his tricks—an' he callin' a sale o' Cox's stock, an' gettin' them that come to buy so full o liquor they wouldn't be knowin' a sheep from a pig . . . !"

But in the mutter of talk and laughter that followed Finn sat silent, staring at the floor. Yes—that was Holt. Resource, ingenuity, impudence, daring—the qualities of a leader, but with a kind of blight on them. Where was his heart? Had it ever been with his army, fighting and starving in the Irish hills? Or had there been nothing but a quick, intriguing brain, and a vanity that must be fed? And what was the truth of that business during the *Minerva's* voyage when he himself had been lying ill, hearing the commotion only through a fog of delirium? He said suddenly:

"There was a time on the *Minerva* when he might have took the ship. It was a Spanish frigate opened fire on us, an' he at liberty an' given charge o' one o' the guns, an' six prisoners of his own choosin' to help him. . . . An' there's one o' them was after tellin' me they was only waitin' for his signal—but it never came . . ."

Silence fell again; unspoken, but loud as shouting, the question in Finn's mind communicated itself to the others. *When men who have been with us come to a little ease and comfort, when they are admitted to the outer fringe of respectability, when there is bestowed upon them a shred of independence and a semblance of liberty—are they with us still?* There, in that well-founded doubt, lay the impotence of the oppressed. They could not match the intricate, powerful and exactly organised might of established authority. They had nothing with which to challenge an always functioning and always disciplined power which, from its massive fortress of privilege, could turn a different battery upon them wherever they might seek to breach it. A cry for justice was answered coldly by the courts; a cry of protest brought admonishment from the pulpits; a cry of hunger, if it were answered at all, was answered with a bowl of soup, a poorhouse, and the bitter bread of charity; the ultimate and desperate cry of rebellion was cut short by the crack of muskets. And even then this invincible power had a last shot in its locker. For when a man came on against it dangerously, evading law and force, ignoring clerical rebuke, and spurning charity, there still remained bribery, temptation, the lure of admittance to the fortress. . . . How many had reached the ramparts as attackers, only to slink in by some side door held enticingly ajar, leaving the rest baffled, leaderless, and disillusioned?

Some such thought. was in their minds, and conversation died under the weight of it. But Finn lay awake long into the night, cursing the fate which had sent him to this isolated place instead of to a settlement where he might have been among those who planned . . . ?

*   *   *   *   *

About this time Johnny sought out his brother. He knew Andy's movements by now, and had made it his business to learn, also, the movements of the settler on whose small, isolated and ill-cultivated farm the boy did as little work as possible. Blake liked his pannikin of rum when the day's work was over, and knew where to go for it; Johnny, crouching in the long grass by the ramshackle outhouse which was Andy's lodging,

knew that the cottage held no one save the settler's wife, and waited
alertly, but without fear. Andy, slouching round the corner of the shed
in the gathering dusk, came face to face with a red-headed youth who did
not move a muscle, but sat staring at him with an odd expression of
searching concentration.

"You know me?" he asked, after a blank pause.

Andy was a dull and loutish youth, but he had eyes in his head, and
he could not fail to see that this stranger was oddly like himself. Red
hair, brown eyes, a pale skin burned copper by the sun, features not unlike
his own . . .

He had been only three when his elder brother disappeared; memory
could not help him, save to a vague recollection of someone who was
always being scolded, punished, beaten, always the centre of a commotion,
always in trouble. But he knew the story—he had heard his mother tell
it a hundred times. He was still gaping silently when the word "Johnny"
was spoken, but already he must have been near to guessing, for it came
less as shock than as confirmation.

He looked furtively over his shoulder towards the cottage. He was no
convict, and he was about his lawful business; neither was Johnny a
convict—but Andy felt very strongly that if he had any business it was
not lawful. The very fact that he was alive seemed unlawful. Andy
was frightened. He moved nearer where the shed hid them from the
cottage, and asked in a scared undertone:

"Where you been all this time?"

Johnny waved his arm vaguely towards the south-west. He had his
purpose in seeking out Andy and he did not want to waste time on
explanations. He began to ask questions, angry when the boy seemed
at first too frightened, too stupid, too confused to answer them, but
continuing to ask, to repeat them over and over again, until Andy, as if
hypnotised, made stumbling replies.

Where was their mother?

Up there—up at Mannion's.

How often did Andy see her? Many times? Not many times?

Andy floundered through a long explanation that he went as often as
he could, for his rations left him hungry and his mother fed him well,
and even saved delicacies for him sometimes from the table of the great
house. Once in a month—sometimes twice in a month . . .

Johnny's thick brows met over his eyes in the effort to follow this.
Of all white-man ideas he found time the hardest to grasp, and was still
baffled by the substitution of weeks, months and years for days, moons
and seasons. He recognised the word "month" but could not yet feel
the time which it represented, and he tried to make Andy translate it in
terms of days and nights counted on his upraised fingers, and asked at
last: "When the moon comes you go, when it comes back you go again?"

Andy was too bewildered to argue; he thought that was near enough,
and agreed.

"What day? You go to-morrow?"

"To-morrow's Tuesday," Andy said, staring blankly.

"Next day?"

There was another long struggle for mutual comprehension while Andy tried to explain that work ceased early on Saturdays, and his master some-times gave him leave for the afternoon and the night, provided he were back in time for Divine Service on Sunday, if it were to be held that week, because the preacher came only occasionally . . .

Johnny neither knew nor cared anything about preachers or Divine Service. He made Andy draw strokes on the ground to represent the days between to-day and Saturday, and between that Saturday and another Saturday. When he had that matter settled he wanted to know if Andy slept at his mother's cottage when he went to Beltrasna, and Andy, relieved by so simple a question, nodded. But the next startled him so much that for a moment he could not answer at all.

How many guns and pistols had Mr. Mannion?

Andy, pale with fright, stammered:

"G-g-guns? Why? What d'ye ask that for?"

"I want 'em," said Johnny simply.

Andy's eyes fairly bulged with astonishment and terror. Johnny, observing but ignoring his fear, persisted:

"How many? This? This?" The fingers of one hand and then the other lifted.

Andy did not know. He had seldom been in any but the back portions of the house, but he admitted at last, unwillingly, that on one or two occasions when he had been summoned to Mr. Mannion's study to carry messages, he had seen two muskets and two pistols hanging on the wall. There would most likely be more somewhere else. He did not know.

And where was the ammunition?

Andy had seen boxes in the storeroom when he went there with his mother, but he thought there would be more in the house—he did not know where.

How were the overseers armed?

They carried pistols, but they might have muskets as well in their quarters. "What d'ye ask me things like that for? How would I know?"

Who kept the keys of the convict hut?

Mr. Mannion, and Toole, the head overseer.

Who kept the keys of the house and the storeroom?

Mr. Mannion and . . .

Andy went quite dumb with fright, but Johnny battered down his resistance with a merciless, direct question.

Their mother . . . ?

Yes . . . yes . . . "What devilment are ye up to? Clear out o' this and leave me be!"

Andy could see now whither this catechism was leading, and he sweated with fear. He was not going to have his neck stretched for a long-lost, almost forgotten, and obviously mad brother. It would not do, he was thinking frantically, to tell all this to his mother, for she would never permit betrayal of a son whom she had always loved far more than either of her other children. Some long-felt jealousy may have fed the satisfaction he felt in deciding to tell Mr. Mannion himself. . . . He would be rewarded . . .

And then he met Johnny's eyes again, and saw that for the eyes of a madman they were very piercing, steady and shrewd. He was in such a fog of alarm and confusion that it took him a little time to realise that now he was being asked about the murder of Merrett, almost two years ago.

"Killed, 'e was," Andy stammered stupidly, "by the natives . . ."

Johnny's eyes glinted with something almost like a smile.

"No." He stood up, and Andy retreated a pace without knowing why. Johnny said:

"I killed him." He repeated, tapping his breast:

"I killed him."

Andy swallowed hard. He protested weakly:

"Ye're mad! 'E was killed with spears—native spears."

Johnny nodded.

"My spears. I throw spears good." He half turned to go, and said over his shoulder almost casually, more as a statement than a threat:

"You tell about me, you don't do what I say, I kill you too."

He went, leaving Andy to a terror that was almost superstitious. There was still something about Johnny that struck all his white acquaintances as—queer. They could not more accurately define it. It might show in his speech, perhaps, or his voice, or his manner, or his movements. But above all in an attitude of mind which was sometimes nakedly exposed by what he said—a kind of direct, fantastic confidence which, in a society that lived furtively and thought deviously, seemed like madness. It was as though words spoken in their own tongue were yet incomprehensible. Andy had felt it in that brief, incredible remark about Mannion's firearms: "I want 'em." He turned it over dazedly in his mind as he stood there in the darkening field. "*I want 'em.*" Christ, who was there among the convicts or the penurious who didn't sometimes dream of being armed with the arms of the rich? But when Johnny said "I want 'em" it was plain that wanting them was no day-dream, but merely a preliminary to getting them. He didn't seem to *know*. . . . He didn't seem to *understand* . . .

He didn't seem to be afraid . . .

Where did he come from? Was he—ah!—was he the mysterious stranger who came to the settlement to barter beef, and disappeared again somewhere up the river? Andy nodded to himself. But where did he go? Where did he live? Spears . . . ? He remembered his mother's story of how Johnny had escaped from Sydney once when he was a small child, and lived for a time with the natives; and that memory, linking now with the strange, alien quality he had felt, made his flesh creep. It seemed to say that something had *happened* to Johnny—something more than mere physical adventures—something mysterious and—and—against nature—that made him remote, alien, incalculable, and dangerous . . .

He could come at night, invisible, soundless, and nothing to tell of his coming or his going but prints of bare feet, two native spears, and a dead man . . .

Andy shivered and plunged blindly for the dark shelter of his hovel. He would say nothing—nothing! He would keep out of Johnny's way . . . !

1 8 0 4

There was no need for Andy to avoid his alarming brother, for Johnny's visits to Green Hills were interrupted by the sudden death of Tom Towns. The death itself was no more than an incident quickly over, and it took only an hour or so to bury his body in a little gully not far from the hut. But Johnny had a fancy to make a tombstone. Though there was as yet no church or churchyard at Green Hills, people died there all the same, and were buried, not always in unmarked graves, Johnny had seen and studied a couple of rough headstones, and he remembered them as he stood by the mound under which Towns lay finally imprisoned by the land he had feared so much.

The sandstone cliffs had shed many a handsome boulder during the centuries, and Johnny chose one which was roughly rectangular, and set to work to trim it. When he was satisfied at last, he rolled and levered it with Billalong's help into position at the head of the grave, but all this was a tiresome preliminary. Now came the part which was a labour of love—the cutting of words in the stone. It was not only the pleasure of making letters which inspired him; he felt that a burial called for some kind of ritual, but he knew of none save the native ones which were obviously unsuitable, and could not, in any case, be performed without a tribe. The white-man ritual of writing seemed appropriate. And as he worked he found a sense of unity between his white and his native self, for this chipping on rocks was something practised by white men and black alike. He, however, had better tools than a sharp flint. He had a hammer and a chisel, and he cut the letters deeply and clearly, if a trifle irregularly. TOM TOWNS. When it was finished he studied it with pleasure, and yet with doubt. On the headstones at Green Hills there had been more—but Towns had never taught him about dates, and had, indeed, lost his own sense of the passage of time. Johnny had no idea what year it was, nor could he have written it if he had known. But the stone did look too bare, and pride in his handiwork told him how to fill it. It was a long task. Sometimes his native self grew tired of it, and he yielded to Billalong's importunities and went fishing or hunting, or visiting the tribes, but always his white self drew him back to work with something of the stubborn patience he had brought to his first game on the bank of a creek nearly sixteen years ago. At last there came a day when he stood back and looked at it with pride and contentment.

TOM TOWNS

JOHNNY PRENTICE MADE IT

Now it was done.

It was done, and he was alone save for Billalong. He was gripped by
a new kind of restlessness—the sex-urge of his young manhood, made
keener and more demanding by sudden solitude. Possessed by this new
desire, he turned again to the primitive people among whom, in past
years, he had been prepared for it, and through the first two full-summer
months of the year he returned almost entirely to a life among the native
tribes. For weeks at a time the hut was deserted—but before he left it
some impulse lately stimulated by contact with more acquisitive people,
made him not only lock the door, but barricade the window from within.
The turning of a key, which had been but a ceremony, had become a
precaution.

It was his own need which drove him back to the natives, but this
temporary return to tribal life fulfilled a need for Billalong too. The
boy was fourteen now, and though he had always been made welcome in
the camps of the black men, his life with Johnny had isolated him not
only from the companionship, but also, more importantly, from the
spiritual experiences of his dark contemporaries. He was in the position
of a boy whose education has been seriously interrupted by truancy; for
though he had passed through the earliest stages of his initiation before
Cunnembeillee's death, his contacts with the tribes since then had been
but visits, allowing no time for the prolonged and serious rites which
custom demanded, and he was, therefore, something of a problem to the
tribesmen. It had always been conceded, however, that the white man,
Androo, who had come among them long ago, who had died, and who
now lived again as Dyonn-ee, was a being who could not be made to fit
exactly into their rigid and intricate social organisation, and towards
whom a certain tolerance must be observed. This tolerance, it was now
agreed, must be extended to Billalong. It was to be deplored that he
was so ignorant, and that various aspects of his education had been so
neglected, but he was a fine, strong lad, and it was remembered that he
had endured the lacerations of his tribal marking with praiseworthy
fortitude. They were prepared to take him back into the tribe and do
the best they could at this late stage to make a man of him. He saw little
of Johnny, for he was kept apart from the camp as the custom was during
the important period of the novitiate, and instructed by the old men upon
the duties and privileges of manhood. And in the meantime Johnny set
about acquiring a wife.

This was not accomplished without some difficulties and delays, for
again tribal law was confounded by a case without precedent. There
were long conclaves among the elders of the tribe before it was decided
that the rules governing marriage would not be too seriously violated by
bestowing upon Dyonn-ee a young girl, lately widowed, called Ngili. He
should, of course, have had an infant bride betrothed to him years ago,

but his whole history as the tribe knew it was so divorced from their law that this normal procedure, like Billalong's education, had been neglected. They clicked their tongues and shook their heads over the untidy business, but agreed that since Dyonn-ee must naturally have a wife, only Ngili would do.

There remained the problem of the hut. She must not go there—it was a forbidden place, marked now by two deaths. On that point they were—to the frightened Ngili's relief—adamant. So Johnny remained with the tribe. He was well enough satisfied with Ngili, for she was young, healthy, and good-tempered, and he required no more of her than that she should meet his sexual needs. For the rest, he hunted with the men, attended their corroborees, and spent a moment or two occasionally playing with Cunnembeillee's two younger sons, Gooradoo and Balgundra, now nearly ten and nine years old. Their little sister, Gooburdi, passed her time with the women, and he saw her only from a distance. Their father, Milbooroo, had a new wife now, and two more children, so Johnny found himself adopted as one of this family group, sitting by Milbooroo's fire, eating whatever the day's hunt had afforded, and thinking only occasionally of the white men's world which had beckoned him so urgently a few months before.

But as the days passed to the end of summer, he grew bored. Having found assuagement for one restlessness, he was beset by another. He began to think again of Green Hills—of the white men he knew there, with whom he had just begun to feel some curious affinity that went deeper than his white skin.

He returned to his hut alone. Billalong was still absent from the camp, preparing for a further stage of his initiation, and as for Ngili, she remained with the tribe, and would still be there when he wanted her again. She, as well as the other natives, accepted his departure without comment; he was Dyonn-ee, of whom orthodox behaviour was not to be expected. So, with the turning of his key in the lock, the opening of the door upon the dim, deserted hut, he stepped back again from the primitive to the modern world—fingered his possessions, put on his clothes again, and clumsily cut his wild, red hair. He had no salt beef to barter this time, and was too impatient to prepare it. All he wanted now was to renew his contact with his own people.

* * * * *

Of all those who smelt trouble in the air during the first months of 1804, none smelt it as keenly—or as warily—as Mr. Joseph Holt. Many were the quiet conversations he had in unobtrusive corners with men whom his reputation as a rebel General drew to him now; desperate men, ready to follow anyone who would lead; anxious, timorous men, unwillingly involved, afraid of the consequences of failure, begging this notable authority for his expert opinion upon the chances of success; men who were merely savage, seeking nothing in rebellion but bloodshed, plunder and revenge; grim, earnest men, speaking with bitterness of tyranny, and of freedom with a sober passion.

He spoke with them all, summing them up in his shrewd, inquisitive, amoral mind, adjusting the tone and tenor of his arguments to each in turn, observing their confusions, their hesitancies and their doubts, promising nothing and hinting much, exploiting his legend, hugging to himself with cynical amusement his own resolve that come what might, there would be no flogging-post and no gallows for Joseph Holt.

To his wife at night in the privacy of their cottage he expounded his philosophy.

"I am an old fox! I have learned where the dangers lie! In troubled times, my heart, men are driven into acts which were far from their thoughts. They are caught in a current, and must go with it; like a whirlpool, it sucks them in against their will. That happened to me in Ireland." He laughed, looking down with pleasure at the good meal set out on the table. "Yet once in I gave a good account of myself, and scrambled out not much the worse!"

Mrs. Holt said dryly:

"A good account of yourself is what you would always give. I could give another. Keep your nose out of this business, pray, or you'll find yourself in a new whirlpool."

He chuckled with enjoyment. He liked his wife's sharp temper and her acid tongue, but even more he liked the contemplation of his own sagacity.

"The devil is busy, I promise you! There was one who came to me to-day with a scheme to overpower the military." He snorted scornfully. "A fool, my love, a numbskull like the rest of them! I declare to you, they couldn't overpower the Orphanage!" He grinned, and pinched her as she passed his chair. "Were I not a married man and a devoted father, and were I disposed to lead this revolt, I could make a short job of it." He struck the handle of his knife two smart blows on the table to emphasise his words. "A *short* and *tidy* job!" His eyes were blank and absent for a moment, and he went on ruminatively: "Aye—they've grown careless, these military gentlemen whose business affairs engage so much of their time. They're so inattentive, so lax in discipline that any man of skill, resource, determination . . ."

He fell silent, staring at his plate, half tempted by his own words, his vanity, and the memory of resounding exploits. Was he not "General" Holt?

His wife's glance at him became fixed, and her eyes narrowed. She snapped:

"Keep your skill and resource for other matters! What have we to do with rebellion, pray? We live well enough, and lay by a little besides."

He looked up at her from beneath his brows, and she answered his slow grin with a toss of her head. He said, yawning:

"Well I know it, my heart! With five hundred pounds put by a man loses his stomach for rebellion. I am on the side of law and government." He glanced at her and added slyly: "But who knows? Laws have been set at naught, and governments cast down. When a contest is at hand the wise man prepares to take his stand with the victors. So I listened well to this poor booby who came to me to-day babbling of liberty, of tyranny, of oppression and extortion, of rights and wrongs, and the like. For I've seen what can be done by boobies when they are seized by this phantasy of freedom—even in a country where law and government are strong. Here they are weak—and isolated—and disunited by their quarrels—and but poorly armed . . ." He looked up and met her frowning stare with a broad smile of reassurance. "These are my private thoughts, my love, uttered only to you who are the light of my eyes and my other half." He reached round the table and drew her on to his knee. "To some I say this, and to others that—and keep my own counsel. But to the wife of my bosom I say what is in my mind, and . . ."

She slapped his roving hand away.

"What's in your mind is so devious that I declare I believe you can't always follow it yourself! Tell me plainly, now, what do you mean to do in this business?"

He roared with laughter and pushed her to her feet.

"Away with you, woman! Can I not eat in peace? My intention is the simplest in the world. Like a ship in bad weather, I shall lie to, and let everyone take care of himself."

*   *   *   *   *

Yet intrigue was the breath of his nostrils, and he sniffed it hungrily. It was true that military discipline was lax. It was true that there was discontent among many besides the convicts. The hardships of the poorer settlers, thought Mr. Holt, would provide fertile soil in which to drop the seeds of revolt. Emancipation had not reconciled ex-convicts to authority. He had seen soldiers desert the army to join rebels before now. This was a situation to be watched narrowly, and one in which a man would do well to keep a foot in either camp. It was not impossible that a rebellion might succeed—but it must be well assured of success before Mr. Holt would openly appear in it. He well knew that the Governor regarded him with suspicion and disfavour, and that his proved complicity in a revolt would have serious consequences for him; therefore there must be no proof. He thought with complacency that he could talk his way out of suspicions. So he was careful, when he kept a rendezvous with disaffected persons, to keep it very privately.

Returning home through Parramatta from a visit to the Hawkesbury one Sunday evening early in March, he was not surprised to see certain men standing about in groups and talking earnestly with an air of suppressed excitement. He saluted them—even exchanged a meaning wink with one—but did not stop. It was providential, he thought, that he should be hailed just then by Timothy Holster, an overseer of the convicts at public labour, for if such a man had heard no whisper of impending trouble, then the secret had been well kept indeed. At last, in a nearby tavern over a glass of rum, the man's tongue was loosened.

"Have ye heard the tales goin' round, Mr. Holt?"

Holt shook his head, his expression all innocent enquiry.

"I have spent the day at the Hawkesbury, my friend. What tales?"

The overseer put his glass down and leaned across the table, his eye watchful.

"Rebellion! The rumour is that the Irishmen will rise to-night, and . . ."

Holt waved his hand impatiently.

"Come, come, how often have we heard that rumour?"

His companion admitted with a sharp, sidelong look:

"Aye, we've heard it many a time, an' nothin' come of it. But mark me, Mr. Holt, the military will laugh it off once too often! They say Abbott and Marsden have got wind of something." He leaned closer. "There's a countryman of yours went out to thatch a building at There or Nowhere, an' fell in with another who spilled enough to frighten the wits from him. He said he'd had his fill of rebellion in Ireland, an' he passed on what he'd heard to one who passed it on again to Abbott. An' I saw the Captain an' his Reverence meself not an hour gone with their heads together . . ."

Holt replied with a shrug:

"Then no doubt precautions are being taken." He finished his rum and stood up. He had not failed to note that close, inquisitive stare, and it gratified him to know that in any talk of revolt his name stood as a perpetual question mark. He suspected Mr. Holster of being one who, like himself, would wait to see which way the wind was blowing, and of hankering after a hint, however vague, that "General" Holt might have his own sources of information. No such hint would be forthcoming. "I have every confidence," he declared, beaming down upon his companion with a smile which did not even pretend to conceal its derision, "that law and order will be preserved."

The overseer said sourly, still watching him:

"Take my advice, Mr. Holt, and don't be out late to-night."

Holt replied with dignity:

"Your concern for me is well-meant, my friend, but unnecessary. When disturbances are in the air, an honest man goes to his home—and stays there. And thither I am bound. Good-day, Sir."

He picked up his hat, bowed ceremoniously, and departed, leaving Mr. Holster to stare after him with a mixture of cynicism and unwilling admiration.

*   *   *   *   *

By eight o'clock it was dark, and all was quiet at Castle Hill. The day had been like other Sundays. If the Reverend Rowland Hassall, preaching to his convict flock, had found it perhaps more restless and inattentive than usual, he had returned home to Parramatta with no forebodings other than those he habitually felt for the souls of people so hardened and so graceless.

In the outlying districts everyone was indoors early. Over the lonely miles between Toongabbee and the Hawkesbury only a lamp in the window of some settler's hut braved the darkness here and there, and a small cluster of lights marked the Government farm at Castle Hill. At night the land took back the silence of its centuries, and lay passive as it had done since the dawn of time under the indifferent stars.

Suddenly at Castle Hill flame and clamour burst shockingly upon that silence. To the insurgents the glare of a burning building was their signal, and the great bell which rang them to their labours in the fields now sent out through the still night a wild and urgent summons to rebellion. In the red, leaping light from the flames they assembled, their yells adding frenzy to the roar of the fire, and the mad clanging of the bell. The officers were few and unprepared, the guards only a handful of ex-convict constables who now—either from choice or from fear—were among the rebels, and shouting as loudly as the rest. Up from the swaying mass of ragged, firelit figures, like something created out of their need and the potency of their excitement, was thrust one who stood on an overturned dray, and shouted with clenched fists above his head: "Death or Liberty!"

The bell stopped ringing, and the flames died down, but they left no silence, for the cry of Cunningham was taken up and repeated till the dark fields and sky seemed shaking with it; and in his house nearby the flogger, Ben Donovan, dived beneath a bed, and lay shivering. The few who represented authority confronted simple alternatives—death, flight or surrender. The dark hid many a fleeing figure.

Now there was only one voice to be heard in that small focus of violence surrounded by the tranquil night. Confidence, Cunningham was thinking like a prayer, confidence is what they must have—a stop to doubts, a blow to fears, an end to hesitations. Promises, assurances, not hopes, but certainties—and what matter if the truth were strained to give them? "We are not alone!" he cried, and that was true, but it was not enough. "The whole colony's with us!" he shouted, and that was false, but full of comfort, and he felt the heat of their courage rise till it seemed hotter than the red ruin of the house behind him. "Sydney and Parramatta are already in our hands . . . !" he yelled above the din of their acclamation, and in the yelling almost hypnotised himself into believing that indeed, by now Holt and his confederates were supreme in Parramatta, and Margarot issuing orders from Government House in Sydney. Might it not be so? Had not their plans been laid as carefully as plans might be where communication was difficult and dangerous, and trusty messengers rare? Here at least, had not the secret been well-kept, the surprise perfect, the execution successful? Why not elsewhere too?

"At the Hawkesbury," he shouted, "they're waiting to join us! We'll be more than two thousand strong when we march on Parramatta and plant the tree of liberty before the Governor's house! Then we'll make for Sydney, boys, and find our friends already in possession, and a ship . . ."

The roar of cheering told him that no further words were necessary. Nor was there time for anything but action now, and he leapt down from the dray and gathered about him those who were to be his lieutenants—Johnston, Harrington, Neale, Brannan, Hogan, John Place, Humes, the overseer of the carpenters, Charles Hill, ex-convict . . .

These knew the plan, and now, under their leadership this ragged and undisciplined mob must put it into execution. But it was a mob composed of men in whom rage had been long gathering, and for whom action must be its outlet before it could be anything else. They knew that, and hardly paused in their council of war to watch Ben Donovan dragged out; hardly heard the wretch yelling for mercy; hardly spared a glance for the battered, bloody object which presently lay senseless on the ground.

Now the pent-up hatred had found its violent release, and action must be purposeful. Arms and ammunition must be secured, and new followers recruited. As the roaring flames had matched the crowd's first mood of frenzy, and lit their movements with a wild maniacal glare, so now its fiercely glowing embers matched their smouldering resolve, and made a red circle of still light in which they waited, listened, re-formed into groups; and from which they moved out at last into the surrounding dark.

So through that long night they scoured the countryside in bands, adding to their small store of arms a musket here and a pistol there, a sword, a bayonet, a pitchfork; drawing to themselves single figures which, like ghosts, appeared from the shadows to join them, and no questions asked; or groups which came shouting and laughing, and fell in to march beside them. As the dark hours went by, settlers in scattered farm-houses were roused from sleep to news of terror and confusion. Sometimes a messenger paused only long enough to call his warning: "Fly for your lives—the Croppies are coming!" Sometimes a terrified woman, clutching a baby and dragging a whimpering child by the hand, pleaded for refuge. Sometimes whole families fled on foot for Parramatta, leaving their doors open, and their liquor temptingly upon the table. Yet sometimes the news brought not alarm, but a grim and eager light to the eye of some embittered settler, or some ex-convict with memories of the lash, or some farm servant with a score to pay; and when they left their homes it was not for Parramatta, and the shelter of the law, but across the inky fields, and through the silent woods with muskets on their shoulders or pitchforks in their hands, to join the nearest party of insurgents. And sometimes when the hammering on the door was answered, it was no messenger that stood there, but the rebels themselves, grim and threatening, demanding food, liquor, weapons.

By the time the dawn broke the parties were widely scattered, but there was hardly a dwelling from Baulkham Hills to Seven Hills, from Prospect to Toongabbee, that had not been stripped of its arms; and Cunningham, on the Toongabbee road with upwards of two hundred men, faced the day in a blaze of hope.

*   *   *   *   *

But those who had escaped from the panic of the fire and the bell had carried their tale of terror to authority, and the techniques of authority needed no improvisation. It was barely half-past eleven on that Sunday night when a messenger from Parramatta rode furiously through the streets of Sydney and dismounted before Government House. By that time most respectable citizens were abed, and indeed the Governor himself, limping a little on his gouty foot, was half-way up the stairs when the sharp rat-rat sounded on the door. Yet there were a few people abroad, and others still awake who had thrown up their windows as the sound of galloping hooves went by; and the rider had shouted his tidings as he rode. By the time a sleepy servant hastened to the door of Government House, and His Excellency, scowling, had descended to the hall again, there were already clusters of people in the streets, night-capped heads peeping from windows, fearful women barring doors, and men ransacking their homes for weapons.

The Governor, reading the hastily written letter from Captain Abbott which the messenger delivered to him, began to act almost before his eyes had taken in the last words. William Chapman was summoned, the household aroused, messengers sent scurrying. Mrs. King, her hair in curl-papers and clutching her peignoir around her, appeared in the door-way and cried: "Mercy on us, King, what's to do?"

He said shortly:

"The prisoners at Castle Hill have risen." His eyes were bulging with anger and alarm, his voice sharp and irascible. "William, send word to Colonel Paterson that I wish to see nim immediately." He added, to his wife: "Abbott says they have been joined by many of the settlers' labourers." He turned furiously on a lingering servant. "Dolt, did I not tell you to order my horse brought round? You there, bring another lamp—must I conduct my business in the dark? Where is William?" He thrust Abbott's letter into his wife's hand. "It would seem they have already committed many outrages—read it for yourself. I shall ride to Parramatta immediately. Or as soon . . ." he glared round at the huddled servants, ". . . as these blocks of wood will bestir themselves to carry out my orders! *Where is William?* God in Heaven, can I find no one to . . . Ha! You are there, Sir! Have an order sent to the Captain of the *Calcutta* that his ship's company is to come ashore under arms. And William—damnation, Sir, can you not *wait?*—make it known that all horses in the town are requisitioned for . . ."

Mrs. King, somewhat pale, but ever practical, left him to his shouting and withdrew to summon Jane Dundas.

"His Excellency will be riding presently to Parramatta, Jane. He will require . . . what is that noise in the kitchen?"

"Hannah, Ma'am—she's in a taking and saying she'll be murdered in her bed."

"Tell her," said Mrs. King tartly, "that wherever else she may be murdered it will not be in her bed, for she is not going to bed. His Excellency will require some food before he leaves. She can set about preparing it. Is Miss Elizabeth sleeping?"

"Like an angel, Ma'am."

But Mrs. King went upstairs to make sure. When she descended again—in seemly attire—it was to find Paterson, looking more gaunt and blue-jowled than ever, in conclave with her husband.

"That is settled, then," King was saying. "A company shall march for Parramatta at once under Johnston, Davies and Laycock. I've already directed Captain Woodriff to place his men from the *Calcutta* under your command for the protection of the town. What else is there?"

The Colonel said gloomily:

"There are rascals among us who will be waiting only to hear news of the success of these vile schemes elsewhere before they make trouble for us here. It would be as well to make a search for arms among the inhabitants, and take possession of them."

"Do so, do so," King replied testily, walking up and down the room. "Take what measures you think necessary. Keep a close eye on that fellow Margarot."

"The parade ground is in a commanding position," the Colonel went on with that deliberation which His Excellency's brisker temperament found so irritating, "and our powder magazine just in front of it. With the remainder of the Corps, and the *Calcutta's* company, and the six-pounder we should be able to meet any emergency." He rubbed his dark, rasping chin reflectively. "I shall arm the Loyal Association, and post them here and there in suitable spots. And doubtless it will be best to stop all communication between this place and Parramatta, whether by land or water . . ."

Mrs. King felt a little reassured. Matters were in hand. The first tumult had subsided, the confusion was already reduced to an ordered and concentrated activity. It was after midnight when Lieutenant Hobby rode in from Parramatta with more news, and by that time the Governor, booted and cloaked, was ready for departure. The rebels, Hobby reported breathlessly, were in great force, and advancing upon Parramatta from different directions. King paused in the doorway with his wife, and they looked down the hill towards the water where moving lights and a clamour of voices proclaimed that the men from the *Calcutta* were coming ashore. He said hurriedly:

"I shall ride on—the Provost Marshal and the others will overtake me. Have no fear, Anna. A company is already marching for Parramatta, and I'll send word to Johnston as we pass by Annandale to take command of them. There's no need for alarm—none at all."

The quiet night suddenly stirred to activity, the noise of horses being saddled in the yard, the coming and going of people in the streets, and his own haste were all denials of his words which they both chose to ignore.

*   *   *   *   *

If Sydney were in an uproar, Parramatta was in a panic. Fugitives from Castle Hill and nearby farms had reached the town soon after nine in the evening with tales that set it seething like a disturbed ants' nest. People rushed into the streets to hear the news, and rushed indoors again to tell it. The drums beat to arms. Messengers galloped by on mysterious errands. Mr. and Mrs. Marsden and Mrs. Macarthur, bundling sleepy children into their clothes, fled by water to Sydney. The barracks was besieged by eminent citizens seeking refuge. Mr. Holt, who had gone straight from his conversation with the overseer to warn Mr. Cox of impending trouble, was assiduous in preparing to defend his employer's house.

Of those who remained in their homes there were not a few who awaited events with a mixture of alarm and eagerness. They knew that confusion might well obscure the difference between friend and foe; indeed it had already so obscured their own thoughts that they hardly knew whose friends they were, or upon which side to seek their foes. Even in

the act of preparing resistance, some were conscious of a buried but
persistent hope for the victory of those against whom they bolted doors
and barricaded windows; and they crept out to hide a musket beneath a
shrub, or lifted a floor plank to conceal a sword, or strapped a knife
beneath a trouser-leg.

There was no sleep in the town that night, for people kept coming in
from the surrounding country with reports which were the more terrifying
for their contradictions. The rebels were even now not a mile distant,
and awaiting only a signal from within the town to enter. The signal
was to be, it was said, the blazing home of the Macarthurs—a wily ruse
to draw the soldiers from the barracks to the assistance of their absent
officer's wife and family. They were five hundred strong—seven hundred
strong—a thousand strong. They were murdering everyone they could
find. They were bent on rape and plunder. They were advancing on
Sydney. They were retreating to the Hawkesbury. They were encamped
at Toongabbee. They were even now at the Park Gates. They had
come together in one force so formidably armed that no resistance was
possible. The soldiers had mutinied. Sydney had fallen. The Governor
had been assassinated . . .

Rumour ran mad, and died down only with the coming of the first
dawn light, and the sharp clatter of hooves through the street as His
Excellency with his bodyguard rode in. The news that Johnston with a
company of the Corps was hard upon his heels brought an abatement of
panic, and in the wan light of early morning the inhabitants emerged
fearfully from their homes to watch the soldiers marching through the
town.

Ah, the decision of military discipline! After that night of uncertainty
and creeping fears they were jerked smartly back to their senses by the
rhythmic rat-tat of drums, and the brisk tramp-tramp of marching feet.
The sounds beat out reassurance to those who had feared, and rebuke to
those who had hoped. What can contend with this? This *is*! The
bearing of the soldiers, their every movement, the very colour and dazzle
of their uniforms and accoutrements—bright scarlet, blinding white,
shining steel—proclaimed them men with a destination and a purpose.
Not even the sight of Major Johnston riding at their head—the thought
of the Governor closeted with Abbott at the barracks—the knowledge of a
Parliament far away across the sea, and a King, fabulous as God upon
a throne remote as Heaven—could pierce the illusion. Here was power,
stepping bravely in full panoply. Here were the soldiers, God bless them!
Hurrah! In the exhilaration of the spectacle there died unnoticed an
inner whisper that these men put off their independence when they put
on their scarlet; that this air of decision was in truth mere mechanical
obedience; that the destination was ordered, and the purpose not theirs.

*　　　　*　　　　*　　　　*　　　　*

At this same dawn hour Johnny Prentice nosed his canoe into the
bank under the willows near Green Hills, and, leaving it hidden there,
climbed up in the ghostly early-morning silence to the hut of the ex-
convict, Miller. It was empty. Another, a quarter of a mile distant,

where he had done business sometimes, was empty too, but leaving it, and passing cautiously along the winding track which led from it in the direction of the village, he heard his name called softly from a dense thicket of scrub, and halted. There were three men whom he knew, including Miller, and they were all armed after a fashion—one with a pike, one with a pitchfork, and one with the old musket which had once been his own.

They told him—their eyes fever-bright with excitement—that the great rebellion had already begun. News had come from Castle Hill during the night, they said. They were waiting here for two other men before they set out to join the rebels.

Johnny's heart jumped in his breast. He had returned just in time! Here was release for the clamouring bodily vigour of his new-found maturity, and perfect satisfaction for his vague but powerful urge towards communion with his own kind. It was not only talk he had wanted—nor more possessions—nor the sight of a civilised community—but a purpose which would knit him into this white world which he had once forsaken, and make him an active part of it again.

Weapons? He had none, and for a moment longingly remembered the second musket hanging on the wall of his hut; but there was no time now to think of that. The village was astir, soon it would be broad daylight, and already, so his companions told him, a part of the victorious rebel army must be marching towards the Hawkesbury.

The other men were late; the sun, already threatening a day of scorching heat, was up by the time they arrived, creeping through the bracken from the direction of the river with weapons in their hands, and news on their lips. Another messenger had come in. All had gone well. Cunningham, with some hundreds of men, was in the neighbourhood of Toongabbee, and Humes with a strong force was in the woods near the Hawkesbury road. The search for arms had been successful. The man who had brought these tidings believed that others had escaped from Castle Hill to Parramatta, and that by now the soldiers had been called out. But by the time they could reach the spot the rebel army would surely have swelled invincibly, and had they not friends at Sydney and Parramatta to lead risings there?

Johnny, wild with impatience, listened eagerly. Their words were bold and hopeful, and his whole heart endorsed them. But they were strangers to him, and he saw them look at him askance, mutter to each other, and look at him again. They went apart with Miller, and he saw them arguing, and knew that he was the subject of their argument. A faint uneasiness chilled the warm glow of his comradeship. Doubts? Why? Was he not of their tribe? There were many tribes among the black men, he thought, and sometimes they fought each other. There were two tribes among the white men, and perpetual enmity between them. But no black man, before a battle, doubted a member of his own tribe, as these white men were now doubting him. Johnny's mind strove with this ominous idea. He felt it less as a personal insult than as a flaw in tribal strength—something dangerous, unnatural and evil.

Yet Miller had persuaded them; he saw a gesture at the musket which had been his gift. He was accepted; he was even given a knife which one of the newcomers wore stuck in his belt; and they were moving at last . . .

        *   *   *   *   *

In Parramatta, meanwhile, His Excellency had repaired to Government House. There from the window of the big, high-ceilinged room where once, long ago, Mr. Mannion had interviewed Governor Phillip, King now looked down the hill at the township and its encompassing fields. Frowning, staring unseeingly at the three tall poplars which marked the beginning of the street, he dictated over his shoulder:

"*. . . I do therefore proclaim the districts of Parramatta, Castle Hill, Toongabbee, Prospect, Seven and Baulkham Hills, Hawkesbury and Nepean to be in a state of rebellion, and do establish martial law through-out those districts . . .*"

His blind stare was suddenly attentive; advancing along the road in a little cloud of dust came a rank of soldiers led by three horsemen in scarlet coats. He called to one of the troopers stationed at the door:

"Major Johnston is coming; admit him instantly when he arrives."

He sat down on the edge of a chair, leaning forward on its arms, too nervy to relax, for all his weariness. The dictation continued:

"*. . . I do therefore charge and command all His Majesty's liege subjects to be assisting in apprehending and giving up to the nearest magistrate every person they may stop who is unprovided with a pass, under pain of being tried by a Court Martial.*

"*And every person who is seen in a state of rebellious opposition to the peace and tranquillity of this colony . . .*"

His thought halted on those words, though his tongue went on dictating.

There was no real peace or tranquillity for these rebels to disturb . . . ! They had merely added violence to confusion . . .

The clip-clop of horses' hooves outside . . .

The Governor's face was suddenly suffused with a choleric flush, and his thoughts bolted.

Major George Johnston of Annandale—summoned to put down rebellion . . . ! By Heaven, could not rebellion be of many kinds . . . ?

Captain John Macarthur of Elizabeth Farm—was he not absent from the colony only because he had been guilty of rebellion more subtle but not less dangerous to its peace and tranquillity than . . . ?

A whole parade of military gentlemen, by God, with their own methods of rebellion . . . !

Rebels to put down rebels . . . !

Rebels in scarlet versus rebels in slops . . . !

He found himself on his feet again, shocked by the intensity of his own anger, startled by a flood of resentment which had made him feel for one unbelievable second that his wrath was less hot against the convict insurgents than against those who were to bring them to justice.

Justice . . . ? Justice . . . ?

He glared at the wall while his amanuensis waited with lifted pen. He was thinking of the still frightened fugitive whom Abbott had summoned to give him an eye-witness' account of the scene at Castle Hill. ". . . *so he stood up on a dray, Your Excellency, and called out 'Death or Liberty'* . . ."

Liberty, liberty, the bright beacon that flared out again no matter how often it seemed quenched . . . !

But this was intolerable! What was the matter with him? The fatigue of a long ride at the end of a trying day—a sleepless night—anxiety . . .

He began pacing and dictating again, and Johnston, dismounting at the steps, heard his irritable voice through the open window:

"*And if they or any of them give up the ringleaders to justice it may be an effectual means of procuring them that amnesty which it is so much my wish to grant* . . ."

The Major's mouth contracted in a brief grimace. Amnesty! String the rascals up and have done with them! Admitted by the trooper, he presented himself in the doorway of the long, sunlit room, and stood for a brief moment meeting a rather strange stare from the Governor's sharp eyes.

It was not that either of them consciously recalled the past; this was no moment for memories. It was but the fraction of a second—one of those sharp splinters from a flying instant which can pierce the mind with a brilliance like pain. To the Governor the outlines of the figure on the threshold blurred; it became young George Johnston, twenty-four, fair-haired, fresh-faced, innocent and amiable. From somewhere in his own middle-aged and gout-racked body there looked out Philip Gidley King at thirty, alert, ambitious, and intelligent. Round them, like a dream, was the land before it had become a colony, the land when it was only the land, all trees and silence. The beginning! There was a poignancy in beginnings—and in youth; in a land untouched, and in lives still malleable; in the ghost of a thought that land and life might have trodden the years differently, taken some path into the future which would not have led to a present whose taste was so bitter and unsatisfying . . .

The moment passed, the resplendent uniform in the doorway clothed solid flesh and blood once more. Major Johnston was still only forty, still fair, still fresh-complexioned; but his belt was longer, his innocence he had long ago discarded, and his amiability had become mechanical. Now he was no penniless junior officer; indeed, in the long years when his military activities had been limited to parades and the routine of the barracks, he had almost forgotten that the function of a soldier was to fight, or that military rank was anything but a social and commercial asset. He was by temperament as placid as his sheep, as deliberate as the growth of his Norfolk Island pines at Annandale. He would act only to enlarge his fortune or to defend his property and his class. His round face, whose rosiness had become a trifle florid, wore a slightly aggrieved expression as he stood there awaiting His Excellency's pleasure, for he had not yet entirely adjusted himself to the surprise of finding himself transformed from a soldier by courtesy to a soldier in fact. Yet the transition would be made—was, indeed, being made with every passing moment—for fighting was a routine in which he had been well instructed if not widely practised; an occasion for physical valour which he had been taught to see as something woven into his uniform; a business precluding imagination, with which, happily, he had never been overburdened. With every tick of the clock since he had been aroused from his bed the night before, Johnston the colonial landowner had been not retreating, but joining forces with Johnston the soldier. There was now left only enough that was purely the master of Annandale to realise, in that embarrassing moment of contact with the Governor's too-revealing stare, that this alliance in which they found themselves was official, not personal—and to assert that it was also temporary . . .

King gave him a curt greeting:

"Come in, Major—I have been waiting for you. You have seen Abbott?"

"Yes, Sir. I halted at the barracks to refresh my men."

"He has more news of the rebels? When I saw him he believed them close to the town."

Johnston advanced into the room, his thumbs tucked into his belt.

"His latest information is that there's no sign of them in the immediate neighbourhood."

"What is the strength of your detachment?"

"Two officers, Sir, two sergeants, and fifty-two rank and file. A number of constables and other inhabitants, mounted and armed, are prepared to render assistance. Reinforcements will be sent up."

King nodded restlessly.

"There seems no doubt that the rebels are in different parties. All the accounts I heard agreed on that—if they agreed," he added sourly, "on nothing else." He picked up a paper and handed it to Johnston. "Your orders, Major."

His Excellency's handwriting, never very legible, was wilder than usual; his tone, always peremptory, was sharpened to an even more dictatorial note. The outward show of civility so laboriously maintained through a long antagonism threatened to crack in this tense atmosphere of crisis, and the Major flushed as he took the paper. It was difficult to read, but not quite so difficult as he made it appear, and King, on edge with impatience, felt his temper rising. He fidgeted about the room, twirling his spectacles in his nervous fingers, glancing from time to time at the bulky figure in the scarlet coat, and the face bent over his writing with an expression which suggested that the scribblings of a child would be more easily decipherable. He rapped out at last:

"I suppose you can't read it, Major?"

In the war which the sharp-tempered Governor waged with the officers, his attempts at tact and conciliation were not always successful, even in moments less strained than this. He had no very high opinion of Johnston's intellectual attainments, but frayed nerves now lent his tone a sneer which made his words almost an imputation of illiteracy. Johnston, redder than ever, tossed the page peevishly on the table.

"You might as well have given me Greek," he retorted, "for all I can make of it!"

King picked it up, controlling himself with an effort. He enjoyed baiting people, but this was no moment, after all, for such self-indulgence; he put on his spectacles again and began to read aloud rapidly, his voice high with irritation. Major Johnston was to divide his forces and go in search of the rebels. He was to fire upon any person who attempted to flee when called upon to halt. Johnston nodded, slightly mollified. He had feared that the Governor would hamper his martial operations with absurd restraints, and he was relieved to learn that he might freely use the prompt and final argument of a bullet.

"It seems," King said, looking at him over the top of the paper, "that the main body must be somewhere near Toongabbee. Fugitives who have come in from that district say they are led by Cunningham—who, by the way, has received many indulgences, and deserves no more. They mention also Humes, Place, and a namesake of yours, Major, a certain William Johnston. It's imperative to take the leaders—the rest will then submit easily."

There flickered across his mind as he spoke the notion that this was a strategy he had attempted to employ on other battlefields. *"Take the leaders . . ."* Johnston's own banishment to England. . . . Macarthur's banishment. . . . But these leaders were not so easily disposed of . . .

He continued sharply:

"I've declared Martial Law. You will act as the occasion seems to demand. Offer rewards for information. Promise clemency to those who surrender. And you will send me reports, of course, how matters progress . . ."

Again, under the quick fire of orders, and the imperious tone in which they were uttered, the Major's dignity rebelled.

He interrupted resentfully:

"You need have no fears on that score—we shall soon dispose of them."

"I don't doubt," King snapped, "that the deluded wretches will be put down—but time is important. They have confederates here and at Sydney, and every hour enables them to gather more disaffected people about them. You will march for Toongabbee immediately, Sir, and as fast as possible."

*　　　*　　　*　　　*　　　*

But information flowed not only in one direction, though it flowed more thinly and precariously to the rebels than away from them. Under cover of darkness, and even in the pale light of dawn, there were a few who came by roundabout, deserted ways from Parramatta to the hill outside Toongabbee where Cunningham had halted his men, and where he had spent the hours since daylight drilling and instructing them. In the face of the tidings they brought it was no use, now, to say that Parramatta had fallen; no use to deny that the alarm had been given, or to pretend that the Governor, once warned, would not strike hard and swiftly. The excitement of the night before had waned, the habit of subordination weighed heavily upon the spirit, the shadows of the noose and the flogging-post lay across the thin, bright beacon-light of freedom.

Cunningham, taking stock of his resources, was sufficiently astute to count intangible liabilities along with tangible assets. Two hundred and thirty-three men, a score or so of muskets, a fowling piece, a few bayonets on poles, a pistol, a couple of swords, some pitchforks and reaping-hooks . . .

These were his assets. His liabilities he read here and there in eyes that watched him—uncertain, anxious, furtive eyes already fixed in fascinated dread upon the spectre of defeat.

More numbers, more arms! Humes and his force should have joined them by now. From his hilltop he watched and waited till the murmuring about him warned that it was dangerous to wait longer. They must march themselves—for Hawkesbury where they would surely find supporters, along a road where they might fall in with other bands, and swell their ranks to the numbers that spell power and confidence.

And so Major Johnston, arriving at the hill, found them gone—but only lately gone. In the fierce, mounting heat of the day he pursued them along the Hawkesbury road, riding in advance of his detachment with Dixon, the priest, at his side, and a trooper just behind him. His men had already had a long and gruelling march, and Johnston, hoping to delay the enemy, sent the trooper ahead with a flag of truce to tell them that the Governor was coming. He returned from this errand only to report that they had taken the flints from his pistols and sent him back, declaring that they would hear no terms. The priest, despatched on a similar errand, fared no better, and all the time the two forces, separated only by a mile or so, pushed on along the road beneath the blazing sun, and the Major racked his brains for a new strategy. From one straggler whom they overtook, disarmed and made prisoner, they learned that they were gaining, and Johnston determined to ride forward himself with the trooper and attempt once more to retard them while Lieutenant Laycock brought up the remainder of the force.

He came in sight of them at last, and reined in to stare at the untidy crowd whose motley weapons caught the glitter of the sun through the cloud of red dust raised by their trudging feet. They were tramping—it could not, he thought contemptuously, be called marching—in some sort of rough formation, but as they heard the beat of hooves behind them such semblance of military bearing as they had vanished. A kind of convulsion stirred their ranks as their heads turned; some quickened their pace, some checked, and a low babel of sound broken by a shout went up. The Major rose in his stirrups and let loose his parade-ground voice: "Halt!"

They halted. Perhaps no one could have told whether it were Cunningham's shout or Johnston's peremptory order which stopped them, but they were still, and the dust settled round them. It was not the stillness of drilled soldiers, but rather that of a field of waving corn, rooted to the ground, and yet moving. The Major eyed them with a kind of wondering, calculating scorn. It would be necessary, he thought, only to hold them till his men came up, and then the discipline and efficiency of trained and well-armed soldiers would make short work of them. He shouted:

"Martial law has been proclaimed—you would do well to listen to me carefully! Those captured in acts of insubordination will be severely dealt with . . ."

Someone cried out "Death or Liberty!" and there was a cheer that rose and died uncertainly. Johnston tried again:

"His Excellency offers mercy to those who submit . . ."

A voice yelled bitterly: "We know his mercy!"

The Major mopped his forehead with his handkerchief. In a way he was enjoying this adventure, for he was a soldier, and a man who liked to feel his authority and importance. But it was a long, long time since he had been under fire; the young lieutenant who had seen action in North America, and suffered a wound in the East Indies, was more than twenty years away—a mere memory to the middle-aged Major who had grown accustomed to security and good living. He was very conscious of being within pistol shot of a mob of desperate rogues, and it was not only the heat of the day which was making him sweat. Keep them talking, he thought, keep them talking . . .

He called out:

"Send your leaders to speak with me!"

"Let ye come here to us," a voice shouted, "if it's talk ye're wantin'."

"You're armed," Johnston taunted them, "and I'm within range of your fire. What kind of cowards are these leaders of yours if they'll not come forward? Where is Cunningham?"

His eyes had been upon one who stood in the front rank with a sword in his hand, and who had turned several times to harangue the rest. He was not surprised when this man began to walk towards him, and the ranks opened to release another who was—though he did not know it at the time, and would have scouted the idea that he could have anything in common with so unprepossessing a rascal—his namesake, Johnston. He rode forward a few paces to confront them.

"Your name is Cunningham?" he asked, staring coldly down at the first man. He did not consciously notice—so natural it seemed—that they had both pulled off their hats, but he felt more confident. "You must know," he went on sharply, "that this is madness. His Excellency has been lenient to you, and such conduct can only . . ."

Cunningham interrupted:

"We want no sermons. What have ye to say?"

"I wish only to prevent bloodshed," Johnston told him haughtily, listening for the sound of his approaching men. Cunningham said:

"If blood's to flow it'll not be only ours."

"Resistance will be useless, and will cost you your life. Surrender may save it." The Major's tone became placatory. "If you will cause these deluded men to give up their arms and submit, I'll mention you to His Excellency in as favourable terms as possible."

Cunningham looked up at him with a curious glint in his eyes.

"Ye will, eh?" Suddenly he was in a rage, and his voice rang out harshly. "To hell with ye! It's but a few of us ye see here. We have other bands at large, and friends in many quarters, and we'll hear no talk of surrender!"

Johnston, still listening, shifted his ground and his tactics again.

"The Reverend Mr. Dixon," he urged, "has come once to you already in an effort to compose this matter. He'll come again—point out to you the evils of the course you are pursuing—the calamity it must bring about if you persist. I'm going to fetch him—I advise you, my men, to reason with your followers, and bid them listen to the worthy priest . . ."

The rejoinder to this, as he swung his horse round again in the direction he had come, was so violent, coarse and contemptuous that he judged it better to feign deafness. But as he galloped off he was counting this fruitless conversation fruitful, for his men were now hard upon the rebels' heels. Accompanied by Mr. Dixon, he returned ahead of them for another parley, leaving Laycock to force the already stiff pace of the detachment still harder.

By now the insurgents had formed a line on the hill beyond their leaders, and the Major measured it with his eye as he lent a perfunctory ear to the exhortations of the priest. He did not expect them to be heeded, nor were they. He wanted only to gain time, and when persuasion had been answered by blunt refusal, and negotiations seemed once more at a deadlock, he flung one last question at Cunningham, seeking not an answer, but another precious moment.

"Be damned, you impudent rascal!" he cried angrily, "in Heaven's name what is it you want?"

Cunningham shouted fiercely:

"It's liberty we want! Death or . . ."

He stopped short, staring along the road. The soldiers were in sight, advancing at the double, fast, purposeful and orderly.

A roar of warning, excitement and defiance went up from the rebels. Cunningham and his companion made the first move to rejoin them—but only the first. Johnston felt the Major's pistol clamped to his head, and Cunningham found himself looking into a muzzle with the trooper's steady hand behind it. They were driven back toward the advancing detachment, and the Major was shouting to Laycock, ordering a charge.

Bedlam broke loose on the red, dusty road. The first volley of fire from the soldiers broke the rebel line. Their muskets replied raggedly, their bullets flew wide, they saw their comrades fall. They were not silent like the soldiers, awaiting and obeying the orders of one voice, but torn and bewildered by their own many voices crying "Stand!" and "Flee!" and "Attack!" and "Surrender!"; calling "Retreat to Hawkesbury!" "Charge them!" "They'll mow us down!" "Death or Liberty!" "Make for the woods!"

It became a nightmare in which they were fleeing along an endless road with the pounding of hooves, and the thud of pursuing feet, and the crack of muskets behind them. In the tumult their captured leaders had broken loose. Cunningham, yelling orders, curses, taunts and frenzied pleas to his demoralised forces, ran forward in a last effort to rally them. A few were still pausing in their flight to face the enemy and return its fire, but he saw one hit, and the others waver as the body fell at their feet. He stooped for the dead man's musket as he ran, shouting hoarsely: "Death or Lib . . . !"

A bullet struck him before he could straighten. There was no battle now, but only a rout, and the rebels thought not of resistance but escape. Many left the road and plunged through the trees and scrub—some to elude capture for a time, and some to fall dead or wounded in the dappled light, hearing a dim confusion of fading sounds, tasting in a last moment of consciousness the old, familiar, bitter flavour of defeat.

Cunningham lay sprawled face downward in the dust; the commotion passed over him, and left him lying there.

* * * * *

Johnny and his companions had struck across country, avoiding the few scattered dwellings—though most of these were now deserted—and keeping to the shelter of the woods. Johnny was out of his own territory now, a stranger. As the others came to the wide road and hurried furtively across it he lingered to stare, and they called to him savagely, seeing but another example of his half-wittedness. How long since he had seen a road! And never one such as this—red and straight and seemingly endless, dwindling to nothing between the tall trees!

The sun climbed higher. They fell in with three other men, strangely armed like themselves, and all went on together. But Johnny was worried. There was something wrong. He was afraid—not of the enemy they sought, but of an incomprehensible something in his companions. They were too silent. Preparations for battle should not be silent. There should be noise . . . eagerness . . . ardour. . . . It was inevitable that there should be at the back of his mind the thought of fierce songs, the stamping of feet, the brandishing of weapons, rhythmic grunts and cries to stimulate the warlike spirit. He knew that these were white men whose customs were not those of black men, yet he remained uneasy. It should not be like this. A march to battle should be a progress already triumphant—not a furtive, gloomy trudge with the weight of some un-admitted fear, and the shadow of some unacknowledged doubt upon it. What were these glances that passed from one to another, asking questions where no question was conceivable . . . ?

There were emotions here which he could understand and share—resolve, fury, and revenge. They were proper emotions for men bent on war. But there was something else. He did not understand desperation, but he could feel it, and it frightened him. Here were warriors who had set out in search of their enemies boldly like men, with weapons in their hands and words of confidence on their tongues—but somewhere in them —too deeply buried for their own recognition, but clear and terrible as magic to Johnny's more primitive awareness, was a doubt which peered ahead, looking not at the battle, but beyond it.

His eyes darted from one to another—more like a black man's than ever in their restless, curious, bewildered scrutiny. He could not sufficiently divorce himself from his native thinking to realise that here a battle was not necessarily an end in itself, and that this tribe did not go out to fight another single tribe similar in strength, as a black tribe did. He could not understand that it marched not only against hostile men, but against a hostile power behind those men—a power whose reserves and resources were inexhaustible. He could not see that this power might lose one—two—a hundred engagements—and still remain unvanquished. He only felt a growing confusion of black-man and white-man emotions —an almost superstitious fear of this fatal something which he could feel clouding the ardour of belligerence, and a savage, frustrated irritation against men who went into battle with defeat already in their hearts.

And then they heard, in the distance, away over to the right where the road cut the woods like a fresh scar, a volley of gunfire. . . . And then a faint sound of shouting. . . . And then more shots. . . . And more shouting. . . . And hoofbeats along the road. . . . And from ahead of them among the trees the sound of running footsteps, the crackle of branches thrust aside, the snapping of twigs underfoot. . . . And suddenly a wild figure fleeing towards them, and another, and another, bringing shock and panic with them, crying out: "Run!" "Run for your lives!" "The soldiers are here!" "Cunningham's dead!" "It's all over—run!"

*   *   *   *   *

That Sunday night of terror and confusion had passed quietly at Beltrasna. The isolation which had sometimes seemed a danger had proved after all its safeguard, for the thoughts of rebels had turned to settlements where there were large numbers who might join them, and stores, and many cottages to plunder for arms and food. There was not time to spare for a single great house, particularly as it was well known from reports of Castle Hill men, who had worked there last November, that its convicts were more closely guarded than elsewhere. Beltrasna's turn would come—but it could wait.

It was not till the next morning, therefore, that the news came to Mr. Mannion. He had wondered with some annoyance at the failure of Toole to return on Sunday night from an errand to Parramatta, and had prepared a rebuke for his tardiness. But his first preoccupation that morning was to finish a letter to his mother, for he had heard that the *Calcutta* was to sail shortly, and proposed to send Mr. Harvey to Sydney that day with a budget of Beltrasna correspondence. Entering his study, he unlatched the windows, threw the room open to the bright sunshine, and settled down in a good humour at his writing-table.

"*I have, for the moment, postponed consideration of Conor's return. She is greatly opposed to the idea of quitting the col* . . ." Mr. Mannion made a neat erasure and substituted "me." He did it quite without misgiving, serene in the belief that only the tantrums and vapours of pregnancy had caused a temporary rift in the tranquillity of his married life.

He continued, writing fast and fluently in his elegant, sloping hand: *"Since her health seems improved, and her mood more tranquil, I do not press the matter. Our dear Julia is not yet of an age to be undesirably influenced by the surroundings in which she finds herself—but have no fear that I shall delay sending her home too long.*

"We have not yet heard of Miles' safe arrival in England, though I do not doubt Frances will have sent us word by the first conveyance. When he visits you you will find him well-grown and personable, but I fear you will discern many little gaucheries, and a certain want of discipline. I look to your influence, my dear mother, and to that of my sister, to smooth away any roughnesses of bearing and behaviour, for which we must blame the isolation and the peculiar nature of this place."

He paused for a few moments, considering, and went on at last with a faint frown.

"From Patrick I continue to receive by every vessel supplications that he may return here—which pleases me, you may be sure, no more than it does you, who have been at such pains to procure for him the interest of so many highly-placed persons. Your account of him, and several from my sister, have been closely studied, and do little to remove the anxiety I feel concerning him. The over-sensitiveness you speak of is a trait which was conspicuous in his dear mother's temperament—but is less fitting in him than in a member of the gentler sex. His own letters betray a nature so undeveloped, and so wanting in knowledge of the world, that I find difficulty in remembering that he is now nearly twenty. My sister tells me that the essay he wrote soon after his arrival upon life in the colony, and which she showed to several of her friends, was but the first of many. It seems that the kindly notice they took of it had the effect—little contemplated by her!—of encouraging a veritable flood of literary composition. I now hear that one of his pieces has actually been published!

"I write to him by this opportunity, and point out that since the time when Collins and Tench (what do you hear of him, by the bye?) published their works, there has been an uninterrupted procession of accounts of this place, every Tom, Dick and Harry who has ever touched upon its shores conceiving himself fit to enlighten the world regarding it. Even our notorious pickpocket Barrington, has seen print—if the volume which bears his name is indeed his work, which you would doubt as I do if you could see him now. His mind is totally gone. I have endeavoured to make Patrick realise that only the novelty of this colony, and the fashion for accounts of it, rather than any pretensions to literary merit, can have made his effusion acceptable. I trust that his naïveté will not prevent his seeing the justice of this observation. But when I recollect his assiduous devotion to a journal which he used to keep when he was here, I begin to apprehend that our family has, by some strange freak, produced an incorrigible scribbl . . ."

It was at this point that his pen stopped in the middle of a word, and he looked up in sharp annoyance to see Toole, cap in hand, at the verandah window. Something in the man's appearance and expression brought Mr. Mannion to his feet in the beginning of alarm.

"What is the meaning of this, Toole? Why were you not back last night as I . . ."

But Toole forgot respect in his excitement; he interrupted:

"It's rebellion, Sir! The convicts at Castle Hill rose last night, and they say at Hawkesbury too, and His Excellency has ordered Martial Law in all these districts, Sir, and called out the soldiers . . ."

Mr. Mannion threw his pen down savagely on the table. Here it was, at last! Here was the result which he had always foretold of that deplorable softness and laxity towards the criminal population! He demanded sharply:

"Where did you hear this?"

"It was on the road, Your Honour, I heard about the rising, and I nearing Toongabbee on my way home last night. There was scores of people making for Parramatta, Sir, but it's little sense I could get from them, so I stopped in Toongabbee to learn more, and while I was indoors some rascal stole my horse, bad cess to him . . ."

He shot a nervous glance at his employer. He could have continued the journey on foot to carry a warning to Beltrasna, but he had felt no enthusiasm at the prospect of a long walk alone through a night infested with desperate armed rebels, and he had waited for morning and the arrival of Major Johnston before setting out. He did not want questions on this point, so he gabbled on hurriedly:

"There was hundreds of the rascals near Toongabbee last night, Sir, but they marched off this morning towards Hawkesbury, and before I left Major Johnston came in with a detachment and went off after them, and by now he should have come up with them, Sir, and . . ."

But Mannion, staring down the hill to where a few figures were visible working in his fields, interrupted impatiently:

"Is all quiet down there among our own labourers?"

"Yes, Your Honour—there's been no rumour reached them yet."

"Muster them," Mr. Mannion ordered, "and put them under lock and key—every man jack of them. Send Byrne to me. Wait . . . ! Get that fellow Finn apart and put him in the barn—ironed and well secured. When they are locked up they will smell something afoot, and I want none of his raving talk among them. Post Evans by the huts, and remain there yourself. And if you see any of these desperadoes at large, shoot them."

He went back into the house to seek Mr. Harvey. Together they barred the doors, and closed and bolted the shutters on the windows, leaving a couple on each side of the house from which they could fire if it became necessary to stand a siege. Byrnes arrived and was admitted. Firearms and ammunition were assembled. Ellen and Maria were set the task of bringing in extra food from the storeroom. Conor took the news calmly; her husband would have preferred a few cries, a little trembling—even a fainting fit—but she said only: "I do not think we need alarm Cousin Bertha. She is remaining in bed and keeps her shutters closed. She will not notice if I bolt them." She roamed about the house, pausing in the kitchen doorway to speak to Emma who, she

thought, looked scared and sullen; Maria had evidently been in tears, but
Ellen's tight-lipped expression suggested that such nonsense had not long
been permitted. She peeped into Cousin Bertha's room occasionally to
assure herself that the old lady was still peacefully dozing. She passed
Mr. Harvey, busy loading pistols, noticed that in this hour of danger and
anxiety the look he gave her was all too revealing, and rewarded him,
half-absently, with a smile. She went on to the nursery and played for
a while with Julia, while the nurse made a pretence of tidying the room,
in the intervals of darting out to ask Byrne if any rebels were sighted
yet. Conor saw that she was the least calm of all the women in the
house—but there was no fear in her restlessness. She was the widow of
a settler, and had learned in his lonely hut to handle a musket; she said
at last to Conor:

"Ma'am, tell the master I can shoot as well as any man. There's but
the three of them to guard the house, and another wouldn't come amiss
now, would it, Ma'am . . . ?"

Conor looked at her curiously:

"You would shoot them, Bessie?"

Bessie stared.

"That I would, to be sure, Ma'am, the nasty good-for-nothing rogues!"

"But Toole says they are not only convicts. There are settlers among
them—some whom you know, perhaps, Bessie. Friends of yours . . . ?"

The young woman bridled offendedly.

"No friends of mine, Ma'am, I declare! We lived respectable, my
Jim and me, and I never held with wild talk and trouble-making. Know
your place, I say, and you'll come to no harm. So tell the master, Ma'am,
and beg him let me hold a gun, and I promise there's no murdering rascal
will get to our little lady there except over my dead body!"

So Conor took her to Mannion, and saw her, equipped with a musket,
take up her position proudly at a window.

"You are a good, loyal girl, Bessie," he declared, "and you shall be
suitably rewarded when this unfortunate business is over."

Conor went back to Julia with that word "loyal" hanging in her
mind. Where and what was loyalty? The nursery, like the rest of the
house, was dim and rather stuffy with all its windows closed; the little girl
was restless, clinging to her mother's skirts and whimpering for the
morning walk so unaccountably denied her. Conor sat on the floor and
tried to amuse her, but all the time her mind was struggling. Was this
to be the climax of her bewilderment? Were all her questions to be
answered by the shell of a burnt and plundered house, and perhaps a
row of dead bodies? Her own . . . and even this little body in her
arms . . . ? She held the child tightly in the instinctive panic of maternal
fear, but another part of her thought was almost detached. If this were
to be the answer it was still one which she could not understand, but it
had, at least, finality. Confronting it she felt too tired to wonder any
more.

Only one incident broke the tense monotony of that long day and
night. Towards evening Toole, who had gone to carry a plate of food to

the captive in the barn, came with a swollen and bloody face to report that Finn had made a desperate effort to overpower him and secure his keys. The overseer had scrambled clear, and once out of reach had no more to fear from a man so well secured with chain and padlock to a strong post. The food had been scattered and spilled in the brief struggle. Conor heard her husband remark dryly that the fool had merely imposed upon himself twenty-four hours' starvation as a prelude to the flogging he would receive when all was quiet again. Finn must have guessed, she thought, that his fellow-convicts were making a bid for freedom, and so he had made his own bid, his own mad and hopeless effort to support their madness. Oh, where and what was loyalty . . . ?

It was dawn on Tuesday before a group of armed civilians scouring the country for remnants of the rebel force brought news to Beltrasna of Major Johnston's victory. Mr. Mannion decided that though precautions must still be observed in case stray runaways should appear and attempt violence, the state of siege might be relaxed. Doors were unbarred, and window shutters thrown open again to the fresh morning air. Conor, standing at one of them, heavy-eyed with sleeplessness, saw Finn being marched down the hill to the little yard behind the convict hut.

*   *   *   *   *

It was dusk on Tuesday evening when Johnny escaped back across the river. He dragged his canoe out of the water and set out southward, carring it on his head, for he had heard rumours that there were boats out watching for runaway rebels, and he dared not encounter them.

He had no very clear memory of what had actually happened after he and his companions had touched the fringe of the debacle. He knew that he had been in a rage; that he had tried to wrest the musket from Miller when he felt the panic grip them all; he had a dim impression of himself holding it like a spear, falling into the attitudes and movements of the native war-dance, shouting words that the natives used before a battle, and of eyes staring at him, shocked and startled. And then a sharp, red-hot pain; a flying bullet had grazed his thigh, and blood ran, warm and sticky, down his leg.

To keep his courage high he had become, for a few seconds, purely native; but it was the native in him which was now defeated by that wound. He knew all about firearms; they were no mystery to him. Yet he could not abandon his whole mind and spirit to the black men's way of thinking, and still remain free of the superstitious awe they felt for the white men's weapon; and this sudden assault coming from nowhere, this injury inflicted by no visible hand, had quenched his burning confidence and left him vulnerable to the panic surrounding him.

He had tried to run. For a while someone—he thought it was Miller —had helped him. But then he had stumbled, fallen, found himself alone, passed through a time which seemed full of painful dreaming, and returned to consciousness when the sun was going down, and there was silence all about him.

His leg, stiff and sore, was caked with dry blood and the coarse blue material of his trousers showed a dark stain; but he could walk. He had made his way painfully back to Green Hills, and crept into the village yesterday evening to find Major Johnston already arrived here, and issuing orders for the disposal of the prisoners his detachment had brought in.

He learned that those of the rebels who had not been killed or captured were still at large in the woods. There seemed to be no one about who knew him save Andy—and even Andy did not know that he had been among the insurgents—so Johnny, held by a kind of terrible curiosity, had lingered near the village picking up scraps of rumour here and there. It had been clear enough that all Andy wanted was to keep far away from his brother, but he was not allowed to do that, for Johnny wanted food. It was not much that Andy could give him, but it was something; and when he had eaten he smeared mud over the tell-tale bloodstain on his trousers, and limped back to the village. He saw Lieutenants Brabyn and Davies march in with more prisoners, and learned from whispering by-standers that the Major, invested with power of life and death under Martial Law, was expected to give them short shrift.

He had passed the night alone, hidden in the scrub near the river, and it was the first time he had ever been sleepless. Here in the familiar quietness under the sky, out of sight of township, roof, or any sign of white-man habitation, he had fought a losing night-long battle with the confusions of his thoughts. Somewhere in him there was still hope, for there was still incredulity. It *could* not have happened so. It *could* not be over like this. The woods were still full of armed men, they said. To-morrow . . . to-morrow . . . ?"

But when daylight came at last and he had returned to the village it had only been to find troopers and armed inhabitants setting out in search of more fugitives, and the Major and his officers very much masters of the situation.

So now he stumbled on through the gathering darkness in a kind of daze. His leg still ached badly, and the pain, added to sleeplessness and hunger, slowed his feet. Yet it was not only physical distress which was pinching his face and giving his usually alert eyes a staring, haunted expression. He looked more like the eight-year-old child he had been at the time he deserted his own world than he had looked for many years; and indeed the emotions which were possessing him now were merely a more adult version of those which had driven him to flee twice before from his own people and his own life.

The first time there had been a bare week of freedom, and then ignominious recapture. The second time there had been years, and his return was voluntary. This third time, his whole outraged spirit was crying, would be final. No return! Never—never! He hated them all —the poor as well as the rich; the oppressed as well as the oppressors. From time to time, as he trudged on, he muttered to himself, or burst out suddenly into a fierce, protesting exclamation which was merely the projection into sound of his inner misery and conflict.

There had been no battle. Killing—but no battle. Defeat—but no battle. Those with whom he had allied himself had been routed, and the fact of their abject, ineffectual, panic-stricken surrender possessed his mind like a waking nightmare. It was not the deaths of those he had seen fall which tormented him. Nor was the sense of loathing he felt a recoil from the men who had marched with him. If he had been able to say to himself that they were cowards, his thought would have been clear, however bitter. He knew that they were not cowards. He grappled with the instinct which told him that there had been something more against them than the handful of men in red coats, and because that something was invisible his native half was fearing it even while his white half toiled back into childhood to re-discover its almost forgotten source and meaning.

It was strange—and yet terribly familiar. He had known about it once. Somewhere—far, far away in his own life, he had felt it. It had returned to him like a wave of sickness when he had first set eyes on Major Johnston last night—thick-set, authoritative, swaggering a little, resplendent in his scarlet. It had gripped him when he saw Cunningham brought in, not dead after all; and it had dried his throat and set his legs trembling when he had been part of the awed, restless, silent little crowd that watched the rebel leader's body swing from the staircase in the public store. It had swept over him again when the crowd stood back to let the Major pass—and he had stood back with them. Hands had gone up to forelocks—and his own hand had made the beginning of a similar gesture, as if governed by some atavistic impulse too strong for his control . . .

That had been the climax of terror, and the spur to an almost maddened rage. He had tried to return to his own tribe and fight a battle with it. He had tried to become one of them; but his horror, now, was because he had become one of them all too surely. Superficially he was hating them for the tradition of subservience that misted their manhood, but his real hatred and his deeper fear were for his own instinctive response to it. All the superstition that his long native life had bred in him cried out its simple, primitive warning: "Evil! Evil! Beware!"

It was late when he came, weary and stumbling, to his own place beneath the overhanging rock. Through the trees a little way down the river he had caught a glimpse of the lights of Beltrasna, and his brain, exhausted by its struggle with invisible perils, swung now with a kind of grateful savagery to the simpler hatred of one man, one enemy, represented by those lights.

He would never again unite himself with the white men's world, he thought—but he would visit it! He would challenge and harass it! He would take from it! He had tried to fight it from within, but it was too full of magic. In his weakness, sleepiness and hunger the thought of magic came very easily, and seemed very real. He had learned from his native friends that you cannot attack magic save with other magic, and his brain, sliding off into sleep, searched confusedly for a counter-magic of his own . . .

But it was here. Of course it was here in his own place—his spirit-place where magic had been wrought upon him once to make a man into a child, and where now it was—he could feel it—being wrought again to make a child finally and tremendously into a man. Stretched on the sandy floor, wavering off into the sanctuary of sleep, he felt his identity with this place flow into him like a flood of strength and peace.

*   *   *   *   *

By the end of the week the Governor was able to assure himself and the populace that law and order had been restored. His offer of clemency to those who gave themselves up had had its effect; all through that week, from a few hours after the fatal encounter with Johnston's men, they had been straggling back to the settlements with their arms, and he imagined that the few who remained in the woods would soon be driven in by hunger.

Humes, Hill, and Place had been hanged at Parramatta on Thursday evening; three others, including the Major's namesake, had met the same fate at Castle Hill the next morning; and Sydney had witnessed the execution of Brannan and Hogan. This, he thought, with the addition of corporal punishment for a selected number, and the gaol-gangs or exile to the Coal River for others, should provide a salutary example. Major Johnston and his victorious detachment had returned to Sydney on Friday to be greeted and fêted as the principal heroes of the crisis; and the Governor, having issued a proclamation revoking Martial Law, had himself set out from Parramatta early on Saturday morning, and had been received with suitable ceremony and acclaim on the Parade Ground by Paterson, the Corps, and the inhabitants.

So it was all over. He relaxed for an hour or two in his favourite chair in the Government House parlour, his wife at his side and a glass of port at his elbow. It was all over—but it had been a near thing. Now that the tumult had subsided, and more accurate information was beginning to appear, he was perturbed to realise how close the rebels had come to success. Closer, perhaps, than they themselves had known. So far as he could judge there had been about three hundred and thirty of them under arms—but another day would have doubled their numbers, and he suspected that many of the civilian inhabitants who had assisted in their defeat and capture would have been prepared quite as ardently to support their triumph if a triumph had seemed likely. He was not at all certain, either, that the incident would have ended so satisfactorily if two rebel parties had not lost themselves, and so failed to join the main body. With a little more luck for the insurgents and a little less promptness of action from himself, there might, he thought uneasily, have been a very different outcome.

And was it over, after all? The ringleaders had been Irish, and Captain Piper's guess that His Excellency saw Irishmen in his dreams was not far from the truth. Humes and Johnston had made dying confessions which were valuable if disquieting, and pointed very clearly to the implication of certain persons upon whom King's eye had rested suspiciously for a long time.

He sighed, yawned, and roused himself reluctantly to reach for paper and pencil on the table beside him. The *Calcutta* had already been waiting too long for his despatches, and he must prepare some kind of account of this disturbance to send Home; a few notes jotted down now would assist his dictation of a full report later. But he had had little sleep this last week, and he was yawning again as he scribbled perfunctorily: "... *fully assured of implication of certain artful and designing wretches* ..." He added to that, after a moment: "... *above the common class of those deluded people*," and scored an emphatic line beneath it with a single, angry stroke. He had enough evidence from confessions and the testimony of witnesses to justify prompt measures against Mr. Margarot, and Mr. Holt, and there were others, too. . . . He wrote slowly: "... *hopeful of getting at concealed directors by other means* ..." His pencil, almost absently, traced the words: "*Patience—patience* . . ." and enclosed them carefully in a neat circle. Then he wrote: "*Troopers*," and his wife observed the familiar downward twist of his lips, the wry, decisive smile that meant he was not ill-pleased by someone's discomfiture. His bodyguard of ex-convict troopers—so haughtily resented by Johnston and the other officers—had come out of this affair with credit, and the Major had been compelled to eat his words. This little force should be increased. . . . And more officers and men were needed to man the colony's artillery . . .

But he threw the pencil down suddenly. He was too tired to think of the business any more at present. The worthy Mr. Howe, he thought, would no doubt produce a full and circumstantial account of the whole affair in his next *Gazette*, and that would serve very well—supplemented by a brief commentary of his own—for the information of Lord Hobart. He heaved himself wearily out of his chair.

"I am going to bed, Anna."

"That," remarked his wife approvingly, "is quite the best thing you could do, my love."

*   *   *   *   *

It was as though the colony, having expended its energy in one burst of violence and excitement, subsided now into a plodding routine. The summer was over, the autumn days shortened towards winter. For the Governor they were filled with duties and problems whose number and variety seemed to have increased a thousandfold since those simple days when he had taken his orders from Phillip. His domain was rapidly expanding now, and must expand still more. Lieutenant Menzies was sent to Coal Harbour, taking with him some of the more refractory convicts to work in the mines; perhaps it was with a subconscious hope that by giving parts of this wild country English names he could impose upon it a more English character, that the Governor celebrated the event by naming this mining settlement Newcastle, and the county in which it was placed Northumberland. Colonel Collins, meanwhile, had bestowed the name of Hobart Town upon his miniature colony of a colony at the Derwent, and his latest reports of the situation there were optimistic enough. King turned his attention to plans for the investigation of Port Dalrymple, and the establishment of yet another outpost.

He was disturbed by the presence of American ships in the waters near Bass Strait, and their encroachment upon the oil and sealskin trade which he regarded as the preserve of his own countrymen. He sought instructions from his superiors on this point, and in the meantime pursued his own high-handed methods. He added information that the much-esteemed Chinese delicacy, bêche-de-mer, had been found in abundance on Wreck Reef, and might offer further valuable commercial opportunities. Nearer home, he kept a sharp eye on the progress of the colony's budding industries, and studied carefully the specimens of wool submitted to him by Mr. Marsden. Wool, naturally, turned his thoughts to Captain Macarthur who, so reports from London assured him, was pursuing the subject with his usual pertinacity—encouraged and supported by the demand of manufacturers that Great Britain should be made independent of Spain for her supplies of fine wool. "*I am not unaware*," King wrote to Hobart, "*that applications may be made for ground being granted at the Cow Pastures . . . but I respectfully presume that the preservation of the wild cattle will for many years operate as a bar to any grounds being granted in the vicinity of that place.*"

Such sober considerations of trade and development were, indeed, interrupted occasionally by reminders that he still had opposition to meet from more than one quarter. The old liquor-war went on. By now it was almost like his gout—an enemy lying in wait, emerging into open assault, engaged, partially subdued, and retiring again to await a fresh occasion. And his fear that the rebellious spirit of the lower orders had not been entirely quenched by their recent defeat seemed well-founded. Sparks glowed in the ashes now and then. The incorrigible rogues sent to Newcastle had, he learned, plotted the assassination of their commandant, and formed a desperate and fantastic plan of escape—but it had been discovered and suppressed in time. More disquieting to His Excellency was the knowledge that other rogues—subtler, but no less incorrigible—were still preaching sedition on his very doorstep. Holt had been packed off to Norfolk Island, but Muir and Margarot and Sir Henry Brown Hayes were still thorns in his flesh. A search of Margarot's house for seditious literature had yielded what he described in a private letter as "some very elegant Republican sentiments"; but despite the opinion of the officers, who would have been glad to see this dangerous character banished to the coal-mines, King preferred to keep him under his own eye. The fellow had even had the audacity to declare that he was employed by certain exalted personages to report to them upon the colony, and the proceeding of every person in it from the Governor downwards. King, who knew well how to be scathing, directed that he should be lavishly supplied with writing materials for this task. He hoped sourly that Mr. Margarot would grow as weary of writing as he himself had grown after William Chapman's departure for England in the *Calcutta*, when he had been for a time, until the appointment of Mr. Blaxcell, without the services of a secretary. There was but little advantage, he thought, and endless work in this task that he had begun so eagerly nearly four years ago.

But by the middle of August he could console himself with the thought that he was at least a step nearer to the end of it. The letter he received from Lord Hobart informed him that the King had been pleased to grant him permission to return to England, and that steps were being taken to appoint his successor. To that extent it was satisfactory, but it carried a phrase or two which stung him to sharp comment, if only in the privacy of his wife's bedchamber.

"Listen to this! '*the unfortunate differences which have so long subsisted between you and the military officers . . .*'! Differences! Persecutions are what I have had to endure! Insults, plottings, and slanderous attacks! And that abominable fellow Colnett of the *Glatton* has evidently been busy with his calumnies in London. Had I meekly granted the pardon he asked for that female who cohabited with him, no doubt I'd have been lauded to the skies! Hobart says they seek a Governor who will act in a manner which he's pleased to describe as '*free from the spirit of party.*'" He snorted. "I hope they may find him! They'll soon discover that however free he may be when he sails, he will no sooner have set foot in this place than he must make his choice whether to pursue the path of duty, or become the tool of these scheming rogues in uniform!"

He was glad enough to feel that the end was in sight, if still distant; but he had put too much of his life, and his restless, nervous energy into this colony to face his own departure from it without a thought of its future. Much would depend on the quality of his successors; he hoped fervently that no ill chance, no whim, no secret lobbying, no impatience over the difficulty of finding the right man, would induce the authorities to choose a Governor from those already here.

He worried, too, about his own future. His appointment had failed to bring him, after all, much pecuniary advantage, and the worldly prospect was not bright for his family—soon to be increased. Sydney and Norfolk, he thought with a sigh, must now make their own way in the world—he had done what he could for them. Now he must think of his younger children. He had written to London in an attempt to have the matter of his claim to Phillip's share of the wild cattle recognised and legalised. He had pruned down their estimated numbers from 5,000 to 3,000, and suggested 1,300 as his proper share; and he had declared himself ready to relinquish all claim to these in return for 300 head from the Government's tame herds. But as yet there had been no response. Among the momentous transactions of the Colonial Office, the disposal of a few hundred head of cattle had not, apparently, been deemed important—but it was important to a husband and father not affluent, and in poor health. To hold in his hand the power of granting away land of a kind which had already enriched many, and not to grant it to those whose future he most wished to secure, had savoured, he was beginning to think rebelliously, of scrupulousness at their expense. During this year he did, in fact, subdue his scruples to the extent of granting 2,000 acres to his wife—but the discovery that the grant was not only questionable but illegal, caused it to be cancelled, and left him still at the mercy of anxieties concerning his private as well as his public responsibilities.

He was relieved at least by a reconciliation with Paterson. The Colonel had made two attempts to sail for Port Dalrymple in June and July, but had been forced by wild weather and adverse winds to return. It was October before he departed again, having first gloomily, but with real thankfulness, accepted the Governor's proffered olive branch. *"No animosity, I hope,"* King wrote to Banks, *"ever existed between us; but I cannot help wishing that Paterson had acted from his own ideas. We should then have remained good friends, and some of these disagreeable occurrences would never have happened."*

The settling of the coast by sea-borne expeditions had lately deflected attention from inland exploration, and a botanical excursion by Mr. Caley into the mountains, to an eminence which he had named, in honour of his patron, Mount Banks, did nothing to encourage the Governor, at present, to further attempts. Mr. Caley, having assured him that the roughness of the country was beyond description, proceeded to describe it as similar to travelling over the tops of houses in a town. Such a country, King thought, might well be left alone for the present. Why travel as if over the tops of houses into barren and useless mountains when a ship could bear you comfortably to promising spots upon the coast? It occurred to him, too, that the evil reputation of those wild hills was a deterrent to would-be absconders. The latest muster in July had revealed a total population in the colony and its dependencies of some 8,600 souls, of whom more than 3,000 were convicts, and many more would repay watching. On the whole he was glad that nature had provided a forbidding western wall to his domain.

Often in the midst of his multitudinous affairs—more and more often as the year went by—he wondered about Flinders. *"I hope,"* he had written to Banks in August, *"that Flinders has reached England long before this arrives."* But the passing months brought no news, and the Captain's friends in Sydney spoke of him to each other with a growing uneasiness. By December the botanist, Robert Brown, who had sailed with him in the *Investigator*, was writing to Sir Joseph: *"I need not say how anxious I am to hear from you, and to learn something of Capt'n Flinders, who left this in so small a vessel that we are not without fears for his safety."*

But the year ended without tidings of the young navigator. Mrs. King said frequently: "How I wish we might hear of Captain Flinders!" And the Governor replied as often: "Yes, indeed—and Bass too." For he had expected to hear from Bass at Otaheite, and two years had passed since any word had been received from that island. King attempted to reassure his wife. "They are veterans of the sea, my love, though young in years. We must not be too anxious. The next ship will bring us news of them—letters from them, perhaps . . ."

But he was a sailor himself, and he knew that there were limits to the contest which skill and intrepidity could wage against the ocean. The two names floated like mist across his mind, or clung like cobwebs to the surface of his thoughts. Flinders . . . ? Bass . . . ? Flinders . . . ?

1805

One morning in January of the new year Dilboong, going soft-footed about her work, lingered near the window which opened on to the verandah. Her mistress was out there, reading aloud from the *Gazette* to the old lady, and no native had ever been able to resist a story

"Here's something about the natives," Dilboong heard her say, and then, raising her voice: "The *natives*, Cousin Bertha. I shall read it to you—Mr. Howe always writes so divertingly of them. La, it's about Bennilong . . . !"

"Who, my love?"

"Bennilong. You remember, do you not? He is our Dilboong's father—though to be sure it's a mercy she was not left to his care, for he seems a restless and troublesome character. Can you hear me? I shall move my chair a little closer. There! '*On Wednesday night the FESTIVAL was given in celebration of the approaching GAMES; and as the ancient Bennilong was to withstand the torrent of revenge . . .*' Mercy, I wonder what he has been doing now? '*. . . a number of persons of the first respectability were present at the spectacle.*' I declare I should like to have been present myself!"

Cousin Bertha murmured deprecatingly:

"It would be no sight for a gentlewoman. However . . ." she chuckled naughtily, ". . . we may read of it! Continue, my dear."

"'*At ten o'clock the champions were enlisted, and attended by his partisans, the unclad warrior rushed within the lists. The adverse party, scattered on the shore with spears impatient, hurried to their boats and thence commenced the assault. The flights were in general three in number, the whole amounting to upwards of one hundred spears, all of which he avoided with agility, receiving many through his slender target.*'"

"A little louder, my love . . . ?"

"'*Seated at length, two others rose to bear the shock, perhaps, of vengeance undeserved: when on a sudden the scene became confused. MUSQUITO, pregnant with nectarean juices, rolled like a pestilence among them, discharging random spears in every direction . . .*' La! How amusing!"

Dilboong, duster in hand, crept nearer to the curtains. She had seen her father sometimes when she lived in Sydney; Mrs. Johnson's servants had pointed him out to her when, bemused with liquor, he walked unsteadily through the town. Often she had heard him mentioned, both there and here, but always with a derision which (since there was evidently a mysterious relationship between them) smote her with shame, and a sense of her own worthlessness. Though this story was not easy to follow, she understood that he had been fighting, and that even in battle he was an object of ridicule. Conor was reading again:

"'*Then Collins, like an Ajax stalking forth . . .*'"

"Who is Collins, pray?"

"He is another of the natives, Cousin, who took a white man's name long ago, and has always since been known by it "

"How odd! Well, what next?"

" '. . . like Ajax stalking forth, brought Bennilong to combat, and he, gifted with the matchless subtlety of Ulysses, parried awhile with eloquence untaught, but his antagonist, intent upon hostility, sent forth a whistling spear . . .' " Dilboong clasped her hands, her eyes enormous with apprehension, " 'which, gliding by his arm might seem to share its master's thirst for gore. Repelling and repulsed, with some fatigue the ardour of the warriors gave way to the persuasions of the ancient NESTOR, who, in the person of TERRIBOLONG, harangued the broken ranks, and reason chased MINERVA from the field.' "

Dilboong stood bewildered, straining her ears. Was it ended? What had happened? Mr. Howe's literary style and classical allusions baffled her. Why were the ladies laughing? What of that whistling spear . . . ? She listened anxiously, but Conor had thrown the paper down beside her chair, and was saying with a sigh:

"It is comical, no doubt—but I fear the natives are not as peaceable as they were . . ."

"What did you say, child?"

"Nothing, Cousin Bertha. Would you like to go indoors now? It grows so hot out here. I shall fetch Dilboong to help you."

Her chair scraped on the stone flags. Dilboong fled.

*　　　　*　　　　*　　　　*　　　　*

The old lady must not be alarmed. But it was true that of late Mr. Mannion had several times expressed misgivings about the natives. He was disturbed by reports from his overseers of nocturnal petty thefts, and damage to his property. Vegetables were stolen from the gardens, plants trampled, young fruit trees torn up by the roots. A blanket, a petticoat and two aprons left hanging on a line outside Ellen's cottage disappeared. Fences were broken down. Stones were flung one night on the roof of the overseers' quarters. There were other thefts, not reported—for an axe should not have been left leaning by the chopping-block, nor should a set of carpenter's tools have lain all night in a half-finished shed. Someone had been negligent, too, when a sack of flour was left against the wall on the verandah near the kitchen door—but it was no use being silent about that, for the sack had been cut open with a knife, and the ground, the flagstones, and the very walls were white with scattered flour.

Such wanton, childish, senseless damage was only to be attributed to natives, particularly as there had been many reports during the last few months that they were causing trouble farther down the river. The prints of bare feet in the spilled flour seemed proof, and had been accepted as such at first by Mr. Mannion, as well as by the rest of the household. It was the clean cut of the knife through the sack which gave him pause —until he reflected that by now a few knives must surely have found their way into native hands, even in this remote part of the colony. A native, of course. But this was the first time the intruder had ventured up to the house itself, and he was uneasy.

In February Ellen heard movements outside her cottage in the small hours of the morning. A week or two later Byrne saw what looked like a man moving through the dark near the convict hut. In March Shawn Morgan twice reported the prints of bare feet around the stables. Towards the end of that month Cousin Bertha's footstool disappeared from the front verandah, and Mr. Mannion came to a decision.

Conor was again expecting a child. He acknowledged and proclaimed a husbandly solicitude which desired to spare her all alarms; it was easy, in the circumstances, to ignore the less presentable reflection that here was an excellent pretext for removing her before she became tiresome again.

"There's a very good sort of house in Chapel Row, my love—I inspected it when I was in Sydney last week. It would be but wise, I think, for you to go there with Cousin Bertha for a few months until we have put a stop to these annoyances. The sea air will benefit your health, no doubt. Julia and Bessie shall go with you too, and we shall find you another servant in Sydney."

She answered serenely:

"It will be a pleasant change. I shall like it—and you will be quite comfortable here with Ellen."

He glanced at her suspiciously, but her expression betrayed nothing. He went on hastily:

"I shall miss you sadly, but you will not be far distant after all, and I shall make many occasions to visit you. I don't doubt the good Mrs. King will pay you every attention. You shall have the carriage so that you may drive to Parramatta to visit Mrs. Macarthur and Mrs. Marsden."

It was a golden morning when they set out, and Conor's spirits rose as they travelled the bumpy road, though the triumph she felt was not unmixed with shame for a subtlety she had learned to use instead of the directness more natural to her character. She thought she understood now why females were so often accused of gaining their ends by machinations and intrigues, by exploiting their charms and their tears. "Gentlemen," she reflected, "leave us little else but guile."

Yet she was able to enjoy the small, sedate victory of having used her guile adroitly. She could not defy Stephen's authority, and she did not choose to appeal to it—but it could still be manipulated. The process of manipulation had enlivened these last months, and she had known something of exultation when he said at last: "Conor, I have been considering whether it would not be well for you to go to Sydney for a time." They were *her* words—the fruit of her careful planting and her patient nourishing—but she had schooled her face. The triumphant little smile it should have worn was well hidden behind a mask of astonished and gratified pleasure. "What a delightful notion! Why did I not think of it myself?"

Having established his wife in the house in Chapel Row, Mr. Mannion waited upon the Governor before returning to Beltrasna.

"I have been inconvenienced by the increasing daring of the natives about my property, Sir," he announced. "I'm told you have had similar complaints from settlers on other parts of the river?"

King removed his spectacles and ran his hand wearily over the thinning hair which retreated yearly farther and farther from his forehead. Had he not known that a term had already been set to his exile he would have found these last months almost unendurable. For the Governor-General of His Majesty's territories in New South Wales was but a man, and a family man at that. An illness which had overtaken Mrs. Jane Dundas at a time when Mrs. King was undergoing the disabilities of pregnancy and confinement, and he himself intermittently prostrated by his gout, had added the final stress of domestic discomfort to a much harassed administrator. This reminder of recalcitrant natives moved him now to a moment of almost despairing irritation.

He was rescued from expressing it in an explosion of temper only by that sharp appreciation of absurdity which came to his aid on many occasions. It showed him a picture of himself at which he could smile, however wryly, engaged in an endless series of hostilities on a descending scale from the heroic to the ridiculous. It tickled his sharp humour to reflect that at the top of this scale he was officially if not actually at war with the armies of Napoleon Buonaparte, and at the bottom actually if not officially with a tribe of naked, spear-throwing savages. Between these two extremes raged his war with the officers, his war with seditious political exiles, and his war with the convicts; and of them all the only one he could not fight with a good heart was the one in which his adversaries were too feeble to be taken seriously.

It was true that he had been having complaints about the natives for several months past. He had summoned three of them to learn their grievance, and had been forced to admit himself not only touched by the ingenuousness of their reply, but impressed by its validity. As the Hawkesbury settlements of the white men extended, they had retreated down the river; they objected to being driven from the few remaining parts of its banks where they could find food. They had asked that they be left undisturbed on the lower reaches, and this he had promised them, winning an interlude of peace. But in spite of his confident report to Lord Hobart on the matter, he knew that it could be but an interlude. He realised now that the civilisation he sponsored in this land was a flood which would find its own way. He could dam it back temporarily when it threatened to engulf and destroy the crude communities of the natives —but time, and the pressure of the white men's ruthless need, would break his dams. Already, in his own experience, he had seen those built by Phillip and Hunter give way. The camp-fires had gone first from the bay of Warrung, leaving it Sydney Cove; they had withdrawn from other harbour sites, and back mile by mile from the coast, pursued by the flood which left new names and customs in its wake. On it flowed, a native name surviving here and there, past Parramatta to The Ponds, Kissing-Point, Toongabbee, Prospect, Castle Hill, on again to the long boundary of the Hawkesbury—and here, too, in scattered villages and farms, the light that marked man's habitation had become a lamp in a cottage window, and the camp-fires still retreated.

It was a problem that had gone far beyond his solution. It was not only something set in motion that he was powerless to stop, but something which it was his duty to keep moving. Nevertheless Monsieur Baudin's words sometimes haunted him. *"You will presently remain the peaceful possessors of their heritage . . ."*

All this was behind the frown that creased his brows as he answered Mr. Mannion's question:

"That is so, Sir."

"Murders have been committed, I understand?"

"There have been several shocking occurrences at South Creek and around the Branch. A settler was killed, and the bodies of another and his servant were found buried among the ruins of his burned home. These outrages are apt to occur, I've noticed, at the time when the maize is ripe . . ."

"I assume, however," Mannion remarked with a shade of irony, "that you don't propose we should reconcile ourselves to an annual repetition of . . ."

King reddened and interrupted sharply. He found Mr. Mannion's tone—not for the first time—offensive.

"I am taking suitable measures, Sir, and your sarcasm is misplaced, to say the least of it. I propose to send detachments to the outer settlements, and order that no natives be permitted to approach the grounds or dwellings of the settlers. You say they have been troublesome in your own neighbourhood?"

Mannion related his story. "In past years they have come less and less frequently about my property, for they have not been encouraged, as I believe they have been in other places, by gifts of food. The attempt to treat savages with leniency is something I have never . . ."

King snapped:

"You may leave the general policy of Government on this matter to me, Sir. I have had some experience of these people, and it frequently happens that their passions are excited by the recollection of some injury long past. I have seen them thrown into transports of rage by the thought of something which occurred in the time of their great-grandfathers. This is not to condone their savagery, Sir, but to explain actions which may seem incomprehensible to us. I should be sorry to think that savagery can only be met with savagery."

Mannion replied coolly, with an irritating smile:

"If by savagery Your Excellency means stern measures to protect life and property from their depredations, it would seem that you have already been driven to it."

The Governor made an involuntary, baffled gesture. He wanted to say: "It is not long since that your property was theirs." But he could not say it, for his imagination instantly provided him with Mr. Mannion's ironic and unanswerable rejoinder: "Do you suggest I should return it to them?" He could not invite such a retort. It opened up a whole, frightening sequence of logic which set the events of seventeen years in reverse, dissolved towns and houses and roads and cultivated fields into mist, and erased the white man like a figure from a slate. It showed him for one mad moment the flood running backward, sucking the invaders into this little cove again, and on to a fleet of ghostly ships that silently, with no wind behind them, receded down the shining harbour, out the Heads, beyond the horizon, leaving this ancient and inscrutable land to its silence, its loneliness, and the unchanging life of its own dark children . . .

"I have no alternative," he said irritably. "If these miserable people must be fired upon in order to secure the settlers' property, it is a painful necessity. I tell you, Sir, I regret it. Should you desire it I shall post soldiers at Beltrasna to protect . . ."

"Protect!" Mannion laughed shortly. "I stand in no need of more protection from savages than my own household and servants can provide. The point of my story, Sir, which I have not yet had the opportunity to make clear to you, is that the sack of flour had been *cut*—with a knife. I mention this circumstance in order to drive home the contention I have frequently expressed—that we have no certain knowledge of the fate of convicts who have escaped at different times. I bear in mind, Sir, the fellow who escaped and was long believed dead, and who—three years later—was observed alive and vigorous on the river bank opposite my property."

King frowned, searching his memory.

"I recall the tale. Prentice—wasn't that his name?"

"It was." Mannion leaned forward and tapped the table emphatically. "Others might have joined him. There may be, for all we know, a band of such rascals at large. It may be they who incite the natives, and supply them with knives. I assure you, Sir, I do not regard these miserable savages as a menace by themselves—but taught, inflamed, supported, and perhaps armed by runaway rogues of our own colour, the matter appears in a different light." He rose briskly. "The responsibility is yours; I can but commend the idea to Your Excellency's attention." He bowed. "My wife begs her regards to you, Sir, and hopes to have the pleasure of seeing Mrs. King before long." He withdrew.

The Governor stood still for a few moments after he had left, staring thoughtfully out the window. It was possible, he thought peevishly, that there might be some truth in Mr. Mannion's theory—but if there were, what more could he do than he was doing? Was he to send out some of his sparse military forces to comb the arid and unexplored fastnesses of the mountains in search of hypothetical absconders—and leave his colony depleted of protectors against another such crisis as he had so narrowly averted last year? Absurd! Impossible! He returned with an impatient shrug to his desk.

*   *   *   *   *

The house in Chapel Row seemed small after the spaciousness of Beltrasna, but by the standards of Sydney it was comfortable, and Conor was well content. Not only Mrs. King, but all the other respectable people of Sydney were attentive, and Mrs. Mannion's carriage drove out almost daily. But she did not always go visiting. She was interested in the rapid growth of a town where less than a score of years earlier there had been nothing, and in the busy life that went on in its narrow, crooked streets. She drove through them across the stone bridge that spanned the Tank Stream, up the hill past the unfinished church, out to the high ridge where the windmill stood near the new citadel which His Excellency was building. Here she often sat for an hour or two on those bright autumn afternoons, looking out from beneath her parasol down the long reaches of the harbour towards the Heads, at the crescent of Sydney Cove where the tall masts of ships marked the wharves, at the huddled little town with its haphazard streets, at the buildings scattered over the foreshores with rock and scrub and tussocky grass between. Once, staring across the water at the grey-green trees that clothed the hills of the northern shore, she thought of those other hills, so similar, which rose west of the Nepean near Beltrasna. What a strange, monotonous, unresponsive country, and how difficult to feel at one with it! Must it always be as if seemed now—an adversary? She was chilled by thinking of it so, for it offered to that thought of strife no more response than it offered to her tentative desire for peace, and she felt that if it were to be seen as a foe it must also be seen as one whose ultimate victory was so certain that it need only wait. Those trees . . . ! An eagle soaring above them caught her eye, and her mind, following its flight as it disappeared northward, looked down upon mile after mile of such trees—twenty miles, fifty, a hundred, five hundred, who knew how many . . . ? She said to herself half aloud a name that was more and more being given to those expanses of timbered country which (for their quality took no more account of time than of distance) seemed not only boundless, but eternal. She almost offered that name, as if by admitting the incongruousness of others, loved and familiar, she might pierce the invisible defences which this land set up, and appease it with an acknowledgment of its difference. Yet she could not avoid the feeling that such a gesture was less spontaneous than exacted. It was not an overture, but a first act of submission. One could fasten an English or an Irish name upon a place, and that was warming to the nostalgic heart; or one could leave a native name, and that was quaint, and still acceptable. But when the land took one's language it was taking one's people, and made strange, faint distortions and adjustments so that a word was still an English word, but not quite, there was a hint of forces not to be controlled. Forest—woods—woodland —coppice. . . . She shook her head. They were words which had struggled here for life where alone words can live—on the tongues of the people—and they were dying . . .

That was the bush . . .

Sometimes she would drive along Church Street past the Parade Ground and the Barracks and the military hospital, and occasionally down to the waterfront and the dockyards near Mr. Campbell's wharf; but more often she would bid Shawn Morgan turn south along High Street and follow it till it left the other streets behind and, skirting the burial ground, passed on between the head of Cockle Bay and the Brickfields to swing

westward towards Parramatta. Several times she drove past Annandale
where Major Johnston's long, low brick house stood on its commanding
eminence looking out over gardens, orangery and vineyard; and once she
was taken with a party of ladies and gentlemen to inspect Surgeon Harris'
estate, whose strange name, "Ultimo," seemed always to cause whispering
amusement. Occasionally she made all day excursions to Parramatta to
visit Mrs. Marsden and Mrs. Macarthur, and listened, half-envious, to
their endless gossip of the colony. Their husbands were so deeply involved
in its affairs, their fortunes so irrevocably bound up with its progress, that
the wives seemed to have a place in it which Conor felt she lacked. True,
Stephen had his property and his interests, but their function was only
to make a rich man richer still, and his persistent attitude of detachment
had kept her with a sense of being unrooted. Isolation had robbed her,
too, of even an observer's share in the crowding incidents and rumours
which enlivened the busy days of these two ladies, and she began to
realise as she listened to them how ignorant she was of the colony's affairs.

She found herself even a little in awe of Mrs. Macarthur. This comely,
capable woman in her thirties was so busy with the management of her
absent husband's affairs, so preoccupied with the children who remained
with her, so eager to relate news of those in England, so proudly confident
of Macarthur's omniscience and the success of any plan he might
undertake, that Conor felt her own loneliness and idleness emphasised.
This, she thought rather sadly, was what she had vaguely imagined that
married life in a faraway colony might be—something full of occupations
and endeavours that a wife might share with her husband. For though
Macarthur was absent in the flesh, he was always very present in his
wife's conversation.

"I'm in hopes that Macarthur may be returning quite soon you know,
Mrs. Mannion." "I have found the responsibility very great during
Macarthur's absence—but naturally I use every endeavour, for I should
not wish him to find his affairs in disorder." "I have felt the separation
from my children keenly, though to be sure my mind is easy while
Macarthur is in England with them." "Mary grows a big girl, does she
not? Macarthur will see a great change in all the children when he
returns . . ."

The name was so ceaselessly repeated that it became a kind of dis-
embodied but dominant personality. It not only stood commandingly in
the present, but so hypnotised the imagination that Conor felt herself
drawn helplessly after it into a future which would be thus, and thus—
because Macarthur willed it so. On the other side of the world, it
appeared, this future was being shaped. Macarthur, said his wife, had
interviewed many influential persons in England. Macarthur was attempting to form a company to encourage the production of fine wool in the
colony. Macarthur had resigned his Commission in the Army, and would
henceforth devote himself entirely to this important project. Macarthur
had met with much injustice and opposition, but of course he did not
allow such things to deter him, being a man of extremely determined
character. Sir Joseph Banks had been most uncivil to Macarthur. Many

people were uncivil to Macarthur, which was entirely due to their envy of his superior powers and noble nature. Macarthur had the ear of Lord Camden, who had lately succeeded Lord Hobart, and was applying for a grant of land near Mount Taurus, ". . . near the Cow Pastures, my love, and very well adapted to the grazing of sheep." It was indeed unfortunate for the colony that its Governors had not seen as clearly as Macarthur where its advantage lay . . .

Mrs. Marsden's husband was also greatly preoccupied with sheep; in a rebellious and irreverent moment Conor even reflected that they seemed to engage his attention more than the human beings who formed his allegorical flock. But his wife's conversation was concerned mostly with tit-bits of gossip, and lamentations upon the wickedness of the colony.

"Do you think of returning home soon, Mrs. Mannion?"

"There's no talk of it at present, Ma'am, and I am well pleased to remain here."

"Ah, but you are far from the centres of our unhappy society! Believe me, I sometimes wonder if God has not wholly forsaken this place, which one could not wonder at, to be sure. My husband has frequently remarked that this is a most ungracious soil for the growth of piety. Pray have you seen Mrs. King's new infant, my love?"

"I saw it last week, Ma'am—a dear little girl, and so thriving . . ."

"May it be God's will to spare it to her!" Mrs. Marsden exclaimed with a quick, passing expression of pain that made Conor feel a poignancy behind the conventional words. She stammered:

"Indeed you have been most unhappy, dear Mrs. Marsden, in losing two of your children so—so sadly. I feel for you more than I can . . ."

"My dear," replied her hostess simply, "I cannot question God's wisdom. My husband wrote to a friend that they are not lost, and in that glorious morning of the resurrection of the spirit we shall all be reunited. His words have given me strength to be resigned. But let us talk of other things. You have been at Government House? How is Dundas, pray?"

"I believe she is still poorly."

"So unfortunate, was it not, with Mrs. King in delicate health, and the Governor in the gout again? You must miss Mrs. Paterson from the society of Sydney?"

"Yes, indeed I do, Ma'am. Have you heard how Colonel Paterson is progressing at Port Dalrymple?"

"There have been difficulties, I understand—but where in this extraordinary country are there not difficulties? Mrs. Paterson writes to Mrs. King, I believe, and I hear she says the place abounds in the most destructive creatures. An insect that makes holes in cloth, and perfectly ruined one of the Colonel's coats—and wild cats that kill the poultry—and small animals that eat the potatoes—and snakes, very venomous—and only imagine, my love, some even say they have seen the *Devil* . . . !"

"The . . . the Devil, Ma'am . . . ?" murmured Conor. "Indeed?"

"Ignorance!" said Mrs. Marsden, shaking her head. "Superstition! The devil is present there, I don't doubt, as he is in every hole and corner of this colony, but he reveals himself only in the works of man, and to the eye of grace, Mrs. Mannion. Tell me, have you heard from Captain Piper?"

"No, Ma'am, but I understand he is still at Norfolk Island?"

"He is in command there, since Colonel Foveaux went home. I write to him frequently. I'm told His Excellency had a letter from him not long since by the *Harrington*, which called at the island on the way from Otaheite—oh, la, Ma'am, what our missionaries have suffered in that place in their efforts to spread the Gospel! You should hear Mr. Hassall and Mr. Cover tell of it!"

Conor enquired:

"Was it not from Otaheite that the Governor hoped to hear news of Mr. Bass?"

Mrs. Marsden shook her head solemnly.

"You are acquainted with Mr. Brown, Ma'am? The botanist who came out with Captain Flinders? No? My husband spoke to him but recently, and he was most concerned about both Mr. Bass and Captain Flinders. He declares he believes Mr. Bass must either have been put to death by the South Sea Islanders—which would not surprise me in the least from the tales I have heard of their diabolical savagery—or captured on the coast of Peru. I fear the worst. And I entertain the gravest misgivings also about Captain Flinders. I suppose the Governor has had no word yet? You have seen him more recently than I."

"He did not speak of it, Ma'am," said Conor, troubled.

But upon her next visit to Government House she learned that the news so long awaited had reached him by a couple of days earlier, in a letter from Flinders himself, begun in Timor more than a year past, and finished eight months ago at Ile de France. The Governor had been in a rage ever since he read the sentence which made the long silence understandable. *"Thus far, my dear Sir, I had written to you from Coupang in case of meeting with a ship by which it might have been sent, little expecting that I should have finished it here, and in a prison."* His anger was reflected throughout the colony wherever the news had travelled, but in the Governor's breast it was mixed with, and made more bitter by, a pang of self-accusation. He could not but remember the despatches to the Secretary of State which he had entrusted to Flinders, nor avoid the knowledge that they must have made provocative reading for the Governor of Ile de France. He was, on the afternoon of Conor's visit, too occupied to pay his respects to Mrs. Mannion; it was Mrs. King, hardly less indignant, who supplied the details.

"You have heard about Captain Flinders, Ma'am? King is beside himself! You know what a miserable vessel the *Cumberland* was, and it seems she was leaky, and the pumps so worn out that the Captain was forced to put in to Ile de France—not knowing about the war, you see—and was immediately seized and made prisoner by this infamous Decaen! A monster, my love! He treated the Captain with the utmost discourtesy, and professed not to believe in his Commission and passport because of his coming in so small a vessel, and actually declared he was an impostor!

A spy! You can conceive the feelings of poor Flinders, so anxious to get home with his charts, and to see his wife again! And he became ill with the scurvy in his confinement, and was not even allowed to walk abroad for almost four months. My dear Mrs. Mannion, when I recall the civility with which we treated the Frenchmen when they were here, I am so indignant I almost lose my powers of speech! The Captain himself remarked in his letter to King that the account of such treatment would surprise us, who had lately shown every attention to the *Géographe* and the *Naturaliste*. Surprise! I was dumbfounded, Ma'am, and I thought King would suffer a seizure, he was so angry!" She touched her handkerchief to her eyes. "So amiable and courteous a young man—so gentle and thoughtful! He mentioned me by name—'my kind friend Mrs. King . . .' And he begged his remembrances to all his other friends—of whom you were one, dear Mrs. Mannion—and indeed I wish he could know how we all feel for him in his misfortune."

"He is still imprisoned, Ma'am?" Conor asked, aghast.

Mrs. King wiped her eyes and lifted her hands helplessly.

"So we assume, my love. No doubt the strongest representations will be made. Sir Joseph will surely intervene! And King has already written to this—this creature, Decaen, in terms which should make him blush if he is not lost to all decent feelings. But in these times of war who can say how long it will take to secure his release?"

Conor went home sadly, thinking of the young man who had sat on the verandah at Beltrasna, and said to her: "I grow grey alone, Madam."

*　　　*　　　*　　　*　　　*

A series of events at this time strengthened Mr. Harvey's wavering resolve to quit an employment which was becoming increasingly uncongenial. One was the departure of Conor, which left Beltrasna quite intolerably bleak. A second was Maria. The big, blowsy, ignorant girl repelled that part of him which was fastidious, but he had not lived six years in this colony without discarding some of the naïveté he had brought with him. In a society where the outnumbered women passed their lives in circumstances not designed to foster feminine delicacy and virtue, he had discovered that he was not wholly fastidious. His amorous experiments in Sydney and Parramatta had spread a veneer of disillusionment over his romanticism, but had left him—rather to his surprise—with little sense of guilt. His unwillingness to pursue them, as Maria's manner indicated that he might do when he chose, under the Beltrasna roof, was merely a gesture of homage to Conor. It was *her* roof; here, at least, he must not only feel, but be blameless.

Yet even stronger as goads to his restlessness were daily events which roused in him emotions ranging from uneasiness to disgust, and from disgust to downright horror. He had chanced to see the convict, Finn, on the day after the rebellion, being carried back to the convicts' quarters, bloody and half-conscious. Twice since, when Mr. Mannion, having occasion to desire punishment for his labourers, had thought it time once again to show an appearance of conforming to the law, it had been Mark's task to convey them to Parramatta, submit charges of "idleness and insubordination," and deliver them to the judgment of the magistrate. The impression made on him by the sight he had witnessed at Toongabbee soon after his arrival, had never been effaced, and it came back more and more to haunt him now, till it was almost an obsession.

He sought no solution but a personal escape. His rebellion was no more than the recoil from brutality of a sensitive nature and a kindly heart; his decision, when at last he was driven into making it, was not concerned with ending suffering, unkindness, or tyranny, but merely with tearing himself free of them, and in this he was not conscious of evasion. He had been reared in a gentility which, if poor, was the more obstinately respectable, and its respectability was based upon the acceptance of society as it existed; upon deference to birth, wealth, position and authority; upon the assumption that the law could do no wrong.

One morning, busy at his employer's accounts, he was disturbed by a faint sound behind him, and turned to find Dilboong dusting the furniture, and watching him at the same time from over her shoulder. He was a little surprised to see her there at that hour, for the dusting was usually finished earlier; but domestic irregularities were no concern of his, and he addressed himself again with a yawn to his figures.

His sharp-pointed pen scratched across the page; the neat flowing handwriting and the finely-formed black figures crept down the page while his mind, only half-occupied, wandered off into thoughts inspired by the items on his list.

1 Gentleman's Black Hat £1/5/0

A beautiful hat—but even in his moment of envy he had acknowledged with his incorrigible diffidence that it would not look so well with his own thin and rather pale young face beneath as it did on Mr. Mannion's handsome head.

1 Chest of Souchong Tea £12/12/0
432 lbs. Sugar @ 1/- 21/12/0
20 Gallons Jamaica Rum 16/ 0/0
20 Gallons Cognac Brandy 16/ 0/0

Why was it that Mr. Mannion could drink freely and show never a sign of it, while he must sip with painful discretion? That evening when he had drunk a little too much . . . ! And even through the bemusement that was clouding his senses, and the silly impulse to laugh at nothing, he had been conscious of cold, blue, contemptuous eyes, and shamed by a cold, ironic voice: "You are a trifle indisposed, I think, Mr. Harvey— perhaps a turn in the fresh air would restore you . . . ?"

Even now, more than a year later, Mark's very ears flamed at the memory. He thrust it aside and hurriedly went on writing.

2 prs. Lady's Gloves 10/0

She had showed them to him—held out a hand for him to admire. He had thought wildly of kissing it, and muttered instead that they were very elegant . . .

6 prs. Lady's Hose £2/8/0

His modesty would not allow his thoughts to linger here. They could pass on more happily to the memory of those six skeins of sewing silk at four shillings, and those twelve yards of bonnet ribbon gleaming under her

busy fingers in the lamplight. And to his triumph when she had unwrapped that pink lutestring for which he had scoured the shops of
Sydney, and declared it exactly the shade of her choice . . .

A murmur at his elbow startled him from his day-dreaming, and
caused him to bungle a figure. He looked up, annoyed. As had happened so often during the years when he sat at lessons with Patrick and
Miles, Dilboong had arrived silently beside his chair; it was the fact that
he no longer looked down at her, but must now raise his eyes to her
black, blunt-nosed face that made him realise with a slight shock how
much she had grown.

She did not speak, but her dark, lustrous eyes were fixed on his face
with an expression half pleading and half apprehensive. Looking at them,
he wondered suddenly if she recalled their first journey to this place
together—if she ever remembered those screams—if she ever thought of
the cup of water he had given her . . . ? Did the fact that they had
once, long ago, shared the strangeness of a new experience, leave her—
as it left him—with the curious, irrational feeling of a bond between
them . . . ?

Of course not! A child's memory was short—a black child's almost
non-existent . . . ! He said rather irritably:

"What is it, Dilboong?"

Her hands were clasped behind her back. One of them came slowly
into view holding a torn scrap of paper which she thrust at him, anxiety
and bashfulness dimming her eyes with moisture, her wide mouth stretched
in an awkward smile more painful than her tears. Puzzled, he took it.

"*dear mister miles i hop you com back soon your obedent servent with
respeck dilbung.*"

He looked at her in astonishment.

"What's this, Dilboong—a letter?"

She nodded, twisting one leg round the other in an agony of embarrassment. He held the paper, looking from it to her, and from her to it.
She had watched the boys at their lessons; she had been punished once or
twice for stealing Miles' slate; Mark had even, on a few occasions, found
her writing short words in the dust of the path, and good-naturedly,
thinking it a joke, corrected her spelling and the form of her letters. He
remembered now that he had seen her several times poring over a copy of
Watt's Catechism, and that sometimes, dusting this very desk, she lingered
to peer at the papers lying on it. And the result of all this—the almost
unbelievable result—what that she could write! Very badly, indeed, but
still, comprehensibly . . .

He stared at her again. She must be, he reflected, about thirteen now,
but she still looked childish—lean, angular and ungraceful in the straight
blue frock from beneath which showed broad, bare feet and bony ankles.
He said helplessly:

"Why, Dilboong, I didn't know you could write . . ." and added,
feeling a sudden pity for this crude and lonely attempt at scholarship,
". . . so well."

She murmured almost inaudibly:

"You send'm? You send'm to Mr. Miles?"

It was nearly two years now, he thought, since Miles had gone away; the memory of a black child was not non-existent after all. He asked on a sudden impulse:

"Do you remember coming here, Dilboong? The first time you came here from Parramatta . . .?"

She slipped behind his chair. He felt her hands clutch his coat. She was bobbing up and down, and making noises like the clip-clop of horses' hooves. . . . Good God, what would Mr. Mannion say if he came in and saw this frivolous tomfoolery? Mark swung round hastily, disengaging her hands. Her mouth was one wide, white-toothed grin until something warned her that she had done wrong, and her eyes flew instantly, in panic, to her letter.

"You send'm?" she besought.

"Yes, yes, child, I'll send it. Now go back to your work, or Ellen will . . ."

Mr. Mannion's voice said harshly from the doorway:

"Dilboong, what are you doing here? You have left a pail of water in the hall, and your work unfinished." Coming across to the desk, he caught sight of the torn scrap of paper, with its laborious scrawl, lying incongruously upon Mr. Harvey's precise columns of figures. He picked it up.

"What's this?" He stared at it. He stared from it to Dilboong, dumb and frightened, with her hands behind her and her head hanging; and from her to Mark, hastily risen from his chair. "What *is* this, Mr. Harvey?"

Mark cleared his throat.

"Dilboong has written a letter, Sir, to Miles. She was asking me if I would send it for her."

Mr. Mannion said incredulously:

"Dilboong wrote this?" He snapped: "Have you nothing better to do, Mr. Harvey, than to waste your time in teaching a savage to write, and assisting her with a ridiculous, presumptuous. . . . Dilboong! Remain where you are!"

Mark looked down at the child with a strange feeling that this had happened before. And yes, of course, it had. . . . Here they were, he and Dilboong, once more experiencing a common ordeal. For he felt already that there was to be more to this than a rebuke administered, and accepted. The terror in Dilboong's eyes not only calmed his own nervousness, but substituted for it a flash of anger.

"I did not assist her with this—this letter, Sir, nor did I teach her to write—or only indirectly. She used to watch when Patrick and Miles were at their lessons, and has evidently practised alone. I'm impressed," he added recklessly, "by her aptitude."

Mr. Mannion said contemptuously:

"Aptitude? You call this crude scribble—*aptitude*?" He tore it carelessly in several pieces and dropped the fragments on the table. "Dilboong, I shall speak to Ellen of your idleness and deceitfulness. Go!" He watched her out of the door and turned again to Mark. "Mr. Harvey, I think you know my views concerning the natives—I have spoken of them often enough. It is fatal to encourage in them tastes and leanings above their station, and I should not have thought it necessary to tell you that an attempt at communication between Dilboong and my son . . ."

Mark actually interrupted him.

"When Miles was here, Sir, they were not only in communication but in close and daily contact. They were playmates, and I should not have thought . . ."

"You need not think, Sir," Mannion said sharply, "though surely it must be clear to you that it was precisely to remove Miles from such undesirable associations that I sent him to England. Oblige me, Mr. Harvey, by thinking less, and giving more of your attention to observing my wishes, which is what I employ you for."

Mark realised with sudden acute nervousness that Mr. Mannion had unwittingly spoken words which were a cue—no, more than that—a challenge to him to speak others, long debated and long practised. He still held in his mind's eye the picture of Dilboong's smitten face, the whisk of her blue dress and her bare feet slinking out of Mr. Mannion's presence round the door. He knew that, having shared this ordeal with her, he must share it to the end—but not necessarily the same end; indeed he almost felt that in turning his own peril of defeat into victory, he would somehow be redeeming the abjectness of her submission. He was pleasantly surprised by the firmness of his own voice.

"I have been wanting to speak to you, Sir, on the subject of my employment. I am not—I do not wish to continue it."

Mannion's expression, in one of lesser dignity, and not so commanding a presence, might have been called a gape. He did not want to lose the services of this young man who—until now—had combined a respectful air and a becoming docility with his undoubted usefulness. He said with annoyance:

"Come, come, Mr. Harvey, what's this nonsense? Your duties are not over-exacting. Your salary is adequate—nay, generous—and you have been treated in my household with every consideration."

Mark objected obstinately:

"Nevertheless, Sir, I don't feel that I can continue in my present situation. I'm a tutor, and without pupils I . . ."

"Ridiculous!" barked Mr. Mannion. "It was always understood that your duties would include other matters besides the education of my sons. You can have no possible objection to the necessary adjustments I have made in your work since Miles. . . ."

"The work is distasteful to me, Sir," said Mark abruptly.

"Distasteful . . . ?" Sheer astonishment drove the anger from Mannion's voice. It took only a second or two for the implications of the un-expected, the astounding word to penetrate his mind, and spread over his face an expression of amused, half-contemptuous indulgence. The idea that an underling of his might object to the employment given him on the ground of uncongeniality was so novel, so breath-taking in its presumption, that he could not take it seriously. This was a tantrum, like Conor's tantrums. Youth was tiresome in its emotional outbursts. . . . He drawled with biting irony:

"May I enquire, young man, which part of your duties it is which fills you with such repugnance?"

If he had not sneered and said "young man," Mark's mood of defiance, already beginning to waver, might have collapsed. But he was painfully conscious that he had always been younger than his years, and that even now, at twenty-eight, he had not achieved the assurance and self-confidence of maturity. He felt too that Mr. Mannion had a hundred times driven him back with a snub, an ironical smile, a contemptuous glance, a brusque order too hurtfully reminding him of his dependence, into shamed awareness of his youth and insignificance. Hot blood rushed to his face, and hot words to his lips.

"I'm not a gaoler, Sir! I'm not an overseer of convicts! I was prepared for some secretarial work in addition to my duties as tutor, but I was not prepared for the task of conveying orders for brutal punishments, or reductions in rations already inadequate, or work beyond the strength of the wretches expected to perform it . . . !"

He often wondered afterwards whether the heat of his anger would have continued to sustain him through the wrath he saw gathering on Mannion's face during this reckless speech. For it was interrupted not by the expected thunder of his employer's voice but by the unexpected intervention of Toole—breathless and agitated—from outside the French windows that opened on to the verandah. The anger that his audacity had provoked was deflected with startling suddenness on to the head of the overseer.

"Your Honour, Sir, if you pl . . ."

"Damnation, Toole!" roared Mr. Mannion, "what do you mean by breaking in upon me in this unmannerly fashion? Can't you see that I'm occupied?"

Toole twisted his cap nervously in his hands.

"Yes, Sir, indeed, but beggin' Your Honour's pardon, it's a matter I . . . ye'd not be wantin' delay, Sir. . . ." He stammered and plunged on desperately: "Divil sweep me, Sir, if I can tell how . . . and Byrne but a few yards distant, and the dirty bosthoon ironed as he was, Sir, the way it's no more than a few steps he could be takin' . . ."

Mr. Mannion strode to the window in a fury.

"What? *What?* Stop chattering, you imbecile, and save your explanations till I ask for them! What has happened?"

From behind the table where he still stood, slightly dazed by his own temerity, Mark stared, and could almost pity Toole's distress. The overseer had been running, but the sweat on his brow which he wiped away with his cap was mainly a sweat of apprehension, and he retreated a step in alarm before his master's impetuous advance.

"It's Finn, Sir," he almost wailed. "He's escaped . . ."

* * * * *

The man-hunt, Mark thought with fervent relief as he packed his bags a few hours later, need not concern him. Mr. Mannion, it seemed, had forgotten him in the first tumult of questioning and organisation which followed Toole's disclosure. Yet he must have given a thought some time during those hours to his once unobtrusive secretary, for, returning to the house at midday, he had summoned Mark to hear a withering speech of dismissal.

"I will tolerate neither insolence nor ingratitude from those I employ, Mr. Harvey. The sooner you take yourself off the better I shall be pleased. You have plans, no doubt, for your future, but you will not receive any recommendation from me—nor, I think, would you have the audacity to expect it. Should you return to England I imagine neither Sir John nor Mr. Desmond O'Connor will speak for you after I have acquainted them of your most singular behaviour. If your intention is to remain in the colony you may be sure my account of you will not advance your interests. Now, since I'm occupied with a matter which I assure you is of more moment than your retirement from my service, I will bid you good-day. You are a fool, young man!"

A fool, thought Mark, tortured by a return of his native diffidence and self-doubt now that his mad moment was over. Yes, a fool indeed, for his store of money was small, and his glimpses of the colony such that he could not face the plunge into it which confronted him without dismay. A fool, and a coward too, for now that he was leaving it Beltrasna seemed a haven of a kind—a home, a room, a bed, a livelihood—in a place where such things were not easily won without influence—or audacity. He had thrown away the goodwill which might have procured him the former; and the latter he had never possessed.

Yet when he had watched Mr. Mannion with one of his overseers and three of his free farm servants ride off with muskets and dogs to hunt down a limping man with shackled feet, he felt glad that his lunacy had saved him from being ordered to join them. They would catch the poor devil, of course, before nightfall—perhaps in an hour or so—and there would be another orgy of blood and cruelty in the yard behind the convict hut. . . . He thought, as the Governor had thought before him: "What mad things a man will do for liberty . . . !" And he paused with a coat in his hand, looking down blankly at his half-packed valise. For had not his own action been mad—and in its way a bid for liberty? Had he not felt the authority of his employer like chains on his spirit, forcing upon him a captivity which was, indeed, different in kind from that of the convict, but still captivity? Struck by that strange thought, his mind dwelt on Finn with a new attention, and he paused to wonder about an incident which, till now, he had been glad enough to pass over as being no concern of his.

Working down at the river on repairs to a small landing-stage, his ankles burdened with heavy irons, Byrne but a few yards distant, and a few minutes out of sight while he went to the cart for nails—the man had simply vanished. That was Toole's story. Where? How? Had he, as someone had suggested, made an attempt to swim to the opposite bank, and sunk in midstream, weighed down by his leg-irons? But there had been no splash, no sound of swimming or of struggle, no cry for help as surely there would have been if . . .

Mark, still staring blindly at his valise, began smoothing the folds of his coat with nervous fingers. Perhaps the man had seen that deep water not as a barrier to be crossed, but as a place kindlier than earth . . . ? Perhaps he had not tried to swim . . . ?

He thrust the coat hurriedly into his bag, snatched up a few remaining articles, packed them with careless haste as if he were late for some urgent appointment. He took a last look about the room, and his reluctance to leave it was forgotten. That last unanswered question haunted it, and all this place. He was glad to be leaving it—glad, glad . . . !

A cart which had arrived with stores that morning would convey him and his two bags back to Parramatta. A humble exit with no farewells, for Ellen was down at her cottage, and he avoided Maria. It was not until he was seated uncomfortably on his valise, and jolting down the hill towards the road, that he saw a small blue-clad figure on the verandah, staring after him.

Dilboong . . .

He had forgotten her. And yet she had perhaps more than once played a part in his life which was significant. He waved to her, feeling curiously remorseful—even guilty. Seeing her thin black arm lift in response, he thought: "What way of escape for her?"

*   *   *   *   *

Finn, crouching behind Johnny in his canoe, gripped its bark sides and held himself rigidly still. His heart was thumping heavily, his mind confused by the suddenness and the complete unexpectedness of this amazing escape, and he could think only of the instability of the frail craft, of the deep water, of the heavy shackles on his feet. He could only discipline his body to make no movement which might upset them, watch the rhythmic lift and fall of Johnny's paddle, and strain his ears without turning his head, for sounds of pursuit.

Johnny himself, though not frightened, was perturbed. He had carried a passenger often enough, but it had always been a native, and he had not reckoned on the difference in weight between a slightly built and naked native, and a solidly-built white man wearing heavy leg-irons. There was so little freeboard that the water lapped Finn's knuckles as he clutched the sides, and their pace was but half what Johnny could accomplish when alone. This was annoying, but—to him—not serious. A capsize would merely mean a swim to the opposite bank; it had not occurred to him that his passenger might be unable to swim—and indeed he was not really sufficiently interested in Finn to care whether he drowned or not.

He had been watching the labour at the landing stage for a couple of days, enjoying the thought that he would allow it to be completed before crossing at night to wreck it again with Mr. Mannion's own stolen axe. He spent a good deal of time on the river now, for the baiting and harassing of Beltrasna's master had become a favourite pastime. Sometimes he killed his own food, sometimes he joined the tribe up the river for a few days, and returned with a share of their game; sometimes he supplemented his rations with fruit and vegetables stolen in the darkness from the Beltrasna fields. It was only last night that he had been visited by an inspiration. He had stolen clothes, tools, vegetables, a footstool—anything he could lay his hands on—and he had destroyed what he could for the sheer pleasure of revenge upon the man he hated. But was there anything which would enrage Mr. Mannion more than the theft of one of his convicts?

He had seen at once that such a thing, though risky, was quite possible. The river, flowing north, made a sharp horseshoe bend eastward directly above the spot where the work was being done. Johnny realised that he could be out of sight in a matter of seconds after the abduction—and round the next bend and out of sight again long before a man on foot could plunge through the thick undergrowth to the head of the horseshoe. The spot where the men were working was invisible from the house and the other buildings; the rough track down to the water and the landing stage had been cleared through tall scrub and bracken which rose like green walls on either side of it. He observed, also, that the overseer was lazy. The cart which brought the two men with timber and tools to the scene of their labour was unloaded at the landing stage, and then taken back to higher ground where the horse was unharnessed and tied up in the shade of a tree—visible from Johnny's vantage point on the opposite bank, but not from the water. The overseer had provided himself with refreshment which he retired every now and then to enjoy; Johnny could see him taking a flask from under some sacks in the cart, sitting down in the shade, removing his hat, tilting the flask to his lips, stretching out on the grass for sometimes as much as ten minutes of contented idleness.

The unknown factors, he realised, were the quickness of the convict, and his willingness to be abducted. He had a little doubt of the second, and decided that if the man failed in the first, and made some sound which invited discovery, no great harm would be done; he would merely have to escape alone instead of with a companion. Nevertheless he took particular care to blacken his hair thoroughly with charcoal, and darken his already deeply-bronzed skin still more; if he were to be seen vanishing up the river in his canoe it was important that he be taken for a native.

So very early this morning he had put the axe and a spear and a bundle of food in his canoe and paddled quietly across to the eastern bank. He drew it close beneath the overhanging fronds of bracken and waited, motionless and silent, as the natives had taught him to be when hunting. He heard the cart arrive; heard the two men's voices, and the sounds of their hammering and sawing. Towards mid-morning he heard the overseer's footsteps passing up the track, the sounds he made rummaging in the cart for his flask, and his grunting sigh of relaxation as he sat down to enjoy his spell. It had needed, then, only a few gentle thrusts with the paddle in the soft mud of the bank to bring the canoe round the corner in sight of the landing stage. And the convict, though startled, had not uttered a sound, staring like a man bewitched as it drifted silently

down to him on the current, and the native in it whispered, incredibly:
"*Come! Come quick* . . . !" But it was *not* a native . . . !

Johnny could paddle almost without a sound, but he knew that the
ripples on the water might betray him if the overseer returned in time to
see them before the river smoothed them out. He did not know now
whether they had been seen or not, nor did he know, either, how lucky
he had been that the slow-witted Byrne, rather than the more astute
Toole, should have been on the scene. Byrne, almost dozing, had been
aroused at last not by any sound, but by the unnatural silence—the
cessation of those noises which told him Finn was still at work. Finding
the convict gone, his only thought was of the surrounding scrub and
bracken, and he had trampled and scoured it, calling, cursing, threatening
and suffering a mounting panic for five minutes before he thought of
looking at the river. It told him nothing, for he was by now too distraught and too preoccupied with fear of his master's wrath to notice a
faint, dispersing muddiness in the clear shallows where the canoe had
scraped the bank . . .

Johnny, then, had a good start, and by the time he pushed his canoe
ashore on the west bank about midday he felt certain that his escapade had
been successful. It was only when he saw the awkwardness with which
Finn scrambled ashore that he thought of those leg-irons as a serious
complication of his plans. But Finn, primed with that store of knowledge
which the oppressed accumulated and passed on from mouth to mouth—
master of a thousand stratagems and devices which they used to escape or
alleviate their lot—knew how to solve this problem. He knew that if
one could secure a heavy implement and the necessary solitude to use it,
the iron ankle-ring could be beaten to an oval shape through which, painfully, the foot might be squeezed. He had observed the axe, and had
been careful, while Johnny was occupied with the paddle, to take possession of it.

It was not safe, however, to use it here. The ring of iron on iron
was not only a loud, but unmistakably a white man's sound, and would
carry far down the river where, even now, pursuers might be overtaking
them. The sun was almost overhead when Johnny hid his canoe well up
the slope, and they set off in a south-westerly direction; it was already
half-way down the western sky by the time they reached the top of the
first ridge. The chain which stretched between the leg-irons would allow
a stride of not more than sixteen inches even on flat and open ground.
Here, in rough, hilly and thickly-wooded country, it caught continuously
upon jutting rocks, fallen branches, and tough, low-growing shrubs. Finn
was forced to pause every few steps to disengage it; often he was tripped,
and brought heavily to his hands and knees; the old injury to his leg
became more painful, and his limp increased. He had made, at first, a
few attempts to talk, but Johnny was sullen, and he himself so exhausted
by the effort of walking with his short, weighted, hampered steps in
country where even a native might sweat, and pause for breath, that he
soon fell silent. Twice, maddened by impatience at this slow, laborious
progress, and smarting under the realisation that in so impulsively stealing

a convict from Mr. Mannion, he had provided himself with an unwanted
companion, Johnny walked on alone. But he returned. It was partly
because Finn had the axe, and Johnny wanted it. It was partly because,
beneath the hatred he had conceived, and the enmity he had sworn to all
white men, there still stirred curiosity, and a kind of nostalgia. But there
was also something else which slowed, halted, and finally turned his steps
backward. He had absorbed the native doctrine of responsibility towards
one's tribe, and practised it for many years with the strange assortment of
human beings who had lived under his roof. Cunnembeille and her
children; Billalong; Tom Towns; they had been his tribe, and he had
grown accustomed to leadership. But when, angry and impatient, he
came back to the man he had stolen and then abandoned, it was to find
him struggling on grimly, accepting these reappearances without any
particular sign of relief, breathing in heavy gasps, his ankles chafed by
the irons till they bled . . .

It was nearly dusk when they crossed the ridge at last and descended
into a narrow gully. Finn, sinking down on a flat rock, set himself to the
task of getting rid of his irons. They must be resting on the rock, and the
axe-blows must be heavy. The already raw ankles, mercilessly jarred
and bruised between rock and blow, swelled to shapeless lumps of purp-
lish, bloody flesh. Johnny stood and watched. Sometimes, from pain and
exhaustion, the convict was forced to rest, but he would not release his
grip on the axe. By now Johnny did not want to take it from him; he
did not want to go on alone. He had grown up in the native tradition
that a man who could endure pain courageously was a true man, and his
hostility faded as he watched this grim, determined, self-inflicted torture.
When the second foot was freed at last, and the irons lay bent and
battered on the rock, their eyes met for a moment. Johnny nodded.

"Good. Water there. Come."

Finn could not walk. Partly crawling, partly rolling, partly edging
himself along in a sitting posture, he reached the last slope of the gully
and slid down to a tiny stream which trickled in its bed. He fell on his
face to drink, and then lay beside it with the cool water washing round
his feet and ankles. Already in a semi-conscious state which was half
sleep and half swoon, he swallowed a few mouthfuls of food that Johnny
gave him, and knew no more till morning.

*   *   *   *   *

The colony's most exciting event in the month of June was the return
of Macarthur. *"This arrival,"* King wrote dryly to Banks, *"though long
expected, and the manner he was to be received, caused a little sensation."*

It had, indeed, been sufficiently long expected for the Governor to
prepare, for himself at least, an attitude and a line of action. Information
from London had left him in no doubt that the man whom he had once
described as "this rich Botany Bay perturbator," would return to the field
well armed. He would reappear not as a military officer, but as a private
individual, supported by the influence of personages in the Home country
to whom even the Governor of New South Wales must defer. The situation was not palatable, but it must be swallowed; King was too astute a

man, too vain a man, and too mindful of his own prestige, to allow the colony at large to see his grimace.

He did, however, permit himself the luxury of turning a phrase on his sharp tongue, and the pleasure of guessing it freely repeated with grins and winks and nudges. Mr. Macarthur might be armoured against the sword of his authority, but by nicknaming him "the hero of the fleece," King felt that he had planted a barb of ridicule which drew a little blood.

For the rest, he was urbane. The first boat to come ashore from the *Argo* brought him a civil communication. Mr. Macarthur had a letter to deliver from my Lord Camden, and begged His Excellency's permission to wait upon him at Government House. The disembarkation was impressive, for Macarthur was surrounded by a veritable retinue. He had brought with him his daughter Elizabeth, his nephew, Mr. Hannibal Macarthur, a youth of seventeen, a Mr. Davidson, also armed with a letter from Lord Camden, a Miss Lucas as governess for Elizabeth, and two professional wool-sorters. Lastly, he had brought some valuable merino sheep, and though these were, for the moment, invisible, they were the symbols of his present triumph, and the guarantee of his future success.

It chanced that Mr. Mannion, visiting his wife for a few days, and walking with her in the bright winter sunshine near the Guard House, encountered Mr. Macarthur on the way to his audience with the Governor.

"Our friend," murmured Mr. Mannion, watching him stride across the street to greet them, "seems full of his customary abounding energy. . . . Well met, Sir! We had heard of your arrival."

"My dear Sir! Mrs. Mannion! I am delighted to see you again!"

"And we to welcome you," responded Mr. Mannion. His wife asked: "You have had a good voyage, I trust?"

"Passable, passable, dear Madam!" Mr. Macarthur made an exuberant gesture with a hat no less beautiful than the one Mark had admired, and which its owner was now replacing on his head. "But no voyage could have brought me fast enough to my dear wife and children. And this air! It is like wine!"

Mr. Mannion eyed him amusedly. The crisp sunlit day was indeed exhilarating, but he suspected Mr. Macarthur of being at least equally intoxicated with excitement and triumph. He said amiably:

"You are on your way to see His Excellency, no doubt. We must not detain you, for you are naturally anxious to reach Parramatta as soon as possible."

"I won't deny it, Sir," Macarthur replied, and Conor, watching his face, observed the quick softening of its expression. She said:

"It will be a day of rejoicing at Elizabeth Farm, Sir. I have seen Mrs. Macarthur and your family recently, and they speak of nothing but your return."

"They cannot have been more eager for it than I, Madam." He bowed. "We shall have the pleasure of seeing you there shortly, shall we not? I have much to tell you, Mr. Mannion, of my plans. For the moment—*au revoir!"* He called back over his shoulder: "You must inspect my new sheep, Sir!"

He passed on towards Government House, and Mr. and Mrs. Mannion resumed their walk. "The hero of the fleece," remarked Mr. Mannion, "is in high spirits!"

* * * * *

In the Governor's sanctum the two former adversaries confronted each other across the paper-strewn table with civil wariness. Lord Camden's letters were brief, and it had taken His Excellency but a few minutes to read them and digest their implications. The Committee of His Majesty's Privy Council for matters respecting Trade and Plantations had recommended that every encouragement be given to the establishment of the fine wool industry in New South Wales. Mr. Macarthur, having taken much pains to increase and improve his flocks, was to be granted a suitable area of land in perpetuity for this purpose; and since he had expressed the opinion that the country about Mount Taurus was particularly suitable, he was to be accommodated in this situation. He was, moreover, to be given at least thirty convicts as shepherds, whom he would maintain at his own expense. *"His Majesty's Government takes a peculiar interest in forwarding the objects of this Letter. I am therefore persuaded you will do everything in your power to promote its success . . ."*

King laid the document down, removed his spectacles, and met Mr. Macarthur's challenging dark eyes across the table.

"His Lordship's wishes," he observed blandly, "in this and all other matters, will of course be attended to. . . ." He leaned back in his chair and deliberately introduced a note of friendly informality into the interview. "You are well, I trust?"

"Thank you, Sir, I am."

"And you have left some of your family in England, I believe?"

"Edward and John remain there at school. Elizabeth's health, I'm sorry to say, suffered somewhat in the English climate, and she has returned with me."

"And Mr. . . . Mr. . . . ?" King shuffled his papers for Lord Camden's second letter. "Mr. Davidson . . . ? He proposes to establish himself in the colony—as your neighbour . . . ?"

"He hopes to be granted land contiguous to mine at Mount Taurus, Sir. The advantages to the colony of . . ."

"Quite," agreed His Excellency. "As His Lordship remarks, it is highly desirable to establish gentlemen of respectable connections in our midst. I'm told you have brought out plants of the vine, Sir . . . ?"

"And the olive, Your Excellency." Mr. Macarthur's brows and the corners of his mouth lifted almost imperceptibly in an ironic, enquiring smile. A wintry twinkle in King's eyes responded.

"The emblem of peace . . ." he murmured. "Splendid, my dear Sir! I trust it will thrive in this climate. I understand that you have purchased a ship to be employed in the whale-fishing trade?"

"I have, Sir. It will also provide at suitable intervals a means of exporting my wool to England, and can return with a cargo of articles of use and comfort to the inhabitants of the colony."

King stared at him thoughtfully. This man was to be not only a breeder of fine-wooled sheep, but a farmer, a merchant, and a shipowner as well. The Governor leaned forward, tapping his glasses gently on the table. "I see. You have given careful thought to your plans. Let it be clear, Mr. Macarthur, that obedience to the wishes of my superiors will ever be my aim. With regard to your desire for land near Mount Taurus, however, I must offer certain points for your consideration. I don't know how well His Lordship may be aware that this land is in the centre of that tract known as the Cow Pastures, where the herds of wild cattle resort for water in periods of drought. I had already mentioned these facts to His Lordship's predecessor, Lord Hobart—but I am unaware how far Lord Camden has had the opportunity of considering the matter in the light of my representations."

He paused. Macarthur, watchful and alert, prompted him:

"Yes, Sir . . . ?"

"I would suggest," King continued carefully, "that the final decision might be deferred until I have further instructions. And in the meantime I would be prepared to grant you a similar or larger area on this side of the river if you can find one suitable for your purpose. Moreover, Sir, I would mark out the suggested area of five thousand acres about Mount Taurus, and undertake not to grant it to any other person, or appropriate it to any other use until His Lordship's further commands have been received."

Macarthur smiled and relaxed. Having set his heart upon the land at the Cow Pastures, he thought it unlikely, to say the least, that any search he might make for a substitute area would be successful; nor had he much fear that a decision once made in his favour would be revoked. Holding all the cards, he was prepared to make gestures of co-operation. He replied handsomely:

"Believe me, Sir, I'm at all times anxious to meet your wishes Such an arrangement will be entirely satisfactory to me."

King nodded.

"Very good. I am happy to see you returned, and you may rest assured I shall do all in my power to further your efforts, according to His Lordship's desire. Now, Sir, you must be anxious to reach Parramatta, so I shall not prolong this pleasant interview. Mrs. King will be happy to see Mrs. Macarthur at Government House when the occasion permits."

He rose and offered his hand. Mr. Macarthur took it, bowed ceremoniously, and departed, treading on air.

"So much," King wrote dryly to Sir Joseph Banks, "for our meeting after four years of suspence and vicisitude."

And Mr. Macarthur, for his part, had the satisfaction of assuring Under-Secretary Chapman: ". . . the letter Lord Camden had the goodness to write respecting me has operated like a necromantick spell, and lulled every angry passion to sleep. Peace has succeeded ungovernable rage, and those who were before ready to annihilate each other are now as friendly *in appearance as if their whole lives had been spent in a constant inter-change of kind offices."*

"You did not mention," he asked, looking up from this letter at his wife, "what I told you of the possibility of Sir George Young succeeding King as Governor?"

"Only to Captain Piper," she replied, "and I bade him not breathe a word of it. Do you think the appointment will be made?"

"There seemed no certainty of it. Various rumours were afoot. Banks will be consulted, no doubt. . . ." His slight frown faded, and his absent stare relaxed into a confident and reassuring smile. Banks, though cool at first, had been amiable enough at their last meeting; and the necromantic spell which had tamed one Governor would surely operate as potently upon another. "No matter, my love—no matter!" He bent over his letter again.

*   *   *   *   *

For Johnny Prentice that winter was the strangest, the most disturbing, and yet the most stimulating time he had ever known. His association with Finn was not without its early storms and quarrels, for he was bewildered and resentful at finding his hitherto undisputed leadership and authority challenged. He recognised in his companion a knowledge born of wider experiences than his own; but this had been equally true of Towns, and would not have greatly impressed him had he not also felt in Finn a strength which, far from failing under these experiences as Towns' had done, had grown and hardened. He was for the first time in daily contact with a man whose character made him aware of his own ignorance and immaturity.

It was the difference between the two convicts which confused and therefore sometimes angered him. Towns, ill and broken, had wanted only rest and protection. He was afraid of the land; he was not interested in the natives, and had, in fact, seen little of them, since they would not come near the hut, and he had never ventured far from it; his scoldings and complaints towards the end had been like the scoldings and complaints of a woman to which Johnny, native-taught, had turned a deaf ear; he had been acquisitive and revengeful, but he had been content to satisfy these emotions vicariously, through Johnny.

Finn accepted hospitality, but not protection. As soon as his feet were healed he began, as a matter of course, to join Johnny on his hunting and fishing expeditions, and learned the country quickly. He made friends with the natives. He stood among them at first silent and observant, but slowly he began to respond to their vivacity with a liveliness of his own which flashed out suddenly in a laugh or a gesture, and seemed to surprise himself. On such occasions Johnny felt a pang of something like jealousy, for his own temperament had always been dour, and the light-heartedness of the natives—continually expressing itself in jokes and capers—was a part of their life which he had never shared. But somewhere in this man Finn there was a sense of fun still alive beneath the grimness bred of suffering, a ready wit, an appreciation of the comical which brought him close to these gay savages. They began to call him Coo-mal, brother.

Alone with Johnny, he neither criticised or complained, but there was sometimes a quality in his watching and listening that made the youth uneasy; a glance which irritated him and set him on the defensive; a few words spoken which made him examine his own actions with a curious unsureness.

Finn, like Towns, had tales to tell, but they were tales of events, of places, of policies, of beliefs, of courage and treachery, of ignorance, cruelty, and hope. He had his hatreds, he desired his revenge, he dreamed of possessions—but so differently from Towns that Johnny was bewildered. Finn's hatred passed over individuals almost lightly, to fix itself like a blasting rav upon something wider—too wide for Johnny's comprehension. In the revenge he sought violence was not an end, but merely an incident, and the goal, again, was beyond Johnny's vision. Possessions had a value not their own; but what that value was reminded obscure, and the pride of one who owned a hut, cattle, tools, money and a musket, was teased by doubts.

So the first weeks were full of restlessness and the effort of adjustment. The long, rough trudge to the hut had taxed Finn's endurance almost to its limit, for they had not dared to loiter. Bewildered by the mysterious young man who looked—at first—like a native, appeared in a native canoe, armed himself with native spears, walked naked like a native, and yet was as white as himself, he had made several attempts during the latter part of the journey to learn something of his history. But Johnny was surly and uncommunicative, and Finn too weary to press his questions. The sight of the hut had so dumbfounded him that not even fever and exhaustion could subdue his almost incredulous amazement, but it was not until a couple of nights of rest, and a couple of days of good feeding had restored his energy, that he settled down to a persistent catechism. The fact that his questions were so often the same which Towns had asked only emphasised, for Johnny, the difference in the manner of their asking, and his uneasy sense of being not master of this situation, as he had been of the earlier one.

"Let ye be tellin' me, now," Finn urged, "whose hut this is?"

It was the third time he had asked the question. For the third time Johnny sullenly ignored it. Finn went on craftily:

"I'm thinkin' it must belong to some prisoner from the settlements down the river, and he escaped . . ."

Johnny gave him an angry, suspicious glance and said fiercely:
"Mine!"

"Yours, is it? And who lives here with ye, then?"

"Me," snapped Johnny. "I live here!"

"All by y'self, entirely?"

The boy nodded sulkily. Finn asked after a moment:

"Was it y'self made it, then?"

Silence.

"Was it findin' it ye were?"

Silence.

"It's been here a long time, I'm thinkin', the way it looks inside and out."

Silence.

"How long?"

Johnny muttered irritably:

"Long time."

"Years?"

"Long time."

"How old was it ye were when ye came?"

Silence.

Finn paused to reflect. Several times on their journey he had felt a strange impression that this youth had only the vaguest notion of time as the white man counted it. He had hesitated when Finn asked how long their pilgrimage was to last, made gestures to indicate the rising and setting of the sun. He spoke English, but crudely, hesitantly, leaving out words, fumbling for others, sometimes seeming to forget the English word for such features of the landscape as rocks, trees, twigs, hills, and fallen logs, and using, instead, native words. Was it possible, Finn wondered, that some desperate male—or even female—prisoner had escaped years ago from the colony with a child, and that the child had survived . . . ?

He altered his question:

"How big?"

Johnny hunched his shoulders impatiently. All he remembered was that once he had had to reach up to the latch on the door; he sketched a careless movement with his hand to indicate the height of an eight-year-old child. Finn stared incredulously:

"And who would it be in the name of the Saints was after bringin' ye here?"

"Cunnembeillee."

Finn was baffled. Was that a native name, or a native word? He tried again.

"Y' mother, eh?"

"No."

"Y' father, then?"

"No!"

There was anger in that last denial. Something in the idea of his father was unwelcome. Finn asked:

"What's y' name, lad?"

And then he was provided with an answer which, at a stroke, solved one mystery, and added another. Johnny went to a corner of the hut and came back to stand by the convict with a sheet of paper in his hand. Already he was feeling the pressure of a personality as strong, if not stronger, than his own: to produce and brandish in Finn's face this evidence of his greatest skill, the source of his fiercest pride, was a boast—an instinctive gesture of self-assertiveness. And the impression it made was indeed gratifying. For Finn, holding the paper, stared thunderstruck at a name written over and over again—written well, in a smooth, copperplate hand—*Johnny Prentice, Johnny Prentice, Johnny Prentice* . . .

"Me!" declared Johnny, hitting his breast as if his name were imprisoned there. "Me—Johnny Prentice!"

So that was it! The convict drew a deep, amazed breath of comprehension. That name, Prentice, was a legend not only among the black tribes of the river, but in all the convict huts of the colony. No daydream of escape, no desperate plan of escape was ever complete without it. When courage failed, when hope struggled, when the bright beacon light of liberty flickered, or when the ill-repute of the wild, inhospitable country across the river chilled the heart, someone would say "Prentice." And even if courage still could not rise to the test, if hope still could not conquer fear, if solitude and starvation were still spectres too grim to be confronted, it was known that the thing *was* possible. It *had* been done. A convict had escaped—and survived for three years—and died in the end of his own choice . . .

And Finn, as a Beltrasna convict, knew the further detail which often escaped the white man's legend. He knew from the gossip of his fellowprisoners that Mr. Mannion's housekeeper had been Prentice's wife; he knew that she had had a son who vanished in childhood just at the time when the legendary father was drowned in the river. How it had all happened was still a mystery—but that this was the son of the famous Prentice there could be no doubt. He looked up at the tall, robust, naked stripling, and he felt awe, envy, and compassion. Awe that a child's life, so weak and vulnerable, should have been preserved in a place where grown men failed and died; envy of a life so free; compassion for a life so rude and solitary . . .

And then he realised what, in the shock of this revelation, he had overlooked. The lad could write! Write like a clerk—like a scholar! He himself could not write as well as this . . . !

"Johnny Prentice," he said slowly. "Aye. So that's the way of it. And it'll be your father was after buildin' this hut, I'm thinkin'. But will ye be tellin' me now who was it taught ye the writing . . . ?"

Johnny, a trifle appeased by the evident astonishment and admiration his accomplishment had aroused, answered more readily:

"Tom Towns." Finn eyed him with a frown, uncomprehending, and he added: "Convict. Run away. Come here."

Finn nodded thoughtfully. He remembered now that there had been a good deal of talk just after his arrival of the savage, Pemulwy, who raided the settlers' farms in company with a couple of escaped convicts. There had been rewards offered for the capture of this Tom Towns, but he had never been taken. He asked sharply:

"Where is he now?"

Johnny replied laconically:

"Dead."

And a couple of days later he took Finn to see the grave in the little gully near the hut. Finn stood before it silently, confronting another doubt, and another puzzle. How had this man died? And had a small child carried away with him, and preserved through years isolated from his own kind, the memory of tombstones? He eyed Johnny curiously.

Already he was learning how to handle this strange youth who was by turns shy and aggressive, shrewd and ignorant, hostile and friendly, mistrustful and confiding—but always vain.

"Be this an' that!" he exclaimed admiringly, "it's never a finer stone I did be seein' in all me days, and me a grave-digger once!" He added his next question in the same amiable tone: "Was it y'self killed him, then?"

Johnny shook his head almost absently. He was admiring his handiwork, and the indifference of his denial was more convincing than indignation. Finn persevered.

"Ah, then, t'was the Indians, to be sure!"

Johnny glanced at him and interrupted impatiently:

"Not killed. Sick." He clutched his hands to his chest, coughed, gasped, spat. He looked back at the stone and asked childishly: "Good?"

"It's the way I'm tellin' ye," Finn assured him. "Divil a finer did I ever see! And where was it ye learned to make a stone the like o' that?"

Johnny's answer set him thinking again. Green Hills? Then this young man could come and go, visit the towns of the white men, and return unharmed and unpursued to this place? He recalled puzzling things he had seen in the hut—incongruous, unbelievable things—a thimble and a candle-snuffer; a woman's petticoat; a footstool, stained and scratched, but made of carved rosewood, and covered with rich material; a set of carpenter's tools, almost new; and money . . .

He knew enough for the present. He stopped asking questions and set himself to learning this new life and savouring his freedom. Johnny still had his moods. Sometimes, without a word, he vanished for several days at a time; not until Finn visited the tribe with him, and saw Ngili with a plump baby the colour of native honey in her arms, did he learn that his young companion was newly a father. But neither the joys nor the duties of parenthood could hold Johnny to the tribe for long. It was mistrust of Finn which drew him back to the hut at first, but as the winter passed and they settled down to life together, he began to realise that for all its irritations it was somehow a richer life than it had been.

Finn had not the fine, manual dexterity of Towns, but he had a rough, practical ingenuity. He could make and mend and improvise. He used the carpenter's tools expertly, and taught Johnny to use them too, so that their dwelling, which had been falling into decay, became tight and weatherproof again. He matched the boy in energy, and outmatched him in knowledge, so that the unskilled and desultory attempts at cultivation around the hut gradually gave way to a systematic and intelligent husbandry. He did not urge visits to Green Hills—and indeed during these months Johnny went only twice. But he assisted in the preparation of the salt beef—pointed out that the supply of salt was almost exhausted and should be replenished—helped to carry the load as far as the river—and sent his companion off with the casual suggestion that they would live better if they had more seeds to plant.

From the first journey Johnny brought back a little corn, a few potatoes, and some melon seeds, in addition to the salt. Finn knew the colony's agricultural routine, and explained that certain crops should be sown at certain times. Turnips and onions in March, he said: wheat in April and May, peas and beans in May. Mid-winter was the time for transplanting fruit trees. He talked a great deal of fruit, and when Johnny made his second trip to Green Hills late in June he returned proudly with a tiny peach tree which Finn planted carefully near the door of the hut.

Johnny began to learn the months by the calendar of growing things; but he also studied the rough written calendar which Finn hurriedly made when he began to realise that the days were passing unnoticed and unnamed. Thus he began to learn figures, though these confused him after years of reckoning as the natives did on ten fingers and ten toes. He grappled painfully with the concept of a year—a long, long section of life that penned the seasons in a rigid enclosure with a name—eighteen-hundred-and-five. How many of these years in a lifetime? Finn counted backwards, showing Johnny himself growing smaller and smaller so that he felt a superstitious chill, and muttered a native exclamation of alarm and recoil. Tribal memories swarmed in his brain and set him trembling. What were these figures, these marks that were like writing—and yet were not writing, being unrelated to familiar speech? There was magic in marks, in curving lines. . . . Marks on the ground, marks on shields, on rocks, on message sticks, on sacred objects seen only by the old men who knew magic and communed with spirits. . . . What was being done to him with these marks? Could they take his manhood away from him . . . ? He listened, fighting his fear, to an incantation that went with these figures, and watched the corresponding gesture of Finn's hand as it reduced his stature. . . . Sixteen, fifteen, fourteen—now he was only as tall as Billalong!—thirteen, twelve, eleven, ten, nine, eight. . . . The magic ceased, but it held him bewitched, facing a sharp line of division across his life, re-inhabiting a small, small body and finding there a self he had almost forgotten. Alone—frightened, sitting under his rock—a fire—a key—Cunnembeillee—the naked baby Billalong in his arms. . . . He shivered, fighting back from it to his adult body, his eyes avoiding the page with the dangerous symbols. Aie, that was long, long ago! Years? More years than the fingers on one's hands . . . ? Many, many years, then, in a lifetime . . . ?

The next day he was missing, and two nights passed before his return. It had been necessary to find the tribe and Ngili, to assert his maturity and prove his manhood, and exorcise the magic of the figures. Yet he returned to them.

And there was writing. A point upon which they had agreed from the outset was their enmity towards Mannion, and one tale of Finn's, arising out of this, concerned a little book which had been taken from him. Johnny could remember books; Patrick Mannion in the house at Parramatta, having lessons from books . . . his own curiosity . . . his sullen resentment at yet another kind of gulf between them, which had made him pretend indifference when Patrick offered to read to him . . . breathless moments when Patrick was not there, and he had pored over the pictures alone . . . many pictures, but one in particular which had seemed to him the most beautiful thing he had ever seen, of an unbelievable bird called a peacock . . .

Yes, he could remember books but found it hard to understand why Finn should see the loss of one as so important—particularly as he said it had no pictures; why he could speak with less bitterness of a flogging than of that act of confiscation; why it should creep so often into his tales; why he should seem to regard the taking of it as something more than the theft of an ordinary possession. Puzzling over it, it was inevitable that Johnny's mind, at last, should relate it to those sacred objects which the tribes kept so carefully hidden in places set apart, and upon whose existence and sanctity they believed their spiritual welfare to depend. And when he saw Finn writing, and learned that the words he wrote were from this book, he was more than ever inclined to regard it as a consecrated mystery. For they were words quite beyond his comprehension. Leaning over the convict's shoulder to feed his vanity on the sight of letters so much more crudely made than his own, his mind as well as his eyes was caught, and his complacency faded into awed bewilderment.

It was hard to read. He had read no handwriting but his own and Tom Towns', and that incomprehensible fragment dropped once by Ensign Barrallier; even where he could decipher the letter these were words whose meaning baffled him; and even where he understood the words they seemed to be saying something his brain could not grasp—leaving him behind—functioning in some realm of thought where he could not follow.

"Some writers have so confounded society with government as to leave little or no distinction between them; whereas they are not only different but have different origins. Society is produced by our wants, and government by our wickedness . . ."

"Government, like dress, is the badge of lost innocence; the palaces of kings are built upon the ruins of the bowers of paradise."

"Society in every state is a blessing, but government, even in its best state, is but a necessary evil . . ."

He spelled out what he could, and Finn, glancing up at his knitted brows and moving lips, read it out aloud to him. Still it meant nothing. Johnny went off hunting, but several times during the day he puzzled about it. What was writing but the words of one's mouth made visible, so that the eye instead of the ear could receive them? But those words said nothing either to his eye or his ear. That night he brought the fragment of Barrallier's writing, carefully preserved, and showed it to Finn. But Finn could not understand it either.

" 'Tis not in our tongue," he said. "I'm thinking it's French."

Johnny frowned discontentedly. He knew there were two tongues— the white men's and the black men's. But now it seemed there was another—perhaps many more? Yet even words in his own tongue could be incomprehensible—to him. Not to Finn, though. He pored over pages covered with such fragmentary passages as memory had been able to preserve from that long-lost book. *"Oh ye that love mankind!"* He could read it, he could speak it, but it meant nothing, and his bewildered stare said so. Mankind, Finn explained, meant men—all men. And

women too—and children. Love . . . ? There were no words to explain
this mystery, and Finn, with a baffled shrug, at last abandoned the attempt.
He tried once to suggest its meaning through Johnny's relationship with
Ngili, only to realise with a rueful grin that he had invoked the thought
of a very different emotion. He came nearer to it when he pointed to
a native woman caressing her child, and built patiently upon that foundation by drawing Johnny's attention to every human relationship where
affection was involved.

Over the shadowy comprehension that began to dawn in the young
man's eyes there flared a sudden and incredulous anger. *Love* mankind?
All men? Love Mannion? Love the red-coated Major by whose orders
Cunningham had swung from the staircase at Green Hills? Love the
miserable, haunted rebels who had gone out to battle, and fled without
fighting? He made a violent and contemptuous gesture of repudiation.
But sometimes the thought returned to tease him, and furrow his brow
again. Love the natives—Milbooroo, Bee-dal, Murron-ye, Mullungra . . . ?
No anger rose in him at these names. They existed, like the trees; they
offered him no harm nor hindrance, and so he offered them no enmity,
but neither did he feel for them anything like this curious emotion that
Finn had suggested. He loved the pleasure he found with Ngili—but
not Ngili herself. He felt nothing for his son except, occasionally, the
amused indulgence one might feel for a baby animal. He thought fleet-
ingly of his mother, but since the night when he had killed Merrett his
mind had avoided her. It lingered for a moment on Cunnembeillee, who
had been in a sense his second mother—but he had buried her with hardly
a sigh. ". . . *love mankind* . . ." He felt no such emotion. The white
men he hated; the black men he tolerated—and used. So far as he could
understand this thing, he felt it only for himself, his possessions, the taste
of food, the ecstasy of satisfied desire, the excitement of the hunt, the
feel of sun on his skin.

And that was enough. Yet one day when Billalong was accidentally
wounded by a spear he felt the mystery leap at him again, unsummoned.
He was surprised by his own relief that the wound was trivial, unwillingly
aware that there was some quality of warmth in his feeling for his young
half-brother Andy. He did not like the discovery; it threatened his detachment, and made his hatreds feel less whole and perfect.

Such thoughts seemed mere passing incidents in days full of physical
activity, but in the obscure fastnesses of his brain they went on toiling.
And at last memory, deeply submerged, sent a few shadowy emotions like
bubbles to the surface of his mind. There *had* once been someone . . . ?
A black man, gentle, merry, kindly, who had laughed with him when he
was very small, before he ran away; who had carried him shoulder-nigh,
and told him stories . . . ah! . . . *Dinewan boorool diggayah gillumnee.* . . .
Where had those words come from? Where had he been keeping them
so secretly, and why, now, did they leap back to his mind, bringing with
them a name . . . *Arabanoo!*

Long, long before he had learned the native belief that the name of a dead man must die with him, his childish instinct had buried that name because it was too painful to remember. But now he remembered it. Arabanoo, his first friend, in whose company he had known ease and happiness . . . Arabanoo—whom he had loved . . . !

And then, with a shock, came the thought of Finn, who also laughed and talked and told stories; Finn, with whom he seemed to feel something not unlike that half-forgotten companionship. Was it the memory of Arabanoo which had made him recognise this tentatively growing intimacy, or was it the beginning of a new friendship which had sent his mind back to Arabanoo?

Such self-examinations, however laborious, inept and inconclusive, excited as well as disturbed him. If he were made to feel a stranger to himself he was also made aware that in a stranger might be qualities and possibilities undreamed of. He began to discover that his mind could do more than present him with an action to match an impulse. I am hungry—I will hunt. I am tired of being alone—I will go to the tribe. I am weary—I will sleep. I am full of desire—I will find Ngili. I hate—I will steal and destroy . . .

He found, by slow and painful degrees, that he could think of other things besides his actions and surroundings. He could think of invisible things, things unnamed but felt, things that lived within himself. His mind could begin at a point and move forward to another point, and beyond that to another still. It could ask "Why?" and grope among a score of different answers. It could contemplate one "because" and discard it in favour of a different "because." There was a new kind of pride, a new and subtle satisfaction in these halting efforts.

One evening when the days were beginning to lengthen, and the trees putting forth their young, rosy leaves, and the wildflowers budding inconspicuously among the undergrowth, they had their worst—and their last—quarrel.

It began over a trifle; Finn had taken the tinder box to use while Johnny was away hunting in the valley of the Wollondilly. Johnny, returning with a possum for supper, looked for it, and flew into a rage when he saw Finn using it to light the fire. He strode over and snatched it, shouldering the convict roughly aside so that a leaping flame singed his hand. Finn swore and gave the angry youth a push which sent him staggering; he tripped over a pail standing near the fire, and sat down ignominiously in a flood of spilled water.

The faint grin that flickered across Finn's mouth and twinkled for an unwary second in his eyes was good-natured rather than derisive—an overture rather than an insult. But Johnny had no sense of humour, and his vanity, tender from many a prick in the last months, was now given a thrust which roused him to murderous fury. His spears were standing where he left them against the wall of the hut near the door; Finn, with a shrug, was already walking away towards the creek to replenish the pail when something made him turn, only just in time. He dodged wildly; the sharp-pointed shaft whistled past his cheek; he leapt for Johnny and closed with him, and for a moment they swayed and struggled desperately in the gathering dusk. But Johnny, for all his wiry strength, could not shift the grip that held him, and Finn gasped out at last, breathlessly:

"Arrah, be aisy, now! Would ye be takin' me from that divil Mannion to kill me y'self? Be this an' that, it's the temper of old Nick himself ye have! Let y' listen, now, bad cess to ye, while I talk some sense into y' black murtherin' heart! If so be ye're not wantin' me here, I'll go. And what would hinder me, the way I have two hands o' me own like y' father had, an' the heart in me as high as his—an' it's a bit o' this an' that, an' a beast or two I'd be takin' with me, let me be tellin' ye, the way I've earned it an' more, while I've been here! Howld still, now, ye wild animal! Is it a king ye think ye 'are, with y' hut an' y' cattle? Be all the saints ye'll stand and listen while I'm tellin' ye ye're but a child without a child's innocence, and a savage without the brother-hood of the savages down yonder, and a wild beast without excuse for it, and ye'self with a human shape and mind . . ."

The words came too fast, and some of them were strange; Johnny knew they were attacking him, for the tone wounded his striving brain as flying spears wound the body. But he had no skill to return weapons such as these; he felt rage and confidence draining out of him. And Finn, his own shock and anger spent, relaxed his hold and said more quietly:

"Ah, let be, then! An' how would ye be different, the way ye lived alone like a cloud in the air entirely? But I've no mind for a spear in me back, lad, and I'm thinkin' the country's big enough for both of us. So let ye be tellin' me, now, do I go or stay?"

Johnny, released, stood and glowered at him. He glanced at his two remaining spears, and thought of the musket hanging on the wall inside the hut; but Finn was planted watchfully between him and the door, and in any case his impulse to violence had lost its urgency. He turned away sullenly to spread the glowing embers of the fire, and throw the possum on them native fashion, fur and all. The dusk deepened to darkness, and the stars came out. A mingled stench of burnt fur and cooking flesh rose from the fire. Johnny squatted over it on his heels and brooded.

He wanted Finn to go; he wanted him to stay. He wanted to feel himself once more sole master of all he surveyed, but even more than that he wanted to recapture the carefree spiritual self-indulgence of his solitary life—the luxurious self-abandonment to any mood or impulse, the spacious, arrogant egotism which Finn's presence was somehow disturbing. He had acquired all the native habits of waywardness, volatility, living for the moment, without being bound permanently to a tribe where he would have learned to practice them within the discipline of a fixed law. When solitude had irked him, he had visited the black men's camps; when tribal life became tedious he had returned to the hut; when Billalong annoyed him, he had cuffed him into docility; when Towns had nagged, he had ignored him. He had accepted no outer discipline, and imposed none on himself. And suddenly here was a man who made him uneasy by being stronger and wiser than himself. He wanted him to go.

And yet he wanted him to stay. This man whom he had just tried to kill had somehow made life bigger, and painted it in brighter colours. Johnny did not know how, but he knew that he could only have his freedom at a price he did not want to pay. He took up his knife, dragged the blackened carcase of the possum from the embers, and began to cut it up, conscious of Finn behind him in the dark, silent, watchful, waiting. Suddenly he wondered with a shock why he had felt no fear sitting thus, lost in thought, with an enemy behind him . . . ?

This was no enemy . . .

Without turning, he held out a slab of the half-cooked meat.

"Here!" he said sullenly.

Finn took it and sat down.

*   *   *   *   *

The news that Mr. Harvey had been ignominiously dismissed from her husband's employment—for this was how Mr. Mannion chose to represent it—had caused Conor some distress. To be sure, she had often ignored or tormented the young man, but sometimes, too, his presence and his dumb devotion had been welcome, and they had found relief from loneliness in each other's company.

It was, therefore, with a pleasant excitement that, upon one wet, windy day in July when she stood at an upper window in Chapel Row, she beheld him striding past, stealing sideways glances at the house from under the brim of his dripping hat. Oblivious of decorum, she knocked eagerly on the pane, and saw him stop dead as he caught sight of her between the curtains. She beckoned, calling at the same time to Bessie in an adjoining room:

"Bessie! Bessie, Mr. Harvey is below in the street—run down, pray, and admit him!"

By the time he stood in the doorway she was half regretting her impetuosity; Stephen would not be pleased, she thought, to learn that she had received his disgraced secretary. But at her first glimpse of the young man standing on the threshold, awkward and eager, his cheeks still wet with rain and his boots wetter, she thrust her doubts aside. It was good to see him again! She held out her hand impulsively.

"Come in, Mr. Harvey, and be seated! La, how wet your boots are! Draw your chair to the fire, pray. Bessie, take Mr. Harvey's coat and hat to be dried. How fortunate, Sir, that I should have seen you passing, for I declare I wondered if we should ever meet again! Why," she added wilfully, knowing the answer very well, "have you not been to visit me?"

"I—I didn't know, ma'am," Mark replied nervously, "whether you—er—whether my visit would be welcome. The circumstances in which I left Beltrasna . . ."

"Pooh!" said Conor. "I was distressed to learn of it, Sir—but it is no reason why you should desert me."

Desert . . . ? Mr. Harvey flushed to his ears. How many times had he walked this way in the hope of seeing her! How many times had he actually seen her driving in the streets, and drawn back, too diffident to make his presence known! He said fervently:

"I have often desired to pay my respects, ma'am. I—I trust you are well?"

"I am very well, Sir, I thank you."

"And little Julia also?"

"Yes, indeed, and more wilful than ever. She has spoken of you many times."

He looked down at his steaming boots and up again at her face, to find her eyes on him, kind and smiling. It was his turn to speak, but he could find no words, and she took pity on his awkwardness.

"Poor Cousin Bertha keeps her room this last week or so—the weather is so trying to her rheumatism. But for the most part she seems better here than at Beltrasna, and much livelier, and she dearly loves to drive out with me on sunny days to see the streets and the people . . ." She broke off and looked at him attentively. "You have been—indisposed, Mr. Harvey? I think you are thinner than you were . . . ?"

For the first time she found herself questioning a life-long assumption that gentlemen were by nature confident, dominant, and efficient creatures who could look after themselves in any circumstances. She could not follow his swift mental comparison of the Beltrasna table with the fare he had been eating lately, but she felt herself upon unsure ground, and hurried on without waiting for his reply:

"Pray where do you live, Sir?"

"I have—lodgings, Ma'am, in Pitt's Row . . ."

"They are comfortable?"

"They are well enough, Ma'am."

There was a brief silence, but her mind was busy. What did a young man, dependent upon his employment, do when that employment was lost? Seek another position, of course! She asked:

"You are satisfied with your new post, I hope?"

He stammered:

"I am not—I have not as yet secured . . ."

Conor's reflections were less thoughts than lightning-streaks of comprehension, shocking and painfully brilliant. It was almost three months since he had left Beltrasna. Had he enough money for sustenance? But something in the brevity of all his answers, and the embarrassment that had sounded in this last one, warned her that though a gentleman might occasionally find the world bewildering and unfriendly, a tactful lady would not suggest by so much as a tone or a glance that such a thing could be. She went on briskly:

"You are wise, I think, not to accept a position in too much haste. You must find one worthy of your talents, Mr. Harvey."

He looked at her quickly.

"I have wondered—as a matter of fact, Madam, I have long been considering a course—though it may not answer—but it would appear that there is a need for—indeed, Ma'am, I should greatly value your opinion—though to be sure it is inconsiderate in me to plague you with . . ."

She asked gently:

"What is this course, Sir?"

He pulled out of his pocket two scraps of paper—one an old and tattered clipping from the *Gazette*, and the other a sheet upon which she recognised his own fine, regular handwriting. He moved his chair an inch or so nearer to hers, and she bent forward to examine the clipping which he offered.

"You see, Ma'am," he explained eagerly, "as long as eighteen months ago Mr. Howe was writing of the need for a school somewhat different from what is already in existence . . ."

She held the paper up to the light from the window, and read with frowning attention:

" '*Populous as the Town of Sydney is, it may be wondered that the Plan of an Academy has not suggested itself for the Instruction of the more advanced Youth only, without an admixture of children in the very leading-strings of Tuition . . .*' "

He watched her face as she read, forgetting the hardships of the last months in the joy of seeing her again. He was ashamed that caution— he even stabbed himself with the word "cowardice"—should for so long have made him hesitate to take this course which he was now so eager to describe to her. But hitherto he had always been employed. He had counted himself fortunate when his talents could earn for him food, shelter, retirement from the rough world, and a yearly pittance; habit had driven him first to explore those avenues which might lead to security without responsibility. But the commercial houses of the town were already supplied with clerks; a couple of posts offered to him as tutor had been accompanied by the proviso that he would also be expected to assist with other duties which, upon examination, proved to be concerned with transactions which even Mr. Harvey could recognise as dubious; once he had been refused haughtily on the ground that Mr. Mannion had represented him as a person of unreliable character, and he had been too wounded to seek private employment again. He had approached His Excellency in the hope that a post might be found for him as a clerk in one of the government stores or offices, but no vacancies seemed available. He had found a little copying to do in the Law Courts, but the work was intermittent, and his resources dwindled steadily. He had thought with longing occasionally of a return to England, but by now he had insufficient money for a passage; and the presence of Conor in the town—the self-indulgence of a walk beneath her windows—were strong anchors . . .

She lowered the paper to her lap and cried delightedly:

"Why, Mr. Harvey, this is the very thing! Pray, how soon do you propose to open your Academy? And where will it be? And how many pupils will you accept, for it will not do to have so many that you cannot pay them proper attention—at least until you are able to find a suitable assistant—though to be sure you will need more than one eventually, and . . ."

Mr. Harvey threw his head back and laughed—a spontaneous, exuberant, youthful laugh of pure amusement that set her laughing too. .

"Now what can I have said that is so amusing?" She pouted. "It's true that I know little of such things, but . . ."

He cried quickly:

"Oh, madam, I was not laughing at you, believe me, but with gladness because you have made my Academy exist—and not only exist, but flourish so that it needs two assistants—and all in a moment . . .!"

She looked at him with smiling mock-penitence.

"Did I run on too fast, Sir? Come now, you shall see how sober and practical I can be. Tell me your plans. What is that other piece of paper?"

He offered it anxiously, bashful and uncertain again.

"It's an advertisement, Ma'am—but a rough draft, you understand—which I thought of asking Mr. Howe to insert in the *Gazette*. If you can suggest any emendations, Ma'am . . ."

She read it aloud, nodding judicious approval so that her ringlets bobbed against her neck, and Mr. Harvey was hard put to it to fix his mind on his own carefully-chosen words.

" '*Mr. Harvey begs to acquaint Parents and Friends that he is desirous of receiving under Tuition Pupils of the Male Sex above the age of twelve years. They will be diligently instructed in Simple, Vulgar and Decimal Arithmetic, Mensuration, Calligraphy, the casting of Accounts, French (if desired) and the Grammar of the English Tongue. Having had the Advantage of a Classical Education, Mr. Harvey is also prepared to instruct those of his Pupils whose parents desire it in Latin and Greek . . .*"

Conor looked up and sighed.

"My, Mr. Harvey, how clever you are! No, no, don't blush and deny it, for it's true, and makes me so ashamed of my ignorance. I declare I wish I could myself be one of your pupils. Now let us consider carefully, Sir. This is a most excellent advertisement . . ."

"You think so, Ma'am, really . . . ?"

"I do indeed. Yet is there nothing more we can add to make it still better? Think, Mr. Harvey."

Mr. Harvey, raised to a seventh Heaven by that "we," was quite incapable of thought, but he knit his brows dutifully.

"Drawing, Mr. Harvey!"

"Drawing, Ma'am . . . ? I—I fear I am not qualified . . ."

"Oh, nonsense, Sir! Have you forgot the delightful little sketches you made at Beltrasna of the river and the house? I keep them in my album still!"

He said doubtfully:

"I might, perhaps, instruct pupils in the rudiments of drawing, Ma'am, the principles of perspective and so on, but . . ."

"Put it in, pray! Here, next to Calligraphy—it will go very well there. And—mercy on us, Sir, we have forgotten Morals!"

Mr. Harvey looked startled.

"It's true, Ma'am, that an attention to the morals of his pupils is an indispensable part of a tutor's . . ."

"Of course it is! And manners also, and gentlemanly behaviour. Now see, Mr. Harvey, after Latin and Greek you must say *'nor will he neglect . . .'* No, no, that's not right! *'Nor will he fail in attention to their Morals, Manners and External Deportment.'* There! You will be besieged by pupils!"

Mark's smile was slightly rueful.

"I trust you are right, Ma'am."

"I am sure of it. Now where is your school to be? Have you considered that?"

"There's a—a building on the Rocks, Ma'am, which I did inspect. Not exactly a house, but I think it would serve, for I shall not of course be able to afford a very elegant place. It is sound, though small, and in a high and healthy air . . ."

"You must add that to your advertisement, of course. Here, at the end of your first sentence. *'. . . Pupils of the Male Sex at his Academy on the Rocks, whose elevated position in a Salubrious Neighbourhood will be highly advantageous to their Health.'* Now it is quite perfect! You are laughing at me again . . . !"

"A little, perhaps, Madam. But only so that I—I may not weep with gratitude for your kindness . . ."

She felt tears spring to her own eyes.

"I have been very unhappy about your—your departure from Beltrasna, Mr. Harvey. Believe me, I do not for a moment credit . . ." A quick indignation had led her tongue to dangerous words, and it stumbled among them for a moment. "——I do not believe you capable of acting save in the most honourable manner . . ."

Suddenly she was frightened. His eyes were saying too much, as they had often done before, but now she discovered herself responding with a new emotion, strange, strong, and perilously sweet. She jumped up in something like a panic and went to the window.

"See, it has stopped raining for the moment. I must send you away, Sir, for I'm bidden to tea with Mrs. King." She held his hand for a moment as he bade her good-bye, but her eyes avoided his. "I shall look forward to seeing our advertisement in the *Gazette*, Sir. And—and perhaps you will escort me to see the premises for your school some day . . . ?"

When he had gone she sat for a long time before the fire staring into its flames, half happy and half sad. Bessie had to call her three times before she would move to dress for her tea party.

To her pleasure, she found that she was the only guest. Mrs. King had taken a liking to her and found it a relief to talk to one of her own sex without need to keep an eye upon complicated relationships between their two husbands. It was a cosy evening by a bright fire in the Government House parlour—so cosy that His Excellency, looking in to pay his respects to Mrs. Mannion, was tempted to draw up a chair and permit himself an hour's relaxation, and the contemplation of a pretty face.

In her husband's absence, he reflected, Mrs. Mannion talked with animation, and showed a good sense remarkable in one of her youth. He was amused by her questions, and if some of them bordered on the tactless, her ingenuousness robbed them of offence. She begged to know why the

Investigator, having been condemned as unseaworthy, should now have been able to return to England; the state of the ship led on naturally to Mr. Brown's reluctance to use her as a conveyance for his valuable speci-mens, and Mrs. Mannion betrayed a lively interest in the botanical curi-osities of the country. From here they passed to the question of the unexplored fastnesses of the interior, and she urged:

"But surely you will make further attempts, Sir? Why, who knows what wonderful places there may be! It cannot be so impossible to pass the mountains!"

The Governor shook his head indulgently.

"Well-equipped expeditions have tried and failed repeatedly. Bass abandoned the attempt. Barrallier did better, but I see no immediate practical benefits from his explorations. Young Caley, I assure you, spoke with horror of the trials he'd suffered—endless chasms, each deeper than the last, and all so barren and rocky that even the natives don't frequent the place."

"Yet convicts have absconded," she argued, "and my husband does not believe that they all perish . . ."

"Ah, convicts!" The Governor shrugged. "They *may* survive by the mercy of Providence and the charity of the natives if they remain near the river, but only death awaits them in the mountains. Yet they try; it is a kind of madness. I've thought of liberty as a beacon, Ma'am—a bright beacon that draws men towards it despite reason—warning—pun-ishment. . . . Ah, well! They don't find it, unless death be liberty. Nor anything else, believe me. No, no, my dear Madam, we have enough to keep us occupied on this side of the river!"

"I wish I were a man, and I should attempt it myself!"

He laughed heartily.

"Pray don't wish for such a calamity, Ma'am," he protested gallantly. "To your charming sex belongs the far more important task of dispensing domestic bliss."

But his wife, mindful of the fame she had won as the first woman to cross the Nepean, came to Conor's support.

"We are not such weak creatures as they think, are we, my love?"

"He despairs too easily, dear Mrs. King! Why, Sir, the very children are more enterprising! Our Miles has spoken of it a thousand times. And several years ago I heard him talking of it with Mr. Wentworth's son, William, when the doctor was visiting Beltrasna. I vow their plans were all made, and you will live to see them prove your doubts un-founded!"

"I hope it, Ma'am—I do indeed!" He bent forward, chuckling, to poke the fire, and Mrs. King asked:

"Do tell us, Mrs. Mannion, what news you have from the two boys in England? Why, Patrick must be quite a young man by now!"

"He is twenty-one, Ma'am, though I find it hard to think of him so."

"And what are Mr. Mannion's plans for him? He spoke once of the Army, I think . . . ?"

"Patrick seems to have no liking for the idea, Sir. In fact, his interests seem divided between our estate here and literary pursuits. He has written," Conor added with some pride, "several essays upon life in the colony, and one of them was published."

His Excellency astonished her with a sudden roar of laughter.

"What, another of them? It's a veritable disease! Collins and Tench were the first sufferers—and by the bye I hear that Collins' book has recently undergone a second edition . . ."

"And Lieutenant Grant has published also," Mrs. King put in. Her husband snorted.

"Nothing new will arise from *his* pen, my love. Thompson, the surgeon, also threatens, I believe. And I'm told that young Tuckey, who was first lieutenant on the *Calcutta*, proposes to torment the world with his ten weeks' observations." He noticed Conor's slightly crestfallen expression, and leaned forward to pat her hand kindly. "Your young man has chosen a path already well trodden, my dear lady, but I don't doubt he will tread it with more grace than many who have gone before him. Nevertheless, he'd do better to bend his energies to the development of the land, Ma'am, for I don't know where the libraries are going to find a corner for all these antipodean productions."

"I think he may do so, Sir," Conor replied, "for my husband now thinks it will be best to allow him to return. You see, Ma'am," she continued—thinking quickly that here might be a chance to speak for Mr. Harvey, and turning instinctively to her kind-hearted hostess—"he has lost the services of the young gentleman who was his secretary and assistant, and feels that perhaps Patrick might now take his place."

Mrs. King nodded.

"Ah, yes—Mr. Harvey—was not that his name? He was presented to me once. A pleasant and modest young man."

"Yes, indeed," Conor agreed warmly, "and he has now the notion of opening an Academy in Sydney, for which he has, I'm sure, every possible qualification . . ."

The Governor interposed:

"I understand Mr. Mannion was not entirely satisfied with him, however?"

Conor gave him a rather startled glance. There was little, it appeared, that escaped His Excellency's sharp eyes and alert ears. She said hastily:

"I do not know the circumstances, Sir, for I was absent at the time, but I am convinced it can have been but a—a disagreement, a misunder-standing—for indeed Mr. Harvey is a person of the most honourable character . . ."

There was a shade of sympathetic comprehension in the shrewd glance which the Governor gave her. Recalling his own encounters with the overbearing Mr. Mannion, he was inclined to absolve Mr. Harvey of blame. He stood up reluctantly and turned his back to the fire, lifting his coat-tails the better to enjoy its heat.

"No doubt, no doubt. The instruction of the young, Ma'am, is an important matter, and one to which I am ever ready to lend my support. My love, you must bid Mr. Harvey to tea with us one day. And now, dear Mrs. Mannion, delightful as it has been to enjoy your company, I have work to do, and must beg you to excuse me."

He went back to his desk, warmed by her smile. Gratitude was at all times pleasing—not only to his kindness, but to his sense of importance; and conveyed by a glance from two particularly lovely eyes, it was more agreeable still.

* * * * *

Conor's second child, a boy, was born in Sydney early in September. Mannion, who had already decided that this son should bear his own Christian name, was more than a little nettled by her insistence that the infant be called after her father. Among Mr. Mannion's Irish acquaintance Mr. Desmond Moore had not been favourably regarded; it was generally agreed that his death, so soon after his elopement with Conor's mother, had been a fortunate escape for that misguided young woman, and that Providence had been kind to Conor in thus restoring her to her grandfather's roof. Mr. Mannion was unwilling to perpetuate the name of this renegade, but his displeasure left his wife unmoved. Upon his second visit to Sydney after her confinement he found it already accepted and used; he could not, without loss of dignity, insist upon Master Stephen in the face of Bessie's cooing references to Master Desmond.

But the trifle put him in an ill humour; the news that Mr. Harvey, instead of sinking to a suitable destitution, was shortly to open an Academy, and that Conor, accompanied by no less a person than the Governor's wife, had driven with him to inspect the premises, increased it. Conor's stay in town, he decided, had already lasted too long. He discerned in her a revival of that impetuous liveliness, that tendency to chatter, that perverse interest in matters of no concern to a gentlewoman, which had so disturbed him in the early days of their married life. He noted disapprovingly that she had made many new acquaintances, and that, in her little drawing-room in Chapel Row, she received with a lack of discrimination which would be unthinkable in any but a colonial society. The Commissary, Mr. Palmer and his wife were frequently to be seen there, and Conor had made a visit to their fine house at Woolloomooloo. It was fortunate, he thought, that Mr. Palmer's sister and brother-in-law, the Campbells, were absent in England, and he frowned when he heard his wife asking eagerly for the latest news of her "dear Sophia." Mr. Campbell was, no doubt, respectable enough in his way, but it was not Mr. Mannion's way; he had never looked very kindly upon wealth gained by trade. All wealth in this colony was, of course, so gained, including much of his own, so that one was compelled to relax one's standards to some extent, but Mr. Campbell could not even produce a military commission or appointment to a civil office to sweeten the smell of his trading. Moreover, Mr. Mannion—who had benefited by the system the military officers had evolved, and shared the slight embarrassments caused by official efforts to break it—was more influenced than he knew by their dislike of this independent, interloping rival merchant. The truth was, he told himself, that, with the possible exception of the Governor's wife, there was really no one at all in the colony who could be called a suitable companion for Mrs. Stephen Mannion. He was prepared to sanction her acquaintance with the wives of some of the officers, but there were gentlemen who had been presented to her of whose private life he could only hope she was ignorant. Upon this point, however, he was quickly disillusioned; she had gathered gossip upon a variety of subjects, from irregular unions and illegitimate children to legal actions, commercial intrigues and political manœuvres. The seclusion of Beltrasna, he decided, was to be desired.

Conor was reluctant, but resigned. She had more than once prolonged her stay without much difficulty. Cousin Bertha's health was better here, and her spirits incredibly brighter; Conor had earlier provided that pretext for her husband's acquiescence, knowing very well that he preferred his solitude at present, but neither knowing nor caring whether Ellen helped to solace it.

She would have stayed if she could, but knowing she must go she acknowledged a curious spiritual weariness in herself which turned gladly enough towards the quiet loneliness of the river and the fields and the climbing hills. She felt that she had gathered here not knowledge, but the raw material of knowledge, which perhaps in a more tranquil scene she might sort, and turn and consider. She had always realised that the colony was split into warring factions, but now she had lived in the midst of them; and she had been impressed anew by the fact that even within them there was a violent and bewildering instability. People changed sides overnight, incensed by some insult, flattered by some favour, attracted by some prospect of advantage, pressed by economic necessity, goaded by spite, driven by fear. The simplicity of her mind was confused by such chaos, but its curiosity was aroused. It appeared that the prime object was to make money, and a desire to be rich seemed to her not only natural but praiseworthy. Yet there were questions. . . . To obtain wealth by such means as importing or distilling spirits which—so His Excellency assured her—not only ruined the health of the community, but reduced it to beggary by its exorbitant price, was surely shocking . . . ? And to traffic in medicines, as those employed by the hospitals were said to do, imposing upon the ignorance of the sick, who became in the end bankrupt not only in pocket but in health—was not that inhuman . . . ? And there were other methods of enrichment, less simple to understand, conveyed only obliquely by hints, and concerned with business transactions whose devious ways she could not follow. . . . There was so much buying and selling—not only among shopkeepers and merchants, where it was to be expected, but throughout the whole community. Everything, it seemed, was sold by and to everybody—land, animals, food, clothing, tools, grain, produce—and always there seemed to be liquor in the business somewhere, used as a payment—or a bribe—or a threat. . . . It seemed that the most estimable and respected people were involved in it; but when they asked indignantly: "May not a man do as he pleases with his own?" the answer was undoubtedly difficult. . . . And when the Governor was accused of tyranny and despotism . . . ? Where did authority end and despotism begin? At what point did freedom end and irresponsibility, selfishness and greed begin to masquerade beneath its name?

She wondered about Stephen, and whether he, who proclaimed himself so aloof, so independent of the colonial Bedlam, could indeed find a path through the intricacies of its economic life without conforming to its strange methods? Her husband's business conversations with his acquaintances, to which she had always lent an inattentive ear, became suddenly of painful interest. When the drawing-room of the house in Chapel Row was full of company she found herself neglecting the gossip of her female guests to hear what Stephen was saying to the gentlemen. And she realised that though he declined to be openly embroiled in factional disputes, he could not, even if he would, conduct his worldly affairs in splendid segregation.

Her scraps of knowledge made no clear pattern in her mind. They yielded what was worse—an ugly, amorphous impression of rapacity and corruption, of hypocrisy, trickery, slander and intimidation; of a society building up upon a foundation of felons a superstructure which sometimes looked uglier than felony itself, and enforcing its discipline on the lower classes by means which seemed to brand it as lower than they; of a Governor whose power, though vested in him by the King, was yet inadequate against the complicated power of wealth; of an insane, contradictory element, its origin obscure and incomprehensible, whereby some who were against the King's representative in New South Wales, nevertheless enjoyed a mysterious support from the King's representatives in England . . .

She spoke little of these bewilderments to her husband, but enough to annoy and alarm him. So, on a warm spring day she took her seat in the carriage with Cousin Bertha, Bessie and the children, and set out on the return journey to Beltrasna. In the High Street near the Granary and Provision Stores she observed Mr. Harvey, and gave him, along with her bow, a smile which made Mr. Mannion frown darkly. She would have been a model of decorum if he had not frowned; but he did frown, and she saw it, and her temper flared rebelliously. She turned her head towards the young man standing, hat in hand, staring after them, and she smiled again. What was worse, she waved; and what was worst of all, she actually called out, raising her voice clearly in the public street:

"Good-bye, Sir! I trust your school will prosper!"

And then, all the way to Parramatta, she sat silent with her gloved hands folded in her lap, and a little smile on her lips.

* * * *

Her husband, before leaving, had sought another interview with the Governor. He had been profoundly disturbed by the mystery surrounding Finn's escape, and the failure of several armed search parties to discover any trace of him. The sudden cessation of annoyances from the unknown nocturnal prowler, coinciding as it had with Finn's disappearance, increased rather than lessened his uneasiness. It suggested a possible connection; it reinforced his suspicion that there might be other escaped convicts at large, and added the unwelcome notion that they might have means of communication with convicts still in custody.

But His Excellency, though admitting the possibility, shrugged it away. He was more concerned, at present, with the question of illicit stills, many of which were known to be operating in different parts of the colony, and with the ravages of a destructive insect that had invaded the wheat-stacks. He pointed out once more that the chances of survival in the uninhabited country beyond the river were slender, and that the proverbial needle in a hay-stack could not be more elusive than a single man in that vast, inhospitable country. Hunger had driven in the majority of absconders; starvation had doubtless disposed of the rest. He expressed civil regret that Sydney was to be deprived of Mrs. Mannion's charming presence, and he wished Mr. Mannion good-day.

He was at this time engaged in collecting reports on sheep-breeding from a number of the colony's landowners. Lord Camden had required exhaustive information on the subject, and King carefully studied a number of documents before he put them together in a bundle to be enclosed with his next despatch.

He would be able to assure His Lordship that the improvement in the quality of fleeces was quite remarkable; the occasion would be opportune, too, for a reminder that he himself, four years ago, had, with good effect, added four rams of the half-Spanish breed to the Government flock, and that by distributing some of the resulting ewes among the settlers, their flocks had been similarly improved. There were, however, certain prejudices to be overcome. There was still an opinion prevalent that weight of mutton and fineness of wool were incompatible, and settlers who held that the Spanish sheep made a smaller carcase than other breeds were not in a position to renounce the immediate profit to be gained by a sale of mutton to the butcher, in favour of the more distant advantage to be won by breeding for fine wool. He recalled that Mr. Macarthur, in conversation with him, had estimated that the twenty thousand sheep at present in the colony might well increase to five million in twenty years. That opinion could be tested only by time; but what already seemed certain was that this colony might now safely be regarded as an important potential source of wool.

The question, since it evidently engaged the attention of his superiors at home, must engage his also; when Mr. Macarthur wrote to him in October, describing his unsuccessful search for an alternative area of land, and trusting that His Excellency would therefore be pleased to allow him and Mr. Davidson to take possession of the tract at the Cow Pastures, he acquiesced with a good grace but still not without reluctance. "I certainly could have wished," he wrote in reply, "to let the Cow Pastures lie over until my Lord Camden's pleasure was received." But since Mr. Macarthur pledged himself and Mr. Davidson to resign the grants if at some future date the Home authorities so directed, there seemed no grounds for further procrastination, and he directed the Surveyor to measure out two thousand acres for Mr. Davidson, and five thousand for the hero of the fleece.

Nevertheless, the problem of the cattle still worried him. "Having *made the location to Mr. Macarthur and Mr. Davidson, a circumstance in which the interest of the Crown occurs respecting the wild cattle, in the centre of which those gentlemen are now seated,"* he wrote to Camden a trifle incoherently, *"and however much I ought to rely on his assurances that these valuable herds shall not be molested, yet I rather hope than am persuaded they will not in some measure suffer or be disturbed . . ."*

Not only the Crown, but he himself, had an interest in those cattle. He had already unburdened himself to Sir Joseph Banks upon the subject of his financial problems and his fears for the future of his family, and he anticipated the coming of his so-far-unknown successor with mixed feelings. After spending some six hundred pounds a year on his household expenses, and meeting the bills for the schooling and maintenance of his children in England, little remained of his salary of one thousand pounds, and he had declared to Sir Joseph that he was willing if necessary to remain two or three years longer to increase his savings.

It was a sacrifice he would make, if he must, to his paternal duty. But as the heat of the summer increased, and his gout prostrated him once more, and he was besieged not only by the problems of his own domain, but by those of Collins at Hobart Town, and Paterson at Port Dalrymple, and Piper at Norfolk Island, and Mr. Throsby, Commandant at Newcastle, he contemplated the possibility with dismay.

Yet into the exacting and too-familiar routine of his days this strange antipodean world could still suddenly introduce an event to charm boredom away with novelty; the end of November saw His Excellency and his slightly startled wife welcoming an exotic guest to Government House.

The *Buffalo*, it appeared, calling at Norfolk Island to take on stores for Port Dalrymple, had found there a personage who announced himself as Tip-a-he, a New Zealand chief who had already had some intercourse with the white men when whalers visited his shores. Wishing to make the acquaintance of the white chief, Governor King, he had embarked with four of his sons upon a small colonial vessel for Norfolk Island, and requested of the *Buffalo's* captain a passage to New South Wales.

It was a bright, hot day when that vessel cast anchor in Port Jackson, and a curious crowd watched its master proceed to Government House to wait upon His Excellency and introduce his passenger. Chief Tip-a-he, a man of commanding stature and presence, clad in the costume of his country, his face elaborately tattooed, his manner composed and dignified as befitted one great chief in the presence of another, performed the ceremonies of greeting with solemnity, and bent from his great height to touch his nose to King's. He explained that he had long desired to make this journey; he considered that the introduction of potatoes into his domain from Norfolk Island had been a great blessing to his people and —though they had not approved—he did not doubt that other blessings might result from his visit to Sydney.

The Governor responded suitably. Tip-a-he and his eldest son were installed at Government House, and appropriate lodgings found for the other boys, of whom the youngest, a lad of eight years, was evidently the apple of his father's eye. King, remembering another savage, Bennilong,

who had once been a guest within these walls, was struck by the contrast
between that primitive being and this dusky aristocrat. Indeed, Tip-a-he
himself observed the native population of Port Jackson with marked disfavour and contempt. His disdain of a people who went naked, and
showed so little inclination to provide themselves with creature comforts,
was only exceeded by his scorn for their methods of warfare. These
trifling battles, he declared with astonished disgust, were not war! Even
with an adversary on the ground, he exclaimed, these contemptible
creatures did not always kill him! He gave the Governor to understand
that in his own country, where his authority extended over a very considerable area, he had an extremely strong *hippah*, or fortified place, from
which he could defy a rival chief Mowpah on the south, and another
enemy Moodee Whenua on the north. War was a serious matter, not
to be taken lightly as these inferior savages took it, and among his own
people the reward of the vanquished was instant death. He engaged the
Governor in consultation upon matters concerning their respective spheres
of authority. Were all the ships that visited his shores the property of
King George? He listened attentively to a description of the difference
between the English and the American flags, and desired to know whether
it were agreeable to his host that he should greet both with hospitality and
assistance. The Governor assured him that it was, and found himself
listening to a long and indignant tale of how one of his guest's countrymen had been flogged by the captain of a whaler—who, remarked Tip-a-
he coldly, must undoubtedly have been an *emoki*, a member of the lower
classes. King hastened to assure him that such an outrage would not be
repeated; and Tip-a-he, for his part, undertook to see that all white men
were courteously received, and provided with potatoes, swine, fowls and
goats in exchange for such articles as they had to barter.

Matters of state thus amicably arranged, Tip-a-he devoted himself to
the enjoyment of his visit. But such a guest, though novel and colourful,
and not without his small importance in this business of colonial expansion, could not fail to be something of an embarrassment to a well-ordered
household. A tattooed savage close upon six feet high and the father of
fifty-two children, who explained that he had killed one of his wives
because her tongue was troublesome, and expressed the opinion that many
of the women here might with advantage be similarly despatched, introduced an inharmonious note. A guest who, though commonly genial and
jocose, did not hesitate to express himself forcibly upon the many aspects
of white society which he considered foolish or reprehensible, and who
demanded at all times the most scrupulous attention and respect, needed
careful handling. Moreover, the suspicion—which His Excellency's tactful
questions had been unable entirely to dissipate—that he might be a can-
nibal, kept the female servants in a state of unrest which Mrs. King found
trying; and it was even whispered that his outlandish presence hastened
the end of Mrs. Jane Dundas.

She died a few days before Christmas. The Governor, learning from
his tearful wife that the good woman had breathed her last, pushed his
papers aside and went out on to the verandah to stand in the noonday

blaze of heat with an irascible feeling that the whole world was in league to plague him. It was a Sunday, and the town seemed quiet, but none knew better than he how deceptive was this appearance of Sabbath calm. He stood there moodily, a stoutish, baldish little man to whom, in this hot and harassing moment, a domestic disaster seemed even more trying than the endless perplexities of his office. Poor Jane . . . a tower of strength to Anna . . . a ministering angel to himself when he was in the gout. . . . They called him a dictator . . . they should have seen his meekness under the scoldings of that bustling, sharp-tongued, dictatorial angel . . . ! The thought pricked his humour. The comfort of the colony, he thought, in the hands of the Governor; and the comfort of the Governor in the hands of—Mrs. Jane Dundas . . . !

His faint smile was a last tribute to her as he shrugged, and turned back to the house.

*   *   *   *   *

Meanwhile Finn and Johnny had become aware that their retreat was no longer secure. From their own observations, and from the reports of natives who frequented the Cow Pastures, they learned of white men ominously busy in that neighbourhood, not merely arriving in small parties as they had done for years to inspect the wild cattle, and return whence they came, but bringing drays laden with timber and other materials, driving flocks of sheep, establishing themselves with every appearance of intending to remain. To Johnny and his convict companion, the enterprise supported with such benevolent interest by His Majesty's Government was an intrusion that aroused the liveliest alarm.

Since their last quarrel life had gone almost merrily for a time, for the better understanding between them, the fading fear of recapture, and the stimulus of liberty had increased Finn's cheerfulness, and loosed his tongue. He was, as Mr. Mannion had once observed, a talker. Captivity had flavoured his thoughts (and therefore all his words) with bitterness and protest; his tongue had brought trouble on him, and finally that worst affliction of the talker—solitude. But now, with an audience of one, and no man to silence him, the long, painful thoughts of that solitude, and the crowding memories of all his life burst from him in an endless stream of tales, comments, conjectures and descriptions.

The taciturn Johnny was a perfect listener. Pictures of an unfamiliar world dressed in an unfamiliar idiom, decorated with an imagery borrowed from an unfamiliar culture, bewildered but entranced him. There was no word, no sight, no incident but could provide a starting point. A wallaby hunt brought curious accounts of men on horseback who hunted a small animal they did not want to eat; a native chanting the refrain of the frog-song, *Yi kwa e kwa, yi kwa e kwa!* might be answered by a verse or two of some song remembered from Finn's childhood; a reference to the black men's magic might inspire tales of the little people who come on May Eve to beg milk and fire at the cottage door, and of how the wise would hang a branch in the doorway at such times, and cross themselves, crying: "God between us and harm!"

It was not easy for Johnny—accustomed to the native philosophy which bound its superstition so closely with its daily life that they were one—to understand that this white man told of such things as tales that had receded from reality, but still clothed them, in moments of atavistic nostalgia, with an other-worldly light. He was less perplexed by descriptions of a land where the moist air spread itself like a veil between earth and sun, and the grass grew green, thick and high under the hedges, and the trees stood bare of leaves in winter-time. But what he wanted to hear most was of how men lived there.

And he noticed as the months went by that Finn, when he spoke on this subject, would often grow abstracted. He would pause with a sentence half finished, begin another and stop short, sit silent for a while as if his brain were continuing what his tongue had abandoned, speak again, and pause again many times, so that Johnny was left with no coherent story, but only a series of impressions, confused yet vivid.

"It was a bad time then . . . aye, a bad time! Full o' fear an' hunger an' danger. . . . But be the Saints, there was hope, too, an' anger, hot as a fire . . . ! There was songs a man was not allowed to sing. . . . Ah, but they was sung, I'm tellin' ye, for all that! Listen, now!

> " 'Oh, the French are on the sea,
>   Says the Shan Van Vocht,
> The French are on the sea,
>   Says the Shan Van Vocht.
> Oh, the French are in the bay,
>   They'll be here by break o' day . . .'

"But they weren't there, lad. . . . An' the bonfires blazin' on all the hills an' crags. . . . Things might 'a gone different then if. . . . Ah, away with it! Where's the use in thinkin' o' things the like o' that, long past an' done? It's eight—ten years since we were singin' the song o' the poor old woman . . ."

Johnny's brows would meet over his dark eyes in the effort to make sense of such disconnected fragments. For a time, then, Finn might speak with a simplicity that left no room for misunderstanding—of food, of labour, of hunger, escape and pursuit—and as suddenly turn back again to matters whose connection with what he had just been describing seemed too shadowy to grasp. From facts, so clear and comprehensible, he would pass to obscurer things; from labour and poverty to freedom; from potatoes to justice; from castles and carriages to the divine right of kings.

And at such times his talking seemed directed at himself, and Johnny, like an eavesdropper, heard overtones of conflict, and echoes of a nagging self-reproach. He heard, incredulously, a man arguing with himself against his own freedom, deriding it, presenting it to himself as something incomplete, a fraud and an illusion. More and more there came these long intervals of silence and these bewildering monologues when Finn's face became closed, and strained and brooding, his zest for the tasks and pleasures of their daily life diminished, and he seemed possessed by an unquiet spirit.

He began to question Johnny more closely about the country. What lay up there in the valley of the Wollondilly where the white men had explored? What was to be seen from the high hills to the westward?

Johnny had grown up among the natives, to whom their own towri was inseparable from themselves, and the white man's restless urge to explore had lain dormant in him. His wanderings had been governed by the needs of his existence, and—save on that one occasion when Barrallier's expedition had alarmed him to action—confined to his own secluded creek and gully, a few miles up and down the Wollondilly, and his familiar route via the Cow Pastures down the Nepean to the settlements. But he was at least able to tell his companion that not much more than ten miles downstream, the Wollondilly was joined by another river which the natives called Koornong, coming in from the west.

"An' how far is it ye've been up that?" Finn asked.

But Johnny shook his head. He had never been up it at all. Why should he? Game was plentiful in the territory he knew.

Finn grew thoughtful, and Johnny was willing enough to accompany him when he proposed an expedition up this river. They set out early one spring morning when the sun was not yet over the hills, and the steep gorge down which they travelled was dim in the pale light of dawn. Finn —to Johnny's surprise—had insisted on bringing with them a package of salt beef, and the remains of a black bream which had been part of their last night's supper; he explained that there was to be no loitering. Johnny was unaccustomed to such haste, and a trifle put out by it. It was a habit with him by now to watch for the small indications by which a man knew where food was to be found, and on such a trip as this—unpursued by any foe, with no need for care or concealment, and bent upon no urgent business—why should they not travel at their leisure? Hurrying thus one could not watch the creek for eels, or the shellfish which were such tasty morsels; or the trees for possums and bees' nests; or the slopes for wallabies and wombats; or the undergrowth for snakes or lizards. It was one of the stupidities of white men, he thought discontentedly, that they would carry food even in country where food was abundant. Scowling at Finn's back, he decided that they were always in such haste to walk over the land that they could never pause long enough to learn its resources. Here, now, was this man, perversely pushing forward as though there were not a whole lifetime of days ahead! Johnny was bad-tempered by the time they reached the Wollondilly, for there had been a tree a mile or two back which plainly had grubs in it, and he had pulled from behind his ear the thin, hooked stick with which he could so easily have plucked them out—but Finn would not wait. And now, on the broad banks of the river, it would have been pleasant to swim for a while, and then lie and gossip in the sunshine of a world where time meant nothing—but still they must go on. They did not even pause to eat, but munched the salt beef as they walked.

It was not yet midday when they reached the spot where the Koornong joined the Wollondilly, and flowed eastward with it towards the Nepean. To the north and south of it hills rose steeply, wild, craggy and inhospitable, but its banks promised walking not too difficult. They pushed up it for a few hours, and at last paused to rest and eat the remainder of their food. A magpie sang clearly in a gnarled tree whose branches hung over the swift-running stream, and the shadows were growing long; Johnny stretched himself out contentedly on the ground and fell into a luxurious half-doze from which he was roused by the sound of Finn's voice, speaking slowly, and sometimes pausing for so long between sentences that Johnny thought his talking ended.

"Ye'll be thinkin' there's no sense in it at all, lad, the way I should feel a distress on me for livin' free. An' it's a fine thing indeed to work without a master, an' rest when the weariness is on ye, an' see an open door an' pass through it. . . . It's a grand thing to be eatin' well—an' there's sights an' sounds come clearer then than they do to a man with an empty belly. . . . Aye, to be a prisoner's more than to be on the wrong side o' the padlocks. It makes ye deaf in time—it makes ye blind. There's trees the like o' these around the fields at Beltrasna, an' a sky as blue as that up yonder over them, an' I've listened to that bird in the mornings—and I goin' out to work with the irons on me. . . .

"Ye'll say I saw an' heard—but I'm tellin' ye a man can see with the eyes in his head an' still be blind, an' if so be he's not hearin' with his heart besides his ears, it's divil a thing there is in a bird's song but a bit o' chirrupin' . . .

"It's the way he loses more than to come an' go—an' never knows he's losin' it at all. It's the way he never knows what's in himself—an' he took up with the hunger, an' the labour, an' the sufferin' till it's gone entirely, an' the heart in him with it, an' the seein' an' the hearin' . . ."

Johnny sat up on his heels like a native and looked sideways at his companion uneasily. The thought had crossed his mind more than once when Finn was in this mood, that the words coming from his lips were altogether different from his daily conversation. He had seen the old men, the wise men of the tribes sit apart and mutter to themselves like this, and their voices held this same absent, self-communing note, and their eyes saw something that was not the scene about them. And speaking to each other of matters too private or too sacred for the ears of everyone, they fell into a kind of chanting; and addressing some supernatural being their words took on rhythmic cadences, so that the evil spirit might be deceived, and imagine them merely singing. Into Finn's voice, too, there had crept something of this chanting note, and his words sounded less like speech than like a spell . . .

"So it's the way I'm tellin' ye, it's a fine thing to live in a free body—free from the irons, an' the lash, an' the hunger, an' find y' heart again, an' feel the eyes an' the ears in y' head open, an' tell ye sights an' sounds like these . . .

"But can a man be sayin' to the heart in him: 'Show me this, an' then no more—show me that, an' divil another thing'? Ah, it's a sly, strong thing, the heart in a man, an' no rest in it at all! An' if so be he lets it wake, it takes a holt on him like a team o' horses, an' pulls, an' pulls . . .

"An' it sayin' to him: 'Whisht, now, there's a fine blue sky that's over ye, an' a sweet song out o' the tree yonder, an' a good smell in y' nostrils—but is it out of y' wits ye are, an' thinkin' it's all for y'selt entirely? Let ye not be too much at ease,' it says, 'an' y'self tastin' y' little bit o' freedom, an' it turnin' sour in y' mouth, the way there's no sweetness in it for any man alone on the whole face o' the earth.' Which is why there's the distress on me, lad, an' I knowin' there's no freedom for meself while there's other men not free, an' livin' with the shame on me that I forgot . . ."

The silence lasted for so long this time that Johnny grew restless, and went down to the river to wade like a child, stepping from one submerged boulder to another, watching the tiny fish dart between them, and the clear water foaming in the rapids. When he returned Finn was standing with his hand shading his eyes against the westering sun, and looking up this new river curving out of sight among the hills.

"Now there's a grand stream!" he said cheerfully. "An' it comin' down from the divil knows where out of a land so big it's but the rim of it we know! Did I ever be tellin' ye, Johnny, how me little book said a few men might be after makin' a new society in a place the like o' this? 'Let us suppose a small number of persons settled in some sequestered part of the earth . . .' Ah, bad cess to it, it's a poor memory I have, an' the words gone out o' me head entirely! But it's the way they'd be learnin' the weakness o' one man alone, an' makin' laws to bind them to each other—an' they mortal men, to be sure, an' not angels out o' Heaven! An' it's a tree they'd be takin' for their House o' Parliament . . ."

He glanced at Johnny's blank face, and back at the towering hills, and grinned. "There's no lack o' trees, an' as for men, some day maybe we'll . . ."

He turned abruptly without finishing his sentence, and began to walk back the way they had come. Johnny, falling in beside him, puzzled for a few moments over the implications of his unfinished speech, but was soon content to forget it. There was an evening meal to be considered, and he was tired of salt beef. About a mile from the Wollondilly he had noticed a place where the wallabies came down in the evening to drink.

*   *   *   *   *

From that time Finn had begun to urge him upon his journeys to Green Hills. He wanted more seeds, more tools, more ammunition, more firearms, a compass, and even some livestock. Billalong had reverted entirely to the life of his mother's people, and had no wish to return to the hut, but he was willing to paddle down the river occasionally with one or two other young natives, and transport back such articles as could be carried and concealed in the bottom of their bark canoes. Knowing their meat supply in jeopardy, Finn worked like a man possessed to secure as much of it as he could before the invaders of the Cow Pastures made further raids too dangerous.

The white men never knew how accurately their movements were reported to a fugitive in the hills who dared not fire a musket when they were near. They could only make the roughest estimate of the numbers of cattle which roamed the fertile pastures, and never suspected that the black savages who came so guilelessly among them were quick to observe a few strayed from the main herd, and to carry their information to an escaped convict. A young bull calf and a couple of heifers found their way into the gully near the hut to join the descendants of those brought there by Andrew Prentice many years ago. But that was only the beginning of their journey; to get them down into the valley of the Wollondilly was a labour of days; and all the time Finn kept the casks filled, and Johnny plied back and forth between the hut and Green Hills.

He returned with wheat, barley, maize, and seed potatoes. He brought two old knapsacks, a sickle, a few half-worn articles of clothing for Finn, some nails, and a supply of needles and thread. He could get neither firearms nor ammunition, and thought angrily of the musket he had given away. Nor could he persuade the men who came by night to barter with him that his beef was a fair exchange for livestock, so he stole a cock and two hens without much difficulty, and during the following week a male and two female kids. But this last venture was attended with many mishaps. Johnny was almost discovered by the settler whose property he was stealing; Billalong and another native youth who had come down the river to assist him were fired upon in the dark, and narrowly escaped. On the return journey one of the canoes capsized, and its precious cargo was only retrieved with difficulty. By the time they reached their own towri Billalong was arguing that they should be permitted to make at least one meal of their spoil as recompense for so much trouble and danger, and Johnny, angrily objecting, found himself left to complete the business alone. By the time he delivered the three lively animals at the hut, his mood was so rebellious that Finn said no more of livestock.

And all the time activity was increasing at the Cow Pastures, and the danger of such expeditions with it. The natives were tired of them, and alone Johnny could do little. It was Finn who first voiced the thought which Johnny had been holding prisoner behind his lips, feeling that to speak of it might make it true. Leave his hut? Leave his most important possession? All that was white in him resisted the idea, and all that was native reinforced that resistance with a violent recoil from the unknown. Leave his own towri? Leave his spirit-place, the overhanging rock near the river where both Johnny and Dyonn-ee, so curiously intermingled, had always gone in search of peace?

"No!" he said angrily. "Stay here in my place!"

Finn answered dryly:

"It'll not be your place long, the way there's gentlefolk come to be y' neighbours!"

"They don't find me," Johnny declared emphatically. "They don't come here!"

Finn shrugged.

"It's as good as here already they are, an' they but little more than a dozen miles away. They'll not be pokin' an' pryin' yet, maybe, for it's full o' business they are with their sheep an' their huts an' their yards—but they'll come. I'll not be here, lad, an' if ye'll be said by me, ye won't either."

Johnny cried savagely:

"I kill them!" Finn laughed at him.

"Ye talk like a fool! 'Tis no poor settler over yonder, an' he with never a thing between him an' y'self but his two arms an' a musket the like o' yours. 'Tis gentry, I'm tellin' ye, an' where gentry come, they come with arms, an' servants, an' overseers, the curse o' Cromwell on them! Who is it ye'd be killin' then? There's convicts like meself there —but did ye kill one there's hundreds more to take his place. Did ye kill a bull, now, or a fine sheep, an' it with a fleece on it worth a handful o' guineas, there'd be the divil to pay, but ye'd still not stay them. Nay, lad, did ye kill the master himself that owns the land an' the sheep an' the convicts, the business would still go on—an' it's nothin' ye'd have done but rouse all the gentry in the colony, an' they huntin' ye down the way ye'd hunt a wallaby. Is it never seein' ye'll be? 'Tis not men have come across the river—'tis money! Can ye steal on that in the dark an' put a bullet through it?"

Again Johnny found himself confronting a choice. To go with Finn, or stay here—alone? The convict awaited his decision anxiously, for in Johnny's possessions he saw a threat of trouble. The plan in his mind was only half-formed, and he saw no need, as yet, to look beyond its first step—the establishment of himself, with the means of livelihood, in some spot much more remote than this. If he went alone he would need a share of the possessions which his own energy and initiative had so greatly increased; how willing would Johnny be to yield it? And he liked Johnny. Something of the exasperated concern of a father for a wayward son, and something of the interest of a human being in an animal imperfectly domesticated, and something of the mere need for companionship, made him face the possibility of their parting with regret.

Johnny, too, struggled with his own conflicting desires. When Finn announced his intention of exploring the Koornong, the youth surlily refused to accompany him. Left alone in the hut, the time passed slowly. He set out one day to visit the tribe in search of company, and was saved only by the bleating of sheep from walking into the arms of a group of labourers and shepherds. He retreated, alarmed and furious, and sat long by his fire that evening, turning over in his mind this sudden dislocation of his life. He began to look eagerly for Finn's return, and every day brought him nearer to his decision. He counted the nights on the calendar—twelve, thirteen, fourteen, and still no sign of Finn.

On the fifteenth day, about sundown, he appeared. His skin was blistered by exposure and fierce sunlight, his clothes torn, his face gaunt and his body thin, for he was a far less accomplished hunter than Johnny. But he was full of news. He had been, he judged, between thirty and forty miles up the Koornong. He had explored some of the tributary streams, but finding them steep and rocky, had returned always to the river. Once he had climbed out of it to a hilltop a thousand feet above its banks, and from there he had seen more mountains and cliffs in the distance reaching up to three—perhaps four thousand feet. But it looked wild country, he said, hilly, rocky and barren; so he had scrambled down to the river banks again and plodded on. And he had come at last to a place where hills rose steeply to a great raised valley, walled by towering cliffs, and watered by a good stream running briskly down to join the river. He had not stayed to explore it very closely, for his food was running low, but he had seen enough, he said, to make him feel that there a man could live secure for many years. Two men, he added, watching Johnny over the coolamon of milk he was lifting to his lips, would live better still . . .

And Johnny asked briefly:

"When we go?"

*　　　*　　　*　　　*　　　*

But he made one last trip to Green Hills towards the end of the year, upon his own business, and saying nothing to Finn. When Andy went to his hut at night his brother was waiting for him, crouched in the long grass; and when the interview was over, and he found himself alone again, only the money in his hand could persuade him that it had not been a dream.

Johnny wanted clothes—new clothes. Those he had taken from the dead convict were in rags now, and the shoes he had bought from Miller hardly held together. Andy was to get him clothes.

The boy stared at him wildly. Here it was again—that baffling assumption that the impossible was possible! Did Johnny think that clothes grew on trees, or lay by the wayside to be picked up . . . ? And then the money was thrust into his hand. At first it made him feel that his brother was less mad than he had thought, for at least he evidently knew that clothes cost money. But when he looked at the coins in his hand he was more than ever convinced that this was a lunatic. For there was more than enough here to buy what Johnny demanded—a coat, a cap, a pair of trousers, a pair of shoes. Anyone who did not know to the last hard-earned farthing what such things cost *must* be mad . . .

Andy had never handled so much money in his life, but the quick, greedy excitement it roused in him was quenched by fear and suspicion. Was this a trap? He looked askance at his brother, and muttered silently:

"It's too much, ye don't need but . . ."

He subtracted a few coins and held them out. Johnny, barely glancing at them, said impatiently:

"I got more—you keep it."

And then, not realising the excellence of his own strategy, he proceeded to his second demand. Andy cried in horror: "No, no—ye're mad!" But he looked down dazedly at the money in his palm, and his brain was still echoing those amazing words: "*I got more . . .*"

Johnny said fiercely:

"You do—or I kill you!"

Greed and terror battled in Andy. He whispered:

"If I do—ye'll give me more money . . . ?"

Johnny looked at him in faint surprise, having almost forgotten the power of these small pieces of metal, and that a threat of death might be less potent than a promise of riches. There was, in fact, very little more money at the hut, and he had no intention of giving it to Andy, but he agreed indifferently:

"Lot more."

Andy muttered, quaking:

"All right—all right! Sunday. Five days." He held up his fingers. "But how'll ye find 'em? Ye don't know the house—ye can't . . ."

Johnny said coldly:

"You tell. Quick, you tell where, you tell everything, or I . . ."

Andy began to gabble explanations. A small room at the front of the house, near the great door on to the west verandah. . . . No, no, there was no ammunition there—it was kept in the storeroom. Yes, he would have the key to that too—". . . but mind ye, it sticks in the lock—ye turn and lift, like this—and His Honour's late to bed—an' the old lady sleeps ill, so don't make no noise for the love o' God—an' watch out for Byrne —an' don't come while there's lights . . ."

Johnny cut his frenzied warnings short with a gesture.

"No one see. Dark night, no moon. Walk quiet. You put the clothes outside window—I take. You don't be there, I come here next night, kill you with spear like that other man."

He went, without farewells. Andy stood with a sweat on him that was not due to the summer night. He would have to be careful; a labourer's wage did not buy a whole outfit at one time. His purchases must be made separately by different people—he would have to take a couple of others into his confidence and pay them a trifle for their complicity, but without mentioning Johnny. . . . They must think he had stolen the money. . . . And the other business . . . ! Mad, mad, but he was caught in it, he could not refuse. . . . If Johnny were taken with the keys on him . . . ! Andy crept into his hovel, and his hands, as he scratched up the earth of the floor to bury his riches, were shaking violently.

*   *   *   *   *

One Monday late in December Mr. Mannion suffered a severe shock when he entered his study early in the morning. Two muskets and two pistols which should have been hanging on the wall were gone.

He stood staring incredulously. The window . . . ? But it had been shut, locked, bolted on the inside—he had just opened it himself. He had gone round the house last night as his custom was before retiring, and secured every door and window. His hand felt in his pocket for his keys, and found them there; he had taken them from their accustomed place on the table by his bed when he rose not an hour ago. His gaze, blank with astonishment and consternation, wandered to the window again, looked through it at the roof of Ellen's cottage just visible down the hill, and narrowed suddenly. Ellen . . . ? Ellen . . . ?

She looked up from her work at the kitchen table to find him standing in the doorway, glaring not at her face, but at her waist. He remarked strangely:

"You have your keys I see, Ellen."

She glanced down at them and back at him in surprise.

"Yes, Sir—and why not?"

He advanced a pace into the room, shut the door behind him and demanded sharply:

"Have they been out of your possession since yesterday?"

"Why no, Sir." Her voice was half puzzled and half resentful. "I keep them by me always."

"At night?"

"They hang on the wall by my bed . . ." She was angry now, and added: ". . . as you very well know, Sir."

He reddened and raised his voice.

"Don't be insolent! You put them there last night?"

"That I did," she snapped irritably, "and they were there this morning just as I left them."

He stood frowning at her for a moment. Then he passed through the kitchen to the outer door; she saw him cross the yard to the storeroom, take out his own keys, unlock the door, and enter. A few minutes later he returned, pale with anger.

"Someone," he rapped out, "has been in there last night. And in the house. The firearms have been stolen from the study, and some ammunition from the storeroom. No locks have been forced. Only you and I have keys."

Her face went white. Suddenly she was struggling with a terrified bewilderment—for Andy had slept at her cottage last night. He had come after dark, which was unusual; his tale was that his master had refused him permission, but hunger had tempted him to make a surreptitious visit. To avoid being seen he had kept off the roads, making his way through the scrub, and approaching the cottage across the fields. There had been a sharp shower of rain, and he was soaked to the skin; he looked ill, scared, sullen. So she had given him a blanket to wrap about him, and set his clothes and his shoes by the fire to dry while she scolded and fed him. And she had aroused herself a couple of hours before dawn to feed him again before he slunk away in the dark with a bundle of food in his hand, upon the long walk back to Green Hills. . . .

Her love had been reserved for Johnny, but Andy was her son too. And if he were suspected of theft, she would be suspected of aiding him. Maria, too, sleeping here in the house now . . . Maria . . . ? Could Maria have let him in . . . ? Were they all to be accused of theft, turned out, delivered over to the unmerciful law, deprived for ever of the security she had won and kept so bitterly . . . ?

She shot a panic-stricken glance at Mannion. Not only determination to get to the bottom of this mystery, but an unexpected echo from their old relationship—a hint of jealous possessiveness—was in his voice as he asked:

"Were you alone at the cottage last night?"

Anything to keep his thoughts from Andy! Resentment as well as fear buttressed her courage. He no longer wanted her himself, but he dared to speak as though . . . ! She set her hands on her hips, and with black eyes snapping, answered impudently:

"And what if I wasn't?"

He took her roughly by the arm.

"Who was with you, you abandoned . . . ?"

She wrenched herself free.

"Did I say there was anyone?"

He shouted furiously:

"Answer me, woman! Was there anyone with you?"

She had deflected his thoughts from her family to a possible lover, so she lied boldly:

"Not a living soul!"

But she was still frightened. Could Andy have stolen the keys? He had gone to his bed early, but she had sat on in the kitchen mending his torn coat till nearly midnight when the fire in the stove went out, and she was half asleep. She had heard him tossing on his bed while she undressed. Could he, between that time and the still dark hour when she had awakened, have done this insane thing—taken his spoils to some safe place and then returned?

Mannion was saying:

"If that is a lie I shall soon discover it. There has been something afoot here for a long time—this is not the first theft that has been committed. I hope for your own sake that you are not concerned in it. The loss of two muskets and two pistols will not—as you know—leave this house stripped of arms. I have never shared the complacency with which many people regard a colony of felons." She did not seem to be listening, and he went on savagely: "I had assumed some sense of obligation in you, Ellen, for the indulgences you have received here, but I suspect that I was mistaken. Once a felon, always a felon!"

Still she did not seem to hear him. She was thinking of those shoes left by the fire to dry, remembering that when she had finished mending the coat, she had bent, yawning, to pick them up and see if they were dry. They were dry. And they were still dry in the dark early morning when she moved them aside to light the fire . . .

Andy had not left the cottage then—unless he had gone barefoot, and why should he do that . . . ?

It was something in the idea of bare feet that flung the name of her elder son into her mind like a stone. It hit and scattered her labouring thoughts like a blow; there was a sudden roaring in her ears, as if she had heard as well as felt the crash of it. *Johnny!* It was *like* Johnny! Yes, it was not at all like the dull and submissive Andy, but it was like Johnny. . . . Those thefts months ago—all that meaningless damage—that reckless, obstinate, malicious talent for being a nuisance . . . ! But the keys? She could find no glimmer of light in the black bewilderment, but she was convinced that somehow Johnny was the answer. In terror that this knowledge might be printed on her face, she turned away to a shelf behind her, and said breathlessly:

"I don't know aught of it! The keys were by my bed all night." She mastered her panic and faced him again. "What would I want with guns?"

He answered unpleasantly:

"Nothing, I trust, but I am far from sure. There are always conspiracies afoot in this colony. There has been some knavery, and I mean to get to the bottom of it. You will be closely watched, I assure you." He held out his hand. "Give me those keys—Bessie shall keep them in future."

Her face crimsoned with rage as she unhooked them from her belt and tossed them on the table. Bessie! The keys—her one badge of respectability and position—to be taken from her and handed over to that saucy madam who never missed an opportunity to underline the difference between a free woman and an ex-convict, a virtuous widow and a discarded mistress! As he picked them up and turned to leave the room she shot a last retort at him:

"If I'm to wait for Bessie every time I want something from the storeroom, your dinner'll come late on the table!"

She collapsed on to a chair as the door banged behind him.

*   *   *   *   *

He found, however, that for all the confidence of his threats to Ellen, he could not get to the bottom of it. Toole, Byrne and Evans, closely questioned, declared that all had been as usual last night. They swore they had not been near Ellen's cottage. The convicts had been mustered, and every one of them was under lock and key. No suspicious sounds had been heard by anyone, either outside the house or in it. Conor, it was true, missed a scarf which she thought she had left in the drawing-room, but confessed that she might have dropped it from the carriage when she was driving in the afternoon.

Mr. Mannion, baffled, and more perturbed than he would admit, was forced to add one more to the tale of Beltrasna's mysteries.

*   *   *   *   *

And Johnny slept the hot morning away peacefully in a rocky gorge on the western side of the river. He lay on his back in the shade, and round his neck, tucked into the front of his dirty coat, was a scarf of pure white silk, embroidered with an intricate and delicately coloured pattern of birds and flowers; a wreath of pink roses enclosed the initials "C.M." Behind him, well hidden among the rocks, were Mr. Mannion's missing firearms, and a bundle of new clothes; a native canoe was drawn up out of the water nearby, and his spears lay beside him within reach of his hand.

It was well after midday when he wakened, yawned, and lay still, feeling happy and excited. His plan had worked perfectly save for one wild moment when it had seemed that he himself might spoil it. Through a window left ajar a bunch of keys had been dropped to him—and an hour or so later he had replaced them on the sill, and a hand had taken them in. He was astonished that it could have been so simple, not realising how much less simple it might have seemed to one without years of training in the art of quiet movement, and eyes well accustomed to darkness.

In the storeroom he had made a dim light for a moment to find what he sought, for the two small, deeply-set windows faced only the open fields. He had known a second of alarm when, emerging into the night again, and setting his burden down beside him, he had re-locked the door, and found that he could not withdraw the key—but only a second, until he remembered Andy's anxiously-whispered warning.

The back door of the house had opened soundlessly; rooms and passages yawned before him like black caverns; as he came to the front of the house the long-forgotten feel of a carpet under his bare feet startled him for an instant. There was no sound save snoring from a room somewhere near the kitchen. He moved forward slowly with Andy's directions in his mind, his eyes growing accustomed to the deeper darkness of the house. Was this the door? He turned the handle silently and pushed it open an inch, listening. No sound. He entered and waited again, peering round the walls. The room seemed vast—endless; the shape of chairs showed in ghostly pallor; there was a strange fragrance that took him back to the garden at Parramatta where, as a child, he had worked with such hatred and rebellion. Pink flowers on a thorny bush . . . what was their name . . . ? For an instant he lost his grip on reality and stood in a dream, and the dream passed from the memory of a scent to the memory of misery and servitude, so that his mission retreated, his plan faded, the booty he had come to take no longer mattered, and he knew only that he was close to his enemy, and his enemy was sleeping—helpless . . .

A sudden mad blood-lust turned him fiercely towards the door again, and his outstretched hand touched something on the back of a chair. He snatched it away, his heart hammering. What? What? Nothing he had ever touched had felt quite like that. It was more like the fur of a very young animal than anything else, so smooth, so soft, so sweet an invitation to the fingers . . . ! His hand crept out again warily, touched it, lifted it.

In his wonder, rage had faded. This was not the time for his revenge. Finn said they needed more firearms, and he knew of no other way to get them, but it was self-indulgence as well as need which had inspired him in this adventure. Some day he would kill his enemy—but first he would again enjoy the pleasure of annoying and outwitting him. He thrust the soft bundle into the bosom of his coat and moved to the door. This must be the wrong room, for Andy had said the one he sought was not large. He stole across the hall and paused at a door which was open.

No sound came from the room. He entered, listened, closed the door, and almost at once saw the dark shapes of muskets against the white wall. He moved over to them, calling his sense of touch to the assistance of his eyes. His fingers explored with infinite caution; he lifted them down one by one, laying them noiselessly on the carpeted floor. He was grinning to himself as he crept down the passage again, the pistols stuck in his kangaroo-hide belt, carrying the muskets carefully beneath his arm. The gentry made it easy for thieves with their carpets!

He left the house, re-locked the back door, and gathered up his bundle of ammunition from beside the storehouse. The load was heavy—but no heavier than he had carried for far longer distances. Back to the river in the still, brooding quietness of the summer night, tension relaxing under the familiar stars and in the fresh and friendly air, pausing by his mother's cottage on the way to place the keys on the sill and see them vanish, to add to his burden the bundle of clothes that lay waiting. Had Andy whispered a frightened question at him? Perhaps, but he had not paused. What was there to say? It was done, and he had what he wanted. His canoe was a moving shadow on the dark water; his paddle disturbed it no more than a leaping fish.

And now he lay on his back, refreshed and elated, thinking of his triumph, imagining Mannion's rage and discomfiture, imagining his own return to the hut, walking in to lay his spoils before Finn's astonished eyes and say: "They're *his*. I went into his house and took 'em!"

1806

It was from English newspapers that arrived early in 1806, and not from tardy official correspondence, that the Governor learned the name of his successor.

It made him thoughtful. It took him back nineteen years to the time when he had been with Phillip on the *Sirius*, sharing the bustle which preceded the sailing of the first fleet to this colony. There had been some talk then, he recalled, of another voyage in preparation—a voyage to transplant the breadfruit from Otaheite to the West Indies, where it would provide cheap food for the slaves on the sugar plantations. The ship which was to sail on this voyage was the *Bounty*, and its commander was young Lieutenant Bligh . . .

"Breadfruit Bligh" . . .

That had become a name about which controversy gathered, opinions clashed, advocacy grew heated and denunciation violent. It had rung throughout England sixteen years ago when the sensational story of the mutiny on the *Bounty*, and its commander's epic voyage in an open boat became known. King, on his arrival in England from Norfolk Island in December of 1790, had heard the echoes; for Bligh's *Narrative of the Mutiny on His Majesty's Ship Bounty* had recently been published, his Court Martial had but lately ended with his honourable acquittal, and he had only a few days earlier been promoted to the rank of Post-Captain.

Since no seaman could fail to be interested in such a naval *cause célèbre*, the young Philip Gidley King had thought of it in the few idle moments of those three eventful months. But he had been far too busy with his own affairs to give it much attention—courting his Anna Josepha, arranging his affairs, battling with illness, and finally getting married.

Now, suddenly and strangely, that old story became significant again. What was the truth about this William Bligh? The man who had turned his defeat into the triumph of that astounding boat voyage, was certainly a hero; but the man against whom his crew had dared to raise the desperate banner of mutiny—what was he? The victim of a set of worthless rogues —or a monster of cruelty? A strict but equitable commander—or a bloody tyrant?

"Bounty Bligh" . . .

And now? The Fate which spun the thread of Bligh's destiny, King reflected sardonically, must surely have a fondness for alliteration! Bligh of Botany Bay! It was indeed interesting to speculate upon the outcome of contact between that man and this place, for Bligh seemed one about whom storms gathered—and here, if anywhere, was a stormy climate. Quite recently, King remembered, there had been rumours of another Court Martial which he had faced as Captain of the *Warrior*. He had suffered nothing worse from that, it appeared, than a request that he should learn to moderate his language; but the impression grew that life in the vicinity of Captain Bligh was unlikely to be tranquil.

Thus the present Governor of New South Wales, holding in his mind a clear and hard-won picture of this vexatious colony, tried to imagine the impact upon it of its Governor-elect. Himself a naval officer, he could not but condemn mutiny, nor (trained in the harsh naval discipline of his time) could he view tales of tyranny very seriously. Against Bligh it might be said that he was passionate, indiscreet, intolerant and overbearing. In his favour it must be said that he was a great navigator and cartographer, a bold explorer, and a man of remarkable determination and endurance. King suspected shrewdly that it might even be the uncompromising violence of his temper, no less than the stubbornness of his purpose, which had gained him this appointment. For doubtless Sir Joseph Banks had had a finger in it, as he had in most matters that concerned the colony, and Sir Joseph was something of a martinet himself. So great a personage, of course, imposed his will by methods more subtle and dignified than those which a naval commander must use towards his crew; yet King fancied that similarities could be discerned between the notable scientist and scholar, and the sailor who had become one of his favourite protégés. Both were men of active and enquiring mind; both self-confident to the point of arrogance; both sticklers for discipline, and sternly exacting in their requirements from subordinates.

King smiled to himself rather wryly. Sir Joseph was his own good friend and patron, and had been pleased to commend his efforts as Governor. But he had also taken him to task for leniency, and deplored the frequency of his reprieves. By now the authorities in England must be well aware that the Governorship of New South Wales was no sinecure. Had they—prompted by Sir Joseph—decided that so turbulent a colony required a stronger hand? Had they envisaged a recalcitrant community subsiding into apprehensive docility at the mere mention of Bounty Bligh?

King hunched his shoulders sceptically; his successor would need more than the severity of a tyrant. That, perhaps, could keep the lower orders down—but would it cow that privileged section of this society from which the most troublesome opposition had always come? Before taking office he had drilled himself in patience. "*I have been obliged to bear and forbear very much,*" he had told Sir Joseph—and had Sir Joseph raised an eyebrow? Yet no; for it had been Sir Joseph who had urged his reconciliation with Paterson, and commended him for putting up with the temperamental Mr. Caley. Rightly or wrongly, he had attempted patience, and he was not a patient man. He had striven—not always successfully—to control his asperity, and to keep his mordant humour from expressing itself in injudicious witticisms. From what he had heard he doubted if Captain Bligh's temper would be even as amenable to control as his own.

Well, who could say what policy would answer best? In five long, difficult years he had achieved something—but how much less than he had so confidently expected! He had settled large numbers of emancipated convicts on the land, steadily reducing the numbers rationed from the Government Store. He had rescued many children from lives of depravity. He had at least embarrassed the monopolists by fixing prices, and encouraging trade from outside the colony to compete with them. He had regulated the currency, brought more public land under cultivation, assisted the settlers to improve their livestock, established new outposts, sponsored new discoveries, promoted small industries . . .

But the military and their adherents were still his powerful foes, and their rancour only increased with prosperity. Illicit stills continued to deluge the colony with potent and injurious spirits. Most of the poorer settlers kept body and soul together, and no more. Many of his regulations were transgressed, and his attempts to bring the transgressors to book defeated by a conspiracy of silence. There were still the machinations of political exiles to be feared—and indeed five more prominent United Irishmen, including the notorious Michael Dwyer, had lately arrived to swell their ranks. Joseph Holt, too, had returned from Norfolk Island in February, and though his wife was reported to have swooned with joy upon beholding him, the Governor was less enthusiastic. Intrigues and swindling still caused endless litigation, and on this question of the law His Excellency had always felt himself at a disadvantage.

He had long ago assured Lord Hobart that he believed he had never departed from the dictates of strict equity between man and man, but he felt himself unable to decide legal points with a legal nicety, and disliked carrying responsibilities for which he was unqualified. And only recently Mr. Macarthur had further disturbed him by hints that all his orders and regulations were, in fact, illegal, and could not be regarded as binding unless sanctioned by an Act of Parliament.

He muttered something that sounded like "Fiddlesticks!" Since copies of all local regulations were sent to the Minister for the Colonies, and had been duly approved, and since it was obvious that no order could ever have been preserved without them, he was perturbed by the suggestion mainly as an indication that his old enemy was still probing for joints in his armour. The question had been raised, he reflected cynically, only when Macarthur desired to contest regulations against the landing of spirits; during the regimes of Grose and Paterson, when orders had been framed for the benefit of the monopolists, he had not seen fit to cast doubts upon their legality. Yet the composition of the Courts, and, in fact, the whole legal situation, troubled him a good deal. Was there not in the whole of Great Britain, he thought testily, one competent and upright lawyer they could send him? Mr. Atkins was a very broken reed—not only because his knowledge of the law was little greater than the

Governor's own, but because his intemperate habits and unstable character failed to inspire that confidence and respect which the office of Judge Advocate demanded.

It was all very well for discontented persons to invoke for their own purposes the sacredness of English law, and claim it as all-sufficient for the government of this colony. Circumstances, conditions, unforeseen crises, and the peculiar composition of its society all forced an administrator into swift and summary adjustments. Captain Bligh, King thought sourly, would discover all these problems in good time. Captain Bligh would find here a form of rebellion not supported by pistols and cutlasses, but by money and influence. Captain Bligh would find here an adversary . . .

His Excellency, staring into space, almost grinned. Captain Bligh would find Mr. John Macarthur—and the encounter would be one to watch with a lively interest—from afar.

*   *   *   *   *

For the moment all was going quietly enough. But at such times the Governor had learned to feel wary, for disturbance was always just round the corner, and the quarter from which it would come, and the form it would take, could only be conjectured. This time it came from the heavens in the form of a deluge that swelled the Hawkesbury from a placid river to a fierce, yellow, destroying torrent.

The *Sydney* was due to sail for Calcutta shortly, and King was tied to his desk preparing despatches to send by her. Mr. Arndell, acting as Magistrate at the Hawkesbury, kept him informed in a series of letters which, throughout the month of March, he read with a growing dismay. In the first few days it was already apparent that the crops would suffer severely, but information that the river was falling made the Governor watch the sky with an anxious hope. By the nineteenth, however, Mr. Arndell was reporting that continual rain threatened returning floods, and King, reading his hasty note dated a few days later, was forced to realise that the colony faced a considerable disaster.

"*The flood is now approaching a very dangerous height. All the settlers are repairing to the high grounds as fast as they can be brought off . . .*"

Still the rain poured down, and the tone of Mr. Arndell's communications became more urgent.

"*I am very sorry to inform Your Excellency of the dreadful damage done by the flood which is now ten feet higher than was ever known before, and rather increases a little yet. Some lives, as well as almost all the stock, wheat, etc., is lost, although every exertion has been used to save the people with all the boats we could get, and the whole exhibits a scene of horror and misery not to be described . . .*"

King threw the paper down and paced the room in a mood of nervous exasperation. The devil take this barbarous land with its droughts, and fires, and floods! Had he not enough to plague him without this? At last it appeared that the water was really falling, but only with the abatement of the flood could the full extent of its havoc be learned. On that terrible Friday night when it had reached its highest level, settlers

and their families had awakened to find water lapping round their beds.
They had scrambled to what safety they could find—into lofts, only to be
driven thence to the roofs; on to the tops of wheat-stacks that floated
away beneath them; into the branches of trees, to crouch through the
long, cold hours under pelting rain, firing guns to attract attention to
their plight. Rescue boats struggled through the dark; shouts, screams,
and the wailing of children sounded thinly through the noise of flood and
downpour; the lowing of panic-stricken cattle, the clamour of horses,
goats, sheep, and squealing pigs made the night hideous. Lanterns glim-
mered faintly across acres of black water; buildings collapsed, adding
timber, furniture, and household possessions to the floating debris; hundreds
of wheat-stacks sailed down the river; no one knew, as yet, how many
human beings had been swept away.

When it was over, and reports had been submitted, there remained for
King the task of relating the melancholy tale to Lord Camden. He was as
devout a man as his respectable situation demanded, but it was in something less than a mood of Christian meekness that he described "the
calamity with which it has pleased the Supreme Ruler of events to visit
our agricultural settlements." This business would jeopardise the food-
supply. The reserve of Government wheat, with what could be grown
in areas unaffected by the flood, would furnish a bare sufficiency until
the next harvest—but the ration must be reduced. It was a long time
now since there had been a serious shortage of food, and the Governor's
chagrin was mixed with a rebellious feeling that the ways in which the
Supreme Ruler saw fit to move were mysterious indeed.

He himself, it was clear, must move with speed. The *Sydney* must
return from India with a cargo of rice; a vessel must be sent to Madras
for provisions. An offer of assistance, at first on acceptable terms, came
from the captain of an American ship in port; but after consultation with
certain inhabitants of the colony, his price rose steeply, and was accompanied by a request for permission to import liquor. King, muttering
"Vipers!" dismissed him curtly, and contracted instead with the captain
of the *Tellicherry*, about to sail for China, to deliver three hundred and
fifty tons of rice within six months.

They would need it all. Fifteen thousand bushels of wheat and fifty-
seven thousand of maize had been destroyed by the flood, as well as
hundreds of acres of vegetable gardens and more stock than the colony
could afford. But it was no use repining. He had done what he could
to guard against want, and he was gripped by the lassitude of reaction.

He sat at his desk one morning, the clear, autumn sunshine smiling
innocently through his window. His half-finished despatch lay unheeded
before him with its enclosures—the *Gazettes* describing the catastrophe, a
sketch plan showing the areas of inundation, the reports of loss and
damage. He found himself more than ever eager to be rid of this assignment. Nothing but fears for his future and the future of his family
dimmed that eagerness, and the blue, beguiling sky outside tempted his
thoughts to the land—not as an assignment, but as a resource. In his
recent fury with the excesses of its climate he had called it a barbarous

land—but it was a rich land too, a land hardly touched as yet, a land of promise. And none of it was his. But, by Heaven, some of it should be his children's! It owed him that. His mind went to that two thousand acres of pleasant, undulating country which he had attempted to grant to his wife two years ago, and his expression darkened. Improper? Irregular? Against the improprieties and the irregularities he had seen practised here, the determination of a father to provide for his children seemed very blameless. These last weeks had taken their toll of his health, and in the depression of weariness and worry his fears for them sharpened, and his hesitancies were overborne. They should have their acres!

*   *   *   *   *

Wet weather, culminating in the torrential rains and floods of March, had hampered the slow removal of Finn and Johnny to their new retreat. Several reconnaissances of the Koornong had made them familiar with its course, and with the tributaries that joined it. Its direction, roughly west for some twenty miles above its junction with the Wollondilly, was changed by an almost right-angle bend to the north, and from here the spot which Finn had chosen was, he judged, about another ten miles upstream. He had half wished to push on farther still, but he feared to increase the distance they must transport their livestock and belongings. There were one or two places on the river banks that tempted him; he did not know that in passing them by he was repeating the history of Andrew Prentice, who had left the pleasant Nepean, and rejected the equally pleasant Wollondilly for his wild hiding-place in the hills between them. Official exploration was along the rivers; that was enough. Some day an expedition would follow the Koornong. He could only be at peace in some spot where it might pass him by, unsuspecting.

So, on the first of several journeys late in 1805, they had made straight to the place Finn had marked down and, climbing some sixteen hundred feet up a steep hill east of the river, found themselves in a high valley at least ten miles long, and varying in width with the curves of its Koornong boundary. To the south, rough, hilly country enclosed it; to the east and north it was hemmed in by vertical cliffs that shot up another fifteen hundred feet to some unknown tableland. Its floor was undulating, and for the most part heavily timbered. There were places where the size of majestic trees promised good soil, and at least three creeks, fed by water-falls from the cliffs, found their tortuous way down across it to join the river.

But Johnny, who judged territory very simply by its food-yielding capacity, observed it without enthusiasm. All his skill as a hunter was needed here to keep them alive, and in the week they spent seeking a permanent site for their new home, Finn realised that in any attempt to undertake this enterprise alone, he would have fared badly. Near the southern end of the valley, in a pocket sheltered by a low hill to the south and west, and close to a clear, swift-running stream, he halted at last, and said soberly:

"We'll be findin' naught better than this, Johnny, an' the time goes by. We'll be gettin' to work an' makin' a roof over our heads."

From that day the ageless silence of the place was broken by the sounds of labour. They had brought an axe and a few tools with them, but the shelter which was to serve for the present must be a mere bark and log humpy, for Finn was in a fever lest their old retreat should be discovered before they could remove their possessions. One of them at a time, it was decided, must return to the hut, while the other remained here to complete their rude dwelling, and begin the clearing of the land.

The year was almost over when Johnny left upon the first of these errands, and it was mid-January by the time he returned, heavily laden with a miscellaneous load which included not only food, salt, and tools packed in one of the casks, but that incongruous object made of rosewood and embroidered satin upon which Cousin Bertha's feet had once rested. Finn stared at it and bit back the jibe that rose to his lips. After all, the lad had also brought a fat wild duck which he had captured native-fashion on the river during his journey, and they would eat well that night.

But in the weeks alone he had been thinking as well as working, and his thoughts were anxious. As he swung his axe at the huge trunks of the trees he told himself that the soil yielded slowly, if surely, and in the meantime they must live. It was clear that this place was not to be compared with the Wollondilly valley for abundance of game. So far he had seen no kangaroos, and few wallabies. One old, slow-moving wombat provided a few substantial if tough meals, and there were some small animals he had not seen before, which launched themselves by night from tree to tree, as if on wings. Wild duck were to be seen, but not often, and his marksmanship was not good enough to bring down the smaller birds. Their stream yielded nothing but frogs, and these he often ate. Fish and eels from the river were his best supply of fresh food, but even these were scarce, and he grudged the time spent in catching them. He husbanded the small supply of salt beef which Johnny had left with him, and was hungry all the time. He tired easily at his labours, and at night he lay awake, thinking.

They had seen no natives, nor any indication that they ever frequented the neighbourhood; that, he realised, was the surest sign of poor hunting country, and his fears for their own livestock became an obsession. His first words to Johnny when he returned were questions about their welfare. Had he secured the fowls in their enclosure near the stream, safe from prowling native dogs? Was the little pool that afforded them drinking water still full? Had he left them grain to supplement their pickings? Were the goats safe, and had he seen the cattle in the Wollondilly valley? Johnny assured him that all was well, but he left for the hut himself next morning.

February had begun when he returned, bowed beneath the weight of another load. He had found the livestock safe, but he would know no peace till they were removed, and he had pushed his pace so that by the time he saw the smoke from the damp branches Johnny was burning, he was almost exhausted. He had been soaked to the skin often, and hungry often, and tired all the time, but his spirits rose as he dumped his burdens on the ground, and turned to see what Johnny had accomplished. It was less than he would have accomplished himself, for Johnny had not yet grasped the importance of time, nor developed an ear for the insistent call of labour. But he had made progress with the clearing, and added some sawn logs to the pile, and begun to prepare a small plot for a garden. And there was a wallaby for supper. Even if Johnny did nothing else, he thought, he was indispensable as a provider of fresh food. He sighed, stretching himself out thankfully on the ground.

"Aye, ye've done well, lad. An' now I'm thinkin' we'd best both go back to the hut an' fetch up the beasts, for it's never a quiet moment I'll know till they're here safe an' sound. There's some bits an' pieces there still, but what we can't be bringin' with us next time we'll leave, an' trust to luck they'll still be there when we're wantin' them. 'Tis the animals we must have, before some pryin' devil sets an eye on them." He looked round at the tranquil, lonely scene, at the smoke drifting like a blue dust through the last slanting rays of sunlight, at the felled tree trunks, and the piled logs, and the young man squatting silently at his side. "There'll be more of us one day," he said slowly. " 'Tis but a beginnin' we're makin', an' we'll be havin' others to help with . . ."

Johnny interrupted sharply:

"More?"

"Aye—more like meself, ready for anythin' if so be they face it as free men. I'll not be troublin' me head yet how we'll get them, but . . ."

Johnny's eyes had begun to snap angrily.

"No more!"

Finn sat up. It had not occurred to him, possessed as he was by his dream, that Johnny could have failed to understand the scattered references he had made to it, dreaming aloud. He said quickly:

"What else is it we've been speakin' of these months past? Now let ye listen to me! Haven't I been after tellin' ye there's no use a man can make of his freedom but to set others free? It's the way it was written in me little book, lad—'O receive the fugitive, and prepare in time an asylum for mankind.' 'Twas said of a nation, to be sure, an' here we're but two men with a few tools an' a few beasts an' our four arms—but we can be makin' a refuge all the same . . ."

Johnny jumped up and looked about him with a glance of searching and suspicious alarm, as if he expected to see their sanctuary already invaded. He rarely wore his clothes, and the fading golden light painted his body to a ruddy brown, and flamed in his red hair. He looked a savage—and yet Finn had seen enough of the natives to know that they were less savage than this youth could be, who was still governed by hatred and mistrust and impulse.

Johnny said violently:

"No men come here! No men come take my things! My hut, my cattle!" His arms waved in passionate gesticulation at the scattered tools. "My spade, axe, guns—everything mine!"

Finn scrambled to his feet, slow and ungainly, prematurely old and grey. There was no menace in his movements, or his voice, but Johnny's eyes grew hostile and defensive. Finn said, watching him:

"An' what was it made them yours, then?"

Johnny claimed fiercely:

"I took 'em!"

" 'Twas y' father took the most of them," Finn replied dryly. "An' some ye traded for salt beef—an' who was it taught ye that? Tom Towns, it was, a poor divil the like o' what will come here an' share in what he helped ye to get. An' some ye took, I'm not denyin' it; an' meself ye took too, an' does that make me yours? No, be all the Saints it doesn't!" He bent forward and shot out a sudden question: "Let ye be tellin' me, now, what ye think o' that fine gentleman ye were after stealin' me from? Come, now, is it a grand fellow he is entirely?"

Johnny made a wild gesture of rage and irritation.

"You know!" he shouted angrily. "You know I hate—I kill some day . . . !"

"Now what would ye be wantin' to do that for?" Finn asked contemptuously. "An' he so like y'self it's y' own brother he might be! 'My house!' he says. 'My land, *my* cattle, *my* tools, an' seeds, an' animals! *My* servant, Matthew Finn,' he says, an' it's *my* servant Johnny Prentice' he'd 'a been after sayin' if ye'd not escaped from him—an' he with divil a care for those that go naked and hungry by his door! Aye, it's much he has, an' but little ye have—but it's the same greedy heart in the both o' ye!"

He turned abruptly, shaken by his anger and dismay, and left the youth standing there. He walked away blindly, climbing the hill till he could see a loop of the river like a fine silver ribbon to the north, and the high hills across it still touched with the radiance of the setting sun. He stood there for a long time, thinking, seeing the battle ahead of him as one not only with a harsh and untamed land, but with a wild and undisciplined heart.

There was too little to divide—and in any case Johnny, the food-provider, was necessary to his plan. Somehow he must hold together the few assets upon which he had built his fantastic dream—for every one of those assets depended on the others. Johnny's youth and strength and long-trained native lore were indispensable. Upon the animals, the tools, and the seeds, they both depended. But only Johnny, brooding and raging down there by the smouldering fire, could tell how much—or how little—he depended on Matthew Finn.

Warm as the evening was, the convict shivered slightly. What was passing in the lad's mind? Was he thinking that he had lived well alone once, and could do so again? Was he looking at the loaded musket, and telling himself that one shot would rid him for ever of a companion who threatened to become troublesome, and secure his possessions against the intrusion of other, unknown men? It was a strange fate, Finn thought, that his life should hang on the impulse of a human being who was neither white nor black, neither good nor evil, a creature untaught, a-moral, governed as simply as a plant or an animal by his own immediate needs. But it could hang on nothing else.

He saw that now with a frightening clarity. Bleakly, his shoulders bent and his head hanging with fatigue, he confronted the knowledge that he was of no further use to Johnny in the battle for existence. He had two strong arms—but to a being with no conception of time what did it matter if two pairs of arms could work faster than one? Such practical knowledge as he possessed of husbandry and the handling of tools he had long ago passed on. His presence, indeed, was a danger. For Johnny was himself no convict; even if he were discovered, and the articles he had stolen along with him, it was possible that his strange history might buy him clemency. But as an associate, an aider and abetter of an escaped convict, his case would be different. Did he realise that?

Nothing, then, was left to hang in the scales against this threat of a development he did not want but a few, subtle, intangible and invisible things not likely to weigh heavily with so primitive a creature. Finn rubbed his hand wearily over his gaunt, bearded cheeks. Even to himself these things seemed nebulous in the face of the bitter fight for mere survival. Friendship . . . a mind that could move in unfamiliar directions . . . a tongue that could clothe thoughts in words, tell stories and sing songs . . . a goodwill that might, perhaps, breed goodwill . . .

It was frail armour against a bullet in the dark—or maybe a spear. . . . For the twilight had deepened to night while he stood there, and a few stars showed between the clouds, and the dying fires shone redly at the foot of the hill. He began to descend, subduing the instinctive impulse to move quietly, for there was nothing here which could be solved by a duel. There was no sound save the croaking of frogs in the stream, and while the fear of sudden death brought a sweat out on his body, his mind was wondering absently if that were the last sound he would hear.

He was halted by the smell of scorching fur and flesh. Johnny was cooking the wallaby . . .

Did that mean . . . ? Finn drew a deep breath and went on. He stumbled out from the scrub on the hillside to the clearing, and saw Johnny's silhouette against the glow of a fire. He knew that he must have been heard, for the boy's ears were as sharp as an animal's, but the figure did not move. He went on slowly, passed round the fire, stood opposite, and still Johnny ignored him, poking with a stick at the carcase that lay sizzling on the embers. The loaded musket and a knife lay at his side.

Finn sat down stiffly. An overwhelming weariness added to his mood of fatalism; he did not move even when Johnny's hand went out for the knife. But the boy only held it, stabbing its point aimlessly into the ground and keeping his eyes on it while he asked sullenly:

"Fugitive—man running away?"

Finn stared at him, and said: "Aye, that's it."

"Tom Towns run away—come to my hut. I give him food. Sick, can't hunt. I give him food long time "

"Aye, lad," Finn agreed heavily. "Ye took him in an' fed him. 'Tis true."

The momentary glance that Johnny shot at him before fixing his eyes once more on the knife was darkly resentful, and yet somehow appealing.

"Not like *him*," he said vehemently. "Not like Mannion?"

Finn felt his weary mood of resignation stabbed by a swift, reviving hope. By God, this boy was not a mere animal after all! He had been searching his heart and questioning his own behaviour—however clumsily. He could resent a charge against his humanity . . .

Suddenly Finn's memory thrust a picture of Mannion at him—an elegant, handsome, commanding personage, immaculately attired; he looked across the still glow of firelight at the figure it illumined—naked, dirty, with a wild thatch of red hair, and sulky, brooding eyes. Even at such a moment he could feel the humour of Johnny's indignant denial, but it was this proof that the difference went deeper than mere outward appearance that animated his voice, and lit his eyes with an involuntary smile. He said soothingly:

"Nay, then, it's wrong I was, for ye're not like him at all, the way ye've been sharin' with two men already, an' they fugitives like I'm tellin' ye of . . ."

Johnny threw the knife down petulantly.

"You say more . . . one word . . . asy . . . ? You say make asy . . . ?"

"Asylum, it was. A place to go, for him who's runnin' away."

Johnny lifted his head and stared across the fire with an expression that was clearly a challenge.

"We make it here?"

"We make it here," Finn replied.

"No!" exclaimed Johnny loudly.

"Yes," answered Finn, and waited for rage, for the knife, for the crack of the musket. But Johnny only picked up a bit of charred wood and tossed it into the fire; a few sparks shot up and died in the darkness. After a long silence he said with a note of grievance:

"When you go away up there I think better I kill you."

Finn exploded:

"An' why didn't ye, then, the way there's a loaded musket by y' hand, an' meself unarmed entirely? Divil sweep ye, why don't ye kill me now?"

And then Johnny clasped both hands over his breast with a wild, uninhibited gesture that seemed strangely poignant in one usually so impassive and reserved. He cried bitterly:

"You talk, talk, talk—I listen *here*! You talk things I don't know!" His head drooped down, his hands caught it between them, his fingers thrust themselves into his tangled hair, his body rocked backward and forward despairingly.

Finn, startled, leaned forward to peer at him. Not all the physical efforts he had made seemed as exhausting as this spiritual struggle. Was he to confront a dangerous and ruthless man—or to humour a frightened child? He dragged himself to his feet and pulled the carcase from the fire. The smell of it, despite his hunger, started a sickness in his stomach, but he reached for the knife and began to cut it up, while Johnny lifted his head and watched miserably.

"Words, words!" exclaimed Finn, hacking at the half-raw flesh. " 'Tis the divil of a talker I am, to be sure, an' the tongue never still in me head! Well, 'tis a better use I can be findin' for me mouth now, an' me desthroyed by the hunger! An' y'self too, the way ye've been swingin' the axe from peep o' day till dark. Take this then—an' there's no need we should be speakin' o' that business for many a day, for 'tis not to-morrow or next week or next month we'll be sparin' a thought to it, an' we with enough to keep us busy for a year . . ." He glanced sideways quickly. ". . . two years, maybe. Three years . . . who can be tellin' such a thing?"

Johnny took the words into his mind and strove with them. Time, time, that bewildering white-man concept! That white-man habit of peering forward into a future so distant that the mind groaned under the effort of reaching it! A year—two, three years . . . ! A problem thrust so far away was no longer a problem, but a kind of story. Finn could see by the slow clearing of Johnny's brow that fear and suspicion were growing faint in a mind to which only the present seemed urgent.

He stretched himself out on the ground with his food, and fell asleep before he had finished eating. But Johnny squatted by the fire till the last red ember winked and died, and the wind rose, scattering the ashes on the ground, and the ragged clouds across the sky.

                    *   *   *   *   *

They were back at the hut by the middle of February, and spent almost a fortnight in preparations for the final departure. They stripped the hut of everything movable, taking locks and hinges from door and window—even pulling rusted, hand-made nails from the wood, and setting them carefully aside. Certain articles particularly dear to Johnny's heart were so jealously preserved that Finn was reminded of a child he had once seen being evicted with her parents from her home, and clutching to her breast a few strangely-loved fragments of wood and rag. He and Johnny had no use for a candle-snuffer, nor for a thimble far too small for their fingers, nor for a silken scarf, nor for the little wooden carvings which had lain for years on a dark shelf in the hut. It was unlikely that they would ever need the money that was so carefully tied in a piece of rag, and bestowed with Johnny's new clothes in a smelling cask. That curious necklace made of human hair and buttons from a soldier's coat had hung undisturbed on a nail ever since Finn's arrival, and he had never even seen Johnny glance at it; but now it was taken down with the care due to a sacred object, and hung round its owner's neck with his key. The pencils—one worn to an inch-long stump—were packed with the scissors and smaller tools, and every fragment of paper, whether blank or covered with writing, was rolled up and thrust into the cask with bags of seed and grain, cooking utensils, and a few native-made articles, relics of Cunnembeillee's housekeeping.

They dug the few remaining potatoes from their patch and placed them with a supply of salt beef in a haversack to provision their journey. Johnny added a dried leg of wallaby, and some pieces from the trunk of a tree-like fern which was good eating when roasted. Interwoven green twigs made a crate in which the fowls could be carried. The goats had already been turned loose in the Wollondilly valley with the cattle, and at last nothing remained but to sleep one last night in the place which had been Johnny's home for nearly fourteen years.

Though the weather had been unsettled for weeks, this night was fine, and Finn slept outside. But Johnny lay on the floor of the dismantled and partly-wrecked hut, and felt misgivings swarm in the darkness. It was when night came that the white-man habits of thought which he was gradually learning wore thin, and he felt the magic and mystery of the natives come close to him. He knew that it was not only his hut that he was leaving, but his spirit-place far down the river, and for once it seemed that his white friend was less wise than the black friends who understood that a man's spirit took root in his own towri, and grew like a tree. He had tried to crush this vague fear of his uprooting, but it was strong in him now, and he put his hand to his breast where the key lay, and the necklace of buttons. Here were the symbol of his hut and the symbol of his ancestry, his link with Cunnembeillee who had brought him to his tribe, and with all his past; while they were with him he felt a little protected from that utter isolation which white men seemed to regard so lightly. He had been glad when Finn's fear that a column of smoke might betray them made him decide not to burn the hut before they left it, for while it stood some part of Johnny which would remain here had still a habitation.

But he had made one decision of his own, and he had said to his companion earlier that day:

"I come back soon, one day, fetch Ngili."

Finn, far from objecting, had agreed quickly. It had already occurred to him that a lusty young man could hardly be expected to leave his woman, and he desired anything that would keep Johnny content. Besides, he thought, native women were no idlers, and Ngili would contribute both food and work in the first critical months. It even crossed his mind that her presence might safeguard them from hostility if natives did appear, and perhaps preserve a bond between them and the tribe into which Johnny had been more or less adopted; and who could say that might not some day prove useful?

They left at dawn next morning, but before they had been walking five minutes Finn declared he had left the tinder-box behind, and sent Johnny on while he returned to perform a last task. In the gully behind the hut he stood looking at the tombstone for a moment. It was better, he thought, that no evidence should remain to identify Johnny with this spot when it was discovered—as it surely must be before long. Yet he knew that this stone with its rudely-carved words was something in which his young companion took a peculiar pride, and he had not dared to suggest defacing it. There was no time for that now; the most he could do was to disguise it, and he dragged it down, its inscription flat against the earth, and kicked a few dead branches over it. Lying thus, half-hidden, it seemed to the casual eye nothing but a slab of rock. The falling leaves and bark would soon mask it and the slight mound on which it lay.

He rejoined Johnny at the junction of the creek and the Wollondilly. The cattle and goats were rounded up, and they set off down the river, driving the animals before them. A cow and one calf were missing, but there were still seven cows and five calves. The three goats kept close to the herd, and the crate containing the fowls was part of the burden on Finn's shoulders. They could not, he was thinking, drive the cattle faster than seven or eight miles a day in this kind of country—and indeed the weight of their own loads made frequent halts necessary. But he watched the sky uneasily, and determined to push on with as little delay as possible, for the clouds were threatening, and already creeks and rivers were running deeper than usual from recent rains. They must keep as much as was practicable to the north bank of the Koornong, which became, with the river's swing northward, its east bank, for upon this side their goal lay, and if the river rose it might be days before they could cross it. He remembered with relief that though at least three sizeable rivers joined it from the south and west, it was fed upon this side only by smallish creeks. Nevertheless it was impossible to keep the cattle always on one bank; they crossed and re-crossed the river at shallow fords, avoiding those places where scrub and rocks and fallen trees barred their way, or seeking a greener pasture on the opposite side.

For the first two days the little expedition made good progress, though the sky was overcast, and there were several showers of rain. The fowls were let out to peck and forage once or twice a day, and Finn gave them a handful of wheat now and then. It was on the afternoon of the third day, when they were taking advantage of a long stretch of easy, grassy walking on the south side, that the downpour began. Finn, alarmed, said urgently:

"It's now or never we must be gettin' the animals back across the river, lad, or we're like to be stranded on this side. Divil sweep me if I ever saw rain the like of it!"

They were only just in time. Before nightfall the Koornong had overflowed those grassy banks. The cattle and goats had made off into the hills, and the two men, streaming with rain and sweat, were clambering arduously along the steep slopes, with a torrent raging below them.

They could find no better shelter than a burnt-out tree that night, and huddled together, shivering in their soaked clothes. At daybreak the rain was still pouring down, but they were glad to move, though progress had become a struggle through wild, precipitous country that dipped down to a succession of small creeks—now deep and fast-flowing—rose again in rocky terraces to a ridge-top, and plunged once more to another minor torrent. The temperature dropped suddenly; Finn's injured leg began to cause him acute pain, and he limped more than ever. Twice they were stopped by creeks too swollen to be crossed, forced farther and farther up into the hills in their search for a place to ford them, so that they found themselves far from the river, confused, with neither sun nor stars to guide them.

The animals had long ago disappeared. "Sure, they'll be makin' their way back to the river an' the good grazin' when the water falls," Finn said wearily. "It'll be runnin' off fast in this steep country, an' there's little more rain can be left in the sky now."

But there was more, and beneath it the bewildering country seemed to abandon such distinctions as it had ever made between one spot and another. Scrambling, stumbling, shivering, hungry and sleepless, Finn and Johnny plunged on through an unchanging world of sodden earth, streaming tree-trunks, slippery rocks, drenched scrub and muddily foaming creeks, bearing in their minds one thought, clinging to one solitary guide —the river. To lose it was to lose direction; and however the obstructing streams and the contours of the land pushed them away from it, they toiled back to where they could see it on their left, thundering away to the sea.

On the fifth night they crouched against a rock wall which gave them some protection from the wind, but little from the rain. Sleep was impossible, and despite their fatigue they would have preferred to struggle on, if merely to keep warmth in their bodies; but in this steep country where cliffs appeared at the feet almost without warning, they dared not move in darkness. At daylight they set out again. Their food supply was meagre, and must be husbanded. Finn, his leg stiff and painful, walked ever more slowly. Johnny, who had not been trained in foodless marches by the natives for nothing, suffered less, but he looked longingly at the fowls sometimes; bedraggled as they were, they were well fed, and in better case than the men. Finn saw his hungry glances and guarded them with a kind of dazed obstinacy, but Johnny said nothing.

On the sixth morning they found at the foot of a cliff line an overhang beneath which there was just room to lie, and they slept for a few hours, and woke to find the rain abating. They ate most of their remaining food and plodded on, a little refreshed. Finn was tortured by what he feared was rheumatism, and hoped might be merely a cramp caused by cold, exposure, and the weight of his burdens, but he had emerged from the semi-stupor of the last two days, and his eyes were thoughtful as he watched Johnny walking ahead of him. Throughout the journey the boy had maintained a stoical calm, enduring the assault of the elements with a detachment that was almost like indifference. No physical hardship, it appeared, could provoke him to the anger that one threat of coercion, or one hint of ridicule aroused so easily. Finn's memory of these past days and nights had the unreal, fragmentary quality of a nightmare, in which impressions flashed with vivid inconsequence from an obscure background of effort. He seemed to recall that once—in a terrible dawn hour when night had been endured, but morning promised no relief—he had shouted and cursed aloud, half raving with pain, sleeplessness, and hunger. And he had seen Johnny's face, gaunt, but utterly impassive, turning to look at him for a moment, and then turning away. He had felt then— for he was far past thinking—a curious reassurance. In this appalling land he was a stranger, but Johnny was at home. He took the onslaught of the weather as the trees and the rocks took it. Quieted, somehow, by that calm acceptance, Finn's moment of rage and panic had passed.

They had no idea how far they had come. Only the river, still occasionally visible far below through gaps in the trees, told them they were still on their course. Towards evening the rain ceased for an hour, and there were a few watery gleams of sunlight through the tattered clouds. At dusk, when it began to rain once more, and the prospect of another night in the open confronted him, Finn saw Johnny halt, stare, and turn with a shout. He tried to quicken his pace, but his legs had by now discovered a dull, limping rhythm of their own, and he could not vary it. He hobbled to where Johnny stood on an outcrop of rock, and looked downward over their wide valley with its surrounding rampart of cliffs. A few hundred feet below, at the foot of a long slope of scrub-covered hillside, he saw a few felled trees near a stream, and a small, square hut of bark and logs.

His knees gave way for a moment. He sat on a rock, shivering, and wondered if this miracle had happened just in time. Could he have survived another night? His whole body ached, his injured leg made every step a torment, his feet were blistered, he was chilled, and burning hot. The quick-falling twilight was coming down like a curtain over the blessed sight below.

Johnny announced:

"Get good food tomorrow." He stared ruminatively towards the river. "Snakes—always plenty snakes in flood. Soon we find the cattle, eh?"

Finn agreed drowsily.

"They'll be back to the river, an' the goats'll stick with them, I'm thinkin'. We'll find them when the weather clears . . ."

Johnny was still staring towards the river.

"Big flood like this one—down there by Green Hills—make wheat no good . . . ? Vegetables no good . . . ? Kill animals, men . . . ?"

A note of vindictive pleasure in his voice made Finn peer up at him, but in the gathering dusk he was only an outline against the sky. "I go now, quick," he said. "Make fire. You come after."

He vanished down the slope and among the scrub. Finn hoisted himself painfully to his feet and followed. Down there in the hut he would find shelter, food, warmth, and sleep, sleep, sleep . . .

*   *   *   *   *

One of the last purchases Conor had made in Sydney was a handsome journal, bound in red morocco leather, and provided with a brass clasp and a key. It was Mrs. King who had inspired this happy thought.

"I regret leaving Sydney, Ma'am," Conor had sighed. "At Beltrasna I find myself often at a loss how to pass the time."

"You should keep a journal, my love," Mrs. King responded promptly. "It's a great resource, I assure you, and passed many an hour for me on board the *Speedy* when I might otherwise have been moping."

Conor brightened.

"Patrick used to keep one when he was here, and it was certainly a great resource to him—his nose was always in it! You are quite right, Ma'am. I shall keep a journal."

So now she sat alone in her room, the door carefully closed (for it was her fancy that this journal should be very private) and scribbled busily:

"*April 26, 1806.*

"*Very wet weather this week, Toole says roads almost impassable. Last Sunday was observed in Sydney as a day of Thanksgiving for the* great Victory of Lord Nelson. This we learned from a Gentleman but recently come to the Colony, Mr. Gregory Blaxland, who rode hither to visit Mr. Mannion. He wishes to observe the methods of Agriculture in this Country, as he intends to settle here with his Brother, who has not yet arrived. Also learn that Mr. Marsden is in ill-health, and hopes soon to return to England, and that much Interest is being taken in the Appointment of Captain Bligh to succeed Governor King. Cannot hear anything of Mr. Harvey, and did not care to ask Mr. M. who was in Sydney yesterday.

"Sadly miss the life and gossip of the Town, though found some of the ladies rather finical. Try to occupy my mind with books and am reading 'The Adventures of Caleb Williams' by Mr. Godwin, which was among a parcel my grandfather directed his bookseller to send me. Am struck by passage: 'the law better adapted for a weapon of tyranny in the hands of the rich than for a shield to protect the humbler part of the community against their usurpations.' Can this be True? Indeed should be sorry to think so, but must confess many things I heard in Sydney seem to support it. Also read again 'The Romance of the Forest' and found pieces of Paper from book belonging to the convict Finn. Felt Disturbed, and wonder what befel him when he escaped from here. Have read and pondered the few words again, and cannot help feeling that they disclose a mind of some Sensibility. Have placed the fragments in this Journal, and shall keep them there. Should greatly like to hear news of Mr. Harvey.

"Julia very Wilful and Disobedient—Stephen indulges her too much. Desmond this morning sat up quite unaided—Bessie says very Forward. To-day Ellen came to me in great Agitation, saying she was no longer Trusted by Mr. M. who still suspects her of being Involved in the theft of Firearms some months ago, and begging me to Intercede for her, for she greatly fears to lose her Position here. Could not deny that Mr. M. seems unfavourably disposed towards her of late, but think he finds her too useful to think seriously of Dismissing her. Was sorry for the poor Wretch, and am surprised at myself for feeling no Animosity towards her that she was so Disobliging once, and for the other Reason. Promised to speak for her, and she wept, and talked much of her elder Son who was lost years ago, and declared that if she had been wanting in Respect to me it was because her Sorrow had made her Bitter. Said that she had been transported here with her Husband because she aided him in stealing when their child was hungry, and cried: Ma'am, you have a son too—would you not steal for him? Was greatly Distressed, and searched my Heart, and am bound to say I would. Told her she must now think of her other Children, and not mourn always for one so long Dead, and she looked at me very Strangely. Indeed she is in all respects a Strange Woman, but I think not Bad, though I should hardly know how to excuse her Conduct were I asked. Think I shall write to Mr. Harvey . . ."

On this sentence, which seemed to have written itself, she paused. It was curious how often she thought of Mr. Harvey now, and always with an eagerness that quickened and warmed her heart. She had never felt so when he was here; only the blank made by his absence told her how much she had relied on his unobtrusive and not very stimulating company. Were human beings so perverse that they valued only what they had lost? The question turned her thoughts to her husband, and her eyes clouded. For he, too, who had seemed to value her so little when her heart was open to him, had become far more attentive now that it was closed. He was often by her side now that she no longer wanted him; having chilled her, he now demanded warmth; having curbed her eager tongue, he now complained of her silence. It was too late, she thought sadly. The hurts of years cannot be assuaged by sudden attention and indulgence, nor a relationship revived which has died a slow death from a million tiny wounds.

Stephen, she thought, was growing old. To her twenty-five years, fifty-two seemed a venerable age. His greying hair, the deepening lines on his face, the twinges of pain that sometimes attacked him when he stooped, were, perhaps, warnings of the bleakness of unloved old age, and he was beginning to claim the reassurance of her devotion. She leaned her head on her hand, tracing fine, aimless lines in the margin of her journal. One injury in any life that could never be atoned was the mutilation of first love. For at that time one was all possibilities. That first, unreserved opening of the heart admitted something with the power in it to reduce unworthiness and magnify virtues; to stimulate energy and reinforce courage; to awaken in the most egotistical a capacity for selflessness, and endow the most foolish with a potential wisdom.

She had never loved Stephen, she thought, but she had been ready to love him, and in her readiness she had become, for a little while, more than her young and ignorant self. She felt obscurely that the bruising of those latent qualities was a wrong not only to herself—and perhaps not even within the compass of her forgiveness. Was it for her to say: I forgive you for robbing life of what it had lent me? I forgive you for taking and wasting that which another man might some day have valued?

Her cheeks burned and her heart beat a little faster. Oh, yes, there could be love again! But there was no return to that first inspired receptiveness when all things seemed possible, no joy quite free of sadness, no confidence undimmed by doubt, no faith entirely whole. She brushed her hand across her eyes and pushed the Journal aside. She took a sheet of paper and a new pen. She wrote carefully:

"*Dear Mr. Harvey . . .*"

And then, as if the written words had revealed to her for the first time how dear he was, she felt a kind of panic, dropped the pen, tore the paper in small fragments, and rested her head on the table to weep.

*   *   *   *   *

It was but a week or two later that a card arrived from Mr. and Mrs. Palmer, begging the company of Mr. and Mrs. Mannion at their house on May 29th. With it came a note from Mrs. King, assuring Conor that, should she and her husband be able to accept the invitation which she believed Mrs. Palmer was sending, a welcome awaited them at Government House.

Mr. Mannion glanced at the Palmers' card, and dropped it rather disdainfully on the table. He had, of course, encountered the Commissary many times in the way of business; but it was Conor's regrettable want of discrimination in receiving during her stay in Chapel Row which had, no doubt, prompted this invitation. He shrugged. After all, one must accept colonial standards to some extent, and Palmer, by reason of his very long residence in the colony, and his increasing wealth, was—by those standards—a person of some importance. He asked resignedly: "Would it amuse you, my love?"

Conor assured him quickly that it would. She was lonely, and hungry for company, but the thought had flashed through her mind, too, that she *might* see Mr. Harvey.

"We shall go, then," Mannion declared, and added, to ensure that his indulgence did not pass unmarked: "It is not altogether convenient, for the rains have delayed my sowing for the harvest, and I have much to attend to here. But I strive to please you."

He felt aggrievedly that she was difficult to please. She had been very quiet of late—silent and withdrawn, as if brooding about something. Women! Perhaps that shocking news of the murder of a stock-keeper only a few miles away at Prospect had disturbed her. All the more reason, he thought impatiently, for a little junketing to distract her mind from such sordid matters. And after all, he could employ this visit to Sydney usefully in making arrangements for the building of his "town house."

They found Mrs. Macarthur and her two daughters also staying at Government House, so there was plenty of feminine chatter, and Conor was at first innocently pleased to find such evidence that old enmities were forgotten. Among the children—two Elizabeths and two Marys—it was clear that it had never been thought of. Mary Macarthur and Elizabeth King, both eleven years old, were inseparable, and Elizabeth Macarthur, at thirteen, seemed to desire no greater happiness than to nurse the year-old Mary King. Yet Conor, talking to their mothers, imagined that she could discern beneath their amiable and lively conversation a certain constraint. It was as though this pleasant companionship which both enjoyed were shadowed by the knowledge that the feud between their husbands was still alive, however decently it might be buried for the moment.

She seemed to feel, in fact, a curious blight upon the society of the town, and an air of underlying anxiety among all her friends. Her host was rarely visible in the drawing-room. "He is beset with a number of vexatious problems," Mrs. King explained, and added with a sigh: "which, to be sure, he always is, but now more so than ever." Conor began to realise that the consequences of the flood—which had seemed to her but a wild, exciting spectacle to be watched from the safe height of her hilltop —were very serious. Rations had been reduced, and Mrs. King confided that the Governor feared they must be reduced still further, "which makes the people so discontent, my love, and King is greatly worried lest there should be—disturbances. He has ordered that everyone must stay indoors in case of alarm, and those found idling about the settlements after sunset are to be imprisoned—but I fear there is much murmuring."

Reduced rations were not, of course, for Mrs. Stephen Mannion and her friends, but she perceived that this setback to the colony's agricultural progress had its effects even upon them. She had evidence of it one day (and confirmation of her suspicion that there was an unadmitted tension between the two ladies at Government House) when she visited Parramatta with her husband, and encountered Mr. Macarthur in the street. He asked eagerly after the health of his family.

"And my dear Elizabeth? She is subject to sore throats, unfortunately. Pray remind her, Mrs. Mannion, to wear a scarf when she is out of doors. But I need not fear—my dear wife watches over her devotedly, and I shall see them all in a day or two when I am in Sydney. . . ." And then, even as Conor's heart warmed to him for his fatherly solicitude, she was suddenly and disagreeably impressed by his next words. His eyes hardened, and his voice became contemptuous and vindictive as he turned to her husband.

"Well, Sir, we're at last overwhelmed by disaster, are we not? A little common prudence and foresight—a little more encouragement to those who are in a position to cultivate their lands and maintain their stock in a large way, and the weight of this calamity would have been but slightly felt. However," he continued with a sneer, "*our friend* at Government House is to escape the consequences of his mismanagement, it seems. What a scare for the new Governor! It will be left to him to remedy matters as best he can."

"There is no news as yet when he is to arrive," Mr. Mannion remarked. Macarthur replied:

"It must be soon, I imagine. Marsden and his family are to return home with our ci-devant King. Well, those who can get off are fortunate. I said so to Piper when I wrote to tell him of this disaster." He bent forward confidentially. "By the way, Sir, I'm considering a new venture. I have purchased a brig . . ."

"I had heard of it," murmured Mr. Mannion.

"There is a trade in sandal-wood to be established in the Feegee and Friendly Islands. The master of an American vessel but recently arrived declares he has collected one hundred and twenty tons of it without difficulty. An American, Sir! Are we to permit Americans and other foreigners to reap benefits which should belong exclusively to British subjects?"

"No, indeed," agreed Mannion. "They are but little known, are they not—these Feegee Islands?"

"Their navigation is said to be intricate and dangerous. Flinders had intended to survey them, I believe. But I tell you, Sir, I burn with indignation to think that so lucrative a trade should be left in the hands of foreigners—of men whose loose and immoral characters threaten to produce the most fatal effects upon the rising generation! And who, if left to themselves—mark my words!—will attempt to capture the whole trade of the colony. I'm determined, Sir, to rescue it from their hands!"

Mr. Mannion enquired:

"You have spoken of it to the Governor?"

"I'm preparing a memorial to submit to him soon. Naturally I shall require some co-operation from him in the matter of stores. And I ask no more than I am prepared to give. I propose to offer accommodation and every facility on board my vessel if he should wish to send an officer to make a survey—provided, of course, that it would not interfere with the mercantile part of the enterprise." He added with a smile: "I think I shall obtain his concurrence. I'm not without my friends in England."

Mr. and Mrs. Mannion proceeded from this interview to the Marsdens' house, where Conor found her hostess full of excitement about their forthcoming departure.

"So very fortunate, my dear," she whispered, "that Captain Bligh has not arrived sooner, for I'm not much more than a month from my time, you know, and can now expect to be confined before we leave. Our dear Anne was born at sea in the midst of a storm—what an ordeal!—it's what I should never wish to experience again, I assure you! You have seen Mr. Fulton? He has arrived from Norfolk Island to do my husband's duty—though to be sure no one else would exert himself as Marsden has done. He was backward and forward in all weathers between here and the Hawkesbury, and occupied for days at a time after that terrible flood. Your property did not suffer, I believe?"

"The lower fields were inundated, Ma'am, but the house and the other buildings and the greater part of the land are above the level which floods would ever reach."

"You are to be envied. The havoc and distress in the Hawkesbury district were beyond description. Marsden told me many of the settlers have not a grain left, nor a place to put their heads in. Mr. Palmer lost nearly the half of his wheat, and my husband lost his brick barn and all the wheat he had saved, and indeed I think there is hardly anyone but has suffered some loss. I fear there will be a great scarcity during the winter."

Yet when the day came to repair to Mr. Palmer's celebrated mansion at Woolloomooloo, Conor could see no signs of scarcity. It was truly, as Mr. Howe said in his *Gazette*, an elegant entertainment, and the select assembly which graced it met again next day for another, equally elegant, given by the officers of H.M.S. *Buffalo*. Floating in rowing-boats over the blue waters of the harbour to Garden Island under a warm sunlight pierced pleasantly by the light, sharp breeze of early winter, and entertained with music from the band of the New South Wales Corps, Conor found it hard to believe in that other dark, grim face that life turned to her now and then. Yet she could not altogether forget it; and when the time came to return to Beltrasna without so much as a glimpse seen or a whisper heard of Mr. Harvey, she felt more forlorn than ever. But His Excellency, at parting, said rather brusquely:

"I wish I could accompany you, Mrs. Mannion. I envy you your happy seclusion at the Nepean!"

*   *   *   *   *

He left his wife, Mrs. Macarthur and the children to speed the parting guests and returned to his study for another perusal of a note from Captain Abbott which had just been brought in from Parramatta. Second only to the economic consequences of the flood, the problem of illicit stills was again exercising his mind. Several had been seized and destroyed earlier in the year, and he had expressed to Camden a hope—more faltering than his words suggested—that the summary banishment of their operators would end the practice, "at least for some time to come." He was not really surprised that it had failed to do so, and his further order, issued about a fortnight ago, had added tempting rewards to those who would lay information. Certain persons of property were, he knew, furnishing sugar and grain, and the thought of these foodstuffs—now doubly precious—being diverted to such a purpose, made him furious. He picked up from his desk the flask which had accompanied Captain Abbott's letter, and sniffed at it with a wry grimace.

Joseph Holt again—confound the fellow! King stood with the flask in one hand and the letter in the other, his eyes skimming Abbott's brief sentences. Servants of Holt had been discovered in the very act of distilling. *"Never was a place better selected and more secret . . ."* Trust that sly rogue! *"The whole of the apparatus I have got . . . about half a gallon of the new liquor, and seven casks containing about 300 gallons of wort. Holt has ackn'ged the material &c. to be his . . . has given me information where there are several others, and this night promised to put me in possession of one which he thinks is now at work . . ."*

King tossed the letter on the desk. Well—that should dispose of a few more at least. And indeed, before a week had passed, three others had been seized. The Governor flew into a rage when Holt's excuse was reported to him, for the culprit's demeanour, though respectful, had been injured, and flavoured with that subtle hint of effrontery which he knew so well how to employ. He had sustained great loss, he declared, in being sent—for no crime whatever—to Norfolk Island; and since no remuneration had been offered him to compensate for such hardship, he had conceived himself justified in making the best use he could of the products of his own farm. His Excellency swore, but was compelled to swallow Mr. Holt's impudence for the sake of Mr. Holt's assistance. And that gentleman himself, being able without difficulty to furnish the four hundred pounds required of him as security for his future good behaviour, remained at large, while his assigned servants paid for their complicity with a flogging, and prompt despatch to Castle Hill.

Yet the Governor knew, despairingly, that he was merely quelling symptoms without attacking the ill. And how these symptoms multiplied! How endless their ramifications, and in how many different shapes they appeared! Riding abroad through the settlements he observed neglected gardens, and wrestled with the thought that scarcity and hardship bred the desire for that temporary escape which liquor could supply; that alcoholic indulgence in turn bred demoralisation and attendant idleness; that idleness manifested itself in untended gardens where vegetables should be growing—and thus brought the vicious circle round to scarcity again. How to break it? Orders, penalties! Those who did not cultivate their plots, he scolded, would be deprived of them. Those who did must not have their industry brought to nothing by the improvidence of others who allowed fences to fall into disrepair, and livestock to stray. He raged and brooded. Where was that spirit of co-operation by which alone a community, in its terrible and inspiring interdependence, could be kept prosperous and stable? He tried to impose it. Orders, penalties! His carriage broke an axle in the deep ruts of the road from Sydney to Parramatta, and set him raging again. This was a public road, was it not? Were the inhabitants indifferent that their vehicles should be damaged, and their horses lamed? Must they not be made to help themselves? Orders! All carts and waggons not otherwise loaded must take a load of brickbats from the brickfields and drop them where directed by the overseer. . . . Penalties! ". . . he is to report those that do not choose to obey . . ."

He was the Governor, and he must govern. Yet exasperation with the defiance, the idleness, or the grudging service of the governed mounted in him every day. Had they no sense of duty? No regard, even, for their own interest? What was the cure for this enmity, this apathy, this mistrust which stood like a wall between his intention and his achievement? Only once, when he was too busy dictating another order to notice it, save as a meaningless caprice of his beleaguered brain, two words appeared and hung there for an instant like a picture—two words printed on either side of the sheet at the top of a half-forgotten letter . . .

"Liberté." "Egalité."

He rubbed his hand irritably across his brow. How hard it was to concentrate! How easily irrelevant fancies invaded the overtaxed brain! Mr. Blaxcell's pen was poised, his eyes enquiring. King marshalled his thoughts sternly, and went on: ". . . do hereby direct and require that every person convicted thereof be fined in the penal sum of four hundred pounds sterling, and imprisoned for the term of six calendar months . . ."

Orders—penalties! What else?

*   *   *   *   *

Towards the end of the first week in July he found, upon his return from a few days in Parramatta, that the ship Fortune had entered the port with unwelcome convicts, and welcome news. This vessel, he learned, had performed part of its voyage with H.M.S. Porpoise and the Lady Madeleine Sinclair, upon which Captain Bligh was travelling, and the arrival of the new Governor could therefore be regarded as imminent. King, well-schooled in the delays and uncertainties of ocean voyaging, set himself to wait, and pray that no further major crisis might develop before he resigned his authority into other hands. A week passed and another, and a third; and then one cold night in early August came news of a fresh rising of convicts at Castle Hill. Again His Excellency set out upon a midnight ride; again Major Johnston was ordered to follow with a detachment. But this time the alarm was groundless, and King, returning cold and weary to Sydney on the following evening, had only one more night to pass before the news arrived which he so eagerly awaited.

BOOK III

GOVERNOR BLIGH

H.M.S. *Porpoise* and the transport *Lady Madeleine Sinclair* reached Port Jackson the next day.

Captain William Bligh stood alone on the deck of the *Sinclair*, his feet planted apart to brace him against the roll of the vessel and the sharp tug of the wind, his hat under his arm, his eyes narrowed, and watering slightly in the wintry air. From here, as they passed into the harbour, there was nothing but the flagstaff on South Head and a few nondescript buildings clustered about it to provide him with an impression of the colony he was about to govern, and he spared them only a glance, which hardly interrupted the procession of his thoughts. For he was making, as he stood there, his final preparation for the office he was about to assume, and his method on this, as on previous occasions when he had known himself committed to a different task, was to marshal what knowledge he had of it, and measure it against his knowledge of himself.

His hair, which had been black in youth, was greying now, and he was growing stout. But at fifty-one he was still active, and an almost Spartan temperance of habits had preserved his health. His complexion had kept—even through a sailor's life of exposure to sun and wind—something of its natural fineness and pallor, and his strikingly blue eyes were still clear and bright. His body, he knew, was his ally. It had seen him through a four thousand mile voyage in an open boat after the mutiny on the *Bounty*, subsisting day by day on a mouthful of water, an ounce of salt pork, an ounce of bread, and an occasional teaspoonful of rum. He did not suppose that the colony of New South Wales could make any greater demand than this upon his physical endurance, so he wasted no more thought upon it, and turned instead with a kind of sober ruthlessness to an examination of his spiritual capacity.

Here he found within himself both an ally and an enemy. He acknowledged his impatience, his irritability, the arrogance of his pride, the violence of his temper, the mischief often wrought by his eloquent and ungovernable tongue. Yet he knew that these were the faults of his virtues. Filled with a passion for efficiency, he was impatient of slovenly performance; driving himself without mercy, his irritation flared against idleness; knowing his own qualities, he felt contempt for those who did not share them; conscious always of the responsibilities of his command, his rage loosed itself against those who failed him, and his tongue flayed them with bitter words. He admitted his explosive temper as a fault, but held with stubborn pride that it did not explode unprovoked; and there remained always at the root of his self-analysis a wondering sense of outrage that it should be provoked so often.

For he was a good commander. He knew that, not only from searching his heart, but as a fact supported by the most ruthless examination of his behaviour. When he had told Sir Joseph Banks that he never crossed the seas without preparing for his voyage with care and foresight, he had told nothing more than the truth, and his care had extended to his crew.

He had not sailed with Cook without learning that attention to the cleanliness of their living quarters, and even to the liveliness of their spirits, were ingredients of success no less in importance than discipline and navigation.

A frown—involuntary reaction to an old bewilderment—puckered his brow for a moment. How many commanders took, as he had taken, endless trouble to provide fiddle music for their men each evening? How many regarded it as a part of duty to dispense merriment as well as food? Captain Bligh's sense of humour was not strongly developed, and he had never yet been able to understand why an order to be cheerful should be less infallibly obeyed than an order to hoist sail. To the man who ordered fresh food to combat scurvy, ordered dripstones to filter water, ordered fires in the galley for warmth, and awnings on the deck for shelter from the sun, it seemed natural to order, also, certain hours set aside for "relaxation and mirth." And a sour look during those hours, or a foot that tripped less than nimbly to the measures of the half-blind fiddler, had roused in him the exasperation of a parent whose child fails to appreciate the benefits bestowed on him. "Why, you damned scoundrel!" he had bellowed, "will you not dance? Would you defy me, rascal? Dance, damn you, dance!"

His energy had raged at indolence; his ambition had looked with scorn upon inertia; his austerity had condemned abandonment to the ease and voluptuous delights of a South Sea paradise. His tongue, leaping too fast and too fluently to invective—even his hands, goaded by anger to an extravagance of vehement gesture—had spread hatred and resentment around him. Yet after seventeen years he had not yet learned how rarely men could look beneath the outer manner for the inner motive, and he still nursed his bitterness towards the mutineers who had cast him adrift with eighteen others, to live or die.

But only one had died. To the end of his life he would assert his right to cherish the "inward happyness and peculiar pleasure" which had sustained him during that terrible voyage. Arrogance—yes, he would not trouble to deny it. There were situations in life which could only be met by certain qualities, and he had known at the time—and still knew —that when he set out across the ocean in a deeply-laden twenty-three-foot boat, having no map and little food, relying only on his memory, his knowledge and his arrogance, he was sufficiently well-equipped. His arrogance had asserted supremacy not only over fellow-castaways, but over bad weather and high seas, over hunger, cold, cramp, sleeplessness and death itself. Yes, he was arrogant; he would not be standing here at this moment if he were not.

And, standing here, what did he confront? He pulled out of his pocket a creased and well-thumbed letter from Sir Joseph, and ran his eye over it for the hundredth time.

"*At present King, the Governor, is tired of his station; and well he may be so. He has carried into effect a reform of great extent which militated much with the interest of the soldiers and settlers there. He is, consequently, disliked and much opposed, and has asked leave to return.*

"In conversation I was this day asked if I knew of a man proper to be sent out in his stead. . . . I immediately answered: As this man must be chosen from among the post-captains I know of no one but Captain Bligh who will suit, but whether it will meet his views is another question.

"I can, therefore, if you chuse it, place you in the government of the new colony, with an income of £2,000 a year. . . . King, who is now there, receives only £1,000 with some deductions, and yet lives like a prince . . . but I could not undertake to recommend any one unless £2,000 clear was given, as I think a man who undertakes so great a trust as the management of an important colony should be certain of living well and laying up a provision for his family . . ."

Bligh looked up from his page. The vessel was running up the harbour now—the noble harbour of which he had heard so much—and his seaman's eye was appraising and appreciating it while his memory still recalled his patron's words. To lay up a provision for one's family was an important consideration—particularly when it was a family of six daughters. The beauty of the scene before his eyes awakened a familiar regret that his wife's dread of the sea should have prevented her from being at his side to share it. The thought of so long a separation from her had made him hesitate before accepting this appointment. Nor had the worldly wisdom of Sir Joseph's hint that his daughters might find eligible husbands in the colony greatly impressed him; the one he had brought—his stately, dark-eyed Mary—was already married, and accompanied by her husband. A fear that his naval career might suffer from this interlude away from active service had perturbed him too—but that matter had been satisfactorily adjusted. Two thousand pounds a year was a salary not to be lightly cast away. Bligh was a careful man in money matters; a captain who was also the purser of his ship, and expected to supplement his pay from the profits of the pursery, learned to be parsimonious, and to regard certain perquisites as the rightful reward of his position. This new post, no doubt, would also provide such perquisites. He had made his decision, and he had no doubt that he could command a colony as effectively as a ship.

Justice, energy, discipline. Of the many tasks which his Instructions laid upon him there was none, he thought, which could not be accomplished with the aid of this trinity of virtues. The peace and security of the colony—the safety and preservation of the public stores and livestock—the cultivation of lands—the distribution and management of the convicts—the conciliation of the natives—the observance of religion—the encouragement of free settlers—the granting of land—the establishment of townships—the control of the liquor traffic . . .

He frowned. He had talked with Sir Joseph and others who were in touch with the colony, or returned from it. He knew that Hunter had been recalled for his failure to fulfil this particular instruction. Yet, after all—Hunter! He recollected that fifteen years ago when he had anchored in Table Bay during his second bread-fruit voyage, he had found there the Dutch snow *Waaksamheyd* with Hunter on board. He had heard a

good deal of the colony on that occasion, and had formed no very flattering opinion of the man who had later become its Governor. A dull
fellow, without sufficient intelligence or steadfastness of purpose to follow
a line clearly laid down for him. For was not the instruction perfectly
explicit? "... *we do therefore strictly enjoin you, on pain of our utmost
displeasure, to order and direct that no spirits shall be landed from any
vessel coming to our said settlement without your consent . . ."*

Captain Bligh, who exacted literal obedience to his own orders from
his own subordinates, was at all times ready to obey his superiors with
similarly unquestioning zeal. He had said so plainly in his address to the
Court during that business of the *Warrior* only last year. "I candidly
and without reserve avow," he had declared, "that I am not a tame and
indifferent observer of the manner in which officers placed under my
orders conduct themselves in the performance of their several duties; a
signal or any communication from any commanding officer have ever been
to me an indication for exertion and alacrity to carry into effect the
purport thereof . . ."

And here in his Instructions was a plain command from no less a
person than his Sovereign. He would obey it. And he would see that
he was, in turn, obeyed.

*   *   *   *   *

His first glimpse of Sydney caused him a pang of disappointment for
which, he realised, the beauty of its harbour approaches was responsible.
One should not enter so noble a haven only to find so insignificant a town.

He stood beside his daughter while the *Sinclair* cast anchor in the
cove, and studied it silently. Mary, dear child, was full of excitement;
and well she might be, for the voyage—what with her illness, and bad
weather, and the atrocious conduct of that ruffian Captain Short of the
Porpoise—had been a trying one. He patted her hand as it lay on the
rail beside his own. She cried eagerly:

"Look, Papa, there's a boat coming out to us!"

He glanced at it and nodded, but his eyes went back to the town. It
sprawled over the low hills, scattered and shabby, its patches of grass
winter-faded, its skyline broken only by a couple of windmills, a couple
of flagstaffs, and a fringe of ragged trees on the eastern shore. It had an
air of awkward immaturity, at once pathetic and repellent. Where
streets were suggested by rows of buildings, they had a curious aimlessness,
a haphazard lack of direction; the town, like a gauche child, over-conscious
of its hands and feet, seemed unable to control them. Clusters of buildings by the water's edge, and wharves jutting out from them, bore witness
to mercantile activity which seemed incongruous when the eye, in the
same glance, took in a farther sweep of untouched, rocky shore where a
naked savage stood at gaze with a spear in his hand. H.M.S. *Buffalo*,
lying at anchor nearby, was part of a familiar world which dimmed as a
bark canoe came into sight, and its black occupants lifted wooden paddles
to salute them. Captain Bligh had seen many strange lands, many odd
communities, and many kinds of savages—but always in passing. The
knowledge that this land was to be his home for some years, this com-

munity his to govern, these savages a part of his responsibility, lent his scrutiny an almost painful intentness. Here was a place not only to be observed, but lived in; a people not only to be appraised, but lived with. His eyes, searching the scene, were searching for himself in it.

The boat they had seen putting out from the shore had reached the vessel by now. The two gentlemen who came aboard introduced themselves as Major Johnston, of the New South Wales Corps, and Captain Houston of the *Buffalo*. They conveyed Governor King's congratulations to Captain Bligh upon his safe arrival, and explained that His Excellency hoped for the pleasure of a private visit from him later in the day.

Bligh acknowledged these civilities with the jerky bow of the shortish and stoutish man.

"My compliments to His Excellency. Glad to avail myself of his invitation." He drew Mary forward. "Permit me to present you to my daughter, gentlemen. Mrs. Putland."

The Major and the Captain, straightening from their bows, allowed their eyes to linger appreciatively for a moment. They saw a small head set proudly on a long, graceful neck, a high, white forehead, a pair of dark, heavy-lidded eyes, a straight nose, and a shapely mouth which suggested more than a little determination. The stocky, fresh-complexioned father, thought Mr. Johnston, looked what he was—a sailor; but whatever he might lack in grace and dignity as the occupant of Government House would be found in this imperious young beauty.

"How glad I shall be to go ashore!" she exclaimed. "Is that Government House, Major?"

"It is, Ma'am."

"Pray point out to me the other principal buildings, Sir."

"Gladly, Ma'am. The windmill you see on the hill behind Government House belongs to the Commissary, Mr. Palmer. The Parade Ground and the Barracks are up yonder a little to the right, near the Church—which is not yet completed, however. Up there, Captain, on the western hill are the fortifications which were commenced some two years ago. The site, you notice, commands the town, the harbour and a considerable extent of the surrounding country. But perhaps of more interest to you, Ma'am, will be the building you can see there below the Church—the Orphanage, Ma'am, which is largely the benevolent concern of the ladies of the colony . . ."

"The wharves," remarked Bligh abruptly, "seem to be in some disrepair—except that one yonder with the dwelling and other buildings nearby."

There was a slight pause.

"That is Mr. Campbell's wharf, Sir," Johnston explained with a hint of coldness in his tone. "He is a merchant—at present in England, but expected here shortly . . ."

Bligh said "Ha!" and shot a quick glance at him. He had picked up a good many fragments of gossip about the commercial feuds of this place, and he knew that the officers of the New South Wales Corps had not welcomed the appearance of independent traders who threatened their monopoly. Already, in that moment of silence, and that faint chilling of the Major's voice, he seemed to have touched the fringe of such a feud.

*   *   *   *

When the new arrivals stepped ashore His Excellency was at the wharf to greet them, and escort them to Government House. Mrs. King, in whom there had stirred momentarily a twinge of jealousy of the handsome young woman who was to supplant her, and whose modish gown made her conscious of how long she had been absent from the world of fashion, succumbed quickly to her natural kind-heartedness, and drew the girl down beside her on the sofa.

"How thankful you must be to have the voyage behind you!" she cried. "Are you affected by the motion of the vessel, my love? I am not myself, but I am so great a coward that I'm always a prey to a thousand fears when at sea."

Her husband enquired, drawing a chair forward for Bligh:

"You had a stormy passage from the Cape, I believe, Captain?"

"Damnable, Sir!" Bligh glowered. "The whole voyage—abominable! If not stormy weather, damned stormy situations! That fellow Short—intolerable behaviour! Disputed my authority! Fired a shot across our bows, Sir, when I altered the course of the *Sinclair*! And another astern . . . !"

Lieutenant Putland turned from the window to add sharply:

"And made me do it!"

"Gracious Father!" exclaimed Mrs. King, clasping her hands.

"Yes, indeed, Ma'am," Mrs. Putland corroborated. "Putland was the officer of the watch on the *Porpoise*, you see. But can you conceive such inhumanity as making a man fire upon his own wife? For I assure you he ordered a third shot prepared to fire into us—did he not, Putland?—unless we bore down immediately!"

"A low fellow!" Bligh's face had reddened with anger, and his blue eyes were fierce. "A deuced violent, vicious, evil-disposed rascal! I shall have him court-martialled, Sir. My daughter's health suffered severely from the distractions caused by his outrageous behaviour!"

But Mrs. Putland protested quickly:

"It was you who suffered, Papa." She turned to her hostess. "I am ashamed, Ma'am, that I should have added to Papa's burdens by my own fears. But I was indisposed, and often quite alone—for Captain Short kept Putland so much on the *Porpoise*—and there was only Papa to attend me, for my maid was ill also . . ." She smiled with a sudden and unexpected impishness. "All the same, I declare that sick as I was I could not refrain from laughing to see him so busy at our cabin fire making my sago and barley-water! And we were sometimes merry enough—were we not, Papa?—playing backgammon as well as we could, with the board slipping and sliding . . ." She looked round the long room, sighed contentedly, and turned to the Governor. "But that's all past now, and oh, how good it is to sit in a room again, with a big fire on the hearth! You are very comfortable here, Sir, are you not?"

"He is not comfortable anywhere of late," Mrs. King interjected ruefully. "He has been most unwell, with the gout flying about him so that he has little rest at night . . ."

King waved his hand irritably.

"My health is indifferent, it's true. And it has not been improved, I assure you, by the cares of office."

"H'm!" Bligh glanced at him keenly. "You find the post of Governor exacting, Sir?"

"Exacting!" King laughed unmirthfully. "Though I'd not wish to damp your spirits at the outset, my friend, it's but an act of charity to warn you that this place is a veritable Hell!"

Mrs. Putland's eyes went quickly from His Excellency's face to Mrs. King's, and thence to her father's. He was sitting in the attitude she knew so well, his feet planted squarely in front of him, his hands resting on his knees—but ready to move suddenly in expressive and emphatic gesture—his head held up, and still, but with a suggestion of listening alertness, his eyes attentive. Her momentary qualm subsided. All her life she had known that Papa was equal to any emergency. All her life Mama had assured her and her sisters that there was no ill-fortune, no opposition, no malice or perfidy which Papa could not overcome. And it was true. One of the early recollections of her childhood was the tale of that wicked man, Fletcher Christian, who had conspired with other rogues not only to murder Papa, but to smirch his honour; and Papa, by his valour and nobility, had frustrated their evil plans, and emerged victorious. . . . She looked at Governor King with a hint of pitying condescension. Poor man! He had done his best, no doubt—but he was not Papa!

She rose to join her husband where he stood staring out at the harbour, and Mrs. King came to stand beside them and point out the different spots of interest. Lieutenant Putland contributed but little to the conversation, and his wife's eager eyes clouded as she looked at him. He was not robust, and had been troubled of late with a distressing cough. She looked out at the brilliant sunshine and reflected hopefully that this climate, which was said to be so beneficial to health, would soon restore him. How blue and sparkling the water! How strangely dull, by contrast, the tree-clothed shores opposite! How odd those crude native canoes, and—la!—was not that one yonder on fire?

"No, no, my love," laughed Mrs. King. "The natives frequently light fires on flat stones which they keep in the canoes, and cook the fish as they catch them."

"Mercy, how strange!" cried Mrs. Putland. "Pray come, Papa, and look . . ."

But when she turned the room was empty. The Governor and the Governor-elect had withdrawn for a private interview.

* * * * *

Bligh was thinking as he followed his host to the study that Sir Joseph had evidently understated the case when he wrote that King was tired of his situation. He was more than tired of it—he was defeated. He would make no such admission, but during their long conclave over the stacks of papers on the desk, Bligh thought that he betrayed it in a defensive irascibility, an over-emphasis upon his difficulties, a sharpening of his voice and manner when he spoke of abuses not yet overcome, a shadow of hostility beneath his air of eagerness to co-operate with a successor who might succeed where he had failed.

But later, watching him sink into an armchair near the fire, and draw a stool forward to support his foot, Bligh amended his first impression, acknowledging that this man might be beaten not by his task alone, but by his task combined with bodily ill-health. It was a welcome reflection; conscious of the rewards of his own temperance and physical self-discipline, he counted to himself at least one advantage over his predecessor.

He said abruptly:

"A Hell, you said, Sir. I will stand, by your leave. Prefer it. Pray enumerate your devils. The liquor traffic we have spoken of—among the first of them, eh?"

"I've got it down to a considerable extent," King replied. "At some later time we shall go more fully into the measures I've adopted. For the present I shall say only that every effort is made to circumvent them, and one needs a hundred eyes like Argus to detect the machinations that are employed. A word upon another matter . . ."

A restless movement of his shoulders, and a sudden nervous twitch of his mouth betrayed to his companion's keen gaze a man ridden by an obsession. Bligh paced the room with his hands clasped behind his back, and let the silence extend, knowing that one who speaks from an emotional compulsion speaks unguardedly, and reveals much—not only of his subject, but of himself. And King went on at last:

"We have many troublesome characters here. The ordinary felons—they are one thing. But this place has been deluged with disaffected persons—predominantly Irish—who need careful watching. Keep an eye on Maurice Margarot, Sir—the last of his particular set, thank God, for the others have either died or left the colony. An intriguer, who has done his utmost to assassinate my character. . . . And a certain Michael Robinson, a lawyer—and a disgrace to that honourable profession! He was taken into the Judge Advocate's office, and there succeeded in keeping the whole town in a state of continual litigation and discord. I judged it best to pack him off to Norfolk Island—where I also sent another Irish rascal called Maum. No Governor's dignity or reputation can be safe with such miscreants at large. You've heard of the notorious Sir Henry Brown Hayes, I don't doubt? A fellow of unsurpassed arrogance, embittered towards me because I've treated him as the felon he is. He had a house in Sydney, and some three years ago purchased a farm which he calls Vaucluse, near the South Head, but he can't live quiet and has been forward in every secret attack upon my character. I sent him also to Norfolk Island, but judged it wise to separate him from Maum—for while they're in association their heads will be together concocting lying and slanderous attacks upon my administration to send home. He's here now—for the moment only, as I propose sending him to Van Diemen's Land. There are others of the same sort—you will soon discover them!

They openly boast of being employed in sending home secret information upon the state of the colony. Margarot had the effrontery to declare that he is authorised to report upon my conduct to no less a person than . . ." King glanced round to assure himself that the door was shut, and then leaned forward to whisper an illustrious name. He sat back, glaring, and flung his hands out in an angry gesture.

"You see, Sir! The lower class felon is bad enough. But these incendiaries who have been in better circumstances—and some in situations of high respectability—come here burdened by no sentiments of loyalty to the authority of the King's representative. From their superior station in life which they have so disgracefully betrayed, they meet with some attention, and believe me, not one of them would scruple to inflame those more ignorant than themselves should the opportunity occur . . ."

Bligh said "H'm!" again, and planted himself with his back to the fire. He had learned a little about a few people in his domain, and a good deal about the Governor he was to succeed. King was morbidly sensitive to an attack upon his dignity. He expected deference. He was nervous of these educated rebels and exiles, and apprehensive of what they might say of him in their unofficial despatches to their friends at home. He was often harsh in his judgments and his punishments—not because he was by nature ruthless, but because to defy his authority was to wound his vanity—and that must be revenged. Captain Bligh had already heard, during this interview, something of the insurrection at Castle Hill, and of the hangings and floggings that had followed. His Excellency's passing reference to several punishments of one thousand lashes each had set the erstwhile Captain of the *Bounty* pondering. He had been reared from childhood in the Navy; he took floggings for granted, and the severity of these particular punishments did not so much shock him as halt his thoughts for a moment upon the knowledge that he—the tyrannical monster against whom his men had mutinied—had never ordered more than forty-eight to any member of his crew upon that ill-fated voyage . . .

Yet he conceded that a colony was not a ship. Upon a ship each man had his appointed place and duty; but in this colony there seemed to be no recognisable pattern . . .

He frowned. He liked a pattern. It was clear that his impression earlier in the day of skirting a feud had been correct. He had already learned much from King—notably that no relationship existed between any two classes—and hardly even between any two individuals—which did not contain at least the elements of a feud. That did not dismay him. He was by nature belligerent, and had never hesitated to fight out an issue. But he liked to have the issue clear. He liked black to be black, and white white. Evil men should be neatly ranged on the side of evil, while good men opposed them stoutly from the stronghold of virtue. And since virtue, to Captain Bligh, was synonymous with duty, and duty had always seemed to him, as a naval officer, a clear and well-lighted path, he was angered and confused by a tale in which values shifted, allegiance veered, men were found now upon one side, and now upon another, and the name of duty was infallibly invoked to justify a score of contradictory aims.

Where then was the pattern? He liked order. He liked to have a chart, a compass, a well-disciplined crew, and a destination. Well, the first he had. His Instructions should be his chart. And the compass his own resolve, pointing inflexibly towards duty. His destination was the day when he should quit this colony, honourably relieved of his responsibility, secure in the knowledge of a task successfully performed. There remained the crew . . .

"You are about to make an annual muster, I think you said?"

King nodded. "It's proceeding."

"What is your estimate," Bligh asked, "of the total population?"

"Something about eight thousand—of whom the great majority, of course, are in Sydney, Parramatta, and the Hawkesbury districts."

Bligh abandoned his metaphor in some haste. A crew of eight thousand was something which a tidy-minded seaman could not contemplate, even as a wayward fancy. His thoughts jumped from this amorphous, unknown community to a single member of it, of whom he had heard much; and as the name of John Macarthur crossed his mind he had a curious, fleeting impression that another—Fletcher Christian—walked beside it like a shadow.

He began to pace the room again.

"Your personal account of some of the leading inhabitants would be of value to me," he suggested, and King, refreshing himself with a sip from the glass at his elbow, was nothing loth to oblige him. As he talked Bligh stumped about the room, halting now and then to stare, gesticulate, or explode into a brief outburst of profanity. And the Governor, sprawling back in his chair, observed him sardonically, quite unaware that history was repeating itself. Hunter, watching King as Governor-elect, had thought bitterly: "He will learn!" And King, watching Bligh, was wondering as he talked how long it would take this turbulent colony to wear down that restless vigour, to slow that active step, to assail that arrogant self-confidence, and to match that evident vehemence of temperament with its own intractable violence. His dry and rather malicious humour found a certain enjoyment in favouring his successor with brief, pungent sketches of the military and civil officers, and he gave his sharp tongue free rein. He described his Lieutenant-Governor's placid and peace-loving disposition against its tormenting background of strife; he sketched Major Johnston cynically: ". . . one of our leading nabobs—the squire of Annandale. An easy-going numbskull, popular with his men, a tool in the hands of those more quick-witted than himself . . ." He touched upon Abbott: ". . . a reliable officer who does his duty and keeps out of trouble—as much as anyone can do in this place . . ." He mentioned Piper: ". . . commanding at Norfolk Island just now, in the absence of Foveaux—an agreeable young man who behaves more honourably than most . . ." He dismissed Palmer with a shrug. "He does well enough as Commissary—though better still as miller, farmer, shipowner and cattle-breeder. 'Little Jack' they call him in the Corps, where he is not greatly in favour." He spoke indulgently of Arndell, caustically of Surgeon Jamison, Mr. Wentworth and Mr. Atkins: ". . . an old reprobate, Sir, who knows less about the law than I do!" He described with an irritated contempt some of the junior officers of the Corps, but spared a tribute to Mr. Robert Campbell. "It will be a good day for the colony when he returns. A man of some character, Sir, and in my opinion the only merchant whose dealings have been upright . . ." He chuckled over Harris: "Our hearty friend Pat Ultimo—a bluff, rough, engaging fellow who enjoys a bottle with his cronies . . ." He recounted the labours and explorations of Mr. Caley: ". . . by no means of that placid temperament one might expect in one who spends his time amid the beauties of Nature. I have endured him for the sake of our good friend Sir Joseph, who finds him useful. Indeed Sir Joseph himself declared to me that had Caley been born a gentleman he would long ago have been shot in a duel—and he may yet meet that unhappy end if he remains here, where gentility is a curiously ill-defined quality."

Perversely, he had omitted the name which was in both their thoughts. His sharp tongue passed on instead to a piquant dissertation upon the origins and private lives of various leading members of the community; but Bligh's expression remained one of intent and unsmiling concentration, and King was forced to enjoy his wit alone. "It has been suggested, Sir, to lock up all unmarried females until they can obtain husbands, but I fear . . ."

Bligh interrupted:

"And Mr. Macarthur? I've been favoured with some accounts of him . . ."

Suddenly the note of bitterness behind King's jibing tone sounded more clearly.

"Ah, yes! Our hero of the fleece! Jack Bodice! You must judge for yourself, Sir. You'll have ample opportunities to do so, for you'll meet him at every turn. Poor Hunter called him a busybody—and other names less mild. Patience, my dear Sir! You'll be suitably greeted by the principal inhabitants when you have taken office—and foremost among them you may be sure will be found Mr. Macarthur." His Excellency took a sip from his glass, and added with a kind of meditative zest: "With the manner of a turtle-dove, the cunning of a fox, the stubbornness of a mule, and the rapacity of a shark!"

"Rogues have cooed at me before now," snapped Bligh, "and I have known them for rogues." He returned to the fireplace and stood with one arm along the mantelpiece, frowning at his host.

"And the free settlers? They shall be my main concern. What temper are they in?"

King shrugged.

"In general a surly one. The flood has occasioned a good deal of distress. And there are some among them who were strongly tinctured with the pernicious democratic spirit of the times before ever they left England, and who have introduced it among their fellows. I've been swift to check such tendencies when they appeared, but they are a danger to be borne in mind. " He yawned. "I have almost completed a full statement of the affairs of the colony, Sir, which may serve to inform you on many matters. Allow me to escort you upon a tour of the grounds before the evening grows too cold. The ladies will perhaps accompany us . . ." He hoisted himself painfully to his feet. "Upon your formally taking office, Sir, I propose to retire to the Government House at Parramatta until such time as the *Buffalo* is ready to sail. There, I need hardly say, I shall be at your service. And any attention my wife can pay to your amiable daughter . . ."

He ushered his guest from the room, still talking.

    *   *   *   *   *

A few days were to intervene before the new Governor formally superseded the old, and Bligh spent them at Government House. While the ladies occupied themselves in preparing for the change in tenancies, Mrs. King initiated Mrs. Putland into the complexities of colonial society, enlightened her in confidential undertones concerning domestic irregularity in certain households, warned her that this tradesman was an extortioner, that lady a malicious gossip, most of the gentlemen likely to thwart and embarrass her Papa as much as they could, and everyone sadly given to unprincipled intrigue. And over the paper-strewn desk behind the closed door of the study the retiring Governor and the Governor-elect held further long and exhaustive discussions upon the administration of the colony, and measured each other as they did so.

It was not difficult, while every hour's conversation added fresh proof of the burdens a Governor must assume, to agree that a man who under-took so onerous a task was entitled to more generous recompense than his salary provided; and during those few days Bligh became, by a scratch of King's pen, the owner of three properties comprising some thousand acres of his new domain. King spoke of the grants he had made to his children, and of cattle and other stock which he would leave behind him in the care of Mr. Rowland Hassall. Bligh said roundly:

"If Macarthur and Davidson and Blaxland and others are to have land so lavishly granted them, I conceive that we may claim similar indulgences —with more reason. I shall take the question up with Sir Joseph. Like yourself, Sir, I have a family to consider."

King nodded. He had plans for another grant to his wife, and was pleased to find that his successor saw eye to eye with him in this matter. They had enough in common to ensure amicable relations, and the differences they discovered caused no friction, since each believed that they favoured himself. They combined in deploring the unrestful spirit which was infecting the common people with such rebellious notions, and in the conviction that a firm hand was needed to keep them down. They shared a belief in the rightness and efficiency of their social order, its natural and inevitable cleavage into upper and lower classes. They were at one in their regard for their common friend and patron, Sir Joseph. If King privately considered that Bligh was a humourless fellow, Bligh found King's satirical flippancy misplaced. When the conversation touched upon the imprisonment of Flinders, King, aware of a momentary tension, decided with inward amusement that Bligh was not guiltless of jealousy towards the young man who had rivalled him as a navigator; and when it revealed how far beyond control the liquor problem still remained, Bligh told himself with complacency that King, for all his bold words, had allowed himself to be duped and intimidated.

Mutual esteem thus pleasantly salted with a few inward reservations, the interviews passed so satisfactorily that upon the day appointed for the formal transfer of authority, the ceremonials passed off in an agreeable atmosphere of cordiality. Guns thundered a salute as Bligh left the *Sinclair* to board the *Porpoise* and hoist his pennant; they thundered again when he left the *Porpoise* for the *Buffalo*, which received and farewelled him with further salvoes. Startled gulls rose wheeling and screaming from the quiet harbour; natives came down on the rocks to stare, and the populace of the town assembled to watch him step ashore at the Government Wharf. The New South Wales Corps and the Sydney Loyal Association, under arms and with the colours of the regiment flying, lined the path leading from the wharf to Government House, and through this lane King, attended by the Civil staff, passed down to welcome his successor as though they had never met before. Compliments and congratulatory speeches exchanged, they returned together to the house, where the civil and military officers were gathered to meet and greet the new Governor. But despite the pomp and parade—despite the ritual of loyal welcome—the new Governor, as he acknowledged each introduction, was noting names, remembering rumours, studying faces, and thinking to himself: "Enemy . . . ?" "Friend . . . ?" "Enemy . . . ?"

*   *   *   *   *

A happy reunion was taking place meanwhile at Elizabeth Farm, for one of the passengers upon the *Porpoise* had been the Macarthurs' eldest son, Edward. His mother studied this seventeen-year-old lad whom she had not seen for eleven years with a kind of incredulity. How the years had flown! The sight of him took her back to a time when she had been the young wife of an obscure lieutenant, and he an ailing infant; when this country, which was now so securely their home and the source of their prosperity, had been all strangeness and wonder; when Governor Phillip, inviting her with his stiff courtesy to dinner at Government House, had assured her that though the other guests must bring their own bread, there would always be a roll for Mrs. Macarthur.

She laughed at the quaint thought that bread had once been so precious, and then sighed, astonished to discover in herself a faint nostalgia for that time of their humble beginnings as colonists. She had found it pleasant, for all its uncertainty and hardship—studying botany with the grave and thoughtful Mr. Dawes, picking out tunes on Mr. Worgan's piano, strolling by the harbour shores with that amusing Captain Tench, exclaiming over the odd customs of the natives, gathering wildflowers and collecting shells from the harbour beaches. . . . How young and carefree she had been!

And how seldom, in the busy, intervening years she had spared more than a passing thought to comparison of the past and the present! How gradually the strangeness and the wonder had merged into acceptance, and the unfamiliar had grown commonplace! Observing the transformation in dear Edward (though even now he did not look robust), she realised as if for the first time the deeper transformation which those years had wrought in herself.

Disturbed by a sudden sharpening of that dim regret for an uncomplicated past, she disciplined her thoughts. What miracles Macarthur had wrought, to be sure! How wonderful his grasp of affairs, which had raised them from poverty and obscurity to wealth and influence! Surely it was obvious that the views of a man who could so rapidly advance his own fortunes were worth attention? Why, then, she wondered, should he meet with so much hostility? For even the joy of having Edward once more beneath the parental roof could not blind her to the fact that there was an increasing unrestfulness in the air, and that the very tolerably serene relationship which had lately existed between Elizabeth Farm and Government House was threatened once again. Macarthur had very grave misgivings about Captain Bligh, whose reputation as a martinet had preceded him; and among all the friends who gathered at her house she observed the same uneasiness.

Were they never to enjoy peace? She knew that there was discontent among the settlers—that black looks often followed her husband, and that vulgar and offensive jests were made about "Jack Bodice." Observing her comfortable and well-ordered home, its thriving gardens and orchards, its flourishing fields, its sleek, well-tended livestock, she thought rebelliously that if only the man by whose wisdom, energy and enterprise all this had been achieved, could replace the bunglers who had reigned at Government House, all would soon be well! How was it that an ungrateful colony should treat so scurvily one whose singular talents and lofty principles it ought surely to cherish and admire?

She was no politician. Her husband—a pattern of all wisdom and virtue—was busy prophesying woe, and she did not doubt that now, as always, he was right. She noted that he, with his customary magnanimity, was prepared to do his part in obliterating the memory of past differences with the late Governor and establishing cordial relations with the new one, for he signed, on behalf of the free inhabitants, addresses to both King and Bligh which could not have been more amiable and conciliatory. Confidence was expressed that the new Governor would promote the happiness of all deserving people (and who, thought the mistress of Elizabeth Farm, more deserving than dear Macarthur?) Assurances were given that the signatories and those whom they represented would regard the laws with reverence, and cheerfully acquiesce in such measures as His Excellency might deem necessary. What more, thought Mrs. Macarthur innocently, could any Governor expect or desire?

Yet the atmosphere was not tranquil. To add to Macarthur's anxieties, Captain Abbott had sent him news that a band of runaway convicts—dangerous desperadoes, four of whom were armed with muskets—were in the neighbourhood of the Cow Pastures, and bent upon destroying his cattle. Doubtless they would be apprehended by the party Captain

Abbott had sent in pursuit—but it was all very disturbing. And somehow Mrs. Macarthur felt a little put out by the way Mrs. King and the
newly-arrived Mrs. Putland had taken to each other, and were always
exchanging visits. Mrs. Putland was generally allowed to be a charming
and accomplished young lady, but reports of her father were conflicting;
Mrs. Macarthur, from her own observation, considered that his manner and
deportment left much to be desired, and would reflect little credit upon
Government House. Some, it was true, found him civil—but others
declared him to be intolerably rude; some described him as a lively and
interesting conversationalist—but others deplored the coarseness and profanity of his speech; some told of courteous attention to their requests—
but others asserted they had met with nothing but vulgar and overbearing
abuse.

Upon one thing, however, all were agreed: he was no idler. Before
the middle of September arrived he had descended upon Parramatta,
scoured it from end to end, pried into public works and institutions,
harangued the officials, catechised the inhabitants—and passed on to inspect
the agricultural settlement at Castle Hill, leaving the town still quivering.
To Mr. Macarthur and his friends such determined zeal boded no good;
wherever they foregathered the opinion was already being expressed that
they had exchanged one tyrant for another who might well prove worse.

*   *   *   *   *

King, now installed with his family in the Government House at
Parramatta, took to his bed. It seemed unlikely that the *Buffalo* could
sail before the end of September, and for the moment he abandoned himself to his gout, and continued his intercourse with Bligh by letter. He
was tired, ill, and in almost continual pain—even his right hand was
sometimes unequal to the task of writing. His wife was his amanuensis
until Mr. Marsden recommended to him a young man called James Hardy
Vaux—that same picturesque convict who had once regaled Mr. Harvey
with an account of his adventures—and with this assistance the ex-
Governor was able to employ himself in the arrangement of his private
papers and accounts, and watch the colony from afar with a grateful sense
of detachment.

It persisted even when, partially recovered, he visited Sydney early in
September to greet the Patersons, who had arrived on a visit from Port
Dalrymple. His faint feeling of chagrin at being no longer the fount of
authority was overborne by the luxury of discarded responsibility, and he
watched his successor's abounding energy with a certain cynical amusement.

Bligh had taken prompt measures to allay the distress of the smaller
settlers; Government, he announced, would grind corn for individuals
provided they paid every eleventh bushel into the public stores for the
relief of impoverished Hawkesbury families; bullocks from the Government
herds would be slaughtered to provide fresh meat which need not be paid
for until after the coming harvest. The more fortunate inhabitants were
invited to assist by delivering contributions of food into the stores, and
individuals were exhorted not to hoard grain.

King watched the inauguration of a daily routine at Government House

which would have taxed the strength of a man much younger than Bligh
—and indeed his secretary, the nineteen-year-old Mr. Griffin, often
emerged from long hours in the study looking wan. Soon after daybreak
His Excellency was abroad inspecting the town, and returned to spend
another hour before breakfast receiving reports, petitions and complaints
from anyone who chose to wait upon him. From breakfast-time till a three
or four-o'clock dinner he was closeted with Mr. Griffin, and frequently
disappeared again in the evening for another two hours at his desk. His
table, for King's taste, was over-simple. The ex-Governor, very conscious
of his own failing health, and the contrasting vigour of one four years his
senior, remarked rather acidly to his wife that Captain Bligh was a man
who made vices of his virtues.

*   *   *   *   *

Late in September, on the eve of setting out upon a longer tour of
inspection, Bligh was presented with another address which gave him food
for thought. He paused in his preparations to re-read certain passages
with close attention. The free inhabitants of Sydney begged to state their
ignorance of the former addresses to King and himself lately published in
the Gazette, and signed, ostensibly on their behalf, by Mr. John Macarthur.
". . . nor do we hesitate in saying that it never was our intention to
address the former; and that we consider such addresses being signed for
us by a person undeputed and unauthorised as an infringement on our
rights and privileges . . ." Bligh ruminated. They had not desired to
present farewell compliments to King. And they were evidently no friends
of Jack Bodice. ". . . we beg to observe that had we deputed anyone,
John Macarthur would not have been chosen by us, we considering him
an unfit person to step forward upon such an occasion, as we chiefly
attribute the rise in the price of mutton to his withholding the large flock
of wethers he now has to make such price as he may choose to demand . . ."
The Governor, pondering this fresh evidence of discord, finished his
preparations for departure and made his farewells to his daughter.

"How long will you be away, Papa?"

"A week at the least—there's much ground to cover, and a devilish
amount of confusion and mismanagement to be overcome if accounts are
true. But you'll not be lonely with the good Mrs. King. When does she
arrive?"

"To-morrow, Papa, and of course I shall not be lonely, for there's a
great deal to be done here, and I want to collect some shells to send Mama,
and no doubt there will be callers . . ."

"Recollect, Mary—civility to all, but no particular attention to anyone.
Government House must not lend itself to any party." He kissed her.
"But you should have some companions of your own age, my dear, for
I fear you must miss your sisters."

"There is Mrs. Mannion who lives somewhere near the Nepean, Papa,
and several other ladies among the officers' wives—oh, I shall find friends
soon, never fear!"

"Later," he promised, "when I have things in better train, you shall
accompany me on a tour of the country. And, Mary—see the man who

was to prepare an emu egg to send your Mama, or it may not be ready. Good-bye, my love, and pass your time pleasantly."

The long ride to the Hawkesbury seemed twice its length, for there was much for the Governor to see. The little cavalcade which attended him was frequently halted while he paused to inspect a field, a hut, a dilapidated barn, a bridge damaged by the rising of its creek, a vegetable garden, a litter of pigs in a settler's yard. Several times His Excellency dismounted and vanished into some modest dwelling, whence his stentorian voice could be heard rapping out questions, and from which he presently emerged with the family at his heels, the man startled and awkward, but with the dawning of a bewildered and uncertain hope in his eyes; the children all stares and bashful grins; the woman, quicker to recover her wits, ready with a bobbing curtsey, and "God save Your Honour!" Sometimes a settler working in his field, or a housewife spreading clothes on a bush to dry, was peremptorily summoned to an interview by the roadside.

"What is the quality of your soil, my man? How many bushels did you harvest last year? How many do you expect this year? What labour do you employ? Are you aware that you can procure seed maize from the Commissary at Parramatta? Are these all your children, my good woman? Do they attend the school? They must do so. The boy looks puny. Hungry? Confound it, Ma'am, your name should be on the list of the storekeeper at the Hawkesbury—you can be furnished with meat immediately, for which you will pay in grain when your harvest is got in. You, sir! Your barn needs repair—see to it! Child, come here! What is your name? Do you say your prayers? That's well, that's all very well, but you should comb your hair also—it looks very ill so tangled . . ."

His mood changed and his tone varied, but his energy never flagged. Not only those whom he encouraged and commended, but those whom he fiercely rebuked were left shaken—lifted by his vitality from the dull and unhopeful monotony of their lives. Sometimes he left resentment behind him; sometimes a black look followed him as he rode off; sometimes a man, smarting from the lash of a merciless tongue, cursed under his breath as he turned back to work. But even for these the day was not as other days. Something had happened; there was a new force in the land.

And Bligh rode on and on indefatigably, barking his questions, roaring his rebukes, snapping out brief commendations, inviting complaints.

"If you have grievances, state them! Damn it, am I a magician? The door of Government House stands open to any man! Good-day to you— and let that fence be mended before I pass this way again!"

At the Hawkesbury he found himself possessed of yet another address. The settlers and inhabitants petitioned for an end to *"that painful monopoly and extortion heretofore practised,"* and a free and open market at which everyone could buy and sell. And they too, like the inhabitants of Sydney, disowned Mr. John Macarthur as their representative. Of the two hundred and forty-four signatures to this document, nearly half, Bligh noticed, were made with a cross; it was growing every day more

apparent to him that—whatever ultimate benefits the colony might expect
from Macarthur's wool-growing experiments—the poor and lowly saw him,
here and now, merely as one whose machinations kept their bellies empty.

*   *   *   *   *

Returning after an arduous week to Sydney, he continued his investigations in the town. Mr. Harvey, bent over a pile of copybooks one morning early in October, heard a stir and a rustle among his pupils, and looked up to see the Governor at the doorway He rose in some confusion, and his class, in obedience to a hurried gesture, rose too. Bligh, observing in one practised, all-embracing glance, the humble schoolhouse, the gaping, poorly-clad children, and the nervous young schoolmaster, left his attendants outside and advanced briskly into the room.

"Good-day, Sir," he said briefly. "You are Mr. Harvey, I suppose?"

"Yes, Sir. I'm honoured that Your Excellency . . ."

"I have heard of you from Mrs. King. I'm making a tour of the educational establishments of the town, Sir. These are all your pupils?"

"All but two, Sir."

"Where are they?"

"One is suffering from the flux, Sir, and the other had the misfortune yesterday to be bitten by a venomous spider."

"Ha! What lesson are these children engaged upon?"

"English Grammar, Sir. They are . . ."

"An important subject, Mr. Harvey. A facility for expressing oneself in our beautiful mother-tongue is a valuable accomplishment . . ." For a second His Excellency's sharp gaze became absent; he cleared his throat loudly, and added a qualification addressed as much to himself as to Mark. ". . . when exercised with moderation and restraint, Sir." He bent over the nearest desk, and his finger pounced. "A blot! Your name, my lad? Eh? Speak up, speak up, I'm not going to devour you! A beautiful language should be written fairly—you hear me? No blots! Neatness! Order! You have such books and materials as you need, Mr. Harvey?"

"I have almost no paper, Sir, which is of course unavoidable, since I know it is extremely scarce, but I have been unable to obtain sufficient slates . . ."

"I shall see what can be done. What was your employment before you established this school, Mr. Harvey?"

"I was tutor to Mr. Mannion's sons at the Nepean, Sir."

"Ah. The lads returned to England, I believe—and so you were left without a post—hey?"

Mark flushed slightly.

"No, Sir. I continued for some time in Mr. Mannion's employment in a—a different capacity." He met the Governor's eyes and, with a hint of angered pride, forestalled the next question. "I believe it has been said that I was dismissed. That is not true, Sir. I resigned."

His Excellency's keen gaze was disconcerting, but Mark continued obstinately to meet it. Bligh said sharply:

"I'm concerned only with the manner in which you conduct this school, young man, and I see as yet no reason to believe you unequal to the task."

"Thank you, Sir," responded Mark stiffly.

Bligh glanced at the pupils.

"Step over to the window with me, if you please.   Now, Sir—you are able to make a subsistence?"

Mark reddened and answered rather shortly:

"Yes, Sir."

"Your pupils seem to be all from the lower orders."

"Yes, Sir."

"Why," asked the Governor—unnecessarily, since he knew very well —"is that?"

"The respectable inhabitants," Mark explained simply, "do not care to have their children mix with the children of convicts and ex-convicts, Your Excellency."

"You must, then," pursued Bligh, watching him attentively, "teach the one or the other.   Why do you choose these?"

Mark felt, and actually displayed, a hint of temper.

"I do not choose them, Sir.   I am willing to teach anyone.   But even if I were able to obtain pupils from among the free people, these whom you see here would continue in ignorance—since if I accepted them also as pupils I should lose the others."

"And the parents of these are able to pay you for your services, Mr. Harvey?"

Mark looked rather sulkily at the floor.

"Most of them are ex-convicts who have obtained situations when their time was expired, Sir," he explained unwillingly.   "They pay with some regularity.   And others who are still convicts, and earn something when their government task is done, pay a little when they can . . ."

"And yet others," Bligh persisted, "nothing at all?"

Mark, goaded into annoyance again, looked up sharply, but the ruthlessness of the Governor's questions was not reflected in his eyes, and the young man's resentment faded as quickly as it had flared.   He shrugged, and ventured a faint smile.

"Exactly, Sir."

Bligh studied him in silence for a moment.

"You are acquainted with Mr. Robert Campbell?"

"No, Sir, though of course I know him by repute."

"H'm!   And what does repute say of him, pray?"

Mark felt some surprise, and hesitated for a moment.   He had learned that a young man who desired to avoid trouble in this place could best do so by keeping his opinions to himself, and he was more than a little taken aback that the Governor should ask such a question about a prominent citizen of one so humble as himself.   But his education had been progressing since he came to Sydney.   In the cheap eating houses which he frequented he had come to understand many things about the colony's economy, and—encouraged by a curious feeling of confidence in his questioner—he answered with a spirit that surprised himself:

"It's said that he is the only honest merchant in the colony, Your Excellency. It's said that he has frequently advanced sums of money to the distressed, and supported them against—against financial oppression. I have heard that the cost of his wares remained unchanged in times of scarcity when . . . when others, Sir, were charging prices ruinous to the poor . . ."

"Ha!" Bligh nodded. "I have heard the same story, young man. I have also had some conversation with Mr. Campbell since his return, and my impression of him agrees with these flattering reports. Should he have room for the services of a clerk during those hours when you are not engaged with your pupils, would the situation meet your wishes?"

"Yes indeed, Sir!" exclaimed Mark fervently.

"Good. I shall speak of it to him. His business is extensive, and will —I trust—increase. I make no promises. If he desires your assistance, he will send for you." The Governor halted Mark's eager thanks with a peremptory gesture, and asked: "How long have you been in the colony, Mr. Harvey?"

"Over seven years, Sir."

He lowered his eyes, instinctively hiding the dejection and nostalgia which they might have betrayed. But despite himself there had been the shadow of a sigh in his voice, and Bligh, who by now had observed him very thoroughly, from his too-pale face and his too-thin hands to his almost threadbare coat and his patched shoes, had heard it. He said— and a kindly sympathy sounded through the normal brusqueness of his tone:

"Exile—hey?"

Mark replied rather stiffly—for he still hated to be pitied:

"I find interest in my work, Your Excellency."

Bligh clapped him on the shoulder.

"Well said! And God bla . . . er . . . bless me if there is a nobler work than the instruction of the young. Books, Sir, and the knowledge to be derived from them, are among the first blessings of our civilisation. You agree?"

"I do indeed, Sir!"

"Good. I have never made a voyage without books, Mr. Harvey. An active mind need fear no idle . . ." he shot another glance at the young man's face, ". . . or lonely hours if there are books at hand. I have studied science, mathematics, astronomy, history . . . you are familiar with Hume's *History of England*, Sir? Good! And the works of Dr. Malthus on the principles of population?"

"No, Sir, I fear I . . ."

"I shall lend it to you. He has a chapter upon the rise and fall of population in new colonies which you will find of interest. Land, readily available, he regards as the most powerful factor for a rapid increase. Those who take part in the building of a new society need a varied knowledge, Mr. Harvey. I have been studying Dickson's *System of Agriculture*, and I have a mind to certain experiments in that direction. A poisonous spider, you said . . .?"

"Sir . . . ? Oh . . . yes, Sir, the child who . . ."

"He has received medical attention?"

"I understand so from his brother, Your Excellency."

"Good. I have an instructive volume on venoms and poisons—though doubtless there are creatures in this country quite new to the science. And the Bible, Sir?"

"The—the Bible, Your Excellency? I do, of course, regularly instruct . . ."

"Instruct—yes, yes, of course, naturally the moral and religious guidance of the young must be attended to. But *read*, Mr. Harvey—read aloud! The Scriptures are an inexhaustible spring of noble language. That child has dirty hands, Sir!"

Mark murmured guiltily:

"Yes, Sir, I . . . er . . . I fear that boys . . ."

"You must insist upon cleanliness, Mr. Harvey. It is indispensable to health." He waved his hand at the class, motionless as statues, round-eyed and open-mouthed. "Be seated!" His voice—as always when he had an order to give—was the voice of the quarter deck, and it smote them down on their benches like grass before a gale. "Very good, Mr. Harvey, I shall not further interrupt you. You have a proper appreciation of your responsibilities, I believe. Apply to me if you need assistance." He turned upon the class, and a quiver ran over it. "Boys! Attend to your tutor, and persevere with your studies. No more blots! Neatness! Cleanliness! Good-day, Sir!"

Mark, with a civil little speech of farewell dying half-uttered on his lips, saw His Excellency's hand trail gently over the tow head of the child nearest to the door as he strode out into the sunlight.

* * * * *

Though not a particularly introspective man, Bligh was too intelligent to omit from any assessment of his problems that very important factor which was himself. This was an uneasy place. He had felt it from the first moment of his arrival, and privately, to his friend Sir Joseph Banks, he had already confessed that had it not been for the company of his daughter and son-in-law, he would have felt "completely forlorn." He occasionally spared, therefore, a few moments for rather impatient self-analysis, and realised that one name was already beginning to stand apart in his thoughts, pricking him like a barb whenever he heard it. And he heard it all too often.

He received Mr. Macarthur among his other callers at Government House with a determined civility; when he felt his irritation rising under the cool, observant, calculating stare of that gentleman's brown, narrow eyes, he endeavoured to shake himself away from it and stand apart, studying, in the development of a mutual hostility, not only John Macarthur, but William Bligh.

He was a hot-tempered and intolerant man, this William Bligh, but he was not vindictive. He was resolved that no favour or discrimination should be shown to anyone, and that his personal relationships should rigidly reflect his impartiality. It was true that he flew into violent rages sometimes. It was true that his command of words was not altogether an asset, but too often a fatal fluency which took possession of his tongue and poured from it an uncontrollable stream of language to which a hard, seafaring life had added rich stores of profanity. But it was also true that between his rages he could be calm, reasonable, serene, even genial—and he had no intention of reserving his more volcanic moods for Mr. Macarthur. Yet for all this carefully considered resolve, the air became electric when they met.

Only Bligh himself knew how relentlessly he had been dogged for years by the spectre of the *Bounty*. Opposition had always enraged him, but since then the word had come to mean—or at least to hint—mutiny. Instinctively he had learned to measure any man who seemed likely to oppose him as a potential leader of mutiny; and there lay always at the back of his mind the prophecy about Macarthur which King had made, and had repeated warningly to him. "*That man will one day set this colony in a flame* . . ."

A challenge! At any challenge William Bligh stiffened, bristled, and prepared to do battle. He knew that Macarthur—though no longer a soldier—still provided the directing brain for that trading monopoly of which the military officers formed the core. He knew that his own Instructions threatened its privileges, and that its members were already busy, as a first step, in spreading such tales of him as might damage his standing and his popularity.

King had spent some time explaining to him the conditions under which Macarthur held his land at the Cow Pastures, and his own belief that such a grant would never have been directed if the importance of the area to the wild cattle had been fully realised. Macarthur, it seemed, had been fortunate that the distance from England was so great, correspondence so slow, and Secretaries of State so occupied with more momentous affairs, that the disposal of a tract of land on the banks of a river in the Antipodes might well escape consideration for a time. Camden had been succeeded by Castlereagh, and Castlereagh by Windham—but still no definite instructions were forthcoming, and Jack Bodice remained in possession.

Continually confronted by fresh evidence of this man's power and influence, Bligh scowled and fumed. The fellow, he thought irritably, was in possession of altogether too much! But the unadmitted fact which pierced deeper than his well-founded reasons for hostility, to goad his human pride and temper, was that Macarthur was invariably and infuriatingly in possession of himself. He was a cold man, where Bligh was hot; he schemed quietly where Bligh noisily ordered; he used words with a subtle venom where Bligh used them with reckless vehemence; he dropped an oblique, provocative phrase where Bligh rapped out a string of oaths. And (with an air of condescension which Bligh found intolerable) he exploited his long residence in the country to suggest that no newcomer, no tyro such as a lately-arrived Governor, could understand its needs and problems as they were understood by Mr. John Macarthur.

So, from the contact of two dynamic characters bent upon two incompatible ends, sparks flew. Small sparks at first, hot and stinging, but quickly extinguished, and possible to ignore. And then, suddenly, out of the tranquil blue and gold of a spring morning, came an explosion that shattered precarious and unreal formalities, and left them enemies.

*   *   *   *   *

His Excellency had ridden up to Parramatta for a few days' visit to the Kings. Rising early, as was his custom, he went out into the garden of Government House where, strolling alone in the slanting sunlight, he found his solitude invaded by the man who was never long absent from his thoughts.

Mr. Macarthur, spruce and elegant in his blue coat, his well-cut breeches, his polished boots and his snowy linen, approached down the path with that air whose arrogance was so subtly masked by a ceremonious courtesy that it almost—but not quite—defied resentment. His hat was in his hand as he bowed, and his tone a nice blend of geniality and respect.

"I trust you will pardon this intrusion, Sir. I was told that you were here, and seeing you in the garden, apparently disengaged, I have taken the liberty . . ."

Bligh answered brusquely:

"At your service, Mr. Macarthur. What is your business?"

"Pray don't let me interrupt your walk, however. The morning is perfect, is it not? If I might take a turn with you . . . ?"

"Delighted," replied the Governor gloomily.

Mr. Macarthur fell into step beside him.

"May I enquire after Mrs. Putland? And her husband?"

"My daughter is well. I can't say the same for Putland."

"I'm concerned to hear it, Sir."

Bligh, conscious that the serenity of his mood was in danger of being shaken by the very presence of this man, made an effort to be amiable.

"Your daughter's health is improved, I trust, Mr. Macarthur?"

"But little, I regret to say. She is a great sufferer. This house is charmingly situated on the rise of the hill, do you not think so? Governor Phillip, I recall, was but marking out the plan of the town when I arrived in 1790. To have seen the colony grow," pursued Mr. Macarthur urbanely, "from nothing to its present state, gives one a feeling of being peculiarly identified with its welfare."

Bligh glanced at him obliquely and said: "H'm!"

Mr. Macarthur paused beside a laurel bush.

"These shrubs and trees have made astonishing growth—but the fertility of the soil in this neighbourhood is such that gardens . . ."

Bligh, irked by this small-talk, interrupted:

"No doubt, no doubt! But you did not come to talk of gardens, I suppose?"

Macarthur acknowledged smilingly:

"No, I confess it. I came, Sir, to speak of a subject which—as you may have heard—occupies much of my thoughts . . ."

Bligh scowled, and words sprang unguardedly to his lips.

"Which subject, pray? I understand your interests are varied—and may be said to include anything which can be bought and sold."

Macarthur's smile became a trifle bleak.

"I have engaged in various enterprises, Sir—all of which I think I may say have contributed something to the progress of the colony."

"Yes, yes!" snapped the Governor irritably. "Yes, indeed, very well, Sir; we need not go into the matter of the progress of the colony, for which, I assure you, I have my own plans. What is this subject that so engages your attention?" He added angrily, before Macarthur could reply: "Wool! I make no doubt of it! I hear on all sides that you have been very active in that line!" He flicked the tall grasses with his cane as he walked, and his step quickened. Mr. Macarthur kept pace with him, but his voice became slower, colder, more formal.

"I have spent years in improving the quality of my fleeces, Sir, and with a success which I flatter myself will in time make this colony an important source of fine wool. During my absence in England . . ."

Bligh stopped short and glared at him.

"Whither you were sent under an arrest, Sir!"

Macarthur bowed frigidly.

"Whither—as you say, Sir—I was sent under an arrest. And—as I add—most unjustly. And where—as I was about to observe, Sir—I was able to persuade my Lord Camden and a Committee of the Privy Council that my experiments were worthy of some support. Upon my return I waited upon Governor King, who was kind enough . . ." and here the hint of a sneer crept into his voice, ". . . to express his pleasure in affording me every assis . . ."

"Damnation!" roared Bligh, and his eyes began to snap dangerously. He knew the history of this smooth rascal! He knew something of what Hunter had endured from him. He knew that King had been forced to accept the humiliation of seeing an enemy return from exile not only unchastened, but re-armed. He knew all this—and Macarthur knew that he knew it. And here he came—no doubt with requests which, for all his suave tone, were demands! He came with courteous phrases on his lips, and black schemes in his tortuous brain! He made an insult of the deference he pretended to the Governor's authority while he plotted to destroy it! And his words, like the viper he was, had a sting in them! ". . . to express his pleasure . . ."! By heaven, there had been little pleasure for King in that interview! The cane slashed angrily at a shrub, and His Excellency's voice rose:

"I know what Governor King has done, Sir, and why! I have talked with him—and with others—and you may be sure I have learned much! Well, Sir?"

"I had hoped for continued support from Your Excellency," Macarthur said, his face growing paler as Bligh's reddened. "My sheep and my cattle . . ."

Bligh turned on him in a fury.

"What have I to do with your sheep, Sir? What have I to do with your cattle?" He waved his cane fiercely in the air before Macarthur's face. "Are you to have such flocks of sheep and such herds of cattle as no man ever heard of before?" He brought the cane whistling down against his boot with a snap like a small report. "*NO, Sir!*"

They stood still in the sunlight facing each other. Macarthur said, his eyes narrower than ever:

"I understood that the Home Government had recommended me to Your Excellency's notice." His voice became very slow and offensively distinct. "It is interested in my concerns."

Bligh's colour darkened till it was almost purple. Did this unscrupulous, mischief-making upstart dare to *threaten* him?

"I have heard of your concerns, Sir!" he shouted. "You have got five thousand acres of land in the finest situation in the country—but, by God, you shan't keep it!"

"Indeed?" Mr. Macarthur's chin was up, and the outward thrust of his lower lip had never looked more truculent. "I hold it on the recommendation of the Privy Council, and by order of the Secretary of State. Even you, I think, must concede my right to it."

His Excellency's voice became a bellow.

"Damn your impudence, Sir, would you teach me my duty? Have a care, for I warn you I'm looking out for you! I'll tolerate no opposition from a parcel of meddling villains who would set themselves above the Governor of the colony—God blast me if I will!"

His hands, reckless and expressive as his tongue, made a violent gesture that swept into oblivion all who might have the temerity to oppose him. Through the fog of his rage he saw Macarthur's face dimly as a pale, frozen mask of enmity, and snapped his fingers at it with ferocious contempt. But his fury had reached its climax, and was passing. There had been hundreds of quarrels in his stormy life. He was as accustomed to the sound of his own voice roaring as to the sound of roaring winds in the masts and rigging of his ship—and like the wind his voice flayed and shook and strained what stood in its path, and passed on, leaving tranquillity. Or so he would have it. But men were not ropes and spars, and his tongue dealt wounds that were not always easily healed; suddenly he felt a curious impression of an event somewhere in his past life which was overtaking him again . . . a momentary confusion in his mind which changed Macarthur's pale, inimical face into the face of Fletcher Christian . . .

The illusion faded, hardly realised. He blinked, made an exasperated gesture, and said harshly:

"The first and most pressing necessity of this colony, Sir, is to promote its agriculture, but I need neither you nor anyone else to teach me the importance of sheep—a matter which I shall attend to in my own time, and according to my own judgment."

His anger was a fire, still alight, though its flame had leapt and subsided. Macarthur's was a subterranean flood, icy and invisible. He answered calmly:

"Naturally, Sir. I don't doubt it. It occurs to me, however, that if —as I suspect—you find my claims extravagant, you have this very morning an opportunity of making your own investigations. I have a flock of some seven or eight hundred sheep at Elizabeth Farm not a mile from this spot, Sir. May I suggest that you examine them? You are returning to the house? With your permission I shall accompany you to pay my respects to Governor King and Mrs. King before departing."

But Mr. Macarthur was invited to breakfast, and over the table the conversation about sheep began again, and continued with some irascibility. Bligh, smouldering, strove with his thoughts, his suspicions and his resentments. Already the details of the altercation were fading from his mind, but he was left with a sense of conflict as real and exhausting as a bout of fisticuffs, and he knew that it was unfinished. Devil take the fellow and his sheep! It was not necessary for this conceited parvenu to harangue him on the subject of wool! He was well aware of its importance, and of the Home Government's interest in the matter; fully prepared to give his attention to this as to all other aspects of colonial development. It was not Macarthur as a sheep-breeder whom he resented, but Macarthur as a pretender to excessive power, and as a disrupter, through his turbulent personality and his financial machinations, of the colony's peace, and its precarious economy. . . . "Damned impudence!" he thought, staring moodily at the tablecloth. "Meddling upstart! Tradesman!" But he would not have it said that he had declined Mr. Macarthur's invitation.

It was mid-morning when he rode up to Elizabeth Farm with King and Captain Abbott. As they walked across the wide, grassy paddocks the sheep, grazing under the benevolent sun, made a pleasant picture. Not one of the gentlemen consciously contrasted their appearance of rural placidity with the controversy they had inspired not only here but on the other side of the world; but they all knew that a battle of wills was raging over those woolly backs.

"It has been said by some," remarked Macarthur—well knowing that to Bligh "some" would mean his friend Sir Joseph Banks—"that the grasses of this country are rank and reedy, and quite unsuitable for sheep. Only ignorance—or malice—could put forward so fallacious an opinion. The natural pasture is rich and sweet, and abundant in all seasons."

Bligh grunted non-committally. Abbott referred to the depredations of the wild dogs, and Macarthur replied quickly:

"The remedy for that, Captain, is more shepherds."

Bligh shot him a dark, exasperated glance. His immediate task, as Governor, was to feed the people, to encourage the cultivation of crops and gardens, to alleviate the hardship of a new colony, never self-sufficient, and just now suffering the results of a calamitous flood. Was he to withdraw labour from the small agricultural settler and set it to watching Mr. Macarthur's sheep? And he had not missed the oblique reference to Sir Joseph, who, whether right or wrong in this particular instance, was his friend—and no admirer of Macarthur. His mood was touchy as he bent to examine the fleeces; he stood fidgeting impatiently while the others estimated the value of the wool, and speculated as to the probable increase in the flocks at the end of ten years. Ten years! Damn it, in the meantime the colony must eat! His sharp eyes had observed and appraised Mr. Macarthur's domain as well as Mr. Macarthur's sheep; he did not grudge the prosperity he saw, but he suspected the use that would be made of it, and his temper was rising again.

". . . do you not agree, Sir?" Captain Abbott was saying.

"Agree?" he retorted. "Of course I agree! Why, in God's name, should I not agree? Why do we stand here like a bunch of nincompoops discussing that which is evident?" He saw Mr. Macarthur's supercilious eyebrows lifting and burst out furiously: "Death and damnation, I don't doubt that fine wool can be produced in this country . . . !"

"I rejoice to hear it, Sir," Macarthur replied. "This morning I gathered the impression that you considered my hopes in this direction ill-judged."

"No such thing!" fumed Bligh. "You'll oblige me, Sir, by not attributing your own meanings to my words!"

Macarthur shrugged. Abbott, who disliked scenes, studied his boots. King, reflecting not without a shade of malice that Jack Bodice and Bounty Bligh were losing no time in coming to grips, turned to lead the way back towards the house.

The Governor's temper was sufficiently subsided by the time they reached it to permit of his remaining a few moments to pay his respects to Mrs. Macarthur—though a certain constraint in the manner of all four gentlemen warned her that there had been trouble. She looked anxiously at her husband, but the mere sight of him was, as always, reassuring. There were a few flecks of grey in his dark hair now, though he was still under forty, but the confidence of his bearing, and his straight, arrogant stare told her that not even this notorious tyrant Bligh could daunt him.

His Excellency, riding away alone, felt the events of that bright morning shadow it with menace. He told himself angrily that support for the legitimate endeavours of any man would never be withheld. Requests, however tiresome and unreasonable, were to be met and examined—though even a saint might be excused a show of impatience sometimes . . .

But this morning he had felt a request coming at him with a challenge concealed in it, and it was a far bigger challenge than it pretended to be. . . . Not merely a challenge concerning some sheep and a tract of land, but a challenge to his whole authority. . . . A first skirmish with a man who had defied and frustrated two Governors, and was preparing to engage a third . . .

William Bligh, cantering briskly through the township of Parramatta, was vowing grimly that Mr. Macarthur would find the third a match for him.

*　　　*　　　*　　　*　　　*

That year, so full of uneasiness and privation in the settlements, had been a year of achievement for Finn and Johnny in their lonely mountain retreat.

There was a hut now, larger than the one they had deserted, with a strong palisade of logs about it. There were small patches of cultivation on the cleared land. The goats and most of the cattle were still left to roam the river banks below where the feed was better, and four new calves and three kids ran with them—but a couple of cows found grass enough round the little creek that flowed by the hut. There was even a note of peaceful domesticity, provided by a fat, year-old baby with a copper-coloured skin and a glint of red in his grease-darkened hair, who played among the pecking fowls and chickens by the door. For not a month had passed after their final establishment before Johnny, with a laconic "I go get Ngili," had vanished, to return with his native wife and their son, Kooree.

It had been a good year on the whole, though one of arduous labour, and not without its hardship and its hunger. To four—and sometimes five—human beings this remote, high valley had become a tribal home. Billalong, restless and volatile, came and went as the spirit moved him, acknowledging Johnny as the head of his ill-defined family, but returning with the nostalgia of native gregariousness to the larger communal life of his mother's tribe, and the camp-fire of his step-father, Milbooroo. If Ngili felt the same call, she gave no sign, and during the winter months when food was scarce and the spoil of Johnny's hunting meagre, her contribution had been welcome. Finn had learned to eat the curious morsels she brought home, and be thankful for them.

The winter had been hard altogether, for they had been unprepared for the cold of this high country. They wore every garment they possessed, and still shivered. Johnny's new clothes were soon shabby and earth-stained, and the few remaining rags he had acquired by barter at Green Hills were shared between the others. Ngili, who suffered more than any of them, went incongruously clad in the petticoat which Johnny had stolen from outside his mother's house at Beltrasna, with Conor's silken scarf—now stained and greasy—wound about the upper part of her body, and a man's tattered coat on top of it. A few possum skins, roughly sewn together by Finn, covered Kooree's small body, but he spent most of his time cradled in Ngili's arms, and drew his warmth from her. There was only a ragged pair of trousers left for Billalong; but he disliked clothes in any case, and preferred to disappear during the winter months to the warmer climate of the plains.

In the mornings the ground was white and hard with frost, and the surrounding tablelands that towered above it sometimes blanketed in snow. Finn and Johnny had clambered one day up a narrow gorge that cut through the sheer cliffs, to emerge at last after several hours of arduous climbing upon a plateau where the wind had a cutting edge, and set them shivering, with the sweat of their exertions still upon them.

Johnny, who had no recollection of having seen snow before, stared almost unbelievingly at the drifts piled against rocks and fallen logs, at the trees, unfamiliar beneath their shroud of white, at the ice-filmed pools and the ferns delicately frosted with a brittle powder that seemed at once to freeze and to burn his fingers.

There seemed nothing to be found on these wild heights—nothing to be used. And yet they lingered, huddled behind a rock to escape the flaying wind, held by wonder and a kind of awe. Here even the ordinary processes of seeing took on a new quality. The air had a clarity, a transparent emptiness through which sight leapt across miles of tangled hills and valleys to a far horizon where the sky came down to meet them —and yet it was not empty. An unearthly, luminous blue filled without dimming it, as though the sky itself had come down to bathe the earth, and paint it with the colour of infinity   Near at hand the eye saw shrubs and rocks and twisted tree-trunks, dead branches with brown leaves fluttering in the wind, fallen logs blackened by the fires of summer, harsh, sandy soil from which small plants grew sturdily; far below it saw the undulations of the valley flattened, and great trees spread on the ground like a carpet; beyond, to the farthest limit of vision, it saw a vast confusion of hills and valleys; but all these things—these real and understandable features of a landscape—seemed less real than the one overpowering fact of blueness. It was silence made visible, space and eternity made visible. The wind roared without disturbing its quiet, tossed the tormented trees and left it motionless.

Beauty, immensity and silence, so moving to the restless human mind, affected the two men strongly but differently. Johnny, still bound in moments of emotion to his native experience, felt a sharp uneasiness. There were tales about these mountains. Tribes which crossed them moved fast, and lingered as little as possible. Country inhospitable to man was not so by accident. In their close identification with the land the natives felt less that an area was poor hunting country to be avoided than that its barrenness was designed to warn them they were rejected, and the place reserved for those strange spirits of whom the legends told. And though Johnny's life with Finn had dimmed his always rather perfunctory acceptance of native superstition, he felt fear in his heart now, and shuddered, not only with the cold.

Finn, with no thought of spirits or malignant powers, was shaken too. His first response was a kind of exaltation—a sense of power and enlargement in himself to match this vastness which, by invasion and the building of a hut, he had claimed and possessed. But upon this bold thought of possession his elation faded, and his confidence ebbed. What were they that they had dared to invade this awful solitude? Giants, or pigmies? What was it in this scene which brought at one moment a mad exhilaration, and in the next a smitten humility?

If there had been anything in it to threaten him, he would have feared it less. If there had been towering snow-clad peaks to shed an avalanche upon him—if there had been impenetrable jungle to entrap him—if there had been waterless desert to torment his thirst, or savage animals to lie in wait for him, the natural resistance of physical fear would have roused his hardihood, and spurred him to defiance. But the snow lay only a few inches deep on the high, flat tableland; the trees that clothed the hills and valleys were not jungle, and nothing moved in them but timid wallabies, clumsy wombats, shy birds and unaggressive snakes. To man this land was not hostile, but indifferent, and its indifference assailed his spirit with a loneliness more wounding than any hardship. The colour that lay over it like the bloom on a ripe plum—so mild, so pure, so lovely—had terror in it too. Its subtle, fading changes from a translucent azure on the sunny ridges to amethyst in the folds of the hills, and cold purple in the deep creek beds, seemed only to emphasise its omnipresent sameness. The whole scene spoke of a secret inviolability, an inscrutable, timeless waiting that dwarfed his effort and his human life. He stared at it dumbly with blank eyes, referring it not to his halted brain, but to his awed and striving spirit.

Not this day or any other day was he really to feel at peace with it. But he took, almost unconsciously, one step on the long road to the union of a land with its invaders. For the thought which came painfully at last was not a resolve upon conquest, but a sober hope for sufferance; he forgot his determination to live in this place, and found instead a hope that he might live with it. He shook himself to his feet as from a dream.

*   *   *   *   *

But now, with spring passing into summer, life was easier. Cultivation, so far, had yielded little save potatoes and a few other vegetables, but these, added to fish, eels, birds, an occasional wild duck and a rare wallaby, had provided during the last couple of months a diet which did more than blunt the edge of hunger. There had been bitter arguments about food during the winter. Ngili in particular saw no reason why they should go hungry when a cow could so easily be killed, or a plump kid, or even a fowl; and Billalong, when he was there, supported her vehemently. But Johnny, to Finn's astonished relief, agreed that the livestock must be preserved, and silenced Ngili with a disciplinary blow on the head which she accepted as matter-of-factly as he dealt it. Billalong was less amenable. Once he did kill a hen, and the belabouring he received from Johnny was ended only by Finn's intervention.

He departed in a rage after this incident, and was seen no more for weeks, but when he returned at last his friendliness and his infectious merriment were unchanged, and—as usual—he did not come empty-handed. He brought more than food, however; he brought news. Settlement at the Cow Pastures was progressing, though escaped convicts plundered the flocks and herds from time to time, and the shepherds, nervous of these desperate and hungry men, were sometimes careless. The natives were no longer welcome in the towri which had once been theirs; the white men shouted and gestured them away. Billalong, however, who was nothing if not audacious, and who had learned from babyhood that laughter and light-heartedness disarm hostility, had ignored scowls and threats, and continued to haunt the outskirts of the white men's establishments, laughing, talking, gesticulating, and even making himself useful occasionally. By now he was received with a shrug and a grin.

He never thought of his parentage and had, indeed, no recollection of his white father. He knew only that somehow he was more successful than the other natives in his contacts with the white men, and that their attitude to him—a dark-skinned, naked stripling whom they had learned to call Billy—was indulgent. He had found also that his two small half-brothers were an asset. Gooradoo and Balgundra were now twelve and eleven years old, sharp-eyed, keen-witted, inquisitive little boys who loved nothing better than to stand at gaze near one of the mysterious white men, puzzled by his clothes, awed by the strange object in his mouth which he set alight so that clouds of smoke issued from between his lips, and noisily amused by his curious language. Flanked by these two—so obviously innocent and harmless—Billalong's own youth was emphasised. They were but three ignorant savage children, less shy than wallabies, and no more important.

They had even been near a house where a white man lived who was called—according to Billalong—Dae-bee-ton, and had seen another white man arrive, evidently a person of great importance, accompanied by several others, including one whom they had heard addressed as Mar-den . . .

"Marsden?" asked Finn sharply. His memory of the man known in the convict huts as "the flogging parson" darkened his face for a moment.

Billalong nodded. Balgundra, he explained, had crept to the kitchen door and asked for food, and he had heard the servants talking. The important visitor was called Gubna . . .

"King?" Finn prompted, but Billalong shook his head. "Ply!" he declared, and laughed uproariously at the ridiculous name. Finn scowled at the ground, wondering. A new Governor? But Billalong was continuing his tale. A great rain had come, and the visitors had been unable to recross the river for several days. . . . Here both Billalong and Ngili went off into a fit of laughter, overcome by amusement at the helplessness of these white people. Taking pity upon them, Billalong continued, he had at last summoned a couple of other natives who had helped him to construct a bark canoe, and in this the important person and his companions were ferried across one by one, and their horses were swum after them. And the man Ply had bestowed upon him as a reward . . . *this*. . . . He disengaged from his matted hair a fragment of soft bark which he carefully unwrapped to display a copper coin. Finn took it from his hand.

"It's money, lad."

Billalong nodded vaguely; he had seen the pile of similar useless objects which used to lie on a shelf in Johnny's old hut. But when Finn, tossing it ruminatively on his palm, added with a grim little smile: "It's half a loaf of bread," he stared. Bread? He knew what bread was. He had been given scraps by the shepherds, and Balgundra had returned from the kitchen of Dae-bee-ton's house with a handful of it. This was not bread! He shook his head in laughing denial; he seized the coin and pretended to bite it, and threw it down with exclamations of disgust. But Finn went on, as if speaking to himself: "Half a loaf of bread . . . but maybe not so much if the baker can make it less . . . maybe but a quarter of a loaf . . ."

He stood up and kicked it savagely into a corner, his face dark with a sudden rage of memories. It lay there forgotten till Kooree, exploring on all fours, discovered it; Ngili snatched it when it was half-way to his mouth, and threw it outside; Billalong saw it, and left it lying; but Johnny, cautious and acquisitive, picked it up, and added it carefully to what remained of his own hoard.

And Finn, reflecting upon Billalong's tale, asked many questions. He began to dream of sheep. Why should it not be possible on those lonely pastures, where the flocks were guarded by a few shepherds, for three boys to . . . ? He talked long and earnestly to Billalong, with Johnny acting as interpreter where the lad's sketchy knowledge of English failed. A beginning had been made, Finn pointed out. Some day there would come a time when a few beasts would stray a little distance from the flock, hidden by a fold of hill or a clump of scrub—and Billalong would be behind them turning them into the hills, over the plateau, down into the valley of the Koornong—and so here . . .

Billalong, an eager listener at first, grew restless. There was excitement in outwitting anyone, but the remainder of the plan sounded intolerably dull. Sheep, he complained, were uninteresting beasts. They were not like kangaroos, whose fleet, bounding gait was a challenge to the hunter, and who matched their strategy and knowledge of the land with his own. Sheep moved slowly, slowly, exasperating in their stupid acquiescence, and one who would tend them must follow at their pace—slowly, slowly. . . . He demonstrated, his pantomime so comic that Ngili became almost hysterical with mirth, and Kooree waved his fat arms and laughed too, and Finn chuckled despite himself, and even Johnny grinned.

After this interlude of levity it was difficult to bring Billalong back to serious discussion. He became angry and impatient. He did not like sheep. Was he, Billalong, already developing into a fine hunter, to walk endlessly day by day behind dull animals which he must not spear? He shook his head violently.

Finn considered him thoughtfully. He had succeeded in holding together this curiously assorted little community by the acknowledgment that temperaments differed, and that each possessed its own value. Along with incessant improvisation to maintain physical existence, he had been forced to direct, unobtrusively, a series of psychological adjustments and compromises.

Ngili, in what she regarded as her own natural tasks—the care of Kooree, and the daily foraging for minor articles of food—was efficient and methodical. But in many other small routine tasks she was exasperatingly unreliable. She was quite ready to carry water in buckets from the creek for the hut or the plants, but she frequently forgot to do it; she liked feeding and tending the fowls, but would often neglect them unless reminded; when the men were felling trees she worked with a will pulling the smaller debris into heaps for burning—but only for so long as it amused her. Finn had discovered that a rebuke at such times turned her sullen, but a laugh, a jesting threat, or a playful slap on her plump shoulders sent her scuttling back to her task with shrill giggles.

Johnny, indispensable as the skilful hunter, was steadily developing also into a white-man worker whose dogged persistence was ever more rarely interrupted by the native impulse to nonchalant idleness; but his temper was still uncertain, and his vanity resented any show of authority. Finn learned that "we shall do this" was fatal, but "shall we do this?" won quick co-operation.

Billalong was merely a gay and improvident native whose land had always been trusted to supply the needs of to-morrow. He could work for short periods like a man possessed, but he needed the constant stimulation of company, conversation, and approval. He could not endure solitude, monotony, or routine. But Finn, acknowledging that his incorrigible light-heartedness leavened their life with merriment, left him to his own carefree devices.

And himself? He was the intermediary, who must span the gulf between their world and his. He was the one who must press here and yield there, give and accept, teach and learn, be subtle and direct, old to curb their volatility, and young to match their laughter. Above all, he must live as they did, in the present, without losing for an instant his own vision of the future . . .

And in that future they must have sheep. Sheep were not only food, but wool—and wool was clothing. Some day there would be others here whose rags would not last for ever. . . He had watched Ngili twisting string from bark and human hair; he recalled that there were—unless death had released them—two men in the Beltrasna huts who had been weavers by trade; but even failing them, his own knowledge would suffice. . . . So when he next spoke of sheep he made it clear that Billalong need perform no more of the undertaking than to manœuvre a few up into the hills, where he himself would be waiting to take charge of them. But not yet. There was still much to be done here, and for the present, he decided, Billalong's youth and wayward energy could be more usefully employed in felling trees than his guile in stealing sheep. It was best to let him come and go as he had always done, urging only that during his visits to the Nepean he should maintain, and if possible increase his contacts with the white man.

In the meantime, then, he remained, and work went on. As the weather changed from spring warmth to summer heat the clearing round the hut spread up from the creek over its eastern slopes, and a perpetual haze of smoke from felled trees hung over the valley. There had been good rains that spring, and between the charred logs and ragged stumps the native grass made a thin film of green over the earth. A small field of wheat was in ear, and a patch of turned ground was ready for the planting of turnips, pumpkins, melons, and seed potatoes.

But Finn, in the midst of his labours, and despite the exultation he felt for what was done, was sometimes oppressed by an acute loneliness. He was free. He had not only cheated death in this alien land, but he was building life with a purpose. He had companions. They shared his work, and with the relaxation of bodily hardship there were even interchanges of thought, of jests, the sense of a tightening bond between them, a growth of communal union.

Yet sometimes it all seemed shadowy. Sometimes he felt his greater age not only as a matter of years, and was shaken by an irritable resentment of their youth and heedlessness. What did they know? Better to seek companionship of a wallaby—a true animal which would not mock one's solitude with the illusion of a common humanity! Even Johnny, white as himself, and speaking his mother-tongue with ever-increasing fluency, was, he felt, shut away from him by ignorance of life as it was lived in the cruel, turbulent, inspiring world that he had left.

They asked for tales, and he gave them tales. And in the telling he could see from their rapt, blank eyes that events and people, so real to him, were being transformed into legends. That they—incapable of relating such tales to any familiar life—were adjusting and distorting them, stripping them of incomprehensible detail, reducing them to a false simplicity.

They learned his songs. The quick, subtle native ear received them and the native gift for mimicry reproduced them with an accuracy which he had at first found amusing, but which now often chilled him with its parrot-like inhumanity, angered him with its incomprehension. Ngili, who crooned endlessly to her baby in her own tongue, would not join in these songs, but she sat listening, beating a rhythmic accompaniment on her bare thighs, and sometimes uttering, with her wide grin, a sudden babble of sound in whose meaningless syllables he would, with a shock, recognise familiar words. To Johnny, indeed, many if not most of the words had meaning—but what was the meaning of this meaning to one who knew nothing of the circumstances in which they had been born, or the events they celebrated? To Billalong they were merely sounds, and since among his mother's people sounds carried their own emotional significance, they underwent, when he sang them, an eerie metamorphosis that struck Finn dumb, staring and listening, half-unbelieving, faintly repelled by these parodies of songs that were dear to him.

But Billalong, oblivious, chanted lustily:

> "I met with Napper Tandy
> And he took me by the hand,
> And he said, How's poor old Ireland,
> And how does she stand?
>
> She's the most distressful country
> That ever yet was seen,
> For they're hanging men and women there
> For the wearin' of the Green . . ."

In such moments life, to Finn, became unreal and intolerable. This vast, silent, blue-haunted, empty place was a dream from which he would wake to see the Irish countryside. It was not possible that a song so identified with the passion and the sadness of his people should be transformed into the chant of a savage; that its words, so burdened with tragedy he had known, and suffering he had shared, should become mere mispronounced and uncomprehended sounds, rising through the indifferent air with no more purpose or resolve behind them than the brazen chorus of the cicadas, now awakening to summer . . .

Stabbed by his knowledge of their origin, he felt an irrational fury at his own isolation from the scenes and circumstances that had inspired them, a maddened impatience for the time when he could sing them once more with men who felt their poignancy. Outraged by the unconcern of his young companions, he would begin to sing too, suddenly and angrily, not with Billalong, but against him—as if by drowning the boy's voice with his own he were drowning this untroubled ignorance with his own bitter comprehension.

> *"When laws can keep the blades of grass*
> *From growing as they grow,*
> *And when the trees in summer-time*
> *Their colour dare not show,*
>
> *Then I will change the colour*
> *That I wear in my caurbeen . . ."*

But the crisis would pass, leaving him full of a grim self-contempt. Had he left that world behind? No, by God, it was on his heels! And he would crush down the pain of memory, and call heartily to Billalong:

"Ah, it's a grand song, and well ye sing it! Let ye be fetchin' the axe now, an' show me how ye can bring down that tree yonder . . ."

1807

Though difficulties in victualling and re-fitting the *Buffalo* had several times delayed the departure of the ex-Governor and his family, Bligh—anxious to send news of the harvest—delayed her sailing still further. The report which he was able to give when he addressed himself to his despatch early in February was less encouraging than he had hoped.

The flood, the dearth of seed, the wet season and the ravages of the moth had all combined to make the wheat crop disappointing, and even with the addition of the maize, now being gathered in, there seemed a prospect of prolonged scarcity. The *Sydney*, which King had so hurriedly despatched after the flood, was hourly expected with its cargo of rice, and Mr. Campbell was about to send a brig to China for more, but these were expedients for a crisis; Bligh was not anxious to discourage the growing of grain by wholesale importation. He had himself purchased a farm at the Hawkesbury, and placed it under the care of that enterprising ex-convict, Andrew Thompson, whose floating bridge Conor Mannion had so often crossed on her drives abroad. Most of the settlers, he considered, were sadly deficient in agricultural knowledge, and his farm should serve as an example to them of what might be accomplished in a small area by industry and intelligent cultivation. He concluded his account of the food situation on a philosophic note: "*We must therefore struggle through until the next harvest, which will teach the settlers to be more provident and industrious than by any admonition whatever.*"

Mr. Griffin reached for a fresh sheet of paper, and His Excellency, after pausing for a moment to arrange his thoughts, passed on to the subject of the wild cattle. This, naturally, brought him to Macarthur, and he was frowning as he dictated a carefully calm paragraph:

"*On this subject I beg leave, Sir, to refer to Governor King, who can point out, as he has done to me, the bad consequences which will attend giving grants in that neighbourhood . . . while there is abundance of land on this side of the river which is very eligible . . .*"

He rose and crossed the room to throw the windows wide. The day had been hot, but with the evening a cool southerly breeze had set in, and he stood for a moment enjoying it, and looking at the lights of the *Porpoise*, anchored in the cove. The *Buffalo*, with the Kings and the Marsdens on board, was down the harbour, and ready—at last—for sea. Bligh was glad of it. The necessary functions and formalities which must attend the ex-Governor's departure had occupied more time than he was willing to spare them. A week ago King had given a large dinner-party on board the *Buffalo*, and yesterday Government House had been gay with lights and music for a farewell dinner and ball. He considered it moodily. A very splendid entertainment, no doubt—in fact, dear Mary declared Mrs. Paterson had assured her it was the most elegant and tasteful ever held in the colony—but he had not enjoyed it. He was a frugal man

458

who disliked lavish spending, and he moodily suspected that it had cost too much; but he was also a forthright man with no great gift for dissimulation, and the empty civilities of social contact with those whom he knew to be his enemies were irksome to him. He had performed them as amiably as he could, but there were moments when his manner became forbidding, his tone curt, and his remarks edged with sarcasm. Between himself and Mr. Macarthur there was now an armed and watchful truce, but several times when that gentleman stood apart conversing with his erstwhile fellow-officers, the Governor's eyes had followed him with a smouldering suspicion.

Macarthur . . . Macarthur . . . how that name recurred! His mind, wandering from his unfinished despatch, had left it there, and through ruminations upon the previous day's festivities, had come full circle to confront it again! He turned back to the room and the patiently attentive Mr. Griffin.

"Where was I? The Cow Pastures . . . h'm . . . yes. . . . Continue: *'The sheep in time will increase in number and quality, both in the carcass and the fleece; but the latter is not an object which everyone can yet entirely attend to. Herdsmen are scarce, and if a few individuals were to have all the servants they pretend should be allowed them for this pursuit, the agriculturist would want his labourer, and the inhabitants grain for their common consumption.'* "

Young Griffin's pen scratched swiftly. His Excellency dealt with reforms, and the obstacles in their way; he touched on the health of the people, and the gratifying increase in marriages; he passed on to the perennial problem of liquor, and began to pace the room as he dictated, his brows lowering over his blue eyes. Mrs. Putland opened the door a crack and peeped in, but seeing Papa occupied, withdrew quietly. Griffin, in a momentary pause, wiped his hot fingers on his handkerchief and stifled a yawn. He had been very late to bed last night, after an exhausting day. Bligh continued:

"*. . . farmers are involved in debt and either ruined by the high price of spirits, or the high price of labour which is regulated thereby; while the unprincipled holder of spirits gets his work done at a cheap rate, and amasses considerable property.*"

He came to a halt again by the window, and stood with his back to it, his eyes fixed in grim concentration upon the wall above his secretary's head. "*I have considered this spirit business in all its bearings, and am come to a determination to prohibit the barter being carried on in any way whatever . . .*"

His voice quickened, and Griffin's pen raced desperately.

"Your pardon, Sir . . . '*it is absolutely necessary to be done to bring . . .*' "

"'*To bring labour to a due value, and support the farming interest.*' You have that now?"

"Yes, Sir," mumbled Mr. Griffin, but was presently left behind again. "'*. . . the strong temptation . . .*'?"

Bligh glared at him.

"Damme, Sir, is your hand paralysed? Where are we? *'The strong temptation it holds out to settlers and other inhabitants to erect private stills, which tend to destroy not only the grain, but the industry and morals of the people . . .'* "

And presently the secretary, to his boundless relief, was aware of silence. He flexed his aching hand and stole a glance at the Governor. Bligh was still staring at the wall over his head, and there was an expression on his face which would have been recognised by many men who had sailed with him. *"I am aware,"* he continued presently with harsh deliberation, *"that prohibiting the barter of spirits will meet with the marked opposition of those few who have so materially enriched themselves by it."*

There was another silence. His Excellency seemed plunged in thought, from which he emerged at last to follow Griffin's wistful gaze to the clock.

"That will do for to-night. We shall continue to-morrow, directly after breakfast if you please." He pulled at his coat collar. "It's devilish hot indoors still—I've been sweating like a pig all day. Find Mrs. Putland and tell her I shall take a turn in the garden—she may wish to join me. After that I have further business to attend to; leave instructions that I'm not to be disturbed."

He stepped out on to the verandah and stood waiting till his daughter's hand slipped beneath his arm.

"More work yet, Papa? Indeed, I don't know how you can continue like this without impairing your health."

He answered, drawing her with him down into the dark garden with its mingled scents of salt water and growing things:

"By virtue of two great blessings, my love—a robust constitution, and the companionship of a devoted daughter."

*   *   *   *

Mr. Mannion, though he had no particular liking for King, considered it but seemly to join the other leading inhabitants of the colony in paying his parting respects. Colonel and Mrs. Paterson were shortly to leave again for Port Dalrymple, but for the moment (since Mr. Mannion's town house was not yet quite completed) their hospitable roof was available, and Conor, with a new gown for the ball packed tenderly in its own box, had accompanied him to Sydney.

Her mood was festive if her husband's were not, and the eagerness with which she greeted each fresh social occasion merely increased his gloom. He was uneasy about the future of the colony—by which he meant, like many others, the future of his own interests in the colony—and conversations with Mr. Macarthur, Surgeon Jamison, Major Johnston and Mr. Gregory Blaxland did nothing to reassure him. But he had his private worries too. He seemed to suffer an endless series of petty, interlocking grievances. Occasional sharp twinges in his back when he stooped reminded him that he was no longer young, and consciousness of his advancing years unpleasantly emphasised Conor's youth and the widening breach between them. More and more he was bored by the narrowness of colonial society, and displeased that Conor should find it so absorbing. There were all kinds of tiresome and sordid details which claimed his attention now that there was no Mr. Harvey to whom he could delegate them; and the mere thought of Mr. Harvey brought other resentments in its train. He was affronted by Conor's refusal to accept his judgment of that ungrateful and ill-advised young man, and though he had almost decided long before Mr. Harvey's exit to permit Patrick's return, he now chose to believe that his secretary's defection had upset his plans, and forced his hand. Patrick was a grievance in himself. But since he seemed determined to throw away the advantages to which his birth entitled him, craving instead an obscure life in an unsavoury penal colony, let him at least fill Mr. Harvey's place and make himself useful. Mr. Mannion's only solace was his daughter, for Miss Julia, at five, was the idol of her papa. Perhaps some remnant of the chagrin he had felt when Conor declined to bestow his name upon their son, increased his partiality for their daughter, and he had developed towards her an attitude of doting indulgence which she was quick to exploit. Yet even she became a source of dissatisfaction sometimes when he contrasted her present environment with that which was her birthright; and not infrequently she was the cause of differences between himself and Conor.

He was, therefore, in a bad mood on that bright day in February when the *Buffalo* at last set sail, and his restless feeling that this colony was fast becoming the kind of place in which no gentleman could live with any peace and dignity, blossomed into a conviction as he watched the Kings preparing to depart for a civilised world.

Standing on the deck of the *Buffalo* amid the throng which had gathered to speed the ex-Governor and his wife, he felt a nostalgia which was not to be ignored. The day was sunny, the scene gay and exciting, but he surveyed it sourly. The vessel was crowded with ladies and gentlemen, and surrounded by a swarm of small boats laden with people of the humbler sort who had come to farewell members of the ship's company, or merely to enjoy an outing. From here on the harbour, under a hot summer sun, and out of sight of the town, the place wore its most prepossessing aspect, but it had no charm for Mr. Mannion. He was tired of it. It had not been amenable of late. It surrounded him with incidents and situations which could not have arisen, he felt, in the ordered communities of the old world. It launched death upon his overseer out of the night; it harassed him with nocturnal prowlers; it snatched one of his convicts, leaving not so much as a ripple or a footprint to explain his vanishing. It kept secrets from him, haunting him with the thought of some stranger who had crept softly through his house while he slept. It had a dangerous power to disturb relationships—master and man, man and mistress, husband and wife, father and son. It bred presumptions, discontents, and rebellions. He thought of Dilboong—a savage, forsooth, learning to read and write! And Julia . . . ?

It was at this moment that he made his decision. For Julia's sake—not, of course, for his own—he must break with this life. He conjured up a vision of his daughter's golden curls close beside the black locks of her willing slave, Dilboong—his daughter's arms clasped tightly about the neck of a black heathen, little better than an animal, and her only playmate! She must be saved from the contamination of this place. She, at least, must put it behind her for ever at an age when she would not bear away memories with her . . .

A crescendo in the chatter about him interrupted his thoughts, and he looked up. It was time for the visitors to leave the ship, and Mrs. King, with tears in her eyes, was distributing embraces among half a dozen ladies who clustered round her. Colonel Paterson, saturnine and reserved as ever, was exchanging a melancholy handshake with her husband, while the bluff Surgeon Harris, his ruddy face shining from the heat and commotion, waited impatiently for a parting word.

"I'll be after you as soon as may be, my dear Governor," Mannion heard him say, "for I doubt this place'll be to my liking with you and your good lady gone. I'm a miserable fool with the pen, but damme, I'll get off to Ultimo where it's quiet, and write you news of all that goes on —and no fault of mine if it makes sorry reading . . . !"

Mannion, at King's elbow, intervened:

"May I wish you a safe and speedy passage, Sir?" He glanced at the surgeon's retreating back, and added: "I think I'm not the only one who would gladly be your fellow-voyager."

King looked ill, but the excitement of the occasion had lent him a touch of his old, sharp animation. He eyed Mr. Mannion shrewdly.

"You are tired of our Antipodean paradise?" he enquired dryly. "However, you are fortunate—you can leave it when you will." His eyes strayed to Bligh, who was bowing stiffly over Mrs. King's hand. "We shall meet you and your amiable wife at home, perhaps, when—um— Paradise has become quite insupportable . . . ?"

But when Mr. Mannion retired, and King was left for a few seconds alone, his eyes became momentarily abstracted as he stared across the water. And though he was devoutly thankful to be leaving the country, he suddenly felt glad that there was some of it which was his. "Australia . . ." The name that Flinders wanted it to bear flashed into his mind, and brought with it a stab of angry pain. It seemed a kind of tribute to that ill-fated man to farewell this land with the name he had given it, and King's mind showed him a picture of its sombre, tree-clothed landscape, its quiet, unyielding hills, and the scattered settlements from which, in time, would come a posterity to call it home. The uneasiness he had felt about those grants to his children, and another with which Bligh had recently indulged him, had almost ceased to disturb him, and now he thought of them gladly as a guarantee of his share in the future of this land. There was even the ghost of a twinkle in his eye as he recalled the naming of his grants to Bligh, and Bligh's to him. His successor— that over-serious fellow!—had ponderously immortalised his participation in two great naval battles, and paid tribute to his wife's maiden name by christening his new properties "Copenhagen," "Camperdown," and "Mount Betham." But he, picking up the pen and bending over the outspread plan, had—with a last, tired flash of his sardonic humour—scrawled upon his new share of Australia: *"Thanks."*

* * * * * *

Governor King had left just too early to hear further news of Flinders—though it was only the news that he was still a prisoner at Ile de France. Three days after the departure of the *Buffalo*, the *General Wellesley* came into port, but she bore more than these unwelcome tidings. The *Sydney* and the *Tellicherry*, which King had so hastily sent away after the flood to bring grain to his stricken colony, had both been lost, but this newly-arrived vessel carried a cargo of some two hundred tons of rice and wheat, which Bligh was thankful to purchase.

He already had enough troubles without a continued food shortage. He suspected fresh plottings among the Irish convicts; ever since that night before his own arrival, when King had ridden out upon a false alarm, there had been rumours. A colony, unlike a ship, was not easily scoured from end to end, and Captain Bligh was already feeling the disadvantages of so scattered a command. But although no arms had been found, and no acts of violence committed as yet, he thought it sound to demonstrate at the outset his determination to permit no disturbances of this kind—particularly when it appeared from the evidence of informers that a ringleader was Michael Dwyer, one of those dangerous State prisoners against whom King had warned him. Not until these miscreants had been arrested, and subdued by flogging and banishment, could he turn his thoughts freely to other matters.

He was far from satisfied with his civil officers. Mr. Gore, who had travelled with him from England, was zealous enough in the office of Provost Marshal, but his personal character, in Bligh's opinion, left much to be desired. Mr. Palmer, the Commissary, seemed friendly, and disposed to support him. Among the magistrates he sensed that Johnston and Jamison were hostile, though relations were still outwardly cordial; and between himself and Harris, who was Naval Officer as well as magistrate and surgeon to the Corps, there was already that antipathy which makes itself felt in men of incompatible temperament. Mr. Grimes, the Surveyor, was altogether too friendly with Mr. Macarthur for Bligh's liking; and the Judge Advocate provided a spectacle which might have seemed ludicrous to anyone but a Governor who saw danger in his weakness and incompetence. For, since Mr. Atkins, together with six officers of the land or sea forces, comprised the Criminal Court, and since, except when there was a ship of war in port, no naval officers were available, this ineffective, elderly tippler was the Governor's only legal counterbalance to the overwhelming influence of the military faction.

He became more convinced as time went on, and he sounded the public opinion of the colony, that alarm on this score was not confined to himself. The people did not like this linking of the military with the civil power and with the Courts of Justice. His own opinion, gaining strength with every week that passed, was that the New South Wales Corps had already been here too long. Its members—and not only of the lower ranks—had formed highly undesirable connections with the convicts; their ownership of goods and land, or their trading pursuits, caused them to neglect their duty and—even worse—to use their official status to further their private ends. Troops sent to this country, he decided, should be constantly withdrawn and replaced before they became a dangerous nuisance.

It was one morning barely a month after King's departure that the Naval Officer waited upon him as was customary with the invoice and papers of a newly-arrived vessel for his inspection. Bligh's face darkened when it appeared that among the cargo were two stills, one directed to Captain Abbott, and the other to Mr. Macarthur. He glared from Mr. Harris to the master of the vessel, and Mr. Griffin read storm signals on his brow.

"Mr. Macarthur is the owner of the *Dart*?"

Harris replied briefly:

"Part-owner, Sir, as I understand."

Bligh threw the papers down on the table angrily.

"It's devilish strange that after his long residence in the colony he should be unaware of the repeated orders forbidding the setting-up of stills. Mr. Harris!"

"Sir?"

"You will see these stills landed and placed in the Government Store until such time as they may be sent back to England. Mr. Macarthur is in error if he imagines that the laws do not apply to him!" He swung his hand out in an abrupt gesture of dismissal that swept a pile of documents to the floor. "That's all!" he added testily. "Oblige me by attending to the matter immediately, Mr. Harris!" He stamped to the door, slammed it shut after them, and glared at his secretary. "Damnation, what are those papers doing scattered over the carpet? Can't you do your work in an orderly fashion, Sir?" He paced the room restively, while Griffin, with scarlet cheeks, restored the papers to their place on the desk. But presently, bending diligently over his work, he felt the Governor's hand clap down on his shoulder.

"There, pay no heed, I upset the thrice-damned things myself. You do your work well, boy. It's that accursed malcontent, Macarthur, who tries my patience beyond bearing. Come now, we had done with seventhly, had we not? '*Eighthly: No person or persons belonging to any of the ships or vessels to throw dirt, rubbish, ballast or otherwise . . .*'"

Mr. Griffin, his young cheeks pink again, but now happily, scribbled with a will. He was aware, however, of a certain preoccupation in the Governor's manner during the remainder of the morning. Bligh was incensed by what he regarded as an act of defiance—and it was by no means the first hint he had received that Mr. Macarthur was disposed to be intractable. He had heard several reports of the wrath which his order forbidding the barter of spirits had roused among the officers, and Mr. Fulton had repeated to him a comment from Macarthur which, he suspected, might have been meant to reach his ears. "Such measures would not be tolerated were there fifty men of spirit to be found in this place!" Bligh, recalling other indications of a rebellious temper, brooded

over this new incident of the stills as he worked; but nothing warned him
that it was the preliminary to a series of legal battles in which his enemy's
oblique methods of attack were to harass him for the remainder of the
year.

By the next day he had dismissed it from his mind, and settled down
to conferences with Paterson, now on the eve of returning to Port
Dalrymple. The Lieutenant-Governor's eagerness to depart was obvious.
He had left his little settlement short of food, and was determined not to
sail from Sydney until he could be assured of a supply to tide them over
at least a few months. The arrival of the *General Wellesley* had solved
his problem, and now—nervously sensitive to Sydney's growing atmosphere of discord—he breathed a sigh of relief, and bade his wife pack
their boxes. He had had his fill of storms in King's day; those which
seemed likely to gather about Bligh's head would not, thank God, involve
him! Let Johnston deal with them! He had suffered much ill-health,
and as he sat down to his conclave with the Governor his dark, gloomy
face was more cadaverous than ever. The despatch of food was arranged;
His Excellency's attention was once more drawn to the inadequacy of the
military forces, and the white-ant-ridden state of the gun carriages; minor
matters were discussed and disposed of. And then, with melancholy
matter-of-factness, the Colonel ventured a personal request:

"The fatigues I must undergo lead me to believe I cannot expect a
long life, Sir. It would relieve my mind were I to know that in the
event of my death my wife would receive a grant of land in this country.
I think," he added, recalling his duel with Macarthur, his clashes with
King, and the thousand tumults with which this colony had tormented his
peaceable soul, "I've earned it."

Bligh agreed. Comforted by the assurance that the grant he requested
would be forthcoming, the Colonel retired. "We're getting off in time,"
he remarked morosely to his wife. "If I know anything of this place—
and of my brother officers—and of Bligh's temper—there'll be nothing but
a continual uproar. I'll be glad to put a stretch of sea between myself
and Sydney!"

    *   *   *   *   *

It was early in April that Bligh welcomed to the colony a highly-
respectable and affluent new settler and his family. Mr. John Blaxland
had already been recommended to him by Sir Joseph Banks, and any
friend of Sir Joseph's was worthy of his attention. He entertained the
family daily at Government House, and Mrs. Putland was instructed to
send out cards of invitation to a large dinner party in their honour.
Since Mr. Blaxland had been the bearer of presents to her from her
Mama, including a gown immensely superior to anything which had ever
been seen in the colony before, she was most happy to arrange an occasion
for wearing it, and the party passed off merrily. Bligh was aware, however, that Mr. Blaxland's brother, Gregory, who had arrived in the colony
last year, was not satisfied with the treatment he had received from King;
nor did he forget King's warning that he might find himself much plagued
by that gentleman. His manner remained cordial, but he was teased by a

suspicion that these wealthy settlers with their large demands and their influential sponsors overseas, would cause him more trouble than the humbler farmers whose interests he was determined to advance.

Only in the outer settlements among these people could he feel that there was any real support for his administration. "By God," he was heard to say more than once, "I'd rather sit down with a settler at the Hawkesbury than with one of the officers!" Sydney, he declared roundly, was nothing but a sink of iniquity. Private soldiers, borrowing some of the arrogance of their superiors, swaggered and quarrelled; sailors from the ships in port came ashore to carouse, and returned to their vessels ruefully with empty pockets. Merchants—such as Simeon Lord, and his partners, Kable and Underwood—waxed rich while their clients sank to penury. The Courts were encumbered with endless lawsuits. For too long the demoralising effects of the rum and merchandise monopoly had taught the people to snatch what they could by fair means or foul.

By degrees the pattern he had sought began to emerge; he was able by now to distinguish his friends as well as his enemies. There were few enough in the upper ranks of his colonial hierarchy, and of these he counted Mr. Robert Campbell and Mr. Palmer as the most reliable. The missionary Mr. Oakes—now Head Constable at Parramatta—might be counted on his side too; and the Reverend Henry Fulton appeared to have redeemed his foolishness in being connected with the Irish rebellion by exemplary behaviour, and earned the pardon which King had bestowed on him. Bligh looked askance at rebels, but he was forced to see what other Governors had seen before him—that much as he might disapprove of such people holding official positions, he must suffer them, for there was no one else.

He flew into a violent rage some weeks later when he learned that only the heads and worms of the stills imported on the *Dart* had been placed in the store. He sent for Harris and berated him fiercely. Mr. Macarthur had been permitted to take the boilers home, Harris explained, for the purpose of removing medicines which had been packed in them. Bligh bellowed, threatened, and repeated his orders that the complete stills were to be impounded—suspecting angrily, from the expression on Pat Ultimo's rubicund and fleshy face, that he was issuing instructions to one who would rather oblige Macarthur than obey the Governor. That suspicion was still sharp in his mind when he subsequently dictated a brief order to Mr. Griffin: *"His Excellency, having thought proper to dispense with the services of John Harris, Esq., as magistrate and Naval Officer, is pleased to appoint Robert Campbell, Esq., to fill those stations."*

*   *   *   *   *

Invitation cards from Government House brought the Mannions to Sydney again early in June. It was the first time the family had been able to dwell beneath its own roof in the colony's capital, for Mr. Mannion's "town house" was just completed. Secure in his possession of Beltrasna—than which even Mr. Palmer's mansion at Woolloomooloo was no finer—he had been content here with a plain, solid building of free-stone, squarely facing the street, with a door and six windows symmetrically placed. Conor found it dull, and regretted that its situation permitted no glimpse of the harbour, but the busy life of the town flowed past it, and there were so many people to visit that she was seldom at home.

She had accepted with a numb, unhappy resignation her husband's decision to return to Ireland. No arguments she could advance moved him, and she was unwilling to plead. It would not be yet, she consoled herself, for Patrick had been given leave to return and take charge of his father's colonial interests; they could not depart till he had arrived, and received the many instructions and exhortations which Mannion was preparing for him. But even now he might be on the way, and Conor felt that her reprieve was short.

The great occasion of their visit was to be a ball at Government House in honour of the King's birthday. It seemed to Conor that Sydney was more unrestful than ever, and comments about the Governor almost invariably waspish. All his orders, innovations and activities were either reviled or sneered at. There were even slighting remarks about the bells which had just been put up on the Church tower, and of which His Excellency was said to be very proud. Surgeon Harris called them "the Governor's iron pots," and it was true that they were too small to be heard at any great distance, but on the morning of His Majesty's birthday Conor was awakened by their modest clamour, and found them cheerful as they rang successive peals throughout the day.

But perhaps it was her mood which lent them magic. For Mrs. Putland had mentioned to her that as part of the celebrations her Papa was to receive at Government House all the schoolmasters of the town and their pupils, and Mrs. Mannion had been promptly and unrepentantly guilty of duplicity.

"How charming a sight that will be!" she exclaimed. "I quite dote on children, Ma'am, don't you?"

The hoped-for invitation had been instantly forthcoming, and she was walking in the garden with her hostess when the ranks of children with their pedagogues turned in at the gates of Government House. She had a glimpse of Mark, unobtrusively bringing up the rear with his handful of ragged urchins, and her heart leapt.

"Here they come, Ma'am! Mercy, what a number! Pray let us go and watch them being presented."

Across the children's heads as they stood shuffling in uneasy silence before the Governor she caught Mark's eye, and bowed smilingly. She saw his flush, and the quick lighting of his eyes; perhaps Mrs. Putland did too, for she asked:

"Who is that young man, my love?"

"His name is Harvey," Conor replied sedately. "He was tutor to my husband's sons some years ago. May I present him to you later?"

She was surprised to find that the interval before this could be accomplished passed entertainingly. His Excellency was in his most genial mood. His loud voice, his magnificent uniform, his august presence and the glories of his house at first smote the children with awe. But by degrees, as they realised that the fierceness of his manner was but mock-ferocity—that his lurid threats were uttered with a twinkle in his eye—that his sudden and alarming gestures to pluck them to his side were merely for the purpose of patting their heads—they relaxed, responded with grins to his sallies, and at last were laughing. By the time he had done with them they were crowding about him to pull audaciously at his sleeve, and their clamour threatened to drown even his stentorian voice. But when he waved them back and held up his hand for silence, silence fell; long years of practice had taught Captain Bligh how to command discipline.

"Good!" he declared. "It may be that you are not a set of worthless rascals after all! Hey? It may be that you are not dunces and simple-tons! Some of you work very neatly. You shall each have a present in honour of his gracious Majesty. Do you like fireworks? Come, come, have you lost your tongues? They wagged fast enough a moment since! Do you like fireworks?"

A fervent chorus cried: "Yes, Sir!"

"Then to-night you shall see some. When it gets dark you shall all go out of doors and watch, and you will see a sight such as you never saw before! Silence! Attention, if you please! Recall your duty to His Majesty, mind your tutors, and study your books with diligence—or I promise you I shall cut you up into small pieces, and feed you to the seagulls—hey? Now be off with you!"

Giggling, nudging each other, shooting last glances from bright, in-quisitive eyes at the great man, the elegant ladies and gentlemen, and the splendid house, the pupils began to file from the room as the Governor turned to their masters for a few parting words. Conor was disturbed to feel her heart beating a little faster. From across the room she heard Mr. Harvey's familiar voice:

". . . thank Your Excellency for your recommendation . . ."

Bligh's answer boomed out clearly:

"Glad to be of assistance, young man, to you or any other who does his duty in an upright manner. Good-day to you, Sir . . . wait . . . you have spoken to Mrs. Mannion . . . ?"

There was a murmur from Mark, and then they were beside her, and the Governor was saying:

"Mr. Harvey, Ma'am, wishes to pay his respects. Mary, permit me to present Mr. Harvey. . . . Confound it, that child yonder—indisposed—worse than puppies, by God! Pray attend to it, my love. . . . You will excuse us, Ma'am?"

They were together—and alone, despite the still crowded room. Accus-tomed to finding him tongue-tied, Conor was surprised to hear Mark say at once:

"This is a great happiness, Madam. I did not think to find you here."

"We are in town for a short time, Sir." To her confusion she felt herself blushing, glanced at the long windows beside them, and said hastily:

"It is a trifle chilly indoors, is it not? Shall we step on to the verandah, Mr. Harvey?"

She was thinking as they stood side by side in the sunshine facing the harbour that he had changed—yet her quick glances discerned no outward difference. She could think of nothing to say, and knew a moment's panic. He was so diffident and retiring—how awkward and disappointing if her own ready tongue failed her, and a miserable silence fell upon these precious minutes!

"Shall we exchange news?" he asked. "I have little—but that little is good."

He *was* different! Feeling a vague dismay, she glanced at him again. The devotion she read in his eyes was no new thing. Nothing was added to it—but something was gone, and she realised—again with that sense of panic—that it was humility. He was more self-possessed, his manner, in some subtle way, more assured . . .

She answered eagerly:

"Let me hear it, pray!"

"I have another post, Ma'am, which occupies my time when school is over. His Excellency was kind enough to speak for me to Mr. Robert Campbell, and—well, Ma'am, I am more comfortably circumstanced than I was before."

"Oh," she cried, "I am glad! I'm well acquainted with Mr. and Mrs. Campbell, you know, and Mr. Campbell's nephew was presented to me only yesterday. This is indeed good news, Sir!"

"And you, Madam? Does all go on as usual at Beltrasna?"

"At present, Sir. But here is something that will interest you—Patrick is returning to the colony! Are you not surprised? In the latest letter we had—which was some months ago—he said he was hopeful of securing a passage quite soon. Will it not be exciting to see him again? My, Mr. Harvey, can you imagine him a young man of twenty-three?"

"It is difficult." He looked down at her smilingly. "But I find it even more difficult to realise that my own age was less than that when I first arrived here, Madam, just eight years ago."

She laughed and sighed in a breath.

"So long? We are well-tried colonists, are we not?" The knowledge that her own colonial days were numbered struck at her happiness like a blow. She began: "However, I fear . . ." But she could not speak of it —not just now. She asked instead:

"Tell me the news of the town, Sir. Your reports at least I can rely on, for I declare those I hear from other people are so conflicting, and often so charged with malice and ill-feeling, and so—so *uncharitable*, Sir, that I cannot place reliance in them."

He said slowly:

"You were always interested in affairs, Madam. I have often recalled how indifferent a bearer of news I proved once." She saw him frown. "Now, perhaps, I could be more informative, but I fear I could not make a pleasant tale."

She replied sadly:

"The tales I hear have never been pleasant, Sir. But tell me of your life here. What do you do, how do you fill your leisure? Who are your friends?"

"Friends? This is a poor climate for friendships, Ma'am. That you have honoured me with yours is something I shall ever—be grateful for. But I have acquaintances. Since the insertion of my first advertisement in the *Gazette*—*our* advertisement, if I may call it so—I have become fairly intimate with the printer, Mr. Howe. He's an active and amusing fellow, and an unfailing source of information upon what goes on in the town—and indeed throughout the colony. And I have made the acquaintance also of a Mr. George Suttor, who . . ."

"Oh, yes, I have heard of him, I think. Has he not a property where he grows excellent grapes and oranges?"

"Yes, Ma'am, near Baulkham Hills. He is a trained horticulturalist who came out some years ago in charge of a consignment of plants and fruit trees for Sir Joseph Banks. I see him but seldom, but he is a man of lively intelligence and strong opinions, and I find his company stimulating. In an eating house which I frequent, I encounter other people, and pass some time in conversation. It is not," he pursued reflectively, "very refined or edifying conversation, but I hear many interesting things . . ."

He paused, and she prompted him:

"What kind of things, Sir?"

For the first time she saw him look at her with eyes that were absent, nd forgetful of her beauty. He said slowly:

"You called me learned once, Madam, but I have been a pupil of late —and no child has ever found his lesson more bewildering . . ."

Wondering, she met his eyes now without embarrassment, for they were still oblivious of her.

"But . . . but you make progress, Sir?"

"A little."

She glanced through the open windows and lowered her voice.

"There are the *strangest* reports abroad concerning the Governor! He's called a tyrant and an oppressor and heaven knows what besides! There are even whispers that he appropriates Government stock to his own use at his farm, and that he won't permit sc much as a pig-sty to be built without his orders, and that he's determined on the ruin of all respectable people, and that no person in an official situation can feel his post secure, and that he makes use of the most shocking and offensive language to all who dare approach him, and Mr. Macarthur told my husband . . ."

Mr. Harvey made a sharp gesture that halted her flood of words.

"I've heard such tales myself, Madam. But since I came to live in Sydney I have learned that there is usually a purpose behind slanders. I'm an obscure person, in the confidence neither of His Excellency nor of those who are his opponents, but I have mingled with the common people of the town, and with those who come in from the outer settlements. From them I hear very different tales. The farming people in particular mention him in terms of gratitude, and Mr. Suttor speaks highly of what he has already accomplished." He stopped for a moment, and then went on, frowning: "Yet I have heard one or two of these same poor settlers, in the presence of some wealthy man, or the friend or agent of some wealthy man—to whom, perhaps, they owe a debt, Ma'am, or who by his influence could bring trouble upon them—calumniate the Governor merely because they know such calumnies will be welcome . . ."

"But," cried Conor indignantly, "how base! Such duplicity is surely . . ."

He interrupted:

"Poverty is an effective destroyer of morals and integrity, Madam. And so, indeed, are wealth and power, though with less excuse. And when I have sometimes felt repugnance that the poor should lend themselves to such ignoble shifts, I have reflected that they do so—for what? For what, Ma'am?"

"I suppose," she answered hesitantly, "to protect themselves . . . ?"

He nodded.

"To protect their families, their few acres, their meagre daily food, their little livelihood. Fear is their taskmaster, Ma'am. But when the rich and powerful employ means no less contemptible, it is not to safeguard a little, but to make much—more still."

They both fell silent, pacing side by side in the bright sunshine, watching their two shadows move across the flagstones. He went on at last:

"My pupils, Madam, are the children of convicts and ex-convicts. I have one whose father, still a prisoner, is employed when his Government labour is done, and from that employment earns a little. I don't know," he added wearily, "what the offence was which caused him to be sent here. I only know that he seems a worthy enough fellow, and his son—though a vexatious rascal sometimes—shows an aptitude for his lessons. This man, Madam, came to me last week to say he was not able to bring me the small sum which is all he is able to pay for the child's attendance, because the free man for whom he worked would not give him his wages. Yet that free man, though not wealthy, is wealthier than I—and a Croesus, Ma'am, compared with my pupil's father . . ."

"A debt?" asked Conor, bewildered. "But surely debts must be paid? Are not the Courts . . . ?"

"Mr. Campbell tells me a convict cannot sue or be sued in the Courts. He has no means of recovering a debt."

"It seems unjust," Conor said doubtfully. "Many things, Sir, seem to me harsh and unjust. And then I ask myself—must not the laws be obeyed? And is it, therefore, unjust that those who have broken them should be punished?"

Mr. Harvey smiled slightly.

"If all those who broke the laws in this colony were so punished, Madam, there would be but few free men. And again: if we allow that this convict must accept as part of his punishment the refusal of his employer to pay his wages, must this punishment extend to his child, who is guilty of no crime? For if I decline to teach him without payment, he remains in ignorance. And if I teach him without payment—which of course I do, Ma'am—I am the sufferer."

Again they walked in silence. Conor said at last:

"In Ireland, Mr. Harvey, I gave no thought to these matters, but here I have found that they occupy my mind frequently. Tell me, Sir—in a place such as this, where there is so much land, and it produces so abundantly—why should there be poverty?"

"I do not know," he replied simply. "Do you recall the advertisement in the *Gazette* which I showed you once, and which spoke of pupils 'in the leading strings of tuition'? I feel myself but such a pupil when I confront these problems. His Excellency was kind enough to send a servant up to me with a book he had promised to lend me, and I have studied it with some care. The author quotes the views of Mr. Godwin . . ."

"La!" cried Conor eagerly, "I have read a book by Mr. Godwin, Sir! But pray continue . . ."

"This author does not appear to be in agreement with Mr. Godwin's views, Madam, but I confess I found myself somewhat impressed by them. Mr. Godwin holds that the vices and weaknesses of society are due to the injustices of their social and political institutions, and that if these were remedied, and men's minds enlightened by a more general diffusion of learning, the temptation to evil would be removed."

"The book I read," Conor replied, "aroused some such thoughts in me, though I confess I cannot see how such a thing is to be accomplished. I think," she added naïvely, "that my grandfather would not have been pleased had he known that it was in the parcel his bookseller sent me. His mind is very strongly set against any changes in society." Suddenly she was moved to speak to him of her childhood. "I was very small when my father died, Sir, but I learned early that he was not to be spoken of in my grandfather's house. Once I asked my Mama why, and she said —with tears in her eyes, Mr. Harvey—that he had sought to change things which grandpapa wished unchanged. I did not know what things she meant—nor do I now—but I have sometimes wondered of late if his mind, too, was disturbed by the sight of so much misery . . ."

Mr. Harvey was appalled to see a glimmer of moisture in her eyes. He stammered, forsaken all at once by his assurance:

"I have distressed you, Madam—pray forgive me! When I have been alone I have often recalled how we used to speak sometimes of such things, and I have indulged myself with the fancy that we might do so again. And now I have most selfishly presumed too far upon your kindness, and plagued you with my thoughts upon matters which no lady . . ."

Conor burst out impatiently:

"La, Sir, you sound like . . . like all other gentlemen! If I am a lady, I am not a booby, I hope?" She relented, touched by his smitten look. "But there! I *am* a booby! I know it, and so I seek to join you in these leading-strings you speak of. Pray tell me more about the Governor. You think there is no foundation for all these rumours?"

"I don't know," he answered rather desperately. "I know only that

I have seen too much purpose behind rumours in the past to give much heed to them. There is a foundation at least," he admitted ruefully, "for the charges of profanity. I have heard sailors on shore leave at Mrs. Stables' tavern, and I assure you that His Excellency can match . . . but enough of that! What I can tell you of my own knowledge, Ma'am, is that the Governor is a man whose mental attainments are remarkable, and one capable of much kindness, though it may be masked by a blunt manner. If I were disposed to prophesy, I should venture the opinion that before another year is out we shall see the colony benefit greatly by his . . ."

"Not I!" she cried suddenly, and turned away from him in distress. He repeated slowly and fearfully:

"Not . . . not you, Ma'am . . . ?"

"We are to leave here soon," she said in a low voice. "We return to Ireland, Mr. Harvey, as soon as Patrick arrives."

There was so long a silence this time that she found it unbearable, and lifted her head to look at him; for a few seconds, with no words and needing none, they faced each other in a kind of terror. Then, from behind them, through the long windows came His Excellency with Mrs. Putland, Mr. Griffin, Mr. Fulton, and a group of other ladies and gentlemen. Mrs. Mannion and Mr. Harvey turned mechanically to meet them.

"Why, confound it!" barked the Governor, staring up at the sky with the knowledgeable gaze of a sailor. "There's foul weather brewing —we'll have rain blowing up before nightfall, mark my words! And the children won't get their fireworks after all!"

A chorus of disappointed exclamations arose from the ladies. Mrs. Putland linked her arm in Conor's, and shivered prettily.

"Come indoors, my love, to the fire. I declare it's quite dark and cold with the sun gone!"

Conor looked up rather dazedly at the black clouds scudding in from the east.

"I had not noticed . . ." she said confusedly. "Yes . . . quite dark . . . quite cold . . ."

*   *   *   *   *

It was barely a month later that Mr. Harvey, walking down towards the High Street after school was over, felt a touch on his arm, and turned to confront a tall young man whom he did not for several seconds recognise as Patrick Mannion.

"Mr. Harvey . . . you can't have forgotten me, Sir?"

Mark took the outstretched hand.

"No, indeed!" Yet despite Conor's reminder that his former pupil was now twenty-three, it had startled him to find the boy a man. And on the heels of that shock came another that whitened his face and so altered his expression that Patrick exclaimed laughingly:

"What's the matter? I am not a ghost!"

Mark forced a smile.

"I was astonished to see you—though I should not have been. Mrs. Mannion told me you were expected." But he was thinking that now, quite soon perhaps, she would be leaving the colony, going away across the sea, out of his life for ever . . .

"You are grown, Patrick," he said slowly, "but not changed, I think?"

"I don't know, Sir. One is always changing, isn't one?"

Mark looked at him quickly.

"That is true. And yet—not so much changing, perhaps, as adding . . . ?" He smiled. ". . . and subtracting! Your studies have gone well, I hope?"

"Oh, well enough!" Patrick looked round restlessly, and said, as if on an impulse: "You're at liberty, Mr. Harvey? Will you walk somewhere with me? Back up the hill to Dawes' Point, where we can see the town and the harbour? I want to talk to someone, and . . ." his sudden, rather shy smile made him again the boy whom Mark remembered, ". . . who better than my tutor?"

My tutor. . . . The words took Mark back to Beltrasna, and that scene with Mr. Mannion in his study. He said with some reserve:

"I don't know if you are aware that I left your father's employment in circumstances which . . ."

Patrick flushed slightly and made an impatient gesture.

"I have had letters from my father, of course. But I imagine I am now of an age to choose my own company."

Bold words, thought Mark, studying him. If they had been spoken by Miles there would have been a finality about them; but a certain ruthless self-confidence in the younger son was lacking in the elder. Patrick had always been a sensitive lad—amenable, affectionate, docile. . . . Yet it appeared that he had been very persistent about returning to the colony . . .

"I am free for an hour," Mark said, "and I'll gladly go with you if you wish it. You came on the *Young William*, of course—I heard she had arrived to-day."

They climbed the hill together, Patrick looking about him at all the changes that had been wrought in seven years, and plying his companion with questions.

"The Church is unfinished even yet? You have not been at Beltrasna, of course, Mr. Harvey, but you say you have seen my family lately? They are all well? I have a new brother and sister to see, have I not? And poor Cousin Bertha—she is still alive? When I spoke to my grandmother of the fine climate here, and the healthy air, she said it must indeed be miraculous if it had preserved Cousin Bertha so long. Where is your school, Sir? Over yonder? I must see it some day. I shall be coming often to Sydney, I suppose. There are many new buildings since I left. Whose house is that? How many inhabitants are there now? I believe there are some gentlemen of means arrived lately as settlers. There was a Dr. Townson on the *Young William*—a scholar who has written several books—he has come out to settle, and he has a brother already in the colony who was once an officer in the Corps. I assured him that there were great opportunities here . . ."

It was not until they had reached the grassy headland that he passed from general to personal matters; and then he burst out rather abruptly:

"My father did not wish me to return here, Mr. Harvey."

"So I understand," replied Mark.

"He wanted me to join the Army. And when I was unwilling for that, he said that if I wished to manage estates I might go back to Ireland —but I did not want that either. And then my grandmother and my aunts all became very busy trying to interest influential persons in gaining me important appointments. . . ." He pulled off his hat and threw himself down on the coarse, short turf. "Pray sit down, Mr. Harvey—it will be warm here till the sun goes. I did not want any of them, Sir! I wanted to come back here!"

Mark sat down beside him and asked curiously:

"You like the colony so much? Why?"

"It isn't the *colony*! Not—not *this* . . . !" He waved his hand at the town below them, and the vessels in the cove. "It's not even Beltrasna, except that it's so quiet and secluded—though I like the place well enough. . . ." He twisted a blade of grass round his finger. "To tell you the truth, Mr. Harvey," he declared at last with the pompousness of self-conscious youth, "I'm not interested in worldly affairs at all!"

Amused, but slightly startled, Mark hid a smile, and asked:

"No? Then what line do you intend to pursue? The—er—the Church?"

"No," said Patrick, frowning at his blade of grass. "Well, perhaps. . . . It might be the Church—some day . . . I have thought of that. You asked me about my studies, Mr. Harvey. I am interested in—in the things of the mind, Sir. In the soul, perhaps—why not?" His voice held a hint of defiance.

"Why not, indeed?" responded Mark. "But I understood from Mrs. Mannion that you were to take charge of Beltrasna when she and your father return to Ireland. You will find that, I think"—his tone was dry—"a very worldly task."

Patrick looked at him doubtfully.

"You think so? But I *could* not remain in England, Sir. You can have no idea how they were all about me, declaring I am the eldest son, and must do this and that. . . ." His blue eyes were rebellious. "I have been reading much, Sir—and writing also. I have had several poems published, and some short pieces of a philosophical nature. . . . And I thought that here—at Beltrasna—when my fath . . . when my family is gone home, I should be alone, and able to devote myself—without neglecting my duties to the property, you understand—to . . ."

"To writing poetry?" enquired Mark. He felt a stab of pity that was not only for this young man, but for the young man who had been himself eight years ago—as naïve as this, as hopeful, as full of unformed aspirations—and even younger. . . . He said almost harshly:

"You say you are not interested in worldly affairs. But they are interested in you, and they will give you no peace—not even here. Less here than elsewhere, perhaps."

"I confess I cannot see why," Patrick replied rather distantly. "If I prefer to devote my leisure to study and literature, and the cultivation of my mind, I see no reason why I should be unable to do it."

Mark said wearily:

"If it is retirement from the world that you want, believe me you might have found it more easily in some seat of learning, or some country vicarage, or even in the heart of London than here. We live very close to 'worldly affairs' here. They crowd about us—wealth, poverty, hunger, greed, ignorance, vice, debts, lawsuits—they will all be your concern, Patrick, when you find yourself master of Beltrasna . . ."

"You speak as if my father had not overseers," Patrick interrupted with a hint of resentment. "Naturally I shall not neglect the estate, and naturally there will be matters of finance and—and discipline to attend to. But I shall be surprised if I am unable to find time for other pursuits more congenial to me." He looked at his companion with an expression in which chagrin was mixed with a bewildered appeal. "I had imagined you would regard such an aim with some approbation, Mr. Harvey."

Mark said hastily:

"God forbid I should seem to—to scorn or deride a preoccupation with the things of the mind, as you term them. I, too, dreamed of such things when I was your age, and imagined I need dream of nothing else. I, too, read books, and studied the philosophers and divines. I even wrote a poem once!" He laughed shortly, staring down at the grass, plucking it up between his fingers, throwing it away and plucking more. Patrick said coldly:

"Well?"

"I was not interested in these 'worldly things' either. Once, for a few hours, when I first arrived in this place, they tempted me. It all seemed so—so easy here—so large and clean, so empty and untouched. . . . You remember Dilboong?"

"Of course." Patrick stared at him in surprise. "Poor hideous Dilboong! What has she to do with it?"

"No matter. . . . I learned that it was not easy at all—or clean. I tried to turn my back on it—to find peace in teaching Mr. Mannion's sons to read and write and cypher and read the classics. . . . But the world caught up with me, and I was compelled to turn and confront it. Yet again, finding it ugly, I tried to run away—and ran straight into its arms. An unfriendly embrace."

"I don't understand you." Patrick's tone was still aloof. "You find it ugly and unfriendly—yet you would not wish me to avoid it?" Mark hit the ground violently with his flat palm.

"You *cannot* avoid it! Oh, yes, it's true that I was a young nobody, and you are the son of Mr. Mannion! In London, perhaps, with a wall of wealth about you, you might have forgotten it—pretended that it was not there. But in this place unless you be blind and deaf, you cannot ignore it—especially now."

"Why especially now?"

Mark asked abruptly:

"You go on to Beltrasna immediately?"

"To-morrow," Patrick said restlessly. "I'm to stay with the Townsons to-night, and leave for Beltrasna in the morning. Why do you ask?"

Mark stood up, brushing the grass from his clothes.

"The colony is in a very unrestful state. You will hear of it from your friends, no doubt, and from your father. There is considerable opposition to Governor Bligh. I think—I feel that there may be serious trouble here shortly."

"There was always trouble," Patrick said impatiently. "And there was always opposition to the Governor, whoever he might be. I can recall a thousand tales of quarrelling when I was here before. I don't propose to embroil myself in any such sordid bickering, I assure you."

Mark said, looking down at him thoughtfully:

"That is a resolve I think you will find it difficult to adhere to—without denying the mind and soul you seek to cultivate. You laugh at me . . . well. . . . I shall say no more. You have not told me of Miles. He was in good health when you left England?"

Patrick scrambled to his feet.

"When was he anything else? He is a great favourite with my aunts and my grandmother. They call him 'our young colonial'—but," added Patrick with a wry little smile, "they also declare that he has far more spirit than I, and should have been the elder son. I wish he had been. You must go back to the town, Mr. Harvey?"

"I fear I must." He asked as they walked down the hill: "Will Miles, then, enter the Army, or accept one of those important appointments which you have crossed the seas to avoid?"

Patrick forgot his annoyance, threw back his head, and shouted with laughter.

"That's a jest, Sir! And a secret also, which I shall entrust to you! I truly believe that they think he will! He smiles, enjoys his life and their attentions, and does not undeceive them. But to me he has confided his great ambition. He's but a lad, of course," added the elder brother tolerantly, "barely seventeen, and full of romantic fancies—but I declare he seems in earnest . . ."

"What is this great ambition then?" Mark enquired. "Will he also disappoint them by wishing to return to the colony?"

"Not only that!" declared Patrick, still chuckling. "He is resolved to come back to the colony—and be first across the mountains!"

Mark laughed.

"Well—who knows? It is like Miles—he was always full of grandiose schemes. We shall go down this path, I think—it is in my way to Mr. Campbell's. What are you looking at?"

"I was trying to recall where our house used to be, long ago when we first came to Sydney. Somewhere over there, I think, not far from where the Church stands now. . . . I used to come up here to play with—with a boy called Johnny. He was Ellen's son . . ."

"Ah, yes," said Mark. "The lad who died . . ."

Patrick glanced at him quickly.

"Disappeared."

"The same thing," said Mark idly. "He was but a child, was he not? He could not have survived long, poor lad."

"It would be—unlikely," responded Patrick, and was silent till they reached the High Street where it ran along the harbour shore. Mark paused.

"I must leave you here. I'm glad to have seen you, and to have learned your plans."

"Though without approval, I fear!" Patrick smiled, but Mark thought with compunction that his voice betrayed a hurt.

"Do not mistake my—my misgivings for disapproval," he urged. "I am in a somewhat despondent mood. Convey my respectful greetings to Mrs. Mannion—I think your father would not welcome them. We may meet again when you are in Sydney?"

"I trust so." Patrick's manner was polite, but formal. Mr. Harvey wondered ruefully as he turned away whether the young man were regretting that he had revealed himself so unreservedly; whether he had kept through the years of his absence the memory of one Mr. Harvey, and returned to find another, who had disappointed him.

*   *   *   *   *

As an acquaintance of the well-informed Mr. Howe, Mark was among the first to hear the news which reached the colony early in July of Captain Flinders' release on parole from long imprisonment. With that exception he heard nothing pleasant, for every week seemed to bring forth some incident which provoked gossip, argument, and even brawls in the houses and taverns, and on the street-corners of the town. And it was curious, he reflected, as one contentious matter succeeded another, how consistently the name of John Macarthur appeared—not always, indeed, as a central figure, but somewhere in the story. It was common talk by now that though the decencies of formal intercourse were still somewhat stiffly observed, there was no love lost between Jack Bodice and the Governor.

Knowing glances were therefore exchanged when a public notice declared that a certain escaped convict was believed to have concealed himself on board Macarthur's vessel, the *Parramatta*, when she departed on a trading voyage to Otaheite. No one suspected Mr. Macarthur of complicity in such an escape; but everyone assumed that should the fact be proved on the vessel's return, he would be as unwilling to forfeit the bond which the law exacted to guard against such abscondings, as the Governor would be willing to enforce it. With the *Parramatta* far beyond their ken across the Pacific, no immediate developments could be expected from this source. But the business of Andrew Thompson's debt to Mr. Macarthur, for which he was haled before the Civil Court, provided an alternative entertainment.

The agricultural community in particular watched the progress of this case with a lively interest, for the colonial system of calculating monetary transactions with the settlers in terms of bushels of wheat was a matter which affected them deeply. They were not concerned with the legal intricacies of the question. They perceived only that the right of a creditor to claim payment at a time when wheat was 28/- a bushel, of a note drawn up at a time when it was 7/6 a bushel, was being questioned —and those copies of the *Gazette* which debated the question were eagerly sought. Mark was more than once pressed into service to read aloud to a group of illiterate but keenly attentive settlers, the rounded periods in which Mr. Howe—who was recognised, of course, as the mouthpiece of His Excellency—denounced this practice. "*It is evidently dangerous, however,*" he wrote, "*for an individual to bind himself in payment of any specific number of bushels of an article to which unforeseen events may give a tenfold value—and Shylock still insists upon his bond.*"

There were winks and nudges, Mark noted, over that. No one doubted the identity of Shylock, nor failed to recognise him again in the gentleman signing himself "An Oculist" who, in the next issue, argued that the literal tenor of every engagement should be fulfilled—and austerely exhorted the Editor to refrain from "calling names." It was openly said by many that Jack Bodice was the more vehement in this prosecution because the defendant was His Excellency's farm-manager, and Mark heard nothing but satisfaction expressed when the Governor cavalierly disposed of the matter by dismissing Macarthur's appeal. But to the poor there was always drama in a clash of wills between the rich, and they whispered to each other with pleasurable excitement that the family at Elizabeth Farm no longer visited at Government House . . .

Mark listened with forebodings. He had lived long enough in the colony to be affected by the current belief that Macarthur was an ill man to cross. Chance made an occasion for him to learn something of Bligh's attitude towards his arch-enemy when, sent by Mr. Campbell with a paper for His Excellency's signature, he presented himself one evening at the door of Government House. Bligh's servant, John Dunn, admitted him rather doubtfully, explaining that his master had but just returned from Parramatta, and was taking supper with his family and some friends. If Mr. Harvey would be seated . . . ?

Mark took the proffered chair. Through the half-open door of an adjoining room he could hear the clink of glass and china, the sound of voices. Bligh's carried with its customary and almost embarrassing clearness, but of the others only a sentence or two here and there was to be heard. They were discussing the Dr. Townson who had been Patrick's fellow-voyager on the *Young William.*

"Well, we shall see, we shall see!" The Governor sounded irascible. "Since he came with a letter from Sir Joseph I've done what I could to make him welcome. He claims land—but brings no order from the Secretary of State—nothing but a letter stating it's the Minister's intention he should be accommodated, and expects me to act on that! King did so, but I give no such grants without specific instructions from the Principal Secretary—and so I told him. He seems discontented, though he has brought with him a pretty pack of stuff which I don't doubt he'll dispose of with great profit. And I've permitted him to occupy land pending a decision, and given him four convicts for eighteen months—but

I wager he'll consider himself ill-used, like the Blaxlands, and lend a ready ear to that rapacious, unscrupulous set that delights in fomenting discord . . ."

Mrs. Putland's voice murmured something inaudible. Bligh's, raised in anger, cut in upon it:

"Macarthur? You may be certain of it! By Heaven, that fellow is intolerable! His only aim is to slight and belittle me! The colony would be peaceful enough if he were out of it—and I would to God he were! Would you not think that a man of his property could live quiet?"

Mr. Griffin's voice enquired:

". . . while you were in Parramatta, Sir?"

"See him?" exclaimed Bligh. "Indeed I saw him! And was he ill? Was he confined to his bed? Was he suff . . . ?"

A little clamour of questioning cut off the end of his sentence, and released Mary Putland's voice:

"*Has* he been ill, Papa?"

There was a thump and a clatter, as though the Governor had pounded the table with his fist.

"No!" he roared. "I'm trying to tell you, if you'll be so good as to permit me to speak! His wife came to call on me at Government House. 'Mr. Macarthur sends his apologies,' she says. 'He would have wished to pay his respects, but he is indisposed.' I express my regrets. I am all civility. I desire to treat the cunning, perfidious, disputatious knave with every courtesy. I give myself the trouble of calling at his house this morning to enquire after his health—which I trust may be such as will bring him to an early grave! And while I am speaking to his wife—in he comes from riding, no more indisposed than I am, damn his lying soul, and looking me over with that insufferable stare of his! 'I have just been riding round my farm,' he says! By God, I let him see my displeasure! I told him that I found it strange—*damned* strange—that he should be so well when only the day before he was too ill to call on me! What . . . ? Say . . . ? He said nothing, but his impudent smile said much! His wife blushed and showed some confusion, as well she might, and tried to tell me it was the first time he had ventured out of doors. Eh . . . ? Absurd, Mary! Humbug! I know well enough that he wanted to noise it abroad that though he does not call on the Governor, the Governor calls on him!"

Mark, with his paper duly signed, took his leave half an hour later and walked back towards Mr. Campbell's wharf, pondering. He felt that the stir of conflict and hostility in the air was quickening. It was like a wind rising, and forming itself into a spinning circle from which there was no escape. Men's minds and emotions, as well as their worldly transactions, were caught up in this whirling ring of greed, fear, enmity and suspicion. That mutual confidence between individuals which made life—so it seemed to Mark—dignified and secure, was being broken down by an unwholesome mistrust. No word or glance or gesture, now, but could be construed by minds tormented into morbid sensitiveness as insult. No incident too trivial, no means too base or paltry to employ if an enemy could thereby be discomfited even for a moment . . .

His Excellency was neither a patient nor a modest man . . .

How useful that could be to those who wished to goad him into unwise words and reckless acts . . .

It was dark as he made his way along the High Street past the Public Wharf and the Hospital. Under the wintry stars the water had a cold, black sparkle, and the breeze that came from it caused him to button his coat more closely round him. Near the house of the Assistant Surveyor he fell in with Mr. Howe, and walked on, only half listening to that gentleman's conversation. The depression which had been growing on him since his last rudely-interrupted meeting with Conor was increased by his uneasiness at the colony's unsettled state. This place had never seemed more malign. Without the knowledge that it harboured Conor, how would it be endurable? He was alternately exalted and cast down, wildly happy and blackly despondent when he recalled the dream-like moment when their eyes had met, and said—what? He did not know, and hardly dared to conjecture.

". . . so Wentworth's under arrest," he heard Mr. Howe saying, "and he'll come before a Court Martial in a day or two . . ."

Wentworth? The tidings passed through his indifferent mind, but the name took him back to a long-ago morning when he had galloped from Beltrasna to Parramatta; when he had sat fidgeting at a window with the surgeon's young son at his elbow. An odd child . . . what was his name . . . ? William . . . William Charles. . . . The years passed, and these children grew up. Patrick, twenty-three; that silent lad who had ridden the long miles to Beltrasna behind him, surely fifteen or sixteen by now . . .

He thought suddenly:

"I have been here long enough! There's nothing for me here . . . !" And, shocked by a desperate feeling that without Conor there was nothing for me anywhere, he hardly heard Mr. Howe's good-night.

He was so weary of strife, and so preoccupied with his own troubles at this time, that he paid little attention to comments upon Mr. Wentworth's arrest, Court-Martial, public reprimand, and subsequent suspension. It all seemed, he thought with distaste, very complicated, very tiresome—and very typical. He sat eating the broth and boiled mutton which Mrs. Stables provided each day at twelve, hearing the conversation about him dimly, through the fog of his unhappy thoughts.

"Abbott tells Wentworth to take two convicts back into the hospital, an' Wentworth says he won't, so . . ."

"'E don't say nothin' of the kind! 'E says the Governor ordered 'em out o' the 'ospital, an' 'e won't take 'em in agin without the Governor says so."

A settler interjected sourly:

"Put about at havin' his workmen took from him, if I know anythin'. He's had men still on the books of the hospital workin' for him on his farm for weeks. Oh, he's not the only one! All the doctors do it—and we can whistle for our labour! The Governor's agin that. He says when they're well enough to work they go on Guv'ment labour, or back to the settlers that had them before. So now they're tryin' to pull him into their quarrels, and make out he's interferin' in the hospital."

Another man said disgustedly:

"It's a made-up business to my way of thinkin', and there's more to it than meets the eye! Like all that goes on among that lot—they've their reasons for everythin' they do!" He leaned across the table and tapped it with his knife. "Where *was* Abbott when he sent that order to Wentworth, tell me that? At Jack Bodice's—that's where!"

Mark glanced up from his meal. How that name found its way into every disturbance . . . !

*   *   *   *   *

Though every hour brought forth its new vexation, and though the days seemed hardly long enough to contain their multitude of petitions, complaints and acrimonious disputes, there were certain definite orders from the Home Government which Bligh must execute. The removal of the inhabitants from Norfolk Island to Van Diemen's Land had long been mooted; the island had proved an expensive settlement, and its lack of a good port made communication difficult in bad weather. Bligh, working late one night—having dismissed Mr. Griffin to his bed—settled down to draft a letter to Captain Piper on this subject.

". . . *As I now think it proper to send you Mr. Secretary Windham's letter on this head, you will be thoroughly acquainted with the whole that is to be done . . ."*

Where was the copy of that letter . . . ? Confound it, the papers mounted like towers! Rummaging among them, his hand slowed, and fell idle; he sat leaning over the desk, resting his arms on it wearily, a frown of anxiety between his brows.

Putland's health was going from bad to worse; the symptoms of a consumption were unmistakable. He was confined to his room now . . . there could be no more large entertainments for a time . . . Mary had no heart for them, poor child . . . it was a sad time for her, distressed by her husband's illness, distracted by her father's cares . . .

The conviction that she must soon face bereavement was always in his mind—a sombre background to the explosions of ill-will and the lightning-flashes of conflict which burst about him without respite. Lately the pipe-maker had been at work again, and a copy of one slanderous lampoon lay among his private papers . . .

There would always be something they could seize upon . . . anything would do . . . an irritable word, a rebuke, a dismissal, an appointment, a new regulation, those leases in the Government domain. . . . There was an instance! His orders concerning the removal of six houses had been eagerly used to inflame opinion against him. A damnable business that a man must be plagued with the effects of his predecessor's negligence . . . ! He scowled more darkly than ever, turning it over in his mind. Phillip had marked out, as directed by his superiors, an area in which no leases were to be granted; King had permitted the erection of six houses; now it was for him to bear the opprobrium involved in restoring Crown lands to the Crown! He had given the occupants notice early in the year that they must remove—he had lately extended the notice till November—he had promised them alternative leases in other parts of the town—what more could he do? Could they not understand that in a rising colony some regular plan must be adopted, some attention paid to the development of the town, some preference given to public utility over individual convenience . . . ? What did the contumacious rogues want? By God, they wanted him to sit with folded hands and do nothing! There was that fellow Whittle, a Sergeant-Major in the Corps—and well in favour, no doubt, with his superiors!—who seemed very active in sowing discontent . . .

The Devil take them all! There was nothing to be gained by sitting here and paying them the compliment of brooding over their iniquities. They were like the wind, and the rain, and the cold, and the high seas, and the pangs of hunger that had assailed his every waking moment years ago, when the area he commanded was an open boat, twenty-three by seven feet. He had declined to admit those things as antagonists to be feared; he had bent his whole energy to the task at hand. This he would do again, let these new enemies shriek and rave as they would. Settle each matter as it arose. And the matter in hand at the moment was Norfolk Island. He picked up his pen again.

By the time he had finished his draft it was long after midnight, but he stepped out on to the verandah for a breath of air before going up to bed. The winter was over; feeling the benevolent air of early spring on his face, his thoughts turned to the outer settlements and the farmers.

Yes, he had made good progress there. Some of the more intelligent settlers were already seeing the advantage of cultivating ten acres well, rather than a larger amount in the old, slovenly way. He was seeing that they got their labourers, too, and that they could buy cattle and other livestock from the Government at half the price charged by private sellers. The barter of liquor, though not entirely suppressed, was greatly reduced, and his currency reforms were protecting honest people from the machinations of knaves . . .

His mood was more tranquil as he stumped up the stairs to bed, the faithful John Dunn at his heels. Yet as he traversed the silent passages to his room he thought again of the tireless forces ranged against him, and the fancy crossed his mind that this sleeping house was becoming rather like a beleaguered fortress.

He had occasion to recall that image very soon. Enmity now raged, and intrigue was directed not only against himself, but against any man who frequented his house on a friendly footing. Provost Marshal Gore, whose official duty it was to execute many of the Governor's orders, could not hope for long to escape drawing upon himself the wrath of the Governor's foes; and he had no doubt that the two individuals who now launched charges of theft and fraud against him were but puppets of others who remained carefully in the background. They were shrewdly chosen. The ex-convict merchant, Underwood, partner of Mr. Simeon Lord, was cherishing a grudge against Bligh, who had lately caused him to be imprisoned, and he was willing enough to accuse any adherent of the Governor of uttering a forged note of fifteen shillings value. The gaoler, McKay, whom the Provost Marshal had often had occasion to reprimand and threaten with dismissal for cruelty to prisoners, was happy to discover an opportunity for revenge, and his mistress was duly persuaded to allege that Mr. Gore's purchase of a trifling ornament was in fact a theft. But Bligh, who by this time was expert in looking behind fact for motive, had no intention of allowing his adherent to be victimised, and himself discomfited.

Atkins, his legal adviser, was a broken reed. It was unfortunate—it was altogether damnable—but the only person in the colony who appeared to have any substantial knowledge of the law was a certain George Crossley, one-time attorney of the Court of King's Bench—but now, alas, an ex-convict. Bligh's private thoughts of the Government which left His Majesty's representative to administer one of His Majesty's colonies without the assistance of a properly-trained lawyer, were blistering. Legal advice he must have, however, and if his Judge Advocate could not supply it, he must get it where he could. Mr. Crossley was summoned.

Outrage! Monstrous and unwarrantable affront to decency! Loud and fierce rang the denunciations of a Governor who profaned the Courts of Law by the employment of so despised a creature. Louder and fiercer still was the uproar when it was discovered that His Excellency, instead of permitting Johnston to nominate the six officers who, with the Judge Advocate were to comprise the Court, proposed to nominate them himself; rumours reached the Governor's ears that the Major, incensed by this usurpation of what he regarded as his sacred privilege, was doing what he could to influence the officers beforehand. Mr. Gore, his case prepared by the opprobrious Mr. Crossley—who, however, much as he had forfeited his respectability, still knew his law—was acquitted. The mysterious failure of the gaoler's mistress to appear in Court in support of her charge was explained by Surgeon Jamison, who produced a certificate declaring that the lady was in the throes of labour. His Excellency, snorting sceptically, was disposed to think that she had taken fright at the hornet's nest she had aroused—or perhaps that her sponsors feared she might not prove a sufficiently reliable witness. Less tactful than savagely triumphant, he ordered the Church bells to peal in celebration of his victory—for no one supposed that the victory was only Mr. Gore's. Yet when Major Johnston and Mr. Jamison waited upon him a few days later, he made a not altogether successful attempt to be conciliatory.

"Do you propose, Sir, to take the command of the regiment from me?" Johnston enquired with haughty sarcasm.

"Nonsense!" Bligh said testily. "I conceive it is my duty as Governor to appoint members of the Court. If you think you have the right to do so, Sir, and not I, then I shall write to England for instructions. Or you may write yourself, and I shall of course abide by the decision whatever it may be. Let us not be at odds upon this matter." But he felt no particular desire to conciliate Mr. Jamison; his eyes were frosty and his voice edged as he addressed that gentleman bitingly:

"I hear your patient has not yet been delivered, Sir. I trust her condition causes you no concern, for her labour appears to be inordinately prolonged!"

Jamison flushed angrily; he began a retort, but Johnston, fidgeting, interjected:

"We were speaking of your—your intervention, Sir, in matters which I consider my concern. I shall be compelled to make representations to the Commander-in-Chief . . ."

"Do so!" snapped Bligh. He had no patience with fools, and the master of Annandale annoyed him. He glared contemptuously at the Surgeon. "You waste your time, gentlemen—and mine. I wish you good-morning!"

A few hours later Mr. Jamison's name, also, disappeared from the list of magistrates.

*   *   *   *   *

Yet it seemed to Bligh that he had no sooner disposed of one malevolent plot than another raised its head. "It will be some time before I feel at home," he had written to Sir Joseph after his arrival—but now, a year later, he seemed farther than ever from peace. And behind every uproar, he discerned the same assailants.

Sometimes he felt that their present machinations were less formidable than the effects of their past predominance. The morals of the community, he thought angrily, had been utterly corrupted. High and low alike had not scrupled to use any means that might advance their worldly interests, but the poor had for the most part sacrificed their integrity, and gained nothing in return.

There was no cure but an orderly and regular form of society in which industry, frugality and honesty were duly rewarded. All his efforts since his accession had been directed to this end. His exhaustive inspection of the colony, and his careful estimate of the needs and resources of the agricultural community were parts of a plan which was already maturing with good effect. No longer need the settler accept, in return for his wheat, liquor or any other goods of which the private trader wished to dispose, at an enormously inflated cost. Now, armed with an order upon the Government store, he might receive such articles as he wished, and pay for them after his next harvest with farm produce at a fixed price. But measures which were contributing so effectively to the welfare of the settlers were leaving the private dealers with quantities of now unprofitable merchandise on their hands; and denunciations of the Governor and his policy became daily louder and more virulent. In this thunderous atmosphere Bligh, accustomed to literal and immediate obedience, confident of his own ability and intelligence, impatient of obstructions, delays and criticisms, felt his fury and his determination rise together. He was defied by persons whose position—and possessions—permitted them to oppose him almost with impunity. He could rebuke, denounce and threaten them, he could deprive them of magisterial rank, and embarrass their financial dealings, but he could not clap them in irons and be done with them. He could counter their moves, but he could not still their mutinous tongues, and he was acutely conscious that he was the butt of a deliberate campaign of traducement and vilification. He was a man who liked to stamp his way in a straight line through life, receiving orders and obeying them, giving orders and seeing them obeyed, thrusting obstacles aside, quelling insubordination with a routine punishment, and counting the incident closed. Intrigue and the subtle weapons of slander tormented his pride, frayed his nerves, rubbed agonisingly on that raw spot in his mind where the word "mutiny" stood like a malignant phantom. His temper became shorter, his tongue sharper, his mood almost morbidly suspicious. Sometimes, leaving the room where his son-in-law lay dying, he knew a wild, baffled feeling that the relentless, invisible hand of calumny was not less ominous or irresistible than the approaching hand of death.

One Sunday morning late in September there occurred an incident, trivial in itself, which yet added fuel to the fire of enmity between the Governor and the military, provided the gossips with another tit-bit, and furnished Mr. Harvey, a startled spectator, with corroboration of his theory that the whispering campaign was having its desired effect of goading His Excellency's pride to extremes.

It was a morning when spring had reached its fulness of perfection— drowsily warm, and yet with no hint of summer's enervation in the air; a golden day full of sparkle and enticement, when only orders, devout-ness, or a stern sense of duty could have lured the feet to Church. Bligh's sense of duty, however, was stern enough; arrayed in full uniform, and with his daughter on his arm, he arrived punctually, took his accustomed seat, and gave due attention to the service. It was but half over when he observed with astonishment that Mrs. Putland was showing signs of distress; her cheeks were alternately pale and red, her gloved hands moved nervously; she cast one quick glance over her shoulder and, to his con-sternation, burst into tears. He bent towards her anxiously.

"My love . . . ? You are indisposed . . . ?"

She shook her head, her handkerchief clutched tightly to her mouth to stifle her sobs. He patted her hand, conscious of sidelong glances from the congregation, reflecting painfully that no doubt she had been suddenly overcome by the thought of her husband's illness, and that too much confinement to the house had depressed her spirits. Full of concern, he followed her when, unable to control her agitation, she rose and hurried from the Church amid a stir and a rustle and a curious turning of heads. In a small adjoining room he found her sunk upon a chair, and sobbing unrestrainedly; she clutched his hand as he bent over her.

"Oh, Papa! Mercy, I am ashamed that I should make such a s-s-spectacle of myself, but indeed I could not . . ."

"There, there!" he fussed soothingly. "What ails you, child? Come now, dry your eyes! You are distressed about our dear John, is not that it?"

"No, Papa—I m-m-mean I *am* distressed, of course, and perhaps that is why I . . . but it is not that, Papa . . ."

"You are faint, then, my love? I shall send for the carriage . . ."

She nodded vehemently.

"Oh, yes, pray do! I am not faint, Papa, but I should like to go home.

I c-could not . . ." a fresh burst of tears made her voice almost inaudible.
"I could not go back in there, indeed I *could* not!"

He asked sharply:

"Why not? What happened to distress you? Come, Mary, I insist
that you tell me . . . ?"

She wailed:

"The s-s-soldiers! They were staring at me, Papa, and laughing and
making faces, and I was so put out of countenance that I . . ."

Bligh's face reddened dangerously. He strode to the door and sent a
bystander scurrying for his carriage.

"Immediately!" he roared. "Bid Mrs. Putland's maid come with it!
Damn it, don't loiter! Must you stand and gape at me?"

Rage already had him in its grip as he returned to his daughter, and
the tender words with which he consoled her were strangely interspersed
with sudden oaths and angry exclamations. By the time he had handed
her into her carriage and stalked back to his place in the Church, his
mood was savage, and no countenance was ever less lit with Christian
piety and meekness. His dear Mary! His beloved daughter! Must they
now strike at him through her? Were the insults of a set of worthless
knaves to be directed at her even while her husband lay at death's door?
Here was the result of the abominable and mutinous conduct of the officers
reflected in the outrageous deportment of the men! He turned his head to
glare at them. God damn and blast their infernal impudence, they were
staring at him too! Staring, grinning, hastily averting their eyes, wearing
that unmistakable expression of men or children who have a secret joke
to be hidden from the eye of authority . . . !

He could scarcely await the end of the service. On its last word he
rose in his fury, grabbed Ensign Bell by the arm and stalked down the
aisle to confront the culprits, closely followed by a startled and apprehensive Lieutenant. The soldiers stood shuffling and agape as he bellowed
out his charge.

"There! That man! And that! And that ugly knave yonder who
is trying to hide his villainous face! And this scoundrel here! By God,
Lieutenant, I shall require some explanation of this atrocious conduct!
Bid Adjutant Minchin wait upon me at Government House immediately,
Sir!"

Minchin, duly presenting himself as required, to find His Excellency
still fuming, was glad enough to escape from a tirade that battered him
like a heavy surf, with orders that Major Johnston was instantly to be
informed of the flagrant misbehaviour of the degraded wretches under his
command. The Sabbath peace thus rudely disturbed, mended itself by
degrees. Mrs. Putland recovered her equanimity, and passed the evening
quietly with her father. The violence of his rage had, as usual, abated,
but he was still resentful—less of the offence itself than of the background
he suspected. The New South Wales Corps! A pretty set! What
respect towards himself was to be hoped for from its rank and file when its
officers so shamelessly opposed him? What discipline was to be expected?
He recalled the pungent sketches King had given him of the origins of

some of those officers, and muttered an obscene epithet which he believed still flattered them. And when Mr. Minchin reappeared in answer to his summons next morning, the Governor, though cool enough to begin with, was still in an ominous mood.

"Well, Sir?" he barked. "What have you to tell me of that monstrous incident yesterday?"

Mr. Minchin was placatory. A drummer, he explained, had observed a hole in another man's cap, and had stuck a feather in it. That was all. But Bligh, glowering, still waited. Mr. Minchin continued:

"The other men saw it, Sir, and laughed. Then they feared they would be seen by the officers, or by yourself, Sir, and that their—er—levity would be considered—er—unbecoming during Divine Service, and looked towards where you and Mrs. Putland were seated . . ." Bligh's expression was growing ever more forbidding, and Mr. Minchin plunged on laboriously: ". . . to observe whether they had been detected, Sir, and . . ."

"Stuff and nonsense!" roared the Governor. Mr. Minchin protested: "I'm sure, Sir, there's not a man in the regiment would wish to cause the least offence to Mrs. Putland . . ."

Bligh began to tramp irritably about the room. Somewhere in his mind was the thought that this story *might* be true. Some part of him, human enough, recognised the power of trifles to amuse idle minds—recalled from his own childhood the tedium of Church attendance lightened by some paltry incident—remembered an apprehensive glance flashed at teacher or parent . . .

But that part of him was no longer robust and confident; it had been poisoned by the unwholesome atmosphere of this place. The soldiers were his enemies . . . they had been the enemies of his predecessors . . . the air was full of slanders, scurrilous jests, and sneering innuendoes . . . it was not the first time that petty insults had been used against him . . . there was that lampoon . . . King had suffered under them too . . . King had warned him . . .

And there was purpose behind it all. That was the harsh and ugly fact which his brain acknowledged, reinforcing his suspicions and goading his emotions. There was implacable purpose . . .

Hostility—opposition—defiance . . .

Mutiny . . . ?

He turned upon Minchin fiercely:

"A miserable excuse! A patched-up, cock-and-bull story! By God, Sir, if anyone dares to offer me an insult I'll have his head off! A feather in the rascal's cap! You might as well tell me there was a feather in his——! Don't come to me with such a tale, Sir! I know the sort of miscreants they are! Convicts!"

"About seventy of them have been convicts, Sir," Minchin said, storing every word in his memory assiduously.

"Jail-birds!" shouted Bligh. "The creatures I saw in Church were jail-birds, and a disgrace to their uniform—in which they but match those of higher rank, Sir!"

That, thought Minchin with relish, would go down well with Johnston, and Abbott, and Will Lawson and Nick Bayly . . . ! He asked woodenly:

"Have you any further orders, Sir?"

Bligh waved him away violently.

"Take yourself off, for God's sake! And tell Major Johnston I expect to see him on this business—and he'll do well to come prepared with something better than a damned, nonsensical, ill-contrived, lack-witted, twaddlesome tale of feathers!"

*   *   *   *   *

Here was more material for the lampooner. A lively sample of his art, likening His Excellency's outburst of temper to the frenzies of a mad dog, found its inevitable way to Government House. It provoked a storm of wrath so alarming and exhausting that Mr. Griffin quailed when a week or so later two more appeared, and effectively interrupted the morning's work. He watched apprehensively as Bligh read the first of them, noting the now familiar suffusion of his ruddy complexion with angry blood, hearing rage lift his resonant voice and loosen his fluent tongue in a thundering cataract of words.

"Hell and damnation!" Bligh leapt to his feet and began to stride about the room. "Must I continue to suffer these intolerable effusions of vulgar spleen? Am I to be the victim of coarse, malicious slanders for ever?" He halted and glared at his secretary; but Mr. Griffin—though the blue lightning of His Excellency's eyes seemed almost to accuse him of responsibility—knew better than to answer such rhetorical questions. He bent nervously over his work while the flood dinned about his ears and the furniture quivered as words were fiercely emphasised by a fist which hammered wherever it might fall. "Am I to be the butt and plaything of a set of villains plunged in infamy? Flunkeys! A disgrace to the uniform they wear! A parcel of *vampires*, sucking the blood of honest men! Creeping, cowardly poltroons who impugn my character with their gross, offensive calumnies! By God, I'll teach them! Let me but lay my hand on the malignant, seditious, venomous, skulking *reptile* who has the damnable *effrontery* to insult the King's representative with his filthy—lying—*poisonous* . . ."

The silence was so sudden and unexpected that Mr. Griffin glanced up in alarm, the thought flickering across his mind that His Excellency must have so excited himself as to bring on an apoplexy.

But Bligh was standing quite motionless in the middle of the room. The two papers were in his hands, and he was staring fixedly at one of them. His colour was still high, and by contrast his eyes seemed more fiercely blue than ever, but they had an absent look. There was nothing unusual about him except that frozen stillness, that unnatural silence, and that queer, faraway stare. Mr. Griffin began to write again, stealing a covert glance now and then. Bligh was angry—yet he did not move or speak. That was so unlike him that his young secretary felt a hint of the fear with which he might have observed some monstrous reversal of a natural law. In anger, His Excellency stamped, raged, pushed chairs about, flung out his hands, swore, waved his cane, shook his fist, shouted, thumped tables and banged doors. Now he merely stood staring at that paper. As if, for all the robust solidity of his flesh and blood, he were, somehow . . . *not there* . . .

It was but a few moments—though to Mr. Griffin it seemed an hour —before he moved. He came back to his chair at the desk; they resumed their work where it had been interrupted. His voice was crisp and decisive as ever, though his manner seemed abstracted, and he paused sometimes. An hour later he gathered some papers together and despatched Mr. Griffin on an errand to the Judge Advocate; and Mr. Griffin, rising, found himself able by craning his head slightly to read what was written on the topmost of the two papers. It was very brief. *"Oh tempora! Oh mores! Is there no CHRISTIAN in New South Wales to put a stop to the tyranny of the Governor?"*

*　　　*　　　*　　　*　　　*

Bligh sat alone at his desk. Mr. Griffin had come close to the truth when his nerves betrayed him with an impression that he was looking at someone who was not there. For Bligh had been on a long journey through space and time as he stood with that second paper held before his eyes. He had been lying in bed in his cabin on the *Bounty*; he had felt the uncertain moment of awakening horribly prolonged, and it had merged at last not into the normal clarity of a daily routine, but into an incredible nightmare which was nevertheless reality. He had felt naked bayonets at his breast, rough hands forcing his arms behind him and tying them with cord; and through the pale, dim light of the hour just before sunrise, he had seen Fletcher Christian's face looking down at him . . .

All that had happened long, long ago, and far from here. Yet just now he had suffered the terrible shock of the man who feels that space and time have betrayed him—that there is a mysterious identity between *then* and *now*—a spectral confusion between *there* and *here*. . . . Where was Fletcher Christian? No one knew. But his name had come into this room, and it had seemed to Bligh that he came with it. For centuries of civilisation lay thinly over the primitive belief that a man and his name were indivisible. Idly, without heeding it, Bligh had heard once that a native of this place had years ago asserted his friendship with the first Judge Advocate by assuming his name. *He is Collins; I am Collins; we are one.* Idly again, with no more than a passing interest, he had learned that when a native died, his name died with him. Odd customs of a savage race! Yet when the ill-omened name of Christian had stared up from the page at him, its owner had been there too—shadowy, but real— not only a bitter memory from the past, but an ominous augury of the future . . .

*　　　*　　　*　　　*　　　*

Surgeon Harris, mindful of his promise to the Kings that he would keep them informed upon the state of the colony, conceived that he now had an almost embarrassing wealth of news. He betook himself, therefore, to Ultimo, whose sequestered quiet, he hoped, would aid him in the task of committing his thoughts to paper. As one of the largest landowners in the colony, he was no idler even now that his functions as Magistrate and Naval Officer had been stripped from him; but his energies were expended upon business, conviviality, and his duties as Surgeon to the Corps, and he had little time or taste for letter-writing. Here, however, in this favourite retreat upon the outskirts of Sydney, where his herd of spotted deer roamed incongruously in haunts once sacred to the kangaroo, and the social distractions of the town were far away, he braced himself for the effort of composition. Rather to his surprise, he found the iniquities of the Governor so congenial a theme that his pen flew.

"*My ever honoured and most respected Madam,*

"*I know you will expect a very long letter with a very circumstantial account of New South Wales since your departure till this period . . . but alas, New South Wales and its directions are so totally altered that had I ten times the abilities of description that I possess I would be at a loss; for you know I am a miserable hand either to write or describe, and cannot do half justice to the misery and oppression that now reigns in this once happy and delightful spot.*"

That, he thought, squaring his elbows and taking a fresh dip in the inkpot, should whet her curiosity! He began to think he might enjoy this task. To Pat Ultimo, who liked good food and good liquor, whose town house was always noisily thronged with his boon companions, and who found even his weekly reading of the *Gazette* something of an intellectual strain, Bligh's administration, though obnoxious, was less galling than his austere mode of living, and his Fellowship of the Royal Society. In Harris' breast there lived no cold and calculating enmity such as Macarthur's, but rather an irritated antipathy—an impulsive and involuntary malice. He would enjoy telling that devoted wife, Mrs. King, how her husband's measures were being reversed . . .

"*He has turned every person who held the least appointment under Gov'r King from every situation whatever they held, and is surrounded by a few who find it in their interest to do whatever he may dictate. And God himself only knows,*" scribbled Mr. Harris with relish, "*the horrid measures that are adopted; it is completely the reign of Robertspere or that of the Terror. . . . Poor King is but a miniature picture when compared to this great man. When he moves it's like that of a great planet— nothing less than his coach and four in waiting, six or eight light horsemen with a serj't, two or three footmen or outriders, and he himself riding in a small sulky with a canvas awning over him. . . . That poor miserable unhappy fellow Putland is in the last stages of consumption; and if the rest of the family were in a like state it would, perhaps, be a good thing for John Bull. At least may they be so who was the cause of sending such a reptile here. I have heard much said of Bounty Bligh before I saw him, but no person could conceive that he could be such a fellow. . . . He has been every day getting worse and worse, and if some steps are not soon— nay, very soon—taken, this place is ruined. Caligula himself never reigned with a more despotic sway than he does . . .*"

Gratified to find how readily the words flowed from his pen, he wrote on industriously, hardly noticing how the hands of the clock crept round. "*The greatest swindler, the most absolute thief and cheat (and who is the Gov'r's friend) is Gore, the Provost Marshal . . . the honest Crossley has*

*got two bullocks and a cow for pleading and assisting Gore at his trial.
. . . Mr. Wentworth has been tried and reprimanded. . . . McKay, the
gaoler, is broke, and has been in gaol some weeks past. . . . When the Gov'r
went last to Parramatta and Hawkesbury he sent down word that no
Civil Court or judicial proceeding should be carried on during his absence,
and that, with afterwards selecting the officers for particular duties, caused
the Major to wait on him to explain the cause for such order, and he felt,
like all great men in authority, indignant. Johnston informed him that he
would write to the Commander-in-Chief with his interference with the
private detail of the regiment. Thus you may see we are not travelling
on velvet. Jamison, who accompanied the Major, was broke from being
a magistrate a few hours later. . . . I probably could make interest to get
at Bligh's despatches, as I am told they are full of the beautifications he
has made at Sydney . . ."*

By this time Mr. Harris' hand was aching, and he was very thirsty.
He rose, yawned, and went in search of refreshment. He had made an
excellent beginning, but a man could not sit writing all day long. He
stood at the window, glass in hand, and ruminated, his mind toying with
words that he had written. "*. . . if some steps are not soon taken . . .*"
Steps . . . ? Who could take steps? Only the Home Government, by
recalling Bligh. . . . Could that be brought about? Mr. Harris was
inclined to think it could. His circle of acquaintances was large, and he
had heard many of them declare their intention of writing to the home
authorities on the subject of the Governor's tyrannical conduct. Jamison
was fuming; the Blaxlands were loud in their complaints; Townson poured
out the tale of his wrongs to anyone who would listen; Wentworth was
smarting under his rebuke and dismissal; Johnston was sulking, and Abbott
was glum . . .

As for Macarthur . . .

Mr. Harris sipped his wine reflectively. A queer fellow, Jack Bodice
—a deuced strange, slippery, dangerous fellow! Quiet—in a way. He
rarely raised his voice—and yet, dammit, all the noise in the colony seemed
to come from him! Out of the Corps now—and yet somehow not out
of it. His finger was there—and everywhere, by God! No one would
be happier to see the Governor recalled . . .

Mr. Harris was not subtle, but he had his shrewdness, and he felt
Macarthur's influence behind the rising clamour in the Corps. Jack
Bodice would fight the battle of the wealthy—not for their sakes, but
because their battle was his own; they would support him—not for his
sake, but because he was a resourceful general in their cause. Harris
grinned to himself, recalling King's nickname for his arch-antagonist. One
thing was sure—this colony, big as it was, was not big enough to hold
Bounty Bligh and the hero of the fleece for very much longer—but
Macarthur would be worsted if he could not get the Governor recalled . . .

Unless . . . ?

Mr. Harris' eyes bulged, and he emptied his glass at a gulp.

*   *   *   *   *

The Governor was not wrong in suspecting that the feuds of the *élite* produced repercussions among the lower orders. Poverty, injustice and venality had produced their inevitable crops of sycophants, ready to say what their superiors wished to hear, swear to what their superiors desired to prove, and ally themselves with the cause that promised immediate advantage. Bligh's determined policy and vigorous measures might dismay his enemies, but his hot temper and his reckless tongue were on their side. The fire of rebellion was alight from the moment when they realised how seriously he threatened their supremacy, but he himself, in moments of suspicion and irascibility, provided them with the fuel to feed it.

He did not trouble to hide his contempt for the Corps. He knew that many of its rank and file had been recruited from military prisons, and that forces for colonial service were often regarded as a convenient means for the disposal of men too troublesome for the regular army. And they, for their part—having basked so long in the reflected glory of their influential officers, and learned the power of a red coat to set them above the felonry among whom they might so easily have found themselves— were jealous of their status. Friction between Bligh and Johnston rallied them quickly to the side of their Commanding Officer, for the master of Annandale was not only easy-going and personally popular, but their shield and buckler against that autocratic naval disciplinarian, Governor Bligh. Minor scenes became a commonplace as hostility mounted; and wherever a group of soldiers gathered there were those to spread tales which lost nothing in the telling.

". . . he comes to my house and asks me who give me leave to build it. 'Major Johnston,' says I, 'two years since, before Your Excellency come to the country.' 'Damn Major Johnston!' says he, 'and Paterson too! I don't care a damn for them,' he says, 'and no person shall have two houses and others go without!' "

"Aye, we've got a tyrant over us, and no mistake! There's Joe Bramwell now—he was comin' in from the bush in his horse and cart, and he sees the Guv'nor riding towards him with his bodyguard, so he pulls into the side of the road and salutes, and Bligh's horse takes fright and rears, and Bligh flies into a passion and calls Joe a tremendous b——r, and bids the guard take him to Government House. And when he gets there Mrs. P. comes to the door and tells him he should·be careful never to meet the Guv'nor on the road . . ."

"Did ye ever hear the like! So the roads is all for him now—be damned to him!"

"And did ye hear how he says the convicts should wear red jackets, for that's the colour for villains . . . ?"

"And keepin' that lot from the Church in the guard-house because they laughed and upset the feelin's of his lady daughter."

"I knew the way it was goin' to be from the first. I seen it long ago when he comes to the Battery one morning and demands to see the men's arms. Flew into a fury, he did; and pulled the flints out and dashed them on the ground, and roared out at me that they're a disgraceful set of useless vagabonds, and not fit to have arms at all . . ."

"Johnston's in a rare takin', I tell ye! I heard him and Minchin and Bayly talkin'. He's goin' to appeal to the Commander-in-Chief . . ."

And Johnston was, indeed, at that moment, writing to the Secretary of His Royal Highness the Duke of York:

"As an officer in command of a regiment, I feel much concerned that so painful a task should be imposed on me as to be obliged to beg the interposition of His Royal Highness the Commander in Chief between Governor Bligh and the corps have the honour to command . . ."

*   *   *   *   *

At Government House, two days later, Mr. Campbell and Mr. Griffin were deep in their usual daily routine of business with His Excellency. The morning was far advanced before Bligh, having disposed of the more pressing matters, threw his pen down and addressed himself to Campbell.

"Those stills that came out in the *Dart*—they can go back on the *Duke of Portland* when she sails shortly. Harris let Macarthur take the boilers away, you recall, and I repeated my order that they be lodged in the stores complete. Be so good as to see that they're shipped aboard the *Duke of Portland* immediately, Mr. Campbell."

Mr. Griffin coughed.

"Sir . . ."

"Eh?" Bligh turned his sharp gaze upon the young man enquiringly.

"Er—I'm not sure, Sir . . . I doubt if the boilers were ever replaced in the stores, Sir. I think Mr. Macarthur still has them in his possession."

Bligh stared.

"Nonsense! I gave Harris orders to place them there months ago! Kindly attend to it, Mr. Campbell."

Campbell nodded imperturbably, but there was a glint in his eye. He had not forgotten the difficulties thrown in his way by Macarthur and his coterie of officer-traders when he was first attempting to establish his business nine years ago, and he shared Mr. Griffin's suspicion that Bligh's order had not been obeyed. He said grimly:

"I'll attend to it, Sir."

Bligh pushed his chair back and stood up, rummaging amongst his papers. Mary had seemed very low in spirits at breakfast; the thought of her pale, anxious face had been troubling him throughout the morning's work. "Where's my pen, confound it?" he demanded. "Hand me some paper, Griffin, if you please. I'll write a letter in the parlour, and sign those when I return."

His step was slower than usual as he left the room, and the door closed so quietly behind him that Campbell and Griffin exchanged a glance, and shook their heads.

"All the same," said Griffin, "I don't believe they *are* in the stores."

*   *   *   *   *

Mrs. Putland was sitting at her escritoire in the parlour, looking sadly at the sheet of paper before her, upon which she had, as yet, written no more than:

"Sydney, New South Wales,
"October 10th, 1807.

"My dearest Mother,
"I take the first opportunity to thank you for the kind presents you sent me by Mr. Blaxland . . ."

She had never wished that Mama were here more passionately than she did now. To those who had sailed under that redoubtable martinet, Captain William Bligh, it might have seemed astonishing that almost the last words of his wife to their twenty-three-year-old daughter should have been: "Take care of your Papa, my love." But Bligh, like many another man whose family is composed of devoted females, was, in their eyes, not only a superior being to be served and revered, but also something of a child to be cherished and defended. Mama was a wise, spirited and intelligent woman who had never hesitated to leap to the defence of her husband when he was attacked, and Mrs. Putland mournfully felt herself but a poor substitute. She had done her best, but she was growing frightened. There were powerful forces at work here to harm him, and she knew that he was being sorely tried by them. For herself, too, she would have liked the comfort of her mother's capable presence, for Putland was now so seriously ill that she had almost abandoned hope of his recovery. Papa was encouraging, and scolded her when she despaired, but . . .

She looked up as the door opened, surprised to see him appear with his writing materials, and set them out on the table by the window.

"I'm tired of that room and that desk," he grumbled, pulling up a chair and seating himself. "I must get a letter off to Sir Joseph, and I'll write it here—I'll not disturb you."

"Disturb me, Papa? Of course not!" She knew very well that his coming here to join her was an offering of sympathy—an attempt at companionship. No doubt Mama had said to him: "Take care of Mary." She felt tears smart behind her eyes and picked up her pen hastily:

". . . the Gown is indeed very elegant, and I received it without its having sustained the least injury . . ."

Bligh glanced across the room at her dark, bent head, and sighed as he drew the thick sheets of paper towards him. He stared absently out the window for a moment, arranging his thoughts, and began to write rapidly:

"My Dear Sir,
"There is a doubtful opportunity which now offers by which I can let you know that I am well, and inform you that from great exertions the Colony is recovered from a deplorable state, indeed I can give you every assurance of its now raising its head to my utmost expectation. The Public Buildings carry an aspect of their value . . ."

A tear-shaped blot fell from his pen, and he cursed under his breath. He had forgotten the blotted copybook in Mark's schoolroom, but he found himself thinking of young Mr. Harvey, and while the front of his mind continued to dictate the words he wrote, the back of it was wondering why sober, honest, and industrious people were so seldom to be found in that rank of society where influence made itself felt. A colony composed of Mr. Harveys and respectable hard-working settlers such as some of those worthy fellows at the Hawkesbury . . . ! The idle fantasy fused with his conscious thought:

"*In the Interior I feel satisfied that the same emulation exists among the Inhabitants, and their industry materially increasing great exertions have been made to till the land, and the ensuing Harvest promises well.*

"*The discontented are checked . . .*"

He turned the page over to write on its other side, but for a moment his pen remained idle. Were they checked . . . ? That doubt hung in his mind throughout another paragraph, and emerged but faintly disguised as he passed on to discuss the high price of meat. "*It is owing to a few wealthy Persons who have got great Property; but as we are encouraging deserving persons the benefits Government wish to bestow will become more equally distributed . . .*"

Mrs. Putland was writing:

"*Papa is quite well, but dreadfully harrassed by business and the troublesome set of people he has to deal with. In general he gives great satisfaction, but there are a few that we suspect wish to oppose him; as yet they have done nothing openly, tho' it is known their TOOLS have been at work sometimes; that is they are trying to find something in Papa's conduct to write home about, but which I am sure from his great circumspection they will not be able to do with honour to themselves. Mr. McArthur is one of the party; the others are the Military Officers, but they are all invited to the house and treated with the same politeness as usual.*"

She looked across at her father. He was bent over his paper, his pen moving fast:

"*But the most material thing to be done is to make everyone confident he will enjoy a just and upright Government—remove without delay the very unfit and very disgraceful Judge Advocate—change the N.S.W. Corps and send them to India . . .*"

"Confound the thing!"

"What is the matter, Papa?"

"This pen—I can scarcely write with it . . ."

"I have a new one here—don't move, pray, I'll bring it to you. My, how much you have written!"

Returning to her own chair, she watched him turn another sheet over to begin scribbling again without pause. How remarkably energetic he was! Dearly as she loved writing to Mama, her own words came tardily to-day. She must give news of Putland of course; yet must she add to the anxiety which would already be aroused on Papa's behalf by her last paragraph? Mama must be told of such things in order to prepare her to seek Sir Joseph's aid in counteracting any wicked machinations which might be attempted in London—but upon other matters one must sound as hopeful as possible . . .

Bligh was near the end of another page.

"*If Government supports my Dignity and determination things will go on all right, and let them be aware of this, as I am not here for my ease or comfort, but to do justice, and relieve the oppressed poor settler who must be the support of the Country, and are honester men than those who wish to keep them under.*

"*The same characters you had suspicions of in Governor King's time are now existing; but Government House is alike to all—and what it should be—but no particular intimacies—that has been the ruin hitherto . . .*"

Mrs. Putland was still searching for words both truthful and reassuring, and the ink on her pen had dried unused many times; she dipped it once more in the inkpot, and wrote slowly:

"*I wish I could tell you that Putland is as well as my Father; since you last heard from us he has been continually ailing, and has every symptom of a Consumption, for these two months past he has been confined to his room, but is now, I trust in God, gradually recovering . . .*"

And Bligh, stealing a glance at her, was stabbed from his own official preoccupations by her forlorn expression. "*In the midst of all this,*" he wrote sadly, "*my beloved daughter's Husband is in a dying State—they have been an inestimable Treasure to me, but we must lose him . . .*"

He gathered up his pages with a sigh and leaned back in his chair to read them over. He recalled the wording of previous letters, wondering if he had expressed his determination emphatically enough, reflecting that wherever the fate of the Colony was debated, the great Sir Joseph's opinion was sought; thinking of others also busy with correspondence, but telling a very different tale. . . . And suddenly, snatching up his pen, he began to write again with vehemence:

"*Remember, my dear Sir, I never failed in anything I undertook, be assured still of my high sense of Honour and Dignity in the present Instance . . .*"

Not involuntarily now—not in a shaken moment of emotional crisis, but deliberately, he dragged the image of Fletcher Christian from his mind and set it up at the head of a long line of men with whom he had come into collision during his tempestuous life. His conflicts with them no longer seemed tribulations to be forgotten, but triumphs to be remembered; and, if necessary, repeated. "*I think,*" he wrote, "*that Providence would never have allowed me to have passed so much of time among bad People if it had not been for some good end.*"

Mrs. Putland's skirts rustled across the room, and her hand rested on his shoulder.

"Have you nearly finished, Papa? We shall need to make haste if these are to go by the *Aurora*—she sails to-day, does she not?"

"I'm all but done." He wrote a few concluding sentences and stood up, stretching himself wearily. "Are your shells for Mama ready? I'll give these to Griffin—and then you must take a turn with me in the garden." He looked at her sharply, and pressed her hand as he took her letter. "You are too pale, my love. We shall see Putland well again soon, never fear—and I shall get the better of my enemies too." He looked up impatiently as a servant appeared in the doorway. "Well, what is it?"

"Mr. Mannion wishes to see Your Excellency."

"Very well, very well!" The Governor's tone was irritable. "Show him into the drawing-room, and I shall be with him presently." The thought of Macarthur's persistent antagonism crossed his mind again, and he turned back to his daughter from the doorway to quote himself with sudden fierceness: "Mark me, Mary—I never yet failed in anything I undertook!"

He found his visitor standing by the window, hat in hand, and gestured him to a chair.

"Be seated, Sir. You wish to see me?"

Mr. Mannion had no intention of permitting his own courtly manners to be frustrated by the Governor's brusqueness.

"I thank you, Sir, but I shall not detain you more than a few moments. I trust I find you well?"

"I'm always well, God be thanked."

"I hear that Captain Putland, however . . . ?"

"Putland is still confined to his bed." Bligh fidgeted, and forestalled the next question. "My daughter is as well as can be expected in the circumstances. Your business, Mr. Mannion?"

"I come to you with an old anxiety, Sir—one which I have taken the liberty of mentioning to your predecessors on former occasions . . ."

"Yes?" snapped Bligh.

"Some time ago one of my convicts disappeared—in a very mysterious and incomprehensible manner. Despite an extensive search, no trace of him could be found."

"Well? He is not the first, and I doubt if he'll be the last. There have always been absconders."

"Quite so." Mr. Mannion's voice was dry. "That is my anxiety, Sir. For many years I have held the view that such rascals might form themselves into dangerous bands—and indeed there have been numerous instances, as you must know, of these bush-rangers, as they are coming to be called, preying upon settlers in the outer districts . . ."

"When such a thing is reported, suitable measures are taken," Bligh answered testily, and Mannion lifted his hands and shoulders in a faint, annoying gesture of resignation.

"Very well, Sir. I conceived it but my duty to report to you the escape of this fellow Finn. He is a trouble-maker of the worst kind—an Irish rebel of '98, transported for his seditious actions, and quick to engage in the same kind of villainy here. I was compelled to keep him apart from my other labourers to a great degree—he was forever talking, inflaming their minds against authority, inciting them to rebellion, causing me more trouble than all the rest together. I had reason to punish—er—to cause a number of them to be punished on his account, and it would not surprise me if they were glad to be rid of him. I, however, would rather have such rogues where I can see them." He bowed. "That is all, Sir. I merely wished to acquaint you that the man is at large—it is for Your Excellency to determine . . ."

"Quite so," Bligh agreed shortly.

Mr. Mannion took his leave, reflecting that His Excellency was a boor.

*   *   *   *   *

With so much to tell, Mr. Harris' letters to the Kings had become incredibly voluminous, and occupied much of his time. But at last they were finished, and it was with the satisfaction of one who has brought a vast labour to a satisfactory conclusion that he glanced through them before sealing them for despatch.

To King—of whose generous table and well-provided cellar he had wistful memories—he had unbosomed himself upon the subject of Bligh's regrettable abstemiousness:

"He is determined that I shall be sober, for I have not had a glass of grog in my house for some months. Indeed I begin to think it is a very good thing for me, for it not only prevents my house from being continually full, but saves me much money; and I begin to think I shall be rich yet, which you know I much want. . . . I applied for four gallons of the brandy by permit, not being able to drink the aq. dent., which was tore with this very polite message: 'That fifteen gallons served the Gov'r's house twelve months, and he thought thirty ought to serve mine.' I do not think he told a lye when he said fifteen gall's serv'd his house twelve months, for I suppose three would at the rate I have seen it brought to table and drank at his house. My house has a set of thirsty souls that come to it. Besides, the masters are of a different temper."

He shuffled through the closely-written pages. He seemed to have given all the gossip; rumour said now that Macarthur was preparing for battle over those stills—but that tale must wait another occasion. Paper was becoming desperately scarce, and Pat Ultimo had realised at last that his stock would be exhausted if he did not call a halt. *"Was I,"* he had written despairingly, *"to detail you every strange event that has happened since you left us, a quire of this paper would not be enough . . ."*

Now that it was done he felt his satisfaction shadowed by regrets. There were still so many rich and scandalous morsels that he might have added. . . . He sealed his bulky package with a frustrated feeling that, even in this notable feat of literary endurance, he had not been able to keep pace with the speed of marching events.

*   *   *   *   *

It was very curious of Mr. Harvey, Patrick thought, to speak so warningly of life at Beltrasna. True, his father was in a forbidding mood and lost no opportunity of reminding him that he had been a sad disappointment; but he had been prepared to suffer that for a few months before his family's departure would leave him in welcome solitude. He was interested in re-discovering the home of his childhood, and in seeing it, now, as an adult responsibility soon to be entrusted to him. He set himself to learning about it with so much enthusiasm and good temper that even Mr. Mannion was disarmed, and remarked to Conor that perhaps a few years in the colony would be fruitful after all.

"He was always a mild lad—biddable enough, but something too irresolute. He will learn here to exercise authority, and that softness will not answer. And no doubt he will also learn to value those surroundings and associations of a cultivated society which he has chosen to cast away. My decision to bring him back here was wise."

Conor looked at him, but made no comment; she was accustomed by now to the expert manner in which he adjusted the truth to prove himself infallible. In July she had found herself pregnant again, but she was not so well as she had been before Julia and Desmond were born, and a kind of dull resignation had taken possession of her. She dreaded the future, but for the present was thankful to have Patrick in the house—a third person who eased, to some extent, the constraint between herself and her husband.

And Patrick for his part was well content. Once, greeting Ellen upon his return, he had remembered the secret that they shared, and had imagined that he saw in her eyes a similar flash of recollection. He had debated with himself whether he would speak of it—ask her if she had ever heard further news of Johnny—but he did not do so. If she knew nothing, she had nothing to tell; and if she did, perhaps it were better that he should remain ignorant. He found her changed—less sharp, less active, and with a subdued hint of fear in her manner. He soon saw that she was out of favour with his father, and being now a young man who could look back over the years with a more worldly comprehension, he suspected reasons connected with their previous relationship, and distastefully dismissed the matter from his mind.

He made friends with the children, and combined with his father in spoiling little Miss Julia, who was enraptured by the sudden appearance of a tall, handsome and indulgent brother. In other respects he found little change in the household. Two new domestics, both wives of free labourers who worked upon the property, had supplanted Maria—now married to one of the grooms, and living in a small cottage at some distance from the great house, where she appeared only twice a week as laundress. Dilboong, indeed, had surprised him. At sixteen she was, he supposed, still ugly; a native could hardly be anything else. But she no longer went barefooted, and a white apron tied over her blue dress disclosed a trim waist and a figure which, if a trifle skinny, was appealingly free and graceful in its movements. Imperceptibly, by her very unobtrusiveness, she had become necessary to the household. Cousin Bertha depended on her; the children ran to her a hundred times a day; her white, bashful smile was always ready, and in the mornings the sound of her voice crooning one of the children's songs as she swept the passages was the first sound that Patrick heard. She was shy of him, and flattened herself against the wall as he passed, but one day when he spoke to her of Miles she seemed to forget her fears, and asked eagerly:

"He come back here? Not long time?"

"Some day," Patrick answered carelessly. Pricked by a wayward memory, he laughed, and added: "He was going to teach you to read, was he not?"

"I learn," she replied, nodding soberly. "I read book, write too." She added humbly, with quick embarrassment: "Not good."

"What do you read?" he asked, surprised and amused. She answered simply:

"Poetry."

"*Poetry . . . ?*" He stared. "What poetry?"

She pulled a small book from a pocket beneath her apron and showed it to him. He read "*Original Poems for Infant Minds,*" and burst out laughing.

"Ah, yes, I see! Children's poems, eh? So you read these to Miss Julia, eh? Very good, Dilboong! Mr. Miles will think you very clever!"

He went away, still laughing, without having seen the quick flare of joy in her eyes.

*   *   *   *   *

It was one evening in October when his father, at the end of an hour's work over farm accounts, stayed him as he rose to leave the study.

"One moment, Patrick. There's a matter I must discuss with you." He fingered the papers and account books for a few moments. "I wish to give you the most solemn warnings before leaving you to a task whose anxieties—nay, dangers—I think you are not fully aware of. As you know, I have always been gravely concerned by the light-hearted manner in which abscondings are regarded here."

"Yes, Sir?"

"There have been incidents in the past years which I have found most disquieting. I've already told you of the theft of my firearms from this very room. Let me again impress upon your mind, Patrick, that the house *was not broken into.* It was entered by means of a key—and not mine. The only other was in Ellen's keeping. Bear in mind, also, that the murder of Merrett occurred *outside Ellen's cottage.*"

"But that was a native, Sir!" Patrick protested.

"I know, I know! There is no mystery about the reason for Merrett's presence there—these convict women are uniformly depraved characters. But an overseer was killed by a native. Why? If we were to say that an overseer was killed by an escaped convict the motive is plain—revenge. Overseers are naturally hated by the rascals they supervise. Therefore I conceive a possible connection between the native who actually performed the deed and some outlaw who incited him to it. It is supposition, but it is based upon a study of the ugly realities of this place. And since the totally inexplicable disappearance of my firearms, I do not rule out the possibility of a connection between Ellen and some villainous runaway, though how it can have been established I'm at a loss to know. Yet they are all sly and deceitful, Patrick. Their cunning is incredible. Ellen may have connections we know nothing of."

"But not with natives, Sir," Patrick objected. "She has always hated them—why, she can't even bear Dilboong to touch her!"

"No, no, not with the natives—her aversion to them is obviously quite genuine. She greatly disliked my introduction of Dilboong into the household. But she may be in league with absconders, and they in turn with natives, and . . ."

But for a few seconds Patrick did not hear him. A vague, fleeting thought had stirred in his mind. Johnny—almost a native . . . ? Johnny and Ellen . . . ? But his father was continuing:

"The official indifference to the problem of the natives is almost as scandalous as the carelessness with regard to absconders. I have told you also of the thefts and damage committed here over a period of months. At that time I endeavoured to implant in Governor King's mind the idea that these two classes—violent, dangerous, escaped criminals, and ignorant, inhuman savages—may disastrously combine in daring acts of outrage against the property and lives of settlers in outlying districts. But my warning fell on deaf ears. Therefore I warn *you*, Patrick, and entreat you to be incessantly on your guard."

"Yes, Father, I shall take every precaution."

"That's not enough!" Mannion exclaimed almost querulously. "What is required is a complete apprehension of the sort of characters you have to deal with. I tell you that with the exception of Toole I don't even wholly trust the overseers. The corruption of this place in unbelievable, and in the past I have more than once had occasion to suspect cheating or disloyalty on the part of those whom I had placed in positions of trust. Ellen is a case in point. I was strongly inclined to dismiss her after the incident of the keys, but on second thoughts I preferred to keep her, since she is useful here, and is, I think, too frightened now to attempt treachery. At all events, nothing more has happened since that time. Except . . ."

He broke off, his expression dark and brooding. Patrick prompted him: "Yes, Sir . . . ?"

"There was the escape of the convict, Finn . . ."

Patrick asked in bewilderment:

"But how could Ellen have been concerned in that?"

Mannion began to walk nervously about the room.

"I don't *know!*" he exclaimed. "I see no possible way in which she can have been concerned. She has no direct contact with the convicts. So far as I am aware she knew nothing of this man, nor ever spoke to him. Yet how did he escape? *How?* I have asked myself that question a thousand times, and I can find only two answers. Either he attempted to swim, and drowned, weighed down by his irons . . ."

"But there would have been some sound, Sir—some sound of struggle, a splashing, a cry for help—the overseer was only a few yards . . ."

"Yes, yes, I agree that drowning is unlikely. And the only explanation which remains is that—he was taken off in a boat."

"A—a boat . . . ?" Patrick echoed, amazed. "But what boat? Where would a boat . . . ?"

Mannion came abruptly to a halt, and leaned his hands on the table, glaring at his son across it.

"Will you never understand, Patrick? *There are criminals at large!* They may have stolen a boat from one of the settlers down the river—or they may be in league with the natives, and it may not have been a boat, but a canoe. This damnable country is infested with rogues and vagabonds, and not all of them are in custody!" His face was flushed, his voice edged, his brow suddenly shining with perspiration. "These desperate villains they call bush-rangers now—these miscreants who have been harassing Macarthur at the Cow Pastures—who knows how many there may be, or where they hide? May not Finn have joined them?" He came back to the table and hammered on it with his closed fist. "I have spoken of this a hundred times! I warned Hunter! I warned King! Only recently I warned Bligh! There has been a most criminal carelessness on the part of those in authority." He sat down and wiped his forehead with his handkerchief. "And now I warn you. Never relax your vigilance, I beg of you. Watch Ellen, and do not trust her—there is no loyalty in these people. The present overseers are reliable enough if they are closely watched, and I shall send you more men of trustworthy character when I reach Ireland. But recollect this—you are attending closely . . . ?"

"Yes, Sir."

"Felons are felons—and not less so when their time is expired. They must be *kept down*, Patrick, and no relaxation of discipline permitted even for a moment. You hear me?"

"Yes, Sir," said Patrick again, eyeing his father's flushed face curiously. This man, betraying tension in his every tone and movement, was not the confident and omnipotent Mr. Stephen Mannion of his childhood. Several times since his return he had seemed to glimpse, beneath the suave manner and the authoritative bearing of his father, an indecision that masked itself with sharper and more frequent orders, an uneasiness not quite concealed by a great show of confidence, an attitude towards the country which declared itself as hatred, but might be—fear? After all, he was growing old. Patrick spoke almost soothingly:

"I shall remember what you say, Sir. You are fatigued, I think—shall I lock up the house for you before I retire?"

"Yes," said Mannion, rising wearily. "Yes, do so, and bring me the keys."

*　　　*　　　*　　　*　　　*

Johnny, at that moment, was busy working on additions to the hut. It was nearly two years now since they had moved to this place, and he did not know at what stage he had ceased to resist Finn's plan for bringing strangers to join them. Slowly his emotions, his memories and his almost forgotten ambition—once hopelessly in conflict—were fitting together to form the picture of an attainable future. Once there had been two emotions, irreconcilable; longing for contact with his own people, blasted by the shock of that abortive rebellion, had been submerged in hatred of them, their communities and all their ways—yet the longing had remained. Indignity, servitude, and a hated master had inspired him to escape, and memories of those things had held him aloof—yet there was no satisfaction in aloofness; he wanted not only to escape from them, but to defy and even to vanquish them. And once there had been an ambition —to grow rich and powerful, a man of many possessions . . .

That was something he had almost forgotten during the years when natives had been his only companions. But now it was coming back to him, curiously altered in its shape. Now all these confused and conflicting desires seemed to fall together in a pattern of possibility. He did not realise that he was no longer merely a vehicle for undisciplined impulses, but he knew there had been a change in himself, and he recognised Finn as its author. He saw now that he could become one of a community of white men, and still reject the community he hated. He was beginning to see—though as yet dimly—that the mere establishment of such a community was a kind of victory over "them." He saw very clearly—for this was easier—that in taking his recruits from Beltrasna he would be revenging himself on the master he had hated. And, looking round this wide valley awaiting cultivation, observing the increase of their livestock, gloating over the small flock of sheep they had successfully stolen from the Cow Pastures, he realised that the ambition he had almost discarded had come quietly to rejoin him. He was already a man of increasing possessions.

And there, in that question of possessions, was the strange thing that Finn had done to him. When, and how? When and how had he ceased to resent the thought of sharing what he owned? Sometimes he remembered the wild, inner conflict he had endured on that night when Finn had first explained his plan, and it seemed that this thing had begun to happen to him in the moment when Finn walked out of the shadows to the fire, and he himself—with a knife and a loaded gun beside him—had sat still, and done nothing.

But it had gone on all the time. How he could talk, that Finn! What tales he could tell! And though they were not about Johnny Prentice, or the shadowy strangers who would come to this place some day, or even about this country, yet they were, somehow, about all these things . . .

Sometimes, listening, Johnny had felt defensive, and even frightened. He had gone back in memory to the tribal camp-fires when the voice of the youara-gurrugin told tales of ancestral heroes, and of things that had happened long ago; and the men sat silent with the red light on their faces, and the present fed from the past, and the hearts of the living were wrung and stirred and changed by the hearts of those long dead. Oh, yes, it was true that there was wizardry in words! The natives knew it—and Matthew Finn knew it too. He had said as much once, when he was talking of his little book.

" 'Twas a friend o' mine give it to me—a grand fellow, full o' learnin'. 'Twas himself taught me the readin' an' writin'. All afire with the throubles o' me country, I was, and remembering me mother's tales o' the famine back in '39 when the people was dying off like flies—an' they without a potato to their pot. Seein' the distress about me, I was, an' listenin' to those that talked o' what was done in America an' France to put down tyrants. An' there comes a night when we're met with some others to make plans, the way all the countryside's afire with rebellion, an' singin' the song of the Shan Van Vocht . . ."

An echo came faintly to Johnny through his thoughts; his hammering took on a rhythm, and he sang to himself in a tuneless undertone as he worked.

"And what colour will they wear?
Says the Shan Van Vocht,
And what colour will they wear?
Says the Shan Van Vocht.
What colour should be seen
Where our fathers' bones have been
But their own immortal green?
Says the Shan Van Vocht . . ."

". . . an' there's one says to me: 'Matt Finn, ye'll never be a leader, the way ye're too ready with y' tongue an' too slow with a pistol entirely!' That went to me heart like a blow, lad' an' me with the sound of a grand speech I'd made still in me ears! But when we were alone again this friend o' mine sees the distress that's on me, an' gives me the little book, an' says: 'There's them that fight with pistols, lad, an' bold brave boys they may be, but their fightin' ends with their last breath. It's the way a bullet goes into a man's body, an' there's an end—but a word goes into his mind, an' let ye be tellin' me,' he says, 'where's the end o' that? For he's passed it on, Matt, before he dies, into another mind, an' from there it goes into a third an' there's no end to it at all.' So I take the book, lad, an' I read it, an' I see that it's the truth he's speakin'. I'm not knowin' where's the man that wrote those words. Under the ground, maybe. I'm not knowin' where's me little book they took from me. Ashes, most like. What matter? The words are still in me mind, an' in thousands more. Some o' them have been passin' into your mind, me fine boy, the way ye've heard me say them so often . . ."

It was true. Johnny rarely thought of them consciously, any more than he thought of his food once he had eaten it—but like his food, they were moulding him. He was barely thinking of them now, but they were there, passing into his nerves, his blood, his muscles, driving the hand that held a hammer and the hand that held a nail, building a new room on the hut, an asylum to receive the fugitive.

By now they were often planning the business. Twelve sheep had been stolen early one morning several months ago. Finn and Johnny, taking charge of them from Billalong in the wild country west of the Cow Pastures, had driven them hard that first day to put as much distance as possible between themselves and the searchers who would surely come after them when the animals were missed at nightfall. But they had seen nothing of pursuers—perhaps Billalong had succeeded in setting them upon a wrong trail—and the rest of the journey had been made in little over a week. The sight of the tiny flock grazing between the stumps and logs of their cleared acres had given them new heart. Now they felt secure, and began to speak of the future. Johnny could see for himself the prospect of more labour than two men could accomplish, even with the erratic help of Billalong and Ngili.

Finn said once:

"There's three men often in me mind, Johnny. All lifers, so they'll still be there most like—unless they're dead. There's Will Howett, a weaver, an' George Humfreys that was a farmer back in Devon once, an' young Danny Murphy that got in throuble before he learned a trade —but a fine boy with strong arms an' a strong heart in him. Aye, those would be the three I'd be wantin'—but there . . . ! Divil sweep me if I'm seeing how we can pick an' choose . . ."

And again:

"There's a power o' work to be done in this valley, lad—an' we needin' more than two pairs o' hands now . . ."

And lately:

"The time's come for some plan. I'll not think o' this man or that— it's how to get any o' them, lad. How . . . *how* . . . ?"

"I get 'em like I got you," Johnny suggested casually.

"Arrah, it's not so aisy! It's not often they're workin' at the very water's edge the way I was. They're scattered round the farm, it might be a mile from the river, with an overseer always there, an' he with a pistol in his belt, bad cess to him! If I could but get word to Humfreys, now . . ."

"All right," said Johnny in his phlegmatic way, "I find him. I tell him what you say."

Finn glanced at his young companion with a faintly disturbed curiosity. He felt that there was something in this kind of direct audacity, this apparent failure fully to understand the efficiency, or adequately to fear the vengeance of the master-class, which was almost childish—or (as Andy had once thought) half-witted. He realised suddenly that Johnny's attitude to the world he had left *was*, in fact, childish; for all the superficial knowledge he had since accumulated, he had remained in his relationship to it the child he had been when he left it. The lad had the rather pathetic courage of ignorance. No memory of shackled feet, of brutal taskmasters, or of the flogging-post shrivelled his heart with fear. His knowledge of servitude was buried deep in the confused, lost world of early childhood, and even there it was a memory of spiritual, not physical wounds. And over it he had built up in the years of his native life a habit of fearlessness, a strange, innocent, unassailable assumption of freedom . . .

And was not that a kind of strength? Had it not already permitted him to succeed in escapades which a man with more mature and bitter knowledge might have shrunk from attempting? Finn, feeling his own courage as something desperately preserved in the face of perpetual fear, his own will to freedom surviving only by the painful and unceasing effort of a spirit scarred and battered, looked at him with a kind of envy.

"How?" he asked.

Johnny answered easily:

"Oh, I find a way. Maybe like a native—maybe like a white man. Maybe in the dark—I don't know. When I get there I find out how. I stay on the other side of the river a few days, watch, go across at night, maybe. I find this Humfreys—you only tell me what he looks like."

"A big man, he is," Finn said slowly, "with a black beard on him, an' black eyes. An' a finger missin' on his right hand here, the way he got

it cut off with a scythe. . . . Listen, now, Johnny, this is the way of it.
If ye can find him, say ye come from Matthew Finn. Say these words
to him: 'a storm in Bantry Bay'—he'll be knowing then that ye do come
from me. Tell him what we're plannin', lad—but don't tell him where
we are. For the love o' God, not a word o' that to any livin' soul! For
if things go wrong, we're not wantin' the soldiers on to us. Tell him
we'll be comin' . . ." He paused.

"When?" asked Johnny. But Finn was silent for a few minutes,
thinking hard.

"We'll be waitin' till near the end of the harvest. There's hot weather
then, an' we'll take a time when it's dry, an' the grass burnt up with the
summer, an' we'll cross the river an' set alight to the grass an' the bracken
near the lower fields. There was a fire one time before, an' every man
brought from his work to help put it out an' save the crops—all confusion,
an' smoke, an' rushin' here an' there—that's the way it'll be again. Tell
him to be waitin' for a fire the like o' that at the end o' the harvest—an'
when he's hearin' three pistol shots, to break an' run towards where they're
comin' from—him an' any others he's been after tellin' of it. But not
more than four or five. Say that's left to him—for there's those in the
gangs not to be trusted. Tell him we'll be there, lad—with three muskets
an' two pistols . . ." He broke off again, frowning. Johnny looked at
him enquiringly, and he added: "But we'll still be on the wrong side o'
the river."

Johnny waved that away.

"Canoes. I get those easy. I see Milbooroo. Billalong, Gooradoo,
Balgundra—they all little boys, black little boys; no one thinks anything
when they go down the river in canoes."

"By God, an' that's the truth, lad! Four canoes, eh? Two men can
go in each, if there's that many get away besides ourselves."

"Maybe." Johnny shrugged. "White men don't paddle canoes good,
maybe they turn over an' drown, maybe they get across."

Finn nodded.

"Aye—we can't do more than give them the chance, I'm thinkin'.
Billalong can be goin' down the day before, and the gossoons along with
him, all in their canoes. . . . An' they can be landin' on the west bank,
the way they'll be in no danger whatever comes, an' by night we'll join
them. An' the next morning before daylight we'll go across towin' the
empty canoes, an' hide them in the bracken, an' wait till we judge it's
time to set the grass afire . . ."

He fell silent, his anxious eyes fixed on the ground. Johnny, to whom
all was settled—and being settled, as good as accomplished—whittled
at a piece of stick unconcernedly until his companion grasped his arm
suddenly, and spoke again with emphasis.

"Now let ye listen to me, boy. This is a plan for desperate men—
but be all the powers, it's hardly a plan at all, the way we must be waitin'
to see what the moment brings. . . . If blood must be shed, it must, but
I'd have ye remember it's not for killin' that we'll be there. Whisht
now . . . !" He stayed Johnny's threatened interruption with a vehement

gesture. "It's no tenderness I'm feelin' for the skins o' Mannion nor his overseers, the curse o' Cromwell on 'em! If so be the need should come I'll put a bullet in 'em an' care less than if it were a wallaby! But mark this—it's no battle we're after wantin', for they'd win it as sure as the sun shines in the sky yonder. We'll not be there for that—but to create a confusion, an' escape—with one man, or two, or three, or whatever—an' with our own skins whole, lad. Let ye not be forgettin' it."

He looked hard at Johnny, and his grip tightened on the young man's wrist.

"An' there's another thing. Whatever comes—*get y'self away!* Ye hear me? Howld y' tongue, now, an' look about ye! What is it ye're seein'? Look! Fields with crops in 'em, an' good cleared land with sheep grazin'. There's goats an' fowls, an' cattle down there by the river, an' behind us there's a hut with y' woman an' child in it. I tell ye, Johnny, I'm not minded to go into this business with the fear on me heart that there'll be neither one of us to come back to it all, the way we've worked an' suffered to make it . . ."

Johnny pulled his arm away angrily.

"We come back—me, you, the other men . . ."

"Aye," agreed Finn wearily, "that's the way of it. . . . But if so be aught should go amiss, lad, ye'll come y'self. Remember now, that was me word. Remember it if ye see that the plan is failin'. Don't be stayin' if by stayin' ye may be taken. Come back with me—or with another—or with more than one—or come back alone. . . . But *come* . . . !"

* * * * *

The Court House was full on the Saturday morning towards the end of October when Mr. Macarthur brought forward his complaint that Mr. Campbell's nephew had illegally dispossessed him of certain property in the shape of two copper boilers, valued at forty pounds sterling.

He was well pleased to have an audience. There were those who whispered that he had contrived it, desiring that as many as possible should hear and be influenced by his denunciation of the Governor. Others, more favourably disposed to him, declared that the crowd had gathered spontaneously—a throng of humble and downtrodden people, anxious to discover from the outcome of this case whether private property might with impunity be snatched from its owners by an abominable tyrant.

To Mark, standing inconspicuously at the rear of the room, it seemed that most of the comments he heard betrayed little sympathy for the champion of their rights; but there was no doubt that as that gentleman rose to his feet to speak, a hush fell upon the murmurous room.

Macarthur was in no hurry to break it. Matters had gone well enough so far. The Bench of Magistrates comprised Mr. Palmer, Major Johnston, and Mr. Atkins—". . . and who knows," a man beside Mark had muttered, "which way that wavering old toper will lean?" And indeed, thought Mark, Mr. Atkins—fumbling and shaking and pale as his neckcloth—looked extremely unhappy.

Mr. Campbell's nephew had related how he took possession of the

boilers, and Mr. Griffin had described the incidents leading up to the
case. Mr. Harris, adroitly questioned by Macarthur as "a medical gentleman accustomed to chemical operations," had deposed that the body of
a still was no more suitable for distilling than any other pot or boiler;
and Mr. Jamison had given evidence that he was present when the boilers
were seized. And now Mr. Macarthur, having requested the Judge
Advocate to make a written record of his speech, grasped the lapels of
his coat, settling it carefully about his shoulders, adjusted the high white
peaks of his collar, looked slowly round the Courtroom, and finally
allowed his eyes to rest for a moment with cold, disdainful menace upon
the nervous countenance of Mr. Atkins.

"I have produced evidence," he began mildly, "to prove to the Court
that two coppers or boilers of stills were taken out of my house on
the 22nd instant without my consent." He paused and fixed the
Governor's young secretary with his eye. "Mr. Griffin has declared in
evidence that the Governor told Mr. Campbell, Naval Officer, to take
these bodies of stills and ship them on board the *Duke of Portland*. By
the acknowledgment of the respectable young gentleman Mr. Robert
Campbell, Junior, he was told by his uncle to execute that command . . ."

He paused again and made a slight gesture, as if to say that, having
disposed of tiresome preliminaries, he would now come to the substance
of his argument. But again he was in no haste to do so, and allowed
the silence to gather a tense expectancy. He had done with the cold
recital of events; he had done, in fact, with the whole trivial business of
the boilers. Now he was concerned with the real issue between himself
and Bligh, in which this absurd squabble was important only as he could
make it so. Now he was concerned with a colony psychologically dis-
organised by rumour, confused by slander and enmity, dry tinder, he
hoped, for the spark of emotional rhetoric which he knew how to apply.

When he spoke again his voice was so changed that there was a little
start and stir amongst his audience. His personality was something he
had learned to use as a musician his instrument, his anger something that
could be played soft or loud, his enmity something that could be muffled
or released with a sudden crash of noise, as he released it now.

"It would therefore appear," he declared, his voice carrying a ring
like struck metal, "that a British subject, living in a British settlement,
in which the British laws are established by the Royal Patent, has had
his property wrested from him by a non-accredited individual, without
any other reason being assigned than that it was . . ." his voice dropped
to a tone that was almost gentle, and in that utter silence more effective
than a shout, ". . . *the Governor's order!*" He allowed that to sink in.
He allowed the extending silence to breed an unspoken word—*tyrant*—
tyrant—tyrant!

When he spoke again, addressing himself to the Bench, passion was
muted as suddenly as it had been sounded; defiance, having roared, was
driven back like a tiger to its cage. A slight inclination of the head, a
resigned lifting of outspread, empty hands, proclaimed him a wronged

man, submitting himself with becoming dignity to the decision of the Court.

"It is therefore for *you*, gentlemen, to determine whether this be the tenor on which Englishmen hold their property in New South Wales."

He sat down.

Mark, lingering when the crowd dispersed, saw Mr. Macarthur surrounded by his adherents, and receiving their congratulations upon his victory. He saw Major Johnston, looking well-pleased, mount his horse and ride off for Annandale. He saw Mr. Atkins, followed by a clerk with a sheaf of papers, emerge from the Court House with Palmer, Campbell, Griffin, and Gore. As they passed him and made their way up the street towards Government House, he thought that the Judge Advocate walked among them less as a companion than as an elderly schoolboy, detected by his fellows in some unforgivable act. Campbell's expression was thunderous; Gore and Palmer were exchanging comments in an angry undertone, and young Mr. Griffin's face was positively scarlet with wrath. There would be a formidable outburst of rage from His Excellency, Mark thought, when the verdict was made known to him.

But he was wrong. Bligh was angry, and his manner showed it clearly enough, but he listened in grim silence while the Judge Advocate —the papers fluttering in his unsteady hands like leaves in a wind— read aloud the proceedings of the Bench. His Excellency's fierce blue eyes grew fiercer still as he leaned forward to catch the words of the verdict, over which Atkins, in his agitation, was stumbling badly:

"*The Bench is—er—of the opinion that Mr. Robert Campbell Junior was not authorised to take the boilers . . .*" He darted a glance at the five inimical faces surrounding him, and his voice quavered to a halt.

"Ha!" said Bligh. "Well, Sir. Continue!"

"*. . . he not being either a magistrate or a Naval Officer, nor did he receive any orders from the Governor to that effect . . .*" Mr. Atkins fumbled for his handkerchief and passed it nervously over his mouth. "Signed," he mumbled, "by Major Johnston, and . . ."

". . . and yourself!" snapped Palmer.

". . . and Richard Atkins!" muttered Gore.

". . . and one who should blush to declare it!" cried Griffin indignantly.

"You may well hesitate to name him, Sirr!" interjected Campbell's cold voice, with a fierce Scottish roll of the final "r".

Bligh silenced the clamour with a wave of his hand, and Atkins floundered on:

"*Mr. Palmer is of opinion, as Mr. Campbell Junior acted under the orders of Mr. Robert Campbell, N.O. Senior, he is justified in what he did.*"

Bligh did not move. He sat with his elbows resting on the arms of his chair and his hands clasped before him, leaning forward slightly, his forbidding stare never wavering from the Judge Advocate's face. It was the other gentlemen who exploded. Griffin was fairly stammering with wrath and excitement:

"I declare to you, Sir, that Macarthur's speech was inflammatory in the highest degree. He had no other purpose than to incite the people to hatred and ill-will against you . . ."

"The fellow's a villain!" Gore added hotly. "And thanks to our friend here . . ." he eyed Mr. Atkins malevolently, "he'll be further encouraged in his villainy . . ."

"Neverrr," declared Mr. Campbell, his r's vibrating with a rich and contemptuous emphasis, "have I obsairrved so disgrraceful and rrepulsive an exhibition of trreacherous pusillanimity . . ."

Mr. Atkins, weakly protesting, wilting under this chorus of indignant reproaches, was nevertheless disturbed most keenly by that silent, remorseless stare of Bligh's; it beat on him like a searchlight, and made him feel naked. He had never been comfortable in this legal function of his, and lately, since the tempo of strife had quickened in the colony, and shown signs of expressing itself with increasing violence in the Courts, he had become almost panic-stricken. "I was not bred to the law . . ." he mumbled querulously, but no one took any notice. He felt ill-used; life had treated him with abominable unfairness by pitchforking him into a duty for which neither training nor character equipped him, and in which, it appeared, he was to be forever in the centre of an uproar. He was almost in tears when Bligh got to his feet suddenly, and the tumult faded as he moved.

"Never mind," he said abruptly, still staring at the Judge Advocate with that expression which so bitingly mingled curiosity and contempt. "Never mind, gentlemen—it will do."

Atkins, interpreting the note of finality, and the abrupt, glacial silence as dismissal, withdrew miserably to assuage his wounded feelings with a much-needed drink.

*　　　*　　　*　　　*　　　*

Mr. Griffin was yawning over his papers. The Governor had prepared a despatch of such inordinate length that his secretary, who had already been at work upon a fair copy for the greater part of the day, felt that he would never reach the end of it. The face of the country had been described, the quality of the soil and the methods of its cultivation discussed; the means employed by Government to aid the settlers, the traffic in spirits, the nature of crops and pastures, the climate, temperatures, winds and rainfall, had all been touched upon. The bad character of many of the prisoners and ex-prisoners had been deplored, and the opinion expressed that only from the next generation was any great improvement in virtue and morals to be expected. Mr. Griffin had reached His Excellency's observations upon the settlers, and for a moment the notion flashed in his mind that perhaps all the turmoil that raged among the eminent and prosperous inhabitants was superficial. Perhaps it was out there in the country districts that the important things were happening —the easing of the burden on small farmers, the unspectacular reforms that assured them, by degrees, a little security; the slow fusing of men with the earth; the settlers *settling* . . .

"*Classes of plain, sensible farming men, of moderate expectations, are the most valuable to come here. Such as the Blaxlands, who lately came out, become so speculative as to care for nothing but making money. They endeavour to monopolize under a principle of buying as cheap as they can and selling dear . . ."*

Griffin came back to turmoil. He was too young and too impatient to hold that fleeting vision of centuries, against which this scrambling for wealth had seemed trivial. It was too clamorous and imminent—fierce, threatening, arresting to the mind and the eye, like a fire in the night, beyond whose glare you could not see, or even remember, the quiet, dark background of the earth.

"As to the civil officers, I must in point of duty, as in honour, object to Mr. Atkins, the Judge Advocate . . ." Mr. Griffin's pen moved more briskly as he mentally endorsed the words he wrote. *". . . he has been accustomed to inebriety; he has been the ridicule of the community; sentences of death have been pronounced in moments of intoxication; his determination is weak; his opinion floating and infirm; his knowledge of the law is insignificant, and subservient to private inclination; and confidential cases of the Crown, where due secrecy is required, he is not to be trusted with . . ."*

Griffin pursed his lips. He knew that Mr. Atkins had been seen deep in conclave with Mr. Macarthur a few days before the recent Court case, and that he had been complaining bitterly to several people since of his deeply-wounded feelings. Almost automatically his pen copied a paragraph about the military, but his attention was caught and fixed by the words: *". . . there is no remedy but by the change of military duty, a circumstance which can only prevent a fixed corps becoming a dangerous militia . . ."*

Dangerous was not too strong a word, he thought soberly. Hostility had gone beyond mere obstructionism, and the Governor knew it. That speech of Macarthur's had proclaimed him to the whole colony not only an enemy of His Excellency, but an enemy now openly defiant; and it was plain to the least observant eye that he was rallying the Corps about him . . .

*   *   *   *   *

In the first week of December Macarthur's schooner *Parramatta* returned to Sydney. The convict who had escaped in her—and who, by now, was safely on another vessel bound for America—would have marvelled, and perhaps rejoiced, had he known that he, one of the lowliest in the colony, was to provide another pretext for battle among its highest.

Bligh, convinced that the master, John Glen, had connived at the escape—a belief subsequently confirmed—directed promptly that Campbell decline to pass the ship's papers for entry, place the vessel under arrest, and declare the bond forfeited. Mr. Macarthur countered immediately with a letter to Glen, asserting that since he considered himself dispossessed of the schooner, its master and crew were no longer to look to him for pay or provisions.

Events moved fast in the heat of rising tempers and personal animosity. The master and crew, abandoned without money or sustenance, came ashore in violation of the local regulations. Mr. Atkins, summoned to Government House, found Bligh in his most belligerent mood.

"Campbell tells me that Macarthur has stopped the wages and provisions on the *Parramatta*," he said curtly. "Devil take him for a mischief-making incendiary! I see through this! No matter! Be seated, Sir, and give me your attention. Glen has shown Mr. Campbell a letter from Macarthur to that effect. He came here to deliver a copy to me also —but I sent him about his business—a damned scoundrel abducting prisoners from the colony! Then he goes on board and reads this letter to the crew, and they come ashore—doubtless to the great satisfaction of that unscrupulous manufacturer of tumults and commotions! Now, Sir! I desire you to send for the master and mates and crew, and take their depositions. Immediately, if you please!"

Mr. Atkins obeyed. A few hours later, apprehensively aware of fresh storms about to break, he was writing to Macarthur:

"Sir,
   "I have it in command from His Excellency the Governor to acquaint you that the master mates and crew of the schooner *Parramatta* have violated the Colonial Regulations by coming unauthorised on shore, and that in their justification they say you have deprived them of their usual alowance of provisions, and that they have no means of subsistence on board your schooner. In consequence of such their representations, I request your attendance at Sydney to-morrow morning at 10 o'clock to shew cause for such your conduct.
                                        "I am, etc.,
                                        "R'd Atkins, J.A."

It chanced that Mr. Macarthur was entertaining Mr. Mannion and Patrick to a glass of wine when this letter was delivered to him. Excusing himself, he read it, and passed it to his elder guest with a shrug.

"You see, Mr. Mannion? This is tyranny, naked and unashamed. Do you know, Sir, that Bligh has deliberately caused the *Parramatta* to be moved from a safe anchorage to one where she is in hourly danger of going ashore? He has placed constables on board her, though it has always been the custom before to place a military guard in such cases. In this we may see his inveterate enmity to the military, Sir—and in my opinion there will be an open breach ere long, for the soldiers are in a resentful mood. It is no new thing—I have seen it coming for a long time. A month since I wrote to Piper at Norfolk Island, and assured him that the Corps was rapidly galloping into a state of war with the Governor."

Mannion studied the letter with some disquiet, and passed it to his son. He knew very well that if the soldiers were in a resentful mood it was one which had been carefully fostered by his host. Wealth, position and worldly interest in the colony placed him on Macarthur's side, but the instinct of one born in the ranks of privilege made him mistrustful of a policy which was rapidly taking shape as rebellion against His Majesty's deputy. It was highly disconcerting to find himself thus torn between two loyalties which, in all his previous experience, had never conflicted. He asked curiously:

"You will—obey this summons, Sir?"

Macarthur laughed shortly.

"I assure you I shall do nothing of the kind. I have already declined any further responsibility for the schooner. Am I to bear the expense of paying and victualling the crew of a vessel over which I have no control? I tell you, Mr. Mannion, someone must meet this tyrant with firmness, or we shall all be undone. This is but part of a studied plan, Sir, to oppress all respectable members of the community. My own ruin is determined upon. Of this I have the most incontrovertible proof."

"Indeed?" Mr. Mannion's reluctance to talk politics was overborne by curiosity. "May I ask what it is?"

Macarthur drew his chair forward and lowered his voice.

"*Written* proof, Sir, in the hand of no other person than that notorious rogue Crossley—a known and convicted perjurer, whom our Governor sees fit to take into his confidence! I possess a paper, Sir, which this perambulating disgrace to his profession drew up following the case I brought against young Campbell. You may recall that on that occasion I conceived it my duty to speak plainly—for which I am accused in this paper of seeking to libel the Governor, to bring him into contempt, and to incite the people to hatred by what it chooses to call scandalous, wicked and seditious words! I'm informed on good authority, Mr. Mannion, that upon the very day following that Court case, the Governor sent Griffin and Crossley down to Palmer's at Woolloomooloo—a conveniently secret and secluded location for the hatching of plots!—and there the three of them with their heads together concocted this complaint against me, the ingenious Crossley decking it out in legal phrases."

Mannion was deeply intrigued. Secret and secluded as Woolloomooloo might be, it was evidently not beyond the all-seeing eye and the all-hearing ears of Mr. Macarthur. And that was surely a very curious paper for him to have in his possession . . . ?

"You were fortunate to obtain this document, Sir," he observed with no more than the hint of a question in his voice. Macarthur eyed him sharply.

"I was indeed. It was no less than an act of Providence, Sir. For once the disgraceful habits of the abominable Crossley served a useful purpose, for it was while he was carousing with a certain worthy fellow known to me that he boasted in his cups of what was planned to bring about my downfall, and drew this paper from his pocket. His companion, with great presence of mind, was able to—er—secure it, and brought it forthwith to me. I assure you, Mr. Mannion," pursued Macarthur nobly, "my horror and indignation were not alone for myself, for I realise that the Governor's malice will not be satisfied with making me its victim. Others will share the same fate. I speak frankly to you, Sir, and to your son. We have endured this man long enough—there must be a change soon."

Patrick, astonished, began:

"But, Sir, by what means . . . ?"

Mannion interrupted quickly:

"I trust the home authorities will see the necessity, Mr. Macarthur. I'm told that many complaints have been sent to England."

"Almost every person of any pretension to credit and respectability," Macarthur replied emphatically, "has protested. Townson—Fitz—Wentworth—both the Blaxlands; Minchin and Harris have written in very plain terms to King, and their remarks will, I hope, find their way to official quarters. Johnston has complained to the Commander-in-Chief. Jamison tells me he has stated to Castlereagh that nothing will induce him to continue serving in the existing circumstances, and many others . . ."

"Doubtless these gentlemen will be attended to." Mr. Mannion rose. It was obvious, he thought, that opposition to Bligh was developing into an organised attack, and that Macarthur was its spearhead. Would the ambitious and imperious nature of this man be content with the hope that written protests might in time bring about the Governor's recall? *Dared* he be content with that? He was becoming very deeply involved, and his refusal to appear to-morrow as requested by the Judge Advocate would involve him further still. Was he planning something else? Would he stop at anything? Mr. Mannion would himself be glad enough to see Bligh go, but he had no intention of being implicated in . . .

He cut the thought off. He did not know what was brewing, and he was determined not to know. He must warn Patrick to extreme circumspection . . .

He said:

"We will take our departure, Sir—with thanks for your kind hospitality. I must reach Beltrasna by nightfall, and Patrick goes on to Sydney to transact some business for me. I fear I shall be leaving him a grave responsibility in peculiarly difficult and unsettled times."

Mr. Macarthur turned a considering gaze upon the young man. There was no very promising ally here, he reflected; this unfledged lad appeared to be without much interest in matters which affected him more deeply than he knew. But he would learn—and what better mentor than himself? He said cordially:

"If I can be of any assistance to your son, Sir, he has only to command me. I have weathered many storms in this colony," he continued, turning to Patrick with all the compelling power of his personality in his smile, "and I can claim to have learned at some expense how to conduct my affairs and guard my rights. Should you at any time after your father's departure feel the need of advice, pray come to me."

"Thank you, Sir," Patrick answered, entirely won by that smile. "You are very kind."

Mr. Macarthur, having sped his guests at the doorway, was left standing alone with Mr. Atkins' letter in his hand. He re-read it, stood thinking for a few moments, and went indoors to compose his reply.

* * * * *

The result of it, as Patrick learned during his few days in Sydney, while the town buzzed with the sensation, was that Oakes, the Chief Constable, had been despatched to Parramatta with a warrant for Macarthur's arrest. Some said the constable had been received with civility and offered a glass of grog; some declared that he had been roundly abused. But there was no doubt about the fact that Mr. Macarthur had declined to be arrested.

Mr. Oakes had been in a lamentable state of indecision. To lay hands upon the great John Macarthur was something which he was loth to do—particularly since that gentleman had got the better of Governors before, and might do so again. And then what might not be the consequences for a luckless constable who had been over-zealous in the performance of his duties? Mr. Oakes, admitted from the darkness into the lamplit parlour at Elizabeth Farm, stood twisting his hat in his hands, acutely dismayed and embarrassed. He had never before been called upon to arrest a gentleman like this, who stood so straight, and forbidding, with his black brows frowning over his dark, angry eyes, his expression a withering mixture of arrogance and contempt, his son and his nephew beside him, his wife pale-faced watching from across the room, his younger children peeping through the door, his servants straining their ears from the kitchen, all the evidences of his wealth surrounding him. Mr. Oakes, having delivered his warrant, waited in an agony of apprehension. Mr. Macarthur, calling for pen, paper and ink, sitting down at the table to write his reply, standing up again to read it aloud with haughty and disdainful emphasis, hypnotised Mr. Oakes by the sheer force of his pride-ridden self-confidence. Its first words—an apostrophe to the unwelcome intruder—transfixed the constable like the gaze of a rattlesnake.

" 'Mr. Oakes. You will inform the persons who sent you here with the warrant you have now shewn me, and given me a copy of, that I will never submit myself to the horrid tyranny that is attempted till I am forced; that I consider it with scorn and contempt, as I do the persons that have directed it to be executed.' "

He tossed the paper on the table, his eyes still menacingly on Oakes' face. For once his anger had almost mastered him, and fury shook his voice a little as he said:

"If the person directing that warrant had served it instead of you, Mr. Oakes, I should have spurned him from my presence. If you come a second time, come well armed, Sir!" He controlled himself with an effort, and smiled, but the smile was stiff. "Let them alone," he said to his nephew and his son; he looked across at his wife, and reassurance softened his rigid smile. "Let them alone—they will soon make a rope to hang themselves!"

He bent to scrawl a date and a signature on the page, and pushed it across the table to the constable.

"You're a poor man, Mr. Oakes," he said dryly, "and you may give offence by returning without your prisoner. You had best go to Captain Abbott—tell him I decline to obey this infamous and illegal warrant, and ask his advice how you should act."

Oakes picked the paper up uncertainly.

"You wish me to take this, Sir?"

"By all means," Macarthur assured him briefly.

"Shall I not call upon you in the morning?" suggested the constable almost pleadingly. "You will then have had time to consider . . ."

"*NO!*" Macarthur turned on him violently. "Do I not know my own mind? Take it now!"

Mr. Oakes took it, and made his way in great agitation to Captain Abbott's house. The Captain was in bed, and refused to get up, but the constable spoke with him through his bedroom window.

"Mr. Macarthur declines complying with the warrant, Sir!"

"The devil he does!" exclaimed Abbott, resting on one elbow and peering into the night.

"He's given me a paper, Sir, setting out his objections. I can't see to read it, but it's couched in—in violent terms, Sir—'horrid tyranny' and the like—and expressing scorn and contempt of the people that sent it. What shall I do, Sir?"

"Mercy on us!" cried Mrs. Abbott from behind the shelter of her husband's recumbent form. "Now there'll be a to-do!"

Abbott ran a hand through his dishevelled hair, and swore in an undertone. Jack Bodice, he thought, was on the warpath with a vengeance! He had been apprehensive about the growing feud, but unable to keep aloof from it. He was an officer of the Corps and—though he had but little liking for some of his fellows, and less for their methods— he could not disentangle himself from his natural alliance with the military faction.

"There's no need for violent measures, Oakes," he said uneasily; "the warrant doesn't call for that."

"Shall I go back to Sydney in the morning, then, Sir?"

"Yes, yes, that would be best. Devil take it, man!" exploded the Captain peevishly, "I'm not disposed to be plagued with such matters at this hour! If Mr. Macarthur bade you take the paper to the Judge Advocate, then take it, and leave me to my sleep!"

Mr. Oakes, with muttered apologies, faded away into the night.

* * * *

Macarthur lay awake till almost daylight. He had talked long with his wife after they retired, and she had fallen asleep at last—troubled, but confident, as always, of his wisdom and rectitude. He himself felt no desire for sleep; his brain was active, stimulated, whetted by anger and a sense of crisis. He lay thinking, planning, considering his position.

The flaring of his temper in the interview with Oakes had been spontaneous enough, for the threat of arrest and public humiliation had outraged his pride. But no matter into what temporary emotion a situa-tion might betray him, there was always a subtle and calculating mind at work in John Macarthur. He had never for an instant lost sight of the fact that behind the merits of any single dispute or charge lay the fundamental war of policy between Bligh and the monopolists. That war was largely expressing itself in a series of battles between the Governor and himself, and it was clear from the document so fortunately secured from Crossley, that his enemy was no more in a mood for compromise than himself. Good, he thought, let there be war; and he set himself methodically to the task of weighing his peril against his advantages.

For he was in peril now. The disputes in which he had so far been involved were minor ones in law—the business of the promissory note, the business of the stills, his argument about the forfeited bond for the escaped convict, his responsibility for the unlawful landing of the *Parramatta's* crew. But now, to-night, in his defiance of a magistrate's warrant, in his written accusation of "horrid tyranny" against the civil authorities, and his declaration of scorn and contempt for the King's representative, he had taken a long stride forward into a position where he might be charged with an offence not minor at all . . .

He turned over—carefully, so as not to disturb his wife—and lay on his back, frowning thoughtfully into the darkness. Would his adherents stand firmly by him in so grave a matter as a charge of sedition?

His frown relaxed. It was always possible to sway those who possessed with the fear that their possessions were endangered. Not only the officers, but most of the rank and file of the Corps owned property—land or livestock. Useful preliminary work had already been done during the past months in stimulating this fear. He thought of the six householders who had been told to remove their dwellings from the Government domain. He thought of the soldier to whom Bligh had declared that no man should have two houses and others go without. He even thought of an order to destroy straying dogs in the town. Nothing was too trivial if it could be used to feed the suspicion that Bligh was bent upon interfering with private property. He thought of the settlers. They were, almost to a man, for Bligh and against himself—but even that could perhaps be turned to account. He had heard a rumour that they were preparing to petition the Governor for trial by a jury of the people—and the Corps could not fail to see the blow to its influence which would be dealt if justice were no longer administered by soldiers . . .

His thoughts lingered on the Courts. If he were brought to trial before a Criminal Court—and he almost certainly would be—there could be little doubt of his acquittal. Six officers, and the Judge Advocate. . . . Unless they were frightened by the seriousness of the charge, he could count on the officers. But was it enough to be acquitted? Bligh and his policy still there, and gathering strength with every month that passed . . .

He stirred restlessly and threw back the coverings; even a single blanket was often too hot on these December nights. He would never be safe nor satisfied till Bligh was gone. His mind played with tentative thoughts of a plan so bold and dangerous that even some of the Governor's bitterest opponents might well shrink from it. His scornful mouth curled even more scornfully. Perhaps this very business that was now brewing could be manipulated to increase their bitterness, and still their qualms? That—and every other circumstance that offered, however, trifling, must become fuel to feed the flame of animosity towards Bligh till it became a raging bonfire. He rummaged in the darker recesses of his memory where—half-forgotten, but never quite discarded—he stored miscellaneous fragments of information, scraps of conversation, oddments of scandal, rumour, or anything else which, of no immediate value, might some day be useful.

There was that debt which Atkins owed him—a little matter of twenty-six pounds. But since it had been drawn fifteen years ago there would be by now a handsome addition of interest, and the salary of a Judge Advocate was not large. It was fortunate that he had not sued for its recovery long ago—this was a much more opportune time. To challenge the probity of the Judge before whom he was to be tried would open up useful avenues of attack—he could intimidate Atkins—he could protest the injustice of being tried by a debtor . . .

And there was that land that King had leased him only a year or so since, near the Church in Sydney. A mistake on King's part, he thought with a faint smile, for an order made by Phillip in 1792 had reserved an area of which it was part as Crown land—and King had not only granted leases within the boundary for five years, but renewed them for another fourteen. And it was well known that Bligh was full of grandiose notions for improving the town, and pleased with his completion of the Church and its "iron pots" . . . ! Yes, that was a good line to pursue. . . . Harris, also, had a lease within the boundary—and Jamison—and Paterson. . . . Arbitrary interference with private property . . . tyrannical disregard for the rights of respectable citizens . . . fear, fear, yes, he would draw them together . . .

And suddenly—surprising himself—the quick, exultant confidence he felt formed itself into an inward laugh that actually broke through his lips and sounded, startling and quickly stifled, in the quiet room. For he had seen that in everything he had done or might do his arch-enemy was also his ally.

Bligh—who tried to rush bull-headed through the subtle mazes contrived by John Macarthur! Bligh—who lost his temper! Bligh—who could be irritated, pricked on to precipitate measures, spurred to reckless, violent language, tempted to rash, unguarded expressions, goaded to a fury that could be made to recoil upon his own head! Look at him! Listen to him! Is not this the appearance—are not these the manners of a tyrant . . . ?

Outside in the still, warm hush of the summer dawn he heard a cock crowing; the sky between the curtains was already paler than the framing darkness of the room. To-day he would go down to Sydney—but not in answer to that impudent demand from Atkins. From now on every word would be a barb, and every move a goad . . .

He turned over on his side, and slept.

*   *   *   *   *

Mr. Oakes set out from Parramatta for Sydney before daylight, and it was but six o'clock when he arrived on the Judge Advocate's doorstep. Mr. Atkins, sleep barely banished from his eyes, took one look at the document which the constable proffered, and was instantly and most unpleasantly wide awake.

He listened in mingled amazement and alarm to Oakes' graphic account of his reception the previous night. "Flew into a passion, he did, Sir, and swore he'd never submit. Says to me: 'If you come back, come well armed, for there'll be blood shed!' Wrote this paper, Sir, and tells me to bring it to those who sent me."

"God bless my soul!" Atkins, clutching a gown over his nightshirt, and running his fingers nervously through his wild grey hair, re-read the incredible missive. "You'll have to wait, Oakes," he said peevishly. "I must see the Governor. I can't do anything till I've seen the Governor. Don't stand there, man! Go away! Come back later—no—wait—I'll send for you when I want you . . . !"

He dressed hurriedly, and in the pale early-morning sunlight hastened through the quiet streets to Government House. His Excellency had not yet risen; Mr. Atkins, too flustered to wait, went home, and within half an hour received a summons that brought him scurrying forth again. Bligh was in the garden, and heard the story quietly enough, but his face reddened dangerously, and his eyes were fierce. "Send for Oakes," he commanded, and began to tramp angrily up and down the paths. Atkins, returning from his mission, found him studying Macarthur's written defiance as he walked.

"There's the indictment that Crossley made out after that business of the stills," he said, glancing at Atkins but speaking half to himself. "That —and the *Parramatta* affair—and now this. . . . What was it Oakes told you that he said? 'They will soon make a rope to hang themselves'? By the eternal God!" he shouted so suddenly that Atkins winced, "he's made his own rope, and I'll see he hangs on it!"

When the constable appeared Bligh turned on him sharply.

"Well, Sir! So you didn't fetch him, eh? You permitted yourself to be duped and brow-beaten. No matter, no matter, it's done, and there are steps to be taken. You shall walk with us, and relate everything that passed, down to the smallest detail, Sir. Atkins, you will convene a bench of Magistrates for this day to hear Mr. Oakes' depositions. Now, Mr. Oakes: you arrived at his house . . . ?"

*   *   *   *   *

The constable's deposition was discussed at length later in the day by the Bench. Major Johnston, ill-at-ease among his fellow-magistrates, Campbell, Palmer and Atkins, could not but agree that the charges were serious. He was not the first or the last man who, willing for another to fight his battles, yet grew nervous when his champion fought too boldly. "Damnation!" he thought uneasily, "Macarthur's going too far!" He watched gloomily while a second warrant was prepared and read.

". . . and whereas the said Francis Oakes came this day before a Bench of Magistrates . . . and deposed on oath that the said John McArthur had refused to obey the said warrant, but treated it in the most contemptuous and disrespectful manner; these are therefore to authorise and require you to take into your custody the body of the said John McArthur, Esq., and him safely lodge in His Majesty's gaol until he shall be discharged by due course of law . . ."

*   *   *   *   *

Patrick, returning to Beltrasna on the 18th of December, had much to think about. During the whole of his stay in Sydney there had been no subject for conversation save the sensational developments of this bitter feud. Dramatic stories had been told of the search made for Macarthur before he was finally discovered sitting with several other gentlemen in the house of Mr. Grimes, the Surveyor-General. Patrick himself had seen him passing under arrest through the streets to the Judge Advocate's, and had learned from one of the gentlemen in whose bail he was released, that he was to be brought before a Bench of Magistrates in the morning.

That was two days ago. Yesterday there had been more excitement and another storm of discussion when the Bench committed him for trial at the next Criminal 'Court, and again released him in the bail of Mr. Garnham Blaxcell and Lieutenant Bayly. Patrick's acquaintances in the town were all fervent Macarthur sympathisers, and loud in their indignation; the picture they painted of a persecuted but indomitable upholder of free men's rights against the machinations of a despotic Governor was so colourful and romantic that Patrick felt himself stirred, and for the greater part of his ride home his mind was still occupied with these high and exciting matters. He was even tempted to daydreams of himself actively involved in the politics he so disdained.

But as he cantered along the road between Toongabbee and Beltrasna he seemed to leave it all behind. He sniffed the pleasant scent of the surrounding bush, and promised himself that when he reached home he would walk down to a secluded spot he knew on the river bank, and wash the dust and heat of the road from his body in the clear water of the Nepean. He was very conscious of his youth and strength to-day, for among the officers and gentlemen of Sydney he had realised that in a colony where women were formidably outnumbered, moral standards relaxed, virtue surrendered to overwhelming pressure, and a personable young man with money in his pocket might find amorous adventure with no trouble at all. He had found it, and his blood ran warmly.

Nearing home, he was surprised to meet one of the overseers galloping along the dusty road towards him. He reined in and lifted a hand, but the man hardly paused as he called a hurried explanation.

"It's the mistress, Sir—she's been taken ill, and the master's sendin' me for one of the medical gentlemen. His Honour told me to ride as fast as I can, Sir . . ."

He was gone, lost in the cloud of golden dust that pounding hooves flung up into the late afternoon sunlight. Patrick stared after him with troubled eyes for a moment, and then turned for home and spurred his horse to a canter. He dismounted at the steps, threw the reins to young Morgan who ran to attend him, and hurried into the house.

He learned from Ellen that Conor had been taken ill a couple of days previously, but now seemed so much worse that they had become alarmed.

"Can I see her?" he asked.

"I think she's sleeping, Sir. Bessie's with her."

"I see. Where's my father?"

"He was called out to attend to something in the east fields, Sir. He'll be back shortly."

He left her and wandered restlessly about the house. Cousin Bertha was not to be seen. He put his head in at the nursery door where Dilboong was attending to the children, and gave Julia a package of candied oranges and other confections which he had brought for her, but he was in no mood for childish prattle, and resisted her entreaties to remain and play with her. Besides, looking at Dilboong, he felt an impulse so quickly stifled that he did not identify it, and knew only that he wanted to get out of the room.

He stood on the verandah and looked down across the fields, moody and depressed. It had been a fair season, but the grass had a tired, scorched look, and only where crops were still standing was there any real green. The harvest was well under way, and most of the wheat was stacked, but the maize in the fields towards the northern end of the property would not be in for some weeks yet. He wondered if the eggs of that destructive fly which had made its appearance some three years ago were already hatching its voracious grubs in the wheat-stacks; and how long it would be before the plough entirely superseded the laborious hoe throughout the colony.

In one of the lower fields he saw that a gang of men was at work, with Toole in charge, sowing a field from which wheat had recently been harvested, with maize. He frowned. He knew that this was quite a general practice, designed to get two crops from the same ground in the one year, but he had been listening to a good deal of talk upon agricultural matters, and knew that there were those who deplored such forcing of the soil. When the direction of affairs was altogether in his hands, he resolved, he would not permit it; and as if in challenge to that audacious thought, he heard his father's brusque voice behind him.

"So you're home, Patrick. Come into the study—I wish to speak to you."

He had just come in from riding, and he looked hot, dusty, and ill-tempered; he wiped his forehead with his handkerchief as he sat down at the desk and waved his son to a chair.

Patrick began:

"There's a great uproar in town over Mr. Macarthur's . . ."

"Never mind that now!" Mannion's voice was irritable. "You can tell me of it later. At the moment there's a more urgent matter, closely concerning ourselves. Shut the door, if you please. I'm disturbed, Patrick. I'm seriously disturbed . . ."

Patrick, having closed the door, sat down again and asked:

"What about, Sir?"

"Toole has discovered a plot," Mannion said abruptly, "among our convicts. It seems he had cause to find fault with that miserable fellow Driver who, when threatened with punishment, fell into a panic and offered to give certain information in return for clemency. He declares that a man named Humfreys was sent by Toole to get a bucket of water from the river when the men were working down there, and was accosted by a native in a canoe, who told him that he came from Finn . . ."

"Finn? That was the man who escaped?"

"The same." Mannion picked up a pen, played with it for a moment, and threw it down. "Driver says he was not admitted to Humfreys' confidence, but gained his knowledge by listening to him whispering with another convict when they thought him sleeping. He says he could not hear everything, but gathered that this Finn—in company with confederates, no doubt—proposes to attempt the release of some of our convicts."

"How?"

"Presumably by 'armed attack."

"Did he hear the time mentioned?"

"He says it was to be at the end of the harvest—which is far from being as definite as I could wish. The signal is to be a fire in the fields, and three shots in rapid succession. More than this he does not know."

"But the other men?" Patrick suggested. "Humfreys and the man with whom he was whispering—can't you learn more from them?"

"No," said Mannion grimly.

Patrick asked, his voice rather uneasy:

"You—have tried?"

"I have tried. Toole has been attempting to—persuade them to speak all the morning. Humfreys admits nothing except that he did speak with a native, but was unable to understand him. That much he could not have denied, for Toole himself, and all the gang, had seen the native fishing about the river for several days, and Toole saw the canoe paddled over to the bank where Humfreys was. He called to the man not to loiter, but thought nothing more of it—for which I have censured him severely. It should be understood by now that I wish the natives kept away from the property altogether, and particularly from any communication with the convicts. In any case, that is all I can get from Humfreys; and both he and the other man declare that Driver is lying, and that no such conversation as he describes ever passed between them."

Patrick said doubtfully:

"Perhaps he is lying. Merely inventing a tale in order to escape punishment . . . ?"

Mannion rose and threw the windows open, his expression scowling and preoccupied.

"I do not think so. It is the mention of that accursed rogue Finn that disturbs me. I had occasion to discipline him on several occasions, and he nursed a rancorous hatred towards me. If ever there was a violent, rebellious, seditious, ill-disposed rascal, it was he! This is precisely the kind of devilish plot he would hatch. Moreover, Driver is not an astute man—in fact he is little better than a half-wit. Why should he introduce that rascal's name into a fairy-tale? For God's sake, Patrick, stop tilting your chair! Can't you sit still?" He added abruptly, after a pause: "Come here."

Patrick stood beside him at the window. He waved his hand at the landscape.

"Somewhere into those hills that abominable felon vanished—and others like him. Where are they now? Dead, I am glibly assured on all sides! The country is barren, I am told—no man can exist there! I am not convinced. We know nothing of what lies beyond the mountains. The thought has preyed upon my mind, Patrick, that while we sit here in unbelievable complacency, a veritable colony of depraved characters may be forming—nay, even associating with native women, and raising a brood of monstrous progeny half-felon and half-savage! And meditating God alone knows what violence and outrage. Here is a hint of it. More than a hint! It amounts to proof of what I have always contended!"

Patrick asked tentatively:

"What makes you think there is a gang concerned in this? Were any numbers mentioned?"

"There was specific mention of no one but Finn, so far as that doltish fellow Driver can tell me. But he must have confederates—no man would attempt such a thing alone. Since his messenger was a native we may suppose he is friendly with some tribe—perhaps living with it—but there is no doubt in my mind that he must have joined forces with other desperadoes escaped from the settlements. And as the signal is to be three shots, they are evidently armed."

Patrick still looked dubious. He had begun to recognise his father's determination to be right at all costs, and it was surely a trait which might affect his judgment in this matter. He had been prophesying peril from armed bands ever since Patrick could remember; and it was unlikely he would regard even the vaguest rumour with much scepticism if it seemed to bear out one of his predictions. It was possible, of course, that there might really be such a plot; but on the whole Patrick was inclined to think that the terrified mind of Dan Driver had conceived it. He asked non-committally:

"What shall you do, Sir?"

Mannion made a harassed gesture.

"I shall question Humfreys and the other man again—and perhaps two or three of the other convicts, though there is no evidence that they know anything of the business. Damnation take it, we're busy, and the harvest upon us—I can't have my men incapacitated just now! If I can discover nothing else I shall order incessant and unremitting vigilance. I shall use every possible precaution. These villains shall not take us unawares. I shall expect the most complete co-operation from you, Patrick."

"Of course, Sir," said Patrick rather resignedly. His father flung himself into his chair again.

"And now—illness! You met the man I sent to Parramatta, I suppose? By God, life is nothing but trouble lately! And you bring news of more from Sydney?"

Patrick began to relate the dramatic story of Mr. Macarthur's arrest. Mr. Mannion's face grew gloomier than ever as he listened.

1 8 0 8

From that day life at Beltrasna became so disagreeable that Patrick more than once wished himself back in London. The week after the disclosure was filled with feverish activity. Mannion toyed with the idea of laying the whole business before the Governor—but he was avoiding Bligh; he was avoiding the whole explosive situation in Sydney. Nor did his memory of previous interviews with Governors on the subject of out- laws encourage him to believe that his tale would meet with proper attention, particularly at this time. He reflected also that, having once invited official notice, he would be bound to deliver Finn and such other miscreants as he might capture into official hands for punishment—and he had other plans for them. He preferred to handle the whole matter himself, and set to work.

He scoured the colony for additional men—not convicts or emancipists, but free men who had served other masters reliably, and might be trusted to earn what he paid them. These secured, he posted watchers along the river bank at night, to give warning of suspicious incidents. Finn was minutely described to all who had not known him. Firearms were in readiness. The convicts were even more closely watched and guarded, and they worked in irons.

But day followed day, and nothing happened. The harvest was practically over, and Mr. Mannion grew ever more restless and distrait as Christmas passed, still uneventfully as far as this outrageous plot was concerned, but not without other trials.

Conor's poor health and listless attitude of indifference to himself had darkened several months, and with this threat of trouble hanging over him he would have wished to send her again to Sydney. But her sudden collapse had ended in a miscarriage from which she was recovering but slowly, and not yet strong enough to undertake so long and rough a journey. She had been removed during her illness to the small bedroom which had once been Mr. Harvey's, and there she remained, pale and tired, with little to say to him when he spent a dutiful half-hour by her bedside.

News from Sydney, too, was more and more disturbing, but though it increased Mr. Mannion's uneasiness, the thought of that impudent scheme which he had uncovered dominated his thoughts. To him every day that dawned was surely the one upon which the ruffian, Finn, would attempt to carry out his foul design, and he could neither rest nor allow others to do so. He permitted his overseers no leave, kept his free labourers about the property, and curtailed their ration of spirits. Their mood, too, grew tense, and their tempers frayed as they reported signs of re- belliousness and unrest in the convict hut. At night they could hear the men singing—always one song, and they knew it well:

"Jem Stag is my name, I'm the Major's own boy,
Swear away, swear away so steady,
My pastime of late is with lives for to toy,
For that sport, Sir, I always am ready;
I will swear black is white, day is night and all such,
For to hang and transport each reformer,
And my reasons for this are 500—not much,
Swear away, swear away, right or wrong, I say,
'What do you think of Jem Stag the informer?'"

Strange accidents began to befall Dan Driver. A pitchfork tore a
gash down his leg; the wheel of a dray ran over his foot; a falling tree
missed him by inches; his fingers were crushed by the blow of a sledge-
hammer. The overseers never saw these things happen, nor, it seemed,
did anyone else. Dan himself was far past explaining anything. He
was nothing but a walking terror; his stupidity was passing rapidly into
imbecility, and he only babbled when questioned. All the time, wherever
he worked, fragments of that song came to his ears.

"I pray you don't think that I'd blush at a lie,
Swear away, swear away so handsome . . ."

He began to scream and run. To scream without words, and to run
without purpose. At any hour those screams might begin, and the overseers, swearing furiously to mask the chill they felt, would pursue him,
cuff him into silence, and fling him back into the hut alone. Mannion,
hearing him from the house, would start up with an oath and slam the
window shut; Conor, roused by them from a fitful doze, would shiver
and weep; Patrick, contending with the final stanzas of a poem celebrating
the ennobling influence of the arts, would fling his pen down in despair,
his mood destroyed. And Toole, passing on his round of inspection late
at night, would hear that devilish chant again, a relentless and incessant
murmur from behind the log walls of the hut:

"My trull's saucy name it was shop-lifting Nan,
She for Botany sailed with Peg Horner,
And the family name I'll keep up while I can,
Swear away, swear away, right or wrong, I say,
'What do you think of Jem Stag the informer?'"

It was all very different from the serene and pleasant life which
Patrick had imagined. His father, besieged from all directions by actual
or threatening troubles, became increasingly short-tempered and exacting.
He was obsessed by suspicion, unwilling that the smallest task should be
performed without his supervision, reluctant to permit his son any but a
subordinate part, irritable, over-particular, nagging, obstinately insistent
upon his own methods. There were long hours when Patrick was idle,
and his thoughts turned to lively company, exciting events, and alluring

pleasures in Sydney. His father said roundly:

"Certainly not! Have you no sense? These villains may descend upon us at any moment, and we need every available man at hand. I'm astonished, Patrick—nay, shocked! Do you wish to return and find your home burned to the ground, and your family murdered? Kindly don't interrupt me! You have no conception of the lengths to which such blackguards will go. Besides, as I have repeatedly told you, matters are in a very unsettled state at Sydney, and I will not permit you to become involved in—er . . ."

"In what?" demanded Patrick sulkily.

"In any kind of intrigue. This place reeks of it, and always has. Macarthur and his followers are undoubtedly forming a cabal against the Governor. I don't altogether blame them, for he's an intolerable fellow, but I suspect them of planning measures which—however provoked by his arbitrary behaviour—are most unwise, and what I would not wish my son to appear in. You will remain here."

Patrick remained. The long, hot summer days passed slowly. He could not concentrate upon his poem. His duties, beneath the prying and censorious eye of his father, became irksome. He had no one to talk to. He visited Conor in her room sometimes, but when the conversation passed from daily happenings to more general and abstract subjects, they were both aware that they could not pursue it far without reaching conclusions which implied criticism not only of Mr. Mannion, but of themselves, and all their life; constraint fell upon them, and finally silence. Cousin Bertha could not hear what he said, and was too old, in any case, to be congenial company. The children were but children, and Ellen he avoided. There remained Dilboong. It was not conversation that he wanted from her— and she did not dream of denying the young master anything he might demand.

For Conor there was nothing left but her journal. When the house- hold was asleep she rose and fetched it from a locked chest, opened it with a tiny key which hung on a ribbon round her neck, and wrote far into the night. During the early months of her pregnancy she had neglected it, unable in her lassitude and intermittent attacks of nausea to face even this small exertion. But by Christmas she had begun to feel stronger, and a re-awakening interest in life drove her to the book which had become her only confidant. Her fine, pointed writing was unsteady in the earlier entries, for she was still feeble, and tired easily, but it grew firmer as the weeks passed.

"December 26th, 1807.

"This is the first day I have been well enough to write for some time. Yesterday Julia's seventh birthday. Feel it strange that I am not more Distressed that I should have lost my poor unborn babe, but cannot pretend to any great grief.

"Learn from Stephen that a most remarkable Plot has been discovered, involving the convict, Finn, who has formed a Desperate plan to abduct other convicts from Beltrasna. Am at a loss to know whether to take this

Seriously, since he has become so devoured by suspicions that I sometimes think his Discernment is impaired. Nevertheless am bound to admit that there may be some Foundation for his fears on this Occasion. Frequently speculate upon how Finn has passed the time since his escape, and in what wild and Awful surroundings. Feel that if he seeks the escape of others, he must surely conceive that life 'n the Wilderness, however Rude and destitute of Comforts, is to be preferred to their situation here. Ventured to express this thought to S. but he replied that Finn's only object is to increase his Band, for the purpose of pillaging and murdering the Settlers."

*   *   *   *   *

At Government House, too, Christmas had passed sadly, for no one could longer pretend that death was not very near to Captain Putland. On the fourth day of the new year Bligh took his weeping daughter in his arms, and led her from the room where she had kept so long and sad a vigil.

For all his robust constitution he felt weary as he accompanied the funeral procession up the hill to the Church. His eyes were grim as he looked at the ranks of the New South Wales Corps, turned out in full array to pay formal respects to the son-in-law of the man they would so willingly destroy. Major Johnston, as one of the chief mourners, wore an expression of decorous melancholy, and the uniforms of his men made a brave splash of scarlet in the hot, almost blinding light of the mid-summer day. The Governor, receiving expressions of sympathy and condolence, was bitterly conscious of their emptiness; he knew that the veil of routine ceremony so decently spread over naked warfare for these few hours would soon be withdrawn.

He had no time to think of his grief, though it stabbed his heart when he saw his daughter's pale face and reddened eyes. His study had become something like the headquarters of a general in the field, and he was seldom absent from it. Campbell, Palmer and Griffin were constantly with him. Atkins, with Crossley at his elbow, was deep in the business of drawing up the indictment for Macarthur's trial. Gore and Fulton came and went, bringing news and rumours of enemy manœuvres.

Macarthur was employing the interlude of his bail so actively that the town lived in a perpetual tremor of gossip and speculation. He had already launched his attack upon Atkins, and his memorial to Bligh had dwelt upon the unhappy effects which might be produced upon the morals of a community if its Judge Advocate should resist payment of a just debt. The Governor's cold reply that the Court of Civil Jurisdiction was always available to injured creditors, and Atkins' hot assurance that he had every intention of paying, were both, so far as Macarthur was concerned, irrelevant. He was discrediting Atkins, and goading Bligh; the time being short, he prepared as many goads as possible for simultaneous use.

It was only four days after the funeral that Bligh learned of another manœuvre in which he instantly discerned an ulterior motive. Arrangements had been made by Johnston, he discovered, for Abbott's transfer from Parramatta to Sydney in an exchange of duties with Captain Kemp.

"A fine scheme!" he said to Palmer with angry contempt. "Abbott's a magistrate—and in this way they hope to gain a preponderancy on the Bench. Is it supposed that I'm so simple as not to see through their ruse? Oh, very well, very well, I can contrive artful plans too! Let Abbott come—but we shall no longer require his services as a magistrate!" He laughed shortly, and then remarked: "I'm informed that the great trouble-maker himself has come down to live at Sydney for a time—so that he may be more favourably placed for sowing discord, I don't doubt! Let him come! Let them all come, let them lie, let them whisper, let them fabricate and distort! I shall show them who governs this colony, by God!"

But Macarthur was allowing him no respite. Upon the next day tidings were brought that he had begun to fence the land which King had leased to him near the Church. Bligh flew into a passion.

"Devil take the scoundrel and his infernal mischief-making! No one knows better than he does the situation in regard to those leases! Why does he choose *this* time—and he under arrest to be tried by a Criminal Court!—to take steps which he knows I cannot permit? This is nothing but flagrant and deliberate provocation! It is calculated to set me at defiance and inflame feeling against me. Griffin! Where's the Surveyor-General? Find him! At Ultimo? I don't care where the devil he is—find him! Send for him—bid him wait on me immediately!"

Mr. Grimes, who had but recently returned after a long absence at Port Dalrymple, had taken up his abode with Mr. Harris. But unlike the Surgeon, he was still employed in a civil capacity, and in this capacity now found himself at odds with his good friend Mr. Macarthur. He was neither disconcerted nor taken by surprise, however, for this latest move in Jack Bodice's spirited campaign had been an open secret in the anti-Bligh camp for several days. It was with his tongue snugly tucked in his cheek, therefore, that he obeyed the Governor's summons, received his instructions, and withdrew to write a letter.

"I am directed by Governor Bligh to inform you that he has particular orders respecting the ground contiguous to the Church; that he cannot allow any person to build near it; that he is sorry to inconvenience Mr. Macarthur, but that any situation he may fix on to an equal extent, the Governor will allow him to occupy it, or that he may await the decision of His Majesty's Ministers on his claim to his present lease."

Macarthur, smiling quietly to himself, replied in his smoothest phrases that it had given him inexpressible concern to discover that his occupation of the site in question should be obnoxious to the Governor. Rather than seem disregardful of the wishes and instructions of persons entitled to the highest respect, he was, he declared earnestly, most willing to make the sacrifice required of him, with no other condition than . . ." His smile broadened a trifle as he concluded.

Bligh, when this letter was submitted to him, erupted again.

"So he'll deign to accept the land between Blake's and Jamison's, will he? Devilish noble and self-denying of him, I declare! Immured in the seclusion of Parramatta as he has been—withdrawn from the world like an anchorite, attending to his own affairs and interfering with nobody—he's doubtless unaware that this lot is on the foreshores of the Cove, and reserved for the Government boats' crews! Great God in Heaven, I have known some hypocrites in my day, but never one to equal this! Be so good as to inform him, Mr. Grimes, that this land is not available!"

Macarthur, impeccably patient and long-suffering, bowed to the Governor's decree, and named two other lots, equally unavailable. Bligh, with increasing irritation, refused them, and pointed out a situation at the end of Pitt's Row which Mr. Macarthur might have if he desired. "Nevertheless," he raged, "it's nothing but a farce! There are innumerable good situations unoccupied. He doesn't want them—he wants only to flout and obstruct me!"

He was a man who did not take kindly to being flouted, and as the soldiers of the Corps continued to fence the disputed land, he sent for Johnston, and peremptorily ordered him to stop the work. Macarthur moved briskly about the town, speaking eloquently and indefatigably of this fresh interference with his private concerns.

"I have been put to great expense over this business. You can see for yourself, Sir, that many of the post-holes are sunk in solid rock. My daughter's health demands residence in Sydney—but it grows increasingly evident, does it not, that the legitimate activities of respectable people are no longer to be tolerated? However, we shall see! Tyranny must be met with firmness. I'm in no mood to submit to this kind of arbitrary conduct on the Governor's part . . ."

*   *   *   *

Mark Harvey, walking up the hill on his way to school next morning, saw that passers-by were loitering curiously about Mr. Macarthur's land, and a little knot of people had gathered. Macarthur himself was there, deep in conversation with Abbott and Kemp; and Mr. Divine, the Superintendent of Public Labour, was riding up and down near the partly-completed fence. The three gentlemen were watching him, and as Mark paused he saw Macarthur—with a bleak smile, and a few words over his shoulder to his companions—advance towards the Superintendent and accost him in a clear and carrying voice:

"You seem interested in my property, Mr. Divine. May I ask if you have any instructions regarding it?"

Divine looked down at him sourly. He found himself remembering a day in 1790 when—having arrived himself only a fortnight earlier—he had gone down to the shore to watch newcomers disembarking from a vessel that had just come in. Among them had been a young lieutenant named John Macarthur—a nobody, with not a penny in the world save his pay, but even then with a stare that he recalled—a bold, dark, arrogant stare . . .

It was confronting him now—seventeen years bolder and more arrogant! Jack Bodice had come a long way, while Nicholas Divine, who had supervised convicts in England—still supervised convicts. The Superintendent felt that he would be glad to see that pride brought low, and he answered shortly:

"I have, Sir."

He knew of the rumour which had reached Bligh that the soldiers were again coming forward to continue the fencing, and he knew that his own presence here was the Governor's attempt to checkmate that move. "My orders are," he stated, "that if any post is put up, I'm to pull it down." He stared away over Macarthur's head, ignoring the bystanders, but not oblivious of the excited stir and murmur among them. No one, however, was more conscious of an audience than Mr. Macarthur, nor possessed of keener dramatic sense. Without moving his eyes from the Superintendent's face, he played to staring eyes and gaping ears.

"Indeed?" he responded. "This must be instantly decided."

He removed his coat, folded it carefully, and laid it over a pile of timber. He pulled the sleeves of his fine linen shirt up a little, that their cuffs might not be soiled. He walked to where a few posts lay scattered on the ground, and studied them for an effective moment. Mr. Divine watched him from the corner of his eye. The onlookers nudged each other and whispered. Kemp said gleefully to Abbott: "I'd give a month's pay to see Bligh's face when he hears of this!" But Abbott, wishing he had not chosen this day for a visit to Sydney, responded only with an anxious grunt. Mr. Macarthur lifted a post, and set it upright in the nearest hole.

Mr. Divine dismounted without haste, and removed it.

"Governor's orders," he remarked phlegmatically as it clattered to the ground across its fellows. His manner was official, but the light of battle was in his eye, and he added cryptically: "When the axe is laid to the root, the tree must fall! I shall be back, Sir."

He mounted and rode away. With that parting promise of fresh developments, Macarthur and most of the little crowd lingered, but Mark, with pupils awaiting him, hurried off. He was deeply perturbed. He had but few acquaintances among the military, but the soldiers were always about the streets, and in the shops and taverns of the town, and he had overheard enough lately to recognise an ominous change in their deportment. Could it be otherwise, he thought, when two of their officers stood by and watched so open a defiance of the Governor? It was being said by some that if Macarthur were convicted at his coming trial, he would be heavily fined and imprisoned; a few even spoke of the pillory. But others declared with the cynicism born of long experience as observers of Jack Bodice's stormy career, that none of these penalties would overtake him. He would be acquitted. Would he not be tried by a Court of officers, they asked, and were *they* likely to bring ruin on one who had served their cause so well?

Mark, trying valiantly to keep his attention upon his class, wondered what fresh sensation he would hear of when he took his accustomed seat in Mrs. Stables' eating-house to-night. As he passed the Church on the way home, he noticed that the post-holes had been filled in, and the timber

removed. A round to the Governor, he thought, and then hesitated.
Was it . . . ?

Macarthur counted it a round to himself. He had another tale of
tyranny to tell. He was, on the whole, well pleased with his progress.
He had led his adherents step by step until now even those who hung
back could hardly withdraw. He had appealed to fear and cupidity; he
had raised the cry of loyalty to the Corps; he had provoked Bligh to
public conflict with him. He had even hinted to Johnston and Abbott
that a tyrant who refused to be intimidated might be deposed, and though
they were nervous, they had listened. But come what might, he had
urged, it was of the utmost importance that they should all both be, and
publicly appear, united. The monster must learn that he had men of
determination firmly combined against him.

Major Johnston called upon the Governor.

"In Governor King's time, Sir," he explained, "it was the custom in
the Corps to hold a regular mess dinner. The officers are anxious to re-
establish this pleasant arrangement. I suppose that in doing so we should
not meet with any objection from Your Excellency?"

"None at all, Major," answered Bligh, civil but watchful. "When
do you propose to hold it?"

"The day after to-morrow has been suggested, Sir. The twenty-
fourth."

"I see," said Bligh, and saw, indeed, very clearly. On the night
before Macarthur's trial the Corps would assemble with its friends for a
friendly and convivial gathering—including, doubtless, the six officers
whom he had nominated to comprise the Court, and the two gentlemen
who were Macarthur's bailsmen. Perhaps, he thought grimly, they would
even invite Macarthur himself . . .

He said curtly:

"Very well, Major. I trust you will spend an enjoyable evening,
and . . ." he could not resist it, ". . . find absorbing topics of discussion."

Johnston's complexion was normally red, and the Governor could not
be sure if it grew redder; the fellow, he thought, was so obtuse that his
blank expression might be unassumed. He replied stolidly:

"Thank you, Sir. You'd still further increase my indebtedness if
you would give me a permit for a pipe of wine for the mess?"

"By all means, Major," Bligh agreed. "There was some twenty-two
thousand gallons came in a week or two ago on the *City of Edinburgh*. I
ordered it all into the store, since it would be most undesirable—as I'm
sure you would agree—for so large and sudden a deluge of alcohol to
descend upon the community—but we can spare a pipe of wine for the
Corps, Sir!"

    *   *   *   *   *

The colony as a whole went about its business quietly enough. Like
all small communities, it relished its parochial gossip, and tales of war
between the Governor and the Corps were passed eagerly from mouth to
mouth. But the poor, though they might take sides in the argument with
their neighbours, had been bred to believe that high matters of policy

were for their betters to decide. The rank and file of the Corps, occupied with their own small affairs and their routine military duties, cursed Bligh, and left the rest to their superiors. The settlers, busy with the harvest, reminded each other of measures he had taken to improve their lot, and hoped for the rout of his enemies. The more lowly townsfolk would bestow their allegiance according to their personal interest and the expediency of the moment. A tradesman, dependent on the patronage of the officers, was an officers' man. A labourer or artisan employed by, or indebted to, or otherwise financially involved with any of the Governor's opponents, was his opponent too. Jack Bodice and his friends were not loved for their own sake—but few men dare quarrel with to-morrow's daily bread.

Nor will they, as a rule, quarrel with to-morrow's little luxuries. The mess dinner having been arranged for the recreation of the officers, Mr. Macarthur—benevolently anxious to provide the rank and file also with a little innocent revelry—accosted Sergeant-Major Whittle in the street.

"Good-day, my friend," he began genially. "Your good wife is well, I hope, and the children?"

The flattered soldier saluted.

"Fair enough, Sir, thankee, though there's my youngest not so well. Her mother says she's feelin' the heat, like."

"No wonder," observed Mr. Macarthur sympathetically. "Very trying weather it is—thirsty weather we might say!"

"All weather's thirsty weather, I say, Sir!" remarked Whittle, and went on gloomily: "Though more so now than once, before a certain person come here, Sir!"

"That reminds me, Sergeant-Major," Macarthur said, ignoring the innuendo, "I'm about to make a purchase of wine, and it has occurred to me that the good fellows in the ranks should share in the little celebration the officers are having to-morrow night. I could let them have some at a very low price—and I'm sure they'll gladly drink to Major Johnston and their officers—eh?"

"That they will, Sir!" Whittle agreed enthusiastically. "And to yourself, Sir, if I may make so bold."

Macarthur's smile was sad, patient, and deprecating.

"That might not be wise, my friend! I'm in disfavour at the moment, as perhaps you know."

"They'll not care for that, Sir," Whittle assured him. "Come what may on a certain occasion in the Court House . . ." he winked meaningly, ". . . they'll drink to you, Sir, take my word for it!"

"Very good, then," said Macarthur briskly. "Will you supply me with a list of the non-commissioned officers and privates who would like a few gallons for their own use? There will be no hurry for payment, you may tell them, and the price will be low."

"I will for sure, Sir, and bring it you myself. Many thanks, Sir, and good day to you!"

Macarthur acknowledged his salute, and went on his way.

* * * * *

Conor had recorded the passing month in her journal.

"*January 2nd, 1808.*

"*Have been unable to write for a few days, but feel stronger now. Patrick came to sit with me for a time this afternoon, and I fear he is cast Down, and finding the seclusion of Beltrasna not to his Taste. Hear there is great Tumult in Sydney owing to the ill-feeling between the Governor and Mr. Macarthur, whose trial is to take place this month. Bessie says it is rumoured there will be Bloodshed if matters not composed between them, but surely this is Idle talk. Here all is governed by Stephen's anticipation of the Plot, and when he comes to see me he is no sooner seated than he Starts up, recollecting some order he must give, or some task he must overlook, and I declare I am not sorry, since I have nothing to say to him.*"

"*January 4th, 1808.*

"*When I open my journal its leaves fall apart where I placed the fragments from the little book which once belonged to the convict Finn. Have read them so often that I now have them by heart, and am frequently reminded of them when pursuing other Thoughts. S. very discomposed this morning and wearied me with endless talk about the evil nature of felons, and the deceitful Conduct of Ellen. Found it strange that he should speak to me of deceitfulness and Ellen in the one breath, and was tempted to say so, but thought it not of sufficient Moment.*

"*Nevertheless, am myself not undisturbed by the thought of this Plot, and trust we may all be Preserved. Recall the conversations I had with Finn long ago, and am teased by the thought that he was not altogether an Evil man, though now planning so wicked an Attack upon us. Feel myself unable to see clearly what is Right or Wrong, which causes me much Agitation of Mind. Would dearly love to see Mr. Harvey and talk with him again. Recall that Governor King once spoke to me of liberty as a Beacon which draws men's feet in search of it, and wonder if the desire for it drew Finn from here, and now draws him back to secure the liberty of others. Also recall the words in his book, and am almost persuaded this must be so, but cannot reconcile . . .*"

Here tangled words, scratched out and re-written, more words attempted and in turn rejected, betrayed a struggle with elusive thoughts—a fruitless struggle, finally abandoned. "*Feel very poorly,*" concluded the neat but wavering handwriting, "*and am unable to put my Thoughts in Order.*"

"*January 10th, 1808.*

"*Bessie says the convict who gave information of the Plot now quite deranged in his Mind. Have several times heard him uttering horrible Cries . . .*"

"*January 16th, 1808.*

"*Weather very hot and Oppressive. Patrick moody, and showed great agitation this afternoon when the convict Driver began to scream. Fear*

*he has something Preying on his mind, and seem to discern something
strange in his manner to Dilboong. S. came in this evening before retiring,
and seemed disposed to display Affection. Asked if I do not find this
small room too dark and confined. Felt some Alarm, but feigned an attack
of faintness, and all passed off well . . ."*

"January·22nd, 1808.

*"Feeling very much better, though still fatigued if I remain active too
long. However, do not wish to appear too Robust at present, and consequently spend much time in my room. Patrick now declares he believes
the Plot was either the fabrication of a crazed Mind, or that it has been
Abandoned. S. also beginning to incline to this Belief, and has dispensed
with the services of some of the extra Men he engaged, but still insists
upon Watchfulness and Prudence, which makes us all very Uncomfortable, and causes much Dissatisfaction among the overseers . . ."*

*"To-day S. and Patrick have received Invitations to a Mess Dinner
to be given by the Officers of the Corps on the twenty-fourth. S. has
declined, and Patrick very put out . . ."*

*   *   *   *   *

There was little in the town of Sydney as a rule to provide an atmosphere of jollity, and the regimental band playing outside the Barracks
drew a crowd up the hill on that hot January evening before Macarthur's
trial. Bligh had under-estimated his enemy's shrewdness when he suspected that he might make one of the gathering indoors. His plan was
mature by now, and he had no intention of affronting the proprieties to
the extent of social intercourse with those who were to be his judges next
day. Nor did he wish to lend colour to any subsequent suspicion that the
Corps was met to plot rather than to eat, drink and be merry. He was
not present at the dinner. He took pains, in fact, to be where scores of
people could see him, and testify, if necessary, that he was not. Straight,
urbane and arrogant as ever, he strolled back and forth on the Parade in
the warm summer night, watched by many eyes, whispered about by many
tongues, but to all appearances lost in enjoyment of the music, and contemplation of the starry sky.

He was well represented, however, indoors. His nephew, Mr. Hannibal
Macarthur, and his eldest son, Mr. Edward Macarthur, were there, besides
his friends Garnham Blaxcell and Nicholas Bayly, in whose bail he had
been released. It was a noisy and hilarious gathering, and liquor flowed
freely. Major Johnston was attempting to drown his misgivings, for the
plan which had been expounded to him was making him very nervous.
He had spoken of it to Abbott, and Abbott had given him little cheer.

"Confound it, Major," he had said, "I don't like it! You may be
right—there may be mutiny if you don't take this step—Macarthur says
so. . . . Damn it all, I think he's right—the Corps is in a restless state,
and the Governor's given them good cause. . . . But mark me, Sir, if you
do this thing I advise you to send instantly afterwards to Paterson,
and give the command over to him—and then go home with the Governor

and account for what you've done. Otherwise it'll be said you did it to get the command yourself, and there'll be the devil to pay. Well . . ." he concluded, brushing it all away from him with a violent gesture, "I don't go down to Sydney till the twenty-seventh—I'm here at Parramatta—and damned glad to be out of it . . . !"

But Johnston, presiding over the banquet, was advancing willy-nilly to the very heart of it, half frightened, half exhilarated, hardly knowing how he had got there. He joined in the rather feverish laughter, and capped the bawdy tales, and wiped his heated face with his napkin, and beat time to the music—and drank.

Once he fell silent for a few moments. His eyes became unfocussed, the room faded away, and his mind fumbled for a memory. A tent . . . God in Heaven, he thought peevishly, why am I thinking of a tent? But there *was* a tent . . . and a queer, lonely, eerie noise that came from the darkness outside. . . . There was himself, young George Johnston, one of the first explorers of the colony, rising on his elbow to listen. . . . There were White and Collins sitting up too, and his own voice, queerly hushed, asked: "What is it?" And there was Phillip clambering to his feet and going outside to look . . .

Strange! It had all been strange then—the whole place damned strange, unfamiliar, unfriendly, uncaring. Pushing on foot through strange country, hearing strange noises in the night . . .

No more of that! A carriage outside to take him home to Annandale. Noises! An owl! Knew it well enough by now! Not strange any more . . .

But he leaned forward moodily, pushing his glass to and fro in the wet circle it had made on the table, and knew that it was still strange. Here, in this hot, crowded, noisy room, it had suddenly thrust at him the sensations of twenty years ago. He felt lonely and startled. He was no more at ease in this place and this situation than he had been long ago in that dark tent, surrounded by the unknown woods.

But he was here, and there was no escape, and the wine was passing. Kemp, beside him, was already showing signs of having drunk too freely, and Johnston laid a restraining but not altogether steady hand on the bottle the Captain was tilting over his glass, and muttered rebukingly: "Look here, Kemp, recollect to-morrow!" To-morrow there would be a trial; the six officers who were to sit upon it would need all their wits about them, and must not appear in so grave a rôle with the marks of carousal too clear upon them. . . . But Kemp had risen waveringly, and had joined some of the others in an impromptu dance, and the laughter and applause were deafening. Good fellows, Johnston thought bemusedly. Wonderful fellows in the Corps, every man of them! Shameful treatment they'd had from Bligh—shameful! Commanding Officer—must stand by them . . . must uphold dignity of the troops . . . grand fellows . . . !

He clapped, and laughed, and drank.

*   *   *   *   *

Bligh was in his study betimes next morning, awaiting the magistrates who had been summoned to attend him on this momentous day. Palmer, arriving at eight o'clock to find Griffin, Atkins and Crossley already with the Governor, was soon followed by Campbell. Mr. Fulton, from Parramatta, and Mr. Arndell from the Hawkesbury were admitted a little later, and the arrival of the Provost Marshal completed the small band of Bligh's adherents.

Already in the streets and about the Court House people were gathering, and by ten o'clock a crowd had assembled. Campbell, Palmer, Griffin and Fulton walked down from Government House, and the throng round the door parted to admit them. Provost Marshal Gore and his constables, conventional adjuncts of the Court, were in their accustomed places, and a buzz of excitement marked the entry of the prisoner with his two bailsmen, Blaxcell and Bayly. Mark, pushing his way into the crowded room, noticed that Macarthur's very passing left a trail of disputation behind; soldiers were arguing hotly with civilians, and he heard a muttered: "Down with Bligh!" swiftly answered by: "Down with Jack Bodice!" Major Johnston was nowhere to be seen. Some said that his chaise had overturned while returning from the dinner last night, and others declared that, overcome by liquor, he had fallen out of it; in any case, he remained in seclusion at Annandale while his officers prepared to do battle with Governor Bligh.

There was tension in the air. Everyone looked restless, Mark thought, save the cause of all the turmoil, who sat studying a sheaf of papers, and lifting his head now and then to stare about him with aloof but observant eyes. Campbell, Palmer and Griffin were talking earnestly, their heads together; Blaxcell and Bayly had stepped aside to converse with a couple of junior officers; almost every well-known person in the town seemed to be present, and Mark could see Mr. Howe pushing through the crowd near the door. He looked round, wondering if Mr. Mannion or Patrick might have ridden in for the occasion, but he could see no sign of anyone from Beltrasna.

A sudden hush made him turn again. The six officers and Mr. Atkins had appeared, and were taking their seats at the table. Kemp, Brabyn, Moore, Laycock, Minchin and Lawson all looked sallow after their evening's dissipation, but their scarlet uniforms advancing in a row were a bright note of colour in the dingy room, and a little ripple of sound that was near to applause came from the soldiers to greet them. The Judge Advocate, too, had attempted to fortify himself against the ordeals of the day, but he was sober enough; his haggard pallor was due less to alcohol than to a sleepless night and a lively apprehension. He arranged his papers before him, smoothed his grey hair nervously, called for silence, and rose to administer the oath to his six colleagues. This formality concluded, he turned to Captain Kemp as the senior among the officers, and, offering him the Book, was preparing to be himself duly sworn when Mr. Macarthur rose.

"May I be permitted, gentlemen? I wish to state an objection to the Judge Advocate sitting on this trial."

The decorous silence was instantly broken by a hum of comment from the spectators. Atkins waved a rebuke at them, and replied quickly:

"By the terms of His Majesty's patent this Court cannot be formed without the Judge Advocate, and I therefore . . ."

The officers, half rising in their seats, drowned his words in a clamour of argument, dominated by Kemp's voice calling out roughly:

"You're no more than a juryman, Sir, and one of ourselves. Read your objections, Mr. Macarthur—we'll hear them before swearing in this—er—Mr. Atkins."

Noise swelled in the room; hostile groans clashed with cries of approbation. Muttered altercations broke out around Mark, and a tall, sunburned fellow at his side said darkly: "There's a plot behind all this—and the redcoats are in it!"

Mr. Atkins, still excitedly protesting, had left the table and withdrawn to a form at the side. Macarthur was on his feet again, and the room grew quiet as he began to read from the papers in his hand.

" 'Gentlemen: It will, I am convinced, excite your surprise, as I think it must that of every impartial man, to hear that I am brought a prisoner to this bar, utterly unacquainted, except from rumour, of the accusations against which I am to defend myself . . .' "

"Shame!" cried a voice from the direction of Sergeant-Major Whittle. "Ar, get along!" snarled Mark's sunburned neighbour. "He'd defend himself agin the devil!" A ripple of laughter and a stir of anger eddied round the room for a moment. Mr. Macarthur's voice continued, clear and loud. He complained that he had already protested to the Governor against Atkins, and requested that a disinterested person should preside at his trial. "And where's he?" came sotto voce from the man at Mark's elbow. "We're all for ye or agin ye, Jack Bodice—an' I'm agin ye!"

Mr. Macarthur's objections to Mr. Atkins, it transpired, were six in number, and all impressively garnished with rhetoric. Mr. Atkins owed him money which, screened from the operations of the law, he was unjustly withholding. Mr. Atkins had for years cherished a rancorous inveteracy against him, John Macarthur, whose life and conduct, he hoped, was a public satire upon the Judge Advocate's. Mr. Atkins regarded him with vindictive malice because he had once given evidence to prove him a swindler. Mr. Atkins had combined and associated with that well-known dismembered limb of the law, George Crossley—and here Mr. Macarthur's voice took on a tone of fiercely righteous indignation; he produced a paper from his pocket and flourished it above his head.

" 'I have also proof in my hand in the writing of the veteran practitioner Crossley which will convince the most sceptical mind that other schemes have been agitated to deprive me . . .' " his voice gathered intensity, " 'of my *property, liberty, honour and life!* Here it is, gentlemen . . .' " He passed it to the Bench, and his next sentences were lost to Mark in the buzz of comment that rose.

" 'This precious document,' " continued Macarthur, his tone growing solemn, " 'came into my hands, as it were, by the interposition of Divine

Providence. It was dropped from the pocket of Crossley, and brought to me . . .' "

"If that weren't lucky for ye!" interjected Mark's neighbour sardonically. Macarthur was passing on to enumerate his fifth and sixth objections, and attention was divided between him and the object of his attack who, half rising now and then as if to protest, was making vague, agitated, ineffectual gestures with his hands.

" 'It will not, I presume,' " Macarthur read on, coldly ignoring him, " 'be denied that the Judge Advocate, from the composition of this Court, combines the character of Judge and juror, and that it follows as an indispensable consequence that any objection which applies to either character is strictly applicable to him. All that is, therefore, for me to do, is to lay before you the legal authorities on which I ground my right to challenge.' "

He shifted his position, rearranged his papers, and proceeded to a series of lengthy and imposing quotations from Tytler, Burn and Blackstone. The room was hot, and growing hotter. The onlookers began to fidget and murmur. Macarthur read on, unperturbed. He could afford to lose their attention for a few minutes while he built some apparent substance into his edifice of defamation. He could capture it again when he chose, and he did so in a peroration addressed to the officers, but directed at the public.

" 'Gentlemen, it would be an unpardonable waste of your time, and an insult to your understanding, to press upon you more authorities, for these I have submitted are clear to the point.' " The moment had come again for emotion, and the austere voice in which he had recited his gleanings from the law books, warmed to a rich and passionate appeal. " 'You will now decide, gentlemen, whether law and justice shall finally prevail against the contrivances of George Crossley.' " He flung his hand out dramatically towards the crowded room. " 'You have the eyes of an anxious public upon you, trembling for the safety of their *property*, their *liberty*, and their *lives*. To you has fallen the lot of deciding a point which perhaps involves the happiness of millions yet unborn. I conjure you . . .' " he cried, both hands imploringly outstretched towards his friends on the Bench, " 'I conjure you in the name of Almighty God, in Whose presence you stand, to consider the *inestimable value* of the precious deposit with which you are now entrusted.' "

The audience was alive again, stirring restlessly like water about to boil. Partisans of either side muttered angrily at each other. Atkins got to his feet, shaking a bundle of papers aloft, and trying to speak, but Macarthur had not quite finished and his voice carried over the rising swell of sound.

" 'For my own part,' " he declared with truth, " 'knowing you as I do, I have no apprehensions. I feel assured that neither expectation of reward or favour, nor dread of persecution, will influence your decision. It is to the officers of the New South Wales Corps that the administration of justice is committed; and who that is just . . .' " he asked with an ineffable expression of nobility, " 'has anything to fear?' "

Uproar broke out. Mr. Atkins, goaded beyond endurance, his voice high and quavering with rage, cried furiously:

"How dare you, Sir! You are attempting to obstruct the course of justice! This is no legally-constituted Court without the Judge Advocate in his place! I shall commit you, Sir, for such contemptuous language . . .!"

Kemp stood up and thumped the table with his fist.

"*You* commit?" he roared derisively. "*You?* No, Sir, I will commit *you* to gaol . . . !"

His words were drowned in the commotion. Atkins stared wildly round the room. The soldiers were growing excited, pushing and being pushed, climbing on benches, engaging in fierce altercation with those about them. Atkins waved his hands distractedly, and shouted above the increasing din:

"I order the people to disperse! This is no Court!"

There was an uncertain wave in the direction of the doors; the six officers were on their feet, and lifted their voices in angry chorus:

"Wait! We *are* a Court! Stay, stay, tell the people not to go! Wait!"

Atkins grabbed his hat and signalled violently to Gore.

"The proceedings are adjourned," he babbled frenziedly. "It is no Court, I tell you! I shall withdraw! You cannot continue in my absence . . ." Leaving his papers on the table, he clapped his hat crookedly on his head, made for the nearest door, and vanished. The Provost Marshal, determined to denude these transactions of their last semblance of civil authority, ordered the withdrawal of his constables, and followed. The noise was tumultuous as Palmer, Fulton, Campbell and Griffin also rose and pushed their way angrily from the room. Macarthur sprang forward and cried loudly:

"Gentlemen, gentlemen, am I to be cast forth at the mercy of a set of armed ruffians—the police? I have information from my friends that I shall be set upon as I leave this Court. I appeal to you for protection! I ask you, gentlemen, for a military guard! I'll warrant my enemies will not easily get at me then!"

A cheer went up from the soldiers. The officers were consulting together. The time was eleven-fifteen, and the day growing even hotter. The room was less crowded now, for some had left despite the officers' plea—either in sympathy with the Governor's cause, or fearing to be embroiled in trouble, or merely seeking respite from the heat. The hubbub died down, the gentlemen on the Bench loosened their collars and mopped their brows as they composed a letter to the Governor, enclosing a copy of Macarthur's speech, and declaring that they, after mature and deliberate consideration, had decided that his objections to the Judge Advocate were good and lawful. "*We further pray Your Excellency's protection*," they added, "*in the execution of our duty, having been grossly insulted and threatened by Richard Atkins, Esq. . . .*"

This letter despatched by messenger, a lull descended. The Governor's study, not half a mile away, had wakened to activity.

*   *   *   *   *

Mr. Atkins and his companions had arrived, breathless and perspiring, to find Bligh busy at his desk. He listened to their tale calmly enough, betraying impatience only when, in their excitement, they all spoke at once.

"Stop, stop, for God's sake! Griffin, fetch Crossley in—he's somewhere about." He picked up a pencil and addressed himself to Atkins. "Now, Sir, begin again. Everything that passed, if you please—in order!"

When the story was done he sat studying his notes for a moment and then looked up at Crossley who had entered behind the Secretary; the ex-attorney came forward to speak in his subdued and deferential tone:

"The position is clear, Your Excellency. As Mr. Atkins has already informed them, there can be no Court without the Judge Advocate. The Imperial Statute provides that the Court shall consist of the Judge Advocate and six officers of His Majesty's land or sea forces. Without the former, Sir, there is, in law, no Criminal Court." Fulton interjected: "I have yet to hear that the allegations of a prisoner ever set aside a Judge of the Court."

Bligh nodded, tapping his pencil thoughtfully on the page. A babel of discussion broke out, from which there emerged the opinion of Mr. Crossley that the officers, in taking upon themselves to adjudicate without the Judge Advocate, would be guilty of a treasonable offence. On the heels of this pronouncement, their letter arrived, and was read aloud by Griffin. Another lively debate resulted at last in a reply scribbled by Bligh and passed to Crossley for comment. The Governor ran a finger round under his collar, and glanced at the clock. It was half-past noon, and the heat of the day at its fiercest. He said testily:

"Open that window, Griffin—need we all stifle? Who brought that letter?"

"Ensign Bell, Sir," Griffin replied, letting a rush of hot but fresh air into the room. "He's waiting outside."

"We shall not keep him long. Give me that paper, Mr. Crossley. Now, gentlemen, listen if you please: '*I do not consider the Court to be formed without the Judge Advocate, and when legally convened I have no right to interpose any authority concerning its legal acts. I therefore can do no otherwise than direct that the Judge Advocate take his seat and act as directed by His Majesty's letters patent for the constituting of the Court of Criminal Jurisdiction . . .*' and I quote it," concluded His Excellency with sudden and bitter sarcasm, "in case these gentlemen should never have heard of it before! Make a copy of it, Campbell, and deliver it to Mr. Bell."

"What shall you do, Sir," Fulton enquired when the letter had been sent, "if they still persist in sitting?"

"The papers should be sent for," Campbell suggested, and Crossley nodded agreement. By the time another letter arrived at two o'clock the subject had been talked threadbare, and the Governor's reply was prompt and brief. He declined to reconsider his decision, and desired that all the papers which the Judge Advocate had left on the table should be delivered to Mr. Gore and Mr. Griffin.

But before these two had been absent half an hour on their errand, John Dunn appeared in the doorway with fresh tidings.

"It's said that Major Johnston is ill, Sir. They say he's been taken speechless, and Mr. Harris and Mr. Jamison have been sent for to Annandale . . ."

"Ha!" Bligh nodded his dismissal, and waited till the door had closed behind him. His eyes, meeting those of his companions, found his own scepticism reflected there. "So the Major is ill," he remarked sourly. "I may be pardoned for suspecting that he is not over anxious to appear publicly upon so delicate an occasion. This speechlessness is most timely, since it absolves him of the duty of reprimanding his officers for their insubordinate conduct!"

"I did hear, Sir," Fulton put in, "that he had an accident going home from the dinner last night."

"I hairrd the same story," Campbell remarked dryly, "but his indisposition at this time is too pairrfectly convenient to be credible." He went across to the window and looked out. "Gore and Griffin are coming back—they don't appear to have the papers."

Bligh took the letter which his secretary handed him, and read it in silence. Griffin dropped into a chair and fanned himself with his hat. "They won't give us the papers," he told Arndell in an undertone. "Did the Governor hear about Johnston? My God, it's as hot as a furnace out there!"

He stopped as Bligh, sitting forward in his chair with his elbows on the desk, read the letter aloud, and tossed it down among the litter of papers.

"We seem to have reached an *impasse*, gentlemen. They won't give up the papers, and they continue to demand a substitute for the Judge Advocate." He shot an exasperated glance at that gentleman. No one held a lower opinion of Mr. Atkins than he did, but the stubborn fact remained that he *was* the Judge Advocate, and the Statute made no provision for appointing a substitute. Bligh went on: "Very well. We can do nothing but wait patiently, and see how these rebels proceed. Your opinion, gentlemen?"

The gentlemen, after some discussion, agreed, and Mr. Atkins, with Crossley at his heels, withdrew to prepare a memorial setting out the events of the day. Bligh stood up briskly:

"In the meantime I see no reason why we should starve. You will all give me the pleasure of your company at dinner."

The magistrates exchanged glances as they followed him into the dining-parlour. His mood and manner throughout this trying morning had been quite astonishingly mild. It was as though, with the battle joined, with letters and messages hurtling about him like bullets, and events exploding about him like shells, temper and irritability had given way to a calm and concentrated determination. It was not, Campbell thought, the kind of battle he was accustomed to; but he was engaging an enemy from his desk as obstinately as he had ever engaged one upon the high seas. He even laughed when the meal was interrupted by the arrival of another missive from the officers, this time enclosing a deposition from Macarthur.

"The oppressed gentleman entreats protection," he remarked satirically. "He declares he has information that a large body of men armed with orders to carry into execution a warrant from the Judge Advocate against him . . ."

"Warrant . . . ?" interjected Griffin. "Atkins has given no warrant . . ."

"That won't disturb him," Bligh retorted. "He swears he considers his life in danger—which I wish to God it were!—and therefore declines giving any bail, and prays the Court to put him under the protection of a military guard. And the officers support his plea. Tcha!" He passed the papers to Palmer. "I'll take some more of that mutton. Upon my word, never was there a more touching accord between brothers than between this prisoner and his so-called judges! Griffin, you and Gore shall go down again presently with another demand for the papers."

He spoke but little during the remainder of the meal. He could see the pattern which Macarthur was weaving from this chaos. The objection he had raised to the Judge Advocate could not arise from any fear of a verdict unfavourable to himself, for Atkins was only one of seven. He was deliberately drawing the officers into an illegal procedure, forcing them into a position where, for their own safety, they must continue to support him. Or so they were being made to believe. They were tools, Bligh reflected, of a man cleverer than themselves, and as he sat there, heedless of the conversation around him, he was thinking that when the time came to deal with them he would not dismiss the possibility that they were guilty of an error of judgment rather than of wilful insubordination.

He pushed his chair back and rose; and as he returned to the study, the others following, his thoughts were again of Major Johnston. Where, in this crisis, was the Commanding Officer of these misguided men? Very much in retirement. Invisible. . . . He glanced at the clock as he sat down to compose his letter. Three forty-five. He took up his pen, thinking of words he had written not so long ago. *A dangerous militia.* . . . How true that prophecy had been he was now discovering. He was inclined to think that further argument was wasted, but he wrote a few lines, signed his name, and handed the paper to Griffin.

"Take it down, and take this precious affidavit of Macarthur's and get it properly attested." He looked round the room when Griffin had gone, and asked.

"Where's Campbell?"

Arndell answered:

"He's gone to see if Atkins has finished the memorial, Sir." Palmer, who had dined a trifle too well for a hot day, was nodding in his chair. He straightened himself with a start, and asked:

"What do you propose regarding the members of the Court, Sir?"

"There's no Court!" snapped Bligh. "There are six damned stupid men, playing the game of a cunning knave! . . . Plague take them! I don't know—we shall discuss it later. . . ." He stood up and went across to the window to stand staring out into the fierce sunlight. The harbour lay flat and silver under the glare. The smell of the bush returned on such days as this, when the sun sucked it from endless miles of trees and sent it like a subtle challenge into territory from which it had been routed. It hung in the motionless air, mingling with the smell of dust and the smell of salt water, but more pervasive than either. Bligh breathed it in, and was unaware of it; but behind his harassed preoccupation with the moment's problems, he suddenly felt his exile, and thought sharply of the land itself.

By God, in the stress of administering the settlements he had forgotten the land! What was it? Different eyes saw it differently, and out of that came conflict. A country of small farms? A country of vast sheep-walks? A base for navigators? A paradise for botanists? The site for a tour of duty? A strategic outpost? A market for traders? A source of easy riches? A land of promise? A gaol? It could be used as all these things—and yet it was more. What were they doing to it? Hating and exploiting it! And what was it doing to them? Nothing. Waiting. Ignoring them . . .

Bligh felt a wave of irritation. He had Phillip's intelligence and fortitude, Hunter's conscientiousness, and King's shrewdness; but he lacked the inspired, if fleeting, perceptiveness of the first, he was not stolid like the second, nor armoured in worldly cynicism like the third. He was a clever, serious, energetic man who liked to achieve clearly specified tasks, and his fugitive impression that this land would mould its inhabitants to its own purposes no matter what he might do or leave undone, outraged his masterful and impatient spirit. It seemed to say to him—to William Bligh, who liked to fill every waking moment with business—that there was no hurry. It had endured for thousands of years, and it could afford to wait still while generations of greedy, undiscerning men brawled, clamoured and destroyed. . . . It could wait a hundred, five hundred, a thousand years, till they made their peace with it, coming all the way, accepting its terms. . . . And if they never did, it would still wait—for ever. . . . Not it, but they, would pass . . .

Intolerable! Bligh turned his back on the thought, and fixed his mind once more on the present. He had a duty to perform, and he was being abominably obstructed; he faced the room again. Fulton and Arndell were still arguing about the outcome of this disgraceful affair, and the probable fate of the officers. Palmer was semi-comatose, but interjecting a word now and then. Atkins and Crossley had returned with the memorial, and were discussing it with Campbell. He went across to the desk to join them, and the enigma of the land was forgotten in the intrigues of the settlement.

It was five o'clock before Gore and Griffin reappeared. The papers were still refused, and the officers begged leave to acquaint His Excellency that they had adjourned to await his further pleasure. Bligh smote the arms of his chair with his open hands.

"I've had enough of this! Griffin—a letter to Major Johnston! '*Sir, His Excellency under particular public circumstances that have occurred, desires me to request that you will see him without delay.'* Send one of my bodyguard with it. Send Thorby. Bid him ride as fast as he can."

Griffin hurried out with the letter, and the Governor turned to Gore.

"Where's Macarthur?"

"I don't know, Sir," Gore replied. "He left the Court House with the officers, and surrounded by the soldiers."

They all exchanged glances. Bligh said slowly:

"As Provost Marshal you're answerable for him, Mr. Gore. We, the officers, and Mr. Macarthur himself, all regarded him as being surrendered from his bail this morning, and there has been no legal authority to grant him further bail."

Gore looked alarmed. Crossley suggested:

"A deposition from Mr. Gore, stating that the prisoner is no longer in his custody, and requesting an escape warrant from the magistrates, would be regular, Sir. The magistrates could then grant him such a warrant to re-take the prisoner."

The lamps were lit by now, and beneath the light that they shed on the desk Mr. Gore's deposition was at length duly made and sworn, and the escape warrant prepared. Griffin read it over aloud. " '. . . *to require and strictly charge and command you and every one of you to take into custody the body of the said John Macarthur, and him safely keep and secure in His Majesty's gaol at Sydney . . .'* "

A knock at the door interrupted him. John Dunn entered to announce the return of Trooper Thorby with a message from Major Johnston. Bligh pushed his chair back and hurried across the room.

"Well—where is it?" he demanded impatiently of the man who presented himself, hot and dusty, in the doorway. Thorby recited:

"The Major sends his compliments, Sir, and is sorry he can't write an answer to the letter he got, but he's dangerously ill, and it would cost him his life to come into town, Sir, and his right arm has been tied up, and he's been bled. That's all, Sir."

"Ah!" said Bligh grimly. "Very well, my man—you may go."

* * * * *

While Trooper Thorby was galloping back from Annandale to Sydney, Mr. Mannion was receiving the daily report of his head overseer. He had been keeping the convicts as far from the river as possible, but Toole, impatient to set the western stubble lands to work again, had urged repeatedly:

" 'Tis badly behindhand we are already, Your Honour, gettin' the maize in. We'd not be taken by surprise, Sir, warned the way we are, and with pistols in our belts."

Mannion had yielded at last, for he too disliked seeing his land lie idle, but each evening he questioned the overseer closely. The only incident that had marked this day, Toole assured him, was an attempt by Dan Driver to drown himself; he had been sent down to fetch water, and dragged out of the river just in time, screaming and struggling.

"More trouble than he's worth, Your Honour," Toole said gloomily.

"Best be rid of him, Sir—send him to Parramatta, and let me be gettin'
ye a man who can do a good day's work."

"Not yet," Mannion said shortly. He knew that the overseer's zeal
in this matter marched with his desire for a few days in Sydney, and he
was already half regretting that parsimony had played its part in persuading him to dispense with some of the extra men he had hired. No other
able-bodied man should leave Beltrasna yet.

"Nothing else has happened?" he enquired.

"No, Sir."

"No sign of anyone on the river? No natives?"

"A lad, Sir, sixteen or thereabouts, an' two little gossoons no higher
than this, Sir. Went down the river in their canoes just before sundown,
chatterin' and screechin' to each other like parrakeets, an' callin' out to
us . . ."

Mannion sighed impatiently and cut him short.

"Very well, very well—we're not concerned with children."

* * * * *

The children, at that moment, were enjoying a meal with Finn and
Johnny, a mile below the northern boundary of Beltrasna, and a prudent
mile or so back from the river's western bank. They found their companions silent—but that was not unusual in Johnny at least. Gooradoo and
Balgundra, having eaten, spent the last hour of fading daylight in games.
They laughed, argued, quarrelled and fought, sprawling and struggling
together like a pair of puppies until Balgundra rolled too near the fire,
and leapt up squealing, with the blistered mark of a burning stick across
his thigh. A year or two ago he would have wept unrestrainedly, but
now he was too old for that. There were a few gulps, a few large, crystal
tears on his coppery cheeks, and then a stoical silence—but the games
were over. He curled himself with Gooradoo beneath a sloping rock, and
presently only an uneasy whimper in his sleep told of his mishap. Billalong, squatting on his heels by the fire, consumed the last fragments of a
fish, and related between mouthfuls the tale of the tribe's latest kangaroo-
hunt.

But Finn and Johnny were inattentive listeners. Their journey from
the valley had been difficult, and not without delays, perils and alarms.
It had been necessary to make contact first with the tribe, but settlement
at the Cow Pastures had made that towri dangerous now, so Johnny had
gone alone, while Finn made his way to an appointed meeting place a few
miles farther down the river. Here Johnny had joined them at last,
accompanied by Milbooroo, both paddling canoes; and here Milbooroo
had left them to return on foot while Finn and Johnny continued their
journey downstream. Well above Beltrasna they had disembarked,
and toiled through the rough country on the western side, carrying on their heads the light, bark canoes which still seemed heavy by the
end of the day. Johnny, scouting at night along the banks, had returned
with the disturbing news that there were sentries posted on the Beltrasna
shore, and Finn said, frowning:

"That's a new thing. I wonder, now, can they have got wind o'

what we're plannin'? Not a word would they be gettin' out of Humfreys
—that I'd swear to—but it might be there's others would talk too loud.
. . . I'm not likin' it, but we're here, an' we'll not be turnin' back now.
Let ye be tellin' me again, Johnny—an' make no mistake for the love o'
God!—what it was ye said to Humfreys?"

He was thankful as he listened to the reply, for his young companion's
natural taciturnity. Johnny had seen no reason why the convicts should
know more than the bare fact that Finn would attempt a rescue at the
end of the harvest, and that it would be announced by a fire and three
shots. The preliminary details, he had considered, were no concern of
theirs. Finn nodded his satisfaction.

"Not a word o' Billalong—or the children? Think, now!"

"No."

"Divil a mention o' canoes?"

"No."

"Nor a whisper o' where we come from?"

"No."

"Ah, well then, it's not everythin' they can be knowin' even if so be
they know some. 'Twas in five days ye told the young ones to come?
I'll be doin' some thinkin' in that time."

He had thought, and as he sat silently in the shadows beyond the
firelight, his eyes were on Billalong. They would light no fire, he decided;
that might be, now, to warn Mannion as well as the convicts. The
children had reported this afternoon that the gangs were working near
the river, and close to the northern boundary. Somehow—though he could
not hope they would ever be left unguarded—he must draw away from
them as many of their guards as possible. He began to see that if
Mannion's suspicions had been aroused—and the presence of those
watchers on the river bank suggested strongly that they had—it might be
turned to advantage. A decoy. . . . He looked from Billalong to the
children, and nodded to himself.

*   *   *   *   *

At nine o'clock the next morning the Provost Marshal, armed with his
escape warrant, re-arrested Macarthur, and the town hummed with what
was perhaps the greatest sensation of its history. Jack Bodice was in
gaol, like any common criminal! People gathered curiously, and a wave
of apprehension swept through the ranks of prosperous citizens; if the
great John Macarthur's person were not sacrosanct, who was safe?

By ten o'clock the six officers were re-assembled in the Court House,
but to-day they had no prisoner before them—only Mr. Bayly and Mr.
Blaxcell, taking the oath in profound and agitated indignation, and declaring that he had been forcibly wrested from their charge. Nor, they
added darkly, did they consider his life safe, for he had been delivered
into the hands of a constable formerly a servant in his house, who had
been dismissed for stealing, and who had, in the most sinister fashion,
been summoned upon this duty out of his proper turn. They thought it
unnecessary to mention that however ill-disposed this constable might be
towards his prisoner, the gaoler himself was a staunch Macarthur partisan.

The officers busied themselves in the preparation of further communications to the Governor. The deposition of Mr. Gore, they protested, was
false, and the arrest of Mr. Macarthur calculated to subvert the legal
authority and independence of the Court. They prayed that His Excellency
would restore the prisoner to his former bail, so that they might proceed
with the trial.

To this His Excellency returned no answer. He was weary of reiterat-
ing that they were not a Court, and he was engaged upon measures of
his own which occupied him throughout the morning and well into the
afternoon. Mr. Atkins having completed his memorial, Mr. Crossley
advised that a summons be sent through the Provost Marshal requiring
the officers to appear before the magistrates and the Governor.

Bligh nodded, waved Griffin to the desk, and walked up and down the
room while the document was being prepared. His bitterness against
Johnston was rising, and it burst from him in a few muttered exclamations
as he paced restlessly to and fro. "Ill! Devil take him! A political
illness . . . !" While Griffin read aloud his circular letter to the officers,
summoning them to attend at Government House next morning, Bligh's
brain was already busy framing the sentences of another communication
to the Major. He vanished into the next room almost before the reading
was concluded, and presently returned with a sheet of paper.

"Copy that," he directed, holding it out to his secretary. And within
half an hour another messenger was cantering along the road to Annandale.

*   *   *   *   *

At Beltrasna, meanwhile, the morning had passed quietly. The convicts,
under a strong guard, were working in the western fields. Conor was
sitting soon after midday on the verandah, stitching idly at her embroidery,
Cousin Bertha dozing beside her, when a succession of piercing childish
shrieks startled her to her feet.

Far away across the lower fields towards the southern end of the
property, she saw two small, black, naked figures, followed by a taller one.
They were racing wildly towards the house, yelling piteously as they ran.
As she started down the steps towards them she saw the overseer, Evans,
appear and run to intercept them, and from behind the house came her
husband and Patrick on horseback.

"Remain where you are, Conor," Mannion called. "Are you mad to
run out like that in the heat of the day? It's nothing—native children—
I'll see what's amiss, and send them about their business."

She went back slowly to the verandah, but continued to stare down the
hill to where the group had gathered, and the natives were wildly gesturing. Mannion had dismounted, and set himself to discover the cause of
the uproar, but for a few moments the united admonitions of himself,
Patrick and Evans were unable to quell the roaring and bellowing, the
screeching and shrill lamentations.

Billalong and his two small half-brothers were, in fact, enormously
enjoying this opportunity to exercise the histrionic gifts with which the
race of Murri was so lavishly endowed. They had obeyed Finn's instructions quite literally, swimming the river far above Beltrasna, and running

as hard as they could through the bush till they reached its fields. They were, therefore, genuinely hot, sweating and out of breath; but the terror in their wild, bright eyes, the panic conveyed by the frenzied gesticulation of their expressive hands, were the results of a childhood spent among people to whom the art of mime was a necessary cultural accomplishment.

"Yerrai!" shrieked Balgundra. "Duggerrigai—marrapu, morla marrapu . . . ! Yerrai!"

"Duggerrigai!" echoed Gooradoo, shuddering. "Wee-ree, Wee-ree!"

"Duggerrigai!" gasped Billalong. "Ye ye chobung! Chawa! Korug koa . . . !" He gestured excitedly up the river. The children danced about Mr. Mannion, clutching importunately at his arms and coat tails. He freed himself, shouting in exasperation:

"Be silent! Silence, I say! God, give me patience! Patrick, you understand a few words of this gabble of theirs, do you not? What are they trying to say? What? What? I can't hear you—damn it, you intolerable brats, cease that appalling din . . . !"

"Only two words," yelled Patrick. " 'Duggerrigai'—white man, and 'Wee-ree'—bad . . ."

Mannion's gaze became intent. He addressed himself to Billalong:

"You! Come, now, what is it?".

Billalong pointed excitedly to a wound on his shoulder, from which the blood had run down over his chest. It had been his own idea, and he was proud of it; a young man who had passed through his initiation thought nothing of gashing himself, and the knife had been easily hidden where he could find it again. A little blood was a small price to pay for verisimilitude in this magnificent drama which they were performing. His action was the cue for a renewed outbreak of lamentation from the two small boys, and Balgundra, presenting a view of his hinder parts to Mr. Mannion's gaze, indicated the fresh blister on his skin, and shrieked grievously: "Yerrai! Yerrai!"

Billalong commanded: "Kurria! Kurria gindai kakullego!" The uproar faded in sobs and moans. Mannion asked urgently:

"You have been injured? Men do this? What men?"

Billalong had been warned not to show too great a knowledge of English, but a few words were common property among the natives now.

"Men," he declared, rolling his eyes in anguish. "Men come—bad!"

"Duggerrigai!" groaned Balgundra in corroboration.

"Wee-ree, wee-ree!" wailed Gooradoo.

"White men?" asked Mannion. "How many?" He lifted his fingers enquiringly, but Billalong produced some more English.

"One-two-three-four-many," he gabbled. Mannion indicated his five outspread fingers, questioning with his eyes. Billalong broke into a vociferous torrent of native language. He snatched Mannion's other hand and lifted all its fingers. He added his own, and gestured to Gooradoo and Balgundra, whose twenty black figures were immediately thrust in the air. He cried: "Man, man, man, man . . . !" with a stamp of his foot in a different place each time, so that a veritable army of men seemed to rise like ghosts about them.

Mannion said irritably to Patrick:

"Absurd! These people are habitually given to the wildest exaggeration. It's well known." He added uneasily: "All the same, it would seem there are at least several of them . . ."

"Where are these men?" Patrick demanded of Billalong. "Wutta duggerrigai?"

Billalong turned his head in the direction from which they had come, and thrust his lips out, native fashion. Mannion said quickly to Patrick; "Can you find out if they are armed?"

"Gooroobeera?" asked Patrick, demonstrating in pantomime the firing of a gun. Billalong nodded emphatically. Mannion mounted his horse in haste.

"Tell them—the smaller ones—that they may go up to the house if they wish. The older one shall guide us. Evans, get all the men together and distribute arms among them. Tell Toole and Allen to march the convicts back to their quarters, and remain on guard. Byrne is to stay at the house. Every other man will come with us."

Conor came anxiously to the edge of the verandah as he galloped up the hill and reined in by the steps.

"A stroke of good fortune," he told her hurriedly. "Finn and his desperadoes have betrayed themselves—they set upon those children up yonder, it seems. Of course I can get no accurate information from such ignorant creatures, but it appears the rascals are this side of the river, and not far distant . . ."

"How—how many of them?" asked Conor.

"Impossible to tell. Not less than five or six, I should imagine. Take Cousin Bertha indoors, and remain there yourself. Byrne will be outside —but they will not approach the house. We shall have every man of them within an hour."

She watched him ride off to superintend the gathering of his force before she roused the old lady and escorted her indoors. She stood for a moment listening to the sounds of commotion outside, and then went into the nursery to stand by the window, with Julia clinging to her skirts, and Bessie plying her with excited questions.

"Mercy on us, ma'am, we might all have been murdered! The nasty, wicked wretches! Will the master catch them, do you think?"

Conor watched a small cavalcade set off, the eldest native boy running ahead, and turning often to beckon them on with the curious native downward movement of the hand. There were Mannion and Patrick, and the two Morgans, and five free labourers, including Maria's husband —all mounted, and all armed with muskets and pistols. Behind them, a few minutes later, followed Evans with two other guards withdrawn from the convict gangs.

"Yes, Bessie," she said slowly. "I feel sure he will."

*   *   *   *   *

The convicts working in the fields by the river exchanged furtive glances. Evans, riding down in haste and excitement to speak to Toole, had not raised his voice enough to be heard by any of them, but it was clear that there was something afoot. Two overseers were withdrawn, and followed the returning Evans up the hill towards the house, leaving Toole and a new man, Allen, in charge of the gangs. The convicts all knew of the plot by now. Humfreys had taken no more than two of them into his confidence, but Mannion's questionings and punishments, and what they had guessed from the incoherent ravings of Dan Driver, had long ago let them into the secret. They had been waiting—some with excitement, and some with dread, but few with any hope—for something to happen, and now they kept their eyes on Humfreys. His hoe continued to rise and fall with monotonous steadiness, but he was watching the nearby fringe of bush, and his ears were straining. He had suffered terribly during his interrogations, and now he was wondering if his strength would prove equal to whatever might be required of it. No fire —no shots. . . . And it looked as though Toole were preparing to muster them and march them back to their quarters. What was happening? Why had the guards been withdrawn? Was Finn at hand? Humfreys had been a conspirator before; he knew that plans must sometimes be altered or abandoned; that one must wait with every sense alert for a sign of change or hasty improvisation. . . .

Toole was shouting an order to the convicts to fall into line, and Allen was bringing another group at pistol point from the next field to join them. They were almost assembled when a shot crashed through the silence of the still, hot afternoon; Toole started, stared around, and bellowed:

"Get into line, there! I'll shoot the first man that tries to move away!"

They obeyed as slowly as they dared, listening. Another shot came from the same direction as the first, and the half-formed line wavered. Another, and it broke. Grotesque in the hopping, hobbling gait which was all their shackles would allow, seven of the convicts, headed by Humfreys, attempted to run. Dan Driver began to scream, and floundered across the field after them, his arms waving in lunatic gestures. The others, with a sweat of fear and excitement pouring from their faces, hesitated, weighing their captivity against a bullet in the back from Toole's pistol. It cracked, and one of the fleeing figures fell forward on its face.

"Stop, ye blackguards!" the overseer roared triumphantly. "I'll pick ye off one by one before y've gone another twenty yards! Get back into line, the rest of ye! Watch 'em, Allen, an' shoot the first one that moves!"

He dared not take his eyes from the shifting and dangerously muttering men near him until the second overseer had them herded together, and held motionless by the threat of his levelled pistol; and in that brief time the fugitives had gained some precious distance. Toole re-loaded his weapon and made after them, aiming at the nearest—not to kill, but to halt. He missed, but the shot went near enough to frighten the man— and others. Three of them baulked, turned, gave up, and began to hobble slowly back with uplifted hands. Toole shouted:

"Aye, ye'd best come back, ye scum! Ye won't? I'll soon persuade ye!"

He fired again. Humfreys, foremost of the remaining fugitives, heard

a man close behind him cry wildly: "No use—no use . . . !" He hobbled
faster and more desperately, his eyes searching the bush ahead in an
agony of fear and hope. Finn, Finn, where was Finn . . . ? Behind him,
as in a nightmare, he could hear Dan Driver screaming.

*   *   *   *   *

Finn and Johnny, breathless, broke through to the fringe of the bush
and fell down on their stomachs behind a sheltering log. The wide, sunlit
field was a scene of chaos. One dark figure was lying still; another,
wounded, was crawling out of the line of the overseer's fire; three had
despaired, and were moving slowly back to join the gang that waited,
savagely shouting, but immobilised under the menace of Allen's pistol.
Dan Driver was shambling forward—but aimlessly, pausing now and then
to turn and fling his arms in the air and shriek wild maledictions at Toole,
who was wasting no time nor ammunition upon so worthless a creature.
But two men were still advancing, and the first of them was Humfreys.
They were beyond the cultivated land now, in the strip of cleared ground
that separated it from the bush, where charred stumps and logs stood
black among the knee-high grass. Behind them Toole had halted momentarily in his pursuit, his weapon levelled at the nearest fugitive. All this
Finn saw as he lifted his musket and took aim.

The sound of his shot, and of Johnny's which followed it immediately,
increased the bedlam. A roar went up from the gang, and Allen's voice
was lifted in threats and commands. Toole dived for the shelter of a
stump. Finn cried to Johnny:

"Get ye round through the bracken there, as near as ye can to the
fellow guarding the gang . . ." Toole was taking aim from behind his
stump, and Finn pulled a pistol from his belt and fired hurriedly in his
direction. "Send a bullet near him," he called to Johnny, "no matter if
ye don't hit him. Take his mind from the gang for a moment—an' they'll
be doin' the rest . . ."

Toole's pistol cracked again, and the man behind Humfreys—unharmed, but panic-stricken, collapsed on the ground, turned, and began to
crawl back, with shouts and gestures of surrender. Johnny had disappeared. Finn yelled, hardly conscious that he was yelling:

"Come out o' there, Toole, ye crawlin' viper! Be the powers, if ye'd
but show y' head . . . !"

Dan had tripped and was sprawling on the ground. Toole fired again
from his ambush, but the remaining fugitive still came on. Out of the
high bracken that swept up from the river bank, invading the cleared land
to within thirty yards of Allen and the gang, Johnny's musket spoke. He
was an indifferent marksman, still preferring to hunt with spears, and it
was one of the convicts who received a bullet in the fleshy part of his arm
—but the diversion served. Allen, in a panic, swung the muzzle of his
weapon away from his charges for a second, and it was long enough. They
were on to him like wolves, and Toole, startled by the sound of a shot
from his rear, flung a hunted glance behind him to see his fellow-overseer
go down, yelling, beneath a sea of savagely-flailing arms.

Then, in a few seconds, all the convicts were scattering, and the field was dotted with hobbling, madly-hurrying figures making for the shelter of the bush. Toole, his face grey, reloaded his pistol with shaking hands, but the convicts were intent upon escape, and gave him and his pistol as wide a berth as possible. Dan Driver had scrambled to his feet again; he seemed to be trying to reach Humfreys, stumbling after him with out-stretched hands, the high, shrieking, wordless babble growing hoarse in his throat.

Finn wiped his arm across his streaming forehead and watched the stump where Toole crouched in concealment. Humfreys was still struggling on; Finn could see the sweat on his face now, and hear the loud, sobbing gasps of his breathing. He began to feel the first elation of victory, for there remained only one pistol against him—and that in the hands of Toole, hemmed between his own musket and Johnny's. Why didn't Johnny fire? No matter—it was surely almost over now . . .

And then, terribly, other sounds came from over the low rise of the hill—a shot from near the river bank, shouts, a rattle of returning fire, the beat of horses' hooves. Finn, hearing them, clambered to his feet, a chill running over his body like icy water. The convicts, hearing them, wavered again, their flare of hope subsiding—all but Humfreys, who goaded himself to a fiercer effort and came on like a marionette. And Toole, hearing them, took heart again, aimed at him, fired, and missed. Finn, sheltering behind a tree, and re-loading his musket hurriedly, shouted incoherent words of encouragement while Humfreys gained a few more yards. Then his weapon and Toole's sounded almost simultaneously; Humfreys stag-gered, recovered, reeled a few more paces, and fell.

Finn, re-loading again, stared round him desperately, the sound of those approaching hoofbeats like thunder in his ears. Where was Johnny? Humfreys, groaning, was on his knees, and trying to crawl. Dan Driver was shambling on, talking loudly to himself, oblivious of the approaching horsemen, of Toole, of danger, of anything but some notion, fixed and relentless, in his crazed mind. There were seconds to spare, Finn thought with wild lucidity, for escape or . . . ? He leapt from behind his tree, ran crouchingly to where Humfreys struggled on all fours, and thrust a pistol into his hand. A bullet from Toole's pistol whistled past them as he dragged the wounded man to his feet and made for the bush again, half carrying him. A few seconds, he thought, for the overseer to re-load—that tree—they were behind it, and there was intermittent cover of a sort now. "Go on," he gasped, thrusting the convict in the direction of the bush, and raising his weapon again. But even as he fired he saw the horsemen silhouetted for a second against the hilltop before they swept down on him in a cloud of dust and a tumult of shots and shouting—and he knew that it was finished.

It seemed to him as he was seized that he had always known it could only end like this—with savage voices, a blow, and cords about his wrists. Looking round for Humfreys, he saw a thing happen which seemed strange but inevitable, and told him clearly what he would never learn from any words. The convict had fallen in a clump of thick scrub, and it was Dan who saw him first, and stumbled towards him, still gabbling.

And Humfreys, supporting himself on one elbow, his dark, exhausted face gleaming whitely above his black beard, and his eyes curiously calm, raised the pistol and shot him in the face.

This was the way of dreams, Finn thought confusedly—to fill the mind with ugly shadows besieging the core of reality which stood alone—a small, bright, distant picture of a valley, a hut, a thin plume of smoke, green crops, and sheep and cattle—all enclosed in a blue veil of silence.

*   *   *   *   *

Johnny, his breath bursting in his lungs, lifted his head cautiously above the water and gasped a few saving mouthfuls of air. The ferns and slimy weeds of the river bank were still close about his head, but he was careful that his movements should make no sound, and not even a ripple on the water. He listened. He could hear nothing near at hand, but there were distant noises of commotion in the direction where he had left Finn. His sharp ears had heard the horsemen sooner than Finn, or Toole, or the convicts, deafened by their own shots and shouting, and he had made an attempt to divert the approaching peril. He had plunged down to the river bank and run madly upstream, gaining a hundred yards or so, and then, hearing the riders almost level with him, had fired a shot into the air. It had halted them, but only for a moment while Mannion directed two men to leave the main body and investigate. By the time they reached the river Johnny was up to his neck in it, crouched under the bank and the overhanging greenery. He could hear them tramping about, searching in the scrub and bracken, swearing and prodding with their muskets, and he feared for the safety of his own weapons, thrust hastily into a thicket of ferns. They came scrambling down to the water, and he sank beneath it, profiting now by his skill in duck-hunting, when a man must learn to stay long under water, and move in it as silently as an eel.

They went away at last, and he came up for breath. There was no sound nearby, so he emerged warily and, to his infinite relief, found his musket and pistol still where he had hidden them. He crept downstream along the bank, and at last came to where the field of battle was visible. Plucking ferns to hold about his head, he lifted it slowly and peered through the green fronds.

The gang was being marched away. The dead and wounded were being carried or dragged together. Mannion and Patrick were riding up towards the house, and Toole was mounting a horse to follow. Behind them, between two armed men, his hands tied behind his back, walked Finn.

*   *   *   *   *

Conor was lying on her bed when she heard her husband's order to Toole, and she began to tremble. The sound of shots had brought her in alarm to the verandah, but from there she could see nothing of what was going on. Bessie and the servants had rushed to the door, and Julia, pushing her way past her nurse, had run sobbing to her mother. It was the child's fear, and not the urging of Byrne, who hurried towards them, that made her order them all indoors and follow herself.

But it was over so quickly that she had barely succeeded in quieting the child before Patrick arrived with news that the desperadoes had been routed, and one, at least, captured. The tumult had died down now. The convicts were under lock and key; the dead and the wounded were being carried up the hill; the overseer, Allen, battered and unconscious, had been taken to his quarters; Cousin Bertha had spent the whole time in her room, placidly busy with her embroidery, hearing nothing. Conor, weak and weary, had returned to her room, but the command she now overheard called by her husband from the verandah brought her up on her elbow, shivering feverishly.

So it was Finn who had been taken! Finn . . . and he with no more than mortal flesh . . Finn, whose white face had once stared at her, dreading what she could bring upon him . . . Finn, who had said that men would dare anything for liberty . . . Finn, who had escaped and been hunted . . . freedom hath been hunted round the world . . .

Finn . . . !

She felt sick, and lay back on her pillow, the room darkening around her. But it was not quite a swoon, and her thoughts went on and on through almost half an hour of slowly accumulating minutes in a growing torment till she could bear it no longer. She rose and went to the window. The verandah was deserted, and there was no one in sight. Round the corner of the house she could hear Patrick calling out something about the horses to Morgan, and her husband giving orders about the burial of the dead convicts; their voices died away as they moved off in the direction of the stables.

She pushed the shutters open and stepped out on to the stone flags. The hot afternoon sunlight lay across them, staining them with a golden light, and lending them a warmth which she could feel even through her slippers. She crossed the verandah, stole down the steps, stood hesitating for one more moment of indecision, and then began to run.

The long slope down to the convict hut was cleared of all native trees, and the oaks, elms and poplars which Mr. Mannion had planted were as yet too small and sparse to screen her. She could only pray that she would not be seen, and she left the rough cart-track to take the shorter way across the open ground. The native grass was brown and dry, and sharp little seeds clung to her stockings and her skirts as she ran. She was breathless when she reached the hut; as she came round it she felt a scream rise in her, but had no power to utter it.

Toole was wielding the lash; Byrne and another man whom she knew only as one of her husband's free labourers, stood by watching. She clutched at the wall beside her, feeling her knees fail. The inside of her mouth was dry and rough, her throat seemed closed so that she fought for air, and her eyes stared through a swimming haze at the frightful figure hanging by its wrists to a blood-bespattered post. Sight began to fade; she felt her weight refused by her shaking knees, and leaned heavily against the wall, fighting an increasing darkness. Suddenly something wet struck her cheek; her hand flew up to it instinctively, and came down before her wild, incredulous eyes, smeared with red.

The scream freed itself at last. She saw Toole and the others spin towards her, their faces blank with amazement, and she heard the scream form itself into words shrieked at them in a frenzy of loathing:

"Devils! Monsters! You dare . . . ! You are murderers! I shall . . ."

They advanced a few steps towards her and she retreated, beating them away with frantic gestures. Toole stammered in consternation:

"Ma'am, I beg of you . . . if you please, Ma'am, this is no place for . . ."

She screamed: "Release him!" They stood gaping at her. She stamped her foot and beat her fist against the wall. "You hear me, you inhuman brutes! Release him!"

Toole took another step towards her, holding out a bloody but placating hand.

"Whisht, now, Ma'am, hush! Byrne here will take you . . ."

She sprang at him with so sudden and tigerish a movement that he backed away, but she snatched the lash still dangling from his fingers, wrenched it from his grasp, and slashed it furiously across his face. He roared out an oath and made a violent movement towards her; Byrne grabbed him just in time.

"God Almighty, ye fool! Would ye lay hands on the master's wife?" There was panic in his urgent undertone. "D'ye want to swing?"

Toole stood still with his hand to his cheek; madness had gone out of him, but his expression was ugly. Conor, shaking from head to foot, repeated hoarsely: "Release him!"

Byrne said, looking at her blankly:

" 'Tis the master's orders, Ma'am."

He expected that to halt her, but she barely heard him, for she was trying to think through the horror that was clouding her brain. That thing was a man—it was Finn—he looked dead hanging there, but he must be alive, he must be still alive . . .

She began to speak, but her voice, cracked with screaming, came out as a harsh whisper. She swallowed, cleared her throat, and tried again:

"Take him down immediately. I command it. You will carry him up to the house, and . . ."

Byrne burst out incredulously:

"To the *house*, Ma'am . . . ?" He muttered to Toole: "It's raving she is! Take him down, then—an' he only a score or so short of his thousand—why not?"

They moved towards the post. She did not watch, but stood leaning exhaustedly against the wall, staring across the scorched paddocks, hearing for the first time a strange, savage, animal-like sound that was coming from inside the hut—a sinking and swelling of groans and cries and curses. Byrne, cap in hand, hovered uneasily at her elbow.

"Won't ye be comin' back to the house with me now, Ma'am? Sure, 'tis out of y'self ye are, an' no wonder, Ma'am, seein' what no lady ought . . ."

She jerked round to look at the others; they were carrying their burden towards a small shed beside the hut. She flashed across the few yards that separated them from her so fast that they hardly knew she had moved till she stood between them and the door of that dark, evil-smelling place. She did not heed what Toole said, but his companion paled to hear such words addressed to her. The sight, at close quarters, of their burden had maddened her almost to hysteria, and she raved at them shrilly, her face greenish with nausea:

"I bade you carry the man to the *house*, Sir! The house, the house, the *house*—can you not hear me? I swear if you do not obey me I shall have you flogged as he was—and you too—all of you . . . !"

The third man, his mouth stupidly agape, stared at her in a shocked amazement which no suffering or brutality had ever aroused in him. They were all horrified and shaken. The world they accepted was rocked to its foundations by a rich and well-born young lady who brandished a lash at them and screamed like a fishwife. The red-hot pain of that blow was fading from Toole's face, but not from his mind; his whole thought was concentrated upon remembering that this madwoman was his master's wife, armoured by that fact against the violence he would have liked to inflict on her. It was Byrne who intervened again.

"Faith, Ma'am, just as ye say, to be sure! If ye'll but allow me to pass, Ma'am, I'll be gettin' somethin' to carry him on . . ." He said in a savage undertone to Toole: "Whisht, ye great booby! It's out of her mind she is—an' she shriekin' like a Banshee! Do as she says, for the love of God, an' leave the master deal with her! It's a seizure she'll be havin'—and we held to account for it . . ."

She knew now that they would obey, and she stood aside in the hot sunlight while they prepared to carry Finn up the hill. She felt weak and tremulous now, but she struck away fiercely the arm which Byrne respectfully offered, and began to stumble after them, already wondering with a kind of confused desperation what she must do next. Once more she had intervened too recklessly. She had won—at the cost of nearly all the strength she had—only one skirmish in a war too big for her. She could give orders to overseers—but now there was Stephen. She felt frightened when she thought of him, and, curiously, hardly less frightened when she thought of Finn. Somehow she had become involved in his life—and perhaps his death? Somehow, without ever doing more than reply when she spoke to him, answer when she questioned him, he had claimed a part of her, and would not let it go. What part? She was accustomed to the convention which allowed no thought, action or emotion of a woman to be uncoloured by her sex; this thing which took no account of his sex or hers, but sped arrow-like from his humanity to pierce her own, was too strange to be welcomed, but too strong to be denied.

She felt so weak that her knees buckled and her head sagged forward. She did not see Patrick come hurriedly round the corner and stand aghast for a moment before he began to run down the hill towards them, but suddenly his hand was beneath her arm.

"Good heavens, what is this? Why are you here? You are ill—hurt . . . ?" With his support she reached the verandah at last, where the men had already set their burden down, and Mannion was striding round from the back of the house.

The sound of his voice so startled and dismayed her that she cried out faintly in the pain of having to confront another ordeal with the first hardly ended. But she knew despairingly that she had not enough strength to oppose that voice. It went on as she struggled blindly up the steps, assisted now by his hand as well as Patrick's—went on loudly, angrily, with that terrible, final note of unassailable authority. Sometimes it seemed to fade, but she knew it had not ceased; it was her own brain, escaping intermittently into semi-consciousness, which shut it out.

". . . to permit your mistress to see . . . !"

". . . her command, Your Honour . . ."

". . . must be out of your mind to bring him here!"

". . . wouldn't listen, Sir, and we afraid to cross her the way she was in such a takin' . . ."

". . . a fire sweeping up the field towards the stables, and every man . . ."

". . . now the mistress is safe, Sir, we'll be takin' this rogue back to the hut, an' . . ."

She forced her eyelids open, licked her dry lips, and uttered a few thick, incoherent words of protest which were drowned by Mannion's furious voice.

"Have I not told you, blockhead, that a fire is raging while you stand here and babble! You are needed there! Put him in the storeroom— yes, fool, I said the storeroom! Byrne, be off immediately. Ellen, assist your mistress to her room. Patrick, return to the field . . ."

She felt herself transferred from his support to Ellen's. She was trying to see again, staring at a swimming landscape, at pillars which moved and spun, at Ellen's white cap floating, dissolving and re-forming in mid-air, at the labourer's red face uplifted from the door of the storehouse. She heard him say:

"The key, Your Honour—it's stuck fast, but I'll have it out immediately, Sir . . ."

Mannion roared at him:

"Leave it, imbecile! Could the fellow walk, even if the door were open? Be off with you, and if that fire reaches the stables I'll have the skin off your back!"

Could the fellow walk? Could he even breathe? Conor felt herself lifted in her husband's arms, and heard herself muttering stupidly: "Can he walk, can he breathe, can he see? He can see a colour and smell a scent like any. . . . Can he see, can he hear . . . ?" And then, for a time, nothing more.

*   *   *   *   *

Pat Ultimo was with Major Johnston when the trooper arrived at Annandale with Bligh's second letter. It was just after four o'clock, and the heat of the day was abating, but a westerly breeze had begun to stir, and the air was dry and dusty. Johnston unfolded the stiff white paper and read, Mr. Harris looking over his shoulder.

"*Government House, 26th January, 1808.*

"*Sir,*

"*In answer to my letter of yesterday I received a verbal message by my orderly from you that you was rendered by illness totally incapable of being at Sydney. I apprehend the same illness will deprive me of your assistance at this time; and the Judge Advocate having laid a memorial before me against six of your officers for practices which he conceives treasonable, I am under the necessity of summoning them before me, and all the magistrates have directions to attend at nine o'clock tomorrow morning.*

"*I leave it for you to judge whether Captain Abbott should be directed to attend at Sydney to command the troops in your absence.*

"*I am, etc.,*
"W'M BLIGH."

"The devil!" exclaimed Johnston.

"My God, Major," Harris said, "this matter grows damned serious! Treasonable practices . . . !"

They looked at each other uneasily. Johnston reached forward to secure a blind flapping against the window. Outside he could see the drive that ran down from his house, bordered by its avenue of Norfolk Island pines—growing tall now, and already a landmark in the district. He could see his fine property sloping away from the hill where his house stood, and it was like an argument. Danger, danger . . . ! He looked down at the letter again. Treasonable practices! Yet even if the officers were brought to a trial, would not that Criminal Court also consist of the Judge Advocate—and six other officers? Why, were there even enough officers eligible to sit on such a Court . . . ?

Harris said suddenly, as if pursuing the same idea:

"You know, he might set aside the Court altogether, and invest the magistrates with its powers. By Heaven, he might!"

Johnston muttered the word "illegal," but Harris scoffed.

"Oh, maybe, maybe, but this is Bounty Bligh, Sir! He'll ruin the lot of us—nay, mark my words, he may not even stop at that! He has the power of life and death—we've heard his Commission read! I tell you, when I call to mind the tales I've heard of the fellow's ruthlessness, I . . ."

He broke off in agitation, and stamped up and down the room, his head bent, his heavy jowl sunk in his white cravat, his hands clasping and unclasping behind his back. Macarthur was in gaol, but his strategy was still working; his adherents were between two fears, but that which he had implanted was the stronger.

Johnston turned from the window.

"Where's the man who brought this letter? I'll send a message back by him—find a servant to take it to him, Harris; I'll not appear myself. Damnation! What shall I say? My compliments to the Governor . . . I'm too ill to write . . . I'll get some person to write him an answer in the evening . . ." Their eyes met, and the Major said: "By that time . . ."

He broke off abruptly, and Harris turned to the door as if unwilling to hear the end of that sentence. Johnston called after him: "I'll go to town at once—order the carriage, Harris. I'll drive with you to Ultimo on the way—you said Minchin would be there. . . . We must make haste!"

He stared out the window for another moment when the surgeon had gone. Here it was. The plan had been formed, it had begun to move. He felt less that he was putting it into execution than that it was carrying him forward with it. The shadows of the pines were growing long, and the wind was restless in their branches.

*　　　*　　　*　　　*　　　*

Conor woke to her own quiet room, not only lying on the bed, but clamped down to it by a lassitude so great that a tentative attempt to lift her head sent her off into another swoon. She seemed to come back and go away many times; once she saw Stephen looking at her from the door; once it was Bessie; once Cousin Bertha was there bending over her, and she felt the dry, cool, papery touch of the old lady's hand on her brow. At last she woke alone to see the room clearly, and objects in sharp definition, without a watery haze about them. She lay still and closed her eyes again, but this time consciousness remained with her in the darkness, and her mind began, fumblingly, to work. And as human brains will, in moments of great physical exhaustion, it stripped away everything but one clear, small thought—the thought of a key in a lock. It was the last thought formed, the last picture recorded before her mind had snatched the respite of unconsciousness; and now, returning warily to work, it began where it had left off, but refused, as yet, to go beyond a beginning.

She lay for a time thinking of this key in a lock, and thinking of nothing else. Her mind and her body, like two careful physicians consulting, watched her and waited. Her body warned her mind. "Not yet —give her nothing more till I am ready." Her mind said: "Be quick; I cannot keep the thoughts away for long." Her heart worked, her blood carried strength in slow and gentle pulsations through her passive limbs, her eyes remained closed, isolating her within her body. And at last, delicately, with caution, her brain offered her the thought, "Go to him," and linked it with the thought of the key in the lock.

Now, with this idea of action, her body was involved, but she still lay quietly, waiting for its sanction. Presently she pressed downward with her hand upon the bed, and felt strength in her wrist. She opened her eyes and waited again. She lifted her head from the pillow and listened. The house was utterly silent. The door into the hall was shut, but the curtains moved over the long windows opening on to the verandah. If Stephen were in his study—but no, there had been something about a fire—he would be out in the fields, surely—and Patrick too. It was growing dusk —Bessie would be putting the children to bed. . . . If Ellen were in the kitchen she could not hope to escape being seen while she crossed the yard separating the house from the storeroom . . .

She did not find it strange that she should be furtive in her own home, scheming to avoid the eyes of her husband and her servants. She did not ask herself why she was going to him, or what she would do when she reached him. She knew only that what she had seen had thrown her irrevocably on his side of the gulf that had yawned between them. That was an action of the mind and spirit, and she was not yet sufficiently returned to her accustomed world to separate physical doing from belief. To be with him was a complete act; her body merely prepared to follow a spirit which had already joined him.

She sat up and moved her feet slowly over the edge of the bed. She held her hands against her head to still a passing attack of giddiness, and then stood up, still for a moment to test her balance. She crept to the door, opened it a crack, and listened. Footsteps came down the passage from the kitchen, and Ellen's voice spoke to one of the maids from near the parlour. Conor closed her door softly, knowing that what she had to do must be done at once.

They had removed her gown and stays, and she drew the girdle of her loose wrapper closely about her waist, but without even a thought of indecorum. Her slippers were on the floor beside the bed, but she did not stay to put them on. For the second time that afternoon she pushed the shutters open and stepped out on to the verandah, blinking at the red glare of the setting sun, and breathing the smoke-smelling air in deep, shaking gulps.

She hurried noiselessly in her stockinged feet round the corner of the verandah, and along the south side of the house, but hesitated before turning the next corner which would bring her opposite the kitchen door. Cautiously she peered round it, and caught a glimpse of a slender, blue-clad, white-aproned figure running across the space between the store-room and the house. It was only Dilboong—but what was she doing in the storeroom? But she dared not wait to wonder, and as she slipped round the corner she saw the black girl standing at the kitchen door, staring at her, and put her finger to her lips. Dilboong's round eyes grew rounder, but she did not speak. Conor whispered: "Dilboong—hush!" She saw the swift, faint movement of the black head—so like the movement of a wild animal listening—the whites of the dark eyes flashing a sideways glance into the house; and she saw, too, without thinking of it, that there was a wet splash of spilled water down the front of the white apron. But she had time only to feel relief that it should be Dilboong who had seen her, for she felt that here was someone well versed in fear, in the need for stealth, someone who understood hiding . . .

She limped hurriedly across the rough, pebbly ground to the storeroom door, pushed it open, and stepped into a dimness that defeated sight at first, but from which there came an evil smell of sweat and blood. She stood holding on to the door, waiting for her eyes to see again.

He was lying face downward in the middle of the room, and a faint, continuous sound, as though breathing had become moaning, came from his lips. A pitcher of water and a tin pannikin stood on the floor nearby. She moved forward to crouch beside him, trying not to look at the raw, swollen, bloody mass of flesh which was his back, and whispered his name, peering down at an unrecognisable face. She could see only one eye, and though its lids were not closed nothing but white showed between

them, and he seemed not to hear her. She poured water on a corner of
her skirt and touched his brow with it; she wiped away, without any
feeling of repugnance, the spittle that ran from one corner of his half-
open mouth, and his lips made a movement towards the wet cloth. She
filled the pannikin, lifted his head, and held it against his mouth; he
swallowed clumsily, the water running down his chin. His eyes opened
for an instant, and he seemed to look at her.

She began to think. She must not be found here, but she must win
at least an hour or two to tend him. She looked up at the door. If it
were locked inside, she thought, they might come, and finding it still
locked, think only that someone had taken the key away. If Stephen
came he would think that Toole or Ellen had taken it; if Toole came he
would think that Stephen or Ellen had taken it. If they listened, they
would hear Finn moaning, and know their captive safe. If they found
her gone—as they would very soon—they would search the whole colony
before they thought of looking for her here. . . . Only Dilboong knew
. . . and suddenly, looking at the pannikin in her hand, she remembered
that splash of water on the front of Dilboong's dress, and knew, with a
sting of tears in her eyes, that she need fear no betrayal there.

She rose and crept softly to the door. Across the yard she saw the
native girl still motionless in the doorway, staring at her, and she laid her
finger on her lips as she bent to take the key from the lock with the
movement that Ellen had taught her. A curious, peaceful weakness
possessed her as she fitted it into the inside lock and turned it. She
stumbled back to the pallet, and ceased to think of time. She bathed
Finn's face and gave him occasional sips of water, and all the while her
mind seemed wandering through long corridors of thought, vaguely seeking
some ratification by her brain of the emotion so frighteningly aroused in
her—condemnation and abhorrence of the whole machinery of her society.
She searched, and found nothing; every passage of her mind was blocked
somewhere by unyielding dogmas, traditional maxims, statements, asser-
tions, rules hammered into her since babyhood and tirelessly reiterated by
every authority she had been taught to venerate. She could find no
sanction for her pity. She sought the image of a kindly and indulgent
grandfather, and found his face austere, his voice chilled with rebuke.
She invoked justice, and quailed under the cold eye of a bewigged judge,
clothed in scarlet and the incomprehensible majesty of the Law. She
appealed to religion, and heard the echo of thunder from a hundred
pulpits. And yet, strangely, as she fell back denied and denounced by
every authority she knew, she found a kind of comfort in her outcast
state. She could not refute the only standards which her world had given
her, nor find words even to question them, but she felt a growth of
rebellion in her heart which sustained, even while it startled her. She
had doubted, but never before challenged her society—only travelled with
it, acquiescent in the smooth path it offered—and she was shaken now by
the rage of unreasoning conviction with which she could condemn it. They
could shriek "felon" at her till her ears were deafened; they could preach
the sanctity of the law and the necessity for a submissive lower class; they

could proclaim the right divine of kings, and the right—whatever it might be—of landowners; they could trumpet the sacredness and the frailty of female reputation, the glory of female obedience, and the inadequacy of female understanding; she would not—for she could not—raise one argument against them. She could only retreat, as she was doing now, into her newly-discovered self, and resist. And in that ostracism, she was less lonely than before.

Less lonely. He had recognised her now, though she thought his mind was still wandering. He had moved a hand, once, with a groan, and tried to support himself while he drank; she had put her own over it, and he had looked down with confused, fever-bright eyes as if somewhere in his brain the action had been recorded. And at last he lifted his head an inch or two and stared with a strange fixity at the door.

He began to move. She felt sickness sweep over her at the sight of that appalling effort, and whispered imploringly: "Oh, no, no, no, lie still!" But it went on—that dreadful writhing and struggling that was like the throes of a mutilated insect, and she saw blood breaking out again from the half-dried wounds on his back. She tried to hold him down, but the look he gave her was so much an accusation that her hands fell away, and she could only plead: "Oh, no, lie still . . . pray, *pray* lie still—you cannot move!"

But he was on his hands and knees. She could not bear any longer to watch the agony of this lonely effort, so she put her hands beneath his arms and lifted him. His weight almost bore her down as he laboured to his feet, and she besought him frantically in a whisper: "What is it that you want? Indeed, you are not strong enough to stand! I beg of you . . . !" He stood with one arm across her shoulders, swaying, his head bent; he lifted the other hand in a wavering gesture towards the door and made a step forward. She cried in panic: "No, no, you are mad!" but he made another step. She thought wildly: He is mad, he is delirious, he does not know what he is doing, but if I let him go on he will swoon, and then I can . . ." She supported him for three more steps that brought him to the wall beside the door, and there he leaned, muttering: "Door . . . door . . . open. . . ." And presently, incredibly: "Escape . . ."

Escape? She stared at him in horror. Escape—when he could hardly walk? Escape—in broad daylight? He lifted his head and looked at her, and the command in his eyes so hypnotised her that protestations died on her lips unuttered, and her hand went out to the key. "Open," he repeated thickly, "open, open, open . . ."

Her feeling now was that she had come so far into this wild world of his where she was so much a stranger, and so ignorant before his tragic knowledge, that she must obey. If this were insanity, or the madness of delirium, it made no difference, for she could find no sanity to set against it. Go out and die; lie here and die. She did not think that he could live, but tried to think it, and found herself facing something which frightened her far more than the thought of his death. For he still had, miraculously, a choice, and she knew that—mad or sane, clear-headed or bemused by fever—his choice was right. He could lie here—to live or die—in the knowledge of captivity; or go out and die in the illusion of freedom. She felt ashamed before the clarity of his delirious thought; humbled by the confidence with which he could still see the path he must take; awed by the superhuman endurance with which he could force his wrecked body along it. She opened the door, and they stumbled through.

Sunlight and fresh air smote him with too swift an intoxication; she caught and steadied him as he lurched forward, dragged his arm across her shoulders again, and moved forward as he moved. She did not question his direction, for she knew it did not matter. They crossed the yard, passed beyond the house and out into the open fields. She waited for shouts, tumult, uproar, and heard nothing but his breathing, growing more laborious with every step, each breath a groan. She began to feel stupid with weakness herself; smiled vaguely at the pale blue and saffron of the evening sky; heard a magpie; drew the smell of burnt grass into her nostrils; saw a crane rise from the river, and watched it out of sight behind the trees. They were alone in the world, and there was nothing to do but keep moving through it, nothing to think about but what it showed them.

When he fell she fell with him, and pushed herself up on her hands to look at him without surprise. He lay on his back, his breath choking in his throat, his eyes wide open and fixed on her. She said, nodding: "We escaped—you are free now. . . ." It was not meant for consolation; she did feel that they had escaped, and his eyes told her, before death made them blank, that he had felt it too.

*   *   *   *   *

Mannion found her there, still sitting by the body, soon after six o'clock. The outbreak of fire had alarmed him so much that as soon as it seemed certain they could control it he had despatched Evans to Parramatta with an urgent message for Captain Abbott. It was evident, he thought, that Finn's fellow-desperadoes, still at large, were bent on further mischief, and he must secure the aid of a military detachment in tracking them down. It was about half-past five when he watched the overseer ride off, and turned back into the house—hot, weary, angry and disturbed—to be met by Bessie's tearful declaration that the mistress had left her room, and was nowhere to be found. Every man and woman had been mustered for the frenzied search that followed, and the house was deserted save for Cousin Bertha, Bessie and the children. Conjectures—each more appalling than the last—had tormented Mannion as he sent armed parties off in every direction. It was clear from her amazing behaviour this afternoon that her mind must be deranged by illness. Had she wandered out aimlessly, not knowing what she did? Had she—he froze with horror at the thought— made away with herself? Yet while he searched, scouring the river bank and calling her name, an idea even more terrible had sharpened his alarm to panic. She had been abducted! Finn's accomplices, as a hideous act of revenge, must have taken advantage of the time when every man was occupied fighting the fire, and somehow seized her! They must have found her wandering in a crazed state out of doors somewhere . . . or perhaps even gained the house itself, and snatched her from her room. . . . Within three seconds of framing this ghastly thought, he believed it. God in Heaven, had he not always warned of the dangers of these devilish gangs? Patrick himself must ride after Evans with this frightful tale to reinforce the demand for military assistance. . . . Half maddened and completely exhausted by anxiety and dread, Mr. Mannion had ridden up past the house to summon his son, and found her—here!

He stood staring down at her with rage, incredulity and repugnance struggling together on his handsome face. Her gown had been dragged away from one shoulder by the pressure of Finn's arm; it was dirty, flecked here and there with blood; her hair was in wild disorder, her stockings stained and torn; her face was plain and pallid, her expression dull.

She rose obediently on his peremptory command, and began to stumble towards the house without a backward look at the still body in the grass. Patrick and Byrne were riding towards the house, and spurred their horses to a gallop when they saw her; Bessie had come out from the back door and was staring. Mannion said icily: "You will take my arm, if you please." This dirty, dishevelled, disreputable woman was his wife; his tormented pride demanded that he re-clothe her in the dignity she had so shamelessly abandoned. She crossed the field on his arm, mounted the steps with his ceremonious assistance, entered the house oblivious of Bessie's stares and exclamations, ignored Patrick—running in behind them and thanking God incoherently for her safety—passed through the door which Mannion opened, and fell upon the bed to which he guided her. He stood over her and uttered one sentence—the last she was ever to hear from him:

"You have disgraced yourself—and me."

*   *   *   *   *

Major Johnston had reached Sydney about five o'clock, but it was not to Government House that his coachman was directed. Although so happily recovered from the indisposition which had endangered his life only the previous day, he did not extend to his Excellency the courtesy of a call in response to the two letters he had received, nor make any attempt, however belated, to compose the differences between his Corps and the Governor, but descended from his carriage in the Barracks Square to be instantly surrounded by a clamouring group of his officers. Within a few moments the beat of drums summoning the soldiers to the Square sent a new wave of excitement sweeping through the town.

Rumour had been running wild all day, and the Governor's summons to the six military members of the ill-fated Court had put the finishing touch to panic among the well-to-do. The tyrant, they told each other, was about to strike. He was about to abolish the Courts altogether, and form a new one of three or four of his own adherents, with himself as President. From the decisions of this all-powerful group there would be no appeal, and its first victims were to be the six gentlemen who had so valiantly opposed him during these last two turbulent days. The respectable—which in their language meant the wealthy—members of the community were to be ruined. No man's property, or even his life, was safe.

Look at Macarthur, languishing in the common gaol! Perhaps to be privately assassinated—perhaps even now a dead man!

Few of them, while whispering these dreadful tales, really believed more than the obvious fact that the military influence and the financial supremacy of their group was imperilled; but to justify the desperate remedy they proposed it was necessary to create an atmosphere or terror and crisis. It must not appear that the Governor was deposed to serve their ends, but to rescue a quaking populace from his tyranny. Major Johnston entered the Barracks amid clamorous prophecies of civil insurrection and chaos.

Mark Harvey, after dismissing his pupils for the day, had strolled along to Dawes' Point where he had spent an hour of this long, hot summer afternoon reading, but the drums roused him and brought him hurrying back past the fort and along Church Street to the Barracks. By the time he reached the Square the troops were drawn up under arms, and clusters of curious onlookers were watching the bustle round the door of the officers' barracks. He asked a bystander what was afoot, but the man only shook his head uneasily. He caught a glimpse of the captain of an American vessel now in port, with whom he had struck up an acquaintance the day before, and found himself recalling their conversation. He had assured Mark that only a few days ago the officers had contrived to smuggle spirits from his ship without his knowledge. "Been trying to make me a party to it for weeks," he had said, "Kemp and Lawson and that fellow Minchin. Kemp asks me straight won't I smuggle it, and Johnston said: 'By God, the Governor had best look sharp, or we'll take it from you in spite of him!' And that's what they did, Sir. I tell you they'll take as much as they can get that way—and pay prices it's hard for a poor man to refuse."

Mark frowned. As he watched the commotion that incident seemed significant—not for itself, but because he had realised by now that behind this and all other incidents which had set the place by the ears lately was the determination of the privileged to retain their privileges at all costs. At all costs, he repeated to himself, staring at the ranks of soldiers and their officers clustered round the Barracks door—with whom, now, various well-known private citizens were conferring in obvious excitement. A voice beside him said: "Good evening to you, Sir," and he glanced round to find a master blacksmith of the town whom he knew slightly standing behind him. He answered:

"Good evening, Mr. Langley. There's a great stir going on—do you know the cause of it?"

"They're up to no good," the man declared sombrely. He turned his face suddenly and touched his cheek. "See this, Sir?"

"A nasty bruise," said Mark. "How did you come by it?"

"From one o' those red-coated ruffians over there," Langley said, nodding grimly in the direction of the ranks. "This morning down by the gaol when there was a crowd around after Jack Bodice was put there, where he belongs. Did ye hear, Mr. Harvey, that the Governor's sent for those six officers that was on the court?"

"Yes," replied Mark, "I heard that."

"Well, when I heard it, I points to the gaol, and I says: 'They'll soon be there too!' An' the next thing I know, I get *this!* *And* give it back!" He spat. "There's convicts that are better men than they, for all their gaudy uniforms."

He moved on, and Mark turned his attention to the door of the Barracks, inside which, at that moment, the Major was still the centre of an uproar. From all sides came the cry that he arrest the Governor—that he prevent the massacre which would undoubtedly take place otherwise—that he preserve the peace and order of the colony—that for the tyrant's own sake he must be placed in custody, lest he fall a victim to the fury of the outraged populace—that Macarthur stood in peril of being secretly made away with, and must be rescued; and the clamour condensed into two cries, persistently repeated: "Arrest the Governor!" "Release Macarthur!"

Major Johnston needed no such persuasion. He would arrest the Governor—of course. He would release Macarthur—that, too,. was obviously necessary. Yet it was not only because the plan was already determined upon that he complied with such alacrity to the second of these demands. In this crisis he was conscious of a feeling that though he commanded the troops drawn up in the Barracks Square, they were not his real strength. He would give the orders; his were the scarlet uniform, and the authority; to him, when the business was over, would fall the nominal control of the colony; he would make the gestures—but, like a puppet, he needed the unseen hand to pull the strings. He needed the reassurance of a stronger personality. He needed the support of a man quite ruthless in pursuing their common purpose. He needed a directing brain. He needed John Macarthur.

The order was written; he signed it and saw it despatched. The small room was intolerably hot. Men came and went, and the babel of voices continued unceasingly. He turned to Mr. John Blaxland, who had just arrived.

"I have flown to you for protection, Major," declared Mr. Blaxland. "We are all ruined unless you act."

Someone came in and reported that Mr. Atkins had been seen spying out the situation in the Square, and had scuttled back to Government House in haste. The noise and jeering that greeted this report faded suddenly, and all eyes turned to the door.

Mr. Macarthur stood there, cooler and calmer than anyone in the room, his chin in the air, his dark eyes narrower, and his outthrust lower lip more truculent than ever.

They all surged towards him, but his eyes were on the Major, and Johnston, as if hypnotised by that cold, demanding, enquiring stare, stammered peevishly:

"God's curse! What am I to do, Macarthur? Here are these fellows advising me to arrest the Governor . . ."

With a slight shrug and a wintry smile Macarthur replied:

"Advising you? Then, Sir, the only thing left for you to do is—to do it." His gaze moved to the heated faces of the officers, and he added gently: "To advise on such matters is legally as criminal as to do them."

Johnston caught his arm.

"Come here—this must be discussed—in here will do . . ."

They vanished together into an adjoining room. Macarthur, sitting on the edge of a table, said:

"What is there to discuss?"

Johnston pulled out a handkerchief and passed it over his forehead nervously.

"There'll be the devil to pay! It's rebellion—the home Government won't look too kindly on . . ."

Macarthur said coldly:

"It is not rebellion, but the deliverance of the colony from intolerable tyranny. You act upon the desire and the earnest recommendation of the military and civil officers, and all the respectable inhabitants . . ."

Johnston sent a hunted glance at the door. The group in the next room was noisy, but it was not numerous. A handful of military officers, six of whom had urgent private reasons for desiring the downfall of the Governor; Mr. Blaxcell, Macarthur's business partner, and Mr. Bayly, his close friend; Mr. Wentworth, smarting under his suspension; Mr. Simeon Lord, who had not forgotten Gore's case; Mr. John Blaxland, who conceived himself ill-used by His Excellency; it was not, Johnston felt, a very convincing gathering. Where were the civil officers of whom Macarthur spoke so largely? Grimes would join them, no doubt . . . and the two doctors, Jamison and Mileham . . . but Atkins, Griffin, Palmer, Campbell, Gore and Fulton were all in the enemy camp. The magistrates . . . ? Himself alone. Abbott, though he would acquiesce, was notably without enthusiasm for the project, and in any case sixteen miles away at Parramatta . . .

Macarthur, who had seen his glance and read it, pursued imperturbably: "You act to preserve order, to avert an insurrection of the inhabitants, to protect the Governor himself from the results of his arbitary conduct. That is clear—but in order to make it clearer I can't too strongly urge that you should not proceed without a requisition in writing, signed by all the respectable inhabitants of the colony, and all the free men . . ."

"But . . . !" exploded Johnston. Macarthur stayed the interruption with an uplifted hand.

"I know, I know! The time is short, and if it is to be done it must be done at once. But the requisition can be written immediately, Sir, and one signature at least you shall have to it—my own—though no doubt others will sign it also. The names of military officers are obviously not to be desired; the situation in which some of them find themselves would suggest a motive, would it not? As for the other citizens of the colony, if they don't sign it to-night . . ." he smiled, ". . . they will later."

Johnston mopped his perspiring face rather gingerly, for it bore a few bruises and abrasions from his fall. Macarthur glanced at the sling in which his right arm rested, and remarked amiably as he reached across the table for a pen, a bottle of ink, and a sheet of paper:

"Happily for me, Major, you were able to sign the order for my release. Your injuries will perhaps permit you to sign one more document —that which acquaints Captain Bligh that he is no longer Governor."

He stood up, went through into the other room, Johnston at his heels, and paused at the outer door for a moment looking at the soldiers standing stiffly in their ranks, and the clusters of people watching curiously from a distance. Surrounded by the officers and the few others who had joined them, he turned back to the room, arranged his writing materials on the table, and dipped his pen into the ink. He had had all day in gaol to think, and he wrote fast, without hesitation.

"*Sir,*

"*The present alarming state of the colony, in which every man's property, liberty and life is endangered, induces us most earnestly to implore you instantly to place Governor Bligh under an arrest, and to assume command of the colony. We pledge ourselves, at a moment of less agitation, to come forward to support the measure with our fortunes and our lives.*

"*We are, with great respect, Sir,*

"*Your most obedient servants . . .*"

He spoke it aloud as he wrote, heads craning and eyes peering over his shoulder. He dipped his pen in the ink again, signed his name emphatically, and scored a black, thick, dramatic line beneath it. He lifted the paper and handed it to Johnston with a bow.

"There, Major, is your requisition. Mr. Blaxland—you would like the pen . . . ?" He saw John Blaxland bend over the paper as he turned away, but he was no longer interested in it. Now—or later—it would gather a host of signatures. The time had come to act.

*   *   *   *   *

The last rays of the setting sun were lying across the Square as Major Johnston placed himself at the head of his men. The hot, sullen light blazed on the red coats of some three hundred soldiers, and brightened the faded regimental colours fluttering in the wind. By now a large crowd had gathered, and as drum and fife struck up "The British Grenadiers" and the soldiers began to march down the hill, its subdued buzz of conversation became an excited uproar. It surged after the regiment, and Mark went with it, apprehension in his heart. The urchins of the town—among whom he recognised and rebuked some of his pupils— yelled and pushed in a frenzy of delight at the martial spectacle. They capered wildly about the column of soldiers, beside which, he noticed, Mr. Macarthur, his son, Mr. Harris, Mr. Jamison, the Blaxlands, Mr. Grimes and Dr. Townson were marching.

He questioned one person after another, but could learn nothing. The only scraps of conversation he overheard reflected his own anxious bewilderment. He saw his friend, George Suttor, just ahead of him, and caught him by the arm.

"What's afoot, Mr. Suttor—where are they going?"

The settler, his face dark with anger, replied: "To arrest the Governor!" Mark stared at him in consternation, and he added bitterly: "That's what I hear, Mr. Harvey, and I believe it, for he's clipped their wings more than they care for—and they have force on their side, Sir, if not justice nor honour." He jerked his head in the direction of Sergeant-Major Whittle. "Listen to that!"

Whittle, stimulated by excitement and alcohol, was loudly exhorting his men.

"Come on then, lads, an' do y' duty! Don't spare them!" He smacked at the legs of a pair of jubilant small boys, prancing almost under his feet. "Get out o' the way, children, or ye'll be killed, for there's men's work to do to-night! We'll not spare 'em, lads . . . !" Through the roar of approbation from his men, he could be heard repeating: "Don't spare 'em!" and a voice that sounded like Macarthur's said sharply: "Hush! Hush!"

Mark cried aghast:

"Surely they won't dare to arrest . . . ?"

But the crowd had forced Suttor away from him, and he was borne along with it to the street outside Government House where it halted, surging, shouting, whispering and staring behind the red-coated line of soldiers. Mark, standing near the front, caught a glimpse of Macarthur. He was among a group of gentlemen and officers, rubbing elbows with them, yet he seemed to stand apart. In all the crowd engaged upon this reckless adventure, only he seemed calm. Yet *was* he calm . . . ? Mark stared. The dark face, wearing its normal, faintly supercilious expression, was uplifted in the gathering dusk, and the eyes were fixed not on the Guard House where Ensign Bell was preparing to admit the soldiers, but on the lighted windows of Government House.

Calm? No! Still, but not calm; set like a mask, but not calm. Ambition, pride and triumph were burning like a light behind that mask; from his motionless figure and still face far more than from the confusion and the clamour surrounding him, came violence. . . . And then, in the general movement he was hidden, and Mark was left with a picture, an impression stamped forever on his mind.

That cold, violent man . . . !

*   *   *   *   *

The Governor had received Johnston's verbal message only a few minutes before he sat down to dinner at about five o'clock with Palmer, Campbell, Atkins, Arndell and Williamson. He was in a black mood, and spoke little. The uneasiness they all felt was sharply increased when they heard the drums beat to summon the soldiers to the Square, and Mr. Atkins went out to reconnoitre. He hurried through the still oppressively warm evening up the hill towards the Barracks, hatless, with the wind flapping his coat-tails and ruffling his already disordered hair. He came back even faster, and burst in upon the gentlemen at the Governor's table, almost too breathless to speak.

"Macarthur . . . released . . . out of gaol! Saw him going into the Barracks . . . !"

Bligh leaned forward incredulously, gripping the edge of the table.

"*WHAT?*" he roared. "By whose order? Johnston's? He's there at the Barracks too?" He leapt to his feet furiously and the choicest profanity of the seven seas thundered round the room. "So!" he added savagely, "he's too ill to attend me when I request it—too ill even to write a civil answer to my letters—but not too ill to make his way to the Barracks! Not too ill to lend countenance to rebels! Not too ill to usurp my authority by releasing from gaol a prisoner committed there by the magistrates of the colony! Great God in Heaven, these are pretty soldiers! Paid for the support of His Majesty's Government, they conspire to subvert it! What's afoot in the town, Atkins? Speak, man— don't stand there goggling!"

Atkins wrung his hands.

"God knows, Sir! There are people abroad in the streets—some seem confused and alarmed by what's going on in the Square, but they're quiet enough. I heard a man speak against the officers and a soldier struck him, and there was a brawl . . ."

"Brawl, brawl, brawl!" repeated Bligh, thumping the table angrily. "This damned colony is nothing but brawls—and lurking behind every one of them is that arch-plotter, that arch-mischief-maker, that seditious villain now set at large to continue his machinations . . . ! What is it, Griffin?"

The secretary had hurried in, pale-faced, and Mrs. Putland, following, hastened to her father's side.

"The guard at the gates, Sir—they're priming and loading, and I fear . . ."

Bligh's head was lowered like that of a goaded animal about to charge, and his voice rasped harshly with bitterness and contempt.

"Ah? My personal guard, provided by the Corps itself! Well, gentlemen, it seems that my enemies are resol . . ."

The word died half uttered; for one second they all looked at each other, silent, listening, and Mary Putland's hand tightened on her father's arm. From up the hill there came the beat of drums, and the sound of marching music.

Bligh said slowly:

"No, no—they wouldn't dare . . . !"

He looked round the room to find consternation and alarm in the eyes watching him. He repeated loudly: "They wouldn't *dare* to touch my person!"

Yet he knew they would. He knew it with those nerves that still winced from an eighteen-year-old memory. All his own deep-rooted respect for authority, all his own rigid, undeviating pursuit of duty rebelled now, as it had rebelled then, against the incredible thought. It was not *possible* that a crew should mutiny against its commander! It

was not *possible* that soldiers should rise against the King's representative!
Yet the one had happened long ago—and now, to the beat of drums and
the sound of shouts and music, the other was advancing upon him.

Almost abstractedly, he took his half-full glass from the table and
lifted it high.

"Gentlemen—the health of His Majesty!"

There was a murmur, a clink of glasses being set down on the table,
and then a sudden babel of anxious discussion and advice. Mrs. Putland
murmured tremulously: "Papa—what shall you do?" He glanced down
at her and closed his hand over hers. The sight of her deep mourning
reminded him of his own, and he resolved that, come what might, he
would meet it in his uniform. His brain was busy now. He would ride
to the Hawkesbury and gather the settlers round him—by God, there was
hardly a man of them but would rally to his standard! And in the towns,
too, many would support him . . .

But first . . .

The sea-captain's instinct on a sinking ship to save his log and his
ship's papers turned his thoughts now to documents which must not fall
into the hands of the rebels. Copies of his confidential correspondence
with the Secretary of State, private letters concerning the colony and
persons in it, the account of yesterday's infamous proceedings. . . . These
he must keep secure for the protection of his character, and the confusion
of his enemies . . .

But the enemies were coming nearer, and John Dunn was in the
doorway, announcing with a quaver in his voice that Captain Kemp and
three officers were already loudly demanding admittance. Mrs. Palmer
appeared, and hurried to Mrs. Putland's side; there was a general rushing
to and fro, a clamour of voices.

Bligh said harshly:

"If they are bent on violence we have nothing with which to oppose
them. I shall get off to the Hawkesbury and call the settlers around me.
Mary, my love, retire with Mrs. Palmer. Dunn! *Dunn!* Where the
devil is the man . . .?"

He strode out of the room, calling to the servant who hovered distraught in the passage.

"Tell the orderly sergeant to have my horses ready. Let no one be
admitted!"

He hurried up to his room, Campbell, Palmer and Griffin at his heels.
He flung open a trunk and a bureau and ransacked them for papers,
selecting some and discarding others while Griffin brought his uniform.
They were all listening tensely to the increasing hubbub out of doors
while he changed into it. Gore arrived, brandishing Johnston's order for
the release of Macarthur. The street outside seemed to be astir with
noise and movement, and through it, from the direction of the gates, came
a sound of feminine screams.

"My God, Campbell," Bligh said, struggling into his uniform, "go
down and see what's happening!"

Campbell threw down the Major's order which he had been reading and rushed downstairs. Mrs. Putland had snatched up a parasol and run out to the gates where she now stood fiercely haranguing Ensign Bell, the officer of the guard, who was preparing to admit his men while the main body of the Corps was already marching up the street.

"Have you no shame, Sir? You—who are given the duty of protecting the Governor's person! Will you open the gates to his murderers?" She brandished her parasol at the red-coated throng through the bars. "You traitors! You rebels! You have just walked over my husband's grave, and now you come to murder my father! You may stab me to the heart, but I warn you to respect the person of the Governor! No, no, you shall not open . . . ! Stop! Oh, Mr. Campbell, Mr. Campbell, prevent them . . . !"

But there was no preventing them; the gates opened, and they surged in. Mr. Fulton, valiantly opposing them at the front of the house, held them off for a few moments, but was taken in the rear by another party which entered by a side door. Mrs. Putland brought her parasol down with a resounding thwack across a pair of red-coated shoulders, but their owner gave her no other acknowledgment than a curse; and it was the only blow struck in defence of Governor Bligh.

*　　　　*　　　　*　　　　*　　　　*

In full uniform, and with his Camperdown medal on his breast, he was standing with Palmer at the head of the stairs when the soldiers broke in. It had all happened so suddenly that he could not yet believe that his chance of escape to the Hawkesbury was gone. He had seconds in which to make up his mind to a course of action, and his brain raced. What were his alternatives? Opposition—surrender—escape. The former must be instantly dismissed; he had no force at his command to oppose these rebels. Surrender? To walk quietly downstairs, confront Johnston, and hand over to him without a struggle the authority vested in him by the King? Never! Only in escape was there still a chance; and to escape he must remain free—in a house already surrounded and invaded. Hopeless? By God, he had been in what many men would have called a hopeless situation once before when faced by mutiny—and how had he won through it? By defeating each hour separately, by forcing his way, minute by minute through inimical days and nights, by saying in his heart that the defeat of every malignant second left him still free to engage the next. . . . Yes, that was all his duty for the moment—to remain free . . .

He said urgently to Palmer:

"Go down—delay them—I may yet get clear . . ."

He ran down the passage and pushed open a door at the back of the house. It was a servant's room, divided by a partition and another door from a second inner room, and into this he hurried. A window looked out on to the yard, and he stood at it concealed by the curtain, peering out, measuring its distance from the ground, hoping for a moment until he saw soldiers come round the corner, and heard the indignant voice of Gore from below, and watched him being hustled at bayonet point out of sight. There were soldiers all about the house, and he knew that, for the present at least, the window offered no escape. He turned back to the room and began to arrange his papers hastily. He tried to conceal them beneath his waistcoat, but the bundle was too large. Men were tramping about the house; suddenly he heard them in the outer room, and crouched quickly behind the bed. The door opened, and he heard Lieutenant Moore's voice say impatiently: "Pooh, he's not here! No, I tell you he's not here."

The door closed again and he stood up, a perspiration on his brow, but a quick upsurge of hope in his heart. They had looked into the room —and failed to find him. Very likely they would not come again . . . perhaps he had only to wait, making no sound, and then . . . ?

But no plans were possible. He did not know what was going on downstairs, where his friends might be, what they might have contrived. He could only hold on to the fact that every moment he remained at liberty left him still a chance to seize an opportunity if it came. He began to sort his papers again, tearing some very small and scattering the pieces on the floor, and he noticed as he did so that the dusk was deepening, and already the light in the little room was too poor to see the writing clearly. If he could remain hidden here till it was quite dark he might yet elude the searchers and get away to the Hawkesbury. Anything, he thought fiercely, rather than have another command wrested from him!

For a very long time he stood there, the papers hidden at his breast beneath his coat, his arm held across them, his ears straining, hope growing stronger with every moment that he was not discovered. The room darkened. His mind reviewed bitterly the events of the last two days. Macarthur—flouting the law, declining to give further bail, walking off surrounded by the soldiers . . . was he to permit such a thing to pass? Had it not then became a plain issue—whether the law were to be obeyed, or the whole authority of Government defied by a single individual? He told himself savagely that anything less than the measures he had taken would have been to leave himself Governor in name alone. Yet was this final outrage really the result of that one legal encounter? Had it really happened so suddenly after all—or was there a carefully-laid plan behind it? And did not plans take time? What secret conclaves had there been among his enemies? What had passed at that mess-dinner? What was the truth of this strange illness of Major Johnston's which yesterday threatened his life—but to-day permitted him to march at the head of his rebellious troops? Which only three or four hours ago rendered him incapable of writing—but which now allowed him to sign the order for Macarthur's release? And as Bligh's ears continued to strain for sounds of the search, his mind halted on that name and began to repeat it— Macarthur, Macarthur, Macarthur. . . . Everywhere, at every turn— Macarthur . . .

He turned to the window again. Now it framed a dark square of sky pricked with twinkling stars, and he thought: "Surely I must have been here an hour or more . . ." But the search was still going on; he could hear voices and tramping feet outside. He began to feel the accumulated fatigue of trying weeks leading up to these last two long, hot, exhausting days; culminating in the shock of rebellion, and this seemingly endless wait in a dark, mean little room. He thought anxiously of his daughter; scoundrels as they were, they would not harm her, but the knowledge of her distress and agitation tormented him. Yet he must not move. She, too, and those few others who were his friends, would be listening, counting every moment a victory . . .

He sat down on the edge of the bed and waited—listened—waited . . .

    *   *   *   *   *

Conor, too, was watching the twilight deepen outside her window. After a time she heard voices calling, and thought: They will be going to take him away. She felt numbly peaceful, for it was still strong in her mind that together she and Finn had achieved some kind of triumph, and she rose and went to the window from where she could see Toole and another man crossing the field with spades over their shoulders. There would be but one grave for him and the other convicts who had died, she thought half-absently—and they, perhaps, were already in it. She could just see the two dim figures making their way towards a small hillock north of the hut, and two others who now followed them, carrying a shapeless burden. Her memory went back to the only other burial which had ever concerned her—when her mother was laid to rest with tears, and flowers, and ceremony, and solemn words, among a crowd of mourning relatives, weeping servants, and respectful peasants. Night came as she watched, and she heard the voices of the men returning, and saw them at last as dark blurs, vanishing round the back of the house, leaving her to solitude, and the warm, dry wind on her brow.

She was only waiting for this; she pushed the shutters wide, and once again stepped out on to the verandah—but this time without stealth or agitation. Her unshod feet were sore, and she limped as she walked across the field with her skirts blowing about her legs, and her hair whipping across her face, but she felt no pain, and was not disturbed by any sense of strangeness in what she did. Johnny, lying face downwards on the fresh mound that covered Finn's body, heard her light footsteps, and lifted his head.

He had made his attempt at rescue, and it had failed. He had lit the fire, hoping that every man might be summoned to fight it, leaving Finn alone in some confinement he could break. He had made his way up the river to the southern boundary of the property, and skirted that boundary through the bush; it had taken time, but he dared not cross the fields. He had come at last to a spot from which the hut was visible—only to see Finn's body being carried up the hill, already far away near the house. He was too late, then. Finn was dead. He watched the column of smoke behind the house rise and thicken, but was no longer interested in it. It didn't matter now. Finn was dead, dead, dead. . . . He looked round him at the bush, puzzled by its silence. Death meant a great noise, a great wailing. He felt it in himself, a storm, a clamour raised by Dyonn-ee, imprisoned by Johnny Prentice, so that he felt suffocated, bursting with agony. They were taking him away for burial. Green branches round the body, and kinsmen round the grave. . . . But he remembered Finn's tales. *"Into the ground they go, an' no time for prayers an' no call for weepin' the way they're no further interest to the master . . ."*

The master. Johnny's blank eyes became suddenly intent, and his misery seemed lightened by the knowledge that there was still something he must do. He had turned his back on the cleared land of Beltrasna, and hurried back to the river, and from there downstream to where the canoes lay, still safely hidden in the thick scrub by the river. The fire, he thought, was useful after all, for there was no one near the banks. He had stripped off his clothes, but kept a belt of kangaroo-hide, into which he thrust his pistol. He took a spear, for it might be necessary to kill silently before he could reach his enemy, but when he did. . . . It was very rarely that a smile touched his impassive face, and the momentary grimace that twitched his lips now held little of mirth. He only knew that the idea of killing Mr. Mannion with his own pistol pleased him.

He had spent almost three hours hiding, welcoming the gathering dusk, reconnoitring, waiting. He had seen the last flames of the fire beaten out; he had been startled by a sudden tumult—men mounting and riding off in different directions, shouting, calling, looking for someone. He had taken refuge in the river again when they came down there, and Mannion himself had been within twenty yards of him, calling to his men: "Search the bracken—she may be lying in a swoon . . ." Then he had gone away, and after a time someone shouted from the top of the hill, and the excitement had passed, and there had been quiet again. Such quiet that he had ventured a little way into the fields, creeping and crouching and hiding, and presently, in the deepening twilight, he had seen two men appear carrying a burden, and he had followed, making wide detours, lying still in the grass sometimes, but slowly coming closer. And when they had done their work and gone away, he had come out from his hiding place in the scrub behind a hillock, and climbed up to the grave, thinking that he would not be disturbed there, since dead convicts were of no further interest to the master.

Only to be roused by this sound of footsteps . . .

He slid quickly to the shelter of a few dark, wind-tossed bushes, and from there peered at the blur of white coming up the slope. A woman . . . ? For an instant he thought of his mother, and knew the same panic he had felt years ago when chance had brought him too close to Andy. But this was not his mother. As she reached the top of the hillock he could see that she was young, and he recalled that Finn had spoken once of Mannion's young wife, ". . . a poor lass with a pretty face an' a kind enough heart in her—but of no account, the way she knows nothin' of the world she lives in . . ." *His* woman? Or a servant, perhaps? *His* servant? Johnny's hand gripped his spear more tightly. How gladly, with what fierce happiness and triumph, he would destroy anyone or anything belonging to *him* . . . !

Conor stood beside the grave, looking down at it. She would not have been surprised or disturbed to learn how close she was in that moment to the savage, dark-skinned people who believed that no man should journey from life into death alone. But this she never learned;

she knew only that she must offer some kind of a prayer here, perform some kind of rite, make some gesture which would acknowledge him as a being with a spirit and a spiritual hereafter. Her tired brain groped among its memories of the service for the dead, and could find only: "We commit his body to the earth."

The earth. She sighed, and behind her Johnny rose soundlessly, his spear poised. She lifted her head and looked at the huge, dark, waiting land whose earth now covered him, at the fields—wide, black, empty expanses—at the hills beyond the river, a silhouette against the sky. The words she found were addressed not to any deity, but to the land; they came from no burial service, but she accepted them as the prayer she sought, and spoke them aloud: "O receive the fugitive, and prepare in time an asylum for mankind . . ."

Johnny's tense arm slackened, the spear sank to his side; amazement and sudden, overwhelming grief held him transfixed. Finn's words . . . why did she speak his words . . . ? Motionless, in misery and bewilderment, he watched her walk quietly back across the fields till the white glimmer of her gown was lost in the darkness.

Yet he was not long alone before grief, becoming intolerable, merged into hatred again. The woman, by speaking Finn's words, had released others in his mind till the night was full of them, and he felt them fighting his desire for revenge. ". . . get y'self away! I'm not minded to go into this thing with the fear on me heart that there'll be neither one of us to come back . . ."

He looked down at the fresh earth and argued with it. Aye, I'll go, never fear, but there's a thing to be done first. The voice in his mind urged: "Don't be stayin' if by stayin' ye may be taken . . ." He resisted it angrily. I'll not be taken! I'll go back—but not leavin' him alive!

He stared at the one light visible from the house on the hilltop, and with that mad, direct audacity which had startled Finn and Andy, set out to reach it. Long years of native training made his caution instinctive. He could use the smallest cover to the greatest advantage, he could merge with shadows; his eyes were confident in darkness, and his ears, trained to hear even the stirring of a grub in a log, missed not the faintest sound. He did not need to think of a strategy of concealment; to one who had hunted his food since early boyhood, it was a perfected art.

He came close to the house at last, and lay behind a pile of sawn logs, looking and listening. The kitchen door was shut, but a rim of light showed underneath it. A man with a musket was pacing up and down along the southern wall, and as Johnny watched another came towards him from between the back of the house and the storeroom. Mannion, it seemed, was not relaxing his vigilance. The light he had seen from the hillock was gone now; someone had closed the shutters of a room. All those along the southern side of the house were closed, and from between their wooden slats only pale yellow bars of illumination showed.

Johnny moved down the hill again, skirting the house at a distance, and came round to the west side and slowly up to Conor's rose-garden, from where, crouching behind the arbour, he saw that one long window was open, its lamplight streaming out beyond the stone pillars of the verandah on to the path that skirted it. On the steps that led up to the front door a man was sitting with a musket across his knees. The lighted room was the one from which he had stolen the firearms, and voices were coming from it, though he was too far away to hear their words.

A little to his right, and close to the path of lamplight—so close, indeed, that a fringe of their leaves was touched by it—he noted a thicket of tall, dark shrubs, and began to crawl towards them. From here he had the light between himself and the sentry on the steps, but the other man who patrolled the south side was approaching, and he froze into absolute stillness as the footsteps reached the corner and came on round it, and a voice called softly: "Byrne!"

The man on the steps rose and went to meet his fellow-guard; they conversed for a few moments in tones that were low, but not low enough. A figure appeared at the lighted window, and Mannion's voice said angrily:

"Byrne—where are you? Damnation, you are there to watch not to gossip! Brown, get back to your own side of the house and stay there. Great Heaven, can I never have obedience to my orders?"

He disappeared again, and Byrne, hurrying back to the steps, began pacing up and down before them. The other man withdrew to the south side of the house, and Johnny listened to his footsteps, but his eyes never moved from Byrne. When they had twice receded, twice returned, and were for the third time receding, he stood up, well screened by the bushes, and rustled their leaves sharply. Byrne halted, glanced towards them for a moment, and resumed his pacing. Twice more Johnny waited, motionless, for the other guard to approach and retire. He rustled the leaves again, and Byrne stood still for a moment and stared before turning away with a slight shrug. But he began pacing the whole length of the house now, passing through the light and glancing at the bushes as he passed; nothing stirred them now save the wind, and each time his scrutiny was more casual. At last he went by without looking, humming idly under his breath, and Johnny let him pass like that three times, waiting for his approach to coincide with the retreat of the other guard. As Byrne stepped for the fourth time from the lamplight into an obscurity that momentarily confused his eyes, a black shadow moved in the bushes, a hand went over his mouth, and a spear beneath his ribs.

*   *   *   *   *

In the study Mannion was talking to Patrick.

"Evans should have reached Parramatta an hour ago, and I hope to God Abbott doesn't delay, for . . ."

Patrick asked moodily:

"His men may find nothing if they come. I can't understand, Father, why you feel so sure there must be more of these . . ."

Mannion's voice held the high note of overstrained nerves.

"Are you a half-wit? We have taken *one man*! Do you imagine this audacious plot can have been attempted by one man alone? Didn't those native children speak of many men?"

"We didn't find them," Patrick answered rather sulkily, "and it was odd the way that elder boy disappeared so suddenly."

"Of course we didn't find them! They had already made their way down the river to where their confederate was finally captured. It passes my comprehension how you can fail to see the peril we still stand in. Of course it was a gang! Who lit that fire? Nay, did we not ourselves hear a shot from near the river as we rode down? Did I not send two men to investigate it?"

Patrick shrugged.

"No one was found there either."

"No!" Mannion retorted. "And shall I tell you why? Because I am surrounded by fools who cannot conduct a search efficiently! They come back to me and say there was no one there! What, then, was the sound we heard? Was it a fish barking, pray? Was it a lizard exploding? Tcha! It was a shot, and where there is a shot there is a man. Where could he escape to? Could he swim the river without being seen? Is he a fish? Or a bird, to fly over it? I tell you he was there somewhere, concealed in the bracken and the underbrush, and those damned incompetent numbskulls let him slip through their fingers . . ."

"Yes," Patrick admitted, "there must have been another there. But it occurred to me, Father, that the fire may have been started by that elder native boy. It would not be the first time they have attempted to burn crops and grasslands. Toole swears that—save for the one shot that wounded Allen—there was only Finn firing, and we saw no sign of any others. It's my belief," he concluded rather defiantly, "that there was one other, and that when he heard us returning he thought only of making good his escape, and is now many miles away . . ."

"Having first deliberately attracted our attention by a shot?" Mannion got up and walked irritably about the room. "If you cannot talk sensibly, Patrick, pray don't talk at all! I tell you there was a gang, and God only knows where they are now, or what devilish revenge they may be planning. Yet to my dying day I shall be glad that thrice-damned, seditious, treacherous blackguard Finn got his just deserts, for a more dangerous vill . . . What was that?"

"I expect it was Byrne, Sir, on the verandah. If you don't want me any longer I shall go to my room." He added hastily: "I shall not go to bed, of course. If Captain Abbott sends a detachment, I dare say it might arrive by ten o'clock."

Mannion, left alone, went across to the window and called:

"Byrne!"

There was no answer. He called again, stepping out on to the verandah; as he did so he saw a figure move just beyond the light, and said testily: "Damn you, why don't you answer when I . . ."

He saw then that the figure was naked, and his first confused thought was of the native youth he had interviewed this morning, and who, perhaps, had returned with other tidings. . . . Yet a flash of caution and suspicion turned him quickly back towards the window in a half-formed fear of native treachery, native collaboration with outlaws . . .

A low, harsh voice said commandingly: "Stop! Turn round!"

It was close behind him. Partly amazement at those unexpected English words, and partly incredulous anger that anyone should dare address him so peremptorily, made him swing round. He saw a tall, lean, naked young man standing in the lamplight, a pistol in his right hand. His hair, washed clean of charcoal by the river, blazed redly; his dark eyes were fierce and ruthless, and like ... whose ...? The last activity of Mannion's brain as the shot split the silence was not actual recognition, but a confused, striving impression of familiarity. He crashed forward on his face, the pistol clattered on the stone floor beside him; and Johnny was half-way across the path before his victim hit the flags.

But Ellen, passing along the hall, had heard the shot, and rushed into the room. As she came through the windows she saw the naked figure for a second; as Patrick ran into the study she glimpsed the face, revealed by a momentary backward glance, and saw the gleam of red hair before the darkness hid it. She was standing motionless, staring into the night, when Patrick pushed past her and knelt beside the prone body of his father. From round the corners of the house the guards came hurrying; Bessie and the other servants crowded at the window, and then stood aside to let Conor through. She crouched over the still figure, and asked at last, almost inaudibly:

"Is he dead, Patrick?"

Silence, and the circle of shocked eyes answered her. She whispered: "How ...? Who ...?" There was no answer to that either, but the eyes moved, and her own followed them, to rest on Ellen. Toole picked up the revolver and thrust it at Patrick.

"Look, Sir—it's his own—one of them that was stolen!" Ellen was still staring into the dark, and seemed unaware of the eyes fixed on her face, and growing slowly more horrified and hostile. Toole growled: "He always *said* she'd been in that business!"

Patrick, still crouching over the body, began uncertainly:

"But I saw ..."

Ellen turned and looked at him, and his heart missed a beat. He put his hand over his eyes and tried to think. What *had* he seen ...? Had something moved out there in the dark—or was it only the shadow of those bushes tossing in the wind? He rubbed his palm over his eyes and looked up at her again. Why did her black eyes watch him so intently?

She said tonelessly:

"He saw me do it. I'm not denying it—I had cause to hate him."

Bessie cried out: "Oh, mercy, the mistress—she's going to swoon!"

Conor, as white as her gown, said: "No. But I shall go to my room. Bessie, return to the children—I can hear Master Desmond calling."

The womenfolk were gone, leaving Ellen standing among the men, a strange, wordless conclave still going on between her and Patrick. He said slowly:

"I thought I saw someone ..."

"Well?" asked Toole roughly, shaking her arm. "Was there anyone here?"

"No," she said. The overseer snorted.

"I'll put her in the cellar under lock and key, Sir," he declared. "Aye, I always thought His Honour had the right of it when he says she knew somethin' o' them firearms, an' they vanishin' like they had wings! Ye'll swing for this, ye murderin' she-devil, or me name's not Michael Toole!"

But still her gaze and Patrick's were locked as though they could not break apart. He felt that she was fighting him, fighting the vague, incredible, unspoken suspicion in his mind.

"Very well," he said rather hoarsely, "take her away. And then come back and—remove the—my father indoors. Toole, you remain here. Where is Byrne?"

It was only a few minutes before they discovered him lying hidden under the bushes, and Toole, cursing furiously to hide his panic, held out the bloodstained spear.

"A native—a damned, creepin' savage! My God, Sir—Merrett— an' now Byrne . . .! I tell ye, these black devils . . . !"

Patrick was not listening. A native . . . ? He felt his vague suspicion grow to a monstrous certainty. What must he do? In the face of her confession, what *could* he do? No proof, nothing that he could even swear to having seen. . . . Nothing to back this wild, fantastic suspicion but one glimpse of Johnny, still alive eight years ago. . . . Suddenly he was fifteen again, sitting in the little lamp-lit room with Ellen, staring with awkward, wondering amazement into her eager, hungry eyes. Was it her right to do this thing, was it her right to command his silence with her eyes, those hungry, hungry eyes . . . ?

He said incoherently:

"Post the guards again. I shall watch this side myself. Take—take that away."

*   *   *   *   *

The search for the Governor had already lasted so long that the onlookers outside were growing restless. It was quite dark now, and the soldiers who had been left to keep the populace at a respectful distance had relaxed their vigilance. Mark moved along the street towards the Commissary's Office, from which he could see the tiny room of his friend Mr. Howe among the outhouses of the Government House yard. He scaled the low fence, made his way across it, and peered into the lighted room.

Mr. Howe and his son Robert, now thirteen years old, were standing in the middle of it, staring upward at a pair of legs that dangled from the loft. Muffled curses were coming from their half-visible owner, while a soldier stood below offering assistance, and another contented himself with advice. There was a brief struggle, and the legs waved more wildly; before Mark's astonished eyes Lieutenant Laycock came down on the floor with a crash in a cloud of dust and debris. He picked himself up, clutching at his back and swearing angrily.

"Damn it, I've dislocated my spine! What the devil are you waiting for, you men? Get along and try somewhere else! He's not up there— but by God he must be somewhere!"

He waved them out of the room, pushed past Mark, and followed them, hobbling into the night. The place had been ransacked, and young Robert—a trifle pale, but composed—began to straighten it as his father beckoned Mark in, pointed him to a chair, stood over him, and began to declaim. For Mr. Howe was not rendered speechless, but rather more voluble than usual by rage.

"Take note, Mr. Harvey," he cried, "of what you have seen this night, for I venture to say that never was a more dastardly outrage perpetrated in the whole annals of civilised communities! We have here, Sir, a colony which has been held in grievous bondage by a set of rogues who now descend like wolves upon the Governor because he has lifted up his arm to protect it from their ravenous clutches! And who *are* these people who dare set aside an authority which His Majesty has appointed? To what do they owe the eminence in society that they have so shamefully used? Not to dignity of birth, Sir—not to superior education—not to liberality of sentiment, but . . ." he shook his fist violently under Mark's nose, ". . . to the petty retailing of three-watered grog, Sir! It is a scandal that will resound to the fur . . ."

He stopped, his flush of rage dying to a sudden pallor. Mark started up from his chair. Robert paused, broom in hand, and they all stood motionless, listening to shouts that came from the house, and were echoed by dozens of voices round the garden and in the street:

"He's found! The Governor's found!"

*   *   *   *   *

Bligh had spent close on two hours alone in the dark little room upstairs, and as the time passed he had almost persuaded himself that the search would be abandoned. Had his friends perhaps succeeded in convincing the rebels that he had already escaped? Were they even now pursuing a mythical fugitive along the road to the Hawkesbury?

But suddenly there was a crescendo in the noise, and he heard a rough voice call out: "Damn my eyes, I'll find him yet! Come upstairs, lads—come with me and we'll have another search!"

There was a clatter of feet along the passage; he heard the outer door open, and crouched behind the bed again. They burst into the room, and the light from a candle filled it with huge, wavering shadows. He was not taken yet, but there was only one more very slender chance. The bottom of the bed was a bare eight or nine inches from the floor, but he forced himself beneath it and lay still, cramped and half-suffocated, his heart thumping heavily against the dusty boards. Presently one of the soldiers thrust his musket under the bedstead and began feeling about with it. Resting on his hands and feet, Bligh arched his body the bare inch or two which the bed would allow, to avoid it, but it struck his boot —and immediately the search was over. The last chance had failed, and an excited uproar broke out: "There's something there! Wait while I feel again! Bring the candles! Aye, here he is . . . !"

They dragged him out, and he stood up, breathless and dishevelled, brushing dust and feathers from his clothes, his heart flaming with bitterness. His shirt frill was disarranged, and he could feel his papers slipping; he put his hand up to his breast, and a soldier, threatening him with a bayonet, shouted: "Damn you, take your hand out of there or I'll whip this into you!"

Bligh said furiously:

"How dare you, fellow! Sergeant—keep this man off—I'm not armed! Stand off, all of you!"

The room was full by now. Lieutenant Minchin pushed through the jostling throng, and one of the soldiers warned him excitedly: "Have a care, Sir, he's got a pistol!"

Bligh snapped. "I have no pistol!" To be searched was the last thing he wanted. In the heat of the first assault his life might have been in danger from some half-drunken soldier, but their superiors, he was beginning to realise, designed a different fate for him. It was his character they would seek to murder, and in that fight those hidden papers would be a better weapon to him than any pistol. He understood, too, with a sudden, heart-stopping shock, how they would use the story of his conceal-ment against him. They would attempt to brand him a coward! They would declare he had behaved like a poltroon—he, William Bligh, who had sailed with Cook, and faced all the perils that confront adventurers in unknown seas! He, who had fought at the Dogger Bank and Gibraltar! He, who had won a medal at Camperdown! He, who had been publicly thanked by Lord Nelson after the battle of Copenhagen! He, who had brought his boatload of starving and exhausted men safely across four thousand miles of ocean! Through the confusion of his thoughts, this one thought stabbed like a sword, so painful that he was only half aware of the commotion about him—of staring faces and whispering tongues, of people coming and going, of Griffin's voice calling out something in the passage, of Minchin informing him with a hateful note of triumph that Major Johnston was awaiting him below. They would call him a coward! They would say: "We found him hiding underneath a bed!" How wickedly true words could lie! At the head of the staircase he was vaguely conscious of Griffin's anxious young face, and of his voice, nervous, but warm with sympathy: "Will you take my arm, Sir?" He shook his head absently and went on down the stairs. A coward! Ha! They had deemed it necessary, all the same, to send practically the whole regiment down to arrest this coward, whose only supporters were a few unarmed men and a couple of women! He passed into the drawing-room, which was thronged with soldiers, caught a glimpse of Harris staring at him, moved his shoulders uneasily, feeling his body bathed in perspiration. He could see Campbell, and Griffin was close behind him, but every other face was hostile. *They had deemed it necessary to arrest him . . . !* The thought flashed like another sword, leaping to oppose the one which had been stabbing him. A coward? *There* was the refutation! Was it not because they feared him that they had done this thing—and does one fear a coward? Was it not because he had proved too strong and too deter-mined an enemy that they came thus to overthrow him? His mind cleared and his eyes began to see again. Lieutenant Moore had stepped forward to offer him a paper, and he stood still to read it in a dead silence, with all eyes upon him.

"Headquarters, 26th January, 1808.

"Sir,

"I am called upon to execute a most painful duty. You are charged by the respectable inhabitants with crimes that render you unfit to exercise the supreme authority another moment in this colony; and in that charge all the officers under my command have joined.

"I therefore require you in His Majesty's sacred name to resign your authority, and to submit to the arrest which I hereby place you under, by the advice of all my officers, and by the advice of every respectable inhabitant of the town of Sydney.

"I am, etc.,

"GEO. JOHNSTON,

"Acting Lieut. Gov. and Major Commanding the N.S.W. Corps."

It was but written confirmation of what had already been done, yet the phraseology made his blood begin to pound angrily, and quickened his heartbeats to a painful thudding. And the final words—though still no more than a logical expression of the outrageous and accomplished fact —hit him like a physical blow. *"To William Bligh, Esq., F.R.S., etc., etc."*

He was no longer His Excellency the Governor. The brutal and insulting finality of that address made the writing swim before his eyes. A swell of rage, powerful as the upsurge of an ocean wave, gathered in him, but found no release. Intelligence told him that no outburst of fury, no protest, no denunciation, no threat could help him now; and bodily exhaustion, increased by that sudden flood of emotion, left him depleted of strength, and struggling once more with the old, tormenting illusion that time was out of joint. Mutiny. . . . Where was Fletcher Christian? He should be here, proclaiming his rebellion, signing his action with his presence. Where was he . . . ? He looked round the crowded room, but the face he was seeking was John Macarthur's.

It was not to be seen. The illusion burst like a bubble and left him soberly confronting reality again. This was a different kind of mutiny— not born out of men's bodily passions and desires, not nourished by dreams of Arcadian idleness and pleasure, not really executed, for all the noise and excitement, in the heat of sudden crisis; not recklessly abandoning him to almost certain death. This was a cold mutiny. This was a mutiny born out of avarice, nourished by fear of powers curtailed and privilege withdrawn; wearing a mask of formality, claiming justification, preparing to destroy his honour, while carefully preserving his life. Even meeting him, now that the thing was done, with an outward show of civility . . .

Lieutenant Moore was saying:

"Major Johnston would like to speak with you in the next room, Sir."

Yes, civil enough, but Bligh saw triumph in his eyes. "You see," they said, "I, whom you summoned to appear before you to-morrow morning, now summon you to appear before my commanding officer."

The crowd parted to let them through. Johnston appeared at the door of the dining-parlour, and about him Bligh observed Dr. Townson, Mr. Blaxcell, Mr. Grimes, Mr. Bayly, both the Blaxlands, and Surgeon Jamison.

Young Edward Macarthur was there too, and his cousin Hannibal—but the man whose moment this was—where was he?

The speech which the Major delivered was a mere repetition of what he had already declared in writing, and Bligh listened perfunctorily. He saw young Griffin standing white-faced between two soldiers, and said, almost before Johnston had ended:

"My secretary may remain with me, I suppose?"

Johnston said: "Yes," but added immediately: "Wait! Mr. Bayly, pray go out and ask if it's approved that Mr. Griffin remain with the—er—with Captain Bligh."

Mr. Bayly disappeared, to return a few minutes later with the announcement: "It's not approved of." Johnston said weightily:

"Martial Law has been proclaimed. A committee has been appointed to examine certain persons, including Mr. Griffin. These examinations will commence immediately. You, Sir," he bowed stiffly to Bligh, "will remain here for the present under an arrest. Mrs. Putland has retired to her room with Mrs. Palmer. Sentinels will be placed over the house."

Now there was a stir of activity. A search had begun for papers. Jamison, Blaxcell and John Blaxland had vanished upstairs; Grimes and Townson were roughly demanding Bligh's keys of his servant. "Hand them over immediately—Major Johnston gives the orders now. Come, you know very well where his private papers are kept!"

Slowly the rooms emptied. Griffin was escorted away by Lieutenant Bell. The officers and gentlemen, talking eagerly together, and shooting backward glances at their prisoner, left the house to return to the Barracks, where there was still a requisition to be filled with signatures which few would now dare to withhold, and interrogations of Bligh's adherents to be conducted. Major Johnston bowed stiffly and departed. Soon after nine o'clock Government House was quiet, and Bligh, left alone in the drawing-room, sat staring blindly at the two great portraits of their Majesties which flanked the door into the dining-parlour.

And then, between them in the doorway, appeared Mrs. Putland, and ran to him, crying: "Papa! Oh, *Papa . . .* !"

His eyes, from that fixed stare, seemed faultily focussed. At the other end of the fifty-foot room she looked small, as if advancing towards him from an immeasurable distance. She knelt beside his chair and laid her head on his knee, weeping bitterly:

"My love," he said mechanically, "there—don't weep! You were with Mrs. Palmer all the time I trust?"

"I was with her on the verandah, Papa, and John Dunn was there also, and Mr. Harris came and remained with us, and assured me that no violence would be offered to you. Oh, for that I was thankful, but I still burned with indignation! Was it not violence to break into your house? I tried to keep them from entering the gate, and Mr. Fulton opposed them at the front door, but they burst in through my room, and then we thought every moment that they must find you. They were sure you had gone down to Mr. Palmer's at one time, and they searched there too, taking Mr. Palmer with them. It seems that he and Mr. Campbell, and

Mr. Gore, and Edmund Griffin are all held under arrest, and . . ."

"Yes, yes," he said wearily. "It is done; I must think . . ."

"Those monsters!" she cried in a storm of anger that dried her tears. "Those wicked rebels! How I prayed they might not find you—that you might escape to the Hawkesbury and return with an army of supporters and defeat them!" She looked up at his still, brooding face and asked hesitantly: "What shall you do now, Papa?" For of course he would do something. He was Papa; he was William Bligh, who always emerged victorious from his trials . . .

He said slowly:

"I shall bring them to justice."

His hand moved over her head as he looked down at her. He asked:

"Mrs. Palmer is still here, is she not? And the servants? You should retire, Mary; you are distressed and fatigued."

She caught his hand.

"And you, Papa! Oh, these dreadful weeks have taxed even your strength, do not deny it! Dear Putland . . . and then one stir after another, all trying your patience and requiring your constant attention . . . and these last two days, contending all the time with those evil men —you have not rested, you have hardly slept . . . ! Pray, dear Papa, let me see you also to your room, and . . ."

He said absently:

"Soon, soon. I am tired—I shall go soon." She glanced at the outer door where a sentry was posted, and lowered her voice:

"You preserved your papers, Papa? John Dunn picked up the torn pieces upstairs and burned them . . ."

"Ah," he said, "good."

"What—what will become of us, Papa? What will they do?"

His eyes moved to her face, but he still spoke remotely, as if to himself:

"They will attempt to prepare a case against me to justify their acts. They will not be able to do so, ingenious and unscrupulous as they are. I am a violent man, Mary, and I have made enemies as any man must who will not compromise in the pursuit of his duty. But never doubt, my love; I shall bring them to justice. Now leave me. I want to think."

He watched her go, and remained there, sitting quite still with his arms resting on the arms of the chair, his chin sunk on his breast, his eyes fixed unseeingly on the floor.

*   *   *   *   *

When the crowd outside began to disperse, Mark turned away with them, feeling sick at heart. The officers were going up towards the Barracks again, and he was standing uncertainly, wondering whether to join the groups of people who were curiously following them, or whether to return to his lodgings for a sleepless night, when he felt a hand on his arm. In the dark it took him a moment or two to recognise the overseer, Evans, whom he had last seen at Beltrasna nearly three years ago. He thought at first that the man was drunk, and shook his arm away impatiently, but Evans grasped it again.

"For God's sake, Sir, what's to do here? I'm just this moment arrived —I want to see the Governor, but . . ."

"There's no Governor," Mark said wearily. "He's been overthrown —deposed by the military."

He tried once more to turn away, but Evans still held on to him, and he saw that not alcohol, but haste and alarm were causing his somewhat wild manner. Feeling a sudden apprehension, he cut short the man's exclamations and questions, and demanded:

"What are you doing here? Is aught amiss at Beltrasna?"

"Aye, there's been a peck o' trouble, Sir, and now, with this business here, damn me if I know what's best . . ."

"What has happened?" Mark asked sharply.

"God save us, Mr. Harvey, I don't know where to begin . . . ! Escaped convicts, Sir, headed by that fellow Finn—came down on us this afternoon and tried to free the prisoners—hell let loose for a while, Sir, but we got Finn in the end . . ."

Alarmed, Mark tried to interrupt, but the man gabbled on breathlessly: "Then they set fire to a field, Sir, and it all but got the stables, and the master sent me to Parramatta to ask Captain Abbott to send a detachment, but . . ."

"And did he? Are they on their way . . . ?"

Evans' voice rose indignantly.

"No, Sir—be damned if I could get him to heed me! Queer, he was, Sir—offhand—seemed put about, as if he weren't rightly attending. Cuts me short and goes to the window like he's listening—but it wasn't to me, Sir, for so help me God, I don't believe he heard the half of what I was saying! Tries to send me off—'Come back in the morning,' he says! And I start to tell him again about Finn and his gang, and he fidgets and snaps out askin' me how many of the rogues we've seen. And of course, Sir, we only *saw* but one, and that was Finn, and we laid him by the heels all right, and when I tells the Captain that he roars out to me to be off and not waste his time, that things was in a bad way here and he couldn't spare the men—though for what I could see all was quiet enough at Parramatta, Sir. But since I could get nothin' from him, I come on to Sydney to see the Governor, for His Honour's in a rare takin', and tells me not to come back without . . ."

Mark grabbed him by the shoulder and shook him violently.

"Stop babbling and tell me if all is well with the family! No one is harmed? Your mistress is safe and well . . . ?"

"Safe enough, Sir, but not well, for she's been on a sick bed these weeks past, and Byrne, he says she went down to where they had Finn strung up for a thousand that the master orders, and took on like she was out of her mind. Lookin' like death, he says she was, when His Honour carried her into the house . . ."

Mark was staring frantically up and down the almost deserted street. By the bridge that spanned the Tank Stream a couple of horses were tethered, awaiting the return of their owners from the Barracks; he called over his shoulder to Evans as he ran towards them:

"Get up to the Barracks and see Major Johnston. He has other matters on his mind to-night, but he'll surely do something. I'll go at once—you can find the owner of this beast and say I've taken it . . ."

Evans, following him at a stiff and stumbling run down to the bridge, watched him mount and gallop up to the corner of the High Street, and heard the noise of hoofbeats dying away in the distance.

* * * * *

The hands of the clock in the Church tower at Sydney crept round towards midnight. The twenty-sixth day of January, 1808, was almost at an end, and the colony had completed, in strife and turmoil, its second decade.

There were few left at the Barracks now. Mr. Grimes had inscribed his name tenth upon the requisition long after the arrest, and since then, as Mr. Macarthur had predicted, many signatures had been added; but what they testified was mainly the prudence of joining the victorious side. Macarthur himself was riding home with his son and his nephew, the fierce triumph in his heart already pleasantly softened by the thought of his domestic haven. Ellen Prentice, sitting in darkness on the cellar steps at Beltrasna, with her head resting against the stone wall, was half-asleep. She had forgotten the tall stranger she had glimpsed for an instant in the lamplight, and would never think of him again; a much smaller Johnny was her companion now, and she was not unhappy with memories that were half thought, half dream. Far away up the river, Johnny was paddling through the night, making his fourth and last escape from his own society. Now there was no bond left, no call. Neither curiosity nor revenge would ever draw him to it again; his repudiation was final and complete. It was all behind him, and there was a life ahead in that distant valley to think about. So much of it was Finn that his arms moved fast, and he looked up at the stars, judging the time impatiently, as if he were going to a joyful meeting.

Conor, unable to sleep, had lit her candle and fetched her journal.

". . . so ended this strange and Terrible day," she was writing slowly, for her hand was unsteady with weariness, "and mingled with my horror that poor Stephen should have met his end in so Shocking and Dreadful a manner, is a feeling of release which, were it not that I have sworn to write nothing but the Truth in this book, I should shrink from confessing. Indeed I do shrink from inscribing even here words which seem so Heartless, but upon every other action am able to look back with Tranquility, if with a great degree of Surprise. Even find Pity in my heart for that strange woman, Ellen, his Murderess. In a quieter time will think more of what has Passed, but at present feel that my mind is too confused and my Understanding too slight to form a Judgment. Feel a great desire to talk to someone. May perhaps see Mr. Harvey in Sydney some day.

"No sound of the detachment from Parramatta yet, but am almost persuaded that S. must have been deceived, and there was in truth no one but Finn, for he possessed great courage, and once said that a man would dare anything for . . ."

She lifted her head, listening to the beat of hooves pounding up the hill. She heard Patrick call loudly from the verandah outside her window, and another voice answer him. She sat still for a few minutes, trembling a little while she listened to their quick exchange of conversation. Then, bending over her journal again, she wrote slowly and carefully: "Mr. Harvey has come." And lay down to sleep.

    *   *   *   *   *

The gilt clock on the mantelpiece in the Government House drawing-room chimed midnight, and aroused Bligh from his long brooding. Earlier, he had taken a candle and moved about the house, his shoulders bowed, his step slow, his eyes noting almost abstractedly the signs of its invasion, and his mind hardly deflected by this restless physical pilgrimage through the silent rooms, from the painfully absorbing pilgrimage of his thoughts. So wrapped in his bitter reflections that he moved automatically, he had returned at last to his chair in the drawing-room, and there he sat, his brain turning over and over the events which had brought him to this moment. And because, from now onward, his only aim would be to fight the charges his enemies would bring against him, it framed his thoughts into random sentences which he would address to the authorities in England.

The country became well cultivated, he told them, thinking of the Hawkesbury farms and the harvest just brought in. The settlers and landholders had a market for whatever their labours produced. . . . When ships arrived the usual impositions were suppressed . . . the necessaries they introduced open to everyone's purchase. . . . The people could relieve their wants without being subject to the wicked, monopolising persons who had been making themselves rich on the vitals of the poor . . .

Names marched through his brain like ranks of enemies—Macarthur, Blaxland, Bayly, Townson, Jamison, Grimes, Johnston—and it was already fighting them with the only weapons which could help him in this battle —words. These persons, it was declaring vigorously to those far-away authorities in London, checked in the enormous practice of bartering spirits, became discontented, and the arch-fiend, John Macarthur, so inflamed their minds. . . . It rushed off at a tangent in a flare of anger, crying indignantly: he stands notorious in all the accounts that have been sent to Your Lordship's office since the colony began . . . he has been the disturber of public society, and a venomous serpent to His Majesty's Governors . . . with the settlers he is the most hated person it is possible to conceive . . . his very breath is sufficient to contaminate a multitude . . .

His hands were grasping the chair arm so tightly that his muscles ached, and he relaxed his grip with a sharp sigh. He faced himself and his own faults, looked back on the ruthless directness of his methods, his impatience, his cavalier treatment of obstruction, his hurtful and merciless contempt for vacillation, his violent temper, his unruly tongue, his moments of unjust and unreasonable suspicion. And though he admitted them as failings—ʒ mitted, even, that they might have hastened this disaster and added to its animosity—he could not believe that a more patient man, a more tactful man, would have averted it. No, no, it went too deep. It was a conflict of policy—his against theirs. To meet their demands with concessions would merely have been to invite further demands. The lust for wealth and power was not to be appeased.

But this was what they would never confess. They would not speak of the strength with which they feared he might have defeated them, but of the weaknesses by which he had made himself vulnerable. They would manipulate and distort the truth; and they would cry: "Coward!" His hands closed convulsively on the chair arms again, and he felt a faint, momentary giddiness.

He must fight this thing with words—he must write, and write . . . but how to send home what he wrote? All the colony in their hands, all the outgoing ships at their mercy. . . . They would send for Paterson, of course—Johnston would never dare to do other than hand over his stolen authority at the first possible moment to his superior officer, the Lieutenant Governor. . . . Yet would he not . . . ? Might he not, at all events, delay and delay, using the interval to send home damaging accounts of the man he had deposed? Bligh stared at the floor without seeing it. Somehow he must get his despatches home—but he must use caution, he must find friends. . . . Once before in the history of this colony a Governor's despatches had most mysteriously vanished . . .

Then the clock chimed, and he woke with a slight shiver from his painful concentration, still staring at the floor, but no longer blindly. It must be weariness, he thought, which caused this odd sensation that it was moving under his feet like a boat. . . . It must be weariness that brought this vague hallucination of morning light on endless miles of sea. . . . It must be weariness that fixed in him so persistently the impression that a long, long voyage was beginning. Yet could it be weariness that was awakening, too, another old sensation, gratefully remembered—that "inward happyness and peculiar pleasure" that he had once recorded of another time?

A different kind of voyage, this. A voyage through treacherous currents of intrigue and slander, through whirlpools of conflicting evidence, through storms of enmity, over the submerged rocks of influence, across the icy seas of legality—and so to port. Yet perhaps not even then . . . ? Perhaps still on through time itself, whose horizon no man could glimpse, beyond the years he could still count his own, into others, uncharted. How long? No matter, he thought, pulling himself wearily to his feet, he would fight them to the end of his days, and beyond if necessary, for the final judge was truth—immortal. An austere judge, from whom he would not escape unreprimanded, but into whose hands, nevertheless, he did not fear to deliver himself—and his adversaries.

Some day it would bring them to justice.

THE END

March, 1944—December, 1947.